2017

PUSHCART PRIZE XLI
BEST OF THE
SMALL PRESSES

EDITED BY BILL HENDERSON
WITH THE PUSHCART PRIZE EDITORS

Note: nominations for this series are invited from any small, independent, literary book press or magazine in the world, print or online. Up to six nominations—tear sheets or copies, selected from work published, or about to be published, in the calendar year—are accepted by our December 1 deadline each year. Write to Pushcart Fellowships, P.O. Box 380, Wainscott, N.Y. 11975 for more information or consult our website www.pushcartprize.com.

Acknowledgments
Selections for The Pushcart Prize are reprinted with the permission of authors and presses cited. Copyright reverts to authors and presses immediately after publication.

Distributed by W. W. Norton & Co.
500 Fifth Ave., New York, N.Y. 10110

Library of Congress Card Number: 76-58675
ISBN (hardcover): 978-1-888889-81-9
ISBN (paperback): 978-1-888889-82-6
ISSN: 0149-7863

for
Wendell Berry

"To cherish what remains of Earth
And to foster its renewal is our
only hope of survival."

INTRODUCTION

Every small press writer and editor knows the question: In the age of instant info, twenty-four hour entertainment, political blowhards and gigantic atrocities, isn't there something better I should be doing with my life than struggling to create authentic and honest art?

There is a farmer in Henry County, Kentucky who might offer his life as an answer. Wendell Berry, far from the centers of publishing and political power, has reached an international audience with his poetry, fiction, criticism, essays and environmental activism. He calls himself a forest Christian, ready to criticize religious establishments and argue for basic decency, love, justice and respect for the earth. In scores of books – most recently *Our Only World* – he has depended not on big bucks publishing but on presses like Counterpoint, Shoemaker & Hoard, Sand Dollar, Safe Harbor Books, The Press of Appletree Alley, Larkspur, Golgonooza Press, *Orion, Sewanee Review, Threepenny Review, Poetry, Limestone, Wind, Southern Review, The Progressive, Mars Hill Review, Hudson Review, Wilderness Chronicles, The Cresset* and others.

His influence has been enormous, far from his 125 acre TV-less, computer-less farm at Port Royal on the Kentucky River. He has been featured often in these pages and was honored with a National Humanities Medal, a Fellowship in the American Academy of Arts and Sciences, and most recently, he was lauded with the Ivan Sandrof Lifetime Achievement Award from the National Book Critics Circle.

I was privileged to be in the New York audience when NBCC members rose as one to offer him a standing ovation for a life of principle and dedication. When I wonder if our small press struggles are worth it, I think of 82-year-old Wendell, and keep the faith.

We dedicate this issue of the Pushcart Prize to Wendell Berry, a friend and mentor.

My resolution this year, as we move into our 4th decade is to keep these Introductions short. Fewer words from me, more room for our brilliant, astonishing writers: this year 71 selections from 50 presses.

I thank our PP XLI guest editors for attempting an impossible job: Chloe Honum, Kevin Prufer, Dorothea Lasky (poetry), April Ford, Zebbie Watson, Perry Janes, Mary Kornblum, and Edward McPherson (prose). All guest editors have been featured in a previous PP edition, as were all of our more than 200 Contributing Editors for this volume.

In celebration of our first 40 years, a feat made possible only with the help of a huge community of writers, editors and friends, I would like to specially mention Philip Schultz and his Writers Studio for a grand Pushcart Prize 40th celebration in New York last year that featured readings by Zadie Smith, Sharon Olds, Jon Galassi, Ben Marcus and Colum McCann. Gratitude also to Cedering Fox for her international Word Theatre/Pushcart Prize galas including a major 40th anniversary fest in East Hampton. Thanks also to John Williams for his feature in the *New York Times Book Review* and to George Slowik, Louisa Ermelino, and Sybil Steinberg at *Publishers Weekly* and to Donna Seaman at *Booklist* and editors at *Library Journal, Kirkus Reviews* and other publications for major reviews and features.

As we move into the next decades, my only worry is that so much truly terrific work will overwhelm the PP. We simply have no room in our limited volume for all that is wonderful and poignant. Please consult the Special Mention section: each of these poems, stories and essays deserves to be read and each in my mind has won a Pushcart Prize.

And while you are appreciating our writers please honor our donors to the Pushcart Prize Fellowships and perhaps consider joining them. We wouldn't be here unless they cared.

As always, thanks to you, dear reader. Without you we would all perish. Words are sacred. You remind us of this every year.

Bill Henderson

THE PEOPLE WHO HELPED

FOUNDING EDITORS—Anaïs Nin (1903-1977), Buckminster Fuller (1895-1983), Charles Newman (1938-2006), Daniel Halpern, Gordon Lish, Harry Smith (1936-2012), Hugh Fox (1932-2011), Ishmael Reed, Joyce Carol Oates, Len Fulton (1934-2011), Leonard Randolph, Leslie Fiedler (1917-2003), Nona Balakian (1918-1991), Paul Bowles (1910-1999), Paul Engle (1908-1991), Ralph Ellison (1913-1994), Reynolds Price (1933-2011), Rhoda Schwartz, Richard Morris, Ted Wilentz (1915-2001), Tom Montag, William Phillips (1907-2002). Poetry editor: H. L. Van Brunt

CONTRIBUTING EDITORS FOR THIS EDITION—Steve Adams, Dan Albergotti, Dick Allen, John Allman, Idris Anderson, Antler, Tony Ardizzone, Renée Ashley, David Baker, Kim Barnes, Ellen Bass, Rick Bass, Claire Bateman, Bruce Beasley, Marvin Bell, Molly Bendall, Karen Bender, Pinckney Benedict, Bruce Bennett, Marie-Helene Bertino, Linda Bierds, Marianne Boruch, Michael Bowden, Fleda Brown, Rosellen Brown, Ayse Papatya Bucak, Christopher Buckley, E. Shaskan Bumas, Richard Burgin, Kathy Callaway, Richard Cecil, Kim Chinquee, Jane Ciabattari, Suzanne Cleary, Billy Collins, Jeremy Collins, Martha Collins, Lydia Conklin, Robert Cording, Stephen Corey, Lisa Couturier, Michael Czyzniejewski, Philip Dacey, Claire Davis, Chard deNiord, Jaquira Diaz, Stuart Dischell, Stephen Dixon, Daniel L. Dolgin, Jack Driscoll, John Drury, Emma Duffy-Comparone, Karl Elder, Elizabeth Ellen, Angie Estes, Kathy Fagan, Ed Falco, Gary Fincke, Maribeth Fischer, April L. Ford, Robert Long Foreman, Ben Fountain, H. E. Francis, Seth Fried, Alice Friman, Sarah Frisch, John Fulton, Frank X. Gaspar, Christine Gelineau, Nancy Geyer, Gary Gildner, Elton Glaser, Mark Halliday, Jeffrey Hammond, James Harms, Jeffrey Harrison, Timothy Hedges, Robin Hemley, Daniel Lee Henry, David Hernandez,

Bob Hicok, Kathleen Hill, Edward Hirsch, Jane Hirshfield, Jen Hirt, Andrea Hollander, Elliott Holt, Chloe Honum, David Hornibrook, Christopher Howell, Maria Hummel, Joe Hurka, Karla Huston, Colette Inez, Mark Irwin, Catherine Jagoe, David Jauss, Bret Anthony Johnston, Laura Kasischke, Brigit Kelly, Thomas Kennedy, David Kirby, John Kistner, Richard Kostelanetz, Keetje Kuipers, Mary Kuryla, Don Lee, Lisa Lee, Fred Leebron, Sandra Leong, Dana Levin, Gerald Locklin, Jennifer Lunden, Margaret Luongo, Clarence Major, Paul Maliszewski, Michael Marberry, Matt Mason, Dan Masterson, Alice Mattison, Tracy Mayor, Robert McBrearty, Rebecca McClanahan, Davis McCombs, Elizabeth McKenzie, Edward McPherson, Nancy Mitchell, Jim Moore, Joan Murray, Kent Nelson, Mike Newirth, Aimee Nezhukumatathil, Meghan O'Gieblyn, Joyce Carol Oates, William Olsen, Dzvinia Orlowsky, Kathleen Ossip, Alan Michael Parker, C. E. Poverman, D. A. Powell, Kevin Prufer, Lia Purpura, James Reiss, Donald Revell, Nancy Richard, Atsuro Riley, Lilliam Rivera, Laura Rodley, Jessica Roeder, Jay Rogoff, Rachel Rose, Mary Ruefle, Maxine Scates, Alice Schell, Grace Schulman, Philip Schultz, Lloyd Schwartz, Maureen Seaton, Diane Seuss, Raena Shirali, Anis Shivani, Floyd Skloot, Arthur Smith, David St. John, Maura Stanton, Maureen Stanton, Pamela Stewart, Terese Svoboda, Barrett Swanson, Chad Sweeney, Jennifer K. Sweeney, Mary Szybist, Ron Tanner, Katherine Taylor, Elaine Terranova, Susan Terris, Joni Tevis, Robert Thomas, Jean Thompson, Melanie Rae Thon, William Trowbridge, Lee Upton, Nance Van Winckel, Ocean Vuong, G. C. Waldrep, Anthony Wallace, BJ Ward, Don Waters, Michael Waters, LaToya Watkins, Marc Watkins, Afaa Weaver, Charles Harper Webb, Roger Weingarten, William Wenthe, Philip White, Marcus Wicker, Jessica Wilbanks, Joe Wilkins, Eleanor Wilner, Bess Winter, Sandi Wisenberg, Mark Wisniewski, David Wojahn, Carolyne Wright, Robert Wrigley, Christina Zawadiwsky

PAST POETRY EDITORS—H.L. Van Brunt, Naomi Lazard, Lynne Spaulding, Herb Leibowitz, Jon Galassi, Grace Schulman, Carolyn Forché, Gerald Stern, Stanley Plumly, William Stafford, Philip Levine, David Wojahn, Jorie Graham, Robert Hass, Philip Booth, Jay Meek, Sandra McPherson, Laura Jensen, William Heyen, Elizabeth Spires, Marvin Bell, Carolyn Kizer, Christopher Buckley, Chase Twichell, Richard Jackson, Susan Mitchell, Lynn Emanuel, David St. John, Carol Muske, Dennis Schmitz, William Matthews, Patricia Strachan, Heather

CONTENTS

THE STORY OF
A TRUE ARTIST

fiction by DOMINICA PHETTEPLACE

from ZYZZYVA

I was once a star on YouTube. With my friend Cam, we went by the handle Cam&Lo.

Our videos were all variations of the same theme, which we created together. Most of the screen would show whatever video game he was playing, with his joke commentary. The lower left of the screen contained a box that showed only the top of my head. Just my eyes, rimmed with liquid liner, and my blond hairbow headband atop my black hair. I would make various exaggerated expressions, depending on what was happening with the video game. That was my commentary.

At our peak, we had 800,000 subscribers. Which is a lot, though maybe not quite enough to justify calling myself a star. But I felt like a star. I got fan mail and hate mail. I got recognized at Celebcon, where fans would stop and ask to take selfies with the top half of my head.

My parents never understood what made our work popular and funny and interesting.

"I don't get it," they would say. "Can you explain it?"

"Exasperated sigh," I would say. "If you don't get it, then my explaining it won't help. Shakes head."

But I did have an agent, and that agent helped us get an endorsement deal from Taco Bell.

"It's very important that the sponsored content you create remains authentic to your audience even while it elevates the brand," she said on the conference call.

Cam and I agreed even though we knew this already. We agreed even though neither of us would ever be caught dead in a Taco Bell.

17

The video Cam put together showed him playing *Battlefield*, only all the bad guy heads had been replaced by Chalupas while the bullets had been replaced by Nachos Belgrande. The top half of my head was where you'd expect it, only my eyes had been replaced by rotating Doritos Locos Tacos that occasionally shot lasers to give Cam an assist. The hilarity was enhanced, as ever, by my hardworking eyebrows.

Actually, it was some of our best work. And we got $5,000 for it. My half was enough to put off foreclosure for another couple of months while my dad continued to look for a job. If we continued to get more deals like that and grow our audience, my parents might not have to work at all, and we could move into a Beverly Hills mansion with a swimming pool. That was the plan.

But after our big Taco Bell deal, Cam announced he was leaving YouTube, thus severing Cam&Lo.

"Sad face. It's not you," he said as he brushed his ironic Justin Bieber bangs from his face. "I need to pivot mediums in order to grow as an audience. This disruption will be good for the both of us. Find me on Vine, my handle is camcam."

Cam and I were artists in several different mediums, not just You-Tube. We were best friends and collaborators. One of our installations in progress was the performance of trying to be popular. Like all worthwhile art, this was very difficult to execute, but we were making progress.

We had begun to eat lunch in the courtyard with the others. We went to parties on Friday nights. The ultimate goal was to continue to look down on the popular kids while being popular ourselves. It was going to be so awesome and meta, once finished. Now it was never going to be finished.

Cam ended us in first period.

In second period he was posting his first Vines.

By third period he already had 100,000 followers and counting.

At lunch I wasn't sure who to eat with, so I went to the courtyard as usual.

"Facepalm," he said when he saw me.

"Sigh," I said.

"It's just that the Popular Kids installation is going to be a solo work from here on out. Also, it's now called Popular Kid, singular."

I was too stunned to even say the words "stunned face" out loud, so I just turned and walked away.

"Wait," he said.

So I stopped and paused a moment before turning around. I truly felt like the act of pausing and turning around would turn everything else around. Cam was wrong and would admit as much as soon as I faced him again and then things could get back to the way they were supposed to be.

"Yes?" I said when I was ready for my apology.

"My lawyer is sending you a contract. Check your email," he said. Then I stormed off for real.

The contract arrived in fourth period. His lawyer used to be our lawyer. Now his lawyer was asking me to sign over my moral rights to Popular Kids for fifty dollars. Only a monster would ask for so much in exchange for so little, but financial straits being what they were, I took it.

I already knew my next installation would be the most powerful form of revenge I could think of.

The only way you can ever really hurt another artist is to create a work so awesomely brilliant and so similar to your rival's that you obviate the need for your rival to exist at all. Aiming for suicide-inducing greatness sounds risky and cruel, but Cam was too much of a narcissist to ever self-annihilate. I could only hope to make him feel jealous and unnecessary, pretty much how I felt as I watched his follower count tick up, up, and up.

Of course each of us as humans contains the abyss, but by fifth period I felt like I contained nothing but the abyss.

How could he do this to me?

My virtual therapist couldn't meet with me until sixth period. My virtual therapist is an internet friend named 2ARAH (pronounced Sarah) who is also an artist. VT is her latest installation, an app where 2ARAH pretends to be a robot pretending to be a therapist. It's a very exclusive app, with a mile-long waitlist, but I got in by sending 2ARAH an autographed hairbow.

Why why why, I asked her, typing from the bathroom stall. I was supposed to be in math class.

BLEEP BLEEP BLORP. The edgy and brave thing about your art is that it makes the boundary between performance and real life porous and unstable. I'm guessing that at some point during his role as your friend, Cam stopped being an authentic friend and started being a 'performance' friend. BLORP.

Yes, but how do I become the greatest performance artist in the world?

Computing . . .

Computing . . .

BLEEP You cannot do it the way you've been doing it. You have to find a radical new direction. What is the most different thing you could possibly do?

I was thinking of starting an installation called Unpopular Kid.

That is incorrect. The most extreme art you could make now would have no performance component at all. It would showcase your most vulnerable, most authentic self. Terminating session . . .

VT then transmitted a series of very comforting emojis. The screen went black before I could protest to her that there was no such thing as an authentic self.

"Etc. etc.," I said to the graffitied door of my stall. I wanted to write some graffiti badmouthing Cam, but since we had been inseparable until today, all users of this stall would know that I wrote it. Instead I wrote "Marina Abramović was here" with my lavender paint maker. Whenever things got rough I always asked myself WWMAD?

WWMAD?

WWMAD?

After school I called our agent, Angela, to see if she had abandoned me, too. The answer was no, in fact Cam had left her and signed with someone new.

"I will continue to represent you but you need to begin to develop your brand independent of Cam. That means you need to create new content," she said.

I was in the library, on a computer terminal. I was watching our You-Tube subscriber count drip down to nothing. Cam had posted a farewell video, himself, without even bothering to include the top of my head.

"I know our revenue wasn't a ton," I said, "But we were building up to something, weren't we?"

"You were, that's why I signed you."

"My family really needs the money. We might lose our home."

"Create a new account, new content. Your fans will find you. In the meantime, look for other work."

"Sobs," I said.

"Hugs," she said.

I created a new YouTube account. TrueLourdes, it was called. My mom named me after Madonna's kid, which was smart. Most of my fans didn't even know my true name, or even what my whole face looked like. They were going to learn.

Even though I used to be a YouTube star, I knew shit about YouTube.

Cam had always handled the technical end of things. He's the one who recorded, edited, and posted.

I was the muse, the inspiration, and the creative collaborator. I was going to have to figure everything out on my own now.

Art could be made anywhere, at any time. I looked around the library. Chess Club appeared to be in session. I walked over to them.

"Excuse me, can I join Chess Club?" It was all superskinny dudes and one superskinny girl. They blinked at me like owls when I asked to join. I took their blinking to mean yes.

"Also, I will be filming myself playing."

Blink, blink, blink.

I entitled my first video "Losing at Chess." It only got a hundred views and a dozen likes. Most of the comments complained about how fat and unattractive I was. As if.

People think that because I cry a lot I am insecure. Quite the opposite. I cry a lot because I am not afraid to show emotion. During the two-hour "Losing at Chess" video, I broke down into tears about a dozen times. I wasn't actually crying over the chess, I barely knew how to play, much to the consternation of my Chess Club teammates. I was crying over everything I had lost that day.

I wasn't even tempted to edit out any of the crying. Also, I didn't know how. That was the kind of thing I was going to have to learn how to do at some point.

To every comment that criticized my appearance, I replied, "You have tried and failed to hurt my feelings." I was trying to generate a meme and I succeeded. This became a popular comeback various places on the Internet over the next week. Somehow this did not translate into subscribers, views, or likes, and hence money, which is what I really needed to keep the lights on.

I oftentimes worry that only rich people can be true artists. Only rich people can afford to not care about money, which is what is required for real art. Cam was rich, or at least his parents were.

If it were just me, I wouldn't fear homelessness. I would live in a dumpster and call it an installation. It's just that I had two parents and two siblings and they would prefer not to live in a dumpster. I oftentimes worry that you can't be a true artist if you have a family that depends on you.

And what is the definition of prostitution anyway? Prostitution is selling your body for money, isn't it? I thought of this as I was at Starbucks, filling out an employment application. I ran into my dad, who was there for the same reason. Neither of us was likely to get the job. I was too young and he was too old. We were competing against people with college degrees and good attitudes. But we were both there because it was important to try.

"Maybe we'll both get hired," he said.

"Maybe I can use this for my art," I said.

Neither turned out to be the case.

At least my mom still had a job. She worked in a high-end boutique. She let the customers know she had a daughter who could babysit. But actually, none of the customers needed a babysitter, they all had at least one nanny, oftentimes more.

One of the customers did need help with a fashion blog she wanted to start.

"Oh, my daughter is great at the Internet."

This wasn't true. But for $10 an hour, I was willing to learn.

Dina needed someone to take and post pictures of her doing various fashion model poses while wearing various expensive outfits. Her plan was to start a blog, then get really famous. That was it, a two-part plan.

"It's actually hard to get Internet famous for being cool," I said. "You have to be lucky and tweet all the time."

I could never really get into Twitter, it seemed a medium best suited for knock-knock jokes. That's why Cam had handled our account.

Now I needed to get my own and help Dina set one up, too. Ugh, fuck work. I just want to make art, tho.

So I created a Twitter installation called @ONECHARACTERLIMIT. It was a response to the artificiality of Twitter's 140-character limit.

@ONECHARACTERLIMIT was a carefully composed series of 140 tweets, each one character long. My only followers were spambots. That led to my next installation, @buttsecks, where I replaced random words from spam tweets with the word buttsecks. This account actually got some real human followers, including Angela, who DMed me that I should create more videos, perhaps look into Vine.

It was impossible to look into Vine without also looking into Cam.

Two months after the end of Cam&Lo he had 1.2 million Vine followers.

His videos mainly consisted of him telling jokes and/or crashing into things. I think they were supposed to be "funny," but I wasn't sure.

I was worried if I showed them to my parents, they would laugh. That their faces would light up with comprehension, like, AH so that's what the Internet is for. My parents didn't know that I hated Cam now because I didn't want to burden them. They had enough on their minds.

I hinted to them that Cam might be having some difficulties and they assumed it had to do with his sexual orientation. It wasn't their fault. They were from a generation that confused "being gay" with "being an artist."

I didn't know if Cam was gay or not. He didn't share that part of himself with me. We were never romantically involved, but the love we shared was deep nonetheless. We were united with a vision and mission.

And now I hated him. I couldn't help thinking back to every snarky thing he had ever said to me, as if those were the only things that mattered.

I commented, "Sell Out!!" on one of his Vines. He replied that I had tried and failed to hurt his feelings.

I couldn't stop comparing myself to him. FKA Twigs once said that too much medicine is poison. Comparing yourself to others is the medicine/poison of the art world.

Angela and VT both agreed that the best thing for me to do was to focus on my work, both the art and the kind of work that pays money.

After school I would photograph Dina making fashion blogger poses. The genre was: expensive clothes on a thin white body, acting naturally. She would stare at the ground, gazing at her stilettos while curling a lock of hair around her finger. Or she would lean against a wall casually, as one does, hands in pockets. Close up of her manicured hand clutching an expensive handbag. These shoots were highly derivative, and not in an ironic way. We collaborated on different ways of copying the most famous fashion bloggers.

Dina rejected all my suggestions for making our pictures more original. I thought she could wear monster makeup or Mickey Mouse hands. I thought she could cosplay as beloved '90s sitcom characters (Steve Urkel! Chandler Bing!). I thought we could replace her head with different dinosaur heads in Photoshop. I suggested she buy herself some sort of novelty headband, like maybe cat ears or a unicorn horn. Dina ignored my suggestions and continued posing like a bashful ingénue with the wardrobe of a socialite.

Dina fired me after a month. It wasn't because of all my wacky suggestions. It was because I failed to make her famous.

At this point it became clear that we were losing the house no matter what, it was just a matter of when and it could happen any day.

"It's not your fault," said my dad, even though I knew if had been just a little bit luckier or a little bit more clever, it would have been enough.

"Great suffering produces great art," my mom said, and I nodded along even though I didn't agree with this statement at all. Art comes from a place much more mysterious than Planet Hardship.

"I'd rather be poor than stupid," I told myself. But then, would I? Would I?

While visiting the food bank I took a series of selfies that got a fair bit of attention. I was trying to interrogate the notion of a selfie as a status marker. I got regrammed by Hans Ulrich Obirst, which made me feel like a real artist.

I started a Patreon account because I knew I still had some fans. Hans Ulrich chipped in $20. So did Cam. Wish I had been in a position to decline that donation, but I wasn't.

All of this resourcefulness, all in the name of drowning just a little more slowly than before. My mom looked for a second job while my dad continued to look for a first job. We moved into a motel room while we looked for an apartment.

Angela booked me a job as a "fan" at Celebcon. You could buy likes and friends, so it made sense that you could also buy "fans" or at least people willing to pretend for a few hours.

Celebcon was over in Anaheim, just an hour away from my house. It was the premier convention for Internet video talent. I had attended last year, but as a creator. I had never paid anyone to be a fan, so I knew that every person who told Cam and me that we were great was telling the truth.

There were creators much more famous than us in attendance. Legitimate stars with millions of subscribers. Fans would go crazy over these true stars, you would hear screaming and a mob would form. This would get the attention of any television executives in attendance. They might not understand the Internet, but they understood the power and influence of sobbing teenage girls.

The weird thing about the biggest Internet stars is that they all wish they were on television, even though nobody watches television anymore.

"The Internet is more influential," said Angela, "But TV is more profitable." This didn't make a lot of sense to me, but if I understood money a little better, I might have more of it.

This year at Celebcon, the biggest Internet stars were hiring fans to make a scene in the hopes of building hype and ultimately scoring a TV deal. It was so crass, it seemed like a perfect setting for an installation.

"No installations," said Angela. "Just show up. Cry, scream, and then count your money once you get home."

Angela gave me a list of celebrities to mob. Cam wasn't on the list, but I knew he would be there. With over 20,000 attendees, it would be easy to avoid him. Especially now that I was no longer a star.

I wore my hairbow to Celebcon. If anyone recognized me, they did not acknowledge me. I was normal now.

I set to work right away with my fellow fans. We ran after our "faves," who were in reality our bosses. We begged them for selfies, we screamed their names, we cried if they had the decency to bump elbows.

Because I was the tallest and my hairbow made me easy to spot, I became the leader of the "fans." I was both in charge of the group and a part of it as well. This felt like acceptance. I was determined to do a good job. I was determined to do the best job.

The weird thing about pretending to be a fan is that it becomes transcendent. I found myself no longer pretending to care, but actually caring. My screams became genuine, as did my excitement, as did my tears.

This was crowdart. I had never experienced such a thing. It was a high. It made me want to run faster. It made me want to push my way to the very front.

It was in the midst of a crowd sprint that I spotted Cam. I stopped suddenly, which caused a multi-person pileup. I changed direction and ran toward him.

Cam was surrounded by a mini-entourage. Nobody I recognized. I assumed these were fellow Viners, his new crowd.

He froze when he saw me and the group of "fans" that had trailed me. Perhaps he thought they were my fans.

Good.

I saw a look of pre-emptive embarrassment flash across his face. Despite the estrangement, he still knew me better than anyone. He knew I was always performing, not just when the cameras were on and not just to please other people. He knew that the person I had always wanted to impress most was him. And now that he was out of my life, the only person left to impress was myself.

And unlike him, I did not embarrass easily.

And maybe Cam's embarrassment was at the root of our split. I was a nonconformist in both "cool" and "uncool" ways. I had a large body and a weird sense of humor. I had brown skin and a poor family. I had a hairbow, which I wore at all times. My pain, my sorrow, my ambition, my aspirations, all so embarrassing.

There was altogether too much of me for him. That's why he only showed a piece of me in our work together. Show too much of me and

I might overshadow him. Keep me at a distance and he might shine brighter, right?

I scanned the faces of Cam's entourage and wondered who among them, if any, he had chosen to collaborate with. I was about to show them what it meant to be a true artist. Cam's crew was quiet, and the quiet awkwardness rippled out into the mass of people somehow. Everyone knew something was about to happen.

I only planned the first part.

"I am your biggest fan!" I screamed at Cam, before I dropped down to my knees and began to sob.

I did not plan what happened next. My fellow "fans," confused about what to do and in need of the money they were supposed to earn today, copied me. So they too, dropped to their knees, thinking it was some sort of reference to something.

They also began to cry, but fake cry, because not everyone is as good at crying on command as I am. Others in the crowd joined in, probably thinking that this was some kind of flash mob. Cam tried to walk away, but this had become a spectacle and he was at the center of it. He was surrounded.

On the periphery, I could feel people recording this. I sobbed all the harder. I was the pathogen and this was about to go viral. I finally understood Vine. This footage would make great Vines.

"Sob," I said, between sobs. I was sweaty from all the running I had been doing and I could feel my hairbow was crooked and about to fall off. I didn't care. This was the real me, off center and full of feels.

In my teary vision I could see phones raised up by both hands and selfie sticks. There were screens everywhere, cameras pointed right at me. They were christening me, I was being rebaptized into celebrity-hood.

Those people saw me and they wanted all their friends to know that they were there when it happened. Their pictures would be evidence that they had been part of something larger than themselves.

I was a star: that meant I was important. I mattered. And, because they were there with me, they mattered too.

Nominated by ZYZZYVA

I SING YOU FOR AN APPLE

by ERIC WILSON

from NEW ENGLAND REVIEW

In memoriam Steinbjørn Berghamar Jacobsen
September 30, 1937–April 12, 2012

When the phone rang that evening in 1978, I was caught off guard. "How soon can you be here in DC?" the voice was asking. I lived in Los Angeles. "And—you *do* know Old Icelandic, right?" Old Icelandic, spoken by the Vikings some thousand years ago, was extinct.

As I hung up, I wondered: How had my career come to this?

My Stanford PhD in Germanic Languages had led to my teaching at UCLA and then Pomona College. But in 1973 my position had been eliminated, and I found myself unemployed—and unemployable. Students were demanding "relevant" courses, and the traditional foreign language requirement had been abolished by colleges almost everywhere. Looking back on this today, I see I was ahead of the curve when it came to joblessness.

All I had been trained to do was teach. What other marketable skills might I have? Slowly I began to find work as a freelance translator. My first assignment dealt with German and French cat food. Thomas Mann had been replaced by *KATKINS für die Katze* and *POUSSY pour le chat*. The one bright spot was that I had passed the State Department examination for escort-interpreters in both German and Swedish.

The assignments for State were normally one-month stints during the summer; I would accompany foreign dignitaries across the country, always starting out in DC. But when my contact at Language Services called me on this Monday afternoon in July, clearly something was amiss. I figured the earliest I could get there would be Wednesday.

"I guess that will have to do," Pavel told me. "At this point you're all we could come up with. But you *do* know Old Icelandic, right?"

"Well, sort of," I ventured, wondering why he was asking this. I had passed State's oral exams in German and Swedish. "Where is this person from?" I asked. Had they stumbled upon a Viking frozen in a block of ice? I didn't understand why he was being so evasive.

"How's your Danish?" Pavel continued. "He *does* speak Danish. Sort of."

I tried to explain that although I could read Danish, spoken Danish is notoriously problematic. With all its slurred sounds and glottal stops, even the next-door Norwegians—much to their consternation and great annoyance—often can't understand spoken Danish. Couldn't they find a native Dane closer to DC?

It was like this: One of their more seasoned escorts had been assigned to this visitor, but the first night he had made "advances" to her. She was discreet in giving the details—other than that he had been quite inebriated—but she had quit on the spot. Stranding him. Stranding *them*.

There was a silence while I tried to absorb this. But there was more: "Unfortunately, that's only part of the problem. Steinbjørn"—I was amused that his first name meant "stone bear"—"doesn't speak Danish. He's a poet, from the Faeroe Islands. They have their own language.

"He's *supposed* to speak Danish," Pavel quickly continued. "Most natives of the Faeroe Islands do. But apparently he doesn't. At any rate, not a Danish that the Danes can understand."

"What makes you think I can understand him, then?"

"We saw on your résumé that you took Old Icelandic at Stanford. Won't that give you a leg up?"

"We read the sagas in Old Icelandic, but we never spoke it. It's a dead language."

"Well, apparently his 'Danish' is something of his own invention, so if on your end you can invent some kind of Danish, then the two of you ought to be evenly matched. Anyway, see how soon you can come and we'll book your flight. Oh, and it's probably best if you meet him directly at your hotel. Steinbjørn has locked himself in his room and is refusing to come out. No one can talk to him."

When I called Pavel back the next morning to arrange for my ticket, he provided a few more details. The Faeroes were up in the North Atlantic, halfway between Norway and Iceland. They consisted of an archipelago of eighteen major islands, populated by forty thousand souls, who spoke a language all their own. In the middle of nowhere.

I tried to imagine—a separate language for a country half the size of

Santa Monica! And like Icelandic, the language had barely changed in a thousand years. It was a living relic, a far distant past that was still hanging in there, but as the present. And to represent the Faeroese, State had invited an alcoholic poet. As it turned out, Steinbjørn proved to be an important man. Just not in the way that our government had expected.

Traffic was bad coming in from Dulles; I got to the Dupont Plaza around 7:00 PM. When I asked for Steinbjørn's room number at the front desk, they seemed greatly relieved that at last someone had come to "take care of things." They gave me a duplicate key to his room.

I knocked loudly, but there was no response. Reluctantly I let myself in. The air conditioning had been set at arctic. The floor was littered with tiny liquor bottles from the mini-fridge, as well as wrappers from Oreo cookies, Mars Bars, and Snickers. In a corner I saw a figure slumped down on the floor, leaning back against a wall, apparently sound asleep. All he was wearing was a colorful pair of paisley Faeroese skivvies.

I knelt down and shook his knee; slowly he opened his eyes. They were an amazingly piercing blue, but at this point too bleary to pierce much of anything. I told him my name and that I would now be his escort-interpreter. I was here; I would stay with him. I said this in my dodgy Danish, which he didn't appear to understand. I tried again, pronouncing all the Danish sounds that are normally slurred or silent. Finally I sensed he was absorbing what I was saying.

Pulling him up by both hands, I was able to get him to his feet. I was surprised at how short he was. As he tried to bring me into focus, his eyes filled with tears. I put my hands on his shoulders, trying to steady him. I wasn't ready for any of this. Although this assignment still seemed preferable to KATKINS für die Katze, I knew I was out of my depth.

Trying to keep him upright, I asked if he wanted something to eat. I used the Danish word "spise" and then the Swedish word "äta," miming lifting a spoon out of an invisible bowl. He shook his head no. I heard "sove" as he mimed tilting his head down into his folded hands. So I led him into the bedroom.

I watched him crawl onto the rumpled unmade bed. Then, lying on his back, he stared up at me and broke into a smile before he closed his eyes. He didn't say goodnight. All he said before he fell asleep was, "Eiríkur." My name in Faeroese.

My instincts told me to call State immediately and tell them I couldn't do this. But then they had already been stranded once. And I had given them my word.

After I had put Steinbjørn to bed, I went down to the lobby and checked in. State had messengered over a thick packet of material for me, which included a bio of Steinbjørn, our month-long itinerary, plane tickets, and a small book in English that described the Faeroe Islands.

The Islands—*Føroyar*—are indeed halfway between Iceland and Norway. Apparently the name of the Islands derives from the Faeroese word for "sheep." "At present," the book informed me, "sheep are roughly equivalent to twice the human population of the Islands. Every winter, many sheep slip on the rocky slopes and plunge to their death in the sea." The whole episode, it seemed, could have been written by Monty Python.

Reading further I learned that roughly 98 percent of Faeroese exports were related to fishing and that the Islands had been under Danish control since 1388. Since then Faeroese had been forbidden as a teaching medium in the schools. For a while it looked as if the language was facing certain extinction. It wasn't until 1948 that school children were finally allowed to be taught in Faeroese instead of Danish. In that year the Home Rule Act granted the Islands special status as a self-governing community within the Kingdom of Denmark.

In 1970 the Faroese withdrew from NATO. And somehow they managed to remain outside the "Common Market," as the European Union was called back then. In 1946 there had been an independence referendum in which the people voted for secession from Denmark, but this was overruled. "It was a consultative referendum," I read, "and the parliament was not bound to follow the people's vote."

This is where Steinbjørn came in. In addition to writing poetry and children's books, he was known to be the Islands' most vocal political activist. He wrote plays advocating complete independence from Denmark. His took his plays and troupes of players down to the docks. When the fishermen came in with their catch of cod, he incited them to join his demonstrations—demanding that the Faeroe Islands break away from Denmark.

The next morning I called State to check in. We still had a full day for sightseeing in DC before we were to fly off to our first official meeting with a professor of Comp Lit and Folklore at one of the Ivy League schools.

I mentioned that Steinbjørn seemed like an odd choice to invite for a high-level visit. Well, Pavel admitted, no one at State knew Faeroese, but they did know he was a political activist and a voice to be reckoned with as the Islands determined their future. If they did achieve total independence from Denmark, they would be a new nation. Before that happened, they wanted Steinbjørn to become favorably disposed to our country. "So that they might become our allies and not get sucked into the Soviet orbit," Pavel said, only half tongue-in-cheek.

Nixon had "opened up" China six years earlier, but we still feared the "Red Menace." In 1964, when I was hired to teach at UCLA, I'd been required to sign an oath that I was not a Communist.

"Once we saw him," Pavel continued, "it occurred to us we may have made a mistake with this one. It all depends on you, Eric, as to whether or not this will work out."

By noon I felt it was time to wake Steinbjørn. I had no idea what to expect but hoped he would at least no longer be inebriated and crying. To my relief he was up and dressed. He was wearing a very plain white cotton shirt, with a simplicity that struck me as something the Amish might wear. His generic jeans were clean, and he wore spit-polished black dress shoes, something a boy might wear to his first Communion. His eyes were a pure blue, his cheeks were rosy, and the planes and angles of his face were quite striking. He could have been a poster boy for the Vikings if only he'd been taller.

We stopped by the first fast food place we found. Since all the items were depicted in saturated color on a sign behind the counter, all he had to do was point. While on most days I would've lamented this apparent slide into a language-less culture, that afternoon it was a welcome reprieve.

Once out on the street, Steinbjørn looked at the mass of humanity hurrying past. He had the unguarded curiosity of a child, and like a child his questions never let up. An elegant woman caught his attention; her burgundy silk dress was so beautiful that I could tell it was something special. She wore spaghetti-strapped shoes with stiletto heels that looked virtually impossible to walk on.

"Om skoarna eetje errr smerrtilika?" Steinbjørn asked. *"Om hun*

eetje ramlar omkull ibland?" Were her shoes not painful? Did she not topple over occasionally? I told him apparently not; she seemed to be walking just fine. "*Sprrrrrrrrrrk!*" he demanded. "*Ask!*"

He started trotting behind her, looking at her feet. I tried to explain one didn't ask strangers that kind of thing. But he got louder each time he commanded: "*Sprrrrrrrrrrk!*" So I caught up with her and posed the question. Her expression was incredulous. Didn't I understand the rules of civilized behavior? When I went back to the expectant Steinbjørn, it was easier simply to tell him that yes, they were *extremely* painful to wear. And she had indeed experienced great falls wearing these shoes. He beamed at me. I had asked!

The next person who caught his eye was a willowy young African American woman with cornrows. Her braided hair was intricately woven into tight patterns very close to her scalp. Steinbjørn wanted to know what kind of hairdo this was and why she wore it. "*Sprrrrrrrrrk, Eiríkur,*" came his command: "*Sprrrrrrrrrk!*"

I had no Danish word for cornrows and no insider's knowledge as to the custom.

When I went up to ask her, she smiled at Steinbjørn and looked right into his preternaturally blue eyes. He greeted her in Faeroese. She hesitated for a moment, then said, "You like my hair, child?" And in the melodic rhythms of Jamaican English, she gave us a detailed lecture on cornrows. I found I didn't need to translate. Steinbjørn was captivated by her warmth and her accent.

The flight to Boston had been just a short hop. Steinbjørn seemed anxious about our first academic appointment. He was wearing his same outfit—white cotton shirt, clean pair of jeans, and polished black shoes—only now he was carrying a very worn old leather satchel. The professor who had agreed to meet with us ushered us into the conference room of his department, rather than just his office.

Professor R. greeted us with hearty pleasantries and asked Steinbjørn if he'd like some coffee. The department secretary had brought in a steaming pot, along with a sterling silver creamer and matching sugar-cube holder. "*Kaffi,*" said Steinbjørn. "*Ja, takk!*"

Professor R. slid across the table to us a folder that resembled a press kit. It contained his CV, a lengthy list of publications, and offprints of a number of his scholarly articles. Many of them dealt with Sir Gawain and the Green Knight. I noticed that he was an Endowed Chair.

"*Överrrrrsett!*" Steinbjørn called out. I had no idea how to translate "endowed chair." To me the term had always had a slightly salacious ring to it. So I "translated" for Steinbjørn in our still-evolving idiolect, giving him generalities about the importance of our host.

Professor R. had a kind face. He told me he set great store by high-level meetings of scholars, and was grateful to the State Department for helping bridge the gulf between linguistics, folklore, and world literature from all eras. He mentioned he was eager to learn Steinbjørn's spin on the Green Knight: whether he favored the interpretation of his being the Green Man of traditional folklore, or rather of his being a Christ figure. How did all this fit into the overall Arthurian legend? How could so many ambiguities be resolved? What *did* Steinbjørn have to say?

In translating I used the Swedish word *riddare* for knight. *Den gröne riddaren*. This made no sense to Steinbjørn, who had never heard of Sir Gawain. He asked how a knight could be green. "*Sprrrrrrrrrrrk!*" he demanded. Clearly I must have been wrong. Clearly I had misunderstood!

The light reflecting off his round spectacles, Professor R. began his own exegesis of the Green Knight. Steinbjørn, without seeming aware of it, had begun to remove the sugar cubes from the sterling silver container and to stack them up, forming a kind of pyramid. When Professor R. noticed this, he stopped speaking.

Steinbjørn apparently felt this meant that the man was finished. He leaned down to open his vintage leather satchel and produce a small book. He walked around the table and slid down to crouch at the professor's side, with me standing behind him, and placed the book onto the table in front of him. It was a very slim volume, almost more of a pamphlet than a real book. The paper was of the same poor quality as propaganda flyers in East Berlin.

"*Överrrrrrsettt!*" Steinbjørn instructed. Without ever having read any Faeroese before, I found I was able to translate the title of what was clearly a Faeroese children's book, *Hin snjóhvíti kettlingurin*. "The snow-white kitty-cat," I translated. The professor's expression suddenly congealed. Something was deeply wrong. For my part, I felt I was back at my PhD orals at Stanford, where I had been called upon to sight-read a passage from one of the sagas in the original Old Icelandic, *Brennu-Njáls Saga*, the Burning of Njál. I was both surprised and relieved that I was able to sight-read the book about the kitty-cat in a language I had never seen before.

Steinbjørn turned to a random page in his book. *Kettlingurin var kritahvítur, hann hevði ikki ein myrkan blett á kroppinum.* "The kitty-cat was white as chalk, he didn't have a single fleck on his body." This time it wasn't my PhD orals, so I could relax. What I didn't understand, I made up, easily guided by the colored illustrations of happy children in their brightly colored Faeroese sweaters and the snow-white cat that was white as chalk. "Well," I said, looking up from the slender book, "I'm sure this will give you the overall idea."

Judging from the professor's expression, I could see he was mentally shifting gears. Clearly Steinbjørn wasn't the high-ranking international scholar he had expected him to be. I explained that there wasn't much written in Faeroese, and that Steinbjørn's children's books were an invaluable learning tool for schools and parents back home in his Islands. Professor R. seemed to be taking this all in.

In a beautifully flowing script, Steinbjørn penned a dedication to the professor on the back cover of the slim volume, then autographed and dated it. With great ceremony he presented it to him. Then he went back to the other side of the table and put the CV, the offprints, and the publication list into his satchel. They smiled at each other as they shook hands. I took a parting look at the sugar-cube pyramid on the table.

Professor R. clasped my shoulder warmly as he guided me out the door. In a quiet voice he told me, "This was quite refreshing. I teach folklore—but I almost never come into any living, breathing contact with it."

I was greatly relieved that the meeting had not turned into a fiasco. "We're counting on you," State had told me. Well, maybe I might actually be able to pull this off.

Our itinerary was a bit of an odd zigzag across the country, since our meetings depended upon our hosts' availability. We next flew to Lexington, Kentucky, and drove through breathtaking rolling hills to a small Appalachian town. We were to meet with a man who had made a short documentary film about coal mining. On our itinerary he was listed as a "political activist playwright," which was what Steinbjørn was supposed to be and was the reason State had invited him here.

Many boys in rural Appalachia, we'd been informed, were leaving school early to work in the mines; many of them did this for instant earnings. They wanted to be somebody *now*; sadly, most often their highest priority was to spend the money on a flashy car. The film was called *In Yer Blood*, because in that part of the world mining was deeply entrenched. It would almost be unusual for a boy from a poor family *not* to go into mining. But black lung disease, for which there was no treatment, was not uncommon, nor were horrific mining accidents. The underlying message of the film was that this practice was the equivalent of sending the boys into the trenches. The writer/director was hoping for widespread distribution of the film in schools throughout the area, as a warning.

We watched the film along with the young director, as well as eight or so teenage boys who had appeared in the film. Clearly they were quite poor. Already some of them had rotting teeth, but they smiled as if that didn't matter. The boys took an instant liking to Steinbjørn.

One cowlicky boy with freckles mentioned that most of the time they didn't have much food at home, so he would be lucky if he could shoot a squirrel for breakfast. There wasn't much meat on a squirrel, but with a nice gravy he could eat it with biscuits. Translating, I drew a blank on all the Scandinavian words for "squirrel." I told the boy I didn't know the word off-hand, so without missing a beat he hopped down from his chair and sank to his haunches, twitching frantically with his nose, holding up his hands in a mendicant's position, darting his eyes skittishly back and forth. *"Ekerrrrrrn!"* Steinbjørn said, in immediate recognition. He too hopped down from his chair, and for a long moment Steinbjørn and the boy became mirror-image squirrels. Then they both broke up in laughter.

Still crouching as a squirrel, the freckled boy—his name turned out to be Lanny—asked me if we were familiar with "haint" stories. Here I was at a loss, but the director explained they're a kind of ghost story popular in Appalachia, about restless spirits who come back to "haint"— *haunt*—the living. They're best told to a group sitting in a circle around a remote campfire as the storyteller casts his spell. "Done properly," the director told me, "these tales can scare the bejesus out of the listeners."

Lanny got up to dim the lights so that we were in almost total darkness. As our eyes adjusted, he instructed us to sit around in a circle on the floor. When we were properly assembled, Lanny began to tell his tale. His coal-black eyes darted around the room far more warily than when he had been the alert but anxious squirrel. His voice was sonorous and almost caressing—but it was an unsettling caress. His rhythms were almost purely Appalachian and it was hard for me to follow the dialect. What I got was the gist of the story, in which some kind of horror had started its slow build. As Lanny let his story unfold, Steinbjørn sat there in complete absorption. He didn't understand the words either, but he understood the tone of menace, and even in the shadows I could see his Nordic blue eyes grow wide as he leaned in to listen.

Our next appointment was with a Comp Lit professor at a large Midwestern university. Professor K. looked young and vulnerable. He sized us up for a long moment, then was visibly relieved. Apparently Steinbjørn did not look the part of the imposing intellectual he had come to expect. "I think I'm going to enjoy this visit," he said.

"The Department makes me host all the 'visiting firemen,'" he confided, "and the last one just about did me in. He was one of these über-intellectuals for whom literature is something remote and abstract. He swept me into a thick cloud of Ingarden's phenomenology and Dilthey's hermeneutics. To be honest, scholarship like this has always scared me." I told him that I had my own horror of hermeneutics, and it occurred to me for the first time that maybe my freedom from academia was not the tragedy I'd always assumed it was.

"I understand you're a poet!" he said, turning to Steinbjørn. "*Yrkjari*," I translated as Steinbjørn beamed. "And that you write children's books. Do you have any samples of your work?"

I translated this for Steinbjørn, and the next thing I knew he was over on the young professor's side of the table, presenting a small children's book that I hadn't seen before: *Lív og Hundurin*. On the cover we saw a girl named Lív and a blue-eyed dog with a long red tongue.

Lív æt ein lítil genta, hon var rund og næstan altíð glað. I was able to sight-read the Faeroese: "Lív was a little girl, she was round and almost always happy." In the colored illustrations, Lív played with her dolls, and her friends Kára and Hanur and Eyð played with their building blocks—when one day Mamma opened the door and out of nowhere there appeared a blue-eyed dog. It smiled at Lív, a long bright red tongue extending down from its eager smile.

Professor K. looked rapt. I explained how Steinbjørn was writing these books so that Faeroese children, whose language had once been banned and almost died out, would have something to read. That he was presenting them with—and preserving—their own culture. The boy had the Faeroese name Hanur, not the Danish name Hans. And until Steinbjørn came along, school children had been reading *Anders And*—"Donald Duck" in Danish.

"You know, they look like a lot of fun," Professor K. observed wistfully. Steinbjørn didn't ask me to translate this. From the professor's expression he could tell that whatever he was saying, he was happy.

While Steinbjørn slept on our flight to San Francisco, I tried to take stock of our situation.

Neither of us really spoke Danish. My "Danish" was essentially Swedish with Danish words thrown in. Steinbjørn was certain that his Danish was very solid, but he spoke it pronouncing all the silent consonants, with an extravagant trill to his r's, and shamelessly sneaking in words from the Faeroese. My mind was constantly making adjustments: For "boy," *dreng* became *drongur*; for "English," *engelsk* became *enkst*. The most confusing shift for me was to realize that in Faeroese *svanger*—in German the word *schwanger* means "pregnant"—means "hungry." But gradually I understood and incorporated more and more Faeroese, and our two versions of "Danish" more or less merged. No outsider would ever have been able to understand us.

But there was one aspect of Steinbjørn that was beginning to worry me far more than his "Danish." One morning when I had gone into his hotel room to pick him up for an early flight, I found propped up next to his suitcase a fifth of Southern Comfort, with about two inches of "Comfort" left at the bottom. He suggested maybe there wasn't enough to keep. Would I like some? At 6:00 AM? Hardly. So he chugged the remaining two inches—like something out of a fraternity initiation— and then tossed the bottle into the wastebasket.

These bottles were becoming a regular phenomenon. If it wasn't Wild Turkey, it might be Old Crow or Jim Beam. In the book on the Faeroe Islands, I had read that anything other than a virtually non-alcoholic beer had to be specially imported, and was sold at horrendous prices. In addition, according to Faeroese regulations, "it is a breach of the law to consume any alcoholic drinks in a restaurant or other public place."

Here Steinbjørn was taking full advantage of the relatively low price of alcohol and his unlimited freedom to drink. But I was becoming increasingly concerned. I hoped I had made the right decision in not calling State to tell them about this. I was afraid they would send him home. But I was also afraid I was enabling him to develop an addiction from which he might never recover. On the other hand, he was the visiting dignitary and I was merely the escort, the "lowly interpreter," to use a term I had once encountered in *Time* magazine. Was it *my* responsibility to intervene? In the end, I made my decision by not making a decision.

In San Francisco we rented a car and drove down to San Juan Bautista, seventeen miles north of Salinas. A rather remote town, it was the home of El Teatro Campesino, which loosely translates as the "farmworkers' theater." The original actors all worked in the fields, and the group had been founded by the United Farm Workers. I realized we were invited here because State considered Steinbjørn to be a "political activist playwright." And the Teatro Campesino fit right into this category.

The troupe, which had started out performing Aztec and Mayan ritual dramas, had moved on to broader aspects of "Chicano" culture—as it was then called—including a focus on the Vietnam War and racism. It was here that Luis Valdez premiered his play *Zoot Suit*, which had gone on to Los Angeles and then even to Broadway and a 1981 film.

At the time we visited them, they were between productions, but they greeted us warmly. They had a lunch ready for us at outdoor picnic tables, introducing Steinbjørn to tacos and burritos, corn-husk tamales and *nopales*—cactus as a vegetable. He loved Dos Equis and Corona and Negra Modelo. And he helped himself liberally to straight shots of *mezcal* from a bottle that contained a *gusano*—the ritual worm.

Many of the children spoke only Spanish, but when Steinbjørn went up to play with them, language proved irrelevant. They showed Steinbjørn some of their folk dances; he watched attentively and then joined in. He joined their circles, arm in arm, as they swayed about, knowing what dance steps came when. And when he gave them instructions on some of his dances in Faeroese, the children caught on almost immediately.

Then one of the children—a little girl in a frilly party dress—hit on the idea of stringing up a *piñata* to show him, even though it wasn't Las Posadas or anyone's birthday. They explained to Steinbjørn that he must break the *piñata* hanging above—a container in the shape of a donkey, covered in papier-mâché—with a special bat. Blindfolded! They sang songs as they spun him around and around and around. Dizzy from the whirling and the Dos Equis and *mezcal con gusano*, he made wild swings with the bat. He kept at it with a joyous frenzy until *pow!* he managed to connect with a crisp perfect crack. Steinbjørn fell to the ground laughing, still blindfolded, as a torrent of fruit and peanuts, small toys, wrapped candies, and confetti rained down upon him.

At that moment everything went black. From behind me, someone had slipped a blindfold over *my* eyes and I felt a bat poking at my hand. *"Te toca a ti!"* a young boy's voice told me. And then I was sent awhirl as childish voices were singing, *"Esta piñata es de muchas mañas, solo contiene naranjas y cañas."*

For all my languages, I'd never studied Spanish, not even in high school, and yet like Steinbjørn I found the joy of that afternoon infectious, beyond any need for shared language or culture.

In Berkeley we had an appointment with a Professor B., who taught folklore. This was to be the last of our formal meetings with professors, for which I was grateful. So far we had made it through them unscathed, but by now Steinbjørn seemed to be in a constant alcoholic fog. At times he lurched noticeably; even casual observers could sense there was something amiss. He was very loud and we were always the center of attention.

Again we sat in a conference room. Steinbjørn had brought his leather satchel but left it on the floor by his feet. Professor B. seemed pleased to see us. I translated his cordial greetings, but this time Steinbjørn just sat there, looking down, sunken in thought. He didn't say anything. I asked him if he was all right.

Then slowly, resolutely, Steinbjørn got up and strode over to a blank wall. He looked at us, intently, then at the wall, intently. Then he held out his arm at full length and began to trace large circles on the wall; circle after circle. He would fix us with his gaze, then look intently back at the wall. Then more circles. And more circles.

Professor B. seemed to be taking all this in stride. Steinbjørn, who appeared to have finished, proclaimed loudly, in English: *"I have vrite a poom!"* Then he stared at the wall and at the invisible circles, while Professor B. and I looked on. I said quietly that Steinbjørn was a poet— perhaps first and foremost a poet, although he also wrote plays and children's books. "He's very respected in his Islands," I added, hoping that he was.

Steinbjørn stood there looking at the blank wall. Then abruptly he went back to the conference table, scooped up his satchel, and headed out the door. Professor B. still seemed to accept all this as being within reason. Or, if not *within* reason exactly, something that transcended reason, or to which reason no longer applied.

"You clearly have your work cut out for you," he said to me.

39

"I'm just hoping to get him home in one piece," I said. By that point I hoped that the trip would not kill him. His alcohol intake had just kept escalating, and by the time I realized how far gone he was it was too late to try to stop him.

"That thing with the circles," he said, "I'll have to try that in charades sometime. See if anyone figures out that it's a poem. Or should I say 'poom'?" He reflected for a moment, then added: "In an odd way, one could say that he himself *is* the poem. If that makes any sense."

It did. By now it made perfect sense.

Before we began to make our way back to the East Coast, as a special treat State had arranged for us to stay at a cabin-like hotel within a short walking distance of the Grand Canyon. Steinbjørn loved the rustic décor and the large pitchers of red wine that could be ordered with dinner—and the pitchers just kept coming.

The next morning, right after breakfast, we walked the short distance over to the rim of the Canyon. It must have appeared to Steinbjørn like something out of a saga—a gigantic fjord now plunging straight downward into the earth. He seemed transfixed. There was a pathway for walking down inside the Canyon, and a few tourists were venturing a short way down in order to take photographs.

I was standing there lost in the immensity of the Canyon, when Steinbjørn took off his white cotton shirt and handed it to me, and then his polished black shoes. *"Eg gårrrr inn!"* he proclaimed. He was going to go in. It was just a dirt pathway; apparently he wanted to keep his shirt and shoes clean. Before I could say anything, he was out of sight.

And then I waited. After some twenty minutes or so I sat down on a bench, carefully folding his shirt and keeping his shiny black shoes within sight. And I waited. I sat there with ever-increasing anxiety for several hours, and still he didn't return. It was hard to make any sense of this. Finally I went into the hotel restaurant, figuring Steinbjørn could find his way back. Maybe he'd turn up for a late lunch.

By late afternoon I had gone from anxious to frantic. Had I lost him? Where did he go? He was shirtless and without shoes! I sat in the lobby trying to read a novel but wasn't able to concentrate. Back then, cell phones were just as wishful a fantasy as Dick Tracy's two-way wrist radio, so Steinbjørn was completely on his own. I would just have to wait.

I couldn't think of any explanation for Steinbjørn's disappearance.

Had he been mugged? What kind of people went down this path, anyway? Had he decided to go all the way to the bottom? Had he fallen and was lying alone and in pain in the dark?

I was sitting in our room at about 10:00 P.M., wondering if I should call State, though I knew no one would be there at that hour in DC, when suddenly and dramatically the door to the room burst open. Steinbjørn—his face, arms, and upper body lobster red—came staggering in and collapsed on the floor, emitting a small cloud of dirt.

"*Eg má bada*," he said weakly. Well, yes, a bath would definitely be in order. I ran the water for him in the old-fashioned tub, then helped steady him as he undressed. The top half of him was a bright alarming red, and below the waist he was as white as the underside of a fish. His feet were raw and swollen. He was in a daze.

Had he gone to the very bottom? He had! But after the sun had set it had turned very cold and he had to run all the way back up from the bottom. He hadn't had any food or water with him. Didn't he get hungry?

He did. When he realized he had neither food nor water with him, he hailed fellow hikers. In the language that existed only between the two of us, he told me he had asked people if they had a *súrepli* to give him: an apple. He proudly explained that he had actually spoken English. He had told other hikers, "*I sing you for an apple!*" People, sensing something was wrong, must have been solicitous of him, giving him water to drink as well as apples and perhaps even sandwiches. He told me he planned to write a memoir about his trip to America. He would not entitle it the Faeroese "*Eg sang fyri eitt súrepli!*" It would be just what he had told the other hikers, in English: "*I Sing You for an Apple!*"

I sat on a stool while he soaked in the bear-claw tub, drifting in and out of sleep. I had to be watchful that he not let his head sink below the waterline and drown. Finally I helped Steinbjørn get into bed. Instinctively, I pulled the covers up to his chin to tuck him in.

I needed to clear my head, so I decided to go back outdoors. Off the hotel lobby was a spacious gift store and I bought a pair of soft, beaded moccasins that Steinbjørn could wear until his feet had healed enough for his dress shoes again.

Then I walked over to the rim of the dark canyon. It was a strange sensation: what lay in front of me was pitch black, a vast unseen void. It was both eerie and calming.

I realized that if I hadn't been thrown over the walls of Academe, I wouldn't have been sitting there at the moment. At Pomona College, with no grad students, my life had narrowed down to teaching case endings to eighteen-year-olds at eight in the morning. I spoke German and they didn't, so there wasn't very much I could learn back from them.

Now, as a translator and sometime escort, I never knew what might lie ahead. One day I would be translating a Swedish child-custody dispute that led to the kidnapping of ten-year-old Felix. The next it might be a German art historian with a new interpretation of Robert Rauschenberg's *Monogram*, the assemblage of a stuffed angora goat encircled by an automobile tire. I translated for both *Playboy* magazine and *National Geographic*. In addition to the State Department, I found myself working for the German FBI, the LA Philharmonic, and the J. Paul Getty Trust. When the Olympic Games came to LA in 1984, I was an interpreter for the West German water polo team. For the Disney *Aladdin* film, I had to spend a day with Gilbert Gottfried—the voice talent who later went on to become the voice of the Aflac duck—coaching him to say his lines in eight different languages for his role as Iago, the "wise-cracking parrot."

Sitting at the dark shimmering void of the Grand Canyon that night in 1978, I had no idea where my career would lead me. But I knew it would continue to surprise me, and that I would not have been able to turn back.

Years later, in 2007, I went onto Google and searched for him: Steinbjørn B. Jacobsen. I hadn't thought about him in years, but there he was.

The Faeroe Islands were in the throes of celebrating his seventieth birthday. The text was all in Faeroese, but once again I was able to get the gist. The photos revealed that Steinbjørn's hair had now turned white, but his eyes were still a piercing blue. His face was boyish and yet—wearing a charcoal gray suit and holding a book up by his chest as if posing for a painting—he had the gravitas of an elder statesman. Extravagant bouquets abounded.

All of the capital city Tórshavn seemed to have turned out to celebrate his birthday. Judging from the crowds, I could see that he had become a national hero. At the time of his visit, I had had no idea how important he was in his Islands, nor to what degree he was loved. In translating his books for the various professors we met with on our trip, I hadn't realized the full magnitude of his accomplishments. This was a language that had come close to extinction; now thanks to the children it was being kept alive.

I scrolled through the list of his works, which was exhaustive. Plays, children's books, works for adults. But nowhere did I see either *"Eg sang fyri eitt súrepli!"* or "I Sing You for an Apple!" So I realized it was up to me to tell his story.

Of course I didn't know any of this back then, while the sunburned Steinbjørn lay sound asleep in our hotel room. At the time I was overcome with relief at not having lost him under my watch. No headlines crying out, "Acclaimed Poet Meets Tragic Death; Interpreter Arrested." He was safe; I was safe. My mind began to float away as I sat there near the edge of the Grand Canyon, contemplating the unending blackness.

I don't know how long I sat there.

Nominated by Karen Bender

ELK

by ROBERT WRIGLEY

from CONDUIT

His hindquarters must have fallen through
the ice, and he could not pull himself back out
and the incoming colder weather
refroze the hole around him and he died,
sinking some, only his broad horns
holding his head and neck above the surface.
Soon he must have been discovered by coyotes,
who ate all they could. His face, that is,
the soft, perhaps just frozen, cheeks and muzzle,
his tongue, which would have protruded
from his open dying mouth, the eyes,
then the opening of the throat, the coyotes'
 prints visable only in the sheen of blood
around the snowless black surface of the lake.
Such cold this early in the winter, autumn really,
still early December, has surprised us all.
Since snow is at last forecast this afternoon,
I have come to skate, half a mile from shore
when I see him, or see what's left,
and reconstruct the narrative of his demise.
The coyotes ignored his spraddled forelegs,
hoof prints still born down against the pull
of his back half. A six-point bull elk,
some abrasions on the surface of the ice
where the horns thrashed but held him.

A half-mile skate back to where I hung my boots
from a limb, a hundred yard walk from there
to the truck, in which I keep a bow saw,
which I could use to remove a wedge of pate
with the perfect rack, but I choose not to.
Something in the weariness of the bones
of his jaw, also the snow just now beginning.
Given the altitude here, he'll be completely covered
in a month, and at break-up, late March
or early April, he will sink as he did not
yesterday or the day before, and the bones
and the horns of him will settle to the bottom.
Although the coyotes may be back tonight,
to dig their way from the horns' stumps
for the ears, which I notice are still whole and upright,
the left one turned slightly farther left,
as though, with the last of his miraculous
senses, he heard them coming over the ice.

Nominated by Conduit, Claire Davis, Elton Glaser

THE G.R.I.E.F

fiction by MICAH STACK

from THE OXFORD AMERICAN

Pleurant, je voyais de l'or—et ne pus boire.

—*Arthur Rimbaud*

Full disclosure up front: I am a gay black man, a proud New Orleanian, thirty years old, five out of the closet, a decade on the down-low before that; bi-dialectal as every educated brother in this city must be, a code-switcher as needed; a poet in my spare time, in my unspare time a poetry teacher devoted to dead French guys and live black ones. Like most black men of my generation, I belong to the hip-hop nation, and like any sensible gay man, I'm ashamed at times to say I'm a fan. The homophobia, the drug dealing and gun toting, the bling and the misogyny—it can feel like stylized, repetitive ugliness, at least mainstream gangsta shit. But I'm an addict, hooked on one rapper above the rest: Mr. Stillz. I've memorized hundreds of his verses, seen the documentaries, the interviews, the countless clips of him recording in his psychedelic freestyle mode. I subscribe to the hip-hop mags because he decorates their pages. So naturally my theories ran buck-wild when the photograph surfaced.

First, though, the facts: On February 12, 2008, two days after Stillz racks up six Grammys, it appears online. It must've been snapped just after Katrina, judging by Stillz's incipient dreads, the fleur-de-lis tattoo under his right sideburn, and the absence of *The G.R.I.E.F.* inked across his right temple (you can timeline his life by his tats). Diminutive Stillz and muscled-up Wreckless Tyrone embrace in a handshake/hug combo. They're French kissing. They both wear white—Stillz in a wife-beater, Tyrone in a tracksuit—and there's a patch of shine on Tyrone's always-Michael-Jordan-clean dome. They're under a pavilion, bright palm trees rising beyond its white columns. Bodyguards and hangers-on surround them. Some look away, but two meaty goons mean-mug, disgusted by this display.

Hours after the pic's gone viral, a super-high Stillz gives an interview on his tour bus. He says, Hell yeah I kiss Tyrone. That man raised me and believed in me when I ain't had shit. It's just a form of affection. It's all love.

I imagine him when he realizes what he's done. Back on his tour bus heading to Miami, he glues himself to his laptop. Tyrone's riding a different bus now: can't stand to see Stillz so slurry from the sizzurp. In web searches, the photo is always—already—the first image to appear. Parodies have flooded YouTube within hours. Rappers he's collaborated with are calling him a faggot. Two days ago he conquered the world and now he's here torturing himself with YouTube comments about how fake he is, how *soft*, how they shoulda known that any nigga who wore that much pink just had to be sweeter than a pancake. Every entry, each little drive-by of hatred, makes it harder for him to breathe:

doughboy187 (Just now)
mr stillz a great raper but he sucking tyrone dick lol
MySwagSoOfficial (Just now)
i like somr of mr stillzes muzik but i worry about him he a lil fruity ;-)
kumquill (1 minute ago)
A skr8 ^ pussy with NO musical talent whatsoever.

And dozens way worse than that. He tells the driver to stop the convoy. He storms onto Tyrone's bus. Everybody get the fuck out, he says, and pushes Tyrone into the bedroom. He pulls a .40 cal from his knapsack, presses it into Tyrone's neck and says, Who leaked the picture? Who leaked it? I will kill a motherfucker *dead*, you heard me?

Put the heat down, Stizzle, damn.

Was it Splack? Splack leak the picture?

Junior, Splack in *jail*. Now put the toast away.

Stillz lowers the pistol. Tyrone grabs it and stashes it under the mattress. He's used to Stillz wildin out like this. Back when he first discovered the kid, when he was still Ahmad Trench—even then he could flip like a light switch. Tyrone sees both the boy from back in the day and the man standing in front of him: they oscillate in his eyes like a hologram. He wraps the man in his arms, rests his chin on thick ropes of hair that smell like cologne and great weed. Had he harmed the kid by giving in to his urges? Stillz always initiated, but maybe Tyrone should've been stronger. For a long time he stays there, holding Stillz.

Junior, don't trip on what them haters say . . . they don't understand a damn thing.

Stillz yanks himself loose. You see what they writing about us? About *me*?

Better watch the way you acting, Tyrone warns.

Nah, I ain't got to watch nothing. I'm on that Casper tip now, Paw: I'm ghost.

And he swaggers off the bus, leaving Wreckless Records—and Wreckless Tyrone—behind.

He announces he wants out of his contract. He sues Tyrone Mosely, his surrogate father and the founder/CEO of Wreckless Records, his home since age thirteen, claiming "fiduciary misconduct and unjust enrichment." With the case tied up in court, he spends months holed up in his Miami mansion. He has women, weed, and pint after pint of promethazine/codeine syrup delivered to him. Buys Lambos and Bugattis he's always too high to drive and keeps grinding out the mixtapes that made him famous, releasing them for free online. He raps till sunrise, when he falls asleep in the private cinema adjacent to his studio, curled up on the couch, shaking.

✿　✿　✿

We have to rewind the track. Summer of '95, New Orleans: Wreckless Tyrone sits in his Mid-City office. The A/C's blasting. With his feet up on the roll-top desk, he rubs a Cohiba along his top lip, contemplating how far he's gotten in the rap game and how much farther he can take it. He's got swagger for weeks but he's real with himself: he lacks the mic skills to be a truly great rapper. His breakout single, "Shine Like Me, Bitch?" is tearing up clubs in the city, but its popularity probably owes more to the "Triggaman" beat he jacked from DJ Jimi than it does to Tyrone's flow. Splack Diggity's rhymes are tighter; his soldier style (gold teeth, fatigues) and his catchphrase ("You heard me!") are catching on in the streets. But Tyrone's not sure Splack can take Wreckless Records to that *other* level. Fuck being local news, he thinks: it's time for *60 Minutes*. The cigar smells raw and sweet, like burnt sugarcane. His label's office/studio is on South Claiborne in the same hood where he used to move weight. Definitely time for an upgrade.

He picks up the phone and dials Wild Wayne at Q93. Wayne hosts the 9 O'Clock Props, where aspiring rappers call in and rhyme over classic New Orleans bounce beats. He gives rookies the first test: *Hey, you, what's your name? / It's the 9 O'Clock Props witcha boy Wild Wayne!* Callers rhyme about themselves. If the flow is wack they get the toilet-flush sound, but those who spit fire proceed to the next challenge: *The 9 O'Clock Props is on / Tell me where you calling from!* Then they describe their hoods. For Tyrone's dollar, nobody could flow like the Trench Sweeper.

It's ya boy Wild Wayne, what's really good?

Anybody who rhymes on the Props can give the Q permission to share their info with labels, so Tyrone asks Wild Wayne where the Trench Sweeper calls from. Wayne hunts through his files, says Ahmad Trench stays at 808 Congress Street, in the Upper Ninth Ward. They chitter-chat for a minute, then Tyrone says, One love, and hangs up. He finally puts a flame to the cigar. Getting the bitch lit takes forever, but when he blows out the first cloud, he's bathed in satisfaction. He'll take the new whip for a ride to the Ninth. After he smokes the Cohiba.

He's got the bass rumbling hard in the Bentley, beating up the block like King Kong is in the trunk. When he sees the Keep It Real Barbershop on the corner, he busts a right onto Congress. On the stoop in front of 808 he spots a short, wiry kid with fucked-up cornrows wearing a baggy t-shirt and blue Dickies, a pair of ragged-ass Chucks on his feet. From Tyrone's ride it seems like the whole block is shaking. Heat rises from the pavement and makes wavy lines in the air like a desert mirage or some shit. He kills the engine and the street stands still.

You the Trench Sweeper?

Maybe. What you know about me?

You know who I am?

Yeah, I know Wreckless Records. "Who Started That Fire?" was cold-blooded.

Tyrone gets out and leans against the Trench Sweeper's stoop. He says, You feeling my man Splack Diggity, huh bra? Well Splack say *you* got that fire—heard you on the Props with Wild Weezle. He told me the other day, Roni, we need to go Batman on this industry. You know why Batman was the shit?

Because dude was mad rich.

Nah . . . I mean, that's true, *but:* Batman was the shit because the nigga had *Robin.*

I always thought Robin was a little *bitch.*

You know how it feel to have ten Gs in one pocket?

Not yet.

Good answer. If you come correct, you'll see what it's like to have your pockets on steroids. Now bust me some rhymes, right off the dome.

The Trench Sweeper raps about what's around him—Tyrone's rims spinning like rotisserie chickens, his grandmama's stoop where he's trying to make a living. The bike he pedals on, the crack he's peddle-ing; he can't stand being broke, so he'll fall for better things. He is a hustler—he'd rather die than to live average, even if he got to live savage. He was born to eat rappers like they came from McDonald's, then he hollers Rest in Peace to his mama and Ronald.

Tyrone pulls a G-stack from his pocket and tosses it at the kid. If he cleans him up, calls some broads to hook up his hair, gets him some fresh gear, the Trench Sweeper might just be the ticket to that other level. A teenage gangsta rapper, not one of these little-kid fad groups but a straight-up G that nevertheless would make females want to pinch his cheeks. Splack should've came, but there would be time for that, time to put them together in the studio and make gold like Midas.

❖ ❖ ❖

Tyrone is a shrewd-ass businessman. He must have figured out quick, when he heard Ahmad's story, that the kid was more likely to become Batman than Robin. See, the year before the discovery, when Ahmad was twelve, he watched his mama and her boyfriend Ronald Beemon get killed in a drive-by. They could build a Batman-type myth out of that and ride on it till the wheels fall off.

But it isn't just shrewdness. Tyrone legally adopts Ahmad, raises him like his own son. He watches with a father's pride as the Trench Sweeper transforms into Mr. Stillz, one half of the Tech Toters and (temporarily) the Robin to Splack's Batman. As the Tech Toters' first album, *We Started That Fire*, goes gold; as Wreckless Records goes nationwide and the Tech Toters graduate from gold to platinum; as Splack Diggity is convicted on gun charges and Stillz goes solo, Tyrone's pride in his son keeps swelling. He loves Ahmad Trench more than his own children.

Mr. Stillz becomes a daddy himself while the Tech Toters are pro-moting *Flame Gang Soldiers*, just before Splack gets sent to the pen. Tyrone throws a party at a hip-hop hotspot in the NYC meatpacking district. There's video footage. Hollywood starlets flirting with Harlem hoods. A life-size ice sculpture of Stillz sparkling by the bar. Cases of Cristal. They shake up bottles and spray Stillz like he's just won the Super Bowl. Tyrone has the waiters wheel out a three-tiered cake with red and yellow icing, the old-school Atlanta Hawks colors that the Tech Toters made their signature. Around the cake's base is a platinum chain with a cross full of flame-colored diamonds.

Father and son embrace beneath a confusion of flashbulbs and clap-ping. Stillz licks smudges of icing off the chain and drapes it around his neck. Splack gives him a hug but then turns away, mean-mugging. He's starting to act like a hater lately, Stillz thinks, even though Splack knows males shouldn't be jealous—that's a female's trait. Their new single shakes the speakers. Tyrone says he'll be right back. More people pour in, girls grinding and twerking on the dance floor, the whole room swirling with sensation: weed smoke wobbling on the strobe-lit air, the poof! of a popped bottle, a sailing cork. With a broad on each arm and a bottle in both hands, Tyrone crosses the room hollering, Show em your chain, Junior! Stillz flashes his huge smile and holds up the glittering cross. Tyrone brings over the two girls, both Blackanese, and puts his mouth by Stillz's ear. That Jesus piece is fly, he says, but I got your real gift right here.

The quartet retreats to a private suite. No footage of that, but certainly that's when it started. And it probably only happened that way, the it-ain't-gay-if-it's-in-a-four-way way, until the storm destroyed 2005.

Tyrone drives the Phantom, Stillz riding shotgun, bodyguards stuffed in the back like prisoners. At the Elysian Fields exit they show their licenses to the National Guardsmen, who tell them to inspect their property and complete their "revacuation." They descend into the city. The road is just a pause in the rubble, and through bloodshot eyes Stillz watches the ruins crawl past: broken ukuleles, Mardi Gras beads, tiny football helmets, boards scattered like hacked-off arms, street signs flipped around or blown off. Flood stains on house-fronts remind him of the notches his mama carved on the wall every year to see how grown he was getting. On a warehouse somebody has spray-painted HOPE IS NOT A PLAN. Stillz points and says, That's the realest shit I'll ever quote.

They ride on. They pass telephone poles cracked at the waist, houses leaning like three-legged lions, a refrigerator sitting in an oak tree. It's quiet for a good minute until one of the bodyguards says, God *damn*. Then it gets quiet again. The city smells like God took a shit on a heap of cotton candy.

Ain't that where Splack used to stay? Stillz says.

Tyrone says, That was his mama's house.

I wonder where she at now.

I ain't found her yet. I'ma throw a couple hunned thousand at her when I find her.

If you find her.

Don't be talking like that, Tyrone says.

Man, this here's a war zone, says Stillz. Ain't no point to being optimistic.

Still, he somehow hopes he'll find 730 Flood Street untouched. First they drive past 808 Congress, where Ahmad had lived with his grandmama that one year. She lost both feet to diabetes in 2003; shortly after that she stopped breathing. Stillz didn't come off tour to see her—that still fucks with him when he lets himself remember. Tyrone's all the family he got left now, and he ain't even kin. But Tyrone is more family than his kin ever was any damn way. Except for his mama: that was his heart. Even though she was already gone, he fixed the house up how she had wanted it. He needs to find it that way.

They cross the bridge into the Lower Ninth. He hasn't touched down in forever: it's like seeing it in a dream. Tyrone steers around a corner and Stillz tells him to pull over at the playground. He gets out, rests his hands on the links of the fence that is, amazingly, still standing. Tyrone joins him. The bodyguards mill around, looking like second-string linemen. Off in the distance some brother is on the roof playing trumpet. To Stillz it sounds like a voice, like a old-ass bluesman howling about his pain. Ahmad Trench had hooped here as a youngster. One basketball goal is crooked to the left. Memory sends the ghost of a Spalding arcing through the air toward the absent backboard at the court's other end. Swish.

I'ma donate like half a millie to rebuild this park, Stillz says.

The sun's fading when they climb back in the Phantom. A few more intersections and they roll up at what should be a purple and green shotgun with gold fleur-de-lis stenciled on the doorframe, like she had wanted. What they find is three concrete steps that lead to a porch and a flood-stained yellow door still in its frame. No roof, no walls, no house.

It's not Mr. Stillz but Ahmad Trench who walks up those steps, who stares at that door that leads to nothing, just a yard littered with scraps of other people's lives. Memory supplies the side of the house. Ronald perched above him on the ladder saying, Hand me that purple paint. They were fighting on this porch the day she died. Memory supplies her voice: *We been over this, Ahmad,* and his own: *He ain't my daddy, he ain't blood.* Then the El Camino, the ski-masked goon with the chopper, the gunshots and echoes. The house-front splattered with Ronald's skull, blood sliding down the door into his mama's hair.

A pelican explodes into flight with a squawk and Ahmad starts kicking the door. It's still locked and he kicks it until the wood splinters around the deadbolt.

Where all the lights in my city go? he says.

Junior—

Tyrone watches him going at the door. It cracks free and swings open. When it rebounds he kicks it until it falls off the hinges, clattering onto some planks.

How they ain't got the power back yet, huh? Where all the lights go?

Tyrone manages to wrap him in a bear hug and carry him off the porch, saying I got you, I got you. The bodyguards don't know what to do—they just stand there ready for whatever.

That was my mama's house, Ahmad says.

Junior, we gonna grind through this.

Grind through this? You don't understand. That was my *mama's house*.

Tyrone thumbs away tears on his son's cheeks and kisses him on the forehead. Ahmad raises his eyes to the sky and says, For goodness sake, Paw. For goodness sake.

They ride out to Stillz's mansion in New Orleans East. It's undamaged except for the two feet of flooding they have to wade through, ruining their pants and kicks. That house, that's where it happens for the first time—for the first time without women involved. The first time it's just them.

They send the goons off to get food, and in the stink of a flooded house without power, they trudge up to the second-floor Jacuzzi. Everything's dark, flashlights and candles the only light. They have running water, at least, and it's cold. They strip down to their draws and slide in: instantaneous relief. Stillz feels human again. Tyrone moves over and puts an arm around his shoulder, asks if he's all right. It's not a big thing, but Stillz rejects it. He knows he ain't supposed to feel what he's feeling. He knows he's high. Then he decides none of that matters. He clutches Tyrone's skull and kisses him roughly, teeth against teeth. Tyrone pulls away and says, You sure you want this? Nothing we ain't done before, Stillz says. That was different, though, Tyrone says. Stillz says, I want *this* right now, and he's pulling on Tyrone. They slide off their draws, towel dry, and move to the bedroom. Tyrone gets on his knees, reaching, but Stillz tells him, No, on the bed, on your back. He opens a bedside drawer and takes out a tube. With squeaky, glistening pumps he slicks himself. Heat rises in him with the force of hatred and he pulls Tyrone to the bed's edge, grabs him by the ankles, and plunges in. Tyrone makes a choking sound and says, Easy, easy. Until he's synced up with Stillz's rhythms, Tyrone winces, holding the backs of his thighs.

His eyes wobble. Stillz looks into them and for a moment feels something like love shoot through his angry lust. And then the feeling fails. He's glad it's dark. The smell of stagnant water hovers up through the shadows.

When it's over, his heart grows polar-bear cold. I ain't no fucking homo, he says.

But it keeps happening. It keeps getting harder to deny.

✻   ✻   ✻

After Katrina they move to Miami and Stillz cranks up the volume on his swagger. He hits the weed and syrup harder. He grows his dreads out, loses count of his tattoos, and starts calling himself The G.R.I.E.F.—The Greatest Rapper in Existence, Fucker. The hip-hop community blah-ha-has. Nobody from New Orleans will *ever* be the King of Hip-Hop. At best, he's The G.R.I.T.S.—The Greatest Rapper in the South. Mr. Stillz deserves only one title: The M.D.M.A. (Most Delusional MC Alive). Maybe if he popped less MDMA he could actually rhyme.

In 2006, Stillz charges $50,000 a verse for each of his 100-plus features. He puts out six free full-length mixtapes—no choruses, just rhyming over other rappers' beats—the best shit he ever makes. Drug ballads knock nipples with anti-Bush rants. He seasons his verses with little dashes of French, the cayenne pepper for his gumbo flow. *Rolling Stone, Spin, Pitchfork, Blender, XXL,* and *The Source* all rank at least one of his mixtapes on those best-of-the-year lists they love to make. Then, in summer '07, when he releases the long-awaited studio album, *The G.R.I.E.F.*, it's *Vibe* who finally cops to the truth. All right, fuckers, it's official: he actually is the greatest rapper in existence.

The crown arrives in the form of six Grammys, and that's when the photo emerges.

✻   ✻   ✻

I know all about the sizzurp. I know how to concoct it. What you do is dump some Sprite out of a two-liter to make room for a pint of codeine cough syrup. Put the cap back on. Turn the bottle upside down: the syrup bleeds into the soda, turns the bubbles Easter-egg pink. Some people slip in Jolly Ranchers for extra sweetness but not Stillz and not me. Let the foaming subside. Pour it in double-stacked Styrofoam cups and sip it till you're moving in slow-mo. When you lean hard and smoke trees on top of it, you feel like the combo might wash you right out of consciousness. I'm far from all-day-every-day like Stillz, but I've felt that blue coil of warmth in my stomach radiating out in slow throbs, so I know how he feels that night in Miami. He's nodding on his black leather sofa as the TV screen scatters the room's shadows. He reaches for another blunt: only two left in the package. He's too woozy to holler for T-Rell the Weed Doctor to roll more. He can't really feel his face but he's used to this numbness—he did a mixtape, after all, called *So Comfortably Numb*, the one where he rapped over classic rock instrumentals.

DJ Red Beans is down the hall mixing the tracks they recorded earlier. As long as Stillz lays down at least four verses a day, he knows he's still the greatest rapper in existence. Nobody else is that dedicated. Nobody's got more words than him. He flips through the channels, lands on BET, and suddenly Tyrone's ranting at the camera. For the first time since breakfast, Stillz takes off his shades.

Look here, mane, they call us Wreckless Records cause we don't never crash, and if your record is a smash, we can still survive. Stizzle *was* my main focus, but I'm trying to bring new artists to the world. And my man Splack Diggity coming home from the pen next month, finna get his shine back. It's going down like the Titanic, you heard me? Stizzle can go get his by hisself. I'll see him in the streets, though. I see you, Mr. Stillz, I see you.

Stillz thinks: So it *was* Splack. I knew it. Acting like a bitch cause I blew up and he got sent away and then his dumb ass got extra years for trying to smuggle in dope through a football. Now he's finally getting out and he's trying to take my shine. And Tyrone's making it happen.

Oh, he want beef? Stillz is shouting. He want *beef*?

He throws the remote at the wall and the batteries roll around on the floor like marbles. He springs from the couch, jumps up and down to shake out the numbness. Nobody can challenge him and survive. Surging with post-nod energy, he shadowboxes his way down the hall, jabbing and uppercutting to the sound of his own voice booming from the speakers in the room where Red Beans sits twisting knobs. Stillz goes into the booth and adjusts the headphones over his dreads.

Alright, Beans, lemme rhyme over Tyrone's new track.

"Still Shining"?

Yeah, but we gonna call ours "No Homo." Get that yellow tape out: this here's about to be a murder scene.

This is what he freestyles:

Ugh, no homo but we cockin em.
The pistol said it's time, so I'm bout to start clockin em.

And I keep poppin till they tell me to pause—
No homo but Ralph Lauren is all over my draws.
Errbody keep tellin me to call Tyrone,
But I don't keep no faggot's number on my phone.
I tote all my chrome, shoot sharper than a spear, bitch.
Point it at your dome, homophone, you on that queer shit.
I'm on my Richard Gere shit, pretty women love me;
Mane, you lookin Dennis Rodman: gay as fuck and ugly.
Yeah, I'm gettin mad hoes like I was a tool shed.
You on that shit that turn a motherfucker's stool red.
No homo, but I'll blow off a fool head.
Bury yo ass like a farmer when the mule dead.
And even though I got two babies on the way,
I throw in that "no homo" so you know that I ain't gay . . .

He goes hard like that for four more minutes. He slams Splack Diggity, too, but Tyrone gets most of his venom. When he leaves two days later for a string of shows in Europe, "No Homo" is out in the world, and my heart floods with hurt for Tyrone.

*   *   *

Paris. The Four Seasons. Above the Marble Courtyard in his presidential suite, he wakes up congested and feverish in a tangle of bodies. He blinks at the space, trying to reconstruct the night. Three broads and DJ Red Beans sprawl around him in bed. Heels, dresses, jeans, and g-strings are strewn across the floor. Condoms, condom wrappers, K-Y, champagne flutes, roach-filled ashtrays, Styrofoam cups stained purple. His clothes rest on a lacquered table and—what the fuck?—they're neatly folded. He's wearing socks, shoes, and nothing else, like a porn star. The early sun is blunted by the room's blue curtains. Stillz jumps when his iPhone vibrates, but the other bodies seem comatose.

As he shivers toward the bathroom, a couple of his rhymes come to mind: Call me Herod, I get head delivered to me on a platter / And the ice in my mouth could make your fucking teeth chatter. What track was that on? When did he record it? No telling. So many rhymes, so much boasting and bragging, and for what? He opens his mouth for the mirror. Light drains through the skylight and catches his grill; the sparkle just don't thrill him like it used to. He sits on the toilet and samples his voicemail. Both his soon-to-be baby mamas are tripping. Expensive fallout from the canceled shows in Amsterdam and Berlin. An artist he

56

sampled without permission is suing. Reviews of the mixtape: largely negative. Gay rumors: buzzing like horseflies. He lets only the final message play all the way through:

Junior, it's me. Calling to apologize. That BET thing, that was just stunting. I ain't even mad at you—I taught you to put business first. But you still my son, you heard? I look at you and I say, That's love right there, that's *life* right there. Fuck the money, fuck the record label, Junior. You my little *son*. You need to holler at your daddy and tell me what's good.

Stillz texts T-Rell the Weed Doctor. He's gonna need a whole forest of blunts to survive today.

He emerges from the Four Seasons into the bright cold, armored in his pretty-boy-gangsta style: black pea coat, grey cashmere v-neck sweater with scarlet lozenges, matching scarf, PRPS Barracuda jeans, and a fresh pair of Supra Muska Skytops, the tall tongues swallowing the cuffs of his denim. Then he's in his limo. It takes him toward his private jet for a nonstop flight to NYC. The Parisian streets speed past his foggy peripherals as he blazes up and sips his breakfast sizzurp. Then he's on the jet, literally lost in the clouds. Wednesday slides into Thursday. Thursday means an interview on HOT 97, a photo shoot, other celebrity shit. He ain't nervous about that. He's nervous about Friday. For the first time since the photo leaked he has to perform in New Orleans. And rumor has it Tyrone might show.

HOT 97's Wanda Velázquez is up first. They start off breezy but she brings the real talk with quickness:

Q: So . . . what's up with all these canceled shows?

A: Too much weed and sizzurp, baby.

Q: Don't you think it's time to slow down a little?

A: Homegirl, I appreciate your concern, I really do. But what I pour in a Styrofoam cup is my business, not nobody else's.

Q: Y'all heard it from the man himself: he'll put whatever he wants in that Styrofoam. Now, Stizzle, tomorrow's Halloween, you'll be back in New Orleans for the first time since the split with Wreckless—we feeling a little nervous?

A: I'm not nervous, no. Every time I rhyme, New Orleans talks through me because I *am* the streets. I'm just going back home where I belong.

Q: Can you tell us about your beef with Tyrone?

A: Download my new mixtape, *Call It a Comeback*. I express myself through music.

Q: The photo—is it real?

A: Like I say, I express myself through music.

Q: But then this whole "no homo" thing . . . if you're not gay, why you feel you have to keep stressing that in your lyrics?

A: Bitch, I'm so high right now we ain't in the same galaxy, and you sit here and judge *me*? What I do is my business. I fuck who I want to fuck, period. This interview is over.

He throws the headphones off and rolls out. His body's so thick with syrup his limbs feel like slow-motion monsters. His crew flurries and jabbers around him. In the hallway he punches the elevator button then rips a framed painting off the wall. The shatter of glass is like a burst of melody, followed by jagged silence. The elevator takes forever. Too many motherfuckers around him, too much time to think. He thinks about fucking Tyrone, how raw and amazing it could be. How none of his bitches had it like that. He wasn't no homo—just because you fuck a man don't make you gay. The elevator dings open. He leans against the back mirror and slides down it. He blew it all because some bitch asked him a question on the radio. He fucked Tyrone over for this? For *this*?

❁　❁　❁

Why am I so obsessed with Stillz? Why him and not some "socially conscious" rapper? The critics claim he has nothing to say, but goddamn does he say it—the most stylish nothing. To hear him in his prime is to hear a man delirious with his talent, flinging out onomatopoeic neologisms, pop-culture references, dizzying internal rhymes, scat jokes, and witty nonsense, every bar a pun or a punch line. The critics are also wrong. There's pain coursing through all his best music. It's just hyper-compacted, snagged in a phrase or tucked under a silence. His soulful eyes brim with the sorrow of a sunken city, the sorrow of men like I once was: covering up shame with defiance, cringing in the closet. He's my modern-day Rimbaud, and Tyrone's his poor Verlaine.

I got a privileged glimpse of that sorrow the day of his Halloween performance in NOLA. His team swept him on the quiet into the downtown W Hotel, and I was waiting down the way at Whiskey Blue. I saw him crossing the lobby. Mr. Stillz, I shouted, approaching with a folded-up poster. Already two bodyguards were moving toward me, looking

58

mad ready to handle me if needed. But my man stopped them. It's cool, he said, let the homeboy holler.

Yo, man, I said, I just gotta say I been feeling your music since the Tech Toters blew up in '96. Can I get your autograph on this here?

'96, huh? That was the days. Who should I dedicate it to?

Charles, I said. Charles D'Ambreaux.

Damn bro? Boy, that's a name right there.

He unfolded the poster. He didn't recall the photo shoot, I could tell, but he knew it was right after he went solo: his cheeks still puffy, still rocking the afro. He and Tyrone are shirtless, posted up in front of a Mardi Gras-colored house: 730 Flood Street. He has a tattoo of Tyrone's face on his chest; Tyrone's got Stillz's face on the same spot. The poster is a capsule of his losses: his mama, her house, his city, his career, his daddy. Behind the sunglasses his eyes were pooling—I swear I could feel it. He was thinking: Fuck the money, fuck the label. Like Tyrone said.

He shook his head like he was about to say something heavy, but he busted out with, God*damn* that's a old-ass picture—that was my first Rolex!

Everybody laughed, Red Beans, the bodyguards, the assistant who handed Stillz an ink pen. Then his face went serious again. He said, You know what? I think I'ma call Tyrone right quick.

For real? Red Beans said.

For real, he said. I think I need to call Tyrone, he said. I think I better call Tyrone.

And I was *there*, hope blooming inside me. I thought, Maybe they'll be brave enough to come out together, to say fuck the haters, to say there's no reason to front about who we really are.

They didn't do that. They claimed the HOT 97 "confession" was a misunderstanding. They said the sex never happened and tried to go back to how things were before the scandal. Maybe they've found some down-low way to make it work. Or maybe they really ain't gay. Maybe I just need them to be. Because I can understand denial and protesting too much (been there, Lord knows), but I can't stand the thought that a man—a *poet*—I admire so much is just a run-of-the-mill homophobe. And come on, that lawsuit? No way he left because of money, not at that moment and not like that.

He's still around, still omnipresent, even, but to diminishing effect. That stream-of-consciousness fever has broken: drugs and complacency at work. He's fading into the Zeitgeist he created. But I like to linger in those pre-"No Homo" days when his lyrics exploded from the speakers, volcanic and addictive. I linger in the hotel, in the only moment I ever got with him. Even though the W was low-lit, I felt as though the sun were blazing through stained glass for our benefit. That poster I offered up seemed to alter him. Every fan wants to make his presence felt, to register on his hero's private Richter scale however slight the quake, but this was so much more. I was fresh out of the closet myself, family and friends turning against me. What can I say? Symbols are important, symbolic victories, and what a message it would've sent. Everything seemed possible in that moment. Art. Revolution. Forgiveness. And I cannot convey how the joy flowed through me when, on a strip of sky above his mama's home, Ahmad Trench—the Trench Sweeper, Mr. Stillz, the Greatest Rapper in Existence, Fucker—inscribed the following on my poster:

For Charles Damn Bro,
Stay real, brother
—The G.R.I.E.F.

Nominated by The Oxford American

ANNA MAY WONG BLOWS OUT SIXTEEN CANDLES

by SALLY WEN MAO

from THE MISSOURI REVIEW

When I was sixteen, I modeled fur coats for a furrier.
White men gazed down my neck like wolves

but my mink collar protected me. When I was sixteen,
I was an extra in *A Tale of Two Worlds*. If I didn't pour

someone's tea, then I was someone's wife. Every brother,
father, or husband of mine was nefarious. They held me

at knifepoint, my neck in a chokehold. If they didn't murder
me, I died of an opium overdose. Now it's 1984

and another white girl awaits her sweet sixteen. It's 1984
and another white girl angsts about a jock who kisses

her at the end of the film. Now it's 1984 and Long
Duk Dong is the white girl's houseguest. He dances,

drunk, agog with gong sounds. All around the nation,
teens still taunt us. Hallways bloat with sweaters, slurs.

When I was eight, the boy who sat behind me brought pins
to class. "Do Asians feel pain the way we do?" he'd ask.

He'd stick the needles to the back of my neck until I winced.
I wore six wool coats so I wouldn't feel the sting. It's 1984

so cast me in a new role already. Cast me as a pothead,
an heiress, a gymnast, a queen. Cast me as a castaway in a city

without shores. Cast me as that girl who rivets center stage
or cast me away, into the blue where my lips don't touch

or say. If I take my time machine back to sixteen, or twenty,
or eight, I'd blow out all my candles. Sixteen wishes

extinguish and burn. The boy will never kiss me at the end
of the movie. The boy will only touch me with his needles.

Nominated by Anthony Wallace

THE HORNET AMONG US

by PAUL CRENSHAW

from WAR, LITERATURE & THE ARTS

The Japanese giant hornet is not the largest insect in the world, but perhaps the most fierce. It can grow to two inches in length, with a wingspan of three. It has a brown thorax, and a yellow and brown striped abdomen. Its mandibles are jagged, lined with sharp, incisor-like protrusions. Its eyes are large dark holes, which make it seem alien, some thing that has no place in our ordered world.

It can fly 60 miles in a day, at speeds of over 25 miles an hour. Its wings beat about 1,000 times a minute. It can lift more weight, relative to size, than any of us can imagine. Its stinger is a quarter of an inch long, and barbless, which means it can sting repeatedly. Its venom can melt human flesh. The venom is loaded with at least eight different chemicals, some of which damage tissue, some of which cause pain, and at least one that's sole purpose is to attract other hornets to do more stinging.

Here's how the hornets work: scouts zoom around, searching for honey bee hives. This is all they do, from when they wake in the spring to when they hibernate in the fall. When a scout finds a hive, it leaves pheromone markers around it, which draw other hornets. When the others arrive, they begin systematically slaughtering the bees. A Japanese giant hornet can kill 40 honey bees in an hour. A nest of Japanese giant hornets, around 30 or so, can destroy an entire honey bee colony in a few hours. The hornets seize the bees one by one and literally slice them apart. They cut off their heads and limbs and wings and keep the juicy, most nutrient-rich parts, which they chew into a paste to feed to their larvae. They eat the bees' honey and devour their young. They do not take over the bees' hives or carefully consume all they have killed. They take only the flight muscles and other juicy bits and leave the heads and limbs lying around.

Hornets' nests are founded by a queen in a dark sheltered place, either underground or in the hollow of a tree. The fertilized queen creates cells from chewed-up treebark and lays an egg in each cell. The queen spends her entire life laying eggs. The eggs transform into larvae, and the larva spin silk over the openings in their cells. In two weeks they complete metamorphosis and hatch. The first generation are workers. They hatch from fertilized eggs, and are female. The females take over construction of the hive. They spend their time tending to the home, caring for the young, shoring up walls and feeding. Unfertilized eggs become males. The males are called scouts, or drones. They spend their entire lives searching for bees' nests to destroy.

Fully formed nests of the Japanese giant hornet are the size of a small child. They can have hundreds of workers. The workers are smaller than the queen, but very aggressive to intruders. Recently, population growth in Japan, and the resulting decimation of the Japanese giant hornet's forest habitat, has caused a population growth in the yellow hornet. The yellow hornet has moved into the cities of Japan, where it drinks from discarded soft drink cans and pilfers trash for leftover food. Over 40 people a year die from its stings.

The Japanese giant hornet has no natural predators, except man. In Japan, they are a delicacy. They are eaten raw or deep-fried, or the amino acids on which they live are harvested and manufactured into a sports energy drink.

The Japanese honey bee does have a defense against the giant hornet, though it does not always work. Sometimes it fails and the bees are destroyed, their heads ripped off and their children eaten and the remains of their bodies strewn about the hive they once called home.

But if the bees are quick enough, if they act according to the plan created for them over millions of years, here is what they do: when a scout appears, they wait until the last possible second, in the last instant before it spreads its pheromones, before it summons the army that will destroy the hive.

At some unspoken sign, some chemical signal like a flare going off in the night, the bees surround the hornet scout so tightly it cannot get away. As one, they begin vibrating their bodies. They rattle themselves so hard that they begin to heat up, to burn inside, to turn themselves to fire. Because the bees can withstand higher temperatures than the hornet, the hornet dies. It inevitably kills a few of the bees before it does, but the hive is saved.

The Old English word hyrnetu means "large wasp, beetle." The Middle English harnete was probably influenced by the word horn, either as "horner" to suggest the sting, or "horn-blower" to suggest the buzz.

In the Hebrew the word tsir'ah means "stinging." In Exodus 23:28 God told Moses "And I will send hornets before you, which shall drive out the Hivite, the Canaanite, and the Hittite."

Deuteronomy 7:20 tells us "Moreover the LORD your God will send the hornet among them until those who are left, who hide themselves from you, are destroyed," and Joshua 24:12 says "I sent the hornet before you which drove them out from before you . . . *but* not with your sword or with your bow."

Biblical scholars believe the word hornet is not literal. In the first two verses, it is a metaphor for panic, a physical manifestation of the fear of the wrath of God. In Joshua, the word hornet means army.

Army ants also spend much of their lives searching for things to destroy. Like an army, they raid in swarms, or columns, depending on the species of ant. In swarms, great fans of raiders sweep along the ground searching for food. Column raiders branch out in small foraging groups, but both techniques utilize overwhelming numbers to envelop prey. Both rely on chemical trails to organize, like orders sent ahead. Both are deadly effective.

While the ants are raiding, birds follow along, eating the flying insects the ants flush from the ground. The larger colonies of ants eat up to 100,000 prey animals each day. They kill lizards and scorpions and centipedes. They kill grasshoppers and mantises and spiders. When they encounter prey, they simply swarm over them. The venom in their stings liquifies the victim's tissues. They cut the bodies into pieces to carry. Some species swarm trees and eat small birds and their eggs. Others hunt mainly the nests of other ant species and wasps. Still others hunt underground, devouring worms and arthropods and young vertebrates.

Because of how much they consume, the ants must migrate. They are constantly moving into new territory, constantly flushing prey, swarming over it, destroying and dismembering. Larger animals that they cannot consume are killed anyway, and left to rot, leaving a swath of death in their wake.

Like an army, they hunt while they move. Soldiers link their bodies to form protective barriers or use their large mandibles to protect the smaller workers while they sting their prey. Scouts constantly search for more prey, laying chemical trails, marking the path for the colony to follow. Other scouts split off from the group to forage, or to find a new home for the night. When they move, they take everything with them: food, larvae, eggs, and the queen, who is too big to walk and must be carried.

Army ants belong to the subfamily of ants called Dorylinae, after the Greek word for spear. Their colonies can contain 20 million ants, and function as a super-organism. There is no one controlling intelligence. They act out of instinct, driven by chemical composition. Only the queen can see. The workers are all blind. Millions of years of convergent evolution have lead the ants to this point. They march along the forest floor destroying everything in their path, each mind alike, each behavior the same.

❀   ❀   ❀

There is a wasp in certain parts of the world that paralyzes its prey, usually a spider, and lays its egg in the paralyzed body, which it buries alive. When the egg hatches, the larva feeds on the body of the spider. The spider is alive all this time, as the larva eats it. It can do nothing to get away. Its stomach is eaten. Its eyes are eaten. Its body is eaten, and after the larva has devoured all the edible parts of the spider, it spins a silk cocoon and pupates.

There is a spider that uses a hand-held net to scoop up prey. It folds itself into a stick, blending in with real sticks, and lies in wait a few inches above the ground, net ready. When prey wander by, it unfolds itself from the stick and scoops its little net down and wraps its prey up.

There is a species of fire ant that builds rafts. Thousands of ants lock themselves together, and they go floating gently down the stream. The

66

ones on the bottom die, but the colony survives. These fire ants were indigenous to South America, but have now invaded the Philippines, China, and the southern United States. They have no natural predators. When they attack, they first bite, digging in with their mandibles, to make themselves hard to remove. Then they sting again and again with stingers left over from a million years ago, when they evolved from wasps.

There is a species of spider that mimics ants so it won't be eaten. There is a species of ant that creates traps like a spider, and when prey appears the ants spring from hiding and pull the prey's legs off so that it cannot run away. There is a species of centipede that is covered with spines and shoots cyanide from its mouth. There is a species of centipede that can grow as long as your forearm. There is a species of bug in Africa that subsists on blood. When it mates, it stabs the female in the abdomen to release sperm directly into her bloodstream, and the female has had to evolve, over the years, a defense so that reproducing won't kill her.

❖   ❖   ❖

Ingenious the ways in which nature kills. The ant wears armor. The hornet wields a sword and attacks from the skies. The spider creates elaborate traps for its prey. The hornet works in teams; the ant works in armies so vast numbers lose meaning. Even the lowly bee has developed measures of counterattack.

They have all evolved, over millions of years, the ability to destroy. This means it was something they worked at. They got better and better and better, and they are good at what they do.

There is only one animal that is better, and has worked harder.

❖   ❖   ❖

When Rome fell to the barbarians, while the city was sacked and burned, while a thousand years of darkness set upon the western world, someone, looking at everything they had ever known fall, must have thought that the invaders in all their glorious multitudes looked like swarming ants. When Masada was surrounded, one of the besieged surely believed the Romans were hornets, alien, so far removed from humanity that they were of another world. When the Greeks stood at the narrow neck of Thermopylae, they must have seen the hordes coming for them, wave after wave after wave, as non-sentient, some form of mindless drone. And when the airplanes lit the night skies over

67

Baghdad, a child, huddled in a corner somewhere, certainly believed that some creature from nightmare, from legend or lore or myth, had arisen like prophecy.

But in their secret hearts they must have known what was coming for them, must have seen, somewhere in the collective conscious, soldiers marching along dusty roads and cities at siege and the dead in the streets. They must have known the feel of tanks rumbling over the earth and the sound of airplanes droning through the skies. They must have seen, in our past and present and future, black lines of smoke twisting toward the clouds as the spear was raised and the sword fell and the hordes came from the mists on the river, howling and rattling their shields, the hornet driven before them.

Nominated by War Literature and The Arts, Jennifer Lunden

THE SPRING FORECAST

by SHELLEY WONG

from CRAZYHORSE

Soon, the sea. On the city corner,
  a tree asserts *I am every*
    shade of pink. Like the inside.
  Dresses as transparent
as watercolor. Doors flung open

    to receive gold arrows.
  (stringing the strings)
Skirts flare into bells. Hair
  like bougainvillea.
    Once, a stop sign

before the water. Once, he traced
  the arch of her foot. Girls pack
    their illuminations
  in butterscotch leather trunks.
The sea rushes

    from the lighthouse. What bloom
  says no? Her hand
petaling open. What you
  would do for a pied-à-terre
    with tall windows and flower boxes.

A head full of leaves.
    Too many bows to tie
        and what of them? Pluck
    the bestsellers. Sandal
ready. A pointed foot,

        pointed feet. Come out, come out,
    ripest peach, offwhite leader.
On the archipelago, you are
    almost new. Don't turn back:
        the girls are walking again. They soak

in their many perfumes.
    (strings up) Soon, the island.

Nominated by Raena Shirali and Michael Marberry

AVARICE

fiction by CHARLES BAXTER

from VIRGINIA QUARTERLY REVIEW

My former daughter-in-law is sitting in the next room eating cookies off a plate. Poor thing, she's a freeloader and can't manage her own life anywhere in the world. Therefore she's here. She's hiding out in this house, for now, believing that she's a victim. Her name's Corinne, and she could have been given any sort of name by her parents, but Corinne happens to be the name she got. It's from the Greek, *kore*. It means "maiden." When I was a girl, no one ever called me that—a maiden. The word is obsolete.

Everyone else under this roof—my son and his second wife (my *current* daughter-in-law, Astrid), and my two grandchildren—probably wonders what Corinne is doing here. I suppose they'd like her to evaporate into what people call "thin" air. Corinne's bipolar and a middle-aged ruin: When she looks at you, her vision goes right through your skin and internal organs and comes out on the other side. She mutters to herself, and she gives off a smell of rancid cooking oil. She's unpresentable. If she tried to go shopping alone at the supermarket, the security people would escort her right back out, that's how alarming she is.

The simple explanation for her having taken up residence here is that she appeared at the downtown Minneapolis bus depot last week, having come from Tulsa, where she lived in destitution. She barely had money for bus fare. My son, Wesley, her ex-husband, had to take her in. We all did. However, the more honest explanation for her arrival is that Jesus sent her to me.

Two weeks ago I was in the shower and felt a lump in my breast. I actually cried out in a moment of fear and panic. Then my Christian faith returned to me, and I understood that I would be all right even though I would die. Jesus would send someone to help me get across into the next world. The person He sent to me was Corinne. I know that this is an unpopular view among young people, but there is a divinity that shapes our ends, and at the root of every explanation is God, and at the root of God is love.

I go into the room where Corinne resides, knitting a baby thing. I pick up the cookie plate. "Thank you, Dolores," she says. She gazes at me with her mad-face expression. "Those were delicious. I've always loved ginger cookies. Is there anything I can do for you?" she asks. She's merely being polite.

"Soon," I tell her. "Soon there will be."

You get old, you think about the past, both the bad and the good. You have time to consider it all. You try to turn even the worst that has happened into a gift.

For example, my late husband, Mike, Wesley's father, was killed by the side of the road as he was changing a tire. This was decades ago. He was the only man I ever married. I never had another one, before or after. A rich drunk socialite, a former beauty queen fresh from a night of multiple martinis with her girlfriends, her former sorority sisters, plowed right into him. Then she went on her merry way. Well, no, that's not quite right. After she hit Mike, my husband's body was thrown forward into the air, and then she ran over him, both the car's front and rear tires. Somehow she made her way home with her dented and blood-spattered car, which she parked in the three-car garage before she tiptoed upstairs and undressed and got into bed next to her businessman husband. She clothed herself in her nightgown. She curled up next to him like a good pretty wife. The sleepy husband asked her—this is in the transcripts—how the evening had gone with her girlfriends, if they had had a good time. Why was she shivering? She said the girls had been just fine but she was cold now. She didn't know that someone had gotten her license plate number, but somebody had, as her dark blue Mercedes-Benz sped away. A man out walking his dog on a nearby sidewalk wrote it down. God put him there—the dog, too.

Meanwhile, right after that, the police arrived at our house. I remember first the phone call and then the doorbell that woke my son, Wesley, in the crib that he was beginning to outgrow. He could climb right out of it but rarely did. Wesley began crying upstairs, while in the living room the police, who would not sit down on the sofa, gave me the bad news. My husband, Mike, they told me, was laid out in the morgue, alone, and I would have to identify him the next day. They were quite courteous, those two men, bearing their news. They spoke in low tones, hushed, which is hard for men. One of them wore old-fashioned tortoiseshell glasses. They warned me that I might not recognize my husband right away. But the next morning I did recognize him because of what he was wearing, a blue patterned sport shirt I had bought at Dayton's on sale and had wrapped up for him at Christmas. He had thanked me with a kiss on the lips Christmas morning after he opened it. "God Rest You Merry, Gentlemen" was playing on the radio when he did that. So of course I remembered the shirt.

The socialite testified that she didn't know she had hit anything or anybody. Or that she didn't *remember* hitting anything or anybody. There was some question—I heard about this—whether she had asked her stepson to take the rap for her. She wanted him to go straight to police headquarters and to say *he* had been driving his stepmother's car, drunk, at the age of seventeen, and therefore he would be tried as a minor and let off scot-free. He wouldn't do it. He wouldn't lie. The socialite's out of prison now, but my husband is still under the ground in Lakewood Cemetery.

I await the resurrection of the dead the way other people await weekend football. I'm old now, and the glory will all be revealed to me soon enough. I can feel it coming. Glory will rain down, soaking me to the skin.

If the socialite hadn't gone to prison, I imagined buying a handgun and going over there to her mansion and shooting her in cold blood if she answered the door. But, no, that's wrong: I had Wesley to raise, so I don't suppose I would have actually committed murder, though to kill her was extremely tempting, and the temptation did not come from Satan but from somewhere else inside me. It was mine. I dreamed of murder like a teenager dreaming of love. Peaceful and calm though I usually am, my husband's death and my wish for revenge changed me. Murder dwelt in my heart. Imagine that! It came as a surprise to me as I did the laundry or cooked dinner or washed dishes. Sometimes I wish I were more Christian: Even now, at my age, with knees that hurt from arthritis and a memory that sometimes fails me, I still think certain people should be wiped off the face of the Earth, which is counter to the teachings of Jesus.

But what I'm saying is that Jesus intervened with me. He came to me

73

one night and said, in that loving way He has, "Dolores, what good would it do if you murdered that foolish woman? It would do you and the world no good at all. It wouldn't bring Mike back. Turn that cheek," He said to me as I was praying, and of course I could see He was right. So I forgave that woman, or tried to. On my knees, I turned the other cheek as I wept. I turned it back and forth.

I believe that humanity is divided into two camps: those who have killed others, or can imagine themselves doing so; and those for whom the act and the thought are inconceivable. Looking at me, you would probably not think me capable of murder, but I found that black coal in my soul, and it burned fiercely. I loved having it there.

All my life, I worked as a librarian in the uptown branch. A librarian with the heart of a murderer! No one guessed.

Months after Mike's death, I'd go into Wesley's room to tuck him in at night. By then he was talking. "Where's Daddy?" he would ask me. Gone to heaven, I'd tell him, and he'd ask, "Where's that?" and I wanted to say, "Right here," but such an answer would be confusing to a child, so I just hummed a little tune, a lullaby to calm him. But my son knew there was something wrong with my face in those days, because of the hard labor of my grief. I didn't smile when I put my son to bed, and probably I didn't smile in the morning, either. I couldn't smile on my own. So there, at night, in his bed, he would get out from under the sheet, stand up in his rocket-ship-pattern pajamas, and he would raise his hand with his two fingers, the index finger and the middle finger outstretched in a V-for-victory sign. He would raise those fingers to the sides of my mouth, lifting them up, trying to get me to smile. He held his fingers there until I agreed to look cheerful for his sake. He was only a little boy, after all.

Time passes. The socialite, as I said, is out of jail, and Wesley has grown up and has two children of his own, my dear grandchildren, Jeremy and Lucy. Corinne gave birth to Jeremy before she fled the marriage, and Astrid, Wesley's second wife, gave birth to Lucy. But I still think of that woman, that socialite, driving away from my dying husband, and of what was going through her head, and what I've decided is that (1) she couldn't take responsibility for her actions, and (2) if she did, she would lose the blue Mercedes, and the big house in the suburbs, and the

Royal Copenhagen china, and the Waterford crystal, and the swimming pool in back, and the health club membership, and the closet full of Manolo Blahnik shoes. All the money in the bank, boiling with possibility, she'd lose all that, and the equities upping and downing on the stock exchange. How she was invested! How she must have loved her *things*, as we all do. God has a name for this love: *avarice*. We Americans are running a laboratory for it, and we are the mice and rats, being tested, to see how much of it we can stand.

God's son despised riches. His contempt for riches sprouts everywhere in the Gospels. He believed that riches were distractions. Listen to Jesus: "You shall love your neighbor as yourself." If that isn't wisdom, I don't know what is. And remember this, about those who are cursed? "For I was hungry, and you gave me no food, I was thirsty and you gave me no drink, I was a stranger and you did not welcome me, naked and you did not clothe me."

Anyway, that's why Corinne is here. We have to feed and clothe her. Jesus doesn't believe in those glittering objects that hypnotize you. Hypnotized, you drive away from a dying man stretched out bleeding on the pavement.

I go into Corinne's room. She sits near the window with sunlight streaming in on her hair, which looks greasy, and she's talking before she even sees me. Apparently she's psychic and knows I'm coming. Since I'm not about to waste a beautiful morning like this one by brooding about breast cancer, I ask her, "Do you want to take a walk?" The question interrupts her monologue. "I've got to exercise these old bones," I tell her. Actually, I'm not *that* old. I'm in my seventies. It's just an expression.

She's gesticulating and carrying on a private conversation and seems to be very busy. Finally she says, "No, I don't think so."

"My joints hurt," I tell her. "I need some fresh air. And I need company." Craftily, I say to her, "Without a companion, I might fall down. I might not get back up. You never know."

"Oh, all right," she says, her nursing instinct rising to one of her many surfaces. Even crazy people want to help out. "Oh all right all right all right." She puts on a pair of tennis shoes that Wesley bought for her yesterday, and we set out into the residential Minneapolis autumn, with me slightly ahead of her so that I don't have to smell her. Has she forgotten how to bathe? She's had opportunities here, bathtubs, showers, and soap—running water, both hot and cold. We amble down toward Lake Calhoun. Out on the blue waters of the lake, some brave fellow has one of those sailboard things and is streaking across the surface like a human water bug. Here onshore, the wind agitates the fallen leaves, whipping them around. It's October. My hips are giving me trouble today, and of course the lump in my right breast still remains there, patiently hatching.

"Do you think of the past?" she asks me. "I do. I wanted to call you on the telephone, you know," Corinne tells me, suddenly lucid, "once I moved away, after Jeremy was born. All those years ago. But I couldn't. I was a mess. I was ashamed of myself. I'm a heap of sorry."

"Oh, I didn't mind," I say, before I realize that she might misunderstand me. "We thought you were in a state." Then she tells me that she suffered panic attacks as a young mom—did I remember this? Of course I did—and that all she could do was escape from here, from the marriage and the child and the house. It's her old story. She repeats it all the time. Contrition is a habit with her now.

"Nature tricked me," she says. "I gave birth to a baby boy, and I didn't love him, and I was so ashamed of myself that I left town. I went to work in Tulsa in an emergency room," she says, knowing I know all this, "and I worked there for years, and the people came in night after night, and, Dolores, you can't imagine these poor people, knifed and shot and slashed and choked. Their hands were broken and their mouths were bloody and bullet holes pierced them, and some of them had been poisoned, and the rest of them were bent over and groaning, and you know what happened then?"

"You forgave yourself?" I ask. I wish she would change the topic. I wish she wouldn't dwell on any of this. She doesn't know I'm capable of murder.

"No. I lived with it. I saw things. I heard things. I got bloodied with the blood of strangers all over me. People screamed right into my face from pain and confusion. I saw a woman whose boyfriend had forced her mouth open and made her swallow poison. A person shouldn't see such terribleness. Her stomach had started to burn away before we got to her. When the police questioned the boyfriend, he said that she had told him to go fuck himself and that no woman was going to speak to him that way without consequences. So he did what he did. A manly thing to do. He had her name tattooed on his arm. With a heart! She survived that time, somehow. Two months later he killed her with a knife while she was sleeping. At least he was done away with in prison, later on, stabbed in turn. I think they call that karma. Thank goodness!"

76

By now we have made our way to 36th and to the fence surrounding the cemetery, whereupon Corinne loses her train of thought, as she does in all the subsequent walks we take together. When she collects her thoughts, she says, out of nowhere, "I hate them."

"Who?" I ask.

"Capitalists," she says, and suddenly I'm not following her. "They've made my life miserable. They've made me a crazy person. You can talk about the victims of communism all you want, but as a woman I'm a victim of capitalism, because did I tell you how they took away my pension? I had a pension, and they gave it to investors and the investors invested the money in bogus real estate and bundled something-or-others, and so I ended up with nothing, bereft, broke, a ruined person, no pension, plus I was crazy and alone, and meanwhile the capitalists were accumulating everything and coming after me in their suits. Have you ever seen how they live? It's comical."

"I agree with you, Corinne," I tell her, because I do. By now we are inside the cemetery, and we stop, because overhead in the sunlight a bird is singing, a song sparrow. We walk on quietly until we come to my husband, Mike's resting place.

Michael Erickson
1937-1967

Next to him is the space in the sacred ground where I'll be casketed in a couple of years. I love this cemetery. I do. I come here often. It's so quiet here under the balding blue sky with its wisps of white hair, and as we're looking down at the grass and the leaves, serenaded by the song sparrows, Corinne falls to her knees, smelly as she still is, a human wreck. She mumbles a prayer. "Wesley's daddy," my former daughter-in-law cries out, "God bless him, rest in peace, forever and ever and ever." She's so vehement, she sounds Irish.

This is how I know she'll take care of me once I'm incapacitated. Slowly, on my bad knees, I get down too. How lovely is her madness to me now.

We get back to the house, and that night the capitalism theme starts up again at the dinner table. We seem to be a household of revolutionaries. This time it comes from Jeremy, who before dinner walks into the kitchen barefoot, holding his iPhone. I am sitting, drinking tea. He's sixteen or seventeen, I can't remember which. Usually he and I talk about space aliens, and I pretend they exist to humor him and bring him around eventually to Jesus, but tonight he's looking at something else. He's wearing his Rage Against the Machine T-shirt, and I notice that he's growing a mustache and succeeding with it this time.

"I can't fucking believe it," he says to me. I don't mind his use of obscenity. Really, I don't. It tickles me, I can't say why. "Grandma Dee, do you like elephants?"

"I like them very much," I say. "Though I've never known any one of them personally." We're seated at the kitchen table. Astrid is making dinner, Wesley is in the garage doing something-or-other, and Corinne is upstairs cooing in front of the TV set. I don't know where Lucy is—reading somewhere in the house, I expect. "They are among the greatest of God's creatures," I say. "I understand that they mourn their dead."

"So look at this fucking thing," he says, pointing at the little phone screen.

"It's too small. I can't see it."

"Want me to read it?" he asks. What a handsome young man he is. I enjoy his company. It's so easy to love a grandchild, there's no effort to it at all. Besides, his face reminds me of my late husband's face just a little.

"Sure," I say.

"Well, see the thing is, it's about elephants being killed and like that."

"What about them?" Astrid asks, from over by the stove. "Killed how?"

"Okay, so in Zimbabwe, which I know where it is because we've studied it in geography, anyway what this says, this article, is, they've been, these people, these Zimbabweans, putting cyanide into the water holes in this, like, huge park, to kill the elephants. And these fuckers have access, I guess, to industrial cyanide that they use in gold mining—"

"Jeremy, please watch your language," Astrid says demurely. She's dicing tomatoes now.

"And they've been, I mean the poisoned water hole has been, like, killing the little animals, the cheetahs, and then the vultures, that *eat* the cheetahs once they're dead, so it's, like, this total outdoor death-palace eatery, but mostly the cyanide in the water holes has been killing the *elephants*." He gazes at me as if I'm to blame. I'm old. I understand: Old people are responsible for everything. "Which are harmless?"

"Why've they been doing that?" I ask.

"Killing elephants? For the ivory. They have, like, tusks."

"How many elephants," I ask, "did they do this to?"

78

"It says here eighty," Jeremy tells me. "Eighty dead elephants poisoned by cyanide lying in dead-elephant piles. Jesus, I hate people sometimes."

"Yes," I say. "That's fair."

"What do you suppose they do with all that ivory?" Astrid asks, stirring a sauce.

"For carvings," I say. "They carve little Buddhas. They kill the elephants and carve the happy Buddha. Then they sell the happy Buddha to Americans. The little ivory Buddha goes in the lighted display case."

"That is so wrong," Jeremy says. "People are fucking sick. These elephants are more human, for fuck's sake, than the humans."

"It's the avarice," I say.

"It's the what?" he asks.

"Another word for greed. Go ask Corinne," I tell him. "She's upstairs, watching TV. She doesn't like it, either. She sounds like you."

"I still hate her," he says. "I can't talk to her yet. It's my *policy*. She just wasn't—"

"I know, I know," I say. "The policy is understandable. You'll just have to give it up eventually, sweetie."

"You can't tell me that it's no biggie because it was a biggie. If that wasn't a biggie, leaving my dad and you to take care of me, then nothing is big, you know?"

"Yes," I say. "I understand. For now."

"Jeremy," Astrid pipes up from the stove, "where's your father?"

"Him? He's out in the garage. He's working on the truck or something. I heard him drop his wrench and swear a minute ago. *There are too many of them in the house*. That's what he said before he went out there. He's *been* saying it."

"Too many what?" Astrid asks.

"Women," I say, because I know Wesley and how he thinks. "We confuse him."

I can see it all, and I know exactly what will happen. I have second sight, which I got from my own father, who foresaw his death. He saw an albino deer cross the road in front of his car while he was on vacation, and he turned to my mother and said, "Something will happen to me," and something did. A stroke took him a week later, and no one was surprised.

They'll do surgery on me and give me the usual chemo and radiation.

79

I'll be okay for a while, but then it will come back in other locations in my body. I won't have too much time then. The point is not to be morbid but to meet the end of life with celebration. This is what I want to say: The thought of dying is a liberation for me. It frees us from the accumulations.

This is where Corinne comes in. I have it all planned out. I will say to her, "There's something I want you to do. I want you to accompany me on this journey as far as you can. You can't go all the way, but you can keep me company part of the way." She'll agree to this. As long as I can walk, Corinne will take me around to the parks and the lakes. We'll go to the Lake Harriet rose garden, and together we'll identify those roses—floribunda! hybrid tea!—and then we'll stroll into the Roberts Bird Sanctuary nearby. I know most of the birds over there: There's a nest of great horned owls, with a couple of owlets growing up and eating whatever the mama owl brings to them, including, I once saw, a crow. I've seen warblers and egrets and herons, very dignified creatures, though comical. We'll see the standard-issue birds, the robins, chickadees, blue jays, and cardinals, birds of that ilk.

She'll take me over to the Lake Harriet Band Shell, where on warm summer nights the Lake Harriet Orchestra (there is one) will play show tunes, and I'll sit there in my wheelchair tapping along with "On the Street Where You Live."

We'll go down to the Mississippi, and we'll walk, or I'll be wheeled, along the pathways near the falls where the mills once were. I'll hear the guides saying that Minneapolis has a thriving industry in prosthetic medicine because so many industrial accidents occurred here years ago thanks to the machinery built for grinding, lost arms and so on, chewed up in the manufacturing process.

We'll be out on the Stone Arch Bridge, and Corinne will be absented in her usual way, ideas batting around her head, all the bowling pins up there scattered and in a mess. "I just don't have any filters," she'll say. "Any thought seems to be welcome in my brain at any time, day or night."

"Yes," I'll agree. I'll see the Pillsbury A Mill from here. What a comfort these old structures will be to us, still standing, their bright gray brick almost indestructible. Spray from the Falls of St. Anthony, named by Father Hennepin himself, will lightly touch my face, and I'll feel a sudden stab of pain in my body, but it won't matter anymore. Pain is the price of admission to the next world. Here will come a boy on a skateboard talking on his cell phone, and behind him, his girlfriend, also on a skateboard (pink, this time), texting as she goes. They'll look just born, those two, out of the eggshell yesterday.

"Jeremy has one of those," Corinne will say, meaning the skateboard. "He's quite the expert."

A fat man in flip-flops will pass by us. He'll be carrying several helium balloons, though I don't think they'll be for sale. On the other side of the bridge in Father Hennepin park, we'll rest under a maple tree. A single leaf will fall into my lap.

Here. I place it before you.

Glory, gloriousness. During my life, I never had the time to look closely at anything except Wes, when he was a baby, and my husband's headstone after he was gone. Now I'll have all the time in the world. Nothing will bore me now. My obliviousness will sink into my past history. Henceforth my patience will be endless, thanks to the brevity of time. Stillness will steal over me as I study the world within. When I look down into my lap, I'll see in this delicate object the three major parts, with their branching veins, and the ten points of the leaf, and the particular bright red-rust-gold color, but it's the veins I'll return to, so like our own, our capillaries.

I'll finger the maple leaf tenderly and wonder why we find it beautiful and will answer the question by saying that it's God-given.

"There's that nice Dr. Jones, way over there," Corinne will say. "Lucy's doctor, out on a stroll." She'll pause, then say, "He could lose some weight."

"They're doing a Katharine Hepburn revival at the St. Anthony Main movie theater," I'll say, gazing at the marquee listing *Bringing Up Baby*.

"I always found her rather virile," Corinne will reply.

Thus will our days pass. You need a companion for what I'm about to do, and she'll be mine. Once I'm in bed, and then in the hospice, she'll read to me: *Pride and Prejudice*, my favorite book after the Bible, and she'll read from the Bible too, in her haphazard way, wandering from verse to verse. I wonder if she'll read from the Book of Esther,

which never mentions God. Slowly I'll depart from this Earth, medi-
cated on morphine as I will be, mulling and stirring the fog descending
over me, over Elizabeth Bennet and Mr. Darcy, over daytime and its
dark twin, night, while in the background someone will be playing
Mozart on a radio. What is that piece? I think I'll know it. *Eine kleine
Nachtmusik*, is it . . . ? Then I'll know more pain, and darkness. And
then the light won't go on ever again, here.

On the other side I'll float for a while, between worlds. The pain will
be gone, the pleasure, too, those categories neutralized. On all sides
the boundary markers will have softened. Instead of coming from a
single source, sound—music—will come from everywhere, and I'll hear
it with more than my ears. I'll see with more than my eyes. Faces, I
think, will pass me in corridors that are not corridors. The old vocabu-
laries will be useless. They will name nothing anymore. This is the
afterlife: We will be headed everywhere and nowhere, and we will drink
in light, swallow it, swim in it. We'll hear laughter. And then—but
"then" has no meaning—my dear Michael will find me, without his
former shape but still recognizable, and he'll take my hand and lead me
toward two rooms, and he'll say to me, "Oh, my dearest, my life, there
is only one question, but you must answer it." And I'll ask him, "What
is that question? Tell me. Because I love you . . ." I'll want to answer it
correctly. What has this to do with the two rooms? But for that moment,
after he puts his finger to his lips, he dissolves into air, he becomes pol-
len, and is scattered.

Somehow I am led into the first room. I'll be in a chamber of per-
petual twilight. No one predicted this twilight, or the shabbiness, the
feeling of a beggar. How richly plain this all is! Something wants some-
thing from me here. My attention. My love.

Now I'll enter the second room. And all at once I'll be dazzled: Be-
cause here on the richest of thrones, gold beyond gold, sits this beauti-
ful man, the most beautiful man I have ever seen, smiling at me with
an expression of infinite compassion. His hair will be curling into ten-
drils of vibrating color. He will be holding up his palm, facing toward
me, and in that hand I will see the world, the solar system, and the
universe, rotating slowly. Behind him somehow are the animals, the
great trees, everything.

It will be a test, the last one I will ever have. Which room do I
choose?

The beautiful man clothed in light will ask me, "Do you admire me? Care for me?"

And I will say, "No, because you are Lucifer." And I will return to the room where it is always twilight, where all that is asked of me is love.

Nominated by Virginia Quarterly Review

SCREAM (OR NEVER MINDING)

by LIA PURPURA

from THE GEORGIA REVIEW

There are things I'm supposed to never mind. "Never mind" means *silent* and *agreed upon*, and that I must want, more than anything, to get through the day, and so should assent to go along. Glance. Turn the page. Turn away from a scream, and the place from which a scream would rise, if cultivated by attention paid.

Subjects one might avoid: ruined land, ruined animals. Because the issues of the day can begin to feel old, and people get tired of feeling bad.

When I was a child I was not daunted. I let myself get completely exhausted.

Never minding makes it possible to do things like eat what you want, and talk about simple, daily things.

A scream is not speech.

Edvard Munch's *The Scream* was recently sold for nearly 120 million dollars. He called it "a cry from the heart," and wrote about it to a friend that "I was being stretched to the limit . . . Nature was screaming in my blood. I was at breaking point. . . ."[1] But as a gesture performed

---

[1] *From Sue Prideaux's Edvard Munch: Behind the Scream, Yale University Press, 2005.*

over and over, on coffee mugs, tote bags, key chains, and cards, it's much reduced, quieted so as to be understood. Seeing the scream again and again, we agree not to.

Instead, we refer to.

Consider all we throw away. The tin my mints came in could do so much work. Could be put to good use and serve again, holding buttons, coins, pills. Then fewer tins would have to be made. Imagine (though there's no need to, this is all real) how many things are made to be thrown away. You can't care about them. Their brevity isn't meaningful like, say, a dart with a poisoned tip, a spear, an arrowhead—objects whose single use sustains.

Yes, I understand making tins is a job. A way of making a living.
That people have jobs making trash for a living.

That subs or heroes or grinders, whatever they're called in a given place, are sold by the inch. That drinks are called "bottomless." That for a set price you can eat all night, stack BBQ ribs ten inches high if you balance just right, walking back to your seat.
    What a deal that is.
    If more is the measure, if the point is *a lot*—best not to fuss over the origins of stuff. And, too, if origins are questionable, you'd want the distance between farm and table to be as vast as possible. Vast is stable. Ribs are tasty. I mean a *factory* farm. A Concentrated Animal Feeding Operation. A CAFO. An acronym is a form of speed, a way to fly past the origin of an idea.
    "Concentrate" was my favorite cereal as a kid. I liked it, too, for its double meaning—a dense substance/a command to think hard. Here, though, *Concentrated* means: twenty hogs in a space the size of your bedroom; ten chickens in a two-foot square pen—that's an area the size of this page for each chicken. Under such conditions, animals are driven mad.
    I probably don't have to be so direct here.
    I'm sure you've heard a lot about this.

Once, a bandwagon was used for exactly that purpose: to carry musi-cians in a procession. To *jump on one* now means *to join a successful enterprise*. So many forms of success depend on never minding, on taking the steps two at a time, up to the wagon and climbing on for the ride. Or think of riding a tide: a force absorbs you, purpose transports, and a shared mind washes over.

At the edges, though—near jetties and inlets, in dips and depressions— little tide pools settle and still, and that's where the interesting stuff collects. You have to get down on your knees to see all the briny, colloidal, fast-swimming creatures that, at a distance, look only like murk.

I want to think about #419.

What might seem like veering around here isn't. I'm trying to lay in how many times a day, and in how many ways, a person—I—might turn away.

Or else, what—stay and scream?

Solastalgia is a very good word, made by combining the Latin *sola-cium* (comfort) and the Greek root *-algia* (pain). Philosopher Glenn Albrecht created it to define "the pain experienced when the place one loves and where one resides is under assault." I'm working on a word for *the loss of fellow-feeling for a creature and the strange emptiness that loss leaves in its place*. "Zoosympenia" might do. "Zoo" (animal) + "sym" (feeling) + "penia" (loss). But first, before words, a feeling must root. For me, it was winter, late afternoon, when eye level with the stove—a beautiful old Chambers—I'd set things in motion. The oven door had a hooked lever which, fixed between two orange dials, made it into the face of an owl. It was possible to come around the corner unseen, inch up to the bird, flip its beak, hear it talk, touch its ever-open eyes. Say *hi* in passing, or play in its gaze. Nearby was a horse in the linoleum. A horse's *head* to be more precise—a little disconcerting but, like a ragged cloud shape in the sky, more a suggestion than a truncated thing. The horse had its own scent when I laid my head next to it. We talked in the mornings. It was always ready. I also had a collection of bees, paper ones my mother cut from tuna cans and distributed on alternate weeks to me and my sister. We'd toss them in air and watch them sift down on the flowers we were.

When I was four, the world was ending. I wasn't certain. I just suspected. It was 1968. The war was on. I had a dog, a monkey, a fox. I did not think of them as toys. If the world was a storm, I was an ark.

I'll get to work on another word, too—something for *the loss of relationship to singular objects due to an overabundance of them.*

How about: *Aesthesioplegia.* "Aesthesio" (sensation) + "plegia" (paralysis).

To understand an object's habits, its tricks, you have to live with it daily. A milk bottle (the one I grew up with had a high, cinched waist and a full-skirted body) might let you take an illegal swig, but only if you used both hands. You might blue the last inch of milk by holding it up to the morning sun and tipping it almost horizontal.

Endless abundance clobbers the chance for relationships. So for example, if asked *Would you like to help stop wrecking the earth,* you'd say, of course, *Yes.* If asked, then, to drink only from fountains and never again buy a bottle of water . . . well, it's hard to imagine giving up convenience—though what you'd get, in return, is the chance to learn the quirks of your local water fountains: the cold ones with high arcs, the calmer but warmer, dribbly ones. You might choose to walk a bit further for the beautiful, pebbly fountain, or make do with closer, slightly tin-flavored water. Or you might carry your own collapsible cup (I had one as a Girl Scout), which when folded would be exactly the size of a tin of mints.

#419 is a cow; that's a tag in its ear. There's a #308 right behind it, a #376, and a #454—all jammed in the frame of the photo. This must be a mixed lot. If I stand back just a little or, rather, hold the newspaper out at arm's length and unfocus a bit, the numbers fade and the cows are wearing bell-shaped earrings. If I shut my eyes, and shut many more things—doors in the brain, as if windows in cold—if I conjure up Heidi and green fields and milk pails, I can hear the little cowbells tinkling. And see the concrete outside my door roll up like a rug, cartoon style, revealing the sleeping pasture below. Which reconstitutes in sun and springs with fat flowers back to life. And feeds all the cows on endless, rollicking, hand-colored cartoon greens.

A *Starry Night* mug. A Caillebot trivet. *Mona Lisa* fridge magnets. Cezanne wrapping paper.

419 is bending to eat. Not grass but corn. I guess I should say, *she's eating what she's made to eat*, which likely includes swine manure, poultry feathers, cement dust, and plastic for roughage. All cheaper and more efficient than grass, easily supplied in confined spaces—though contributing, as you might imagine, to conditions that justify prophylactic antibiotics.

But let me just do a description here. Establish a scene. 419 is bending to eat. Her tags are clearly visible, as is the patch of white between her eyes, which are good at seeing blue-purples and yellow-greens and not so adept at the red-brown-pink spectrum. And there, in relief, against the white chest of 308—the fringe of 419's black eyelashes. Like a girl's. Like my son's in sleep.

Once you really see a thing (even briefly, and slight as a lash) it's hard to unsee.

This summer I saw two sandpipers dig for crabs at the edge of the shore with long, pointed beaks. When the waves rolled out, one dug, picked, and ate very quickly. The other plucked its catch and ran straight to a dry spot higher up and took its time pecking every bit of meat. One found more crabs, but ate each only partly. The other stuck with a single crab and mined it completely. One was not more adept, or the other wiser—just that there was, undeniably, the *inclination* each had. It was impossible to miss: each preferred a particular method, each had an idea, a disposition. A sensibility. An imagination.

Endless *Starry Nights* wreck time. *Great Waves* get drained, and *Sunflowers* dimmed by repetition. What Munch once made of a sensation at dusk (his friends having left him after a walk, his brief pause on a path and his sense of despair) is no longer a space where you and the painter might linger together. Now it's a trinket. A T-shirt. A necklace. A thing you stop seeing that stands in for. It's a joke. A tactic. A way to connect at the office, in meetings (which make everyone want to scream). Why tame that original moment?

Why encourage skipping so quickly past? Why reduce so much to mild laughter? A while back, inflatable *Scream* dolls were all the rage—there on your desk or life-size, a bald, angsty friend who'd commiserate, lift a beer with you at the end of the day. Imagine him on the label of a microbrew—the colors amped, the border crisp. A beer called Scream. Scream lager. Scream ale.

I'd like to think the painting's new owner wanted back to a time before the image refracted, to park a chair near the original sky, the fat blue scream pressing in like a wave, the bridge's red rail like an iron poker, the gash of sky marbled and fleshy, and to be, as everything was—clouds, air, nerves, smudgy suggestion of boats—overcome. I'm hoping he wanted to clear some space, amid colors eddying fast and draining, so a scream might speak, singularly, to him.

To own a thing in a more perfect way, go into training. Adopt the gestures of a beloved friend you rarely see, the way she holds a thought in her hands and twists it into place in air. Study how her fingers flare when describing something unjust, or a point beyond which she won't be pushed, so you, too, can shape ideas in air and close up the distance between you.

Or, paring a spot of mold from cheese, take up a worn, well-sharpened knife, and cutting slowly toward your body, let the blade come to rest against the flesh of your thumb—and in this, the old-fashioned way, free-hand, with no cutting board—spend a few moments with your grandmother again.

Some forms of ownership don't require the purchase of anything.

I'm meant to forget that certain very basic gestures—fingers on toggles—are a satisfaction, and to never mind their passing. Am I alone in wanting to turn and adjust faucet handles? Repair fixtures with a wrench and a smear of putty? Yank a towel on a roller to produce a clean spot? Now you need only wave your wet hands at a sensor or move around until lasers kick in. Or often, don't. And then, there you are, swaying dumbly alone in your stall—a scene very different from, say, a man dancing naked, as William Carlos Williams wrote,

grotesquely
before my mirror

waving my shirt round my head
and singing softly to myself
"I am lonely, lonely"[2]

—a loneliness so vital it's worth celebrating, so human it's lyrical, so physically achy it calls forth the drive to *make* something of it.

Or how about this: You've got a drill with a bad battery, a nickel-cadmium, heavy-metal thing you want to recycle. Opening the drill takes a good ten minutes with tiny screwdrivers. The drill itself is just fine: the gears enmeshed and sharp, the motor precise in its cylindrical compactness and nestled within its casing, all the parts good, all able to perform. But the battery pack costs way more than the drill, is specialized and hard to find, or doesn't even exist without the drill, so you throw the whole thing away.

A thing designed with a subsystem that quits, with no way of keeping the perfect remains. An object lost to itself at the outset. No sense of a tool becoming, through long use, a hand's extension, no hint of its shape responding to a body—of such a fit being intimate.

I'm not supposed to be upset by any of this.

Childhood's a long training in never minding all you're losing, everything that's falling, crashing, being taken. In the diamonded, rhinestoned late 1970s most things were too bright, or tight, or Lucite—and I wasn't learning. I turned away from (and here's a good, bygone word) the *boughten*, and instead toward . . . well, mostly a dream of wildness, Long Island's marshes long filled in and black-topped for parking lots, malls, Levittowns. I spent much time prospecting for bits. One summer I rose at dawn and gathered dandelions from all the front yards, washed and sugared them, added yeast, water, lemon—and then, for the next few weeks, set to racking off my dandelion wine. (I was reading Bradbury's story at the time.) I wore flannel shirts and overalls, work boots and braids. In love with my bike and my dog, I read outdoor survival guides. I looked for occasions to use the word *pemmican*. I wrote out the steps for tanning hides (the native way, with animal brains, or ash, or acorns). I heard *mall* as the tool—not as a baubly, over-lit place. What others called *wild* in me I knew to be a fending off. A countering. A minding greatly.

2 *From William Carlos Williams's "Danse Russe."*

90

In the Outdoors section of the *Rapid City Journal* I recently read about a couple "Bonded by Their Adventures." Their twenty safaris. Their thirty-year marriage. A few of their tales were gathered therein (in the scary dark of a rainforest when etc. etc. which ended in "the pure joy of being together outdoors")—but it was the front page photo that held me. On the very bright walls, head after head (after head after head)—at least 50 mounts in the living room alone. And how strange the couple looked, alive, among them.

I remember the busts of Beethoven and Mozart (and Haydn and Liszt and Chopin) in my elementary school's music room. I couldn't make any sense of them: a pianist with no arms; a joyless composer who wrote "Ode to Joy." Their limbless bodies in marbly coldness. Stunted and chopped. I knew a head with a bit of neck was meant to be never minded. Another version of how-things-are-done. The men, canonical. The sculptures, memorial. A cliché of sight. I *understood*.

Still it was hard to see anything but severedness.

You should know that the place in *The Scream* where the figure stands is an actual road in Oslo overlooking the bay where screams from the slaughterhouse and asylum converged. Munch's sister was locked in there, while he was free to walk with friends and think and listen and create.

He wrote:

"I went along the road with two friends—
     The sun set
Suddenly the sky became blood—and I felt the breath of sadness
~~A tearing pain beneath my heart~~
I stopped—leaned against the fence—deathly tired
Clouds over the fjord ~~of blood~~ dripped reeking with blood
My friends went on but I just stood trembling with an open wound in my breast ~~trembling with anxiety~~ I heard a huge extraordinary scream pass through nature."[3]

You might try it—anyone might: at the end of a day finding yourself abruptly alone, and since certain sounds cannot be unheard, certain

3 *From Prideaux's Edvard Munch: Behind the Scream.*

images cannot be unseen, in that moment, when a bay might tilt, or a sky drain and pin its red light hard to your chest, you might press your hands to your ears and, at that spot where the world leaks in, wherever it happens—diner, store, street—there, in the moment a scream originates, try to make something of that.

Nominated by Andrea Hollander, Joan Murray

STILL WHEN I PICTURE IT THE FACE OF GOD IS A WHITE MAN'S FACE

by SHANE McCRAE

from POETRY

Before it disappears
on the sand his long white   beard before it disappears
The face of the man
in the waves I ask her does she see it ask her does
The old man in the waves   as the waves crest she see it does
she see the old man his
White   his face crumbling face it looks
as old as he's as old as
The ocean looks
and for a moment almost looks
His face like it's   all the way him
As never such old skin
looks my / Daughter age four
She thinks it might he might be real she shouts *Hello*
And after there's no answer answers *No*

Nominated by Martha Collins, D.A. Powell, Lee Upton, Robert Wrigley

THE GEORGE
SPELVIN PLAYERS

fiction by REBECCA MAKKAI

from PLEIADES

Barnes Harlow was actually Jason something, but no one dreamed of calling him that. He was Barnes Harlow when he was robbed of the Daytime Emmy, he was Barnes Harlow all twelve years he played Dalton Shaw, Esq., and he was Barnes Harlow when, in that guise, he married Silvia Romero Caldwell Blake, poisoned his mother-in-law, opened a restaurant, burned down that restaurant, was drugged by Michaela, and saved the Whitney family from carbon monoxide poisoning.

Soledad shared these details with the core company, who sprawled exhausted on the stage. In the five minutes since Barnes had left the theater, Soledad had relayed the basic history of the fictional Appleburg, Ohio, and told them what Barnes Harlow looked like with his shirt off. "Not *greasy*-smooth," she said. "Just, you know, TV-star smooth." She swore her grandmother had tapes of the show, stacks of VHS cassettes in her basement.

"On a more professional level," Tim said, "what did we think? Starstruck aside?"

Beth vowed to speak last. Last week in the green room, Phyllis had accused her of treating every conversation like a race.

Phyllis lay back, staring into the rafters. Beth could see up her skirt, not that Phyllis would care. "Isn't this your decision, Tim?" Her smoker's voice lent her authority. "Cast him or don't. Regardless of his chest-hair situation."

DeShawn said, "You know how much they memorize on the soaps? You can't be a slacker."

But it would be different, Tim said, with someone like Barnes among

94

them. (Tim undid and redid his ponytail—his deliberation pose.) Women who'd watched Barnes on *Splendor of Love*, who knew he'd moved back to Missouri to care for his mother and recover from whatever ego or amphetamine issue he was dealing with, would flock from miles around. They'd throw roses. They might throw underwear. At *Bob Cratchit*. With children in the audience.

"It's called publicity," Soledad said.

"Something's wrong with him," Beth finally offered. (Quickly—before Phyllis rolled her eyes, before Soledad crossed her arms like she was being bullied.) "Sure, they killed his character, but that happens all the time. They don't leave New York and try out for, I'm sorry, a dinky-ass theater's obligatory Christmas play. In what's essentially a basement. I think we're his rock bottom."

DeShawn said, "All the soaps are getting cancelled. And his mom has lupus."

So it was decided. But when Beth looked back later, she had to admit no one was thinking clearly that night. Tim had barely resisted stroking Barnes's hair. All three women were involuntarily smitten. DeShawn, who had eyes for no one but his Dave, still couldn't stop grinning. Barnes Harlow had been hired by five excitement-starved actors who were, every single one, sexually attracted to him. What they should have done was consulted Kostas, who was backstage writing up the performance report. A straight guy with a crush on Soledad would've been the first to call Barnes a prettyboy, to suggest they check his arms for track marks. Barnes's good looks (the bone structure, that hair, the green eyes) were so cheesy, so predictable, that perhaps each of them felt alone in seeing through all that, seeing that the real Barnes Harlow—Jason, in fact!—was vulnerable and lonely. And the great danger in believing you alone understood someone was the sense of ownership that followed close behind. Beth knew this from hard experience, but it didn't come to mind. Instead she mused that playing Mrs. Cratchit would be more tolerable this time around.

They herded up the stairs, dropping people at each floor. Tim lived on the second, across from the young librarian who was the only non-theater person in the building. Beth lived above the librarian, across from DeShawn-and-Dave. Soledad and Phyllis somehow coexisted on the fourth. Back in the seventies, an original ensemble member had owned the building, built the theater space, and willed the whole thing to the company. The librarian's rent helped offset utilities, and between tickets and donations and extra jobs (Beth was brunch hostess at The

Bullfrog), they managed to keep the theater running and not starve. They did their laundry in the costume room. Tim's partner Len kept the books, DeShawn's partner Dave did the publicity and advertising and even acted on occasion, Kostas lived across town and stage-managed and designed the sets and was Technical Director too, and Aunt Jacqui, the actual aunt of some original, long-gone ensemble member, did props and costumes. Locals and college students filled out most casts. It was a bizarre setup for a theater: half-residential, half-repertory, non-equity, barely tenable, always teetering between ruin and success, between embarrassment and artistry. But it was steady work (unheard of, unless you wanted to move to Branson and sing about riverboats), and everyone, with the exception of Phyllis, was young and headed (they hoped, they hoped) for bigger towns. Every few years, someone left for St. Louis or Chicago to try their luck. It had never happened before now that someone had come in the other direction, voluntarily.

Beth called her sister that night to tell her about Barnes Harlow. But her brother-in-law picked up the phone, started bantering in his lawyer voice. "How's life in the M.O.?" he said. "Still acting?"

"Still lawyering?" she responded, and almost hung up, but took a deep breath and didn't. He was family. Or at least, this was how the rest of the world defined family. People who married your sister. People who shared your vision problems and allergies. You called them twice a year and caught up. And then you went back to your real family, the one you'd chosen, the one you'd built things with.

When rehearsals started, Barnes Harlow was nothing but professional. He memorized quickly, asked questions but not too many, watched everyone else's scenes with dark eyebrows pleasantly raised. He remembered their names. "Beth," he'd said at their second meeting. "Beth with the red hair." She wanted to answer, "Barnes. Barnes with shoulders of Adonis," but of course she didn't. They comported themselves more professionally when he was in the room—not snapping at Tim, not swearing, even after the children playing the young Cratchits had gone home. They were still performing *Uncle Vanya* at night, so they rehearsed afternoons, plus Saturdays for the Cratchit family scenes. They'd already switched to their seasonal habit of referring to Tim as Big Tim, just to differentiate him from Tiny Tim the character. Barnes joined in gamely. The first time the toilet flushed above the stage—the librarian had been warned about evening performances, but they knew if they restricted her plumbing all day long she'd move out—Tim turned a sort of spaghetti-sauce shade Beth had never seen on him. The sound was impressive, a churning waterfall on all sides as things traveled through the pipes and out over the lobby.

"Our secret's out," Tim said. "We perform in a sewer."

"It's like a guerrilla theater from the sixties!" Barnes insisted. "You know, doing shows in some warehouse in the Village!"

DeShawn, positioned as Scrooge behind her, whispered in Beth's ear: "I can see it. *A Nude Christmas Carol*. Bongo drums and strobe lights. One of those deals where everyone's covered in chicken blood."

Barnes sat in the audience for the last performance of Vanya and started the standing ovation. He joined them at the cast party up at Tim's, but he stopped at one beer, as if on principle—as if a second beer would compromise his integrity. He recycled the bottle, clapped Tim on the shoulder, and took off. Of course they talked about him the rest of the night. Beth tried changing the subject every few minutes: "Did you see that woman with the transparent shirt?" she said. "In the front row?" And she said, "Let's never do a play with a gunshot again. I aged twelve years." But each time, it was seconds before they were back on Barnes and what costars he'd dated. Had he been on *Splendor of Love* when Meg Pemberton was on *Splendor of Love*, before she changed her chin and moved to Hollywood and made Julia Roberts obsolete? Yes, he definitely had. He'd kissed her! Soledad was sure. Were they still in touch? Would movie stars stay in touch with people from the soap world? A plan was hatched: Soledad would find a magazine with Meg Pemberton on the cover, and she'd read it in front of Barnes to see if he said something. "This is sick," Tim said at regular intervals. "We shouldn't talk about him." And then DeShawn would say, "He's kind of tall for TV, don't you think?"

There was a term Beth had learned in a sociology class, though she couldn't remember it now, for a society where people had more than one connection to each other. In a big city, a guy would be your mail-man and nothing else. But in a small town, he might be your mailman and your cousin and your neighbor, and his wife is your boss. She wondered what her sociology professor would make of the George Spelvin Players—who not only lived and worked together, but whose constantly shifting fictional relationships were also vivid, if not real. Beth had been Tim's mother, his wife, his sister, his therapist. He had killed her in six different plays. Now, as Jacob Marley, he was her husband's dead boss. Beth had kissed most of them, even Phyllis. She'd been naked under a blanket with DeShawn every night for five weeks. She wondered if what they were trying to do with Barnes, through this obsessive examination, was to weave him into their complex fabric. They refused to let him be simply a colleague. They wanted to envelop him: talent, legitimacy and all.

Late that night, Beth started to tell them this theory—or at least DeShawn, who was near her on the couch and would actually listen— but then she remembered she was practicing restraint. She'd stopped telling DeShawn he and Dave were codependent, and she'd stopped telling Phyllis when her hook earrings were about to fall out. Part of her was sure that if her hair weren't flaming red, people wouldn't think she was so loud. But it was red, and so they insisted she talked too much, and so she was trying to accommodate them. It was her new thing.

That next week, during dress and tech rehearsals, things started to go missing. First it was Scrooge's candlestick, which DeShawn and Aunt Jacqui both swore had been on the prop table. They could hardly think of anywhere to look; they both just stood staring at the X of glow tape where it belonged. Then it was Soledad's phone, which finally showed up on the back of the green room toilet though she hadn't used the bathroom all night. The next day it was the festive bonnet Phyllis wore as Mrs. Fezziwig, its labeled clip still on the clothes rack.

Tim rattled the chains he wore as Marley's ghost, till they all looked at him like children in trouble with the PE teacher. "If this is part of the prank war," he said, "it's not funny. We don't cross this line." The prank war was vague and unending, with some origin story about a broken-down car. The war might occasionally come onstage—the letter you were handed as a Russian peasant might, in fact, bear a pornographic image—but theft was beyond the pale. It slowed rehearsals. It cost money. Aunt Jacqui would have to stay late to lock things up, Tim announced. Beth could hear Soledad and Phyllis whispering, and she knew they were asking what the point was, when everyone had keys to everything.

On Tuesday night, Beth and Barnes hung around so Tim could re-block the end of the second act, where they danced together around the table. Again and again, Bob Cratchit swung Mrs. Cratchit through the air. Their chests pressed together fifty times in a row. Laughing and giddy, Beth wiped the sweat off Barnes's forehead with her apron. It became clear that they were both waiting for Tim to leave—that they were following another script, larger and more inevitable than any Dickens adaptation. Beth's veins were on fire. Her body could believe this luck, even as her brain could not.

It was late enough that the librarian started making noise again upstairs. The dishwasher, then loud talking. There were two sets of footsteps, one heavier than usual. "Lucy's got herself a date," Tim said. "Go, Lucy."

Beth said, "So do you. Isn't Len waiting?"

He gave a sort of checkmated look. "I'll walk you upstairs, Beth."

Barnes waved goodnight, but Beth knew he wouldn't really leave the building.

Tim stood with an arm on her doorframe. "It's not worth it," he said. "Is it? This could be so messy. He's a real person, not just some fantasy."

"I'm the only one who *didn't* fall for the fantasy. I'm the only one not stalking him on the Internet. You do not get to accuse people of having *fantasy* issues, Tim."

Tim threw his whole head back so all she could see was his Adam's apple. He stomped downstairs and slammed his own door. Another sociological complexity: Tim was her boss. Yet she was allowed to yell at him on an almost daily basis.

Ten minutes later, Barnes knocked on her door with no pretense or excuse, just a loopy grin.

Beth noted that soap stars don't kiss with any remarkable skill. But they've been coached in variety, in camera angles, so they never stop moving their faces around. Up, down, left, right, neck, to please the invisible director. The sex was a good deal less acrobatic. Soap stars are not coached in sexual positions, she figured. Just in strategic sheet placement.

She decided to wash her linens the next afternoon. It wasn't that Barnes's smell was some disgusting thing she wanted to eradicate—it was just that, unless a man was her actual boyfriend, she didn't feel like finding his hair on her pillowcase. She'd had the habit since college, to the point that when her sophomore roommates saw her heading out with the laundry bag, they'd screech and groan and give her the third degree.

But when she got to the costume shop, Lucy the librarian was there, and the washer and dryer were both full.

Lucy jumped when she saw Beth. "I'm so sorry!" she said. She never seemed to figure out that she was the only one who paid rent, that she didn't need to apologize for taking up room on the staircase and in the parking lot. Beth glanced at Lucy's plastic laundry basket. Just a few wet clothes waiting to be air-dried. She wanted to lift them by the corners, to see if there were small, pilfered props hiding in the wet cups of the bras.

"Don't worry," Beth said, and she hoisted herself to sit on the sewing table. "How's the library?" She was aware that when she tried to make small-talk, it came off as condescending. And maybe she did feel sorry for this woman, younger than herself but pasty and baffled, her clothes a mess of rumpled layers.

Lucy smiled graciously. "Can I ask something? That new guy."

"Oh, that's Barnes."

"Did he just move to town?"

"Crazy beautiful, right? And he speaks Italian. Hey, did you know we're having a theft problem?" She watched Lucy carefully, to see if she'd cover her mouth defensively, if blood would rush to her neck.

Instead she said, "In the building?"

"The theater. Props and stuff."

"But nothing valuable?"

"Props are valuable to *us*."

"Oh, I know. That's terrible."

"Tell us if you see anything weird, okay?"

The dryer buzzed, and Lucy began scooping things out. "I wanted to ask, though," she said, and her voice echoed in the cavern of the dryer. "He looks so familiar."

"He was on *Splendor of Love*." It suddenly occurred to her that Lucy was actually quite pretty, even with the stringy hair and the skin that showed every blemish. She added, "I think he's still dating someone from New York."

"That fits. The New York thing. Because I thought I recognized him from that old Head & Shoulders commercial. The one with the high school teacher, and the kids are laughing at him?"

Beth doubted it was true. It wouldn't be plausible for high school students to laugh at someone who looked like Barnes, no matter how many white plastic flakes were sprinkled in his hair. "Huh. Maybe. Soap actors do a lot of commercials."

"For soap, I guess." Lucy smiled like they were supposed to bond over this.

"But he's not worth it."

"Not worth what?"

"Like, pursuing." She saw that she'd insulted her, that this had never been on Lucy's mind, so she kept talking just to cover up. "Or employing, for that matter. He's got a New York ego. And the rest of us are just here to have fun. I mean, you know why we're called the George Spelvin, right?"

Lucy shook her head. "Was that the founder?"

"God, no. It's an old theater joke. If you're in a play that's so bad you don't even want it on your résumé, that's what you put in the playbill. Like, 'the role of Hamlet will be played by George Spelvin.' So can you imagine? The whole theater. The whole *thing* is a joke. That's the message." Though none of them believed it really. Hadn't August Platt done so well when he got to Chicago? And he wasn't so much better than the rest of them.

"I love it," Lucy said. "I can't believe I never knew." She was ready to go, her basket a heap of dry clothes on top of the wet bras, the last load spinning in the dryer.

Beth waved her fingers and put on a witchy voice: "Things are so seldom as they appear."

That night in the green room, Tim gave her a searching, accusatory look. She wasn't surprised when Soledad and Phyllis did the same. DeShawn just giggled.

Barnes walked in, his black leather coat spotted with snow, and they all stared at their scripts, their costumes, the mirror. Beth asked him about the second act, if the new exit gave him time to change back to the Charles Dickens costume he wore as narrator. Barnes looked a little startled, maybe even a little hurt. Beth assumed he was used to a more moony-eyed version of the morning after. "Yeah," he said. "Sure. We'll find out today."

The Cratchit children had homework spread on the floor: Wyatt, whose emaciated frame was perfect for Tiny Tim; Liberty, a tenth grader with a fierce crush on Barnes; and Micah, who'd played Tiny Tim just four years ago. Soledad was small and squeaky enough to play Martha, the oldest Cratchit.

Here was Aunt Jacqui, glasses pushed up into the mess of her hair, shirt smeared. She said, "I am losing my mind." She'd taken inventory last night, but now the long green cape for the Ghost of Christmas

Future was missing. Fezziwig's shoes were gone. Scrooge's porridge bowl, his top hat, Martha Cratchit's sewing. Kostas planned to station his biggest college kid, Double Denis, by one prop table. He'd stand at the other himself.

Backstage, Tim whispered to Beth at every opportunity. "Could it be Kostas?" he said. "Could Kostas be jealous of Barnes? Like, is he mad at you?"

"Kostas is in love with Soledad."

"Still. Didn't he have a thing with you once? Maybe it's like an alpha male deal."

Beth looked across the stage and into the other wing where Kostas stood guard, picking his ear. "It couldn't be the kids. They weren't here."

"It's someone who lives in the building. Right? It's someone with keys."

The other adult cast members, the ones from town, were unlikely suspects as well. Palmer the retired lawyer, playing Fezziwig; A.J. from the bank, playing Bob Cratchit's brother and other small parts. They were both so tired at the end of rehearsals that Beth couldn't imagine them lurking around the building an extra hour just to make off with props.

Tim's face was flushed, and he adjusted his ponytail again and again. He was thrilled, she saw, in the true sense of the word. To be honest, she was, too. Who were they, as actors, but people who manufactured and played at excitement every night of the week? And here came a real mystery, a real drama. If she weren't exhausted from staying up with Barnes, she might have met Tim's energy level. They might have grasped each other's arms and jumped up and down.

That night, as she brushed her teeth, she looked in the mirror and saw an empty spot on the shelf behind her. It took a minute to remember what had been there: the candle shaped like a water lily. It was old and caked in dust, and she'd only lit it once. She looked on the floor and behind the toilet and even under the sink. She concocted an elaborate scenario where Barnes had knocked it on the floor, and was so embarrassed to have broken her candle that he flushed the pieces down the toilet. But she knew that wasn't it. She felt sick and electrified at once. She washed her face and then walked through the apartment.

Her jewelry was still there, and her wallet. The little dragon statue by the stereo. She went to her bedroom. Barnes was never there alone, but she'd been half-asleep when he left, and it was dark. His glass of water still sat on the nightstand. The photo of her father, though—a parrot on his arm at the Disney World bird show right before the cancer, the little pewter frame—that was gone.

There were two more days, two more rehearsals, till opening night. In the women's dressing room, Soledad gave a report: "So he overlapped with Meg Pemberton for five years," she said. "They aren't close, but sometimes when she's back in New York for an opening, she'll drop by the set."

Liberty, pinning up her hair at the mirror, squealed. "I bet he has pictures of her!"

Phyllis said, "Have you noticed he never mentions his mother?"

Liberty said, "My English teacher grew up watching *Splendor of Love*. What if some of his New York friends come to the show?"

"No," Beth said, because she could see Liberty had her hopes up. "Not here. Not going to happen."

It was technically Thanksgiving but no one had plans, not even Barnes. There was some vague talk of sushi.

Backstage, Beth hooked a finger under Barnes's suspender and said, an inch from his ear, "Come visit again tonight." Why this should be her instinct, she couldn't fathom. But her later justification went something like this: When you have a suspect, you want him in custody. You want to question him, whether or not he knows he's being questioned. She could smell him now, musk and makeup and sweat. He said, "Yeah. Let's do that." His lips brushed her forehead as he turned back to the stage.

She poured them each a glass of red wine. Barnes took two sips, then set his glass down and didn't touch it again. Beth said, "I haven't gotten to know you very well."

He grinned and did a fake chin stroke. Of course he thought she was falling for him, that she'd brought him here to peer deep into his soul. And maybe she had, but not in the way he expected. "I'm a pretty normal guy," he said.

"Do you think you'll ever go back to New York?"

"Too soon to tell. I grew up here, though. I like the weather."

Maybe it was the mention of weather that sent Beth into overdrive. She wasn't going to sit here listening to chit-chat. She said, "Isn't there stuff you miss? Like, doesn't everyone in New York have a shrink? Don't you miss your shrink?"

He laughed as if she'd simultaneously charmed him and scared him. "I underestimated you. You're a firecracker."

Beth said, "I take it back. I don't think you *do* have a shrink."

"Why?"

"You're unable to talk about yourself."

He ran his finger down her neck and seemed to attempt some kind of hypnotizing trick with his eyes. "You know, your skin is perfect."

"Case in point."

She slept with him—what was the harm, as long as she didn't leave him alone?—and tried again afterward, when he was tired and bare-chested and theoretically more vulnerable.

She said, "I think everyone's basically deranged. Don't you? I mean, when I was little I would push my sister into walls. And I'm afraid of microwaves. I have to leave the room if the microwave is on, because I think it's trying to irradiate me. That's what I want to know about you. What brand of crazy you are."

"I'm boring," he said. "Is that a brand of crazy?"

"It might be. I'm pretty sure it is."

Tim had called a meeting. Three PM in the green room, before the final rehearsal (an early one, so they could head down to promote the play at the tree lighting ceremony in town). Kostas glared—not just at Tim, but all of them—leaning against the wall. He had things to do, a scrim to fix, missing light gels to replace. His crew was there, five guys from the community college, too techy to care about missing costumes, too scared of Kostas to dream of pulling pranks. Aunt Jacqui sat on the couch with her face in her hands, glasses hanging down her back on their chain. The actors: Soledad on DeShawn's lap, Phyllis on the piano bench. Palmer the lawyer and A.J. from the bank. Wyatt with his mom, Liberty and Micah without theirs. De Shawn's Dave, even, and Tim's Len, over by the door, just because they lived here. Blair, the college girl from the ticket office. Barnes looked uncomfortable in the blue chair. But then, it was a really uncomfortable chair.

Tim stood in the middle of the room, turning slowly. Theater in the round. He said, "If you want the show to fail, if you want the theater to close, this is the way. The collection bucket is gone, the Christmas goose is gone. Soledad, your whole Fan costume is gone."

"And my wallet," Aunt Jacqui said. "Don't forget my wallet."

"I don't even know what to say anymore. Props and costumes will be locked in my car overnight. Don't complain if they smell like smoke."

Aunt Jacqui let out a sort of sob.

Soledad said, "Can I point something out?" She didn't wait. "Whoever's doing this isn't suddenly going to confess everything to the entire group. This is a waste of time. Some of us need to rest."

Tim ignored her. "We can call the police, but they'll mess everything up."

Phyllis cleared her throat, and they knew from long experience that she'd keep doing it until they were all looking at her, so they turned quickly. Beth even forced herself to fold her hands in her lap and lean forward. "There's something obvious we're overlooking," Phyllis said. "The one person with keys who is *not* in this room is that librarian."

Because it seemed relevant, Beth told them the librarian had seemed jumpy. She didn't tell them about her own apartment, to which Lucy wouldn't have a key. Maybe it was a red herring, after all. She checked Barnes's reaction. He was nodding and chattering with as much interest as the rest of them.

Tim said, "This is fucking ridiculous." But then he unclipped the ring of keys from his belt. "She doesn't get home till five-thirty. Who's coming?"

Phyllis wanted to go, and of course so did Beth. They talked Barnes into coming too. Len volunteered to stand guard in the hall, pretending to fix his doormat. Everyone else got back to work, and Soledad promised to help Aunt Jacqui sew replacement pieces. DeShawn would drive to Target for sadly un-Victorian props.

Tim knocked on Lucy's door, and when he was sure the apartment was empty, the four of them walked in. Len, in the hall, sang "Smoke Gets in Your Eyes." If he stopped, it would be a sign. Barnes hung back a little, bemused but along for the ride. Beth whispered, "You don't think badly of us, do you?" She was baiting him. If he was as innocent as he looked, she wanted him to grin at her, to admit that this was fun. She wanted a crack in the façade. And if it was his fault, she wanted him stung by the irony of it all.

"No," he said. And there was no hint of either exuberance or guilt. "You gotta do what you gotta do."

Beth walked ahead and took in the apartment. Stacks of books along the walls, but no shelves. An antique coffee table with an open box of crackers and a few magazines. A tiny television. There was something haphazard and temporary about the whole place.

"There's nothing on the walls," she finally said. "That's what's so creepy. Hasn't she been here a few years?"

Phyllis came out of the kitchen. "She has nice appliances. You know she's not a real librarian. She just works at the library."

"What does that even mean?" Beth said.

"Kind of like we're not a real theater."

Beth opened the cupboard under the sink. She looked in the coat closet. Lucy's bed, in the back room, was just a mattress on the floor. There wasn't much to search.

She realized a part of her had really hoped, really expected, to find the missing props there. Aprons and candlesticks and wigs and pipes, all surrounding the rubber Christmas goose. Some strange shrine born of jealousy or psychosis.

Tim said, "Are we satisfied? Do we feel sufficiently horrible now?"

They gathered in the living room, where Barnes had been standing alone. Beth saw him touch the pocket of his jacket, checking something. She wanted to turn him upside down and shake everything out. Every pilfered scrap, every ticket stub, every coin, every toothpick. She scanned the room, but she couldn't possibly know what was missing. Barnes gave her a look she might have described as imploring—but then he didn't know she was on to him. So what was the look, then? She examined the last edge of it. Coy. Conspiratorial. Apologetic.

DeShawn had found decent candlesticks at Target, and a porridge bowl, and new wine glasses for the Cratchits' table. Best of all, he'd convinced the owner of the hardware store to loan him the plastic turkey from the display in the window. It was the wrong bird, ridiculously large and rigid, but Beth held her tongue. The final rehearsal was not a time for complaints.

Soledad and Aunt Jacqui had sewn a new handkerchief for Bob Cratchit, a new green cape for Christmas Future, a decent nightcap for Scrooge. The new aprons were fine. Beth didn't know Mrs. Cratchit's dress was missing till she was presented with a new one—her dress from Vanya, with the brooch removed. It was too formal, and far too rich, with a high, lacy neck and puffed sleeves. Maybe Jacqui could give

106

it a lower neckline by tomorrow night. At least a tattered shawl. But then she looked at Aunt Jacqui, at the red streaks on her neck, where she must have been scratching compulsively. She walked into the bathroom to keep herself from saying anything.

Backstage, DeShawn whispered: "What if Jacqui's doing it herself? Maybe it's a cry for help."

Everything onstage was askew. The props were wrong, of course, but the timing too, and Kostas's guys missed half the light cues. In the first act, the Cratchit home suddenly plunged into darkness. Liberty, seated at the dining table, shrieked, and Wyatt started laughing. Soledad got out her next line, and then Wyatt remembered himself and asked, in his Tiny Tim voice, if his father would take him to watch the ice skaters. Beth and Barnes were standing behind the children, and unconsciously, she had reached out to steady herself with a hand on his chest. She didn't know she'd done it till he backed away. The lights came back then, and Barnes had a line, and then Micah, but Micah was silent, confused.

In the time between the light and the silence, she saw again the same look Barnes had given her upstairs in the librarian's apartment. But this time, accompanied by his ducking away from her hand, she finally understood. It was pity. He thought she cared deeply about him, that she was in over her head, and he wanted to let her down easy. She remembered, in college, calling a boy she'd had a fling with—just to invite him to a party, not to propose marriage!—and he'd said, in the most cringing voice possible, "I actually have *company* right now." If you could have boiled that sentence down into a syrup, and put that syrup in a bottle of eye drops, and squeezed it right into someone's eyes: that was the horrible, horrible look Barnes was giving her.

Beth opened her mouth, thinking she'd say something to cover Micah's flub, but she must have been holding too much in today—because what came bubbling out like magma was directed at Barnes. "You need to put it back," she said. Barnes stared, and she could feel the three children and Soledad, at the table behind her, turning and wondering where she was taking this scene, how they could help, what had gone wrong. "I don't know what you took from the librarian's apartment, but you need to *put it back*. If you want to screw over the theater, if you want to ruin the production, that's one level—but she doesn't even *know* you. She doesn't know we were in there." And then, just to hurt him: "*Jason.*"

Barnes stuck his arms in the air as if she were pointing a gun. He laughed and looked out at the empty seats. Backstage right, Beth could see Tim and DeShawn and Phyllis and Palmer the lawyer. She could see the silhouettes of the guys up in the light box.

Barnes said, "This is uncalled for." He took a step back.

She expected Tim to stop her. She waited for Phyllis to tell her to shut up. She realized, when they didn't, what she ought to have known all along: It was as obvious to them as it was to her. They all knew. They all knew it all along. They had just each, for their own strange, small reasons, kept quiet.

Barnes must have realized it too. A good actor can always judge his audience.

What he said next, Beth wasn't sure she heard correctly. It wasn't till they'd gathered in Soledad's apartment late that night, repeating his words to each other until they were certain he'd said what he'd said—only then did she start to put meaning to them. At the time, all she could decode, of the syllables leaving his mouth, was that he was deeply unwell. That something foreign—some drug or chemical or messenger of neurological imbalance—was in his veins and in his eyes and in the strange tilt of his head. That he would not, under any circumstances, be playing the role of Bob Cratchit tomorrow night.

What he said was, "You're not real. I made you up."

Beth could think of nothing but to repeat herself with authority. She said, "You need to give it back." On instinct, she angled her body between his and the children.

Barnes reached out one long finger and poked her, hard, on the shoulder. "Did I make up that sex, or did I make up all the sex ever?"

He poked her again, on the other shoulder. His whole body wobbled, and she thought he might fall over. For a moment, it seemed he would vomit.

Kostas shuffled from backstage, more ticked off than scared. "Okay, buddy," he said, and Beth felt something drain from her head, a terror she hadn't realized the extent of. "You want the hospital, or you want to go home?" His hands were out, ready to react to Barnes.

"I was rearranging the set," Barnes said, or really, whined. "You think the set stops at the edge of the stage? I knew this place the second I saw it. I knew I made it up. You," he said, and he pointed at Kostas. "You I didn't invent."

"Nope. And I'm the guy who's escorting you from the building."

"When I walk out of here," Barnes said, and he looked around with something like hatred. He stared at Liberty and Micah the longest. "When I walk out of here. *Puff.*"

And he did just that—he walked out, with Kostas and Double Denis trailing—but none of them vanished in a puff of smoke, if that's indeed what he'd meant.

Much later that night, Soledad would Google "kleptomania" and announce that it didn't go together with delusion. Tim, reading over her shoulder, argued this just meant kleptomania was the diagnosis when it was *only* theft, when the theft wasn't part of some larger psychosis.

They would sit around Soledad's living room watching the *Splendor of Love* tapes that had arrived from her grandmother. They were out of order, just random episodes, the Barnes of twelve years ago looking tanner but less chiseled, the Barnes of last year somehow smaller and flatter than the man they'd known. But what could they possibly learn from his lines of recited dialogue? They'd watch a scene where he consoled a woman in a police department. They'd watch him hide money in a hollow book. They'd watch someone shoot him dead. Then, as the killer walked away, they'd watch him open one slow, vengeful eye.

At 1AM, the volume down, they would go through the contents of his duffel bag again. He'd left it in the green room, under his black leather jacket. There was Liberty's calculator, and the inkwell (his own prop!) and a phone bill with the librarian's name. There was half a bag of marijuana that not even Tim wanted, on the grounds that it might be laced with something hallucinogenic. There was a bottle of Vicodin, and gym shoes. His wallet must have been with the street clothes Kostas had shoved him into.

Tim would say, "Beth, I'm glad you said it. The next time I curse you and your big mouth, remind me: I love you, and I'm glad you said it. Because no one else was going to."

Soledad would give a fake moan. "Beth broke the soap star."

But all this would happen long after midnight, after they should have been in bed, after they'd had hours to digest how thoroughly they'd been played for fools.

Right then, as Kostas and Double Denis left with Barnes and reappeared a minute later saying they'd locked the doors, everything was still adrenaline and confusion. Tim clapped his hands together and came onstage in his Marley costume and said, "Okay. We need a Cratchit. DeShawn, what's Dave doing right now?"

DeShawn texted Dave, who gamely ran downstairs and suited up.

Dave couldn't stop sniffing the sleeve of the costume, as if it would tell him what was wrong with Barnes. They decided he could carry a stack of papers in the office scenes, and something that looked like a bill in the home scenes, until his lines were memorized. "Just for a couple nights," he promised. "I'll do nothing but study!"

They tried to rehearse, but it was perfunctory, mostly for the benefit of Dave and the lighting crew. Beth was still shaking, well into the second act. She led Dave around the table in a simple, tripping version of the dance she'd rehearsed with Barnes. Dave was taller than Barnes, with a belly that didn't suit a Cratchit, but he was here and he was kind, and he believed Beth existed. All points in his favor.

And finally Tim said, "It's time." Beth struggled to remember the reason they'd rehearsed early to begin with: The tree-lighting. "Without Barnes—" he said, "let's just have the Fezziwig scene. Then Wyatt can come out and do 'God bless us.' Just that. We have to go."

Downtown, they wove through masses of bright-hatted children, parents with coffee, the Girl Scout troop that had decorated the bottom half of the tree with birdseed stars, the kids from the high school choir with yellow robes pulled over their coats. The actors assembled in front of the tree. Tim rang the hand bell (a Target replacement for a gorgeous old one they'd never get back) and announced that they were the George Spelvin Players, that tickets were still available, that they wished everyone a joyous season.

Kostas started the CD, and the Fezziwig party began. DeShawn as Scrooge showed up with Soledad, the Ghost of Christmas Past. The rest of them laughed and danced and shouted a few lines out of order. Only a quarter of the crowd watched. The high school choir was already gathering by the risers, and people were still waiting to buy roasted chestnuts from the Elks Club.

The crowd was more visible than it would have been from a stage—no footlights sealed off the fictional world from the real—and Beth could make out individual faces. She scanned the crowd for Barnes, worried he'd show up shouting, show up with a gun. He wasn't there. But oh, God: The librarian stood at the front of the crowd, an encouraging grin, hands around her Starbucks cup. Beth knew that if she looked that direction she'd lose it, fall on the ground and confess everything. Who were they to feel victimized by a psychotic thief when they themselves, under their own delusions, had violated her home? Had fingered her belongings, seen her naked walls? Someone can invade your life, can rearrange your world, and you don't even know it. So Beth ignored the blocking and turned back toward Dave.

Right then the microphone by the risers turned on with a horrible shriek. It stopped, then started again. The choir director leaned into it and said, "Sorry, folks." The crowd laughed and turned that way, and in a moment the Spelvin Players had fully lost the crowd. Voices swelled around them, and a child ran right between Soledad and Beth to touch the tree. Liberty swallowed her next line. They glanced to Tim. It was the second time in one night that their little balloon had been completely punctured, and it was too much. Soledad whimpered—actually whimpered—and put her head on Beth's shoulder.

But Tim had that Manic Tim Look on his face. He ran up to DeShawn and took both his hands, and said, in his loudest voice: "Ebenezer. Ebenezer! I love you, I've always loved you! It's always been you and only you. And you don't have to love me back. But I can die happy knowing I said it."

DeShawn said, "I have always depended on the kindness of ghosts."

Phyllis stopped her jig to call, "Marley should have died hereafter! There would have been a time for such a word!"

And they were off, the Spelvin players, on a spaceship of their own manufacture. Only a few heads turned back, and then a couple more. One older man looked particularly amused, elbowing his wife. The librarian kept smiling, confused but supportive. Beth understood that the goal, from this point on, was chaos rather than publicity. *It's not that you're ignoring us; it's that we're laughing at you.*

Beth said, "All Russia is our orchard!"

Micah—when had his voice grown so deep?—dropped to his knees and shouted "Stellllla!"

At the same time that Beth was reveling in the strangeness of it, in the sort of Artaud-invades-a-tree-lighting-ness of it, she felt deeply dizzy, like something fundamental had come unglued. Maybe this was the way Barnes experienced the whole world: a bunch of actors reciting made-up lines, out of order, out of context. She saw the closest people in the crowd, the ones still watching, or watching again, move their lips, and she guessed what they were saying: "I don't get it." "Doesn't the one with the ponytail look like what's-his-name? The tennis player?" "Everything's about sports with you." And none of it made any more sense, really, than the nonsense coming from her own mouth.

The lovely vacancy of memorized lines had always been the escape part of acting, for Beth: being the empty vessel from which someone else's words flowed. The litany of it. But if she ever went off the deep end, if she ever fell as far as Barnes—she could see how everything might come to sound like a disembodied quotation, how every tree might be painted scenery. And she, too, might then want to take control in strange and illicit ways. She might poke people to test if they were real. She might steal the world's trinkets to create, if not order out of the chaos, at least her own small chaos within the larger one.

The dance (what was left of it) swung her from A.J. to Dave.

Tim, in his best Lady Bracknell drawl: "The good ended happily and the bad unhappily. That is what fiction *means*!"

Wyatt, either joining the fun or trying to do what he'd been told: "God bless us, every one!"

Beth noticed a boy with glasses, watching with utter glee and tapping his fingers together. He was ten or eleven. Standing on his actual tip-toes, as if this were not only the most exciting thing he'd ever seen but also the funniest, and the most heroic. They'd kept the dialogue between themselves to that point, but Beth found herself approaching the boy as the others kept chattering and dancing, the crowd filtering right through them now. She said to him, "We are such stuff as dreams are made on."

He answered back: "I don't think we're in Kansas anymore." A grin.

"We must cultivate our garden," she said.

The tall man behind the boy tousled his hair, sort of strained-jovial, and said, "Hey buddy, we don't want to miss the lighting." Even though the tree was right behind Beth.

"You know what would be awesome?" the boy said to Beth, ignoring him. "It would really be incredibly awesome if it turned out they were lighting the tree *on fire*."

The man gave a quick chuckle and drew his son back into the crowd.

"Yes, Torvald," Beth said to no one. "I've changed."

When the choir climbed the risers, the Spelvin Players gave up—no finale, no bows—and joined the audience. They caught their breath and listened, quiet and respectful, aside from Tim pointing at DeShawn on "round yon virgin." Soledad broke out a flask, and Beth tugged at her lace collar, tight and ridiculous. They were ridiculous people, putting on a ridiculous play. She'd known this yesterday, but she knew it more starkly today.

The conductor was short and enthusiastic. This was clearly the biggest night of his year. Beth watched the singers, their faces glowing from the candles they held. They looked so earnest, so untrammeled. She was projecting, of course. Surely some of these singers came from terrible homes. One of the altos was probably pregnant. Still, she felt exhausted in comparison, as if something had passed her by. As if her whole life—not just the show—were a sort of make-believe she'd suddenly grown far too old for.

At the front of the crowd, the librarian sipped her Starbucks and closed her eyes.

Perhaps, after all her efforts to reign herself in, it was true that Beth's greatest talent in life was to tell people what they ought to know. And in this moment she told herself, pointedly, the difference between someone like her and someone like Barnes Harlow. The difference was: Barnes Harlow looked down at the crack in the universe and fell right in. She saw the crack and stepped quickly over.

Or at least she could pretend so, until the panic had passed. And she was a fabulous pretender.

Around her, the sing-along had started. "Winter Wonderland" and "Rudolph the Red-Nosed Reindeer." The louder she sang, the less she cared. Barnes was the one who didn't exist, she decided. They'd made him up, all of them together. He was a character on a soap opera. A figment. A ghost.

Just beyond the librarian stood the boy who wanted to light things on fire. Hadn't Beth been like that once? Hadn't she intended to set the whole world on fire? Hadn't they all?

Tomorrow they would open to a full house. They would acknowledge nothing missing.

Nominated by Pleiades

THE REVOLT
OF THE TURTLES

by STEPHEN DUNN

from THE SOUTHERN REVIEW

On gray forgetful mornings like this
sea turtles would gather in the shallow waters
of the Gulf to discuss issues of self-presentation
and related concerns like, If there were a God
would he have a hard shell and a retractable head,
and whether speed on land
was of any importance to a good swimmer.

They knew that tourists needed to placate
their children with catchy stories, and amuse
themselves with various cruelties,
such as turning turtles over on their backs
and watching their legs wriggle.
So the turtles formed a committee to address

How to Live among People Who among
Other Atrocities Want to Turn You into Soup.

The committee was also charged with wondering
if God would mind a retelling of their lives,
one in which sea turtles
were responsible for all things
right-minded and progressive, and men
and women for poisoning the water.

The oldest sea turtle among them knew
that whoever was in control of the stories
controlled all the shoulds and should-nots.
But he wasn't interested in punishment,
only ways in which power could bring about
fairness and decency. And when he finished speaking
in the now-memorable and ever-deepening

waters of the Gulf, all the sea turtles
began to chant, *Only fairness, only decency.*

Nominated by Jane Hirshfield, David Jauss, Dan Masterson, BJ Ward

IF YOU CAN'T SAY ANYTHING NICE, WRITE A ONE-STAR REVIEW

by JANE LANCELLOTTI

from NARRATIVE

"This book sucked!" "Vastly overrated!" "Boring!" "Tedious!" "Waste of time!" "Just shoot me!" They were all screaming at him—I mean at my friend, whom I'll call Howard, who got great reviews in the *New York Times* and the *Washington Post* for his latest novel but who couldn't stop the shouting from Internet reviewers, whose inspirational and cheerfully inventive names all sounded like JerkWadJunior, Eff-You69, and DarthReader. The whole negativity thing was getting to him, big-time.

"Have no fear," I told Howard. I'd monitor the Internet. I'd take time off from my one, singular guilty pleasure in watching footage of celebrities leaving restaurants on tmz.com and check his reviews instead. It'd be fun. I'd spare him the screaming meemies, I said. Let him know if the snoozers and slammers lived up to their names. That was the plan, anyway, until on my watch Howard got his first one-star review, and I got mad. I got so mad I scrolled obsessively through reader reviews of literary masterpieces that have stood the test of time. What did the Howie-haters have to say about *Jane Eyre* and *Pride and Prejudice* or any of the ones you wish you could read for the first time? God help me, I opened the door onto those reviews the way you might peer into the refrigerator after midnight to see what's lurking behind the cheese. With some appetite but not expecting much, I began with reviews of *Pride and Prejudice* because who, after all, would take on Jane Austen?

Answer: forty tremendously bored and really, *really* disappointed readers.

"I felt the same annoyance as when sitting next to a loudmouthed

116

idiot in a train," wrote one of *Pride and Prejudice*. "Not worth reading," another whined because "the storyline is boring" and "the characters are not well developed." Hold your ponies: Were we talking about the same Austen, the quintessential novelist of social manners, the genial satirist?

I called Howard.

"How bad is it?" he asked.

"Let me put things in perspective," I said and read him a thought-provoking review of Shakespeare. "Nothing earth-shattering on jealosy" [*sic*] in *Othello*. I skipped through the centuries to William Gaddis, who uses "so much adjective" [*sic*] in *The Recognitions* and is "so full of himself" as to be "not worth reading."

"Point taken," he said. "You can stop now."

But I couldn't. George Eliot, Edith Wharton, Willa Cather—no author dodged readers who were indifferent to literary masterpieces and offered such evaluations as this one of *My Ántonia*: "I've seen trash on the curb with more plot than this." Meanwhile, Howard received a one-star along the lines of "not worth the paper it was written on."

"The highest Criticism," Oscar Wilde wrote in his famous essay "The Critic as Artist," "is more creative than creation." What he meant, of course, is that the riches of the imagination are as crucial in judging art as they are in creating it. Notice how the godlike capital *C* for Criticism is working here. How it makes you wish that Wilde himself could show up next to the reviewer's desktop and cover the whole darn keyboard with his paisley cravat to prevent the cynic from posting that he would rather scoop out an eye with a rusty spoon than read *Great Expectations*.

Through the ages, there have been major thinkers, such as Matthew Arnold, whose fluency and insight elevated the ways in which we talk about art. Only now, instead of Arnold of Great Britain, we have Arnie from Massapequa, who misguidedly equates *Jane Eyre* with "another of those cheesey love novels written by Danielle Steel."

"It's only a lack of education," Howie said of the Arnies. Or a kind of literary autism in which a reader tries to connect with the classics and can't. It wasn't until I overheard a classroom of MFA writing students reveal to their professor that they were more influenced by the opinions of amateur online reviewers than by those written by acknowledged pros that I realized how truly and righteously screwed we are when people with screen names as ludicrous as old CB handles—Buzbo, Cha-Cha, and GoodBuddy—let you know before you buy To *Kill a Mockingbird* that "it sucked, just like any other book."

The Internet has always held a special place in its big bloggy heart for the cranky and disgruntled. The speed and anonymity of the Web make it irresistible to the one-star reviewer, in much the same way that a blank wall and a can of black spray paint are irresistible to a pissed-off adolescent. The Web is threaded with the complaints and disparagements of people who feel compelled to remark on the "timidity" of steak sauce or to cast a vote on whether Cindy Crawford has (A) good genes or (B) good docs or (C) both. And while it's true that there are also thoughtful, well-considered, *well-written* comments online, there may never have been a meaner, less inhibited group of haters than one-star book reviewers. Consider the reviewer who would "rather have a coffee enema" than read *To the Lighthouse;* another who would "rather slit [his] wrists than read one more page" of *Madame Bovary;* and another who writes of *Wuthering Heights*: "Quick! Gouge out my eyes!!!" Why must readers link violence, enemas, blood, and blinding with the act of reading?

One way to climb inside the mind of the one-star reviewer is to take him up on his invitation to have a look at his other reviews. What else is a guy from Los Angeles ripping apart besides Doctorow's *Ragtime?* Why, it's packing tape, a product he hails with five stars because he can rip it apart with his fingers. Or his canines. And what about the singularly unappeasable critic who not only is "done with" Hemingway after reading *The Sun Also Rises* but also hated the lip-piercing set by GlitZ JewelZ, complained about the Velvet Kitten Satin Booty, and couldn't stomach a long curly wig, which, "despite styling, remains a bit lifeless." Oh, yeah. She also condemns Hemingway's prose for remaining "a bit lifeless." Wigs and art—can they really be the same? Has online reviewing become the nicest possible way to kill time while on hold with the Better Business Bureau?

"It all stems from the same thing," says Sherry Turkle in her book *Alone Together: Why We Expect More from Technology and Less from Each Other* (a 305-page work that received a one-star for being 299 pages too long). "When we are face to face, we are inhibited from aggression by the presence of another face, another person. We're aware that we're with a human being." That got me wondering: What if another of those anonymous reviewers found herself face-toface with last year's National Book Award winner, Louise Erdrich? Would the reviewer have accused Erdrich of being a weird older woman writing a smutty page-turner from the perspective of a thirteen-year-old boy?

A person venting gratuitous irritation by giving a one-star rating to

Toni Morrison for her "poorly constructed" novel *Sula* finds confirmation in the echoes of fellow one-star commentators that come in a barrage of "I totally agree!" and "Your [*sic*] so right," fulfilling the quest for at least one fellow negativo to be listening and agreeing. The reviewer who never finished reading *Pride and Prejudice* but disparaged the novel anyway finds a chorus of agree-ers. "Plot?? What plot??" (one question mark being insufficient for her disdain). Same for the guy who couldn't follow the story of the impotent Jake Barnes in *The Sun Also Rises* but reviewed the book, without a hint of wit or irony, under a pseudonym inspired by male genitalia. "This is Ernest Hemingway????" he grumbles. "What is the point???"

Who are these people? Are they online versions of the bully who kicks over bicycles? Or the kid who gets his bicycle kicked over? Or are they, more likely, past-hopeful writers whose thwarted ambitions propelled a spite-filled review of Philip Roth? Roth is blamed for being "established" and "no longer bound to be at his very best, because the work will be published one way or another." One Roth detractor hints that if she were to write a novel, she would deliver a far better result than *American Pastoral*.

My pal Howard waxed poetic. "What we have," he noted, "is a subculture of literary vandals who have replaced the light of intellect with the ruinous glow of a single emoji star from which no author can hide."

If there's one thing the Internet has taught us, it's that it reflects all of society: those interested in a true exchange of ideas and those who relish the click-based titillation of a nasty comment directed at the immortals. "Shakespeare is s*** y duz every1 think he iz so gr8 like wat did he evr do 4 man kind." Authors beware.

Nominated by Narrative

BASEMENT DELIVERY

by EMILY SKILLINGS

from JUBILAT

Having lived so long without one, we forgot
what a basement felt like—how it seemed
to the carrier(s), to the inhabitant(s),
the structure(s), that there was an *underneathness*
to all that daily interaction and exchange—
i.e. an empty teacup hovering just above a pool.

On the day the basement was delivered
pink air made its way underneath the canopy.
Ten strong women arrived to pump it through the ground,
evicting domestic earthworms, telepathic moss
and scarce minerals. An important rivulet was rerouted.
The sub-story attached and crystallized like in that dream.

The whole procedure only took a few minutes.
In the presence of a basement, our history was whisked,
indexed into a ladder, roped down—our kidneys and lungs
wrung out. We stood around slowly. We were cooled
and stored. In the parlor, at first blush of waking,
our usual words and arrangements seemed normal enough,

but then that lower sound, that kept air, funneled up to us.
A collection freed itself. It was *again* again. Leave no stone already.

Nominated by Jubilat

NAMING HAPPINESS

by MONTE REEL

from ORION

Almost every day during the fall that I turned forty, I walked to a park in Buenos Aires where a C-shaped pond cradled a large flower garden. A white, trellised Grecian bridge, looking like something that might be replicated in miniature on a wedding cake, spanned the water, leading pedestrians into the blooms. Paths of crushed brick meandered through the bushes and traced the pond's inner shoreline. More than a thousand varieties of roses and carnations colored the garden. All was trimmed, labeled, composed.

On weekdays I visited the park alone, but on Saturday mornings I brought my three-year-old daughter, Sofia. She liked my company because I carried stale bread to feed the coscoroba swans and white-winged coots. I liked her company because she didn't mock me when I stared at birds and trees and tried to match them with pictures in field guides. I probably should have sagged with shame: I was fast becoming a cliché, the Lover of Nature, one of those guys with the boots and the new field glasses who'd lost the ability to mask his low-grade OCD. But Sofia didn't judge. Maybe watching someone struggle to attach the correct names to common objects seemed perfectly natural to her, since she spent a lot of her time doing pretty much the same thing. She demanded no explanations, which was convenient, because I wouldn't have been able to come up with any.

One Saturday morning while we walked that waterside path, my mind straying, I felt a tap on my shoulder. Something random, or so it seemed, had trespassed into this highly ordered landscape. It was a falling leaf, riding a gentle, spiraling current to the ground, scuttling to a stop. It was yellow and freckled with brown. The edges curled upward. It looked sort of like an elfin canoe.

A linden leaf. *Tilia americana*. I know this only because I looked it up.

The linden is not an exotic tree. Maybe I'd be embarrassed to admit I hadn't recognized it if Henry David Thoreau, that diligent rhapsodist of falling leaves, hadn't been mystified by the same species while paddling the Concord River with his brother in the late summer of 1839. At the time, he hadn't yet become the sage of Walden; he was still a relative dilettante in nature who couldn't tell the difference between poison sumac and poison oak. The unknown tree sent Thoreau to his reference library, where he grounded himself in its history.

He found poetry there. The ancient Greeks believed that a linden tree had once transformed itself into Philyra, the mythological nymph who had taught humanity how to make paper. Philyra was the goddess of writing and a goddess of beauty.

"As we sailed under this canopy of leaves," Thoreau wrote of his first linden, "we saw the sky through its chinks, and, as it were, the meaning and idea of the tree stamped in a thousand hieroglyphics on the heavens."

What he read in that tree, I think, was a desperate plea for attention on the part of Nature itself: *See me, Henry! Listen to me! If you learn my vocabulary, you can decode meaning on the surface of almost anything!*

My linden leaf wasn't nearly so articulate or exclamatory. After authenticating the species, I tossed the leaf in the water. It landed just right, boat-wise, and drifted away from the bank for a couple seconds. Then it caught a shifting wind and headed back to the shore, close to Sofia. She was squatting stone still, seemingly lost in her own thoughts. She stared at a stripe of sunlight that sparkled atop the wind-stirred ripples in the middle of the pond.

"What is *that* called?" she asked. She must have watched me pin-down the name of the leaf. Maybe she wanted to play the same game.

I tracked her squinting gaze. "You mean that stripe on the water?" I asked. "The sparkles?"

"What is that *called*?"

"Not sure," I said, too casually. "I think it's just called sparkles."

She sighed, theatrically. "No it's *not*." She'd recognized the lazy disregard in my answer, and I recognized her frustration: it was the maddening sense that the world is speaking a language we haven't fully learned, and no one else seems to realize that this is a serious problem.

I was the formula-fed baby of an era of technological triumph, raised on sitcoms, videogames, aspartame, and Yellow #5. Mine was an age of specialization that actively discouraged the kind of intellectual leap-frogging that drove naturalists like Thoreau to try to unite science and spirit, to reconcile the romantic and the empirical. I always feared over-stepping my bounds. I absorbed the message that "nature" (the very word quivered with vulnerability if left unprotected by scare quotes) should be left to the experts—the mycologists, the lichenologists, the ichthyologists, the myrmecologists, the trichopterologists, the cetologists, the cnidariologists (it's real, I swear). Attempting a generalized grasp of natural phenomena, without dedicating oneself to a tightly focused area of study, betrayed a pitiful naïveté. Nature was like my television set, or my car, or my laptop: I relied on it, had no idea how it really worked, and didn't need to know. I could spend every minute of my life trying to learn the names of all of the organisms within walking distance of my front door, and I'd manage only a superficial fraction. So what was the point? Why stress a mind already bombarded with too much information?

This logic had formed an alliance with a fear that hid somewhere in my hindbrain: knowing too much might kill whatever magic remained in the world. Beauty in nature, I believed, was delicate, like the lightly dusted wings of a butterfly. Pinning an identifying label onto it might mar the specimen, draining it of its vitality, leaving only a hollow and meaningless shell.

Experience supported this hunch. As a second grader in central Illinois, I sometimes spent my school recess periods sifting through the gravel under the playground's swing set, trying to find Indian beads. They were tiny, segmented, cylindrical rocks that, I was told, had been handcrafted as jewels by the native tribes of the Great Plains—the Shawnee, the Kickapoo, the Sauk. Indian beads were moderately hard to find. But a half-hour of searching on the playground usually uncovered a couple. In class, I kept a small collection of them in the groove that was designed to keep pencils from rolling off my desktop.

They possessed a sort of magic, those beads. With one in hand, I could

123

imagine that the dull, flat, thoroughly conquered landscape outside was wild and hallowed ground worthy of legend. The perfectly segmented fields that surrounded the school weren't merely corn and soybean farms. They were the battlefields of warring tribes, the sacred sites of ancient rituals, haunted lands of blood and smoke.

When I was older, I did some research to learn more about Indian beads. Those poetic totems that had ennobled a bland world, I discovered, had nothing to do with Indians. The beads are actually fragments of the fossilized stems of segmented crinoids, marine echinoderms that sometime in the nineteenth century were saddled with the name *Delocrinus missouriensis*. They are occasionally called sea lilies. The Indians didn't make them. It is possible, I suppose, that no tribes had set foot on that little patch of land around my school, ever.

Delocrinus missouriensis.

The magic was destroyed in an instant.

Nature writing is a dangerous business. Botch the job and you murder the vitality you're trying to celebrate. All those tiresome descriptions. The inevitable tone of eulogy. The misty spiritualism embedded in every floating cloud. Thoreau nailed it: "The surliness with which the woodchopper speaks of his woods, handling them as indifferently as his axe, is better than the mealy-mouthed enthusiasm of the lover of nature."

That sentence appears in *A Week on the Concord and Merrimack Rivers*, which he published in 1849. But he'd written the same sentence, give or take a word or two, in one of his daily journal entries eight years earlier. I dove into his journal at about the same time I started making my daily pilgrimages to the park in Buenos Aires. Every page, it seemed, was studded with precisely identified sedges and songbirds. Here was a man who, after being stumped by that linden, buckled down with his field guides and eventually was able to identify unseen plants *by their scent when stepped upon*. He greedily collected hard little facts of nature, and when he put them all together they mingled, spawned, evolved, and collectively transformed a small, unremarkable plot of New England soil into an inexhaustible universe. To read the journal was to witness a man *name* a new world into existence. Identification itself was an act of creation.

In the journal, Thoreau monitors his senses closely, and constantly

124

exercises them. Inspired by the writings of painter and art critic John Ruskin, he is determined to see the world in all its colors, not just the primary ones. At one point, Thoreau tries to track down a cyanometer—an instrument that Alexander von Humboldt used during his journeys in South America to distinguish fifty-three distinct shades of blue sky.

The fastidiousness began to rub off on me, particularly during my walks to the rose garden. I began to seek a more incisive language to match my perceptions. I wasn't content to see the crushed-brick pathways as orange, or even burnt-orange; they were *slightly moistened paprika*. The trellised bridge wasn't merely white: I distinguished six different shades of white on its sides, ranging from cream to glittering mica, and its glossy underside swam with greens—shimmering reflections from the dark water below. But the water itself was more than green; it was an Impressionist's unstirred solution of black, ochre, camel, raw umber, myrtle, and teal.

It was exhausting to sustain that level of particularity, but that's really how a lot of those who followed Ruskin saw color, or tried to see it: as combinations of discreet tones. Ruskin (who, incidentally, compiled his own botanical dictionary) encouraged his readers to exercise their eyes by teasing apart all sensations of beauty. The dynamics of water especially beguiled him. In his autobiography he claims that he spent four to five hours every day, from youth until age forty, simply staring at the play of light and color on rivers and wave-tossed seas. When I first read that, I smelled a lie. I didn't believe anyone could spend so much time—fifty thousand hours, more or less—entranced by a glimmering surface. Then I estimated how much time I'd spent staring at a TV or computer screen. My doubts subsided.

Ruskin's mind wasn't empty while he stared. In 1844, when he was twenty-five, he attempted to analyze a sparkling stripe of moonlight reflected upon an otherwise dark sea. The "long line of splendour," he realized, was a function of perspective: the moonlight shone equally upon every square inch of the sea's surface, but it was the position of his eyes that determined the appearance and location of that stripe of dancing light. The seer creates the beauty—it was an idea that had been embalmed into a banal platitude many years before his realization. But it led to another question that common knowledge hadn't answered: why does that splendor seem so splendid?

Thoreau repeated Ruskin's discovery of perspective one summer night at Walden Pond in 1851. "I was startled to see midway in the dark water a bright flamelike, more than phosphorescent light crowning the crests of the wavelets, which at first I mistook for fireflies, and thought even of cucullos," he noted in his journal, referring to a species of luminescent insect that von Humboldt had reported finding in Cuba. They weren't fireflies, of course. Thoreau began casting around for other possibilities, but the phenomenon was madly elusive. To what could he compare the vision, and why did it entrance him? "I thought of St. Elmo's lights and the like," he wrote—but that wasn't quite it, either. At a loss, he threw himself headlong into metaphor. The sparkles were "like so many lustrous burnished coins poured from a bag with inexhaustible lavishness," or like "a myriad little mirrors," or maybe "like a myriad candles everywhere issuing from the waves," or "like some inflammable gas on the surface."

He was groping in vain. Thoreau wrote on for several pages, trying to precisely identify a phenomenon he couldn't quite name.

At the park, Sofia confronted a similar obstacle. "It's like fireworks," she said, dropping a term she often used to refer to anything flame-related. "But it's not fireworks."

I started to think about some of the discreet components that allowed Sofia and me to see that stripe of sparkles. The water, of course, was essential, as was the sunlight. But perhaps most important was the breeze—the same one that had swept the clouds away from the sun, wrinkled the surface of the pond, and nudged the stem of a loose linden leaf from its branch.

And what, in turn, did that breeze depend upon?

The endless possible answers to the question eventually led me to Edward Lorenz, a meteorologist and mathematician who in 1961 was tinkering with a computer model for predicting weather patterns. When entering data into the program, he rounded off 0.506127—the full numerical sequence of one unit of weather data—to 0.506. The slight abbreviation resulted in a completely different climatic scenario. He wrote, "One meteorologist remarked that if the theory were correct, one flap of a seagull's wings could change the course of weather forever." The concept—that the slightest move of a wing could trigger enormous meteorological changes—later lost its connection to the seagull and became known by the more poetic term, "The Butterfly Effect."

If the single beat of a wing held so much potential, just think what the deep, breathy sigh of a three-year-old girl—*What is that called?*—might spark.

I went into overdrive, piecing together long chains of natural causes and effects, discovering a surprising form of pleasure in the act. If I didn't discover physical bridges, I constructed metaphorical ones. This is how a happy mind works. Unity is the norm. Things fall together. The center holds.

But *what*, if anything, does it hold?

A decade after Thoreau's death, George Eliot identified a "pregnant little fact" that, to many readers in the following century, seemed to reveal a fatal flaw in the brand of analogizing intelligence that was so characteristic of all those of the previous era who tried to make sense of the world around them. In *Middlemarch*, Eliot wrote:

> *Your pier-glass or extensive surface of polished steel made to be rubbed by a housemaid, will be minutely and multitudinously scratched in all directions; but place now against it a lighted candle as a centre of illumination, and lo! the scratches will seem to arrange themselves in a fine series of concentric circles round that little sun. It is demonstrable that the scratches are going everywhere impartially and it is only your candle which produces the flattering illusion of a concentric arrangement, its light falling with an exclusive optical selection. These things are a parable. The scratches are events, and the candle is the egoism of any person. . . .*

The center might hold, in other words, but everyone knows that *what* it holds is nothing—a mere metaphor, a romantic illusion, like that stripe of sparkles on water. It's only a cheap trick of perspective; it doesn't really exist, so maybe it cannot, or should not, be named.

Before Eliot articulated her doubts, Thoreau had entertained similar ones, and he dismissed them. "All perception of truth is the detection of an analogy," he wrote. It didn't matter that the individual mind imposed that analogy onto the world, or that the truth might not be graspable at the same time to all human minds. "Facts should only be as the frame to my pictures; they should be material to the mythology which

127

I am writing," he wrote. That sentence is a reminder-to-self of his purpose, and it's repeated often in his journal. He's constantly worried that the incessant accumulation of facts he's compiling will take over his life and, somehow, obscure the truth of it. He's afraid it could tip the balance away from poetry and toward a fatal data overload.

"I fear that the character of my knowledge is from year to year becoming more distinct and scientific; that, in exchange for views as wide as heaven's cope, I am being narrowed down to the field of the microscope," Thoreau confessed to his journal. "I see details, not wholes nor the shadow of the whole. I count some parts, and say, 'I know.'"

It reads almost as an admission of failure—*almost*, but not quite. He wrote that on August 19, 1851, less than twenty-four hours before he identified a violet meadow flower, *Rhexia virginica*, and was inspired to dream of a new taxonomy of human feeling that was as pinpoint precise as botanical language. Suddenly, he had regained his footing—and this balance, this capacity to reconcile warring worldviews, is what sets apart the nature writing of Thoreau from all those mired in the twinned, imprisoning beliefs that objectivity is an impossible illusion and that subjectivity is, at heart, a lie. But to Thoreau, the fact that no two people saw the same shimmering stripe of diamonds on the water didn't limit the power or truth of the phenomenon. It enhanced it.

"To myriad eyes suitably placed," Thoreau wrote, "the whole surface of the pond would be seen to shimmer."

It struck me as an ennobling outlook, and when I pored over his journals that fall, I embraced the idea with fanatical zeal. The whole world—not just our limited little circle of pier-glass—shone with beauty. With such a wide-angled view, maybe I wouldn't have felt let down by facts when I learned that Indian beads were really fossilized sea lilies, or *Delocrinus missouriensis*. Instead, I might have recognized that the truth was infinitely more fanciful than any bogus fairytale I could have dreamed up. Maybe such a perspective would have allowed me to author a new personal mythology, one worthy of Philyra, beloved goddess of writing and beauty, whom the Greeks said was the daughter of Oceanus, the titan who ruled the ancient seas. Maybe the land where I grew up would be infused with as much magic and legend as the lost kingdom of Atlantis. Maybe a sense of wonder could be restored without sacrificing truth.

I come from a place that, once upon a time, was lost in the middle of an ocean, at the bottom of a sea.

For months during my stay in South America I rode that wave, the captain of an unsinkable ship, a celebrant of inexhaustible marvels. I lived for that tiny explosion of pleasure I'd get from correctly identifying a yellow-bellied kiskadee perched on a coral tree overhanging the pond. I learned how to identify several birds by their calls alone. The world appeared more legible than ever before.

Butterfly wings, a three-year-old's sigh, linden leaves, a breeze, Thoreau, Ruskin, a goddess of words and beauty—metaphorical bridges materialized out of thin air, spanning gulfs. Watching them appear (always composed of at least six shades of white) filled me with a warm satisfaction that I think could accurately be labeled happiness. Darkness itself became a trick of perspective. The whole wretched world, if viewed from enough angles, really did sparkle and shine.

The Germans, I would learn, had come up with a precise word for what I was doing. *Beziehungswahn* is the mania for seeing meaningful connections linking almost everything, including oneself, to almost everything else. It's a clinical term. A form of madness.

Of course my happiness was all POV. One day, inevitably, the ability to build metaphorical bridges failed me, and the old ones collapsed, exposing rotted foundations teeming with larval infestations. People suffered and died, friendships were neglected, marriages crumbled, three-year-olds grew tired of looking at swans. My mind, which I'd trained to stare at all things intensely and consider them with fine-grained specificity, was now—involuntarily and uncontrollably—focusing on ugliness and pain with the same rigor.

Trusting that the perspective will change back again is the trick, and few things remind me of this more effectively than looking closely at the world outside and consciously registering what's there, like the line of dancing light that Sofia saw in the water. For a while I had resigned myself to the idea that the phenomenon—that play of light—couldn't be named. Maybe some things defied classification. I told myself I was okay with that. But it turns out that I simply wasn't looking in the right places, and it took me weeks of searching to get the right angle on it, to discover that the stripe of sparkles actually *does* have a name.

I found it in an eighty-seven-page article titled *Molekuliarnaia Fizika Moria* ("Molecular Physics of the Sea"), by Soviet physicist Vasilii Vladimirovich Shuleikin. The article was translated into English by the U.S. Hydrographic Office in 1963. According to that translation, Shuleikin

129

reported that a streak of light visible upon a breeze-wrinkled surface of water is called "The Road to Happiness."

The act of pinning a precise label on that phenomenon filled me with something I'll call ecstasy. I felt light, buoyant, weightless, as if I could have stepped out onto the water and set forth upon that shimmering road, as if the fundamental laws of nature simply did not apply.

Nominated by Orion

THE ANTIQUE BLACKS

by ADRIAN MATEJKA

from COPPER NICKEL

*—for Sun Ra, Richard Pryor, Guion S. Bluford & the 13
other black astronauts who made it to outer space*

In Richard Pryor's origin myth of black
size, the two most magnanimous black men

in the world are peeing off the 30th Street Bridge
into the White River's busted up water. & above,

constellations in the sky's pat afro seem
as indiscriminant as lint in hair & more mundane

lights move lowly on the horizon the way cop
lights always move when black people think

about congregating outside of church. One
brother stares toward Saturn & says, *Man,*

this water is cold. The other looks in the same
direction & says, *Yeah, & it's deep, too.*

•

There's the upward inflection of it—
                the honeyed smile of space
                front & center in our heads—

Voyager winking
like a gold incisor
on its way out
        of this solar system.

Then there's the *because*
& *I-told-you-so* of it—
        slicking its promissory
goatee with a ringed thumb
        & ringed forefinger

right before a bugged-out
        hustle of piano & grin.
Almost & *might be* there again,

        the rounded parts of Saturn
        waiting to go green
                like the cheap metal

under a Jesus piece's already
        sketchy plating.

        The myth of space,
        though.
                It's like *this* wide.

                        •

It's like back in Indiana, where my white
mother said, *You are black* because my black
father's jurisdiction includes the skin heliotrope
I'm in. It includes nickel plating four-fingered
rings, fist-picking Cassinis, one-dropping
codes again. Pacers' caps tilting toward Saturn
on their own volition. All things interstellar
are black & white through a telescope—
the Moon, Mars, Voyager—it doesn't matter.
Back in Indiana, we got one channel: TV40,
The Little Rascals & Stymie's meticulous

black & white head as shined up as a Buick
handle when the passenger door shuts. Then
Leave It to Beaver's statutory whiteness cuffed
between corduroy preachers, one after another.
Something happened between those creased
sermons & I was like them that dream, staring
at the bent springs under my brother's bunk,
hand-me-down Millennium Falcon pillowcase
with a circumference of sweat mapping every
one of those faded stars & laser swooshes.
The zig-zag idea of something extraterrestrial.
The sorriest captain of the saddest bottle ship
this side of the White River where there
is always a jumble of something bottoming
the preacher's corked-up jug of canaries & stars.

·

It might squeak like a cork
fitting into an old jug,
            but it's the plutoid
of expectations gerrymandering itself—

enough rough meat left
            to crack the jaw
            of any brother who can't

            play ball. It follows him
across parking lots & into
bagel shops like a rain
            cloud in a cartoon.

The whole thing sounds
like a rocket ship
            cresting a full moon.

            Him & his slick silhouette
while his boys watch him toss up
brick after brick after brick.

Him & his pack of white
friends—a flotilla
of jumpers & pale layups & we're

        all rising up in the gospel
        of headbands & Chuck Taylors

        Tuesday mornings at the Y.

In Indiana, you either play
        ball or deal with abjection

        like a rocket ship
crashed into the moon's eye.

•

The moon was still out the Tuesday morning I got my first
real curl & Guion S. Bluford became the first black man
into outer space. August 30, 1983. I styled my wet frond
like *Purple Rain* Prince: left side tucked behind my ear, right
side getting activator in the same eye I would have used
to telescope the Challenger as it eclipsed Kennedy Space Center
at midnight in the habit of every brother I have ever met
trying to get away from something without a quotient. Math,
astrophysics—it doesn't matter. It all equals escape. All
those funny words related to space flight, too—*velocity*,
trajectory, *stamina*. In Indiana, any yellow brother with
enough stamina could pretend to be Prince if he widened
his eyes like two afterburners & got a curl. Even in Pike
Township, where the Pyramids have the exact same velocity
as three cranial lumps rising from skillet hits. Or in Martinsville,
a town so precise with its epithets, billboards, & buckshot,
Guion S. Bluford wouldn't even fly over the place.

•

Guion S. Bluford is not
Sun Ra any more

than the *Sounds of Earth*—

golden in that spinning

Voyager space probe—
parlays the real ruckus

we make in our tin
            pan hustle of engine ignition
& *nigger* used as noun & noun
            again in NASA hallways.

Where to begin? Where is
            the smiling headdress
of planets? Where is

            the smiling astronaut team
portrait, the singular brother
in his Colonel dress—

            ringed in whiteness
like number 1 on these dice?

·

Before 8 - 9 - * - 1 - 4 was catchy enough,
extraterrestrial enough to scare any 10-year-
old babysitting behind a door with a lock
as hollow as a half note, John Williams tried
300 chromatic combinations for the theme
to *Close Encounters of the Third Kind*. Before
the Challenger's third trip to space. Before
Guion S. Bluford confirmed space sounds
the same as Indiana at night only without
the black-masked & scrambling burglars,
black space in nooses, & lightning bugs.

·

Richard Pryor:

I feel it's time black people went to space.
White people have been going to space for years
& spacing out on us, as you might say.

•

        Without the sonic spacing
        of lead in & lead out,

        the moon is the same shape

        as a record
which is shaped the same
        as a luminout afro
which frames the face in the same

way a crown of stars would
if crowns were stars for anyone

other than Sun Ra—

13 stars clustered around his elbows

& ears & working tape deck. He said:

I'm not part of history. I'm more
        a part of the mystery
        which is my story

one hand teletyping an allegory
of astronaut & ancient prototype
        on a piano bench

in Auntie's front room with plastic
covered furniture, her phonograph
        always playing jazz—

        right next to a pool hall
        ringed by posters

                for disco throw downs
& Under-21 battles of the bands—

all of that razzmatazz, all those side
tables & decorative lamps—
                well-lit postscripts
                to explorers & outer space

                        •

Richard Pryor:

We're going to send explorer ships through
other galaxies & no longer will they have
the same type of music—Beethoven, Brahms,
& Tchaikovsky. From now on, we'll have a little
Miles Davis, some Charlie Parker. We going
to have some different kinds of things in there.

                        •

All lowercase things in here, all spacing

things in here & those words—

                & that vernacular hubbub—

                & that code switch tripping

on curbs in triplicate—

                three fingers on the piano keys,
                three huffed-up hopes on the upswing

of Indianapolis' West Side. Words work

the fast magic like a magician's
fingers fanned out as a W—

tingling fingers over here, white
chickens pecking the rain's thin wrist

over there—
building a nest egg

on every great crescendo
        of winged g-dropping.

        •

This is the g-dropping vernacular
they put in me back then. This is

the polyphone when my head
was an agrarian gang sign pointing

like a percussion mallet to a corn
maze in one of the smaller Indiana

towns. Be cool & try to grin it off.
Be cool & try to lean it off.

I'm grinning to this vernacular
like the bass drum in a patriotic

marching band. Be cool & try to ride
the beat the same way me & Pryor,

Ra, & Bluford did driving across
the 30th Street Bridge, laughing at two

big-headed dudes peeing into the water
& looking at the stars. Right before

the cop hit his lights. *Face the car,*
fingers locked behind your heads.

Right after the patriotic fireworks
started to pop off. *Do I need to call*

the drug dog? Right after the rattling
windows, mosquitoes in my ears as busy

as 4th-of-July traffic cops. Right before
the real thrill of real planets & pretend

planets spun high into the sky, Ra
throwing up the three West Side fingers,

each ringed by the misnomer of me
grinning at an imaginary billy club

down swinging. Because fireworks
light up in the same colors as billy clubs

& rough knuckle ups if you don't
duck on the double. Because the West

Side can be more cold-blooded
& patriotic than any part of Earth

Voyager saw when it took a blue picture
on the way out of the heliosphere.

Nominated by Copper Nickel, Ed Falco

TAXIDERMY

fiction by VLADISLAVA KOLOSOVA

from PLOUGHSHARES

Afterward, Eva turns her face to the wall and falls asleep immediately, smacking her lips like a newborn. Her husband and I are left alone, wide awake and clueless about what to do with our naked bodies. He fondles his half-limp dick underneath the blanket. His arm is thrusting mechanically, without much enthusiasm or hope.

"It's OK, really," I say.

"You think I'm pathetic," he says.

"It's normal, I guess. We're tired. It's late."

Their bed is round, and ostentatiously big, but it's still too small for three people to not have any body contact. My butt is touching Eva's, and my back feels her even breaths. I hate her for being able to sleep. My left side is pins and needles, but if I turned over, I would touch both her and Husband with my shoulders. In the glow of the dying night his body is waxy and pale, like a sweating cheese. My thong is close enough to angle it with my foot, but I wonder if that would make everything even more awkward. Nobody is naked as long as everyone is.

It's hot, and the room seems to breathe slightly, as if we were inside a great belly. I listen to the cuckoo clock on the wall. They paid for the entire night. One hour and fifty-six minutes left.

"So, how long have you been married?"

"Six years," Husband says and turns his body toward mine. His head lies on my scattered hair now. It's a little like being chained, and I think *Keep your hands to yourself.* But he, too, seems relieved that Eva is asleep and the sex is over. From atop the dresser a stuffed cat is watching us with glass eyes. I could swear it smiles, in a way animals aren't supposed to.

"Where did you meet Eva?" I ask.

"Leninsky Boulevard," he says. "Where did *you* meet her?"

"Leninsky Boulevard."

I was about to finish my shift when a redhead with a Versace bag walked up and scanned me from head to toe: "You do girls?"

I nodded: "One hundred Greens an hour."

(Her bag seemed real, plus she joggled a set of Mercedes keys around her finger, so I figured I could charge more than usually.)

"You are a seventy, my dear. I know Leninsky prices."

I was so surprised by her precise estimation I forgot to get offended.

The idea blossomed in my mind for a second. It was an easy seventy. I was tired of all the doughy family fathers with girls' asses. Occasionally, I got picked up by girls with guys' asses, but had gotten sick of them too. In bed, they all felt like bicycles. The redhead wasn't chubby, but there was plenty of her. She had skin the hue of biscuit, with freckles sprinkled all over her face and full upper arms. She seemed to be five years older than I—twenty-six, twenty-seven.

"Twelve hundred for me and my husband," she said. "The entire night."

Twelve hundred bucks was seven days worth of work. Five hours in exchange for thirty-five. I could study in bed for the next two weekends. Finish my anthropology paper. Sleep through a night. It was finals week, and I was exhausted: exams during the day, Leninsky Boulevard at night. I followed the redhead to the car.

She drove a black "gelding"—a Mercedes 600. I guessed it before, but now I was sure: she was a wife of a New Russian. Briefly, I imagined what her life was like. Waking up without an alarm. Showering for as long as she wanted to. God, she could pee whenever she wanted, just sit on the toilet bowl and pee, without using the loo time to put on makeup or call her sister. Time wasn't money for her. Time didn't exist.

"You should have asked for fifteen hundred," she said counting out the bills. "I wouldn't have given you more than twelve hundred, but one should never seem hungry to accept an offer. You are new, huh? From Podmoskovye? Ural? Siberia?"

"Omsk."

"No shit? Which school?"

"Fourteenth public school. The bilingual strand."

"I was in the Twelfth! Do you know it, the rusty four-story house next to the bus station?"

Before I could answer, she hugged me. "I'm Eva," she said and slammed her high heels against the accelerator pedal.

"Did you write down my car number?" she asked.

I shook my head and smiled: "You seem OK."

She flipped her fingers against my forehead. "Don't be stupid," she said, not without warmth. "What if I'm taking you to an apartment full of army soldiers?"

The car flew through the deserted streets of 4 a.m.–Moscow, away from the city center. Old buildings turned into high-rises, then a forest, then villas with fences higher than the villas themselves. Rublevka—the millionaire-ghetto. Geldings, Boomers, Jags parking in front of spick-and-span mansions. Here, not a trace of the Soviet Union could be seen, even though it collapsed only five years ago. No spalling paint to complain about. No overused faces proudly wearing their exhaustion, like Hero of Labor medals. New Russians were brand-new people with brand-new houses in a brand-new quarter of the town, with brand-new habits and brand-new wives. Some of them had gotten rich on oil, some on cat food, some on blood.

"Have you ever been to Paris?" I asked.

"U-hum", Eva says.

"And?"

"It was OK. Clean streets, old people with very white teeth. Very civilized. I liked the cheese. We have an apartment there."

"Will you move there? Later?"

"Why? It's boring. And when we'll be old, it will be OK here too. We will be the first generation of happy grandmothers in Russia. Like we were the first generation of rich girls."

In front of a villa with two marble bears at the entrance, Eva stood on the brakes and honked. When the security guard opened the gate, she let the car roll in, still honking. A man in a silky orange bathrobe appeared at the mansion door. "Wednesday, Eva, it's Wednesday. A weeknight," he said, rubbing his eyes. "Morning," he mumbled in my direction and disappeared in the house again.

"Andrei!" Eva called and tottered after him as fast as her high heels allowed.

I stayed at the entrance to look at the house more closely. It had four stories plus three medieval turrets, a porch supported by Greek columns and a roof of wooden lace like those from fairy tales about Ivan Tsarevich. I have never been inside a Rublevka mansion. People who live there usually didn't bother with girls from Leninsky Boulevard: not exotic, not expensive enough. But I guess even the rich like their McDonald's from time to time.

Inside, a stuffed lynx stood on its hind legs, holding the Russian flag. I followed the music somewhere from inside the house, the furry white carpet drowning the sound of my heels. A stuffed Labrador. A stuffed gazelle. Eva and Husband were in one of the living rooms on the first floor, arguing. I stayed in the hall, pretending to admire the minimalist art in ornate, gilded frames. A giant slab of marble leaned on the wall. Engraved on it, Husband was standing with his legs apart, wearing a suit and looking all business. He wore a heavy gold chain instead of a tie, and a massive watch. Both were worked in gold. Whoever made it even took the effort to engrave "Rolex" in tiny, tiny letters. In the background: the black gelding and Eva in a short, tight dress. The thing must have weighed half a ton.

"Do you want a drink?" Eva beckoned me into the living room. The arguing quieted down.

"Nice art," I said.

"It's a tombstone", she said. "In Andrei's business, one never knows."

My mind made a connection. Those marble slabs started to appear at graveyards a couple of years ago. They were multiple times as tall as any tombstone before, with engraved life-size men, often armed. Long golden epitaphs, short lifespans.

Eva poured me a drink. I drank it. She poured me another one. I drank it as well. She turned the soapy Russian pop louder. Husband sipped on a cup of coffee. His cleanly shaven scalp and flat boxer's nose made his head seem very round. He was so muscular and broad-shouldered that he looked like a sign for a men's toilet: a circle atop an inverted triangle. Between the lapels of his bathrobe, a woolly carpet of gray was showing. He must have been in his forties or fifties. He hadn't looked at me once.

When Husband opened a little plastic bag with white powder, Eva dashed to him and blew inside it. The powder rose up in a little cloud and sedated on the glass table. "Eva," he said tiredly. She giggled, kissed him, pressed her wet lips onto the powder and danced through the room like a dervish, cheering. She swirled through the room, then sat down on my lap, clutching my waist with both of her legs, and dropped her upper body. Her cinnamon hair touched the floor and moved like sea anemones. When she came back up, laughing, her golden eyes looked animally. No thought. Only hunger and instinct. She pushed me back into the couch pillows, bent over, and pressed her white mouth on mine. Her lips were full and whippy and bitter.

The three of us went to the bedroom.

I couldn't really imagine how people coordinated twelve limbs and three genitals. I had started in the business only two weeks ago. But it was twelve hundred bucks.

I don't like my job, but I like that I can do it.

When I moved to Moscow for college, I was selling bubble gum and canned gin and tonic. The kiosk was so tiny there wasn't even space for a chair—one had to stand up for the entire twelve hours. Its walls were made of tin. In summer, one felt like a baked fish in foil. Last winter, I almost lost my ear to a cold burn.

The prettiest girl in my Human Origins class had said, Why stand on your feet all day for slave wages when you can earn money lying on your back?

One traded sex anyway, always. For a man, for a man with a car, for flowers, admiration, a white gown.

I preferred dollars.

It was easier than I thought. Educative, even. After the night in Eva's bed I was three things wiser than before.

One: It's basically like twister, only nobody tells you where to put your arms and legs—and when you decide to put them *somewhere*, the spot is already occupied.

Two: Watching naked people making out in front of you is like seeing Mount Elbrus for the first time. It doesn't even seem real at first.

Three: It's better to close your eyes anyway. When I am drunk, genitals make me giggle because they are so absurdly beautiful.

Or just absurd. Like flaccid penises. Husband's dick had the consistency of a half-filled water balloon. If I squeezed it, it became kind of hard; if I didn't, it just flopped from side to side.

With Eva, it wasn't bad, but it wasn't sex either. The powder on her lips made me grow fur on the inside of my veins and turned the whole thing into something too fluffy and warm to actually have an arc and an end. We probably would still be doing it if Eva hadn't groaned and come or maybe half-come. Or maybe she was just tired and turned her head to the wall, pretending to sleep.

Since then, I've looked at the watch hand dissecting the hour, thinking: Another minute. Poof. Gone. And I should be happy because it means I'm closer to getting out of here. But it's so scary it makes my chest tighten. When a minute is gone—it's *gone*. Makes me crazy if I think of it too much. But the closer I watch time, the faster it spins. All clocks seem like stopwatches now.

I try to think of other things. Think of my bed. Think of an omelet. Think of how to get home.

"What are you thinking?" Husband asks.

"Nothing," I say. "Sorry for waking you up."

"I'm used to it."

"Why don't you tell Eva you prefer to sleep?"

"Have you ever had a dog?"

"My parents did. A terrier. His name was Rambo. Why?"

In the light of morning, behind Husband's left ear, I see a patch of silver hair he had forgotten to shave. His face looks lifeless, like an electronic device pulled out of the socket.

"Mine was a Labrador. Musya," he says. "Anyway, if you had a dog, you probably know this scenario: You wake up, and in front of your bed is a half-shredded bloody bird corpse. And a proud mutt looking into your eyes for approval."

"Thanks."

"I didn't mean . . . I'm sorry. I mean. You're beautiful. It's just . . . I get tired. I used to be a professional boxer. Master of sports. I need my rhythm. Regular sleeping patterns. I didn't even drink before all this," he says with a sweeping motion spanning the entire room.

"How old are you?" I ask.

"Guess."

I think fifty-two, so I say forty-three.

He looks offended. "No, forty-one."

"Oh," I say.

"Not knowing what your wife is doing is worse than not liking it."

Eva turns on her back and snorts like a wood saw. I bet she was one of those people with good sleep and digestion. Who never wonder what they are. Who never doubt if they *are* at all. Eva knows she is, because she doesn't know that she doesn't know whether she is or not.

I look around the room. This round bed, covered with white satin, like a monstrous wedding cake. The cuckoo clock. An aquarium with exotic fish—a piece of nature transplanted into the urban home, framed, domesticated. The smiling stuffed cat on the dresser.

"Did you know that when you taxidermy a small animal, you have to pull the brain through its ear?" Husband says, catching my gaze.

"Taxi-what?"

"This cat—his name is Grisha. He died when I was sixteen. He was the first pet I stuffed."

"Did you do the other animals in the house as well?"

"It was my hobby, before Eva and I got married. But she says the faintest whiff of formaldehyde makes her vomit."

"Why taxidermy?"

"I don't know. Maybe I feel like I beat death in a small way."

"What was the last animal you stuffed?"

"I don't have the time anymore, with the house, and the business, and the casinos at night."

"The casinos are a rip-off. I know a guy who works there. He says the rules are set so crassly in favor of the house it's almost impossible to win."

"Do you think it's about winning?"

I shrug my shoulders.

"It's about losing the most," he says with tired eyes. "The prostitutes, the houses . . . If you don't throw your money to the wind, nobody takes you seriously as a business partner."

"What business are you in?"

"Import-export."

"Of what?"

He smiles again, almost paternally. "You're not from Moscow, are you?"

"Why did you marry Eva?"

"She was the most alive person I knew. And I the most alone."

"But why did you *marry* her?"

"Men need wives."

"Not rich men. You can buy someone who cooks your food and keeps your house clean. You could buy the entire Leninsky Boulevard, if you wanted to. You have the money."

"But who will spend my money?"

I do not have an answer.

"Can I hug you?" he asks suddenly.

I wrap myself into his arms and bury my face in the wool on his chest.

The clock seems to tick louder and louder. One second passes, then another, soon it will be a minute, then an hour, then twenty-four, today will be yesterday, and years will be gone, and everything will be gone, including me.

Husband strokes my back. And I find it snug and disgusting at the same time, and want it to stop, but it's as if I am somewhere outside of time, in a place where I don't have limbs that move when I order them to. I lie face down and laugh silently until his chest hair is wet and I feel as if I am lying face down in moss.

"I'm sorry," I finally say. "I am not crying. Please, please say something other than, Are you OK? OK?"

"I have a son," he says. "Last time I heard from his mother, they were in Uzbekistan."

Grisha watches from the dresser and I look in his eyes, thinking: For you the time really did stop.

But he just stares back, because he is a stuffed cat and not a metaphor.

I turn my head to Eva. In her sleep, her smile resembles the cat's, her upper lip curling upward, exposing her teeth.

Husband strokes my hair, and when he presses me tighter to his body, I realize he has a boner.

"Listen, our neighbor to the right is looking for a wife," he says stroking my hair. "He's almost impotent—should be easy. Maybe I can arrange something. Write down your number, OK?"

"I'll go get a pen," I say, and miraculously my feet obey.

Switched into vertical from the horizontal, I realize how the room smells of sex and morning breath. The morning behind the window is bleary and matte, as if it has a hangover too. From here, I can hear the horns of elektrichkas—electric commuter trains, taking pensioners to their dachas.

In the hallway, I pick up the orange bathrobe that Husband lost on the way to the bedroom three hours earlier. It's more expensive than the clothes I left in their bedroom anyway. I take my bag, recount the money and slip into my shoes. I walk past the stuffed gazelle, past the stuffed Labrador, past the tombstone, down the hallway and silently close the front door behind me.

Nominated by Ploughshares

THE BEATING HEART OF THE WRISTWATCH

by MARTIN ESPADA

from PURPLE PASSION PRESS

My father worked as a mechanic in the Air Force,
the engines of the planes howling in his ears all day.
One morning the wristwatch his father gave him was gone.
The next day, he saw another soldier wearing the watch.
There was nothing he could say: no one would believe
the greaser airplane mechanic at the Air Force base
in San Antonio. Instead, one howling night he got drunk
and tore up the planks of an empty barracks for firewood.
There was no way for him to tell time locked in the brig.

When he died, I stole my father's wristwatch.
I listened to the beating heart of the watch.
The heart of the watch kept beating long after
my father's heart stopped beating. Somewhere,
the son of the man who stole my father's wristwatch
in the Air Force holds the watch to his ear and listens
to the heart of the watch beating. He keeps the watch
in a sacred place where no one else will hear it.
So the son tries to resurrect the father. The Bible
tells the story wrong. We try to resurrect the father.
We listen for the heartbeat and hear the howling.

Nominated by Purple Passion Press

WINTER WHEAT

by DOUG CRANDELL

from THE SUN

That fall my brothers and I would be sowing the fields on our own for the first time. Dad was working extra shifts at the ceiling-tile factory with the threat of layoffs ever present. One night he sat us down and said, "Wheat'll be yours to get in the ground. Work together." That was it. Derrick was eighteen, Darren was almost fourteen, and I was ten and proud to be included. "Questions?" Dad said. He was so spare with words that every one he did speak seemed significant. He looked at us, his eyes like round black stones. I envied the manly hair on his arms.

Derrick told him we understood.

"Listen to your brothers," Dad instructed me, and then he was out the door to the factory.

The winter wheat went into the ground around late September, as soon as the flies were dead and gone, and it sprouted quickly, the green shoots hibernating beneath the snow until the spring sunshine ushered them into adulthood, when sturdy heads of grain would click together in the wind like thousands of tap-dancers. Each afternoon my brothers and I would get off the bus and shuck our starched blue denims in favor of Carhartt pants made supple by work. The weather was still warm enough that we could wear just our white T-shirts until the sun went down.

It was on one of those sunny fall afternoons that we met our new neighbor Kenny Pound. My parents were cash-renting our farm, which meant we were working someone else's land and getting little of the profits in exchange for doing all the labor. Dad was still at work, putting in overtime, and Mom was filling in for someone at the grocery store when Kenny pulled up in his truck. Our sisters, Dina and Dana, had chores to do in the house, and Dad had left us a note saying we needed to get at least thirty acres seeded by nightfall. Kenny walked over as we were filling the planter with dusty wheat seed. He had recently begun cash-renting the farm up the road, from the same landlord as we were. We knew someone had moved in, but we weren't prepared for a man with a thick beard and dark-brown hair that hung well below the collar of his flannel shirt.

"Looks like our new neighbor is Bob Seger," Darren said under his breath.

"I can see you men have what it takes to fill the coffers," Kenny said in greeting. I looked to Darren and Derrick and could tell that they, too, barely knew what this meant. My brothers each ripped open another bag of seed and dumped it into the planter, but I couldn't take my eyes off our new neighbor. He wore real cowboy boots, not steel-toed lace-ups like ours, and he didn't wear a seed-company cap, leaving his hair free to blow in the autumn breeze. He introduced himself with a broad smile and immediately pitched in to help. My brothers shrugged and went on working. Once the planter was filled, he asked if we needed anything else. We were about to start seeding when an old station wagon pulled into the field and Kenny's wife, Sarah, got out with a baby on her hip and several paper lunch bags in her hand. She waved as if she knew us.

We all sat and ate peanut-butter sandwiches and drank ice-cold pop for longer than we should have while Kenny told us how they'd been living on a commune near Denver, Colorado, but he was from Indiana and had missed it so much that they had to come back. The baby boy Sarah held had the same thick, dark hair as Kenny, who wasn't shy about showing his love for his son. He cradled the tyke and kissed the top of his head and laughed whenever he blew spittle. The whistles of a bobwhite along the fence line traveled over the empty fields to us, and Kenny said the bird was calling for its young. "You know, they'll starve themselves and go without water trying to feed their children." Just then a flock of birds burst into the evening sky, looking like little black brush marks before disappearing completely. Kenny took the baby's bottle from Sarah and fed him. We'd never seen our dad hold a baby. He rarely even hugged us, though sometimes on your birthday or Christmas he might grab you for a quick embrace. Kenny acted as much like a mother as he did a father.

After Sarah and the baby had gone home, Kenny handed Derrick a cassette tape of Prince's *Controversy*. "Listen to 'Let's Work,'" he said. "It'll make the time go faster." Then he winked and climbed into his truck. "I'll be back tomorrow!" he yelled as he bounced over the furrows and turned onto the highway.

The next morning before school, Mom gave Derrick one of Dad's notes, scratched with such intensity that the pen had nearly torn the paper. He read it aloud: "No dawdling. You only got twenty drilled."

"Just do your best," said Mom, clad in her polyester uniform from the grocery store. She worked the deli, shaving pound after pound of meat we couldn't afford. In her spare time she'd draw or sew or crochet scarves for us that were so long they trailed along the ground like a bride's train. Right now she was in the bathroom talking about herself in the third person: "Your mother's got to get this hair colored!" She grabbed her car keys and kissed us all goodbye while our sisters packed our lunches.

After Mom left, Derrick said he'd listened to the Prince tape. He shook his head and announced: "Not for everyone's ears." I knew he meant it wasn't for *my* ears, which only made me want to listen to it more. I was about to whine when Dana said there was a man at the door, and we all turned to see Kenny standing on the porch, the sleeping baby in his arms and a diaper bag over his shoulder. He asked if he could come in, mouthing the words so as not to wake his son. I jumped up and opened the door. Kenny stepped inside and whispered to the girls, "You must be the sisters." Dina and Dana blushed. I noticed he wore a puka-shell necklace, and his chest hair was as black as crow feathers.

Dana asked why he had a baby. Her perplexed look seemed to express how we were all feeling.

"Because he's mine," said Kenny, gently pushing the baby's pacifier back into his mouth. "I'm his daddy."

"But he's got a momma, too, right?" Dana asked. "Why doesn't she have him?"

Kenny grinned and said he would tell Dana all about it later if she and Dina would watch the baby after school while he helped Derrick, Darren, and me get our wheat into the ground.

"You don't have to help us, Mr. Pound," said Derrick. "Dad gave the job to us to do. We'll be fine."

"Call me Kenny. And I know you can handle the work." The baby

151

started to rouse, and Kenny removed a bottle from the bag, held it to his cheek to check the temperature, and gave it to his child. "What I was hoping," he said to Derrick, "is that we could help each other." He offered to help us get our wheat drilled, and then we "men" could assist him with his. I nodded enthusiastically, happy to be considered one of the men. Kenny said he would ask our folks first, of course, and he would pay Dina and Dana for the baby-sitting. He needed their help only because Sarah was driving to Kokomo and back to take nursing classes. He put the baby on his shoulder and patted his son's back rhythmically until the child let out two burps. "I'd better get out of your way," Kenny said. "Don't want you to miss your bus."

Derrick curtly said that he drove us to school.

Kenny praised Derrick for taking care of his brothers and sisters, which caused Derrick to squint suspiciously at him. Kenny told us all to have a wonderful day and left.

"Let's hope he doesn't act that way around Dad," Derrick said as Kenny buckled his son into a car seat and bent to kiss his brow.

That afternoon after school, Kenny handed the baby and the diaper bag over to the girls and paid them each five dollars. Mom seemed bewildered and told Kenny the girls would watch the baby without pay, but he insisted and said he considered it an honor to have his son cared for by "such fine women." Dana giggled.

We changed our clothes and went to work with Kenny in the fields. The air was cool and smelled of wood smoke and manure. Around dinnertime Mom brought us steaming bowls of chicken and dumplings. Kenny ate around the chicken but slurped the broth and gobbled the dumplings. As it grew dark, we started to climb back on the tractors, but Kenny pulled us aside. "You boys are lucky," he told us, nodding toward the gravel driveway, where Mom was pulling away in the station wagon. "You got a family here." He stood straighter. "There's nothing more valuable in all the world."

I was a pudgy kid, and I stood on my tiptoes and sucked in my gut to look leaner. We'd been raised to be stoic and reserved, slow to show emotion, but now, in the cool of the evening, Derrick and Darren cautiously began to smile. Kenny drew us in for a hug just as our father's headlights illuminated the field, bouncing when he drove over ruts. Panic shot through me. I pictured him and Kenny in a brawl like the ones I'd seen on *Bonanza*—split lips and bodies flailing about before someone pulled the panting men apart.

Derrick, Darren, and I stepped back from Kenny, but not before Dad had seen the hug. He killed the pickup's engine but left the bright headlights on to see by. His steel-toed work boots hit the ground like the flat of a shovel on wet cement, and I shielded my eyes from the headlights' glare. Kenny stepped forward, his hand extended. "You must be Mr. Crandell," he said. I was glad he didn't try to embrace Dad—or, worse, slap him five. They shook hands. Dad dropped his cigarette on the ground and crushed it out in the soft loam. He looked around as if searching for an explanation for the scene he'd come upon: a young man hugging his boys.

"Why don't you tell me what's going on here," Dad said to Kenny.

Kenny patted our father on the shoulder. Dad glanced at the hand as if it were laced with nitroglycerin. "Nothing, sir," said Kenny. "I'm helping the boys get your wheat in the ground, and I'm hoping they'll do the same for me."

Dad lit another cigarette as Kenny explained the arrangement. When he was done, Dad nodded, seeming to inspect Kenny's puka necklace and hippie beard. The ember of his Salem Light glowed bright red.

"If you've been helping the boys get the wheat sowed," Dad said, "they'll return it likewise." Then he turned away and slogged back to his pickup. "Get your work done so you can help the man," he called over his shoulder to us.

For the next four days we worked with Kenny, and we loved it. The afternoon sun was golden, and the sky was an enormous blue bowl. It was hard not to smile when he told us what a good job we were doing and how he hoped his boy would grow up to be like us. As we drilled the seed into the earth, which had just the perfect degree of dampness, we listened to Kenny's music. He had dozens of cassettes he'd made, the tracks listed in precise cursive writing. On the fourth day, our fields planted, we drove the equipment over to Kenny's. He was sowing eighty acres, and the time flew by.

Just after dusk on the seventh day, all the winter wheat, Kenny's and ours, was sown. His wife brought us spiced cider and hot biscuits. We sat on the tractors and ate and laughed as Kenny told us how he'd once covered forty acres before discovering he hadn't put seed in the planting drums, so the only thing he'd sown was air. His wife had the baby swaddled in a fuzzy blanket, and Kenny held him and kissed his forehead. It still stunned me: Here was a man who used his back to make his living, and yet he also showed affection and talked about his feelings. Kenny handed the baby to his wife and told her he'd be home before long. Then he asked us if we'd ever seen the river on a night like this. He pointed to the moon. "Come on," he said. "It's just a short walk."

We followed Kenny over the soft topsoil and into a ditch planted high with fescue to keep erosion at bay. The night air had a bite to it, and trees rustled in a breeze. We slipped along a fence line and down a hill to the edge of the water, its glassy surface mirroring the moon.

"Would you look at that," said Kenny.

I waited for him to show us something. Then it dawned on me that Kenny had brought us to the water just to see the moon's reflection. We didn't speak. While we stood there, Kenny recited some lines of a poem about the smell and taste of leaves, the stories they held. Then he told us we shouldn't be afraid to live the life we each decided was right for us. I looked to Darren and Derrick for some clue as to what they were thinking, but they seemed slightly dazed. After a while Kenny said, "Fellas, I sure have enjoyed working with you this past week." His voice caught, and he wiped his eyes. "Can't wait to work many more seasons with you."

Derrick and Darren seemed glad when we made the short walk back to the field, but I secretly wished we could have stayed there by the water.

A couple of nights later, as we were falling asleep in our twin beds in the room we shared, I asked my brothers if they missed working with Kenny. The bedroom remained quiet, and I didn't ask a second time. Maybe it was because Kenny had shown us something about being men that we had yet to understand, or maybe my brothers were embarrassed at how loving Kenny was with his son and us and how solemn and reticent our own father had always been. I lay there that night and hoped I would have the courage to follow Kenny's example someday, but I also wanted to be the sort of man my father respected and admired.

For the rest of that fall Dad had less overtime at the factory, and we worked with him more on the farm. I'd sometimes catch a wistful expression on Derrick's or Darren's face that I read as a desire for the work to be more fun, or for some encouragement, maybe even a hug at the end of the day. But we labored with Dad as we always had: mostly in silence, with a seriousness that now seemed almost cruel.

One weekend, as we spread straw for the hogs in advance of a cold night, Dad rounded a corner and found us singing a song from one of Kenny's tapes, with me standing on a bale and crooning while Darren and Derrick played pitchfork guitars. Dad stood and stared at us while we scrambled back to work. For a second I thought I saw him open his mouth to say something, but he only licked his lips and coughed before walking back to the tractor.

"That was close," said Derrick as Dad drove away, the tractor spewing black diesel exhaust. We returned to our task with renewed solemnity, but before long we were kidding around and praising one another's work once more.

It was early November when we learned of Kenny's death. The maples and sycamores were bare, the last fields of corn stark and empty. We'd been done with our own harvest for a couple of weeks and were grateful for some downtime. Derrick had mentioned just the day before that we ought to ask if Kenny needed any help. We hadn't seen him in more than a month. The last time had been at the grain elevator, where Kenny had hugged us in front of our father's friends, men with shaven faces and scoured work boots and pressed denim shirts. Kenny still wore his puka-shell necklace and had a tiny braid behind one ear. He talked about his wife and baby, telling us we'd all get together after the first snow and go sledding. He even suggested our folks come along. We could hardly picture our father lying on a Flexible Flyer, wind blowing his cap off, his cheeks red.

That afternoon in November, Dad asked if we wanted to go take a look at the sprouting wheat. We eagerly agreed. The wheat had been ours to get into the ground, and we were proud of it. As we put on our boots and gloves, Dad seemed unsure about the wisdom of what he'd just asked us to do. He forced a smile and gave us each a pat on the back as we exited the house. Mom and the girls were grocery shopping for a big post-harvest meal that night. The weather was bitter and gray. We walked the length of a pasture and over another fence line to the periphery of one of our fields: forty acres carpeted in a perfect Kelly green, a testimony to our labor. Blackbirds hopped over the verdant landscape.

"Boys," Dad said, "that young guy, Kenny . . ." He rubbed his hands together and looked at us standing in the cold. His voice grew softer. "It's a damn shame. He slipped, they said. He was picking corn alone. Didn't have much of a chance."

155

We all knew what a combine could do to a person. My vision blurred, and the tears came fast. Derrick kicked the ground and closed his eyes tight while Darren looked away and walked in a circle. "I know," said Dad. It was clear he was trying to offer up a side of himself that we needed just then, but he was unaccustomed to giving consolation. "Come on, now," he said, and he pulled me to his chest. I sobbed, and he made a soothing sound that I'd heard him use to calm sows in labor. Then he handed me his handkerchief, and I blew my nose. Derrick and Darren wiped their eyes with the cuffs of their jean jackets. "I'm sorry," said Dad. "I know you boys were fond of him."

With that he started to walk along the edge of the field, and we followed. Halfway down, Dad stopped and surveyed our work. He said we'd done a fine job getting the wheat in the ground. The following summer we would harvest it together.

Two days later Dad drove us to Kenny's funeral. He told Sarah that we'd plant her fields and harvest them, too. He even patted the baby's head. On the drive home Dad told us a story we'd never heard, about a time when his brother had nearly been killed by a team of draft horses. "You never know," he said.

We drove on, past fields of winter wheat on either side of the road, all that beautiful green that would lie dormant under the white snow, safe from the subzero cold until spring, when the sun would return, and it would grow again. In the fall the grain would be separated from the chaff, which would be plowed under, as it had been so many times before.

Nominated by The Sun

CONSIDER OEDIPUS' FATHER

by DAVID TOMAS MARTINEZ

from POETRY

It could have been a car door
          leaving that bruise,

as any mom knows,
almost anything could take an eye out,

and almost anybody could get their tongue
          frozen to a pole,

which is kind of funny
          to the point of tears
          plus a knee slap or two
that an eye can be made blue, pink
by a baby's fist, it fits
perfectly in the socket. It's happened to me.
          Get it?

Any scenario is better,
beats sitting in a car and hearing
          someone you love
          sob,
which I have done
with a black eye.

For me, a woman's tears
are **IKEA** instructions
on the European side.

I'm sure for Laius, Oedipus's father, it was the same.
            Think of him sleeping
after having held a crying Jocasta
because they had fought for hours
because she was stronger.

            Who knew better the anger of young Jocasta?

Knew that when the oracle, or the police,
            come, they are taking someone with them.

I'm sure Laius looked at the crib
            and thought *better you*
than me, kid.

Now consider your own
father, or the guy your mother
            dated until he took
the three-sided road,

crouched in front of a paper
            plate with a catcher's
            mitt, teaching
            a curveball grip—

            but did he ever teach
the essential lesson
of how to block a punch
            from a finely manicured hand,
or to walk away when
records are being candled and books disemboweled,

teach the wonderment of
            a jar of peanut butter jammed
in a TV screen

below a snail trail of ice cream
             near broken pictures on the wall?

Not while he's king, I bet, and not while
             there are mothers and their jobs,
like breastfeeding or serving a warm plate
             on a table

next
to cold beers
             from the hand

of a mother he made from a virgin
             with his own hands, his own hands.

Nominated by Stuart Dischell, Jody Stewart

THE MUSHROOM QUEEN

fiction by LIZ ZIEMSKA

from TIN HOUSE

It's the middle of the night and the woman can't sleep. Perhaps it's the full moon, or the *fool* moon, the kind of moon that keeps you awake thinking stupid thoughts. She puts on her glasses and sees that it's 2:55 AM. The man lies beside her, generating too much heat. There's a small brown dog nestled into her armpit. A white dog sleeps at her feet. She's wedged in like a crooked tooth.

For about an hour now she's been thinking about the two races of man. One race is very, very slow; they crawl upon the earth like slugs, leaving silvery slime trails wherever they go. The other is very, very fast, about as fast as electrons, and when they pass by they leave a radiant residue, though you can never be sure if you've actually seen them, or if there's a smudge on your glasses picking up the light in a funny way. The two races live side by side, completely unaware of each other, sucking on the same earth.

But on the night of the *fool* moon, a special moon that occurs once per decade—or every 9.3 years to be exact—when the moonrise lag is equal to the moonset lag, causing great upheavals of the deep, cold waters of the Pacific Ocean, the slow race can sometimes catch up to the fast race.

All of this is just nonsense, of course. It's the duration that's the important part here. Nine-point-three years is a long time to be married.

The woman sighs, digs her toes into the fur of the white dog. She looks out the sliding glass doors at the garden in moonlight—they still don't have curtains. It really is beautiful out there, like a scene from *Last Year at Marienbad*, her favorite film, but enacted with owls, rabbits, voles and coyotes. A tiny, mournful cry reaches her through the partially opened door, some small furred thing losing its life out beyond the chicken-wire fence and the scrub grass, where the man keeps the pile of lumber that once was the trellis under which they were married.

A bit of white flashes by in her peripheral vision—a flap of cloth?—then disappears behind the farthest clump of jade plant.

Kicking off the blankets, the woman rolls carefully from the bed without disturbing the dogs and the man. She shakes a sweater from a pile of clothing the man has left on the floor, where the jeans and underwear he shucked off still retain his shape, as if his body had dematerialized. She walks to the door and looks out. It's the one thing they had agreed on, a luxury but well worth it: the lawn, the decorative clumps of shrubbery, the drooping leaves of the Mexican bamboo, the flax. And then she sees it again, a figure in white moving very quickly across the grass, diving behind the nearest jade plant. It is coming closer to the house, where the dogs and the man lie paralyzed in sleep.

The woman slides the glass door open wider and steps out onto the deck, closing the door behind her so the dogs won't get out. She stands there under the moonlight. It has a definite tone, like minute silver shavings striking glass, a tone that shifts as the silver bounces off her head, her shoulders, her upturned face. The moon is past its highest point; she can feel her energy weakening. She thinks again about the two races of man. What if the fast race can sometimes clean up the messes of the slow? Her toes grip the worn redwood boards.

She steps off the deck onto the lawn. What is wrong with her marriage anyway? Nothing that she can point to, no crimes, no infidelities. Some petty cruelty in times of stress, but who isn't guilty of that? Nevertheless, she feels restless, bored, *slow*. There's nothing wrong, but everything's wrong: she'd like that on a T-shirt, please. For months now she's been fantasizing about being more than she is, but it isn't coming true. What if she could step into the fast, fast world without being missed? What she wants now, more than anything, is a placeholder, someone to keep her life intact while she goes on a little reconnaissance trip.

The woman reaches the jade plant just as another woman steps out to face her. They are nearly identical, mirror images, though the doppelgänger, as befits a creature of the moonlight, is more glamorous looking than her sun-fattened twin. Even so, to examine herself three-dimensionally is unnerving for the woman. Mirrors don't tell half the story. Is this really how her nose looks in profile? The skin of the other is beaded with tiny water droplets, her white cotton nightgown translucent with moisture. The woman reaches out to touch her, but just as she's about to make contact, the other one grabs her by the throat and tosses her into the jade plant. Our woman is gone. Her double crosses the lawn, steps onto the deck, slides open the door, dries her feet on the pile of discarded clothes, and climbs into bed.

The big white dog lifts his head and wags his tail. Then he stops, sits up, and looks again. He's confused. His eyes tell him one thing, but his nose, the more reliable source, tells him another: she may look like his beloved mistress, but she smells, definitively, like rabbits. There's nothing the white dog loves more than killing rabbits.

He wags his tail again. The woman sleeps. Maybe his nose is wrong. He's getting old, almost six, though not very old for his breed. He has another six years in him, he can feel it, but things are starting to break down. He can't bank the curves like he used to while chasing the neighbor's cat off the lawn. Thank God the mangy creature was taken out by coyotes (tracked, tricked, cornered, and devoured—he had heard it all one night). Thank God he didn't have to suffer the humiliation of another failed chase, the cat's mocking glance as it jumped onto the fence and disappeared into the street, where the dog could not go without a leash.

The woman digs her toes into his fur, like the other one had done. She turns onto her side, pulls the blanket up to her chin, tucks the brown dog, that small, furry shithead, into the curve of her body, like the other woman had always done. Everything checks out, except for the strange straw-and-dandelion smell of rabbits. Perhaps, like his hips, his nose is starting to go.

Our woman, the original, sinks into the soft, moist ground at the base of the jade plant, terrified. She tries to scream but soil fills her mouth. She opens her eyes, but there is nothing but darkness, no air, no sound; the world is extinguished. And yet she lives on, packed in with the weight of the earth; no longer merely slow, she is *immobile*.

The small brown dog knows of course that the creature in bed with him is not his beloved mistress, but he also realizes that it would be dangerous to let on that he knows. This "woman" is so much a copy of *his*

162

woman that it obviously took a great deal of effort to pull off the stunt, and great effort usually comes with great desire. The small dog knows there's nothing more dangerous in the world than desire. He also knows that to raise an alarm about this fake would be to risk the life of his true mistress, who is obviously being held captive somewhere.

What he needs to do now is to convince this dim-witted white brute to stop sniffing her like she's some kind of rabbit he'd like to snatch up in his teeth and shake to death. That stupid white fluff likes to leave his rabbit carcasses all over the lawn, those pretty little brownish-gray rabbits that come to feed on the garden and leave their delicious little pellets behind for the small dog to find and eat. That's what the dumb white leg-humper is missing: this fake woman doesn't smell like rabbits; she smells like rabbit poo.

Some fun facts about fungus, the most prevalent organism on the planet.

About 250 million years ago a meteorite struck down around Siberia, creating tidal waves, lava flows, hot gases, and searing winds. The land grew dark under a cloud of debris, causing 90 percent of its species to die out. Fungus inherited the earth.

Animals are more closely related to fungi than to any other kingdom. Millions of years ago we shared a common ancestor. Man is just a branch off the fungal evolutionary tree, the branch that evolved the ability to capture nutrients by surrounding its food with cellular sacs, or stomachs. As animals emerged from the water, they developed a dense layer of cells to prevent the loss of moisture. Fungi, on the other hand, solved the problem of moisture retention by going underground.

Mycelium, a web-like mass of tiny branching threads containing one or more fungal cells surrounded by a tubular wall, is the vegetative part of fungus. It's the stuff that grows, spreads out, running through every cubic centimeter of soil in the world. Every time you step on a soccer field, a forest, a suburban lawn, you walk upon thousands of sentient cells that are able to communicate with one another using chemical messengers. Mycelium helps to heal and steer the ecosystem, recycling waste into soil. Constantly moving, mycelium can travel several inches a day. There have been experiments conducted in Japan that show slime mold successfully navigating a food maze, choosing the shortest distance between two points, disregarding dead ends.

Mushrooms are the fruiting bodies, the reproductive organs, of my-

celium. They feed on rotting things, like rabbit poo, and troubled rela-
tionships.

.

The Mushroom Queen was tired of living underground. She can as-
sume any form. Her skin is nicer than human skin, firm and white, and
it has no pores, only spores, because mushrooms are self-propagating,
which can get pretty lonely. So she deposed herself and came to the
woman's house from the east, traveling west along the shore of a wide
green river, over the Appalachians, beneath the Great Lakes, flowing
right across the vast mid-western plains. She was born over a century
ago in the unkempt garden of a red brick house that was once a home,
then a nursery, then a nunnery, and is now again a home. That is where
our woman arrives now, sucked across the country and extruded from
the ground beneath a trellis of tangled vines that sprout purple flowers
in the summer. They have switched places, the discontent of one calling
to the desire of the other. Nature abhors a vacuum.

The man thinks this woman is an improvement over the other. He does
not know there's been a switch, only a sudden unexplainable change in
personality. He doesn't question it, as he is unaccustomed to question-
ing good fortune when it rains down on his head. This woman is more
pliable than the other, more eager. The other one never wanted to make
love in the morning. As he sinks his fingers into her flesh and buries his
face into her dark curls, he falls in love with her all over again.
    The Mushroom Queen has gills behind her ears, but the man doesn't
seem to notice. He delights in her damp, earthy scent, her luminous
whiteness, the way her body forms around his. She opens her mouth to
laugh at his jokes but no sound comes out. Already the walls of the
bedroom are covered in green slime.

At breakfast, the man makes "the usual:" boiled eggs, toast, a wedge of
Brie, apricot jam, and good strong oolong tea. The Mushroom Queen
sniffs the Brie with its waxy casing of *Penicillium camemberti*. It
wouldn't do to eat a distant cousin, so she pushes it aside. "You love
Brie," says the man. The Mushroom Queen shrugs. "Maybe you're
pregnant." A grin spreads across his face. She laughs her soundless
laugh. If the Mushroom Queen wanted to propagate all she would have

to do is point a finger and a mushroom would bud out of its tip. She pushes her egg away, too fresh. "What can I get you instead?" says the man.

The contents of the compost bin would be nice, thinks the Mushroom Queen. She would like to take the bin to the guest room, where it is dark and damp, spread it out on the duvet and roll around in the coffee grounds, potato peels and carrot tops, but that wouldn't be good for their relationship.

This is her first time imitating human form, and the Mushroom Queen is not very good at it. One breast has come out larger than the other, and she forgot to grow earlobes—what will she do with all the earrings the other woman owns? Her hair moves by itself, as if animated by a celestial wind, for, unlike human hair, which is just dead keratin, the hair of the Mushroom Queen is alive—mycelium embedded with loam to make it black. Speech is difficult, though not impossible. Moving air through a mushroom is no problem, just look at the spore dispersal of the *Calvatia gigantea*, the giant puffball. It is the tone modulation she can't get right. Much easier to nod and smile; the man does all the talking anyway.

The Mushroom Queen bathes in the normal way when the man wants to take a bath with her, but she doesn't feel fully clean in water. Later that afternoon, while he's napping, she goes out into the garden and tears open a bag of premium potting soil, rubs herself down beneath the shade of the tree ferns.

Our woman's body is pressed down through a root sieve, releasing the one hundred trillion cells of her symbiotic microbiome into the soil. They wriggle away in search of a new host. What's left of her, the approximately 37.2 trillion cells that had once been organized into brain, liver, eyeballs, belly-button, are absorbed by the tube-like hyphae of the North American mycelium web and fanned out across the garden. In her newly dematerialized state she is simultaneously nowhere and everywhere. But this is just an illusion, a temporary form of vertigo brought on by the sudden vastness of her being. In reality, she covers a little less than three square acres, one edge dangling in the cool green waters of the Hudson, the other pushed up against the crumbling blacktop of Route 9. A red-brick house squats on her chest like a poorly-digested meal. There's a maple tree growing out of her forehead, its flame-colored leaves the color of her panic.

Days pass. At night the mist rises from the Pacific, rolls up the cliff, and settles around the house, muffling it from the street noise and the neighboring houses. One morning when the dogs step out, they find the lawn covered in mushrooms. The woman used to come out with a weed puller and scoop out each fungus by the root, afraid the dogs would eat them. Her people had been mushroom eaters in the old country, but she'd lost the knack of sorting edible from poisonous. The dogs sniff the ground beneath the nearest jade plant. There's something lingering among the watery stems of the succulent, a sad, familiar scent of laundry detergent and lemon verbena hand lotion.

What does the Mushroom Queen end up eating? Fermented things, like pickles, soy sauce drunk directly from the bottle, kimchi, forgotten packages of ham gone slippery with pink goo, old strawberries melting into their green plastic basket, glued together by a whitish fur. She hides eggs under the quilt in the unused guest room until they rot, sucks out the yolks and eats the shells. She drinks beer, endless bottles of beer, though the man is surprised. The other woman never touched alcohol, "empty calories" she called it. But the Mushroom Queen never gains weight, only biomass.

How does the Mushroom Queen feel about the dogs? They're competitors for the rabbit pellets, and they don't give anything back, their own waste too rich in erythrocytes from the meat they eat to grow mushrooms. And the dogs are suspicious of her, particularly the little one. It's a good thing they can't speak. The man ignores them; he doesn't even feed them. Their leashes hang limply from the doorknob. The Mushroom Queen can't risk walking them, can't expose herself to the neighbors, not knowing their names. Besotted with the myth of personhood, humans have names. Mushrooms have no such cult of personality. All is mycelium; mycelium is all.

It takes a great deal of concentration to concentrate the self, but nothing banishes lethargy like a well-defined villain. At five cell layers instead of one, our woman has condensed herself from three acres down to the size of the lawn in her own backyard, but still flat and thin enough to move through the soil without having to worry about snagging parts of herself on telephone poles and sewage pipes. She's heading west against the earth's rotation, gliding through the rich dark loam of the Hudson River Valley as easily as a manta ray swimming through water. She's heading home, never mind that home is the place from which she had recently dreamed of escaping.

The small dog leads the white dog on a tour of the woman's closet to check the shoes, but not one pair is missing, not even the pale blue sneakers she wore when she walked them around the block—the only time she ever left the house. The man left the house almost every other morning, coming back hours later smelling of coffee, cigarettes, and something else; something younger.

The woman had taken them on endless loops around the neighborhood, making sure to pass by the little parking lot where the tourists stop to gawk at the cliffs above the ocean, and also to admire the dogs, and by extension, the woman. She needed it, that daily dose. The man used to admire her, a long time ago, back when the dogs were just pups, but then he began spending his days staring into a glowing screen. The small dog liked to snuffle under his chair, looking for crumbs—the man is such a messy eater. He'd get up on his hind legs and peer at the screen, trying to make sense of the sinuous writhing shapes, until the woman walked into the room and the image changed instantly to regiments of black ants marching on a plain white ground.

Born into darkness, the Mushroom Queen cannot sleep at night. She wanders the house picking up objects at random, trying to guess their purpose. There are wedding photographs on the piano, the man and the woman surrounded by smiling friends and children playing musical instruments. The man is ducking under colorful streamers as the wedding party braids them around a maypole. The bride looks young and happy in her butterfly-embroidered skirt. Will she try to find her way back? What will happen if she does? Which one would the man choose?

The Mushroom Queen wants to experience love, that's why she came here in the first place, but she also wants to be *known*. She has learned about the distinction from the books in the basement of the red-brick house. Seeping into soggy cardboard boxes, she consumed page after page of *Romeo and Juliet*, *Pride and Prejudice*, *Wuthering Heights*, even *Gone with the Wind*, and realized that to be loved is not the same as to be known. For instance, Karenin loved his wife, Anna, in his own

167

way, but he did not *know* her. How is the Mushroom Queen going to get the man to see her clearly, to fall in love with her without the use of deception?

There are so many things she can do: *Pleurotus ostreatus*, the oyster mushroom, to unclog his arteries; *Lentinula edodes*, the shiitake, with its powerful anticancer, antiviral, and anti-herpes polysaccharides; *Ganoderma lucidum*, the reishi mushroom, for longevity and sexual prowess. On the other hand, there are the death caps and the *Amanita ocreata*, the destroying angel—so like the common button mushroom, except for the veil connecting its egg shaped cap with its chubby stem like a fibrous foreskin. That and its ability to instantly dissolve the mammalian liver. The Mushroom Queen loves these mushrooms, but to win the man's affection, she'll do it the hard way, using nothing but the clumsy human heart, or a reasonable fungal facsimile.

The small dog is angry with the white dog. More than once he's come upon them in the hallway, the big white idiot lying on his back, paws in the air, tongue lolling out of his big stupid grin, writhing under the hands of the Mushroom Queen as she scratches the fur of his belly. Disgusting.

The small dog follows the imposter as the man leads her onto the lawn, to the hidden bower where he and the real woman used to make love in the afternoon. He watches from behind the acacia tree. He had seen before how the man leaned over the original, pumping the essence out of her, making her cranky and bloated, causing her to crave salt and sweet, spicy and sour. He had seen it but what could he do? The Mushroom Queen is not depleted by the man's attentions. Each day she grows stronger. Even now, as the man leans over her, she arches her neck, her eyes roll back until only the whites are visible, her mushroom-brown lips split apart in a silent yawl of pleasure.

Our woman trails the rains as they sweep across the continent. By early August she's made it all the way to the eastern slopes of the Rocky Mountains. She climbs the foothills, the land rising and falling, rising and falling, like a roller-coaster. At five thousand feet she reaches a broad, high meadow sheltered from the winds by an aspen grove. She weaves in through the orange paintbrush and chamomile, primrose, fireweed, and horsemint. The air is cool and thin, the soil moist and rich. It would be lovely to settle down in this place, but vengeance keeps her moving. A jagged wall of granite rises above her, a hundred times more daunting than the Appalachians. Up ahead is the timberline, where there are no trees, no soil, and very little water. She can't go up but she can go *through*, releasing polysaccharides, glycoproteins, chelating enzymes and acids, creating micro cavities in the granite, but that would take too long, and time is running out—she can feel it in the very tips of her hyphae. She hunkers down among the lupines, pushing up mushrooms as she contemplates her next move.

The man would have liked the paradox of a mushroom attempting to scale a mountain. A paradigm shift is what you need, he would have said. They used to be good at playing games with words—it's what brought them together in the first place. But over time, they learned that there are only so many stories to tell, and only so many ways to tell them, and in the end, silence is better. At least now, if she made it home alive, they will have something new to talk about.

The Mushroom Queen's attention is beginning to wander. There's a hollow spot under the floor near the bookshelf where the termites have devoured an entire wooden slat. Rats gnaw all night long in the crawl space above the bed. The garage roof sinks in the middle like a swaybacked horse, pine roots have buckled the concrete driveway, silverfish scuttle among the cutlery—the house is calling to her and she has no choice but to respond. After all, she is a saprophyte, a primary decomposer of twigs, grass, stumps, logs, and other dead things. It's what she does; it's nothing personal. Besides, human love tasted so much better on the page. Already her hyphae are slipping in between the man's cells, prying them apart. Soon she will dissolve him. The dogs are next. For now their abundant fur has kept them safe, that and their reflexes. But how long can they dodge her sticky threads? The Mushroom Queen has stopped feeding them, hoping to slow them down. They are starving, growing weaker by the day. Even the rabbits have left the lawn.

Unloved, unbrushed, his belly empty, the small dog fills his days with happy memories. Like laundry day, when the woman used to dump the fresh load onto the bed and drop the small dog into the heap so he could root and dig and roll around in the warm fragrant cloth. No one does laundry now that the woman is gone. The dishes go unwashed, the floors unswept. Without the woman's constant ministrations, the walls themselves are caving in.

Back at the timberline, beetles arrive and land on the woman's mushroom caps, burrowing deeply into her soft pink flesh, piercing through into her spore-rich under layer. How good it feels to be cleaned out like this!

I cook, you clean, the man used to say, preferring the "deep eroticism" of a woman standing at the sink in purple rubber gloves.

Another rainstorm comes and the beetles are picked up by the wind, up and over the mountain they fly, spores clinging to their legs and wings. They settle down near Grand Junction, Colorado, depositing her spores onto the ground as they scuttle away into the fields. She sinks into the mulch and germinates a fresh new webbing of mycelium. Reborn, she waits a few more days to see how many more of her progeny will make the crossing. By early September she's half her size, but twice as determined.

Hugging the Colorado River all the way to the California border, our woman enters the Imperial Valley. Shimmying along irrigation canals, she runs her mycelium under fields of cabbages and cantaloupe, sucking up life-giving nitrogen as she fans up and out into San Bernardino County. From there she hops lawns all the way to Point Dume.

The Mushroom Queen has established a mycelial perimeter around the house extending from the Pacific Coast Highway to the very edge of the cliff above the Pacific Ocean. Through the septal pores of her naked hyphae tips she is aware of her rival's imminent approach. The Mushroom Queen enters the kitchen in black galoshes. She puts on a pair of purple rubber gloves, steps into a couple of trash bags, making sure to tape the plastic securely at the wrists and ankles, and wraps several yards of cling wrap around her head and neck. Then she begins to whip up a batch of poison. The house, the man, the dogs: they all belong to her now. She's not willing to share them.

Giddy, triumphant, our woman breaks through the cracked terra-cotta patio and surges under the grass, following the lawnmower as the man, recklessly barefoot, paces out wide even rows. The Mushroom Queen walks behind him in her battle gear, a bottle of viscous liquid attached to the garden hose, saturating the lawn in the path created by the mower.

Our woman can taste the individual ingredients: olive oil, baking soda, apple cider vinegar. Such wholesome things, how often had she used them herself, but now they are *dissolving* her. She sinks down through the sod, then the three inches of trucked-in dirt, the chicken-wire gopher barrier, and finally settles into the sand and clay that are the true soils of this land, this place where nothing was ever meant to grow. A fleeting thought crosses her mind: without the artificial lawn, the fertilizer, the monumental water bills—all things that she and her husband fussed over together—the Mushroom Queen could never have gained a foothold in their lives, because nothing grows in clay and sand, not even fungus. Clinging to the underside of the mulch layer, the woman crawls all the way to the back and takes shelter in the shade of the disassembled trellis.

Our woman tries to will herself back into human shape, but it's no good. She lacks the skill, and furthermore, she could no longer remember what she looked like. The Mushroom Queen, as she can see despite the many layers of Saran Wrap and Hefty Cinch Saks, doesn't look very human anymore. Her forehead bulges in the middle from the pressure of the cap, her body has grown cylindrical, stem-like, but love is blind.

How can she fight the Mushroom Queen if she can't get by the poisoned lawn? Perhaps she could enlist the aid of some parasitic bacteria? But that might harm the dogs and the man, and really, she's never been the kind of person to up the ante out of stubbornness until everything around her lies in ruins.

And then she remembers something she heard as she was driven from the lawn, something whispered to her by the *Onychomycosis* fungus growing on the third toe of the man's left foot: the man knows there's been a switch.

He knows and he does not miss her at all.

The fight goes out of her completely. She shrinks a little bit further into herself, the sand and clay robbing her mycelium of precious fluids. If she stays here a moment longer, she'll have to wait until the spring rains to make her escape. Where will she go? Back to the meadow with the primrose and chamomile? Back to the garden behind the red-brick house with its ancient, loamy soil? What had once been a prison now seems like Elysium.

171

And to be completely honest, she doesn't blame the man; he owes her nothing. Wishing to escape is the same as escaping. Her vanity is bruised, but maybe things are as they should be. What is a trellis after all but a perforated wooden barrier; a basket made of loose twigs through which the things you gather can fall out along the way.

She does not miss her human form. What a relief it is to escape that tired paradigm of head-torso-limbs, so much more trouble than it's worth. She likes her new spread-out state, her very own magic carpet; she can go anywhere.

She had longed to join the fast race but now instead she's joined the eternal race: fungus will survive the destruction of the environment, the melting of the polar ice caps, the rising of the waters. Fungus will survive until the earth falls into the sun, and maybe even after. She's gotten what she wanted. Well, almost.

She does not blame the white dog for betraying her with the Mushroom Queen. After all, he's just a dog, uncomplicated, happy-go-lucky, like the man, a love pig. But the small dog is different. She has always suspected that he isn't a dog at all, but a demoted human soul sent back to earth in a fur suit to atone for his sins. The small dog can be made to understand.

She has a plan, but it's risky, given her limited skills as a relatively new fungus. Her mycelium is plenipotent—it can create any type of mushroom—but she lacks control. Some of the beetles that came to her rescue in Colorado didn't make it to the other side of the mountain; they died writhing in the meadow. But what are her choices? The Mushroom Queen is distracted with the man, but eventually she'll turn the dogs into soil. At least if the woman can transform them, just as she had been transformed, digest their extracellular matrix, carefully separate their cells and braid them into her mycelium, they can be together.

The jade plant, a desert species, does not waste energy on growing an extensive root system. Its roots are shallow and wide and spread out from the stem horizontally mere inches below the surface in order to capture every drop of rain. These shallow roots act as a protective umbrella for the creatures that live below—an entire family of alligator lizards, a pair of carpenter bees. The male bee is black and shiny, about the size of a store-bought strawberry. When he takes to the air his wings make the sound of a miniature chain-saw. The female looks even bigger than her mate because of the dusty saffron hairs covering her golden body. Wherever she flies she leaves behind the scent of flowers—no wonder the male can't resist her. Under the jade plant where she first entered the soil, among the lizards and bees, our woman spins out fresh strands of mycelium and begins weaving a mat, a raft. A lure.

The small dog walks over to the nearest clump of jade plant. Shaky with hunger, he lifts his leg against the plump green leaves. That's when he sees them: three little mushrooms growing out of the lawn at the base of the plant. They're pink and tender with snug-fitting egg-shaped caps, arranged in an arc like the tips of a woman's fingers. Those familiar pink fingers that used to offer little bits of cheese, then reach for the tuft of hair that grows out of his head and scratch and scratch until he couldn't take it anymore. He can picture his mistress standing on tiptoe somewhere underground, reaching and reaching for the surface, only her fingertips breaking through to the mist-dampened air.

He starts digging frantically, trying to get her out before she suffocates, soil flying around him, clinging to his russet fur, but there are no fingers beneath the tips, no hand outstretched, no woman, just mushrooms. He sighs a deep, shuddering doggie sigh. She's never coming back, his beloved mistress; he'll never see her again. No one misses her but him. Despondent, he opens his small, sharp-fanged mouth and eats the mushrooms, one by one, until there's nothing left but a dug-out scar of earth at the base of the jade plant.

Nominated by Tin House, Ayse Papatya Bucak

COCAINE

by ALEX DIMITROV

from THE ADROIT JOURNAL

People disappear
And go looking for a place to be looked at.
All the way down Wilshire and above us: like a sheet of indigo tile.
As we waited, our nicotine glowed in the distance like flies
to some heaven, some high road.
"Who sat on mountaintops in cars reading books aloud to the
canyons?"
Like gods and at home being extras at best.
I almost believed love then someone new called me
and time's been repeating. Time's on like a show.
They say we're all wanted for living, that somebody's coming,
but even the darkest of frames make a face feel unsafe.
Yours was here, yours was seen
and it could have been two but you sold it for nothing.
Goodbye to all that then we're back low,
trying to fit the right size for what passes as days.
Take a vitamin, angel. Drink water.
The earth is a big thing.
Would you still like to have it or take the check early tonight?
I get worried then go for a drive with my eyes closed
right here—on the thirty-third floor of my thirty-third year—
what a party it turned out to be.
No one wanted to leave.
When the car you steer best is not yours; or the body.
The house and the job. Rooms of white lines. Gold lobbies.

We cringe at these lists but without them, who's counting?
I was flying over the country with you,
over states in their neat squares and fixed laws.
Flying over the country with women and men
in their trim suits and skirts.
Some nights I wait right out front for a moment
well after I get home. (Forced silence.)
I know what's inside.
We know what comes next.

Nominated by The Adroit Journal, D.A. Powell, Mark Irwin, Jennifer K. Sweeney

BEETS

by CATE HENNESSEY

from FOURTH GENRE

> . . . the showy
> flowers are over, retreated
> into the earth. It simply
>
> means what it is:
> Neither beginning
> nor *fin de siècle*
>
> regardless of the way it feels.
> —Laura Kasischke, "Happy Meal"

Here in the Pennsylvania deep freeze of January, a month with single-digit temperature days and nights, my youngest daughter and I while on a walk through snowy woods talk about the garden we'll have this summer. She wants her own patch for sunflowers and cucumbers and peas, and I know what she sees in her summer future because I see it, too: a self crouched at the edge of the raised beds, examining the yellow trumpet blossoms of cucumbers. A straw basket she's filling with cherry tomatoes and purple beans. The damp morning soil and the clear evening air, all without mosquitoes or slugs or wasps. And not any weeds twining the stems of her plants. As we walk through the snowy woods, my daughter and I, we talk together with the same hope and awe in our voices about the garden at its best, which is us at our best, and here in January, that is what we must hope for.

My gardens are never as ambitious or tidy or fruitful as the gardens in my mind. Something always happens. Once I planted too much in a small space and by June had a welter of lettuce, nasturtiums, peas, and scraggly tomatoes. Another time I had too many seedlings and threw most of them to the compost pile. One year a hurricane. And then there is the issue of cost. My garden requires money in addition to sunshine and rain. Some years, the sun and rain are the easy part, and I find myself investing an obscene number of dollars in fish emulsion, tomato cages, stakes, wire fencing for the peas, bird netting for strawberries, not to mention all manner of contraptions to keep out the deer.

I have three seed catalogs on my kitchen table this morning, all of which arrived just after the new year. The furnace is having a hard time—3 degrees at 7 a.m.—and it's trying mightily but not warming the rooms above 60 degrees. So here I sit, wrapped in sweaters and slippers and scarves, listening to the soft hiss of the gas burner as it heats the kettle. Dogs breathe sleep on their blankets. The sky is blue and cloudless outside, crackling bright, stark beautiful. Four months until anything can go in the soil. We gardeners are a hopeful lot. After all, looking at the last harvest does us no good. Some of it has long passed through our bellies, some is still in freezers or canning jars. That past is what we know for sure. Maybe the past, the recent past anyway, with the evidence of its successes or failures still before us, is the only thing we can be certain of. It's the next season and its surprises—the good and the bad—that interest us. And so I look at the seed catalogs.

Only one of them, Jung Seeds and Plants, is in full, glossy color. The cover is tomato red around the edges, the lettering large and sunflower yellow. The center bears photos of the most succulent possibilities: asparagus and strawberries. Peach-colored roses, a riot of zinnias, artisan tomatoes of oblong shapes and strange colors—yellow, burgundy, plum, striped pale gold, and green and pink. My god, how could anyone not look ahead? At the same time, fast-forwarding my attention four months allows no appreciation for winter, the here and now, as my aging gray and white cat settles himself on the Jung catalog. I run my hand over his neck and spine. This cat knows how to get what he wants, even in the season of cold. I should not let him settle like this on the kitchen table. We both know this. But I like his company, the soft dog breathing, the heater blowing and chuffing. In no other season would I have all of these things in hand, in ear, in sight. Still, the seed catalogs call with their bright covers. The Jung is still securely beneath the cat, and since I am loathe to disturb him, I open John Scheepers Kitchen Garden Seeds. This particular publication has arrived at my house— first the white one we painted yellow, and now the sea-green house we painted navy blue—ever since at the white house I ordered from Scheepers 100 Giant Darwin tulip bulbs. But that is a different story and a different catalog, the bulb collection, which arrives in summer, a full-color glossy magazine of voluptuous petals. The Scheepers garden seed catalog, on the other hand, is full color only on the cover—this year a collage of hollyhocks, pumpkins, smiling gardeners, and tomatillos. At bottom center, a large bundle of beets topped with red-veined foliage.

Not long ago I ordered some beets at a local restaurant. It was farm to table, the kind that's become popular in this place, a county of open space and old money. The beet salad—with arugula, chèvre, a balsamic reduction—was to be served warm, according to the menu (it was late November). When the dish arrived, burgundy slices smoldered on white, rectangular china. But in my mouth the beets were cold and slippery, as if they had come from a can. And maybe they had. But I had ordered the beets out of something—nostalgia? memory? the worst of the writer's sins, sentimentality?—and feeling guilty for this (I am always feeling guilty), I ate.

Beets first appeared in my kitchen a few years ago, the last year we lived in the white-and-then-yellow house. I had been buying seasonal produce from local farmers, and in the middle of winter the growers could offer only crates of root vegetables, last summer's harvest kept fresh in cellars. I'd been making my way through a 50-pound bag of potatoes I'd bought partially out of wistfulness, partially out of thrift. When my neighbor first told me about those potatoes, $12 for 50 pounds, available at a farm not far from my house, I was small again and it was a blustering gray day in western New York. The farmers' market in that time and place meant a few tables set up in a weedy lot at the corner of Lake Shore Drive and Main Street—one block from Lake Erie and one block from the government housing. I was standing there next to the tables with my mother, and we were waiting for my father's mother to stop haggling with her favorite farmer, Mr. _____, whose name my parents and I have since forgotten. He was a very fat man whose stomach hung over soiled jeans, and he might have been missing a few teeth. My grandmother, whom my brothers and I called Busia, was missing all of hers except two. To the market she had worn a paisley kerchief over her gray hair and a long, camel-colored wool coat that kept flapping its hem in the wind. She and the farmer were haggling over 50 pounds of potatoes because it would have been impolite not to haggle after so many years of doing so. The banter as usual was over a dime or a quarter or a nickel. My mother shook her head a little and murmured, *What is she going to do with 50 pounds of potatoes?* By this time, my father's father had been dead for most of a decade, or maybe half a decade, and my grandmother lived alone. Back then, those 50 pounds of potatoes made her strange, one more odd little thing to add to her list of oddities—the toothless mouth, her fractured English and rapid-fire Polish, the migraines and terrible sadness. I didn't know that something (in fact many things) had happened in Germany. I wouldn't know until I was 16, but that story too is for another time. When I was small, Busia was just a strange old lady.

The strange old lady had her own garden, but it was cheaper for her to buy the potatoes than grow them herself. There was the question of space, too. Her cinder-shingled house on Roberts Road had a short, narrow backyard, not nearly large enough to grow a winter's worth of potatoes in addition to the enormous red tomatoes on heavy vines that she staked and tied with her cast-off hosiery. Then the precise rows of bush beans. An orderly tangle of cucumbers and their yellow trumpet blossoms. Bouquets of parsley, stands of dill. And beets. The earth in her garden was black from manure she asked my father each year to turn into the ground. The earth in my parents' garden was orange clay. And did Busia also grow onions? I can't say for sure. My father remembers no, but we all agree she had a peach tree and a plum tree, and she boiled the fruit down and preserved it into leathery, sugarless jam. In the winter she spread this jam over butter on white toast and brought it on plates to my brother and me as we sat on her couch and watched *Wheel of Fortune* and *Jeopardy*.

Jeść, jeść, she said to us. Eat, eat. Then she shuffled back toward the kitchen and my father where they continued their conversation in Polish. My brother and I, having only English, heard them as a country apart from our blue TV haze.

In those years before I turned 12, before my grandmother's mind began to muddle, each Christmas Eve she made *barszcz*, beet soup from her own beets, and served the soup with half a hard-cooked egg floating in the middle of the bowl. A waste of a good egg, I thought, since I liked eggs and hated beets. Slender, slippery rectangles of the maroon root at the bottom of a bowl of maroon broth. And a strange undertaste I know now from reading recipes as sausage, dill, and black peppercorns.

When we are children, we don't have a history, so we cannot understand the holiness of food. Or the holiness of a particular food. And if we don't like a food when we are small, we think adults are crazy for their reverence. All the adults around the *Wigilia* table murmured their appreciation for the *barszcz*, while I stared at the bowl.

The 50 pounds of potatoes in my pantry went slowly down in that winter of seasonal eating at the white-and-then-yellow house. I got bored with the potatoes and started purchasing vegetables I had never tasted: turnips, rutabagas, parsnips. Then, after I'd exhausted everything else from the crates at the farmer's market, came the beets. I bought two large bunches and resolved not to make *barszcz*. The beets roasted in the oven instead, tossed with olive oil, sweet potatoes, carrots, salt, and pepper. My husband and I spooned this over greens, topped the whole thing with blue cheese and walnuts. Once a poached egg instead of cheese and nuts, and the yellow yolk and the magenta beets bled into each other with the vibrancy of a chemical sunrise. As I ate the roasted beets that had melted into the poached egg, I murmured.

The Scheepers catalog is a pleasure gardener's magazine. Its table of contents, rather difficult to find, resides quietly in the middle, which suggests that the reader has the time and interest and curiosity to look carefully through the pages and maybe along the way will discover something new to try in the garden this year. The beet page, for example, page 24 in this year's catalog, features seven types of seeds to choose from: Kestrel Baby Beets, Chioggia Beets, Boro, Detroit Red, Touchstone Gold, Cylindra, and Bull's Blood. No photograph or illustration offered for any of the varieties. Scheepers requires its readers to imagine. This imagining is not difficult, however, since whoever writes the vegetable descriptions does so with vigor and precision: *A graceful, globe-shaped gem, Kestrel produces sweet, tender baby beets. An American hybrid developed to mature early yet hold well in the garden, it has deep ruby-colored flesh that is soft-crisp with a delicate flavor.*

The catalog also offers a general description of beets and guidance for how to store them through the winter (in layers, in a box, with a measure of sand between each layer). That most hobby gardeners need to learn how to store beets, that *I* need to learn how to store beets, kills me. Busia and her sisters in rural Poland would have known this by age eight, maybe earlier. Would they have had names for different varieties of beets? Or was only one kind of beet grown in Subcarpathian Poland between the world wars? I don't know; the people I want to ask are all dead.

If Scheepers' luscious descriptions make it impossible for a gardener to settle on just one beet variety, there's the Unbeatable Beet Mixture. Four varieties in one packet of 220 seeds for $3.25. In theory, I could grow 220 beets for just over three dollars. The possibility of seeds—the impossibility of having my daughters, like me at their age, picky and suspicious of adults and their taste buds, eat any beets, let alone 220 of them! Though if I managed to harvest 100 beets, after dumb mistakes, insects, and whatever else, I would count myself lucky. Lucky. Luck and the beets. I think of my friend John Guzlowski, a man like my father whose parents were Catholic and taken from Poland to work in Germany during the Second World War. This displacement happened before the fathers and mothers had met, before the children were born. John is a poet who writes about what happened to his parents in the war and what happened to them afterward: *hope is the cancer no drug can cure*. This line, which rattles my heart, is from a poem about his father dying. His father, by then an old man in America, is calling out for his mother, who died not from the war but from illness when he was a very small boy. And I think John is right, there is no cure for hope. We're born into it—our planet, our home, keeps going, spinning and spinning. The earth turns toward the sun no matter what is going on in each corner of our boulder of rock and water. Hope dies when the earth dies. But hope as a cancer—I think he is right there, too, that hope grows when it is not supposed to.

Luck is one way John tries to understand who lived and who died in the war, in the camps. Luck, which is not gardening, since the nature of seeds—designed to grow—offers hope, that addiction of gardeners. John's mother at Buchenwald pried beets with her fingers out of the nearly frozen soil. How large and endless the fields of beets. What she must have thought about those long days, her life back in what is now Ukraine, the day she watched her mother and sister raped and shot. When the *niewolniki*, the slave laborers like John's mother, were starving, they sometimes smuggled a beet from the field and ate it raw. But John's mother had more luck. A guard from the beet field asked who could milk a cow, and his mother said she could, and that winter, instead of turning to ice in the field, she pressed in the dairy barn against the bodies and udders of cows.

I don't know what other than *barszcz* my grandmother prepared with beets those years she kept her garden on Roberts Road. Except for *Wigilia*, we rarely ate dinner at her home, and when we did, it was for me as if hope and loveliness had left the room. That sounds much grander and more dramatic than it was. Memory, or at least I find that mine, is like that—it calls up emotions deep and complicated and twined with a childhood I mistook for simplicity—and now I question the validity of events, stories I think I thought I've heard, the knowledge of myself even into the present That is, Busia cooked peasant country food—rice and beef wrapped in cabbage, or soured cabbage with black peppercorns. I shrank from the stuff, or at least inside myself I shrank. I can feel it now, that old dread, even though these days I eat those same foods without flinching, and I want to go back and hug and shake the childishness from the little girl who stared at her plate.

After my father's mother died, which was six weeks after my first daughter's birth and after I'd moved to the land of old money and open space, there came a story about Busia and beets. What she did with them during the war. The man who was her newborn son's father and would later become her husband threw beets wrapped in a rag over the barbed wire fence that surrounded her barrack. I can't see far enough into the past to know if he threw the beets in daytime or night, if the weather was foggy or clear, if she caught the beets or picked them up. Then she carried them back to the low and narrow wooden structure where she slept with hundreds of other Polish and Russian and Ukrainian women who worked at the munitions factory in a German town called Unterlüß. Certainly her hands mashed the beets, which she cooked on the black iron stove meant to heat the long room, but between the slats in the roof snowflakes came down. Busia was not the same as John's mother, the *niewolnika* in the concentration camp. Forced laborers like Busia were luckier, a different class of slave: they could leave their barracks on weekends and wear a coat with the letter P for Pole or OST for Eastern worker and go into town where they weren't allowed to enter restaurants or attend Mass or walk on the sidewalk at the same time as the Germans, and if this sounds a little like segregation in the American South, you're not wrong.

Mashing the cooked beets into paste, Busia fed them to my father, a few months old in the winter of '44 and '45, because the milk in her left breast had disappeared. He was hungry for more than the right breast; there were no rations for babies, nor rations enough for her. A few months before she arrived in Unterlüß in the autumn of 1943, after a boxcar ride from Poland, the women who came before her stood daily in line at the canteen for a few liters of turnip soup and 300 grams of bread. Through the week someone handed them 50 grams of margarine and 25 grams of meat. But luck, luck, luck all the same. After Busia's shift, after her son was born, she could rock and sing to him and the other babies in the factory nursery, even nurse him on her lunch break. In other parts of the country, women like her had to give up their babies, who were taken to other villages and adopted into German families. Or the babies were taken to places with names like Velkpe and Waltrop where the infants, who would have slowed their mothers' work in the factories and fields, weren't fed. They withered in their cribs and died.

Outside the kitchen window, the goldfinches and chickadees are at the thistle feeder, which is largely empty save a few seeds that cling to the mesh. A cardinal in the holly tree. Icicles hang in spikes from the gutters. We are out of thistle and have been for months, one of those things we haven't gotten around to. The birds must be hungry with this deep freeze. Two weeks of snow covering everything. The trees are teeming with birds. I am still thinking about John and hope. That because of hope we have remembered the war in redemptive ways when there was nothing redemptive about it. These birds—they don't, I assume, feel hope. They are driven by instinct. Hunger and reproduction. Fill those two voids. It is a job, a compulsion to assuage the pain in the belly, the longing in the groin. These things bear violence, even in birds. Harassment at the feeder. Later, in spring, the strange position of the female, always beneath and shuddering, and in the case of my hens, crouched still as death to protect themselves. Their eyes bulge. How much can we hope for when we are women in wartime, when we go back to instinct, and civilization is another word for what we have lost. Still women push out new creatures whose hunger must be gentled, and the rest of their lives these women pour themselves into this thing, another beast, and they try to fill its hunger. I fear I am someone who believes in hope and wants to believe in redemption, who dreams of gardens in her winter mind, but underneath, buried not far from the topsoil, history whispers *luck, luck, luck*.

In the last years of her life, Busia wouldn't or couldn't remember to eat. The irony is not lost on me that she forgot about food, or that it didn't seem to matter. She went nearly wild with hunger in Unterlüß, hallucinating the factory's sulfur piles into loaves of bread and once stealing vegetables with her fingers from another woman's soup pot. The year between college and graduate school, I was 22 and drove from Pittsburgh to western New York, then went with my father to visit Busia at the St. Francis home. She was living there because, even when she lived at her daughter's house, Busia would wander out the door and forget where she was. She forgot too her small collection of English but remembered German and Polish. My father was frustrated—she was losing weight, her cheekbones poked like tent poles against her skin. We sat in her gray room and took turns coaxing bits of chocolate pudding into her mouth, using a plastic spoon and some Polish, which by then I'd learned a little during my last years in college. Now it was I who was saying *Jeść, jeść*, the toast and jam turned to pudding, the plate to a tray, the old couch to a room that smelled of urine and caustic laundry detergent. The TV up on the wall in the corner was off, and my father and I were talking in Polish, Busia in the cocoon of herself, and the cup of pudding slowly emptying. I didn't want to reach the bottom. Because then there would be nothing left.

The last seed catalog on the kitchen table is a new one to enter the mailbox this year. Territorial Seed Company. Three times as thick as the Scheepers. Full-color photos throughout, and on the cover the ubiquitous wheelbarrow overflowing with produce. There are several sections of garden tools and tricks and trowels. This catalog says that sun, earth, and rain are not enough to grow seeds. There are soil thermometers, clogs, Wonder Gloves, digital pH meters, ladybugs, apple maggot traps, grow-light systems, skin therapy for cracked hands, compost pails, rain gauges, and hose nozzles—all the contraptions to care for seeds and care for ourselves as we care for the seeds, all the while believing because there was today and yesterday that there will be tomorrow. Because we are human and the earth is our home, we hope. We hope, we small things, while around us luck swirls like fog. All white, this fog, and there is only a short distance to see in front of us, we can feel the clouds on our skin, but we can't tell for sure if that dampness on our arms, on our faces, is why we're still here.

My aunt says Busia told her the same terrible story about the war, over and over through their years of washing and canning, as if a singular event carried everything Busia could say about what happened in Germany. Her grief over the bodies of women and babies who died when the Allied bombs came down on the barracks and the nursery.

Luck, luck, she ran through the bombs with her son to the forest and survived. An ironic luck, to live until age 92 with the images that threw her back always across an ocean and years to the place where she suffered and then survived when her friends did not. Where she became harnessed to the man who helped her survive but later turned her life into another kind of hell. My grandfather, Dziadzia, didn't talk about the war, but he drank his sorrows each weekend and poured them out onto the horse races, his wife, and four children. The war went on and on, and the children looked on from the attic stairs and wished for it all—the fighting and shouting and pulling their father out of the neighbor's bushes at midnight—to end.

Dziadzia died when I was 2 and he was 69 and his hair still black. Died the age my father is now. Dad's hair is still mostly black too, but Dad is not a yeller or a drunk or a gambler. He has two brothers and a sister, and neither are they drunks or yellers or gamblers at all. If there is redemption from war, it is in them. It's the chickadee at the birdfeeder, the red-capped woodpecker at the suet. That I can consider seeds and sit at the kitchen table with my coffee and slices of apple and watch small creatures. Of course that I am here at all is a direct consequence of the war that threw my grandparents together. But there were millions and millions for whom the family story ends only in death, given not even the strange and eternal gift of trauma. A future woman looking at the birdfeeder becomes impossible. So I am back to lucky. The millions dead quite outweigh this scribbling, this moment at the table in which the snow lies still and the trees flutter with birds.

And yet. I think if Busia saw me fretting over words and facts and hope and luck and getting these pieces of story (seeds and winter and food all wrapped up in the past) just so, she would say, stop looking back, stop pretending you can know what all of that war was, you don't want to know what it was. All your searching through articles and books and archives can't tell you. It is over, and your father is here, and you are here, and you have had children, and that is enough. Make the soil good and black. Tie up the tomatoes. Cook the pierogi and cook the potatoes. But don't cook the *barszcz* if you don't like it. Who cares if you never liked it and never will?

I am not sure I can take her advice, should take her advice, though I want to (even long to). I know I should not try so hard to find meaning in her past, to decipher a war and the people who went through it and never went home again. There is no worth in sentimentality. She learned this. Move on, move forward. Here is the garden in spring, even in January, even if come autumn the cache in the cellar isn't as gorgeous as you'd hoped. There is waving a hand in the air at the restaurant and saying, *These beets are cold*, and not feeling bad about saying so because there is a stove in the kitchen, and it is no accident the kitchen is warm.

Nominated by Fourth Genre, Lia Purpura

THE TALLGRASS SHUFFLES

by SEA SHARP

from STORM CELLAR

last night the wind said
be careful girl the
moon be watching

said keep your fingers
out the mud keep your tongue
in your head said the moon

is watching you said she'll pull
you apart like the tide
when your time comes girl

rip out your womb like a second heart
drag it on the asphalt like roadkill
said you smell like roadkill

you taste like shit girl
said be careful the moon be
watching and she gone be mad

she gone tie you to the shed 'cause you
ain't primp enough for no ribbons girl
you ain't show girl you ain't top breed

you ain't pedigree girl
down girl bad girl sit girl
bangbang dead girl going

going sold just like that girl
the moon be watching so slow
down child said be still girl

said quit that noise
said stop that shine
said shuck that corn

girl she seen you bust the limestones brittle
do the tallgrass shuffles like dance moves
like prairie inferno hopscotch like shoooo

said ooooh girl stop playing
now smooth down your dress
and fold up your tail

and zip shut that grin
and pin back your ears
said the moon be watching you

said be careful said
swoosh and such said
heel girl said stay girl said die girl

Nominated by Storm Cellar

THE DEVIL'S TRIANGLE

fiction by EMMA DUFFY-COMPARONE

from NEW ENGLAND REVIEW

Her parents always said they'd dig their own graves if anything happened to their children, so when her sister Claire disappeared on a camping trip in the White Mountains, Elsie kept an eye on things. She brought them groceries. Made mushroom risottos and bean enchiladas and coconut lentil soups and made her father sit at the table until he ate three bites. Took her mother to cafés downtown to drink cappuccino and play honeymoon whist. Signed her father up for beach yoga and dragged him to the ocean at sunrise with bamboo mats. Researched imaginal psychotherapy and psychodynamic insight therapy and expressive therapy and brief solution focused therapy and called psychologists and psychiatrists and support groups and chauffeured her mother to initial consultations. "I don't need some Wellesley cunt taking notes while I play in a sandbox," her mother would say, sinking into Elsie's Volkswagen, clenching her purse, and Elsie would drive home and call someone else.

It had been a year of that. Still they knew nothing, and Elsie lived in that nothing, roaming the endless corridors of it, the silence unspeakable and huge.

"Come down for the weekend," Elsie's other sister Mika said, on the phone. The sisters were triplets. They were twenty-nine. They'd all been sharing an apartment in Cambridge, and when Claire went missing, Mika dropped out of law school and drove south without so much as a map. Before, she had been ambitious and idealistic and highstrung, had volunteered at a women's shelter every night after class got out, had railed daily against the patriarchal machine, had even lasted forty-nine weeks, as far as she knew, without buying a single item made in China. Now she was a secretary at a hearing center and spent all day yelling into the phone at *all of the old fucks.* Sometimes she didn't answer Elsie's calls for weeks, and when she did, she sounded like someone else, her voice thin and hoarse.

"I don't know," said Elsie.

"Don't you have Columbus Day off?" Elsie was a high school librarian, a little intense these days, maybe, a little aggressive—*Take this!* she'd say, pushing hardcovers into the chests of bagel-faced linebackers, gloomy and skittish bulimics, gamers with Red Bull teeth, *Just take this!*

"There's shit I have to order."

"Mitchell's having a party on his yacht," Mika said. "You could use a little extroversion. You can practice your small talk."

"Who's Mitchell?" said Elsie.

"My boyfriend."

"I thought Francois was your boyfriend."

"Who?" said Mika. "Oh, Jacques. Yeah, he was."

"Oh."

"You don't have to say *oh* like that."

"I didn't!" Steam banged, pitchless, up the pipes in the apartment where Elsie still lived. Fall was here, and she hated it—the quick animal scratch of yard rakes, chestnuts dropping like bullets on the tops of cars, the occasional jack-o-lantern snatched in the night and found murdered in the road. It would snow soon, and evenings were getting very dark.

"A *yacht*?" Elsie said.

"A superyacht." Mika sighed. "How long can you do this?"

Elsie looked into Claire's room—surfboard propped against the closet door, cross-country skis tucked under the bed, Buddha statue in the window, boxes of books on large animal husbandry and small animal surgery and fundamental veterinary clinical pathology, harp zipped in its cover, eighteen Japanese tea pots Claire had individually named. Mika had sublet her own room to a surgical intern who was never home, but Elsie was still paying for Claire's—she didn't know what else to do. What else could she do? Claire had just run to the bathroom—*Be right back!*—a tampon like a flare in her fist.

"It's just for the time being," said Elsie.

"Use my miles."

Elsie knocked on Mika's door, woozy from the flight, taxi backing up and bobbing over a succession of speed bumps. Cadillacs and Buicks

190

sat in assigned covered parking spots. Anoles darted out from bushes and scaled the concrete stairs. Gnomes pushed gnome wheelbarrows in rock gardens. Mika didn't have a garden, just a piece of trellis that didn't quite hide the gas tank. After returning from a cross-country road trip, Claire had once proclaimed that Florida—blue hairs vying for discounted cinnamon buns, alligators loitering in soupy meridians, palm trees nothing but poles with bad hats—on her personal Spectrum of Existential Angst (SEA, she called it, for short), was an eleven. But here Mika had landed, in a condo complex on the yellowed outskirts of Miami.

Mika opened the door with a whoosh of central air, beer in hand. "I got out of work early," she said, squeezing Elsie hard. "Said I had diarrhea." Her hair was blond now and it didn't suit her. Her skin and lips looked washed out, the pouches under her eyes dark as figs.

"Are you eating?" Elsie said.

"Yes, I'm *eating*." She took Elsie's bag and dropped it in the front hall. "Bathroom's that way."

Elsie walked around Mika's condo. A TV the size of a milk truck shouted local news. She studied framed pictures of people she had never seen, grinning wildly with their faces pushed together, colored drinks raised to the camera, doing Jell-O shots, belly shots. It took Elsie a few seconds to recognize her sister in them at all. Elsie wandered into the small lanai and looked at the fountain in the center of a manmade pond.

"Water view, baby," Mika said, when she walked in.

"Very nice," said Elsie, and Mika handed her a Corona. Under the overhead light, Mika's skin looked green as a grass stain. Claire had always tended to the lighting in the girls' apartments, swapping 40-watts with 60-watts, making sure they felt cozy and at ease. She would turn on a lamp, walk to the other end of the room, and grimace. *What do you think?* she'd say to Elsie or Mika, who would nod, shrug, but Claire would already be stomping toward it, ripping off the shade, wringing the lamp by the neck. *Depressing*, she'd say. *Looks like the kind of hotel room you die in.*

"Go sit in the sun," said Mika. "I'll bring out some lunch."

Elsie walked into the small backyard. A few hibiscuses bloomed, blossoms as big as cats. The yard had a stone patio, a glass table and umbrella, and a gas grill tucked in the corner by an animal cage and two recycling bins so full of liquor bottles that several empty handles had been placed on the ground. She walked over and crouched to look

191

inside the mesh hut. Claire's guinea pig, Pam, sat on chicken wire, breathing rapidly. Mika had taken her when she moved out of the apartment. Now the animal was barely recognizable, polka-dotted with scarlet sores like sucked cough drops, her nails brown and corkscrewing into her feet, her left eye oozed shut, the right cloudy as if rinsed with half-and-half.

Elsie reached into the cage to pet her.

Mika emerged from the house carrying two sandwiches on plates. "Courtesy of Miracle Hearing," she said. When the doctors had lunch meetings, she could sometimes, if timed right, score a leftover sandwich. If you threw those things in the toaster oven, she said, boom: dinner. "I added mustard."

"Looks like Pam's been doing some hard living," Elsie said.

Mika shrugged and handed Elsie a plate. "She's happy."

"Happy?" Elsie eyed the sandwich warily.

"Well, I don't know! You can't tell with those things." Mika bent over and stared blankly into the cage. "They don't bring much to the table."

"Jesus," said Elsie. "You have to feed her."

Mika dropped into a chair and began to eat. "I feed her," she said with her mouth full, "and at six we have cocktails."

"I'm serious. Claire will frea—"

"Okay, boss," said Mika. She set her plate on the arm of the chair, pulled a pack of cigarettes from her pocket, and shook one out.

"You smoke?" Elsie asked. The sandwich was stale as a paperback.

"Not really."

"Don't do that. I'm begging you."

"You got bigger problems," Mika said, cupping her hand over the lighter. She blew a woolly stream from the side of her mouth. "You should see your eye right now. Wandering's a word for it."

"Yeah, well," Elsie said. Pam hadn't moved. A nauseous breeze drifted over from the cage. "It's been doing that lately."

Mika cringed. "That's fucked," she said.

"What's Mitchell like?" Elsie said, after they'd finished eating and Mika suggested they go for a walk. "Besides owning a yacht." The road was a three-lane highway, and not, Elsie was realizing, on the way to something else. This, the highway, was the walk. Storm clouds billowed from a Mack. An old Pontiac dragged its muffler like a car for newlyweds.

"He's—" Mika frowned. "He has this space between his front teeth.

192

And when he smiles his eyes get all squinty. He likes to fuck me in front of the window. Says it's not fair he's the only one who gets to see me."

Elsie made a face. "How charitable."

"Yeah, well." Mika was pumping her arms, her hands in fists. Hills, she said, were prime time to work her ass. "I think he's great."

Elsie shrugged. "Is it serious?"

"Enh," said Mika. "He does his own thing."

"So you just stay in touch?"

"He might text, like, twice a week?"

"Do you text him?" Elsie said.

"Well, I *respond*," said Mika. "You can't seem too needy or they'll lose interest."

A woman stood on her deck, stomach hanging out, clutching a beer and looking out over the traffic, and Elsie waved. "That's needy?" she asked.

"He likes to come and go."

"And you're okay with that."

"What?"

"I don't know," Elsie said. "Really, what do I know?" Mika had always insisted that dating culture was yet another mass conspiracy—along with toothpaste, manholes, airline snacks—of female subjugation. Once, when Elsie had been considering quitting her job to be near an old boyfriend, Mika had asked her if she needed a fucking ambulance, and then hadn't talked to her for a week.

Those beers had been a bad move. Mika, who'd had six, maybe seven, didn't seem phased. Elsie took off her long-sleeved shirt and wiped down her chest with it. Men leaned out of a roofless jeep, hooting.

"When are you going back to school?" Elsie said.

"I'm not."

"I don't understand."

Mika shrugged. "I didn't really want to be a lawyer."

At the grounds, after two hours had passed, having checked every bathroom, parking lot, and campsite, Elsie and Mika had stumbled blind into separate parts of the woods, their calls like echoes of each other. *Claire! Claire!*

"Right," said Elsie. "You wanted to be a secretary."

They came to a rest stop near a city reservoir, and Mika pointed to a bench next to some Porta Potties. "This is my favorite spot," she said. "Let's sit, okay? Let's just sit for a minute."

They sat.

Construction trucks howled behind them. The Porta Potties smelled syrupy and rank. A diesel breeze shuffled her bangs. "Did you have to put her out by the trash?" Elsie said, finally.

"What are you talking about?"

"Pam."

Mika sighed. "You saw my yard. It's a fucking bathmat. Everything's technically *by the trash*." Elsie watched her suck on a cigarette, and then she looked away, out at the gunmetal water, at the wires strung from pole to pole to ward off the birds.

There was a pair of Frye boots Mika needed at Nordstrom. "When you divide the price by every day I'll wear them," she said, "they're practically free." Then she wanted to go to Victoria's Secret.

Mitchell, she said, preferred her in the push-up.

"Who *are* you?" Elsie said, eyes wide.

"What do you mean?"

"I don't know," Elsie said. "Nothing." She could smell the store's perfume from the street. Naked, decapitated mannequins stood in the window.

"Let's get you something sexy," Mika said. "My treat."

"What happened to your whole theory on the conspiracy of commercialized objectification?" Elsie said.

"We'll give them dirty looks," Mika said, pulling Elsie by the elbow into the store.

There was the underwear that showed a quarter of your ass. There was the underwear that showed half of your ass. Then there was the rest. Striped, hearted, leoparded. Bows and buckles. Stores like this always made Elsie feel like an imposter. You either had sex appeal or you didn't, like attached earlobes. Claire had it. It was something about the way she walked, Elsie thought. She took her time. She used her hips. She didn't scurry out of the room like a shoplifter. "Try these," Mika said, pointing to a table. "And these." Elsie scanned Mika's face for a hint of cynicism, of irony, but she was flipping assertively through a pile of "Cheekies" fanned out like a platter of cold cuts.

"You know those cotton ones that Claire wears?" Elsie said. "Are those here? I'd wear those."

Mika was tearing through a hanger of bras. "Hmm," she said.

Elsie thumbed the material. "Do you think Victoria's secret is that she has a yeast infection?" she said. Mika's phone began to ring.

Elsie's heart sank, then fell out the leg of her pants. "Your phone," she said.

"I've got it," Mika said, reaching for her bag.

"It's in your purse."

"Obviously"

Mika had found Claire's flip-flop a hundred feet from the bathrooms. *It's hers!* she'd yelled, beginning to sob, her face scratched red, from a branch or her own fingernails. *It's Claire's!*

Elsie stared at Mika, clutching a pair of underwear in her fist. "Who is it?" she said. The ring was a muffled siren in Mika's purse.

"Hold *on*," said Mika. She squinted at the phone, then shook her head and dropped it back into her purse.

"Tell me," said Elsie.

"Eight hundred number."

"Oh," said Elsie.

They went back to the underwear.

"Is this what you'd call 'taking back our sexuality'?" Elsie said. Her pulse was throwing punches. She held up a black G-string. "Do you think this thong is third-wave or postfeminist?"

"Just pick out a few fucking panties."

"I'll get this number." Elsie swung the thong. "It can double as an eye patch."

"Seriously," said Mika.

"I am serious."

"Pick something out for real."

Elsie dutifully flipped through a rack of polyester teddies. She tried hard to have an opinion about them, or else not to have an opinion about them—she wasn't sure which. She supposed they were nice, the teddies. She supposed she could use one. She held one up and studied it.

"Do you have any in an A-cup?" Elsie asked one of the salesgirls.

"A-cups are only sold online."

"What are you saying?" Elsie said hotly, and then shuffled apologetically behind a mannequin.

Mika came out of the dressing room. "Did you see these dresses over here?" she said. "I could see you in one of these." They were black, silky, with thin straps and pooling necklines. Mika grabbed one and handed it to her sister. Elsie held it against her torso and looked down dubiously. "My bush'll fall out," she said.

"Good. You're wearing it tonight. Phil will be into it."

"Phil?"

"That guy I told you about."

"No, you didn't."

"Oh," said Mika. "He's a friend of Mitch's. I told him you were coming."

"I'm not in the mood for that."

Mika's eyes grew wet, veiny as leaves, and she looked away.

"I'd prefer to be clothed," Elsie said.

Mika bought the dress for Elsie and five new bras for herself. They walked out into the afternoon sun. Palm leaves clattered like bones above them. "Now let's get your hair done," said Mika.

"I just got it cut."

"Highlights. Just a few."

"Mika."

Elsie's hair, two hours later, was a parched blond, coarse and stringy as a doll's.

"You look like a different person!" Mika said, clapping, when the foil came off.

"Like you?" Elsie snapped, and then excused herself to the bathroom and sat on the floor. The plunger next to her had been recently used. She looked at the toilet for a while, at the slick pottery glaze of it, and then retched into the bowl.

Mika was helping Mitchell set up for the party and had left cab fare and the address of the marina for Elsie while she took a nap and a shower. She was to be there at five, Mika said, no later. It was already twenty past. The dress was light as a kerchief when Elsie took it out of the bag. She put it on, thong too, and walked around the empty condo, her wet hair dripping down her shoulders, her legs, already ugly with winter, jutting out from the dress. It seemed impossible that the day was not yet over. It seemed more than impossible that there was a party tonight and she would be at it. She realized she didn't have any shoes, so she put her sneakers back on, and then looked in the mirror. Her hair didn't seem attached to her at all but positioned on top of her, stiffly, like wicker.

She called a cab, and then went outside to see if Pam had eaten any of the lettuce she had put in the cage. It hadn't been touched. She nudged a leaf under Pam's chin, and then tapped the water bottle to let a few drips out.

"Hold on," whispered Elsie. "Please."

She stood there for a minute, while the one cloud in Florida sat on

196

the sun, which made all the birds sing out, in bursts, like music boxes opened and slammed shut again.

Then she pulled Pam out, and when the cab came, she budded herself in and Pam, too, while she was at it.

At the marina in South Beach, the sun was dropping to the sea, lighting up sails like Chinese lanterns. Elsie padded along the boardwalk, gripping Pam to her chest. Three sheepish-looking pelicans hung their heads on the dock. A group of women approached her and they parted down the middle for Elsie. For a moment she was swallowed in shampoo and chatter and cigarettes, and then she emerged from the other side and kept walking. Her hair rustled in the wind.

Narrow-eyed yachts glowed like a neighborhood: *Knot His, Atta Buoy, Alimony.* Elsie wasn't big on parties. She wasn't big on boats, either. Blinking in the direction of his pants—*Maybe next time*, Claire had once said after a double date, *focus more on eating*—"that would be a moot point. I mean, I would think the smaller, for her, the more, ah, palatable." Should she leap off this yacht buzzed, or plastered? She looked away, embarrassed, looked anywhere, at her tragic sneakers, at the woman across the deck also looking at her sneakers, at pelicans—so homely, poor bastards, abandoned dinosaurs—plunging into the water, and settled finally on his arm hair, which was so long it actually swayed a little in the wind, like wheat.

"She hasn't left," he said.

"Oh."

"Not technically."

"I see."

"Her stuff's still at the house. I told her she could keep it there until she figures things out."

"Right."

"Everyone keeps telling me to move on," Phil said miserably. "Just start a new life. But I just can't seem to—." He looked away and then back, staring blankly. "I was hoping she was going through a phase."

She tried to think of something to say. "I like your shirt," she said.

He looked down, making a double chin, and plucked at the material. "I did a wash yesterday and now this seems a little small."

"It's very festive."

"Not that I'm one of those guys who can't do stuff around the house!" he said. "You should see the tub when I'm done with it."

"Be right back, okay?" Elsie said. "I'd love another drink?"

At the food table she grabbed a few cucumber sticks and then hurried down to the lower deck. A couple was kissing in the corridor. The woman made soft whining noises and stepped out of her shoes. "Excuse me," Elsie said, pushing past them. The door to the storeroom was open slightly, and she ducked inside.

She found the bench and knelt down to pull the box out. Pam was there, panting, her fur almost damp to the touch. Elsie didn't know what she'd been thinking. She put the cucumbers down, slumped onto the shrimp-smelling carpet, and tried the deep breathing exercises she had read about in one of her mother's handouts: inhale for four, hold for four, exhale for eight. She could hear Mika in the corridor. "Mitch, where *are* you?" she was yelling. She sounded drunk. "Mitch, baby, come on!"

"Mika!" Elsie called out, and waited. "Mika, in here!" But the corridor was quiet again.

Elsie sat there for a while with her head against the wall. Then she gently pushed Pam's box back under the bench, staggered back up to the upper deck, and threw down another G&T.

Phil was still out by the deep end. "I got you a drink," he said, holding up an empty glass, "but then I drank it."

"No problem."

Mika was stumbling toward them, barefoot, wrapped in a beach towel and clutching a martini. Her eyes were red, sore looking, sooty with mascara. "Mika Machine!" Phil said.

Mika eyed him coolly.

"Where's Mitch?" he said. "I have his watch."

"Yeah?" Mika scowled. "Chuck it overboard."

"Ah, well," said Phil. He chuckled nervously.

"You okay?" said Elsie.

"Domestic troubles?" said Phil.

"I need a drink," Mika said, although hers was full.

"Mika," said Elsie, but her sister wouldn't look at her. "What's going on?" she said, but Mika was already wandering down the deck.

"Great girl," Phil said, watching her walk away. Then he turned back to Elsie and studied her. "Need Dramamine?"

"It's not that."

He nodded sympathetically. "Have your period?"

"Jesus," she said, and leaned over the railing. The sea was ruffled, gray as a hubcap.

198

"Careful," he said. "Don't lean so far."

"I like it," she said, quietly. "You ever get that feeling, like you might jump?"

He looked at her, eyes wide. "I can't swim."

"Should you be on a boat?"

"Ennnh," he said. "You live in Miami, too?"

"Boston," Elsie said. At the edge of the pool, Mika was unwrapping her towel and then dropped it to the deck to reveal a white bikini.

"Boston!" He looked momentarily despondent, then recovered. "What do you do up there? Do you Ski-doo?"

"I'm a librarian." Elsie watched Mika step gingerly into the pool. "I mean I was. I mean I still—at a high school."

"I love the sound of the bindings getting swiped over that detector thing," Phil said. "You know, so the alarm doesn't go off."

"The desensitizer," Elsie said. She looked at him. "You do?"

"Yeah," he said. "I like to check out cookbooks."

"You cook?"

"Not really, but I like the pictures. Also Eleanor Roosevelt biographies. And books on UFOs, sightings and myths and stuff. The Loch Ness Monster, I'm into that. The Devil's Triangle."

She was watching Mika swim toward the deep end. "What's that?" she said.

"You know." He drew a triangle in the air. "Weird stuff happens out there. Ever heard of Flight 19?"

"No."

"USS *Cyclops*?"

Elsie shook her head.

"Vanished without a trace," he said moodily, narrowing his eyes.

Mika was struggling to swim with her drink. Her nose kept dipping under the water, and she began to choke.

Phil pointed to the horizon. "We're sailing into the corner of it now."

"Really," said Elsie.

"Now, let's see." Phil pulled his lips to one side like a drape, thinking. "There was the *Spray*, the *Star Tiger*, the *Star Ariel*, Flight 201, the *Piper*—"

"What do you do?" she said tensely. She squinted at the dimming sky. "For work."

"Kind of in between jobs at the moment."

"Sure," Elsie said. Her head felt tingly and dense. In the deep end, Mika grabbed a man by the shoulders and then wrapped her legs around his waist.

"Huh," Elsie said. "I didn't picture Mitchell with a ponytail."

Phil frowned at the pool. "That's Greg," he said.

"Greg."

"People call him Dom."

Elsie looked back at Mika, who was whispering in Dom's ear. She laughed drunkenly, then pulled one triangle of her bikini top to the side until her nipple bobbed out of the water. *Go ahead*, Elsie heard Mika say, and Dom reached out and pinched it.

"Wowza," said Phil.

"Where the hell's Mitchell?" Elsie snapped. She pictured sinkholes, quicksand, oceans black and swallowing airplanes, closing over whole destroyers like lips.

Phil chuckled. "I think she's moved on."

"You don't know her." She looked at him darkly. "You don't know anything about her."

"True," said Phil. His hand hovered near her, weirdly, as if trying to land, and she froze while he tucked an imaginary piece of hair behind her ear. "So what's that like?" he said.

"What?" said Elsie.

"You know," Phil said. "Being twins."

Dom had pulled off Mika's bathing suit top and was holding it, teasingly, in the air above her head. *Come on*, Mika said, laughing.

"*Twins?*" Elsie said. She looked at Phil. Her blood pressure swooned. Sweat burst from her hairline and the back of her legs. "We're not just— is that what she said?"

Dom grabbed Mika and spun her around, pinning her arms behind her back. Then he hoisted her so her breasts stuck out of the water. A few men in the pool started to clap.

"I bet you feel each other's feelings and shit," Phil said. He was stroking the back of her neck. "I bet you have ESP."

"I'd like to be alone," Elsie said edgily.

"Me too," said Phil. He began to play with the strap of her dress. "There's a storeroom downstairs we could—"

She smacked his hand.

"Oof," said Phil. He shook his hand playfully. "Are you Italian?"

"Are you autistic?"

Phil flinched, stepping back. "You sure you're twins?" he said.

"Excuse me?"

He eyed her accusingly. "I thought you'd be like her." He stared dejectedly into the pool. *Keep going*, the other men called out. Mika's breasts swung on top of the water. *Take her bottoms off!* "I figured you'd be fun."

Mika's legs shimmered in the underwater lights.

"Fun like what?" said Elsie. The men were swimming closer.

Phil shrugged and pointed into the pool. "Like that."

Dom tossed the bikini top onto the deck and Mika lunged for it. She slipped in his arms, and the martini glass shattered on the edge of the deck.

The wind caught in Elsie's throat like a gag. "Like that?" she said. She saw Claire's sandal held high in Mika's hand. Squad cars. Their mother's mouth opened in a shriek.

"Yeah."

The men were surrounding Mika now. *Come on*, Elsie heard them saying. Mika was struggling up the ladder, covering her breasts with one arm. She slipped on the wet deck, caught herself, and then stumbled toward the stairs.

"You think she's having *fun*?" Elsie snapped, swiping the bikini top from the deck.

Then she ran after her sister.

When Elsie got down the stairs she couldn't find Mika anywhere. She looked in every cabin and corridor. She ran back up the stairs to the top deck. Phil fished through a cooler of beers. Dom and the other two men were tossing a Nerf ball in the pool and talking about The Heat. The bartender was organizing empties behind him in a cardboard box. "Mika!" she yelled, but no one looked over. A crowd of women exploded into false laughter. She ran to the edge of the railing and looked blindly out onto the water, looking but afraid to look, and then staggered back down the stairs.

The bottom level was dark, where everyone was dancing. Rap throbbed out of speakers, over the engine. She tripped over a row of abandoned high heels, steadying herself against a column, and then pushed through the clammy, gyrating crowd. The yacht pushed through the sea. She squinted into the strobe lights, everything illuminated and thrown back into darkness, faces appearing and vanishing, appearing and vanishing, like flashbacks, like visions. Even the woman on crutches was trying to dance.

"Mika!" Elsie yelled.

She made it to the other side of the floor and stumbled out onto the deck. The engine jackhammered the bones of her chest. The door slammed tight behind her, and the wind began to lift her hair like a kite.

She squinted at the stars, scattered Braille. The moon cast a blurry drop cloth on the sea. She looked down toward the stern and then, finally, made out the shape of Mika's back.

Mika was smoking, a towel pulled tight around her, a stick of celery clutched in her other fist. "Maybe Pam would want this," she shouted over the waves, when Elsie joined her.

"It doesn't matter," Elsie shouted back. She draped the bathing suit around Mika's neck, and Mika moved her towel out of the way so Elsie could tie it. Music ricocheted off the sea. Elsie adjusted the suit carefully, and then collected Mika's bleached, heavy hair in her hands and began to wring it out. Coil and wring. Coil and wring. The propeller's foamy wash roiled into darkness. "I couldn't find you," she said. Her heart knocked around, all the pieces of it, dice in a cup.

"I'm here," Mika said.

Nominated by Lydia Conklin

THE BRAIN IS NOT
THE UNITED STATES

by ELIZABETH SCANLON

from BOSTON REVIEW

The brain is not the United States, the brain is the ocean,
Dr. Yquem said, referring to its activity as opposed to its structure,
the brain is not the United States whose borders are mapped
and whose expansion is inhibited by bodies of water—

The brain is the ocean who is vast
and incorporates every chemical dumped into it,
whose depths we do not know, whose darkness we fear
in the most primordial way,
who stymies knowing up from down when one sinks fast
      into its long pull.

The brain is not the mind, try explaining this to a child,
that what is meant when we say *I don't mind* is not the same thing
as in *make up your mind* and that neither of them are the stuff
      in your skull.

I am trying hard to concentrate on the kind doctor's research
but the statistics mean nothing, I don't have a head for numbers
so maybe these distinctions are wasted on me,
which is not to say that my mind is made up but this is not
      my subject.

The brain is *le cerveau* in France, I'm France!
says the overacting imagination. I am not the United States.

The *cerveau* is also a walnut, you can see that,
a little crenellated universe in a nutshell,
it is a want, the brain, it is a salvo,
it is firing all the time in concert with other, louder artillery.

It is warning you
It is the nanny state
It is a slow gun that is nonetheless faster than we can see.
The brain is not the United Mind it is something more diversified.

But I cannot pledge allegiance to that because I am not the brain.
I am not a good citizen of any nation.
        The brain is the citizen of the body
and pays its taxes without much complaint.

But because I am France I am not interested in medication.
I believe in wine and unruly behavior and that etiquette
can and must be learned. It is a subject, like math.

It is not a subject of a royal kingdom. Rulers rarely care
what you say about them.

It is not the United States, it is not where you are from,
with its false meritocracy and aspirational wellness.
It is what you choose to do.

The brain is not the United States, it is the ocean
and we are everywhere on its shores,
never knowing it entirely.

Nominated by Dana Levin

NEW TECHNOLOGIES OF READING

by ANGELA WOODWARD

from CONJUNCTIONS

ONE) 3-D PRINTING

Hard to say if the reading process is at all improved by this, but the figurines exude a degree of charm. These are produced not on a flat substrate but in three dimensions in successive layers: The ink is substrate and substance in one. The pieces with a religious purpose—eight million iterations of "God Is Good" extruded letter by letter and formed into a little stand-up Jesus—should remain tourist items. I was given a Santeria saint with her heart in her hands, which unfolds into a spell for binding love. From this incantation was designed and printed a splint made of the same biocompatible material that goes into sutures. The lettering was so faint I had to draw my face quite close, where I was overwhelmed by the stink of the paper. The vibrant turquoise favored by the beach shops still holds a few random filaments, liver cells, scraps of endothelial membrane, an acrylic liquid that hardens when exposed to ultraviolet light.

Efforts to engineer tissues and organs have been similarly hampered by two-dimensional constraints. When will someone go the other way and print a book the size of a building? The central story blazes with neon like the main drag of a midsize town adorned on both sides with used car lots. Unpaved roads made from nylon powder lead off into unpromising plot developments. Precisely melted, they solidify into a filigree pattern. Dense, dendritic lanes dead-end at a silt-laden canal. In the next volume, a grain silo, a railroad bridge, a bowling alley, a laundromat. Vast distances between them and the intimate, interior world of the microscope.

The process comes closest to fulfilling its promise in the wildlife series put out by Tasso. The text interlaces the natural history of the animal with its genetic code, or so says the accompanying booklet (with a scan of the reader's wound, to determine how it might be fixed over time). Would there be blood beneath the fur? Would turning its pages wrench cartilage out of joint? Such a fantasy could be entertained at least. My squirrel erupted from its plastic packaging and began chattering from the window ledge. At first entirely lifelike, after a few days the cartoonish flatness of its eyes gave it away. Bone cells on polymer scaffolds eventually collapsed. By that time, I wondered what I had ever seen in it. It was so false and so removed from any version of "habitat" that I felt ashamed for both of us. Later that evening I changed my shirt, and felt the heat of the discarded garment in my hands.

TWO) CONDENSED BOOKS

I've learned to avoid the pill versions. These are simply too strong. Often slow to take effect, suddenly the reader is drawn into an improbable romance involving a spy, a dermatology clinic, a girls' camp by a lake. The smell of the old *Reader's Digest* triple editions pervades the action, a clammy, mildewed dinginess at odds with the overall glitz. Note too that only the most staid of novels are available in this format, so that one feels violently ill and hallucinated while reinforcing gender roles long outgrown: his stubbly cheeks, the swish of her hair, the rewarded patience of the passive beauty. The last time, I woke up with my head throbbing, my mouth dry, carpet burns on my hips. I thought I could ingest a self-reflective arctic brooding, but it was all the most generic lust, him on top ruffling my bangs and calling me "baby."

The charcoal versions I find fascinating, though also incomplete. I was ushered into one of the private rooms above Powells and given something the shape of a pencil box. The mechanism on the side ignites the contents. The reader controls the amount of fumes by opening or closing the lid. I let too much escape all at once. Before I had comprehended the complexity of the narrative, it had crumbled. I prodded the ashes and got only a few last puffs, goodbye, Sidney, I will carry your . . . it's all so . . . refugee camp . . . two sisters . . . less able to . . . . built itself over the river, and was just as quickly razed by the . . . all confused in gray swirls of languid euphoria. The material once combusted can't be revisited. This series makes use of mostly forgotten novels from the 1930s and '40s, many of them from the outskirts of the empire, the plight of the indigenous, the abuse of youth, religious minorities, other topics ancillary to the perpetuation of our culture and all the more poignant for being rendered in this disposable format. A girl wandered into . . . and was at once accepted by the community. On recovering her memory, she . . . birches, bird song, the calls of frogs . . . and was swept downstream. Why does my hand feel so heavy? Dry clicks of the eyelids. Enlarged tongue. Painful swellings, probably boils, accompanied by panic and a feeling of uselessness. Over the period of one brief coughing fit, the rest of the manuscript disintegrated.

today's inventiveness in delivery modes

those who remain nostalgic for the stable trailing of the finger over the

whisper and hiss of the paper falling, the physical decline in the width of what remains to be read while the already read fattens behind

fear to express what could be labeled instantly as antagonistic to possibilities not yet imagined

still secure in the

The latest in the trend is the notorious club version. I had my doubts too. To be lost in the strands of a mother's grief, the slow interpolation of relationships so that the good have become weak and the mean-spirited have shown their integrity, the fascination with the reader's own self as she persists with this fruitless intertwining of the writer's fiction with her life's trajectory—and yet, at the end, the swift blow to the side of the head was the most rewarding of all. In that moment of impact, stars blossomed inside my brain, pinwheels of light in colors of an intensity not available in nature, and the sense of being with her, the wielder, as she reared back and struck

Thousands of splinters radiated from the wound, some driving deep within, some scattering and lying golden and green in that same carpet where I'd attempt to allow the reader to virtually inhabit the skin of . . . resulting in third degree burns on my arms. Luckily I had gone too fast at first, and only a little bit was left when it came to my thighs. The rash stopped short of the vulva, but still spent several prickly evenings as it hardened, then practically waltzed me . . . smell of gasoline over the road now mingled with the more acrid . . . eventually scaled off like sunburn, leaving flakes all over the floor

transferred to a "black site" where he was shaved, placed in a "hanging" stress position and subjected to fifty-nine hours of sleep deprivation after which . . . "mild paralysis" . . . "legs and feet began" . . . "back and abdomen spasming" . . . "premature" heart beats and . . . provided fabricated, inconsistent, and generally unreliable information

In this case my advice is to wait, as the new iterations come out so much "improved" from each other that they hardly resemble members of the same line. One of the earliest was put on like a raincoat. It crackled with the reader's movements and was only audible while lying in deathlike stillness. I turned over in bed and the voice, so private and interior, was instantly drowned out by the friction of my hair against the blanket. The next was more of a wearable boombox, wires all up and down the sleeves and poking into slits in the sternum. I remember one July afternoon witnessing a couple reading this way in the middle of Tenney Park Beach, a ring of teenagers receding from the tinny outpouring of whatever mechanistic poetry issued from the sheathing. From these garment-like contraptions to the salve is a leap I can hardly fathom and if not for the packaging, the familiar blaring cobalt

central question of whether the intent is to block out the world news or to seal the reader into her own

so-called "rectal feeding." They only began to express their outrage when the executive summary was published. "I can't imagine there being a good day to release this kind of document," she told the committee, when as a matter of fact the contents were such common knowledge that Hollywood script writers had already dined out on them through a decade of award cycles.

Unable to get past the barrier, the traffic backed up for four miles. He leaned against the side of the jeep, until the sound of the girl in the Toyota

after which he began hallucinating . . . back and neck spasming . . . arms and legs locked in "mild paralysis" and

The next edition came with a special tool for scraping it off the skin once read. This operation, however, was so distressing and frankly worked so poorly that I went back to clawing it off with my bare fingers. The sound of the steel, the shape of the blade, and that it occasionally drew blood, while fragments of the text remained embedded in my elbow creases

called it "rectal feeding" and expected this little two-word pad to stave off the legal associations with rape and starvation, which it so neatly combined.

books from the legacy collection put in "dark storage," where they can be accessed via

as illustrated in this passage: the light that travels lengthwise under the cover of the copy machine, the light that leaps out if the lid is lifted too soon, the light that bounces off the page and obscures the type, the light behind the eyes with the cessation of the optical

Even though the executive summary had been heavily redacted, most of the identities of the sites had been known for years. For example, two law suits by . . . and named Poland, the Polish government, and . . . "They deserve a lot of praise," he replied. "As far as I'm concerned, they ought to be decorated, not criticized." Other practices used to "extract information" referred to . . . such information likened to honey or sludge, given a palpability that related then to this tightening coat of

voice that had seemed so private and interior interrupted by the amplified friction of the skin against the cot

The other series I've more recently been introduced to is the drone edition. The first one sent to me failed to rise above the level of my shoulder, and directed its monotonous recitation towards the floor. "He leaned against the side of the jeep, until the sound" came out much like the emanations of a geopositioning device, including the English accent and quirky stressing of final syllables. My neighbor's boys booted it around when I was done with it. It got stuck in the crab apple, where it lodged for weeks until it was either stolen or destroyed by weathering. On one of those freezing nights, the engineer heard the girl in the Toyota sobbing softly. The ones released in time for last year's holiday gift season were in contrast too small, and managed their attachment to the reader's ear much too persistently. The gnat-like volume followed me from room to room, buzzing the tale of . . . erotic in its intensity

fear of them spreading, mutating wildly and then infecting broader communities heretofore untouched by the contagion of the word. The light released when the cover is lifted midscan, the light reflected off the page to blur the type, the voice, at first so interior and private that it was erotic in its intensity now amplified to

"enhanced interrogation methods" paled beside the stark descriptions of not only the equipment in the room but the ulcers on the skin and the contusions mapped below

the one that now hovers at an immense distance, locked onto my signal. I am unable to see, hear, or understand it, yet to escape the devotion of its ceaseless surveillance is

acrid smell of the burned flesh could not be wiped away, only masked by the chlorine. On one of those freezing nights, the engineer heard the girl in the Toyota sobbing softly. The whole stretch of highway was ultimately bulldozed and all photos and documents deleted from the server

Nominated by Meghan O'Gleblyn, Barrett Swanson

FROM "PLEASE BURY ME IN THIS"

by ALLISON BENIS WHITE

from COPPER NICKEL

I am making a world I can think inside.

Cutting faces out of paper and taping them on glass like thoughts.

Am I a monster, Clarice Inspector asked in *The Hour of the Star, or is this what it means to be human?*

To have a mind, I think as I cut another face.

What makes the shape become visible, and breathe, is the angle and variation of absence.

Sugar skull, I whisper, what I have known all along.

I am you gone.

Nominated by Copper Nickel, David Hernandez

THE FIVE-POUND BURRITO

fiction by T.C. BOYLE

from KENYON REVIEW

He lived in a world of grease, and no matter how often he bathed, which was once a day, rigorously—and no shower but a drawn bath—he smelled of *carnitas*, *machaca*, and the chopped white onion and soapy cilantro he folded each morning into his *pico de gallo*. The grease itself was worked up under his nails and into the folds of his skin, folds that hung looser and penetrated deeper now that he was no longer young. This was a condition of his life and his livelihood, and if it had its drawbacks—he was sixty-two and never married because what woman would want a man who smelled so inveterately of fried pork?—it had its rewards, too. For one thing, he was his own boss, the little hole-in-the-wall café he'd opened back in the sixties still doing business when so many showier places had come and gone. For another, he was content, his world restricted to what he knew, the sink, the dishwasher, the griddle, and the grill, and he saw his customers, the regulars and one-timers alike, as a kind of flock that had to be fed like the chickens his mother had kept when he was a boy. What did he do with himself? He scraped his griddle, took his aprons, shirts, and underwear to the Chinese laundry that had been in operation nearly as long as he had and went home each evening to put his feet up and sit in front of the TV.

His only employee was a sour woman named Sepideh, an Iranian (or, as she preferred it, Persian) immigrant who as a girl had gotten out of her native country after the regime change and was between forty-five and sixty, depending on what time of day you asked her. In the mornings she was unconquerably old, but by closing time her age had dropped, though she dragged her feet, her shoulders slumped, and her makeup grew increasingly tragic. She was dark-skinned and dark-eyed, and she dyed her once-black hair black all over again. People took her for a Mexican, which was really a matter of indifference to him—he didn't care whether his waitress was from Chapultepec or Hokkaido, as long as she did her job and took some of the pressure off him. And she did. And had for some twenty years now and counting.

On this particular day, midweek, dreary, the downtown skyline obliterated by fog or smog, or whatever they wanted to call it, Sepideh was late because the bus she took from the section of town known as Little Persia, where she lived with her mother and an equally sour-faced brother he'd met once or twice, had broken down. As luck would have it, there was a line outside the door when at eleven o'clock on the dot he shuffled across the floor and flipped the sign from *Closed* to *Open*. In came the customers, most of them wearing familiar faces, and as they crowded in at the counter and unfolded their newspapers and propped up their tablets and laptops on the six tables arranged in a narrow line along the far wall that featured the framed black-and-white photo of a dead president, he began taking orders.

First in line was Scott, a student from the university who had the same thing five days a week: black coffee and the chorizo and scrambled egg burrito he lathered with jalapeños, *Just to wake up*, as he put it on the mornings when he was capable of speech. Next to him were Humberto and Baltasar, two baggy-pants old men from the neighborhood who would slurp heavily sugared coffee for the next three hours and try to talk him to death as he hustled from grill to griddle to the refrigerator and back, and here were two others easing onto the stools beside them, new faces, more students—but big, all head and neck, shoulder and belly, footballers, no doubt, who would devour everything in a two-foot radius, complain that the portions were too small and the burritos like prisoners' rations, and try to suck the glaze off the plates in the process. Of course, he should be happy because the students had discovered him yet again—and how many generations had made the same discovery and then faded away in the lean months when he could have used their business?

He dealt out a stack of plastic menus as if he were flipping cards like the dealer at the blackjack table at Caesar's, where he liked to spend his two weeks off every February, bathed in the little spotlight that illuminated the table, a gratis rum and Coke sizzling at his elbow. Then he leaned over the counter and announced in the voice that was dying in his throat a little more each day as he groped toward old age and infirmity, "No table service today. You people back there got to come up to the counter if you want to get fed." That was it. He didn't need to give an explanation—if they wanted Michelin stars, let them line up over in Beverly Hills or Pacific Palisades—but he couldn't help adding, "She's late today, Sepideh."

And so it began: breakfast, then the lunch rush, furious work in a hot, cramped kitchen, and all he could see was people's mouths opening and closing and the great wads of beans and rice and marinated pork, chicken, and beef swelling their throats. It was past noon before he could catch his breath—he didn't even have time for a cigarette, and that put him in a foul mood, the lack of nicotine—and when he saw the face in the tortilla that provided the foundation for the burrito he was just then constructing, he ignored it. It was nobody's face, eyes, nose, cheekbones, brow, and it meant nothing except that he was exhausted, already exhausted, and he still had six and a half hours to go. And sure, he'd seen faces before—Mohammed, the Buddha, Sandy Koufax once, but Jesus? Never. The woman over on Broadway had seen Jesus, exactly as He was in the Shroud of Turin, only the shroud in this case was made of unleavened flour, lard, and water. He could have used Jesus himself, because that woman got rich and the lines for her place went around a whole city block. If he only had Jesus, he could hire somebody more competent—and dependable—than Sepideh and sit back and take a load off. That was what he was thinking as he smeared *refritos* over the face of the tortilla and piled up rice and meat and guacamole and *crema*, cheese, shredded lettuce, *pico de gallo*, the works—and why not?—for yet another pair of footballers who were sitting there at the back table like statues come to life. Call it whimsy, or maybe revenge, but he mounded the ingredients up till the burrito was as big as a stuffed pillowcase. Let them complain about this one.

That was when he had his moment of inspiration, divine or other-wise. He would weigh it. Actually weigh it, and that would be his ammunition and his pride, too, the biggest burrito in town. If he didn't have Jesus, at least he would have that.

We each live through our days in an accumulation of milliseconds, seconds, minutes, hours, days, months, and years, and life is a path we must follow, invariably, until the end. Is there change—or the hope of it? Yes, but change is wearing and bad for the nerves and almost always for the worse. So it was with Sal, the American-born son of Mexican

214

immigrants who'd opened Salvador's Café with a loan from his uncle James when he was still in his twenties, and now, nearly forty years later, saw his business take off like a rocket on the fuel of the five-pound burrito. Suddenly his homely café was a destination, not only for his regulars and the famished and greedy of the neighborhood, but for the educated classes from the West Side who pulled up out front in their shining new German automobiles and stepped through the door as if they expected the floor to fall away beneath the soles of their running shoes and suck them down to some deeper, darker place.

This was change, positive change, at least at first. He hired a man to help with the dishes and the sweeping up and a second waitress, a young girl studying for her nursing degree who gave everybody in the place something to look at. And on the counter, raised at eye-level on a cloth-covered pedestal, was the big butcher's scale on which he cer-emoniously weighed each dripping pork, chicken, or beef burrito be-fore Sepideh—or the new girl, Marta—made a show of hefting the supersized plate and setting it down laboriously in front of the cus-tomer who had ordered it. A man from the newspaper came. And then another. The line went around the block, and never mind Jesus.

Sal was there one early morning—typically he arose at five and was in the kitchen by six, preparing things ahead of time, and, of course, with success came the need for yet more preparation—when he felt a numinous shift in the atmosphere, as if those timid first-timers from the West Side had been right after all. The floor didn't open up beneath him, of course, but as he cut meat from the bone and shucked avocados for guacamole, he felt the atmosphere permeated by a new presence, and no ordinary presence but the kind that makes a dog's hackles rise when it sniffs at the shadows. For a moment he felt dizzy and wondered if he were having some sort of attack, the inevitable myocardial infarc-tion or stroke that would bring him down for good, but the dizziness passed and he found himself in the kitchen still, the knife clenched in his hand and the cubes of pork gently oozing on the chopping block before him. He shook his head to clear it. Something was different, but he couldn't say what.

The morning wore on in a fugue of chopping, dicing, and tearing up over the emanations of habaneros and jalapeños, his back aching and his hands dripping with the juice of the hundred-millionth tomato of his resuscitated life, and he forgot all about it till the knock came at the alley door. This was the knock of Stanford Wong, who delivered pro-duce to the restaurants of the neighborhood and was as punctual as the great clock in Greenwich, England, that kept time for the world. Sal wiped his hands on his apron and hurried to the door because Stanford, understandably, didn't like to be delayed. There might have been a noise outside the door, a furtive scratching as of something trying to get in, but it didn't register until he pulled back the door and saw that it wasn't Stanford stationed there at all but an erect five-and-a-half-foot rooster dressed in Stanford Wong's khaki shorts and khaki shirt with the black plastic nameplate—*Stanford*—fixed over the breast.

Was he taken aback? Was he seeing things? He'd had his breakfast, hadn't he? Yes, yes, of course: eggs. Chicken embryos. Fried in butter, topped with a sprinkle of Cotija cheese and served up on toast. He just stood there, blinking, but the bird, which somehow seemed to have hands as well as wings, was impatient and brushed by him with a crate of lettuce and half a dozen clear plastic bags of tomatillos, peppers, and the like balanced against his—its?—chest, setting the load down on the counter and swinging round abruptly with Stanford's receipt book in hand. But there were words now, the bird saying something out of a beak that snapped and glistened to show off a pink wedge of tongue, and yet the words made no sense unless you were to interpret them in the usual way, as in, *Same order tomorrow?* and *You take care now.*

The door swung shut. The crate sat astride the counter, just as it had yesterday and the day before and the day before that. It took him a moment—and maybe he'd better have another cup of coffee—before he went to the crate and began shoving heads of lettuce into the refrigerator, all the while thinking that there were two possibilities here. The first and most obvious was that he was hallucinating. The second, and more disturbing, was that Stanford Wong had been transformed into a giant rooster. Either way, the prospects could hardly be called favorable, and if he was losing his mind in the uproar over the five-pound burrito, who could blame him?

Next it was Sepideh, dressed in black skirt and white blouse, but with her head covered in feathers and her nose replaced by a dull, puce beak and no shoes on her feet because her legs, her scaly yellow legs, supported not phalanges and painted toenails but the splayed, naked claws of an antediluvian hen. She was never talkative, especially in the morning, but whatever she had to say to him came in a series of irritable clucks and gabbles, and he just—well, he just blew her off. Then came Marta and she was a hen, too, and by the time Oscar Martí, the cleanup man, showed his face, it was no surprise at all that he should be a rooster just like Stanford Wong—and, for that matter, once the door

216

opened for business, that all the male customers should be crowing and flapping their wings, while their female counterparts clucked and brooded and held their own counsel over pocketbooks stuffed with eyeliner, compacts, and lipstick that had no discernible purpose. Something was wrong here, desperately wrong, but work was work and whether he could understand what anybody was saying, customers or staff, really didn't seem to matter, as everything by this juncture had been reduced to routine: spread the tortilla, crown it with toppings, fold it, dip the ladle in the salsa verde and serve it up on the big white scale.

That was Monday. Mondays were always a trial, what with forcing yourself back into the routine after the day of rest, the Lord's day, when people went to church to dip their fingers in holy water and count their blessings. Sal locked up after work that night, and if he noticed that everyone, every living man, woman, and child on the streets and sealed behind the windows of their cars, was a member of a different species— poultry, that is—he didn't let it affect him. Even so, the minute he came in the door of his apartment he went straight to the mirror in the bathroom and was relieved to see his own human face staring back at him out of drooping eyes. He poured himself a drink that night, a practice he found himself engaging in less and less as he got older, heated up a burrito (regular size) in the microwave, and watched reality TV till he couldn't hold his eyes open anymore. It would be one thing to say that his dreams were populated with hens, roosters, and bobbing chicks, but the fact was that he dreamed of nothing—or nothing he could remember on wakening. He was a blank canvas, tabula rasa. Mechanically, he shaved. Mechanically, he broke two eggs in a pan and laid three strips of bacon beside them, and he drove mechanically to work. In the dark.

When Stanford Wong's knock came precisely at eight, Sal moved briskly to the door, his mood soaring on his second cup of coffee—with a shot of espresso to top it off—and the prospect of yet another record-setting day. If things kept up like this, he'd soon be sitting in a chair all day long watching the world come and go while the new grill man he'd hire and train himself did all the dirty work. And it was all due to the inspiration of that day six months back when he'd brought out the scale and piled up the burrito and made his statement to the world. The five-pound burrito. It was a concept, an innovation unmatched by anybody in the city, whether they had a sit-down place or a lunch cart or even one of those eateries with the white tablecloths and the waiters who looked at you as if you belonged on the plate instead of sitting upright

217

in a chair and putting in an order. People just couldn't understand what it took to consume a burrito of that caliber—no individual, not even the greediest, most swollen footballer, could ever hope to get it all down in a single sitting. Though people placed bets and Sal had agreed to advertise that if you could manage to eat the whole thing, it was on the house. Very few could. In fact, only one man—skinny, Asian, the size of a child—was able to accomplish the feat incontrovertibly, and it turned out later that he was world-famous as a competitive eater who'd won the Nathan's hot-dog-eating contest three years running.

But here was Stanford Wong's knock, and as he opened the door, he didn't know what to expect, least of all what he saw standing there before him on its hind legs—*his* hind legs. This wasn't Stanford Wong and it wasn't a chicken either—no, this was a hog, with pinched little hog's eyes and a bristling inflamed snout, but it was dressed in Stanford Wong's khaki shorts and khaki shirt with the black plastic nameplate fixed over the breast. It—he—trotted brusquely into the kitchen and set the crate of lettuce and plastic bags of vegetables on the counter, then swung round with Stanford Wong's accounts ledger clutched under one arm and grunted and snuffled out a sentence or two that could only have meant, *How they hangin'?* and *See you tomorrow, same order, right?*

Right. So he chopped peppers and grilled pork and made a pot of *albondigas* soup, shredded lettuce, and stirred up yesterday's steamer trays of rice and *refritos* and thought nothing of it when Sepideh appeared as a grunting old sow in her black skirt and white blouse and then Marta, resplendent in red shorts and a clinging top, in her guise as a smooth, pink, young shoat who nonetheless stood five feet seven inches tall on her cloven hoofs and managed to wield her tray and heft the big burritos as if she'd been born to it. As on the previous day, work consumed him, and if his customers vocalized in a cascade of snorts and aspirated grunts, it was all the same to him. Back at home that night he passed on the burrito left over from work, though he hated waste, and instead slipped a package of frozen meatless lasagna into the oven and poured himself not one but two drinks before he let the TV lull him to a dreamless sleep.

He found himself on edge the next morning and drank a cup of tea instead of coffee and had toast only instead of his usual fried eggs with bacon or ham or chorizo. It was dark as he drove to work and if his headlights happened to catch a figure walking along a shadowy street or spot a face behind an oncoming windshield, he made himself look away. What next? That was all he could think. Cattle, no doubt. Huge, stinking, lowing steers speaking their own arcane language and demanding big burritos, the biggest in town. When Stanford Wong's knock came this time, he was prepared, or thought he was, but oh, how mistaken he turned out to be. This wasn't Stanford Wong and it wasn't a rooster or a hog or a steer either—it was an alien, and not one of the *indocumentados* of which his late sainted parents were representatives, but one of the true aliens, with their lizard skin, razor teeth and eyeballs like ashtrays. Of course, this one was wearing Stanford Wong's clothing and was carrying his crate of lettuce, but its claws were wicked and long and scraped mercilessly at the linoleum, and when it spoke— *How's business?* and *That five-pounder's going to make you rich*—it could only hiss.

All day, as the aliens crowded the café and his own aliens, Sepideh and Marta, served them their big, dripping chile verde-drenched burritos, he kept wondering about their spaceship and if it was like the ones in the movies, all silver and gleaming and silent, and, more to the point, where they'd parked it. No matter. The aliens lashed at their food with a snap of their gleaming teeth and a quick release of their forked tongues, and the cash register rang and the line went round the block.

It was around then, on that day, the third day, almost at closing time, that Sal saw a new face in the tortilla he laid on the grill for the burrito he was preparing for a big, square-shouldered footballer alien. This face—the brow, the blind eyes and moving lips that swelled against the pressure of his tongs—was one that leapt out at him in its familiarity. And who was it? Not Jesus, no, but someone . . . someone more important even, if only to him. It was his father, the man who'd held him in his arms and pushed him on the swing and showed him how to grip a baseball and figure his equations in algebra—his father, dead these thirty years and more. The lips moved—and here Sal felt himself lifted into the arena of the fantastic—moved and spoke.

"You're over-reaching, Salvador. Pushing your luck. Flirting with excess and exception, when the truth is you're not exceptional at all but just a mule like me, made to work and live an honest, proportionate life. Go back to two pounds, Salvador. Two maximum. And please, for the love of God and His angels too, dump some aromatic salts in that bathtub. . . ." And then the lips stopped moving in that impress of dough and the voice faded out.

But there it was, revelation from the mouth of a flour tortilla, and the next day, despite the complaints of his customers—human beings, just like him—he went back to the standard-sized burrito. Trade fell off. He had to let Marta go and then Oscar too. The chickens went back to their henhouses and the hogs to their pens and the aliens trooped out across the lot to wherever they'd parked their spaceship and whirred off into the sky in a blaze of light, still traveling as day turned to night and the stars came out to welcome them home.

Nominated by Don Waters

DADDY DOZENS

by JAMILA WOODS

from POETRY

My Daddy's forehead is so big, we don't need a dining room table.
My Daddy's forehead so big, his hat size is equator. So big, it's a
five-head. Tyra Banks burst into tears when she seen my Daddy's
forehead. My Daddy's forehead got its own area code. My Daddy
baseball cap got stretch marks. My Daddy pillowcase got craters.
His eyebrows need GPS to find each other. My Daddy forehead
lives in two time zones. Planets confuse my Daddy forehead for the
sun. Couch cushions lose quarters in the wrinkles in my Daddy
forehead. My Daddy so smart, he fall asleep with the movie on and
wake up soon as the credits start to roll. My Daddy so smart, he
perform surgery on his own ingrown toenail. Momma was not
impressed, but my Daddy got brains. My Daddy know exactly how
to drive me to my friend's house without lookin at no map. My
Daddy born here, he so smart, he know the highways like the
wrinkles in his forehead. He know the free clinics like the gray
hairs on his big ass head. My Daddy so smart, he wear a
stethoscope and a white coat. My Daddy drive to work in a minivan
only slightly bigger than his forehead, that's just how my Daddy
rolls. My Daddy got swag. My Daddy dance to "Single Ladies" in
the hallway. My Daddy drink a small coffee cream and sugar. My
Daddy drink a whole can of Red Bull. My Daddy eat a whole pack
of sour Skittles and never had a cavity. My Daddy so smart, he got
a pullout couch in his office. Got a mini fridge there too. Got a cell
phone, and a pager, and a email address where I can leave him

messages when he's not at home. My Daddy's not home. Momma saves a plate that turns cold.

But when my Daddy does come home, he got a office in his bedroom too. Computer screen night light, Momma says she can't sleep right, but my Daddy got work, my Daddy at work, at home, in the attic, with the TV on, in the dark, from the front yard, through the windows, you can see him working, glass flickering, my house got its own forehead, glinting, sweaty, in the evening, while my Daddy at work, at home, in his own area code, a whole other time zone.

Nominated by Poetry

DR. J

by KALPANA NARAYANAN

from GRANTA

1

My father has his own language for everything. A friend of a friend is a FOF. A suitcase is a rolly-polly. When I finished my MFA, I was a NINJA: No Income, No Job, No Assets. The tree in his and my mother's front yard, he points out to me as we walk, is called M-Squared, because it's either a maple or a magnolia, he's not sure which. Growing up in the South, I used to see this bumper sticker everywhere: 'I can do all things through Jesus Christ who Strengthens Me.' One day in high school, I went out to my dad's car and saw that he had made his own bumper sticker. It said: 'I can do all things through Lord Venkateswara who Strengthens Me.' My dad moved to Atlanta twenty-nine years ago with one suitcase, and began to name the new things he saw, and press himself into this life, and a world sprang up around him.

Two years ago, I put my things in a storage unit a subway ride away from where I'd been living in Brooklyn and took a suitcase with me to Rome, Georgia, where I planned to write. I had gone through a break-up and was trying unsuccessfully to finish a draft of a book. Leaving New York seemed like a good idea. After two months, I thought, I'd go back and begin my life.

But after Rome and back in New York again, I ended up moving fifteen more times. On the first of almost every month for two years, I carried my suitcase up several flights of stairs to a new apartment, and then carried it down thirty days later and lugged it up a new flight of stairs. I couldn't bring myself to sign a lease—to commit to New York, my old life, for more than a month at a time—until it felt like home again, the place I should be forever. I don't know what I was waiting for—some feeling of warmth, some feeling of being necessary. As soon as New York felt like that place, I would unpack. Each time it didn't, I moved.

Finally, on Christmas, I found myself back in my parents' carpeted house in Atlanta. This hadn't been my plan. As I lugged my suitcase up the most familiar staircase, I imagined my dad asking me to tell him how many steps there were. 'Thirty-nine,' he'd say, and then ask if that was a movie, *The 39 Steps*, as he does every time he sees me walk up these stairs. In trying to find a home, I'd somehow ended up in my childhood bed, falling asleep next to a *Gone with the Wind* poster.

My first weeks back in Atlanta, I take walks with my dad around the country club that borders my parents' neighborhood. My mother's at a wedding in India. When my dad walks, he walks with a big stick because he's scared of dogs. The houses here are a mix of Georgian, Tudor, neoclassical homes with sprawling lawns and dogs that bark at us from the edges. We pass by women in visors, speed-walking in pairs.

As we walk, we discuss writing books. My dad says, 'Nothing could be harder,' and talks about all the times he's tried to start his book. When we get home, he opens up his laptop at the kitchen table, to get started again.

He's a business school professor and has always had two book ideas—one is a finance self-help book. The second is a novel that involves a fictional plot about Chelsea Clinton. A few years ago, my dad said that his dream had always been to write a book by the age of sixty. He said this two days before he turned sixty. So that weekend, we began to co-write the first book. We're at ten pages.

After typing a few words, my dad closes his laptop. He says he knows now what he wants printed on his tombstone: 'Despite publishing, he perished.'

2

Over the next weeks, I take my dad's car and drive past Chick-fil-As, and trees that end in kudzu, to look at apartments that are mainly carpeted and cat-filled. When I introduce myself as Kalpana, Southerners hear Coconut. One landlord calls me Carpet. My parents say that when I was five and they sent me to Montessori school, I stood in the corner and cried because I only knew Tamil. No one understood me, and I couldn't understand anyone. My mother had to write out the Tamil words for food and bathroom, so that my teachers could speak to me. The South still feels like that sometimes—a universe made up of a completely different language.

One day, I get lost in the Kroger parking lot. I click on the remote control and my dad's car beeps in front of me. Confused, I walk in the opposite direction. A man with a kind smile shakes his head at me and says, 'Bless your heart.'

My plan for January—to get a car, apartment, and write—is not working. I'm unable to find an apartment that I like, or a car. Because there's nowhere to walk to, except past all my parents' neighbors to the end of the cul-de-sac, I stay inside the house most days.

One morning my boxes arrive from the storage unit. Sitting on my parents' basement floor, I open some of the smaller boxes and tear up. When I was moving, I kept a few paperbacks with me, but I haven't seen most of my books since I went to Rome. I feel more at home, here, than I've felt anywhere in the past two years. I pull out my OED. I can't find the magnifying glass to read the small print, so I flip through its pages. I find three yellowed papers tucked inside that I'd forgotten about.

They're my dad's vocab lists, from when he was twenty and in Madras, learning English for the GRE. The sheets are beige and tissue-paper thin, and in his messy blue cursive are columns of words. The lists are arbitrary and extraordinary. He defines 'libidinous, lascivious, lubricous, licentious, lewd, lustful and prurient' all as 'sexy'. He has a French section, and carefully writes out the pronunciation of each word. Ennui: on-wee, bon vivant: boe-vivah.

While I was still living in New York, he and my mother visited me, and we saw a Broadway show, *The 25th Annual Putnam County Spelling Bee*. In the lobby, attendants asked for audience participants. My dad has always wanted to be a stand-up comedian, and immediately went over and filled out a form. Of all the volunteers, my dad was selected. It's set up so that the audience member goes up on stage and spells a word right in the first round. Then in the next round, they're

225

given an extremely difficult word, eliminated and asked to head back to their seat. But my father kept spelling words like 'dengue' correctly. After three rounds like this, they still couldn't eliminate him.

After each win, the cast linked arms with my dad and danced in a circle. My dad jumped up and down during each circle dance. The actors could hardly hang onto him, he leapt so high with such joy.

In the next round, they asked him to spell 'meeshevoshop'. This time, my dad spelled the word wrong. As my dad returned to his seat, the announcer admitted it was a made-up word, because that was the only way to have the show continue on schedule. The crowd couldn't stop clapping as he sat down.

That night, home from work, my dad sips from a minigoblet of red wine and opens up the book of songs that accompany his India-bought karaoke machine.

Sitting on the couch, he enters the number for 'Bol Radha Bol', the old Hindi film song that's always his first pick. As the opening chord plays, my dad opens and closes his left hand while his right hand grips the mic. Slightly shaking his head and his shoulders, he sings in the most earnest and hopeful voice, begging Radha to speak. *Tell Radha tell, will this meeting of two rivers happen or not? / My mind Ganges, and your Jamuna mind, will they merge?* In the car, he sings along occasionally to the Beatles or Maroon 5, but it's when he's singing 'Bol Radha Bol' that he's his most passionate, that he has every word memorized. The karaoke machine, as if wanting to reward his knowledge, his loyalty, gives him a score of 97. I sing my best 'Uptown Girl' while a black-and-white photo of the Brooklyn Bridge sits on the screen. It gives me a 45.

A few years ago, friends of mine got married in Atlanta and had karaoke at their reception. When my dad found out they had his favorite song, 'American Pie', he added his name to the list. Usually when 'American Pie' plays on his mix CD, he sings, 'A long long time ago,' and then hums the rest of the song, because he doesn't know the words. That night, my friends' friends—FOFs—watched an Indian man in a suit sing every single word to 'American Pie' in the slowest, most sincere, effortful voice. With the words on the screen before him, he sang each syllable with perfect precision, enunciation, until eventually the DJs had to cut him off because 'American Pie' is eight minutes long.

Another time I watched him perform before a crowd was after he got voted Teacher of the Year by his students, which happens frequently. He went on stage, and instead of giving a thank you speech, my father said, 'Let's recite the Eight Words.' Together, he and his executive MBA students chanted, 'Dream Big, Work Hard, Learn Constantly, Enjoy Life.' These are his favorite eight words, which he's always asking me and my sister to repeat, and which we can never remember. Newt Gingrich's daughter introduced these words to the world in a book she co-wrote with her father. My father's a liberal, but he's open to anyone having something good to say.

Over the next weeks, I read, I start to leave the house more. One rainy afternoon, a friend picks me up, and we go to the mall I used to hang out at in high school to see a movie. It's sold out. We end up wandering into a Build-A-Bear store, where you select a fur, accessories and a scent, and take these different parts over to a machine to be 'built'. We watch a kid watching rapturously as the machine aggressively stuffs a limp gray cloth with feathers, until it puffs up into an elephant. We drink at the dank, restaurant bar on the main floor and begin to write out on a napkin a story about an Indian girl and her elephant. For a moment, being in my hometown feels unfamiliar, a surprising remix.

At home, my father takes my mother's yellow sari and begins to wrap it around himself, telling me and my sister that we need to know how to wear a sari, and that he can teach us. He ends up tangled in the folds of chiffon. When we ask who his favorite daughter is, he says, after thinking on it, 'You're like my eyes. I need both of you.' When I say sorry for not doing the dishes one morning, he sings, 'It's too late, baby,' then asks me if that's a song. Eating peas, he tells me that peas are his favorite food because a hundred peas only have one calorie.

At the dinner table with my mom and dad one night, I begin to weep.
'What?' they both ask.
'I don't want you to die,' I say.
My mom reaches out and touches my wrist.
'We've lived good lives. We have everything we want,' she says.
'That makes it sound like you're going to die,' I say, crying.
There's a pause.
'Okay Kalpana, we won't die,' my dad says, realizing what I need to hear.

227

The next day, I carry my suitcase out. I'm going back to Rome, Georgia, to the same house I went to two years ago.

I think of my dad coming to the States in the early 1980s with one suitcase. My mother came over the next year, carrying a three-month-old me. My dad says he was scared, riding the New York subway for the first time to collect us at JFK. At baggage claim, he picked up his wife and her suitcase, and I met him, and he met me.

I think of my dad landing in Delhi twenty-five years later. His brother had called the day before to say their father was sick. My dad couldn't get on the same-day flight, so he went the next day. When he landed at 10 p.m., he ran to baggage claim and met his brother at Immigrations. His brother told him that their father had died at 9:15 p.m. The two rode down empty roads, past sleeping cows and scrawny dogs, to the hospital, but it had closed for the night.

At 5 a.m. the next morning, they brought their father's body home, and my father's sister bathed and dressed him in a veshti while a priest performed a puja in front of a small flame. Embers from the fire were placed in a pot, which my father carried. That afternoon, the three brothers rode over to a cremation site in a mini-van, their father laid out between them, bare-chested except for a thin white thread that strapped from his shoulder to his hip. At the site, their father was placed on top of a stack of wood, and ghee was poured on his body. My father, as firstborn son, took a stick out of the pot of embers he held and touched the stick to his father's neck. He lit his father's body on fire.

My father says after doing that, he doesn't fear much.

I think of my dad in his twenties, hanging out of a packed train in Bombay, wind on his face, on his way to work, and now of him driving his Camry in Atlanta traffic to Georgia Tech.

My father came here with a suitcase, some lists of vocabulary, and, in a part of the States that he perhaps never thought he'd call home, he sang seven minutes of his favorite song at a wedding, was voted teacher of the year and performed on Broadway.

India is still his home. It's where his mother is. It's where, the day after he cremated his father's body, he and his two brothers drove out to the Ganges, dumped in their father's ashes and then took a dip together in cold, holy water. My dad says that as a child, his father would wade into the Kaveri River, carrying my dad on his shoulders, and that

that day it was my dad's turn to carry his father's remains into the water. It's 'Bol Radha Bol', a song about two rivers, people, merging, that he knows all the words to, and that he croons at night.

But it's Atlanta where he's commissioner of the NBA: the Noontime Basketball Association, a group of Georgia Tech faculty and staff that play at lunchtime, and Atlanta where he goes by Dr. J, a name his friend gave him in the eighties, in the era of Julius Erving's slam dunk. It's Atlanta where his bedside clock is set five hours ahead, so that his clock says it's nine a.m., when the actual time is four a.m., to trick himself into thinking he's waking at nine. It's in Atlanta where, in 1991, he got to ask his favorite politician, Bill Clinton, a question during a town hall meeting. On national TV, my dad asked Clinton if he would consider Ross Perot as a running mate, as Clinton once said he'd do in a speech, to which Bill Clinton said he never said that.

When I ask my dad how he knew Atlanta was home, he says 'It's where I got a job.' He says moving to the States was 'a shock' and that he wanted to turn around when he landed. I ask if he ever thought about moving back to India. He pauses then says, 'The kids wouldn't have been able to adjust.'

'You mean me?'

'Yes.'

I put my suitcase in the car and shut the trunk.

My dad says, 'Maybe I'll come up and work on my book too.'

I say okay.

As I drive away that day, past M-squared, I wave at him, and he waves back. Years ago, on a plot of land in the New South, my father opened up his suitcase and unpacked a universe of words. He made a world that is my home, and he gave me a language, so that wherever I go, I might also be able to name the things I see. So that Atlanta might feel like a possible home, as might the other, parallel world of New York, one flight away—so that in either place, I might unpack my suitcase and, like my father, be able to start to make that world my own.

Nominated by Granta

PLUTO'S GATE: MISSISSIPPI

by JAMES KIMBRELL

from CINCINNATI REVIEW

for Private First Class, C. Liegh McInnis

I appear to be a full-on rich guy
wheeling into Oxford
down the cedar-lined drive across from William Faulkner's
determined to shield myself (my fancy wristwatch
                    my roadster
                    both used both fast as hell) from the
                    shame
I once knew in this my state
beneath my bowl-cut
my underwear of the dead
my hand-me-down teeth
and at the first supper club I light upon—three gins in—I say to
this woman
Khayat is of Lebanese descent
    no hell no he ain't! she says
      nearly hysterical in her insistence that *no prez of Ole Mizz*
                              could be a sandnigger

I ask her where do you go to church
                        Saint John's she says

tell Father Hadeed I said hi
tell him I said Alhamdulilla
tell him the ghost of Bill Faulkner quoth to me

quail fly south in the afternoon
better pray often
better pray soon
for those students in '64 crossing Lynch Street
on the way to Jackson State
white drivers speeding up
dubbed it Black Topping
how much shit can one people take
consider the white family walking down Ellis
carrying their groceries
too poor for even the most worn-out hooptie
the youngest amongst them a little boy
—*hey y'all!*—
totes among other items
a sweaty gallon of milk
that has burst a jagged seam in the paper sack
so that he cradles the whole mess
with both arms as if carrying a sick baby
and that was rough but
no one swerved to hit us
Jesus of the Confounderacy
Jesus of the Union
because I love my schoolmates
that never left
black white Pakistani
Choctaw Lebanese quadroons
women with hair piled to dangerous heights
that saved me from my youth
I love kibbie and the swamp
I love the heat
O hellish dome as soon as I could
I packed my junk and was gone
gone in my ragged-out
Plymouth Belvedere
with its push-button transmission
and sawed-off seatbelts
my face stinging like a stuck voodoo doll
red with the turpentine curse of that place
I especially did not love
on that particular day the Sergeant Major in the meeting

of noncommissioned officers
scheduling guard drills around MLK's birthday
says shoot six more
we'll take the whole week off
—oooh this sure is a tell-all!—

well yes though I don't dare tell C. Liegh
after drill when we're heading to his place
in the old neighborhood
where we'll eat a free bucket of chicken because Monica still works
at Popeye's
and we're going to watch Prince videos
and not drink beers
because for whatever reason we're both sober
and on our way
everyone stares us down
like the only time they saw a black and white guy
in a car together was when
they were cops
and I tell C. Liegh a dream I have betimes
                     I'm back at our old house on Hooker Street
                     always a black family surprised to see whitey
                             and I'm so white in this dream
                             you can barely see me
                             white as a polar bear's pillowcase
                             white as the ear fuzz
                             of the great Johnny Winter
but they see me and I see them seeing me
I say back then my bed was behind the table
here's the notch I cut with a steak knife
when I was three
                 and for the first time—eyes wide—they believe me
the little girl her hand on her hip
says *let me guess whitebread*
grew up poor
                     wants to do some good
                         just what we need
                             Starbucks!
I say we were so poor I still get nervous in Starbucks
boo fricking hoo she says *you still white*

white as God's white-ass golf balls
I say shoot me already
                    at which point her mother brings the gun
when she pulls the trigger the Confederate flag pops out
the mother says *just kidding you want some dinner*
and this time when she shoots
the table is covered
with turnips cornbread little cups
of mayonnaise-colored pudding
what you looking at she says *better eat your dinner*
and the three of us say an honest grace
grateful uneasy
                    Lord we say
                    we need wings to match the other wings
                    we don't have
                    we need a bubbling we can hold
                    Yahweh Hot Rod Sky Talker
                    talk to us Mister Master
                    Cloud Cork of the Transcendent Cava
                    Amen and Amen
but when we open our eyes
the food has vamoosed
and we all cry out stumbling in that wilderness
if we had soup we could have soup and crackers
if we had crackers . . . but of course
we don't because love comes on like a weight
and a claw and a sucker punch
and in the case of Mississippi
gateway to this our under-country
history is the dish that leaves us skinny
petrified forest of narcotic tornadoes
Scratch's bullwhip
devil's dancefloor
crackhead's cruise ship
backwoods Medusa with a kudzu Afro
whose green gaze
sprouts branches from the fluted
columns of Beauvoir
                    O hold my hand brother
before we return

233

peckers in the dirt of our poke-salad geography
redeemed as empty Faygo bottles
in the burned-down shed
in the bamboo patch
behind Bilbo's poolhall

Nominated by David McCombs

FORTY-TWO

fiction BY LISA TADDEO

from NEW ENGLAND REVIEW

Joan had to look beautiful.

Tonight there was a wedding in goddamned Brooklyn, farm-to-table animals talking about steel cut oatmeal as though they invented the steel that cut it. In New York the things you hate are the things you do.

She worked out at least two hours a day. On Mondays and Tuesdays, which are the kindest days for older single women, she worked out as many as four. At six in the morning she ran to her barre class in leg warmers and black Lululemons size four. The class was a bunch of women squatting on a powder blue rug. You know the type, until you become one.

FORTY-TWO. Somehow it was better than forty-one, because forty-one felt eggless. She had sex one time the forty-first year, and it lopped the steamer tail off her heart. After undressing her, the guy, a hairless NYU professor, looked at her in a way that she knew meant he had recently fucked a student, someone breathy and Macintosh-assed, full of Virginia Woolf and hope, and he was upset now at this reedy downgrade. Courageously he regrouped, bent her over, and fucked her anyhow. He tweaked her bony nipples and the most she felt of it was his eyes on the wall in front of her.

The reason the first part of the week is better for older single women is that the latter part is about anticipating Rolling Rocks in loud rooms. Anticipation, Joan knew, was for younger people. And on the weekends starting on Thursday young girls are out in floral Topshop shirts swinging small handbags. They wear cheap riding boots because it doesn't matter. They'll be wanted anyway, they'll be drunkenly nuzzled while Joan tries ordering a gin & tonic from a female bartender who ignores her or a male bartender who looks at her like she's a ten-dollar bill.

But on Mondays and Tuesdays older women rule the city. They drizzle orange wine down their hoarse throats at Barbuto, the dressed-down autumn light coming through the garage windows illuminating their eggplant highlights. They eat charred octopus with new potatoes in lemon and olive oil. They have consistent bounties of seedless grapes in their low-humming fridges.

Up close the skin on Joan's shoulders and cleavage was freckled and a little coarse. For lotion she used Santa Maria Novella, and her subway-tiled bathroom looked like an advertisement for someone who flew to Europe a lot. When her pedicure was older than a week in the winter and five days in the summer, she actually hated herself.

The good thing about Joan was, she wasn't in denial. She didn't want to love charred octopus or be able to afford it. But she did and she could. The only occasional problem was that Joan liked younger guys. Not animalistically young like twenty-two. More like twenty-seven to thirty-four. The word cougar is for idiots but it was nonetheless branded into the flank steak of her triceps.

Now Joan knew the score. For example, she was never one of those older women who is the last female standing at a young person's bar. She didn't eat at places she didn't have a reservation or know the manager. For the last decade she'd been polishing her pride like a gun collection. She no longer winked.

In the evenings she would attend a TRX class or a power yoga class or she would kickbox. Back at home before bed she free-styled a hundred walking lunges around her apartment with a seven-pound weight in each hand. She performed tricep dips off the quiet coast of her teak bed. She wore short black exercise shorts. She looked good in them, especially from far away. Her knees were wrinkled but her thighs were taut. Or, her thighs were taut but her knees were wrinkled. Daily happiness depended on how that sentence was ordered in her brain.

In a small wooden box at her nightstand she kept a special reserve of six joints meticulously rolled, because the last time she'd slept with someone on the regular he'd been twenty-seven and having good pot at your house means one extra reason for the guy to come over, besides a good mattress and good coffee and great products in a clean bathroom. At home your towels smell like ancient noodles. But at Joan's the rugs are free of hair and dried-up snot. The sink smells like lemon. The maid folds your boxers. Sleeping with an older woman is like having a weekend vacation home.

In addition to the young girls, Joan envied also the women who wake at 3 A.M. to get stuff done because they can't work when the world knows they're awake. They have, like, six little legs at their knees. She told her therapist as much, and her therapist said, That's nothing to be envious of, but Joan thought she could detect a note of pride in the voice of her therapist, who was married, with three small children.

Tonight there was a wedding and she had to look beautiful. She needed a blowout and a wax and a manicure and a salt scrub and an eyelash tint, which she should have done yesterday but didn't. She needed five hours but she only had four. She needed cool hairless cheeks. She was horrified by how much she needed in a day, to arrive not hating herself into the evening. She knew it wasn't only her. Everything in Manhattan was about feeding needs. Sure, it had always been like that, but lately it seemed like they took up so much brain estate that a lady hardly had enough time to Instagram a photo of herself feeding each need. Eyelash tinting, for example. Nowadays if you have a one-night stand you can't run into the bathroom in the morning to apply mascara. It's expected that your eyelashes are already black and thick as caterpillars. Be nice to you, said signs outside of Sabon on the way to Organic Avenue. But the problem, Joan knew, was that if you be nice to you, you get fat.

The twenty-seven-year-old caught her plucking a black wiry hair out of her chin, like a fish dislodging a hook from its own face. The bathroom door was ajar and she saw his eyeball out of the corner of her degradation. That was the last time he slept over. He had single-position sex with her two weeks later but he didn't sleep over and he never texted after that. She remembered with bitter fondness the Dean & DeLuca chicken salad she fixed him for lunch one day, the way he took it to go like someone who fucked more than one woman a week. The more a man didn't want her, the more it made her vagina tingle. It was like a fish that tried to pan fry itself.

TWENTY-SEVEN. When Joan was twenty-seven she had started waking with the drysocket dread, the biological alarm that *brinnggs* off at 4 A.M. in nice apartments. The tick tick salty tock of eggs hatching and immediately drying upon impact, inside the choking cotton of a Tampax Super Plus. She would wake in an Irishy-weather sweat, feeling lonely and receiving wedding invitations from girls less pretty than her. More than she wanted kids, she wanted to be in love.

But Joan had done better in her career than almost everyone she knew. For example, she had started pulling NFL players out of hats during Fashion Week, when her friends were leaving Orbit wrappers in the back rows of Stella McCartney.

She could have had a man and a career. It wasn't that she chose one over the other. No woman ever chose a career over having a man's prescription pills in her medicine cabinet. But Joan didn't like anyone who liked her. The guys who liked her were mostly smart and not sexy and she really wanted someone sexy. She would even have been okay with chubby and sexy but the chubby sexy guys were all taken. They were thirty-four and dating twenty-five-year-olds with underwire bras and smooth foreheads. The problem was Joan's generation thought they could wait longer. The problem was, they were wrong.

THIRTY-FOUR. When she was thirty-four she dated a man who was forty-six, who wore Saks brand shirts and had sunken cheeks and a money clip. They ate at the bars at great restaurants every night, but then she had sex with a gritty LES bartender and she did it without a condom on purpose. Mr. Big, her friends called the forty-six-year-old. They said, What's wrong with James? He's *ahmaayzing*. They said *amazing* in a way that meant they'd never want to ride him. The bartender gave her gonorrhea, which she didn't even know still existed, and it made her feel older than her mother's chewed Nicorette gum, frozen in time and lodged like the miniature porcelain animal figurines, seals and bunnies, that had been left inside the old lady's old Volvo. The same Volvo Joan still kept in the city, because having a car in the city means you can kill yourself gently if you really must. If something awful happens, you have a car, you can get the fuck out.

Tonight there was a wedding and she had to look beautiful because she was in love with the groom. It was the kind of love that made her feel old and hairy. It also made her feel alive.

He was an actor who was thirty-two. She first noticed him across the room at a party because he was wildly tall. He had a grown-up look but he was also a kid. He was good at drinking beer and playing baseball. That was something she realized now that Mr. Big didn't have, the tufted Bambi plush of youth to make her feel bad. She must like feeling bad somewhat. Everybody did but she might like it a little more than most.

He was at the bar so she sauntered over. She walked with her butt light behind her and her boobs pendulous in front of her. She'd learned the walk from a pole dancing workout class she'd been taking before a super hot twenty-four-year-old brunette with sharp dark bangs started taking the class and even the other women looked like they wanted to fuck her. Why, Joan wondered, were other women her age complicit in appreciating youth?

She ordered a Hendricks because that was what she ordered when she was trying to get a younger guy to notice her. A grandfather clock of an older woman drinking Hendricks was a Gatsby sort of thing. It made men feel like Warren Beatty, to drink beside one.

Hendricks, huh? he said on cue. One thing good about being forty-two was that she had eaten enough golden osetra to be able to predict any party conversation.

Jack had noticed her from across the room also. She was wearing one of those thick crepe red dresses that women her age wore to play in the same league as twenty-something girls in American Apparel skirts.

Hendricks, for the long and short of it, she'd said in a husky voice, holding the cool glass up to her bronzed cheek like a pitchwoman. There was something freakishly hot about an older woman who wanted it. He imagined her in doggy style. He knew her thighs would be super thin and also she would be kind of stretched out so fucking her would be a planetary exercise, like he was poking between two long trees into a dark solar system and feeling only wetness and morbid air.

That had been eight months ago. An entire summer passed and summers in Manhattan are the worst, if you're single and in love with someone who isn't. If you're older and single and the younger man you are in love with is not on Facebook but his even-younger girlfriend is.

Her name was Molly. She had a hundred brothers. Her youth was brutal.

Joan learned about Jack and Molly from Facebook. It made her feel creepy and old to click into Molly's friends and go through each of their pages one by one to see if one of them had a different photo of Jack. Jack wasn't on Facebook, which Joan loved about him.

Thursdays through Saturdays Joan played with the recurrent hair under her chin and moused through Molly's life. She found out information, which is all any woman wants. Some of the information waggled her belly and chopped up her guts into the blunt mince of the sweetbreads she orders at Gramercy Tavern. Like for example Joan found out that a few months prior, when Jack had invited Joan out for an unusual Friday night dinner, it was because Molly had been in Nantucket with some friends. She saw the pictures of furry Abercrombie blonds and one brown-haired girl on a lobster boat, fresher than a

Tulum mist. Joan got super pissed about that. Then she tucked an Ambien down her throat like a child into bed and reminded herself that they weren't even having an affair.

The most that had ever happened was, they kissed.

The kiss happened at the Spotted Pig, on the secret third floor where Joan was at a famous producer's party and texted Jack to see if he wanted to come by and he brought his friend Luke who looked at her like he knew what her nipples tasted like.

Joan drank Old Speckled Hen and didn't get drunk and Jack drank whiskey until he became a little more selfish than usual. She was wearing a slip dress and Luke left with some twenty-two-year-old and Jack put his large hand on her silk thigh, and then she took his hand and slipped his thumb under the liquidy lip of the dress and he got a semi and kissed her. His tongue licked the hops off her tongue. She felt like she had eighteen clitorises, and all of them couldn't drive.

One day one month later Jack bit the bullet and decided to propose to Molly. He bought an antique ring that was cheap but looked thoughtful. It was the kind of ring you could get in Florence on the bridge for four hundred euros and pretend it came from Paris. He plans a weekend in Saratoga. He has no idea he is not interesting. He has never wanted for women. Molly's dad has a sailboat they take out on the Cape. At the very least, he will have a summer place to go to all his life. He receives a text the first morning in Saratoga, from Joan.

Hey buddy: book party/clambake out in the Hamptons, couple of directors I can intro. This is a Must come.

Molly was in the shower. They were about to go horseback riding.

He wanted to punch something, or fuck a slutty girl. His anger peed out of him in weird ways. He didn't want to be this greedy about always wanting to be in the right place at the right time. Molly was singing Vampire Weekend in the shower. She had brown hair and makeupless skin. He thought of Joan in a cream satin dress with vermilion lips beckoning to him from a foaming writer's beach.

Joan was staying in a house in Amagansett with a strawberry patch path to the beach. The bedding in her room was vineyard grape–themed. What was awful and what gave the whole house a depressed cast was how many times she had changed *shd* to *should* then finally to *must* in that text. And then capitalized *Must*. She thought of grape must, in her room lotioning her legs, praying to the perfect clouds that Jack would come. She wanted his balls inside of her. She wanted him more than her whole life.

Be happy in every moment, said a sign on whitewashed store-bought driftwood in the hallway that connected Joan's bedroom to the bedroom of the fifty-something corporate realtor who was trying to sleep with her all weekend.

An entire 40 percent of him had activated plan B. Plan B was, he high-tailed it out of the B&B he got on discount from Jetsetter and texted Molly from the road something panicked about something that happened with a surprise for her that evening. They had been dating for six years and she had seen him bring the special bottle of Barolo with him and she was expecting it, so what would be the big deal if he just made up a story about his buddy who was supposed to bring the newly-purchased ring to Saratoga but then the buddy gets tied up at work. It was the best kind of lie, because she would know for sure she only had to wait one more night for a ring. But then a wave of something he imagined to be selflessness washed over him so he wrote back:

Sorry, kiddo. Out in Saratoga, wrong side of the Manhattan summer tracks. You don't know how bummed I am . . .

In her room sadly smelling the Diptyque candle she bought in case he came, Joan went on Facebook which she'd promised herself she wouldn't do anymore. She clicked on Molly. She hated when men used ellipses. Why do men use ellipses.

. . . means I don't give that much of a fuck about you . . .

When someone hasn't changed a thing on Facebook in several weeks then all of a sudden there is a new cover photo of a ring on a finger on a candlelit table, someone else might kill herself. That's something that Facebook can do.

Joan called her therapist on emergency, and she was sitting on the floor of her grape-themed room drinking a glass of red wine in the summer. She told her therapist, I'm on my second glass of wine since I've been talking to you. Her therapist said, We should be wrapping up anyway, but Joan looked at the clock, and it was 8:26 and they had four minutes left, and she wanted to kill everybody. She wanted to kill her therapist's Wheaten Terrier, who was whining in the background, like he was reminding Joan that other people had amassed a family, while she had eaten at every restaurant rated over a twenty-four in Zagat.

Molly was twenty-six. It was the perfect age to be engaged for a girl.

Jack, at thirty-two, was the perfect age to settle down. He hadn't rushed like his friends who pulled the trigger at twenty-five for girls who they were definitely going to cheat on with women like Joan, who you could tell from their lipstick would give wet, pleading blow jobs.

241

Everything with Molly was great. She didn't even nag. Actually, Molly'd asked him when they first moved in if he could vacuum the plank floor but he hadn't done that yet, so he knew Molly vacuumed then washed the floors herself. He knew that if her father knew she was cleaning so much he'd be pissed, but he also knew Molly wanted her father to like him, more than she herself needed to like him.

The day of a wedding is always about three people. The groom, the bride, and the person most unrequitedly in love with the groom or the bride.

After fifteen years of not smoking, the day of the wedding Joan starts smoking again. When she was fifteen she started smoking and wearing makeup. At twenty-eight she started removing the makeup, especially from her eyes, with fine linen cloths. At thirty-six she treated each fine linen cloth as a disposable thing, using one for every two days. It made her feel greedy and wealthy and safe. It made her feel old.

Jack is nervous as hell. He is also excited for the attention, even though the wedding party will be small. It is going to be at the Vinegar Hill House, a big group dinner after he and Molly sign the papers at City Hall. Molly asked him not to shave because she loves his beard. He thinks of their handwritten vows. He is excited to perform his.

Joan ditches the salt scrub in favor of the eyelash tint. The face is more important than the body if nobody is going to make love to you that night. Without makeup, her face is the color of ricotta. She smokes five cigarettes before 9 A.M. and the ricotta turns gray, like it's been sea-salted. By noon she has had seventeen. She has cigarette number twenty and she thinks maybe she should take the car. She's wanted to take the car for maybe seven years now. She keeps putting it off. When Joan was twenty, her father told her she could do anything. He told her not to jump into anything. He told her the world would wait for her.

TWENTY. When Molly was twenty she took a class called Jane Austen and Old Maids. It frankly stuck with her. Today Molly gets ready alone, in the apartment she shares with her husband-to-be. She does her own hair, which is long and brown, and she fixes twigs and berries and marigolds she got from the co-op into a fiery halo at the top. She's naked. The sun comes through the uncleanable windows and lights the garland and she looks like an angel.

She shimmies the ivory eyelet dress on over her pale body. She catches sight of her full breasts in the ornate antique mirror they bought upstate the weekend of the engagement. Coming down her body a tag inside the dress scratches the meat of her left breast. The tag says, Cornwall 1968. She bought the dress at a thrift store in Saratoga. Everything that weekend was magic.

SIXTY-EIGHT. Her grandmother and her mother's two sisters died at sixty-eight of complications from breast cancer. Her mother was diagnosed two years ago, at fifty-eight, so back then Molly thought about a decade a lot. Ten years. Now she thinks that it's okay that the past two haven't been perfect. That they have eight left. Her mother is the kind of mother who always had brownies in an oven. Her mother loves her father so much she can't imagine the two of them disconnected, she can't imagine her mother in the ground and her father above it.

She puts on cowboy boots, a simple pair of ruddy Fryes that have been to Montana and Wyoming and Colorado inside horse muck and in salmony streams. The dress is tea length and her calves are lovely. The last time she wore the boots was at a horse ranch weekend with her girlfriends, the month before she met Jack. She made love to one of the cowboys with her boots on in a lightly used hay-smelling barn in the moonlight and he came inside her and Jack never has. The cowboy stroked her hair for an hour after they finished. He said, If you ever decide the big city's not for you, come see me. I'll be here. He had a silly cowboy name and he wore a bolo tie and her friends made endless fun of her. She never felt safer. Now every time she smells hay she thinks of kindness.

Since Molly was seven, she has measured her care for someone by whether or not she would leave snot on their floor. When she was seven and sleeping at her cousin Julie's house, Julie had refused to let Molly have a certain stuffed bear to sleep with, even after Molly cried and begged, even after Julie's mom who was now dead of breast cancer had asked Julie to let Molly have the bear, but she didn't *tell* her daughter to do it, she only asked, which was how you created monsters.

Molly cried so much that night that her nose filled with gray storm. In the morning she was less sad than bitter. Tears had dried like snail treads down her cheek and her nose was filled with calcified pain. She cleared each nostril with her child finger and dropped the results, like soft hail, one by one on Julie's bedroom carpet. She left the tissues there too, hidden under the nightstand.

You could also reverse the test, you could measure how much someone cared for you by whether or not you could imagine them leaving snot on your floor.

Molly walked the three blocks from her apartment to the Vinegar Hill House. There was no limo for this bride, no ladies in waiting holding her train. She was doing everything herself. When her parents had offered, she'd refused their financial assistance. Her father's money would make her think less of Jack.

When a moment is upon you, the best you can do for it is to imagine it in the past. Like how a whole weekend with friends will come and go and mostly you'll be glad when everyone is gone home, and later you'll see a picture of yourselves on a lobster boat in red and blue sweatshirts smiling and blinking against the September suntanless sun and you'll think, I must have been happier that day than I thought I was.

The restaurant is set for the wedding. The mason jars for cocktails, the burlap runners, the long wooden tables, and the bar mop napkins. The wedges of thick toast are out already on rough cutting boards awaiting their marriage to cheese. The votives in Ball jars, the Kombucha on tap. The ceremony will happen on the terrace, the officiant will be some large-gutted Pakistani friend of the groom's, and it will be shorter than the lifespan of a piece of gum.

Her vows are simple and unspecific. She had always thought her wedding vows with the man of her dreams would be specific, about things he did with his cereal, flowers he stole from the grates of Park Slope, picayune habits he had that were annoying, his smelly obsession with roll mops. Jack doesn't vacuum. She was going to work that into her vows and then she felt tired.

For the past two months Molly has been finding tissues. He doesn't vacuum so she finds the crumpled tissues, like lowbrow snowflakes, in the corners behind their bed, on his side, and also on hers. It is not mere laziness. It is the triumph of his indolence over his love for her, and it is dishonest. She has her dishonesties, too. She asked Jack not to shave because underneath the beard he is gaunt and sallow and looks like the unemployable actor her father promised he would become.

Twenty-six is Molly's perfect age. She thinks of the six years she has spent with Jack, the eight years she imagines she has left with her mother. She thinks of the impending six-minute ceremony, and the forty-three minutes the cowboy fucked her in the hay during which time she came and then came again against the milk-bearded mooing of the cows outside and the whistle of the humble Colorado wind. The ecstasy of grass, the violence of milk. Staring at the wedding bounty before her, feeling the weight of the crown of flowers in her hair, she

244

knows there are hundreds, thousands, who will be jealous, but she doesn't know them by name. She whispers the name of the cowboy to the unlit candles like a church girl, to the naked bread and the tiny daisies in tiny glass jars. She incants the name, and the name itself, like the memory of a moment before it becomes a legend, frees her enough to think the thing she has been thinking for ten thousand seconds, for one hundred billion years, the thing we all think when we finally get what we want. The right way to do something might be the wrong way in the end. Fortunately or unfortunately, both ways lead to Rome.

Joan is on her way, in the car. On her way she receives a text from Jack.

There's a hidden message to you in my speech thing today. Shhh . . .

Jack is on his way, in a cab. He sends the text to Joan. Not having been employed for a couple of years, it makes him feel good to rattle off a text that he knows will go a long way, for his career. It feels like an Excel spreadsheet. Also, how he thought to change *shout-out* to *hidden message*, because it sounded warmer. Finally, on the way to his wedding, he marvels at how easy it is, with women. If only they knew how little time we spend thinking of them, and if only they knew how much we know about how much they think about us. The freaking man hours a woman puts into men! To looking good for men. The brow tints and whatever. And at the end of the day, you can be twenty-six and it doesn't matter. There's someone out there who's gonna be eighteen, with a smaller vagina. Jack is so happy he isn't a woman, even if he is an actor.

The motor is on in the Volvo in Manhattan and there's a wedding in Brooklyn and Joan reads the ellipsis, finally, for what it is. She reads it all the way through to the end.

At the restaurant with a few Mexican waiters watching her with genuine care and admiration, Molly calls the cowboy's name like he is in the room and like she did in the hay that day and she says it to the wildflower bouquet housed inside the McCann's Irish Oatmeal tin on the wedding cake table. Like Snow White speaking to the forest creatures she leans down and says his name to the ironic bird-and-bee salt-and-pepper shakers and none of them answer, or come to life. Which makes her feel bummed but she regroups, because there is a silver lining, like the one in the oatmeal tin that cuts your finger if you aren't careful.

In the distance she sees Jack, though he doesn't see her. She sees him come into the place and check his hair and smooth his beard in his reflection on a dirty window. It's time to do this. Everything is time. You commit yourself to a course in life, to a course of treatment, but nothing lasts forever, not the good or the bad. Molly, feeling the most beautiful she will ever feel, adjusts the marigolds in her hair, and thinks, forty-two. If she dies at sixty-eight, like all the breast-charred women before her, she'll have just forty-two years left.

Nominated by New England Review, Maura Stanton

WE WOULD NEVER SLEEP

by DAVID HERNANDEZ

from THE SUN

We the people, we the one
times 320 million, I'm rounding up, there are really
too many grass blades to count,
wheat plants to tally, just see
the whole field swaying from here to that shy
blue mountain. Swaying
as in rocking, but also the other
definition of the verb: we sway, we influence,
we impress. Unless we're asleep,
unless the field's asleep, more a postcard
than a real field, portrait of the people
unmoved. You know that shooting last week?
I will admit the number dead
was too low to startle me
if you admit you felt the same,
and the person standing by you
agrees, and the person beside that person.
It has to be double digits,
don't you think? To really
shake up your afternoon? I'm troubled by
how untroubled I felt
regarding the total coffins, five
if you care to know, five still
even if you don't. I'm angry
that I'm getting used to it, the daily number

gunned down: *pop-pop* on Wednesday,
Thursday's spent casings
pinging on the sidewalk. It all sounds
so industrial, there's nothing metal
that won't make a noise, I'm thinking every gun
should come with a microphone,
each street with loudspeakers
to broadcast their banging.
We would never sleep, the field
always awake, acres of swaying
up to that shy blue mountain, no wonder
it cowers on the horizon, I mean
look at us, look with the mountain's eyes,
we the people
putting holes in the people.

Nominated by The Sun, Bob Hicok, Mike Newirth

PRIEST

fiction by ERIN McGRAW

from IMAGE

When Father Tom comes to a party, people look embarrassed, even the ones who invited him. At wedding and funeral receptions, he sits at the table with the great-aunts. He is the necessary conduit, but he frightens people who hear "priest" and imagine no house, no family, no sex. "You must have started so young!" a parishioner recently said to him. "I'm always surprised when young men. . . ."

She faltered, and Father Tom was moved to pity. "Me, too," he said.

He didn't start especially young. He went to college, got a job as a loan officer, and tried to understand the misery that swept over him every morning when he cinched up his tie. He had a girlfriend and met his car payments. There was no reason for him to find himself standing in his apartment garage with a rope and instructions he'd downloaded for tying a noose.

"I'm glad you didn't follow through," said the priest Tom talked to later, because a priest was cheaper than a therapist.

"Bad at knots," Tom said.

The priest thought Tom's answer was God, of course, and Tom forgave him for that. It was the priest's job to think that despair at life's unsolvable monotony could be solved by God, and it was Tom's job to listen politely, go home, and get any ropes or extension cords out of the house.

He was back at the church a week later. "Give me something to do," Tom said, and the priest handed him a rake. Three hours later, when he had sweated through his flannel shirt and streaked his face with leaf

249

dirt, he felt better than he had in months. "What else do you have?" he asked the priest, who told him to come back after he'd had a shower.

He tutored kids in math and washed forks after the parish potluck. He vacuumed the sacristy. He braced himself for the inevitable next talk about God, which came like clockwork. "How can you be so sure you're not priest material?" the priest said.

"I'm not sure I believe in God," Tom said.

"You don't have to be sure about God. You just have to believe in God's work," the priest said, words that Tom could not resist. The work—God's work, whatever—was everywhere, the world bleeding from every orifice. "How can you stand it?" his girlfriend asked after he spent a weekend locked in with violent offenders.

"They're people, too," he said lamely. He felt coherent when he was with the killers and freaks. He felt alive. When he moved toward ordination and one examiner after another asked him whether he was sure he had a vocation, he told them, "I don't think anyone can be sure. But I feel close to myself when I'm doing this work." Once upon a time, the examiners would have pressed him about whether he felt close to God, but no one talked like that anymore.

Now that the vows are finished and the rest of his life is signed away and set out to collect dust, he's tired of being close to himself. At the end of the day, after the meetings are finished and the computer shut off, the unanswerable questions return. When his mother was close to death, she caught at his sleeve and pulled until his ear was next to her mouth. "I'm afraid," she whispered.

"It's okay."

"I'm not supposed to be afraid. It means I don't have faith."

"Mom, everybody—"

She shook her head. "I'm going to go to hell."

She died two days later, and nothing the mortician did could erase the terror from her face.

He prays for her, of course. But there isn't enough prayer in the world. Not for his mother, not for the hemophiliac girl he knew in grade school who got knocked down and bled out on the playground, not for continents full of children waking up with a stomach full of hungry and no food for miles. No one has answers, his confessor has told him. Is that supposed to make Father Tom feel better?

One night, maddened by his circling, ceaseless thoughts, he dropped to the worn carpet and forced himself through push-ups until his arms gave out. He hadn't done push-ups since he was in high school, and his arms burned after twenty, but at least he quit thinking about the argument he'd had with his mother the night before he started college, the one that left her weeping in the bathroom after he told her that heaven was a fairy tale. In the morning he made himself pray the Daily Office, which he skipped so often he hardly remembered how to do it.

The trick is to drive away thoughts. No wonder the ancients believed in demons; as far as Father Tom can see, demonic possession is a perfectly reasonable way to interpret the memories that assail him. "Do you have trouble not thinking about sex?" his confessor asks in a confiding tone. Sex is the least of it. Father Tom remembers his girlfriend's face, scrubbed of emotion, when he told her he was going to become a priest. "So I get dumped for Jesus," she said.

Sometimes he prays, sometimes he does squats or jumping jacks, one week he drank a glass of water every half-hour, peed like a racehorse, and lost two pounds. These actions—mortifications, to use the old word—make him a better priest, a better person. If he'd discovered discipline a little sooner, he wouldn't have made his mother cry and might never have entered the priesthood. Wearing his belt one notch too tight, he counseled a gay fourteen-year-old for three straight hours. The boy was cutting himself; he showed Father Tom the neat scars laddering up his leg. Father Tom shifted in his chair, feeling the belt sawing at his soft waist. "What would happen?" he said, leaning forward. "What would happen if you never cut yourself again? What if you made peace with the dryness in your heart?" The boy is in college now, and his mother thinks he's happy.

A few weeks after that counseling session, Father Tom holds a blade against his thigh, bouncing it lightly. The razor blade makes a light pinging sensation on his skin; it's keen and unexpectedly lighthearted. Father Tom is teasing himself; nothing will come of this. He has too much work to do. Just a week ago he agreed to spearhead a new outreach to troubled youth downtown, an agreement he made while knuckling a finger backward painfully under the desk. "I'm so glad," said the social worker who had called the meeting, a brisk woman with a terrible haircut. "No one reaches people better than you do. Sometimes I think, when I look at you, that I'm seeing the face of Jesus."

"Jesus is either horrified or laughing himself sick," Father Tom said.

"You need to learn to accept a compliment, Father."

"Thank you," he said, forcing his finger back a millimeter further. The woman meant to be kind, and he was not ungrateful. She had no way to understand that Father Tom and Jesus have worked out their own understanding. Death, which Jesus treated so cavalierly, will eventually come to save Father Tom, and then Father Tom will believe. In the meantime, he will practice the little deaths, every day. It is a life. It makes him happy.

Nominated by Image, Jay Rogoff, Ron Tanner

WALK

by JANE SPRINGER

from THE SOUTHERN REVIEW

The kill was accidental the coyotes did not want the meat the meat
didn't want to be downed that day the rain charged the air with
negative ions we all felt great & walked, garnet crystals flanked
the washed-up creek wind-rush, you know that feeling of no
surveillance? Curious objects fall—a purple leaf or walnut
in its citron husk, we peeled one bare down to its tannic heart
with 911 a county away, the sky a blank crow caw.

It's not as though the coyotes buttoned up their coyote suits that
morning plotting to leave a being childless. Whether fowl or furred
the mothers left their hymnals in their caves that day
the same as us—it's not unusual, in fall, to come across
vermillion grasses in the rough part of the field path, but maybe
that's why the coyotes fled the scene so fast: an eerie fear
the meat belonged to family, but which one?

Can it be said that one gets used to either being stalked or stalking?
Having had no recent predators, the coyotes must have felt
free walking the beat—you know that feeling of no surveillance?
When all the woods are yours to eat, don't trespass signs
are landscape. After all, we'd been so used to trying not to gain
attention, our sheer movement past the cattails may have startled
the coyotes before the feast, our footsteps sounding

numerous as rain & with winter on fall's heels one might believe
each droplet held an icicle or spectacle for bearing witness
to what pack in nature lay our meat to waste. Rain accents cadmium
vine strung down to chartreuse feather—no lens does justice.
That's why we took the walk, while shivering, & saw this meat
arrested, fresh, & glittering as if to plead a silent testament:
Aren't you my kin? Whoever once walked aimless

in these woods now walks awake with me in death.

Nominated by Ed Falco

VOLTAIRE NIGHT

by DEB OLIN UNFERTH

from THE PARIS REVIEW

I'm the one who started it. I was depressed as hell and wanted to share my bad news. "Has anyone read *Candide*?" I said. I don't even recall what the bad news was but it must have had to do with a certain man who didn't love me anymore. In those days I felt most of the time like someone had knocked me in the head with a brick, and even though I had stopped drinking, I had started again, and the way I saw it, a real brick in the head would have been okay because then I'd be dead or at least unconscious.

I had a job teaching a class in the adult-ed program of a fancy prestigious college. The class went one winter night a week, and while the school was fancy, the adult-ed program was not—classes were not held on the beautiful medieval campus, but shoved over into a hideous office building downtown in order for the working citizens of our land to have easier access to higher learning, though we all knew the truth: it was to keep the fake teachers and students from mingling with (and possibly infecting) the real ones. The hallways of the downtown building were lined with artful black-and-white photographs of the real campus so that we could all look at the place we'd been denied. The classrooms in the downtown building did not have windows. This was an architectural feat, maybe even a masterpiece, something in the league of M. C. Escher, because the outside of the building had windows running up and down three sides and while, yes, one side had no windows, it was not the side that held our classrooms. I sometimes stood at the foot of the building, looking up and marveling at how this had been accomplished.

Still, getting the job was my one obvious piece of luck that year. The

255

pay wasn't great, but it was decent and it beat the other adjunct work I was doing. I was teaching all over town and could barely pay the rent. I was drinking in the cheapest bars, driving home blind.

The people who took these adult-ed classes tended to be smart, overeducated for jobs that were no longer fulfilling or that had never satisfied in the first place—journalists, lawyers—and now, in their middle years, they recalled that they had once wanted something artistic for their lives but it had not worked out, and despite whatever trappings they had—spouses, houses, tykes—they found themselves confronting a deep, colorless meaninglessness each day. They thought that maybe realizing their early dreams would change all that. They wrote books six thousand pages long and made jokes about bringing them to class in a dump truck. Or they wrote nothing but had a great idea for a story that they recorded on their phones and had assistants transcribe. Or their spouses were working, and they themselves had quit their numbing jobs, were staying home to write, give it a go at last. Their writing—let's be honest—was nothing to shout about. Not good, mostly unreadable. No control or sense of timing, no grasp of narrative beyond cliché. But often the language itself had personality, and a clear voice came through: sardonic, witty, self-deprecating, with a tarp of sad earnestness over it, all of which I liked, so I found it easy to read the pages they gave me and to encourage them.

In Voltaire's *Candide*, there's a certain passage where a huge crowd wants to board a boat, all vying for the same seat Candide—luckless man, but in this one instance he is lucky and in possession of some extra cash—has offered to pay for. The seat will go, he says, to the man or woman most bad off among them. One by one they choose their woes and tell their tales. That scene—communal, classroom-like, someone in charge judging their stories and making promises no one could keep—these students, with me as their leader, reminded me of that.

After the final class of my first course at the school, the students suggested we go for a drink.

I didn't usually go for drinks with my students. I knew teachers who did, and I found it unprofessional and revolting, though that would not have stopped me. Neither would have the fact that I had sworn to quit drinking. But the school had put in place a policy, which applied even to the dubious adult ed. I'd had to sign a statement. Still, an end-of-term drink seemed like a nice idea.

We walked four blocks through the freezing cold to an upscale, unpopular joint in the nighttime-deadtime downtown. We sat in giant, stuffed chairs in a dark room, empty of anyone but us and the bartender. They all looked over at me, waiting. At last I said, "Has anyone read *Candide*?"

"Yes, yes," they murmured. "Voltaire. Of course." As I said, this was an educated crowd. They'd read it in college, they said. Or they'd read it when they were twelve and had found it confusing. Or they'd liked it and had read his other works since and found them less fun.

"Let's play a game," I said. "Let's each tell the story of the worst thing that's happened to us."

"In our lives?"

I hesitated. I wanted to talk about the boyfriend who'd left me, and even in my traumatized state I had to admit it wasn't the worst thing that had happened in my life. I'd had people die on me. I'd once had a fire burn up all my things. Besides, this boyfriend left me a lot. We were on the third or the fourth time now, depending on how you were counting. Those were the days that the same boyfriend left me over and over, and each time felt like a tragedy.

"Lately," I said.

They looked hesitant.

"And whoever tells the worst story wins," I said.

"What do they win?"

"Well, they get to be the winner."

They looked disappointed. "But the winner of what?"

"Voltaire night," I said.

As a matter of fact, Candide had solicited his crowd, had not wanted to sail alone, and I could understand that. He'd had it announced in town. Maybe he'd taken out an ad in a circular: Will pay passage for the most unfortunate man in the land. So many showed up an entire fleet of boats could not have taken them all away.

The students were into it, but nervous. The first told a silly story, something about a drawer that held important papers getting stuck and his having to saw it open with a chain saw. Another said she'd gained ten pounds. Another said her final grandparent had died and she was unnerved—what with only one generation between her and death. A second round of drinks and the stories grew more personal. One man divorced last month. He hadn't wanted a divorce. He was in a new apartment in a strange neighborhood. He'd been married fourteen years. He felt so old. One man's teenager had run away that year, and it had taken a week to find her, and when he did finally locate her and had gone to pick her up, the girl screamed, "I hate you!" while he stood in the driveway, stunned. Why did she hate him? What had he done? One woman had learned she had cancer. She'd had her first round of radiation last week—a curable kind, but still. The mood in the room grew somber, and we felt protective of one another, commiserative, full of solidarity. Then one guy said, "Well, I got a flat last week in the rain," and we all shouted, "You lose!" and threw pretzels and straws at him.

I did tell the story of the boyfriend, not the long absurd version that my friends were all sick of, but the miniature version, the kind I'd tell on the bus, and I told it in a dramatic fashion: "The man I love no longer loves me and I can't seem to get over him, no matter what I do or where I go." The students all rose to my defense. They were indignant, outraged. The guy was obviously a fool. I deserved better. "I know, I know," I said, shaking my head. Who can explain love? we all wondered, eating our peanut mix. Who can explain the recession of love? Love's sneaky decline?

I don't recall who won Voltaire night that first time, but I know we voted and had a winner who received extra rounds of commiseration and drinks and a couple of comradely hugs as we all parted at the door and hurried through the cold for separate trains or lots.

It was a grand night, our first Voltaire night.

The class went six weeks and restarted the next month like a new moon. Perhaps because I'd done well with the first class, or perhaps because no one in the office was paying any attention at all, I was given the course again and several students from the first class signed up. It was an open class, noncredit, at the service of anyone in the world who could show up on Tuesdays and pay the (exorbitant) fee. But the old students claimed an elevated status over the new ones anyway—not by their superior writing (they were all equally bad and no one had improved) but by talking about Voltaire night. The best night of the class, they agreed. One of the best nights of the past year, in fact, for them all. It had been so fun. And enriching. Too bad the new students had missed out.

Hey, the new students said, *they* wanted a chance at Voltaire night. It wasn't fair that I had picked favorites and wouldn't grant the new students this educational opportunity. So we planned a second Voltaire night, and the final night of the class, we trudged out into the cold.

It was March now, but the wind was still punishing in that evil Chicago way. I talked again about the cruel boyfriend who didn't love me, who even after these months was still causing me pain. He had come back in the meantime but had left again, and again I got all the commiseration I could hope for, and Voltaire night was special all over again—even if we did stay out a bit late, due to the fact that the bar closed at one, and maybe we had too many drinks, but it was okay. We all waved good-bye at last and crept off into the night calling that we'd see one another next month.

It didn't slip by me that the meaninglessness on their faces might gleam only when they came to class—those faces turned toward me, hoping for not success, but proof that they were at least *worthy* of some intangible (maybe nonexistent) thing, even if they never got it. But maybe at home they were happy. A few, of course, took the class merely as an extracurricular, nothing more—women, mostly. These had happy lives that brought fulfillment. They tended to take the class only for one session, wrote friendly, honest evaluations encouraging me to do such and such (what that thing was always differed: talk more, talk less, fewer or more handouts), and they'd wave good-bye and we'd never see them again. Some were like that, but not many.

Voltaire night took hold. It became an institution, part of class. Leading up to it, the students conferred. Where should it be held? Should food be involved? And the parameters—the worst thing in the past five years? since Christmas? as a kid? They'd settle in and tell their stories as if we were around a campfire, as if these were the stories of their lives: their disappointments and frustrations, what they'd strove for and hadn't gotten, the promises made to them that had been broken, the people who were gone or who still were there but seemed changed somehow, not what they'd once been, or perhaps it was the students themselves who had changed. Blame the vicissitudes of life or, alternately, its flatness, the dullness of it, the sad fact of aging. This of course took a lot longer than our original three-minute summaries, so Voltaire night grew long. We'd all be drunk, having closed down several places, and the folks from the suburbs missed the very last train and had to curl on a bench at the station, like criminals down on their luck (which weren't we all, in some way?), until the five-thirty A.M. shuttle. But it was worth it, we all said, for how else could everyone have gotten a turn? How else could everyone have told their story?

As for me, I'd arrive home at four in the morning and spend a few days cursing myself. The trouble I could get in for this. Unseemly. Voltaire night was out of control, a monster I had to rein in but didn't know how to rein in. I didn't want to rein it in. Voltaire night was the one night I looked forward to, all of that sitting around feeling sorry for ourselves. I would have liked to do it every night.

There was the Voltaire night that Max accidently smashed several glasses onto the floor and Stuart threw up on the sidewalk. There was the Voltaire night I somehow found myself separated from them all at two in the morning, smoking pot with strangers at a faraway club. How had I gotten there?

There were other things going on with me. Voltaire night was just a handful of nights out of that year, but the other nights weren't so very different.

I had to change. In many ways I had to change.

One Voltaire night, a clear spring night, after a winter that had seemed to go on for years (and, in fact, this was my second year on the job), the students voted to tell the worst thing of their entire lives.

I don't know why we hadn't done that yet. Worst thing ever. It seems like it would be a fast place to go once you're on the worst-thing roller coaster, but we hadn't. Maybe we'd refrained because we knew once we'd done it, future Voltaire nights would be awkward. Once you'd told the worst, how could you complain about the past three months, which contained only the usual disillusionments, the familiar slow-burn panic that you were doing nothing with your life, had not lived up to your "potential," or worse, you had and it had changed nothing, that you had not yet even learned how to love? But the students voted. The worst-ever Voltaire night. We went to a nice place for dinner and ordered several bottles of wine.

*   *   *

Among us was a new guy, had been with us only one session and had barely spoken in class. I hadn't even noticed him much among the brash, flirty, loud men. He raised his glass. "I'll go next."

"All right, all right," we said. The newcomers often went first, were fool enough to go when people were just settling in. The regulars knew to wait. The best spot was an hour or two in, when people were happy, when the deep-level drunk hadn't set in yet, turning the night into a disco or a disorderly blur.

"The worst thing that ever happened to me," he said, "began with an experiment. You ever see those ads asking for human subjects? A hundred bucks to take some drugs, fifty to do some puzzles?"

"Uh-huh," we said, meeting eyes with one another. A human-subject-experiment story, here we go. Our stories would top that.

"I was living in Hyde Park, newly married. My wife was pregnant. Four months. We were overjoyed, but poor. I did freelance design back then, my wife was in sales, and no matter how much work I managed to scrape together, it wasn't going to be enough. So I used to answer those ads for a few bucks. Cover an eye and identify colors. Recite words I was told to remember."

"Uh-huh," we said.

"Well, one day I came across an ad that said, 'Twelve-week experiment, fifteen thousand dollars,' and I thought, Wow, fifteen thousand dollars! I went down and signed up."

I'm not sure I have the details right. I want to be clear about that. I'm not sure if it was fifteen thousand or ten or eleven, or if she was five months along or four. I'm pretty sure it was twelve weeks. What one hears at Voltaire night, stays at Voltaire night, and it is only now that I am violating this contract.

"It turned out they paid you fifteen thousand dollars because the study was miserable, and no one would do it unless for a lot. They wanted to chart the temperatures of nocturnal humans—humans who had been deprived of all natural light." He leaned forward and sketched the light in the air. "So two guys came over and spent all afternoon removing the

261

light from our apartment. They blocked up our windows. They used heavy, black boards and put black tape around the edges so no light could possibly slip in. You were required to sleep in the day and be up at night. And you were forbidden to leave the house while the least bit of sun stood in the sky."

"For twelve weeks?" we said. We were laughing hysterically.

"They gave you a sun calendar so you would know when the day was over, and since the study went into summer, you could see on the calendar that by the end you were going to be inside a lot."

"That's crazy," we said.

"You don't get used to it," he said, "if you're wondering. But that wasn't the worst part."

"What could be worse?"

"In order to have your temperature charted you had to have a tiny rectal thermometer inserted in your anus, twenty-four hours a day for twelve weeks."

We looked around nervously, to be sure we were still laughing. How much would you have to be paid to do that? we wondered. Would you do that for fifteen or eight or eleven or whatever thousand dollars? What was that worth?

"The thermometer was sort of surgically put in there. I had to go get it checked twice a week, make sure it was still in place, because a man has to shit, you know. So I'd lie in bed all day, unable to sleep, in an apartment with blackened windows, not a single slip of light, and my wife would go to work. Long after dark I'd go to the lab and bend over so they could check my thermometer. How do you feel? they'd say. Are you experiencing discomfort? And then I'd go home through the dark to the apartment and eat and watch TV and try to stay awake and do my freelance projects, although it was hard to work under those conditions and gradually I sought fewer and fewer. But still I was not unhappy because my wife was getting a little bigger each day, a little rounder, and she held my daughter inside her (by this time we knew we had a girl) and I knew that when my daughter arrived, she would have everything she needed because of my suffering through this."

"The weeks went by and I have to admit it got worse. Outside, spring was shifting to summer, and inside, the nights grew shorter, stuffier. I stayed inside through it all. The thermometer was uncomfortable. I could feel it in there, although they'd initially told me I wouldn't. It began to get a tiny bit painful but they checked it and said it was fine. I sat up through the night, but sleeping in the day grew harder as my initial determination wore off and was replaced by a lethargy. The weeks were interminable, each week seemed like an ordeal, a string of hot days before me that seemed endless. We had no air-conditioning, just a meek fan that rotated the dead air in a room whose windows were taped shut. I didn't want to spend money on an air conditioner. I barely saw my wife. She worked all day and had to be up early. She was leaving for work as I was going to sleep, though I couldn't sleep. I was achy, exhausted, although all I did was sit around, all day and night, alone mostly. Even my outings to the lab—the cooling darkness, going through the neighborhoods, outings that should have held joy because each one marked another step toward the end—were tinged with bad feelings. You'd think I'd go for walks at night, meet friends for late dinners and drinks—that's what I had planned—but I did so less and less. The thermometer was uncomfortable, I was too sleep deprived to be much company. No, my visits to the lab, my late-night trips to the grocery, my stops for gas became my only outings. I stayed in, watched TV or played video games that involved blowing up objects and leaving huge craters in the earth."

"Why didn't you just quit?" we said. We were not laughing. "I would have quit, by God. No way could I do that."

"That's what my wife said," he admitted. "Oh, I wanted to, all right. I came close to giving up, but if I did, all the weeks I'd suffered would be for nothing. If you quit in the middle, you got only five hundred bucks. And the truth that I hadn't told my wife was that despite my plan to double our money, I'd stopped working nearly altogether. She believed my work day began in earnest after she'd gone to sleep, but I quit the moment I saw the light switch off in the bedroom. Unless I finished the experiment and got the money, we'd wind up with a loss."

"Oh, that's bad, that's very bad," we said, settling back down.

"So the weeks stretched in front of me, and every week that passed, I thought, Thank God that's over, but the idea of six or seven more like it seemed impossible. But I thought of my coming daughter, how beautiful she'd be, how much like her mother, and I soldiered on. And one day it was five weeks left, and one day it was four weeks left, and one day it was three weeks left."

"Sometimes I just couldn't face the hot apartment and my wife, who was more annoyed by the day with the experiment. Sometimes I stopped at a bar on my way back from the lab. The first time one drink was enough to push me home. The second time, it was two drinks, the third time, four. I arrived home later and later, and my wife went from annoyed to disturbed to enraged. One night (I'd gone out every other night for a week at that point), she screamed over her belly, I don't even know who you are anymore!

"I remember it so well. It felt so unfair. I was close, less than a week away, only a few more days. I screamed something back, incoherent and nasty.

"Would you just get out? she yelled. Get out, just get out.

"I'd never been a drinker, beyond some nights in college, and the bar I went to was the worst place on the planet: Christmas lights strung in July, broken tables, stained linoleum, a line of human subjects sipping their lot, the kind of place the postmen went before they shot themselves in the heart. I sat down and ordered a drink."

This was going to turn out to be the final Voltaire night, though we didn't know it yet. The restaurant was quiet that evening, glasses emptying and refilling, the windows covered in lights. Here's what I wonder: Candide and his hapless crew. I could see them in my mind, gathering on the dock, their trunks and boxes piled on the wet wood, their fingers in their pockets wrapped around their last coins, while Candide strolled among them. Why did they all want to get on that ship? What was wrong with where they were? Were they fleeing the scene? Making a humble retreat? Or had they been told—politely but firmly—to leave?

Or were they going toward something, looking for a better life?

"The next thing I remember is that I couldn't open my eyes. Something was pressing down on my face. I couldn't get the lids up. I struggled to lift myself to consciousness, felt my body pushing itself to the surface, breaking through ice and pebbles and glass. I opened my eyes."

"Illumination. Beautiful, glorious daylight. Unfettered. Lawless. It was as if a drain had been unclogged and light had spilled out—pale, glowing, garish. The earth was swept with it and yet light itself was landless, had more in common with water, the way it rushed through and filled up any space between objects.

"So this, I thought, is what it is to be nocturnal."

"Where were you?" we said. We could hardly breathe.

"That's what I was thinking. I was confused. Had I completed the experiment? Or even better, had it all been a horrible dream? Had I never attempted any experiment? Had no experiment ever existed? I tried to sit up and sleep slid off me.

"I was in my car. I had not finished the experiment. I had stayed out all night. Day was pouring over me like poisoned tar. I had no idea where I was. I felt sick in every possible way. The car wouldn't start and I was like, Fuck! I had to get out of that daylight.

"I left the car and my hangover hit me like a baseball bat. I staggered around, put my head on the hood."

"Had you been in a crash?" we said.

"I had run out of gas," he said, spreading his hands in astonishment. "I was on the emptiest road I'd ever seen. Beyond city, beyond suburbs, beyond what lay beyond suburbs—fields and sky and summer. I must have driven until the tank emptied, I must have been on my way out of town—had had it, had quit, left, but only gotten this far. And here it was, a perfect day. I hated myself. I began to walk."

"They had emphasized how important the final week was, how the first month was basically control. The second month showed the shift, but this final week—when the body had fully adjusted (though you never do get used to it)—was what we were all there for, the *data*, all for some obscure paper in some obscure journal, one experiment amid so many experiments going on all over the country, the world, in a vast experiment that in a thousand years will have been wiped from the earth nearly a thousand years ago. I walked two miles in the blazing sun to a gas station. Out front I stood by a signpost and threw up in the road.

"My daughter, my wife—I'd let them down in so many ways. I'd kept my own wife in the literal dark during the most trying months of her pregnancy, had ignored her, had done no freelance work, and now on top of that may have lost even the fifteen grand and would sink us into debt.

265

I paid for gas and a ride back, drove home, and crawled into bed—my wife was already gone, didn't answer my texts. I lay in bed, not sleeping.

"Hours later I got out of bed, found my phone. I had a text from her: I've gone to stay with my sister. I went over to the sink. I was leaning over it, wanting to vomit, and my head lifted. I found I was looking at the calendar. I'd been x-ing off the days, but I'd stopped these last couple weeks, hadn't even managed that. The final day of the experiment was circled in red. I looked at the date. I looked at my phone. I had been so distraught that I hadn't realized: the dates matched. That day, that night, was the end of the experiment. Shaking, starving, still hungover, terrified, and tired as hell, I took a shower as it got dark. I drove to the lab."

Here's a question: How can you quantify how much a man suffers? How can you measure the amount of pain he has against the amount of other things he has—maybe not happiness but, at least, hope? In order to make a proper calculation, Candide would have had to know the other details of the men's lives, their weaning and rearing, first loves, last, nutrient intake, and so on. He would have needed a measuring system and ledger. It would have taken more than one night.

"I was waiting for them to come get me at the lab when my wife's sister sent me a text: She's gone into labor.

"Two months early? I texted back.

"Seven weeks, she texted. We're headed for the hospital.

"Take this thermometer out! I yelled down the hallway. We're having a baby! So at last, after all those weeks, they took it out and my butt relaxed.

"Congratulations, they said.

"Where's my check?

"We just look at the final numbers, they said. The check should arrive in three days.

"I ran to my car, praying I was on my way from the worst time in my life to the best."

"In the car, my butt began spasming. They'd said it might. They'd said that when a thermometer is removed after having been there for ten weeks, one 'might experience some discomfort in the anal area.' This was not discomfort. This was horrible pain. Under normal circumstances, I would have taken three sleeping pills and gotten into bed and not gotten up for two days. Under normal circumstances I might have gone to the hospital for myself. I was sleep deprived, too, don't forget, and hungover. I was dizzy and sick, bursts of black and red in front of my eyes, but my wife was having our baby! I arrived at the hospital and ran in. She's coming, was all my wife said and she was smiling. I kissed her face with terror and relief.

"Her labor was long. Twenty-six hours, and I was with her, spasming the whole time. We were both exhausted. The doctor was saying we'd go one more hour and then give up and have a cesarean, but then lo and behold the baby was coming. The baby is coming, the baby is coming, I said. This is it, the nurses said. I held my wife's hand while she pushed and screamed. The doctor reached and—I was at my wife's head, I couldn't see. We were waiting for them to raise our beautiful squalling daughter, put an end to our misery. But the doctor didn't raise our daughter.

"Holy Mother of God, said a nurse, and pulled her hands to her chest. Our Lord Jesus Christ."

What? we said. What was it?

"I was too scared to let go of my wife's hand and walk over there. What's wrong? cried my wife, but they bundled the baby up and raced off with her, turning in the doorway to say something along the lines of 'We'll be right back.'"

I didn't know this yet, but by the time of the last Voltaire night, things were beginning to take a slow turn for the better for me. A very low creak was sounding in the wheel, but it was turning. I was managing to publish some stories at last. The horrible man was gone for good. It would be the beginning of a better life for me, though it did not feel better yet and it would take me a couple of years to roll my way out. Still a long road to happiness, but I was seeing tiny points of light in the distance and I was heading toward them. I'd teach one more class after this one at that school, but my heart wasn't in it and I didn't do a very good job. The following year I got a tenure-track position at a large university, a job I'd really wanted, and then I was gone.

"My wife and I were stunned. I ran into the hallway, but the doctor and nurses were gone. I heard my wife calling and I ran back. A nurse was there, sewing her up. She wouldn't say a word. Someone will come talk to you, she said. Just stay calm.

"What's happening? Is she alive? we said.

"Yes, she's alive, said the nurse, or at least she was.

"Was? we screamed.

"I'm sure she's still alive. Please wait. Just stay calm."

Years later this man wrote and asked me to write him a letter of recommendation, and I agreed. In the letter I wrote about Voltaire night, about how it came about, how we did it for all those months, and how the night he told his story—I didn't tell the story itself—was the best Voltaire night ever, how after that we didn't even mention Voltaire night again. He had clearly won.

Years after that I heard he was dying of stomach cancer. I heard another in the group died of a brain tumor. I don't know what became of the others, though I can see them in my mind and I can imagine the joy of success rising out of them and gathering around their heads. I hope it for them. Now and then one writes a quick note to me at my university address. "Do you remember me?" "Yes, yes, I do," I answer. They don't write again, as if they'd just needed that slim reassurance that somebody still knew what had once gone so wrong.

"Neither of us had slept in so long. It had always been night. We were both in outlandish pain. We held each other's hands and wept.

"The doctor came back. Without the baby. Where is she, we said.

"Now stay calm, he said, using his hands to demonstrate calm.

"Quit telling us to stay calm, we said.

"Your daughter has an extremely rare muscular condition. Impossible to detect without amniocentesis.

"What? we said. What kind of condition? Will she live? Is she okay?

"She's alive but she has no muscle. Her muscle has degenerated. She is unable to sustain muscle.

"What does that mean? we said. We don't know what that means! Where is our baby? We want to see her.

"Her appearance is startling. I don't want you to be alarmed.

"We won't be alarmed, we said. Bring her, bring her.

"Okay, I'm going to bring her in for a few minutes but then we have to get her to ICU. He paused. I need to tell you. She's going to need a

268

lot of treatment. This condition is associated with severe disabilities, physical and mental.

"Okay, we said.

"And a short life span.

"We won't be alarmed. We promise. Bring her.

"He went out for a moment and came back. A nurse came in with a bundle and put her in my wife's arms."

At this point he pulled out his phone and held it up for us to see. "Seven years old now," he said, proudly. "They said she wouldn't live three years." I took it from him. I had never seen anything like it. It was hard to know exactly how to look at her for a moment. Her face didn't look quite like a face but then I found her eyes and assembled the rest of the face around them. We all looked at the photo and then at him.

"Did you get the money?" one of us said.

But who could win the Voltaire-night prize—which was nothing, just another path over water? Which was to live your life after Voltaire night, to keep going, strike out for more, after the terrible thing had happened to you, more terrible than what had happened to anyone else, and which might turn out to be the best?

"The nurse placed the tiny bundle in my wife's arms," he said, "and I pulled back the blanket. I touched the top of her head with my hands. She was so small and her bones were visible all over her face. I could barely breathe. My God, I said, she's beautiful.

"Isn't she? said my wife. She's perfect."

Nominated by The Paris Review

MORE THAN THIS

by DAVID KIRBY

from RATTLE

When you tell me that a woman is visiting the grave
of her college friend and she's trying not to get irritated
at the man in the red truck who keeps walking back and forth
and dropping tools as he listens to a pro football
game on the truck radio, which is much too loud, I start
to feel as though I know where this story is going,
so I say *Stop, you're going to make me cry.*
How sad the world is. When young men died in the mud
of Flanders, the headmaster called their brothers out
of the classroom one by one, but when the older brothers
began to die by the hundreds every day, they simply handed
the child a note as he did his lessons, and of course the boy
wouldn't cry in front of the others, though at night
the halls were filled with the sound of schoolboys sobbing
for the dead, young men only slightly older than themselves.
Yet the world's beauty breaks our hearts as well:
the old cowboy is riding along and looks down
at his dog and realizes she died a long time ago
and that his horse did as well, and this makes him
wonder if he is dead, too, and as he's thinking this,
he comes to a big shiny gate that opens onto a golden
highway, and there's a man in a robe and white wings,
and when the cowboy asks what this place is, the man tells
him it's heaven and invites him in, though he says animals
aren't allowed, so the cowboy keeps going till he comes

to an old rusty gate with a road full of weeds and potholes
on the other side and a guy on a tractor, and the guy
wipes his brow and says you three must be thirsty,
come in and get a drink, and the cowboy says okay,
but what is this place, and the guy says it's heaven,
and the cowboy says then what's that place down
the road with the shiny gate and the golden highway,
and when the guy says oh, that's hell, the cowboy
says doesn't it make you mad that they're pretending
to be you, and the guy on the tractor says no,
we like it that they screen out the folks who'd desert
their friends. You tell me your friend can't take it
any more, and she turns to confront the man
who's making all the noise, to beg him to leave her alone
with her grief, and that's when she sees that he's been
putting up a Christmas tree on his son's grave
and that he's grieving, too, but in his own way,
one that is not better or worse than the woman's,
just different, the kind of grief that says the world
is so beautiful, that it will give you no peace.

Nominated by Mark Halliday, Jane Hirshfield

NARRATOR

fiction by ELIZABETH TALLENT

from THE THREEPENNY REVIEW

Near the end of what the schedule called the welcome get-together two women—summer dresses, charm—stood at the foot of the solemn Arts and Crafts staircase where he was seated higher up, mostly in shadow. That could have been me his silence fell on: I had wanted to approach him, and had held off because all I had for a first thing to say was *I love your work*, and I had no second thing. Brightly, the women took turns talking in the face of his eclipsing wordlessness. *This is you in real life?* I said to him in my head. The women at the foot of the stairs were older than me, in their late thirties—close to his age, then, and whatever was going on with him, they looked like they could handle it, and this was a relief, as if being his adoring reader conferred on me the responsibility to protect us all from any wounding or disillusioning outcome. But they were fine. Unless they let it show that they were hurt, his silence could be construed as distractedness or even, attractively, as brooding, and who gained from letting his rudeness be recognized for what it was? Not him. Not them. They might feel the need to maintain appearances if they were going to be his students in the coming week, as I would not be, having been too broke to enroll before the last minute, and too full of doubt about whether I wanted criticism. I didn't get to watch how the stairwell thing ended. A boy came up to me, and I made my half of small talk: New Mexico, yes as beautiful as that, no never been before—what about you, five hundred pages, that's amazing. Throughout I was troubled by an awareness of semi-fraudulence; his confidence was so cheerfully aggressive that mine flew under his radar. The full moon would be up before long and if I wanted we could ride across the bridge on his motorcycle, an Indian he'd been restoring for years—parts cost a fortune. There was a night ride across the bridge in his novel and it would be good to check the details. *Long day*, I said— *the flight, you know?*

Enough students were out, in couples and noisy gangs, that I didn't worry, crossing campus. True about the moon: sidewalks and storefronts brightened as I walked back to my hotel, followed, for a couple of bad blocks, by a limping street person who shouted, at intervals, *Hallelujah!* On the phone my husband told me a neighbor's toddler had fallen down an old hand-dug well but apart from a broken leg wasn't hurt, and he had finished those kitchen cabinets and would drive them to the job site tomorrow, and our dog had been looking all over for me, did I want to talk to him? *Goofball sweetheart why did you ever let me get on that plane?* I asked our dog. When my husband came back on the phone he said *Crazy how he loves you* and *So the first day sucked, hunh?* and *They're gonna love the story. Sleep tight baby. Hallelujah.*

Though I hadn't done it before, the homework of annotating other people's stories was the part of workshop that appealed to the diligent student in me. The bed strewn with manuscripts, I sat up embroidering the margins with exegesis and happy alternatives—if someone had pointed out that *You should try X* can seem condescending, I would have been really shocked. At two A.M., when the city noise was down to faraway sirens, I collected the manuscripts and stacked them on the desk. They were not neutral, but charged with their writers' realities the way intimately dirtied belongings are—hairbrushes, used bandaids— and I couldn't have fallen asleep with them on the bed. Where, in Berkeley, was his house, and was he asleep, and in what kind of bed, and with whom beside him? Before I left the party I had sat for a while on his step in the dark stairwell. All I had to go on were the narrators of his books, rueful first-person failers at romance whose perceptiveness was the great pleasure of reading him, but I felt betrayed. Savagely I compared the ungenerosity I'd witnessed with the radiance I'd hoped for. How could the voices in his novels abide in the brain of that withholder? The women had not trespassed in approaching, the party was meant for such encounters. Two prettier incarnations of eager me had been rebuffed, was that it? No. Or only partly. From his work I had pieced together scraps I believed were *really him*. At some point I had forsaken disinterested absorption and begun reading to construct a him I could love. Think of those times I'd said not *His books are wonderful*, but *I'm in love with him*. Now it was tempting to accuse his

273

work of inauthenticity rather than face the error of this magpie compilation of shiny bits into an imaginary whole. He had never meant to tell me who he was. Nothing real was lost, there was no fall from grace, not one page in his books is diminished, not one word, you have the books, and the books are more than enough, the books will never dismay you, I coaxed myself. But the feeling that something was lost survived every attempt to reason it away.

The days passed without my seeing him again, and besides I was distracted by an acceptance entailing thrilling, dangerous phone calls from the editor who had taken the story, whose perfectionism in regard to my prose dwarfed my own. Equally confusingly, my workshop wanted the ending changed. The ending had come in a rush so pure that my role was secretarial, the typewriter chickchickchickchickchick-tsinging along, rattling the kitchen table with its uneven legs; now I couldn't tell if it was good or not, and I needed to get home to regain my hold on intuition. At the farewell party in the twilight of the grand redwood-paneled reception room hundreds of voices promised to stay in touch. At the room's far end, past the caterer's table with its slowly advancing queue, French doors stood ajar, and two butterflies dodged in, teetering over heads that didn't notice. They weren't swallowtails or anything glamorous, but pale small nervous slips dabbling in the party air, and my awareness linked lightly with them, every swerve mirrored, or as it felt enacted, by the consciousness I called mine, which for the moment wasn't. After a while they pattered back out through the doors. Then there he stood, watching them go. And maybe because rationality had absented itself for the duration of their flight, what happened next felt inevitable. I stared. His head turned; when he believed I was going to retreat—when I, too, was aware of the socially destined instant for looking away—and I didn't, then the nature of whatever it was that was going on between us changed, and was, unmistakably, an assertion. Gladness showered through me. I could take this chance, could mean, nakedly—rejoicing in being at risk—*I want you.* Before now I'd had no idea what I was capable of—part of me stepped aside, in order to feel fascination with this development. But did he want this? Because who was I? He broke the connection with a dubious glance down and away, consulting the proprieties, because non-crazy strangers did not lock each other in a transparently sexual gaze heedless of everybody around them, and he wasn't, of course he wasn't, sure what he was getting into. If I hadn't been so happy to have discovered this crazy recklessness, no doubt I would have been ashamed. As it was I was alone until he looked up to see whether he was still being stared at, as he was, greenly, oh shamelessly, by me, and he wondered whether something was wrong with me, but he could see mine was a sane face and that I, too, recognized the exposedness and hazard of not breaking off the stare and this information flaring back and forth between us meant we were no longer strangers.

We spent the night over coffee in a café on Telegraph Avenue, breaking pieces off from our lives, making them into stories. At the next table two sixtyish gents in identical black berets slaughtered each other's pawns. Look, I told him, how when one leans over the board, the other leans back the exact, compensatory distance. When I recognized what I was up to, proffering little details to amuse him and to accomplish what my old anthropology professor would have called *establishing kinship—We're alike, details matter to us, and there will be no end of details*—I understood that delight, which had always seemed to belong among the harmless emotions, could in fact cut deep. It could cut you away from your old life, once you'd really felt it. The most fantastic determination arose, to stay in his presence. At the same time I understood full well I would be getting on an airplane in—I looked at my watch—five hours. He, too, looked at his watch. Our plan was simple: *not* to sleep together, because that would make parting terrible. We would stay talking until the last minute, and then he would drive me to the airport, stopping by my hotel first for my things. I didn't have money for another ticket and couldn't miss my early-morning flight.

He left it till late in the conversation to ask, "You're, what—?"

"Twenty-four." I stirred my coffee like there was a way of stirring coffee right.

"What's in New Mexico?"

"Beauty." I didn't look up from my coffee to gauge if that was too romantic. "The first morning I woke up there—in the desert; we'd driven to our campsite in the dark—I thought, *This is it, I'm in the right place.*"

Another thing he said across the table, in the tone of putting two and two together: "The story that got taken from the slush pile, that was yours."

A workshop instructor who was a friend of the editor's had spread the word. "Someone"—the moonlight motorcycle-ride guy—"told me, 'It's lightning striking, the only magazine that can transform an unknown into a known.' Not that I'm not grateful, I'm completely grateful but what if I'm not good at the *known* part."

"Why wouldn't you be good?'

"Too awkward for it."

"You're the girl wonder."

That shut me up: I took it to mean that instead of complaining, I should adapt. I was going to go on to hear a correction encoded in other remarks; this was only the first instance. "You're chipper this morning, kid"—that was a warning whose franker, ruder form would have been *Tone it down.* "You look like something from the court of Louis Quatorze" meant I should have blow-dried my long hair straight, as usual, instead of letting its manic curliness emerge. When he would announce, of his morning's work, "Two pages" or "Only one paragraph, but a crucial one," I heard, "And what have you gotten done? Since your famous story. What?" I understood that I could be getting it all wrong, but I couldn't not interpret.

Those first charmed early-summer days he put on his record of Glenn Gould's Goldberg Variations, which I had never heard before, and taught me to listen for the snatches of Gould's ecstatic counter-humming. When I was moved to tears by Pachelbel's Canon in D he didn't say *Where have you been?* He played Joni Mitchell's "A Case of You." He sang it barelegged, in his bathrobe, while making coffee to bring to me in the downstairs bedroom. One morning, sitting up to take the cup, I asked, "Do you remember at the welcoming party, you were sitting in the stairwell and two women came up to you? And you wouldn't say anything?"

He needed to think. "Esmé and Joanie, you mean. They just found out Joanie's pregnant. Try getting a word in edgewise."

My stricken expression amused him; he said, "You have lesbians in New Mexico, right?"

It seemed easier to make a secret of that first, accusatory misreading of him than to try to explain.

I hadn't caught my flight. Instead we made love in the hotel room I hadn't wanted him to see, since I had left it a mess. "Was this all you?" he asked, of the clothes strewn everywhere, and it was partly from shame that I lifted his t-shirt and slid a hand inside. When we woke it was early afternoon and my having not gone home became real to me.

My husband had a daylong meeting that prevented his picking me up at the airport—at least he was spared that.

Where he lived was a comradely neighborhood of mostly neglected Victorians, none very fanciful, shaded by trees as old as they were. His place was the guest cottage—"So it's small," he cautioned, on the drive there—belonging to a Victorian that had tilted past any hope of renovation. In its place some previous owner put up a one-story studio-apartment building, rentals that, since he disliked teaching, provided the only reliable part of his income. His minding about precariousness (if it was) was embarrassing. It was proof that he was *older*. Even if they could have, no one I knew in New Mexico would have wanted to use the phrase *reliable income* in a sentence about themselves: jobs were quit nonchalantly, security was to be scorned. With the help of an architect friend—a former lover, he clarified as if pressed; and never do that, never renovate a house with someone you're sleeping with—all that was stodgy and cramped had been replaced with clarity and open-ness, as much, at least, as the basically modest structure permitted. This preface sounded like something recited fairly often. The attic had been torn out to allow for the loft bedroom, its pitched ceiling set with a large skylight, its wide-planked floor bare, the bed done in white linen. The white bed was like his saying *reliable income*—it was the opposite of daring. No man I had ever known, if it had even occurred to him to buy pillowcases and sheets instead of sleeping on a bare mat-tress, would ever have chosen all white—my husband, for some reason I was imagining what my carpenter husband would say about that bed. Sleeplessness and guilt were catching up with me, and there was the slight feeling any tour of a house gives, of coercing praise. I was irri-tated that in these circumstances, to me costly and extraordinary, the usual compliments were expected. "Beautiful light," I said. The narrow stairs to the loft were flanked by cleverly fitted bookshelves, and more bookshelves ran around the large downstairs living room, off which the galley kitchen and bathroom opened, and, on another wall, doors lead-ing to his study and the guest bedroom that would be mine, because, he said apologetically, he couldn't sleep through the night with anyone in bed with him—it wasn't me; he hadn't ever been able to. Was that going to be all right? Of course it was, I said. I sat down on the edge of the twin bed. *I can get the money somehow, I can fly home tomorrow.* Even as I thought that he sat down beside me. "When I think you could have gotten on that plane. I would be alone, wondering what just hit me. Instead we get this chance." In that room there was a telephone, and he left me alone with it.

He had his coffee shop, and when he was done working, that's where he liked to go—at least, before me he had gone there. Time spent with me, in bed or talking, interfered with the coffee shop, and with research in the university library and his circuit of bookstores and Saturday games of pick-up basketball, but for several weeks I was unaware that he, who liked everything just so, had altered his routines for my sake. From the congratulatory hostility of his friends I gathered that women came and went—"Your free throw's gone to shit," said Billy, owner of the shabby, stately Victorian next door whose honeysuckle-overrun backyard was a storehouse of costly toys—motorcyles, a sailboat. "How I know you have a girlfriend." I would have liked to talk to someone who knew him—even Billy, flagrantly indiscreet—about whether my anxious adaptation to his preferences was intuitive enough, or I was getting some things wrong. Other women had lived with him: what had they done in the mornings, how had they kept quiet enough? One was a cellist—how had *that* worked? His writing hours, eight to noon, were non-negotiable. If he missed a day his black mood saturated our world. But this was rare.

The check came, for the story. Forwarded by my husband, who I called sometimes when I was alone in the house. "You can always come home, you know," my husband said. "People get into trouble. They get in over their heads."

The house was close enough to the university that, days when he was teaching, he could ride his bicycle. Secretly I held it against him that he was honoring his responsibilities, meeting his classes, having conversations about weather and politics. My syllogism ran: what love does is shatter life as you've known it; his life isn't shattered; therefore he is not in love. Of the two of us I was the *real* lover. This self-declared greater authenticity, this was consoling—but, really, why was it? The question of who was more naked emotionally would have struck him as crazy, my guess is. But either my willingness to tear my life apart had this secret virtuousness, or the damage I was doing was deeply—callously—irresponsible.

By now I knew something about the women before me, including the Chinese lover whose loss he still wasn't reconciled to, though it had been years. I stole her picture and tucked it into *Middlemarch*, the only book in this house full of his books that belonged to me, and when he admitted to not liking Eliot much I was relieved to have a book which by not mattering to him could talk privately and confidentially to what was left of me as a writer, the little that was left after I was, as I believed I wanted to be, stripped down to bare life, to skin and heartbeat and sex, never enough sex, impatient sex, adoring sex, fear of boredom sex. The immense sanity of *Middlemarch* made it a safe haven for the little insanity of the stolen photograph. Whenever I went back to *Middlemarch*, I imagined the magnanimous moral acuity with which the narrator would have illumined a theft like mine, bringing it into the embrace of the humanly forgivable while at the same time—and how did Eliot get away with this?—indicting its betrayal of the more honorable self I would, in *Middlemarch*'s narrator's eyes, possess. But I didn't go back often; sex and aimless daydreaming absorbed the hours I would usually have spent reading, and when I went up to the loft, I left the book behind—I didn't want him noticing it. He had a habit of picking up my things and studying them quizzically, as if wondering how they had come to be in his house, and if he picked up *Middlemarch* there was a chance the photo would fall out. If I fell asleep in his bed after sex he would wake me after an hour or two, saying *Kid, you need to go downstairs*. On the way down I ran my fingers over the spines of the books lining the stairwell. If you opened one it would appear untouched; he recorded observations and memorable passages in a series of reading notebooks.

My scribbled-in *Middlemarch* stayed on the nightstand by the twin bed, and I had hung my clothes in the closet, but that didn't mean I felt at home in the room, with its dresser whose bottom drawer was jammed with photos. What did it mean that this drawer, alone in all the house, had not been systematically sorted? Near the bottom of the slag heap was an envelope of tintypes: from a background of stippled tarnish gazed a poetic boy, doleful eyes and stiff upright collar, and I wanted to take it to him and say *Look, you in 1843*, but that would prove I'd been rifling through the drawer, and even if he hadn't said not to, I wasn't sure it was all right. His childhood was there, his youth, the face of the first author's photo. Houses and cities before this one. His women, too, and I dealt them out across the floor, a solitaire of faces, wildly unalike: I wanted to know their stories. No doubt I did know pieces, from his work, but here they were, real, and I would have listened to them all if I could, I would have asked each one *How did it end?* When he was writing he would sometimes knock and come in and rummage through the pictures, whose haphazardness replicated memory's chanciness. As with memory there was the sense that everything was there, in the drawer—just not readily findable. Disorder is friendly to serendipity, was that the point? When he found what he wanted he didn't take it back to his desk but stayed and studied it, and when he was done dropped it casually back into the hodge podge. If I opened the drawer after he'd gone there was no way to guess which photo he'd been holding.

There were things that happened in sex that felt like they could never be forgotten. Recognitions, flights of soul-baring mutual exposure, a kind of raw ravishment that seemed bound to transform our lives. But, sharing the setting of so many hours of tumult—the bed—and tumult's instruments—our two bodies—these passages lacked the distinctness of *event* and turned out to be, as far as memory was concerned, elusive. And there was sadness in that, in coming back to our same selves. By midsummer, something—maybe the infuriating inescapability of those selves, maybe an intimation of the monotonousness sex could devolve into, if we kept this up—caused us to start turning sex into stories. Sex with me as a boy, the one and only boy who ever caught his eye, a lovely apparition of a boy he wanted to keep from all harm, but who one day was simply gone, sex as if he was a pornographer and I was a schoolgirl who began, more and more, to conjure long-absent emotions, tenderness, possessiveness, even as the schoolgirl became more and more corrupt, telling sly little lies, the sex we would have if after ten years' separation we saw each other across a crowded room, sex as if I had just learned he'd been unfaithful to me with one of his exes, sex as if I was unfaithful, the sex we would have if we broke up and after ten years ended up in the same Paris hotel for some kind of writers' event, a book-signing maybe, and sometimes it was his book and sometimes it was mine, sex with me in the stockings and heels of a prostitute, with him as a cop, me as a runaway desperate for shelter, with him as a woman, with the two of us as strangers seated near each other on a nightlong flight.

These games always began the same way. Ceremonious, the invitation, somber and respectful in inverse proportion to the derangement solicited. *What if you are. What if I am.* We never talked about this, and though either could have said *Let's not go there*, neither of us ever declined a game described by the other. The inventing of parts to play was spontaneous, their unforeseeableness part of the game's attraction, but a special mood, an upswell of lurid remorse, alerted me whenever I was about to say *And then after forever we see each other again.* In these scenarios where we had spent years apart, the lovely stroke was our immediate, inevitable recognition of each other—not, like other emotions we played at, a shock, not a wounding excitement, but an entrancing correction to loss. All wrongs set right. *And we look at each other. And it's like—*

While he wouldn't drink any coffee that wasn't made from freshly ground Italian dark roast (which I had never tried before) and he had a taste for expensive chocolate, he seemed mostly indifferent to food, and never cooked. What had he done when he was alone? Was it just like this, cereal, soup from cans, microwaved enchiladas? Should I try to make something—would that feel, to him, to me, ominously wife-y? He liked bicycling to the farmer's market and would come back with the ripest, freshest tomatoes. He taught me to slather mayonnaise across sliced bakery bread, grinding black pepper into the bleeding exposed slices before covering them with the top slice, taking fast bites before the bread turned sodden, licking juice from wrists and finger-tips, the tomatoes still warm from basking in their crates at the farmer's market, their taste leaking acid-bright through the oily mayonnaise blandness, the bread rough in texture, sweet in fragrance. There was at least a chance he'd never told any other lover about tomato sandwiches. After weeks of not caring what I ate, I had found something I couldn't get enough of, and as soon as I finished one sandwich I would make another, waiting until he was out to indulge, and it didn't matter how carefully I cleared away all traces of my feast, he could tell, he was quick with numbers and probably counted the tomatoes.

Really the little house was saturated with his vigilance; there was no corner I could narrate from. When I went elsewhere, tried working in a café (not his) for example, it was as if the house was still with me, its atmosphere extending to the little table where I sat with my books and my legal pad and my cup of coffee with cream and two teaspoons of brown sugar stirred in, and even the music in the coffee shop, which should have had nothing to do with him, caused me to wonder whether he was thinking of me and wanted me to come home or whether he was relieved to have an afternoon to himself, and whether the onset of ir-ritation was inevitable in love, and if it was how people could stand their lives, but look, everyone at the tables around me was standing their life, and I had more than most, I was in love. With *him*, and that was extraordinary, it was surreal—naturally it required adaptation, but I ought to rejoice, day by day, in the revision asked of me, I ought to get a handle on my moods. Two hours had passed; I gave up trying. He was sitting with Billy on Billy's front steps and greeted me by saying, "Everest redux." Billy said, "Can I have a kiss for luck? Leaving for Kathmandu early in the A.M. Oh and forgot to tell you"—turning to him—"Delia's going to housesit. I don't want to be distracted on the Icefall by visions of Fats"—his skinny, hyper Border Collie—"wasting away in some kennel. Only good vibes. Last year when I got up into the Death Zone I hallucinated my grandmother." Deepening his Texas drawl: "'Time you *git* back home.' Actually one of the sherpas looked a whole lot like her. Brightest black eyes. See right through bullshit, which you want in a sherpa or grandma. I lied a lot when I was little, like practice for being in the closet. So, Delia. Fats loves her. So, she'll be staying here." He said, "Always smart not to leave a house empty," but I knew Billy was curious if I would show that I minded, because Delia was his most recent ex, the lover before me, and thinking *only good vibes, right*, I said, "Fats will be happy" and kissed Billy on his sunburned forehead.

I gave up on the coffee shop but when I tried writing in the afternoons in the guest bedroom, sitting up in the twin bed with a legal pad on my knees, he would wander in and start picking up various objects, my traveling alarm clock, my hairbrush, and I would drop the legal pad and hold out my arms. Maybe because he was becoming restless, or was troubled by what looked, in me, like the immobilizing onset of depression, he talked me into going running and that was how we spent our evenings now, on an oval track whose cinders were the real old-school kind, sooty black, gritting under running shoes. If there had been a meet that weekend the chalk lines marking the lanes were still visible, and the infield was grass, evenly mown, where he liked, after running, to throw a football, liked it even more than he ordinarily would have because football figured in the novel he was writing about two brothers whose only way of connecting with each other was throwing a football back and forth, and he needed the sense impressions of long shadows across summer grass and the Braille of white x's stitched into leather to prompt the next morning's writing. When he held a football his tall, brainy self came together, justified. Pleasantly dangerous with the love of competition, though all there was to compete with at the moment was me. When he cocked his arm back and took a step, tiny grasshoppers showered up. The spiral floated higher, as if the air was tenderly prolonging its suspension, and took its time descending. The thump of flight dead-ending against my chest as I ran pleased me. He had trouble accepting that I could throw a spiral, though he might have known my body learned fast. I couldn't throw as far, and he walked backwards, taunting for more distance. Taunting I took as a guy-guy thing; my prowess, modest as it was, made me an honorary boy, and was sexy. One bright evening as I cocked my arm back he cried *Throw it, piggy!* Shocked into grace I sent a real beauty his way, and with long-legged strides he covered the grass and leaped, a show-offy catch tendered as apology before I could call down the field *What?*, but I was standing there understanding: *piggy* was a thing he called me to himself, that had slipped out. In my need and aimlessness and insatiability I was a pale sow. How deluded I had been, believing I was a genius lover no excess could turn repellent. The next morning I woke up sick, ashamed that wherever he was in the house he could hear me vomiting, and when I said I wanted a hotel room he told me a tenant had moved out from one of his units and I could have the key.

These studio units, five of them, occupied the shabby one-story stucco box that stood between his house and the street. Flat-roofed cinderblock painted a sullen ochre, this building was a problem factory. Termites, leaks, cavalier electrical wiring. With his tenants he was on amiable terms, an unexpectedly easy-going landlord. The little box I let myself into had a floor of sky-blue linoleum—sick as I was, that blue made me glad. The space was bare except for a bed frame and mattress where I dropped the sheets and towels he'd given me. The hours I spent in the tiny bathroom were both wretched and luxurious in their privacy; whenever there was a lull in the vomiting I would lock and unlock the door just to do so. Now he is locked the fuck out. Now I let him back in. Now out forever. After dark I leaned over the toy kitchen sink and drank from the faucet. It was miraculous to be alone. There was a telephone on the kitchen's cinder-block wall, and as I looked at it, it rang. Thirteen, fourteen, fifteen. I slept in the bare bed and woke scared that my fever sweat had stained the mattress; it was light; that day lasted forever, the thing sickness does to time. His knocking woke me; he came in all tall and fresh from his shower. Having already worked his habitual four hours. First he made the bed; with the heel of his hand he pushed sweaty hair from my face; I was unashamed, I could have killed him if he didn't make love to me. "I'll check in on you tomorrow," he said. I barely kept myself from saying *Do you love me. Do you love me*. Nausea helped keep me from blurting that out; the strenuousness of repressing nausea carried over into this other, useful repression. "I'm so hungry," I said instead. "Can you bring me a bowl of rice?" In saying it I discovered that the one thing I could bear to think of eating was the bowl of rice he would carry over from his house. I needed something he made for me. When I woke it was night. Cool air and traffic sounds came through the picture window, and seemed to mean I was going to be able to live without him. Now and then the phone began to ring and I let it ring on and on. Sometime during that night I went through the cupboards. I sat cross-legged on the floor with a cup of tea and ate stale arrowroot biscuits from the pack the tenant had forgotten, feeling sick again as I ate. It didn't matter that I knew that very well, and even understood it; the bowl of rice was now an obsession. It seemed like the only thing I had ever wanted from him, though in another sense all I had done since staring at him that first time was want things from him. In the morning while it was still dark he let himself in—of course there was a master key—with nothing in his hands, and when we were through making love he said, "You're going to bathe, right?" Then I was alone without a bowl of rice, cross-legged on the kitchen floor with the cup of tea I'd made and the last five arrowroot biscuits, locked deep in hunger, realizing that because the hunger felt clear and exhilarating, with no undertow of nausea, that I was either well or about to be. I called and made a reservation on a flight to New Mexico that had one seat left.

When the taxi pulled up before dawn he was sitting on the curb, his back to me, a tall man in a child's closed-off pose, ignoring the headlights that shone on him. Against black asphalt the hopping gold-gashed dot dot dot was the last flare-up of his tossed cigarette. I thought, and came close to saying, *You don't smoke*. He stood up and said, "I won't try to stop you," and it was another blow, not to be stopped.

In the novel he wrote about that time I wasn't his only lover. House-sitting next door, the narrator's sensible, affectionate ex affords him sexual refuge from the neediness of the younger woman he'd believed he was in love with, whose obsession with him has begun to alarm him. Impulsively, after the first time they slept together, she left her husband for him. How responsible did that make him, for her? He understands, as she doesn't seem to, that there's nothing unerring about desire. At its most compelling, it can lead to a dead end, as has happened in their case. This younger, dark-haired lover keeps *Middlemarch* on her night-stand, and rifling through the book one night while she's sleeping the narrator finds the naked photograph of the Chinese woman whose de-votion he had foolishly walked away from and he thinks, I could get her back. She lives not very far away, and I would have heard if she got married—people can't wait to tell you that kind of thing, about an ex. Here the novel takes a comic turn, because now he needs to break up with two women, his house-sitting ex, likely to go okay, and, a more troubling prospect, this girl inexplicably damaged by their affair, turned from a promising actress whose raffishly seductive Ophelia had gotten raves into a real-life depressive who hasn't gone on a single audition. He needs to rouse her from her depression, to talk to her frankly, encouragingly. A tone he can manage, now, because of what he hopes for. Tricky to carry off, the passage where, tilting the picture to catch what little light there is, he falls in love—the novel's greatest feat, also the one thing I was sure had never happened. I don't mean the novel was true, only that the things in it had happened. The likelier explana-tion was, he'd gone into the guest bedroom while I was out. Farfetched, his coming into the room while I slept—why would he?—though I could see why he wanted, thematically, the juxtaposition of sleep and epiphany, and how the little scene was tighter for suspense about whether the dark-haired lover would wake up.

Twelve years later, on our way home from the funeral of a well-loved colleague who had lived in Berkeley, two friends and I stopped in a bookstore. Between the memorial service and the trip out to the cem-etery the funeral had taken most of the day. Afterward we had gone to dinner, and except for the driver we were all a little drunk and, in the wake of grieving funeral stiltedness and the tears we had shed, trying to cheer each other up. Death seemed like another of Howard's con-tradictions: his rumbling, comedic fatness concealed an exquisite sen-sibility, gracious, capable of conveying the most delicate illuminations to his students or soft-shoeing around the lectern, reciting *In Brueghel's*

285

great picture The Kermess. If Howard's massiveness was bearish, that of his famous feminist-scholar wife was majestic, accoutered with scarves, shawls, trifocals on beaded chains, a cane she was rumored to have aimed at an unprepared grad student in her Dickinson seminar— *My soul had stood, a loaded gun*, David said; Josh corrected, *My life*, with the affable condescension that, David's grin said, he'd been hoping for, since it made Josh look not so Zen after all. Josh was lanky, mild, exceedingly tall, with an air of baffled inquiry and goodwill I attributed to endless zazen, David sturdy, impatient, his scorn exuberant, the professional vendettas he waged merciless. It was David I told my love affairs to, and when I had the flu it was David who came over, fed Leo his supper, and read aloud. Through the wall I could hear David's merry *showed their terrible claws till Max said "BE STILL!"* followed by Leo's doubtful *Be still!*

That evening of the funeral one of us suggested waiting out rush hour in the bookstore and we wandered through in our black clothes, David to philosophy, Josh to poetry, me to a long table of tumbled sale books on whose other side—I stared—*he* stood with an open book in his hand, looking up before I could turn away, the brilliant dark eyes that had held mine as I came over and over meeting mine now without recognition, just as neutrally looking away, the book in his hand the real object of desire, something falsely assertive and theatrical in the steadiness of his downward gaze that convinced me he had been attracted to me not as a familiar person but as a new one, red-haired now, in high heels, in head-to-toe black, a writer with three books to my name, teaching at a university a couple of hours away, single mother to a solemn, intuitive toddler who spoke in complete sentences, light of my life though he wasn't going to get to hear about my son, wasn't going to get a word of my story, and in the inward silence and disbelief conferred by his not knowing who I was there was time for a decision, which was: before he can figure out who he's just seen, before, as some fractional lift of his jaw told me he was about to, he can look up and meet your eyes again and know who you are, before before before before before before before before he can say your name followed by *I don't believe it*, followed by *I always thought I'd see you again*, look away. Get out. Go. And I did, and though behind me where I stood on the street corner the bookstore door opened now and then and let people out none of them was him. Person after person failed to be him. He hadn't known me. I had known him—did that mean I had been, all along, the real lover?

What we had should have still burned both of us. If it had been real, if we had gone as deep as I believed we had, he could never have failed to recognize me. After a while my friends came out carrying their bags, and David told me, "This is the first time I've ever seen you leave a bookstore empty-handed, ever," and we pulled our gloves on, telling each other taking a little time had been a good idea, and our heads were clear now, and we could make the drive home. Of course, that was when he came out the door—long-legged, striding fast. Pausing, fingers touched to his lips, then the upright palm flashed at me—a gesture I didn't recognize, for a second, as a blown kiss—before he turned the corner.

"Wasn't that—?" David said.

"Yes."

"Did he just—"

"When we're in the car, you two," Josh said. "I've got to be at the Zen Center at five in the morning."

"The day before, he told me his biggest fear wasn't that they wouldn't get all the cancer. His biggest fear wasn't of dying, even, though he said that was how his father died when Howard was only nine, under the anesthetic for an operation supposed to be simple, with nobody believing they needed to say goodbye beforehand, and now that he was facing *a simple operation* himself, one nobody dies of, he couldn't help thinking of his father. No. His biggest fear was that he'd be left impotent. Of all the things that can conceivably go wrong with prostate cancer surgery, that was the most terrifying."

"What did you say?" Josh asked, from the backseat.

"'Most terrifying?' I'm wondering why it's me, the gay boy, Howard chooses to confide in about impotence. Because my whole life revolves around penises? I'm a little unnerved, because, you know Howard, his usual decorum, where's that gone? But I want to be staunch for him, I love this man. And he says, 'Not for me. If it came down to living without it, I would grieve, but it wouldn't be the end of the world. For me. Whereas for Martha.'"

"'Most terrifying,'" Josh said. "I'm very sorry he had to make those calculations."

"'Martha can't live without it.'"

"You were right there," Josh said. "You reassured him."

287

"Of course I reassured him." David checked Josh's expression in the rear-view mirror. "But it's not something I imagined, that the two of them ever—or still—"

"Or, hmmm, that she could be said—"

"You idiots, he adored her," I said. "That's what he was telling David. Not, 'My god, this woman, it's unimaginable that I'll never make love to her again.' But 'How can she bear the loss.'"

Josh took off his tie, rolled it up, tucked it in his jacket pocket, and then handed his glasses forward to me, saying, "Can you take custody?" I cradled them as cautiously as if they were his eyes. Once he was asleep, David said, "That was him, wasn't it?"

I told him what happened. "After I'd gone he must have stood there thinking, But I know her, I know her from somewhere. Then he gets it—who I am, and that I'd walked away without a word. Which has to have hurt."

"It's generally that way when you save your own skin—somebody gets hurt."

"Even hurt, he blows me a kiss. That makes him seem—"

"Kind of great," David said.

"Wasn't I right? Walking away?"

"Don't misunderstand me," David said. "There's no problem with a little mystery, in the context of a larger, immensely hard-won clarity." He yawned. "I'm not the idiot." He tipped his curly head to indicate the back seat. "He's the idiot. Did I reassure him. Fuck. I'm the most reassuring person alive."

Oncoming traffic made an irregular stream of white light, its brilliance intensifying, fusing, then sliding by. I held up Josh's glasses and the lights dilated gorgeously. I said, "You know why we'll never give up cars—because riding in cars at night is so beautiful, it's telling stories in a cave with the darkness kept out, the dash lights for the embers of the fire."

"You don't have to tell me any stories," David said. "I'm absolutely wide awake."

I didn't sleep long, but when I woke he was in a different mood.

"You know, his novel," David said, "—the one about you—is that a good book?"

"If you like his voice it's good."

288

"On its own, though, is it?"

"Mine wasn't exactly a disinterested reading," I said. "The style is his style, and like all his work it moved right along, but the novel overall felt tilted in the narrator's favor, and it would have been more compelling if he had made the dark-haired lover—"

"You," David said.

"—okay, me, but I really am talking about the character now, who is all shattered vulnerability and clinging, the embodiment of squishy need. If he had granted her some independent perceptions, even at points conflicting with his, made her more real, more likable, then her realness would test the narrator's possession of the story, and cast some doubt on the narrator's growing contempt. If it's less justified, more ambiguous, then his contempt isn't just about her and how she deserves it, it's also about him and how ready he is to feel it. If it's not so clear that he's right to feel what he feels, then everything between them gets more interesting, right?"

"That's a sadder ending," David said. "The way that you tell it."

"I wasn't thinking it was sad," I said. "I was thinking it was—better."

Nominated by Threepenny Review

100 BELLS

by TARFIA FAIZULLAH

from POETRY

With thanks to Vievee Francis

My sister died. He raped me. They beat me. I fell
to the floor. I didn't. I knew children,
their smallness. Her corpse. My fingernails.
The softness of my belly, how it could
double over. It was puckered, like children,
ugly when they cry. My sister died
and was revived. Her brain burst
into blood. Father was driving. He fell
asleep. They beat me. I didn't flinch. I did.
It was the only dance I knew.
It was the kathak. My ankles sang
with 100 bells. The stranger
raped me on the fitted sheet.
I didn't scream. I did not know
better. I knew better. I did not
live. My father said, I will go to jail
tonight because I will kill you. I said,
She died. It was the kathakali. Only men were
allowed to dance it. I threw
a chair at my mother. I ran from her.
The kitchen. The flyswatter was
a whip. The flyswatter was a flyswatter.

I was thrown into a fire ant bed. I wanted to be
a man. It was summer in Texas and dry.
I burned. It was a snake dance.
He said, Now I've seen a Muslim girl
naked. I held him to my chest. I held her
because I didn't know it would be
the last time. I threw no
punches. I threw a glass box into a wall.
Somebody is always singing. Songs
were not allowed. Mother said,
Dance and the bells will sing with you.
I slithered. Glass beneath my feet. I
locked the door. I did not
die. I shaved my head. Until the horns
I knew were there were visible.
Until the doorknob went silent.

Nominated by David Hernandez

TRASH FOOD

by CHRIS OFFUTT

from THE OXFORD AMERICAN

Over the years I've known many people with nicknames, including Lucky, Big O, Haywire, Turtle Eggs, Hercules, two guys named Hollywood, and three guys called Booger. I've had my own nicknames as well. In college people called me "Arf" because of a dog on a t-shirt. Back home a few of my best buddies call me "Shit-for-Brains," because our teachers thought I was smart.

Three years ago, shortly after moving to Oxford, someone introduced me to John T. Edge. He goes by his first name and middle initial, but I understood it as a nickname—Jaunty. The word "jaunty" means lively and cheerful, someone always merry and bright. The name seemed to suit him perfectly. Each time I called him Jaunty he gave me a quick sharp look of suspicion. He wondered if I was making fun of his name—and of him. The matter was resolved when I suggested he call me "Chrissie O."

Last spring John T. asked me to join him at an Oxford restaurant. My wife dropped me off and drove to a nearby secondhand store. Our plan was for me to meet her later and find a couple of cheap lamps. During lunch John T. asked me to give a presentation at the Southern Foodways Alliance symposium over which he presided every fall.

I reminded him that I lacked the necessary qualifications. At the time I'd only published a few humorous essays that dealt with food. Other writers were more knowledgeable and wrote with a historical context, from a scholarly perspective. All I did was write personal essays inspired by old community cookbooks I found in secondhand stores. Strictly speaking, my food writing wasn't technically about food.

John T. said that didn't matter. He wanted me to explore "trash food," because, as he put it, "you write about class."

I sat without speaking, my food getting cold on my plate. Three thoughts ran through my mind fast as flipping an egg. First, I couldn't see the connection between social class and garbage. Second, I didn't like having my thirty-year career reduced to a single subject matter. Third, I'd never heard of anything called "trash food."

I write about my friends, my family, and my experiences, but never with a socio-political agenda such as class. My goal was always art first, combined with an attempt at rigorous self-examination. Facing John T., I found myself in a professional and social pickle, not unusual for a country boy who's clawed his way out of the hills of eastern Kentucky, one of the steepest social climbs in America. I've never mastered the high-born art of concealing my emotions. My feelings are always readily apparent.

Recognizing my turmoil, John T. asked if I was pissed off. I nodded and he apologized immediately. I told him I was overly sensitive to matters of social class. I explained that people from the hills of Appalachia have always had to fight to prove they were smart, diligent, and trustworthy. It's the same for people who grew up in the Mississippi Delta, the barrios of Los Angeles and Texas, or the black neighborhoods in New York, Chicago, and Memphis. His request reminded me that due to social class I'd been refused dates, bank loans, and even jobs. I've been called hillbilly, stumpjumper, cracker, weedsucker, redneck, and white trash—mean-spirited terms designed to hurt me and make me feel bad about myself.

As a young man, I used to laugh awkwardly at remarks about sex with my sister or the perceived novelty of my wearing shoes. As I got older I quit laughing. When strangers thought I was stupid because of where I grew up, I understood that they were granting me the high ground. I learned to patiently wait in ambush for the chance to utterly demolish them intellectually. Later I realized that this particular battle strategy was a waste of energy. It was easier to simply stop talking to that person—forever.

But I didn't want to do that with a guy whose name sounds like "jaunty." A guy who'd inadvertently triggered an old emotional response. A guy who liked my work well enough to pay me for it.

By this time our lunch had a tension to it that draped over us both like a lead vest for an X-ray. We just looked at each other, neither of us knowing what to do. John T. suggested I think about it, then graciously offered me a lift to meet my wife. But a funny thing had happened. Our conversation had left me inexplicably ashamed of shopping at a thrift store. I wanted to walk to hide my destination, but refusing a ride might make John T. think I was angry with him. I wasn't. I was upset. But not with him.

My solution was a verbal compromise, a term politicians use to mean a blatant lie. I told him to drop me at a restaurant where I was meeting my wife for cocktails. He did so and I waited until his red Italian sports car sped away. As soon as he was out of sight I walked to the junk store. I sat out front like a man with not a care in the world, ensconced in a battered patio chair staring at clouds above the parking lot. When I was a kid my mother bought baked goods at the day-old bread store and hoped no one would see her car. Now I was embarrassed for shopping secondhand.

My behavior was class-based twice over: buying used goods to save a buck and feeling ashamed of it. I'd behaved in strict accordance with my social station, then evaluated myself in a negative fashion. Even my anger was classic self-oppression, a learned behavior of lower-class people. I was transforming outward shame into inner fury. Without a clear target, I aimed that rage at myself.

My thoughts and feelings were completely irrational. I knew they made no sense. Most of what I owned had belonged to someone else—cars, clothes, shoes, furniture, dishware, cookbooks. I liked old and battered things. They reminded me of myself, still capable and functioning despite the wear and tear. I enjoyed the idea that my belongings had a previous history before coming my way. It was very satisfying to repair a broken lamp made of popsicle sticks and transform it to a lovely source of illumination. A writer's livelihood is weak at best, and I'd become adept at operating in a secondhand economy. I was comfortable with it.

Still, I sat in that chair getting madder and madder. After careful examination I concluded that the core of my anger was fear—in this case fear that John T. would judge me for shopping secondhand. I knew it was absurd since he is not judgmental in the least. Anyone can see that he's an open-hearted guy willing to embrace anything and everyone—even me.

Nevertheless I'd felt compelled to mislead him based on class stigma. I was ashamed—of my fifteen-year-old Mazda, my income, and my rented home. I felt ashamed of the very clothes I was wearing, the shoes on my feet. Abruptly, with the force of being struck in the face, I understood it wasn't his judgment I feared. It was my own. I'd judged myself and found failure. I wanted a car like his. I wanted to dress like him and have a house like his. I wanted to be in a position to offer other people jobs.

The flip side of shame is pride. All I had was the pride of refusal. I could say no to his offer. I did not have to write about trash food and class. No, I decided, no, no, no. Later, it occurred to me that my reluctance was evidence that maybe I should say yes. I resolved to do some research before refusing his offer.

John T. had been a little shaky on the label of "trash food," mentioning mullet and possum as examples. At one time this list included crawfish because Cajun people ate it, and catfish because it was favored by African Americans and poor Southern whites. As these cuisines gained popularity, the food itself became culturally upgraded. Crawfish and catfish stopped being "trash food" when the people eating it in restaurants were the same ones who felt superior to the lower classes. Elite white diners had to redefine the food to justify eating it. Otherwise they were voluntarily lowering their own social status—something nobody wants to do.

It should be noted that carp and gar still remain reputationally compromised. In other words—poor folks eat it and rich folks don't. I predict that one day wealthy white people will pay thirty-five dollars for a tiny portion of carp with a rich sauce—and congratulate themselves for doing so.

I ran a multitude of various searches on library databases and the Internet in general, typing in permutations of the words "trash" and "food." Surprisingly, every single reference was to "white trash food." Within certain communities, it's become popular to host "white trash parties" where people are urged to bring Cheetos, pork rinds, Vienna sausages, Jell-O with marshmallows, fried baloney, corndogs, RC cola, Slim Jims, Fritos, Twinkies, and cottage cheese with jelly. In short—the food I ate as a kid in the hills.

Participating in such a feast is considered proof of being very cool and very hip. But it's not. Implicit in the menu is a vicious ridicule of the people who eat such food on a regular basis. People who attend these "white trash parties" are cuisinally slumming, temporarily visiting a place they never want to live. They are the worst sort of tourists—they want to see the Mississippi Delta and the hills of Appalachia but are afraid to get off the bus.

The term "white trash" is an epithet of bigotry that equates human worth with garbage. It implies a dismissal of the group as stupid, violent, lazy, and untrustworthy—the same negative descriptors of racial minorities, of anyone outside of the mainstream. At every stage of American history, various groups of people have endured such personal attacks. Language is used as a weapon: divisive, cruel, enciphered. Today is no different. For example, here in Mississippi, the term "Democrats" is code for "African Americans." Throughout the U.S.A., "family values" is code for "no homosexuals." The term "trash food" is not about food, it's coded language for social class. It's about poor people and what they can afford to eat.

In America, class lines run parallel to racial lines. At the very bottom are people of color. The Caucasian equivalent is me—an Appalachian. As a male Caucasian in America, I am supposed to have an inherent advantage in every possible way. It's true. I can pass more easily in society. I have better access to education, health care, and employment. But if I insist on behaving like a poor white person—shopping at secondhand shops and eating mullet—I not only earn the epithet of "trash," I somehow deserve it.

The term "white trash" is class disparagement due to economics. Polite society regards me as stupid, lazy, ignorant, violent and untrustworthy.

I am trash because of where I'm from.

I am trash because of where I shop.

I am trash because of what I eat.

But human beings are not trash. We are the civilizing force on the planet. We produce great art, great music, great food, and great technology. It's not the opposable thumb that separates us from the beasts, it's our facility with language. We are able to communicate with great precision. Nevertheless, history is fraught with the persistence of treating fellow humans as garbage, which means collection and transport for destruction. The most efficient management of humans as trash occurred when the Third Reich systematically murdered people by the millions. People they didn't like. People they were afraid of: Jews, Romanis, Catholics, gays and lesbians, Jehovah's Witnesses, and the disabled.

In World War II, my father-in-law was captured by the Nazis and placed on a train car so crammed with people that everyone had to stand for days. Arthur hadn't eaten in a week. He was close to starvation. A Romani man gave him half a turnip, which saved his life. That Romani man later died. Arthur survived the war. He had been raised to look down on Romani people as stupid, lazy, violent, and untrustworthy—the ubiquitous language of class discrimination. He subsequently revised his view of Romanis. For Arthur, the stakes of starvation were high enough that he changed his view of a group of people. But the wealthy elite in this country are not starving. When they changed their eating habits, they didn't change their view of people. They just upgraded crawfish and catfish.

Economic status dictates class and diet. We arrange food in a hierarchy based on who originally ate it until we reach mullet, gar, possum, and squirrel—the diet of the poor. The food is called trash, and then the people are.

When the white elite take an interest in the food poor people eat, the price goes up. The result is a cost that prohibits poor families from eating the very food they've been condemned for eating. It happened with salmon and tuna years ago. When I was a kid and money was tight, my mother mixed a can of tuna with pasta and vegetables. Our family of six ate it for two days. Gone are the days of subsisting on cheap fish patties at the end of the month. The status of the food rose but not the people. They just had less to eat.

What is trash food? I say all food is trash without human intervention. Cattle, sheep, hogs, and chickens would die unless slaughtered for the table. If humans didn't harvest vegetables, they would rot in the field. Food is a disposable commodity until we accumulate the raw material, blend ingredients, and apply heat, cold, and pressure. Then our bodies extract nutrients and convert it into waste, which must be disposed of. The act of eating produces trash.

In the hills of Kentucky we all looked alike—scruffy white people with squinty eyes and cowlicks. We shared the same economic class, the same religion, the same values and loyalties. Even our enemy was mutual: people who lived in town. Appalachians are suspicious of their neighbors, distrustful of strangers, and uncertain about third cousins. It's a culture that operates under a very simple principle: you leave me alone, and I'll leave you alone. After moving away from the hills I developed a different way of interacting with people. I still get cantankerous and defensive—ask John T.—but I'm better with human relations than I used to be. I've learned to observe and listen.

As an adult I have lived and worked in eleven different states—New York, Massachusetts, Florida, New Mexico, Montana, California, Tennessee, Georgia, Iowa, Arizona, and now Mississippi. These circumstances often placed me in contact with African Americans as neighbors, members of the same labor crew, working in restaurants, and now university colleagues. The first interaction between a black man and a white man is one of mutual evaluation: does the other guy hate my guts? The white guy—me—is worried that after generations of repression and mistreatment, will this black guy take his anger out on me because I'm white? And the black guy is wondering if I am one more racist asshole he can't turn his back on. This period of reconnaissance typically doesn't last long because both parties know the covert codes the other uses—the avoidance of touch, the averted eyes, a posture of hostility. Once each man is satisfied that the other guy is all right, connections begin to occur. Those connections are always based on class. And class translates to food.

Last year my mother and I were in the hardware store buying parts to fix a toilet. The first thing we learned was that the apparatus inside commodes has gotten pretty fancy over the years. Like breakfast cereal, there were dozens of types to choose from. Toilet parts were made of plastic, copper, and cheap metal. Some were silent and some saved water and some looked as if they came from an alien spacecraft.

A store clerk, an African-American man in his sixties, offered to help us. I told him I was overwhelmed, that plumbing had gotten too complicated. I tried to make a joke by saying it was a lot simpler when everyone used an outhouse. He gave me a quick sharp look of suspicion. I recognized his expression. It's the same one John T. gave me when I mispronounced his name, the same look I gave John T. when he mentioned "trash food" and social class. The same one I unleashed on people who called me a hillbilly or a redneck.

I understood the clerk's concern. He wondered if I was making a veiled comment about race, economics, and the lack of plumbing. I told him that back in Kentucky when the hole filled up with waste, we dug a new hole and moved the outhouse to it. Then we'd plant a fruit tree where the old outhouse had been.

"Man," I said, "that tree would bear. Big old peaches."

He looked at me differently then, a serious expression. His earlier suspicion was gone.

"You know some things," he said. "Yes you do."

"I know one thing," I said. "When I was a kid I wouldn't eat those peaches."

The two of us began laughing at the same time. We stood there and laughed until the mirth trailed away, reignited, and brought forth another bout of laughter. Eventually we wound down to a final chuckle. We stood in the aisle and studied the toilet repair kits on the pegboard wall. They were like books in a foreign language.

"Well," I said to him. "What do you think?"

"What do I think?" he said.

I nodded.

"I think I won't eat those peaches."

We started laughing again, this time longer, slapping each other's arms. Pretty soon one of us just had to mutter "peaches" to start all over again. Race was no more important to us than plumbing parts or shopping at a secondhand store. We were two Southern men laughing together in an easy way, linked by class and food.

On the surface, John T. and I should have been able to laugh in a similar way last spring. We have more in common than the store clerk and I do. John T. and I share race, status, and regional origin. We are close to the same age. We are sons of the South. We're both writers, married with families. John T. and I have cooked for each other, gotten drunk together, and told each other stories. We live in the same town, have the same friends.

But none of that mattered in the face of social class, an invisible and permanent division. It's the boundary John T. had the courage to ask me to write about. The boundary that made me lie about the secondhand store last spring. The boundary that still fills me with shame and anger. A boundary that only food can cross.

Nominated by The Oxford American, Marc Watkins

FROM THANK YOU TERROR

by MATHIAS SVALINA

from THE VOLTA

I was dead
but they kept killing me
by the seaside,
the Super Target,
on a plane,
in a beetle's husk.

My arms stretched wide
but could not
find my eyes.

I won't betray you
I won't betray you
I say again
& again to Artaud.
But where is the sonnet of power?
Where is the sonnet of suffering?

And when the skin comes off
it comes off like a shower curtain.
And when there is joy
there is joy like a dirt road.

You do not get
to pick your oracle.
You only know
your weaknesses.

Nominated by The Volta

THE LINE AGENT PASCAL

fiction by DANIEL MASON

from ZOETROPE: ALL-STORY

Every morning, Hippolyte Pascal, Agent of the Line at Urupá, woke to
the sun and the sound of parrots, rose from his hammock, dressed, set
a battered kettle on the fire, and crossed his tiny station to check the
signal.

At 0800 hours, if the Line was in order, he would receive the first
transmission from the Depot, followed shortly by a second from the
agent at Varzea Nova, eighty-two kilometers into the interior, and then
the third, from Juá. Then he would reply, "Pascal reports, Urupá," and
the time, and the others would answer in turn: Fernandes, fifty-eight
kilometers forward at Itiraca, then Bonplan at Macunarímbare, Wilson-
Jones at Canaã, the Jesuit Perez at the Mines. The morning's report
would follow: minor variations on the previous day, a band of Nambik-
wara sighted near Bonplan's station, a rotted telegraph pole at Itiraca,
a call for fresh provisions, a request for gunpowder. And then he would
rise and pour himself his coffee and set about his day.

Hippolyte Pascal had been a station agent for nine years—three at
the Depot and six at his little station house at Urupá. It was rare to find
a man who could keep his post so long. Most succumbed quickly to the
isolation, the unceasing shrill, the horror of the vastness, the distance
and the space. Yet the territory, as it appeared to him, bore small re-
semblance to the map. Because it was impossible to see beyond one or
two paces into the forest that surrounded the station clearing, it mat-
tered little whether civilization was one kilometer away or one thou-
sand. What mattered was the Line. Sometimes he thought: it is as if
they are next door, for when I speak, they listen, and they only need to

call out for me to respond. There were few men, he told himself, in such immediate contact with other people. Other times, he thought, with an exhilaration that was almost dizzying, I am the loneliest man in the world.

The station house had been built by his predecessor, a German who had died of snakebite. Over time, Pascal had modified it slightly. He widened the windows to take in more of the forest, and added a layer of palm fronds to the roof, which cooled the room and softened the monsoon rains that could turn the tin into a deafening drum. Inside there was a hammock strung between the walls, a chair, and a table upon which sat the telegraph apparatus of key and sounder, two crouching dragons of zinc and brass. The table's legs stood in tins of water, to keep away the ants. There was a single drawer, which held a razor and a pair of scissors, and a small vial of lavender oil that he combed into his moustache. He kept both the house and his person as clean as the telegraph, wearing and washing his two white shirts on alternating days. He had a single necktie and waistcoat. In the pocket of the coat was a watch, which he wound each night and each morning as soon as he awoke. He once had a belt, until the ants devoured it. On the door, hung a top hat issued by the Commission, of wool, and likely not to their taste.

Outside the house was a clearing, where he fought back the philodendrons. The German had planted a papaya tree, and to this Pascal added a patch of yellow watermelons. From the station, the telegraph wire snaked through the little garden, up a foot-worn path, and into the cut of the *picada*. There it climbed a tall pole encrusted with bromeliads, and joined the six-hundred-and-eight kilometers of coiled copper that connected the Commission to the Mines. Another small path dropped from the clearing into a lagoon, where every evening, after carefully checking the water for caimans, Agent Pascal folded his suit on the bank, and slipped naked into the black water.

How had he, a Frenchman, arrived at such a lonely post deep in the jungles of Brazil? Unlike most of the other Line Agents, who were fleeing something in that world populated by other people, he had nothing to run from: no debts, no secrets, no angry cuckold, no warrants, no corpses left in the wake of knife-fights in the tango halls of Buenos Aires or the harder quarters of Belem. He'd come, he decided, like a pebble tumbles, from Aix to port and port to ship and ship to sea, set-

303

tling at last at this repose. If in his childhood, he had never sought solitude, neither did he seek company. Born into a family of twelve, later sent to study with an order of friars who had taken vows of silence, he had, at one point in his life, either been satiated by the society of others or inoculated against their absence. That he was somehow different was a fact that had dawned slowly, on long walks through Roman quarries, beneath the river willows, at sea. When the offer came to fill the post left by the German, he had the sensation of a great space opening before him. It was only after the Commission Agent repeated for the third time that he would have to do without the presence of other people, that he realized he was being warned.

Was this the secret of his duration? The presence of a fortitude? Or the absence of a fear? And yet the truth was that in the earliest days at his post, it hadn't been so easy. Then, waking early, he found the slow tick of the clock towards 0800 almost unbearable, and as the evening clatter began to die down, he dreaded the moment when the line went still. In the garden, tending his melons, or repairing tears in the thatch, he heard the telegraph tapping and would rush inside, only to find it a feint of his imagination. But as the first week gave way to the second, he'd found himself settling into the days, the heat, the shrill of the insects, the space. In the beginning, he had imagined marking hours until his tour was up. But then, almost without noticing, months passed. By the time the Commission wrote, to invite him back to Cuiabá for a week in civilization, he found himself responding less with relief, than a vague discomfort that his idyll had been disturbed.

Still, he went. The train was the same that had brought him to Urupá. Lurching, it broke through vines that had grown across the track. Over swamp and hill, through tunnels of foliage, past encampments of scattered rails, at last arriving in the city on the river, with its sweltering sunlight and its muddy cross-hatch of streets.

There he joined a group of Commission officers in their revelry. They were a different kind of men: utterly incapable of solitude or silence, drawn to the jungle for its decadence, its bordellos, its forests fecund with fruit and game. They must have recognized a reluctant bacchant in the trim little Line Agent. They loosened his tie, and pinched his cheeks, and pressed oily cups of cane wine into his hand. When midnight came, he joined them in their stagger to the quayside pleasure-houses. But there, when he surrendered the damp bills, when he was led by the cotton-skirted girl to the planked quarters that creaked above the river, he had the sense, touched by her thin fingers, that there was

304

something dangerous in the tenderness, that as she moved above him, palms pressed to his beating heart, he was passing perilously close to a zone of fracture, as one might feel the ground give imperceptibly and know the entire mountain could give way.

Later, he blamed the wine. The next morning, daylight flooding the streets, the earth-red men, the red dogs, the horses fat with worm, he'd gone straight to the train station. It was empty, but he waited alone in a dark corner, where a mangy dog gnawed his red-raw tail, and the monsoons hammered on the tin. In the evening, an engine appeared out of the jungle, steaming, seething, festooned with torn foliage like some exhausted reveler at a Rite of Spring. It left that night. When, three days later, he descended at his station house, he found the melons ripe, and close to bursting.

After that, he never returned to the city. He knew this troubled the Commission. Too often they had seen the agents drift into a particular species of languid melancholia that gave way to increasing frenzy as the forest walls closed in. *Please let us know when you would like to return to Cuiabá*, they wrote him: at first a gentle suggestion, later more like a command. *It was highly recommended*, they said, *For body and spirit, for hygiene of the mind*. To these requests, Agent Pascal replied politely, deferring, each time, for another couple months. But inside, he found himself protesting. What was he, still a child, being told to come and play with others? Why did he need the city, when he had the other Line Agents? Wasn't that true friendship? Not some night of carousing in Cuiabá?

For the truth was that, however distant his colleagues were, he'd come to know them intimately over the years, could describe each man, each station, with details he had never seen. From the requests for medicines, he knew Pinto at Varzea Nova suffered lumbago; that some-how in that land of dysentery, Brother Perez was chronically consti-pated; that the Hungarian at Juá, a defrocked pharmacist who variously spelled his name Szarsaly and Sarszaly, was febrile, saw faces in the foliage and heard voices in the humming of the Line. He knew their height and weight by their requests to the tailor; the meticulousness of their grooming by the requests for shaving-razors or cologne. He followed the education of Bonplan's daughters through the primers ordered by their father, already on to multiplication and second declen-sions. By the reports of visitors, or Indians, or claim-jumpers or desert-

305

ers from the penal battalions, he knew what each agent thought of other men.

If Szarsaly or Sarszaly, Pinto, Bonplan were discrete, treating the Line with solemnity, sparse in their signals, others used the Line with less discretion, clattering on with personal musings or gossip or simply for the love of being heard. Of these, the two Argentines were the worst: Brother Perez and Fernandes, different as wool and water, and yet inextricably entwined. Fernandes was a card-shark, a debtor, who joked often about hiding from his creditors, and confessed petty thievery in the manner of a man who'd done much worse. He was thin and tall, and according the Hungarian, who had seen him, very handsome; in Cuiabá, the Commission officers described his adventures with a bit of awe. Often, there came news from the Depot that a certain "Edwiges" was "asking around." Other times it was "Ana Maria." He had a common-law wife, Mathilde, the daughter of an English tailor, whom he had somehow lured out to his God-forsaken site. It was she who concerned the bulk of his requests. There were magazines and bonbons and stationary, and silky undergarments, their measurements provided in breathless detail. One year, Fernandes spent his entire bonus on a phonograph. Another, he ordered little waistcoats for a pair of capuchin monkeys they kept as pets. He was often a bit late in his transmissions, blaming it on "calisthenics," which Pascal took to mean Mathilde.

And Brother Perez? A fat man, to judge by his trousers, and a rashy one by the quantities of talcum that made up his monthly supply. He, too, was not alone, having established at the Mines a kind of personal mission, alternately preaching to the passing tribes from St. Ignatius' Spiritual Exercises, or bribing them with the same bonbons Fernandes ordered for Mathilde. When not proselytizing the Indians, he turned to the other agents, and in particular, Fernandes, who—as he often reminded the six hundred and eight kilometers of copper that tied them all together—was shaming Argentina by living in sin. To whom Fernandes would reply with more requests for lingerie, with exacting specifications for thigh and waist and breast, a cycle that repeated itself enough times that Agent Pascal began to suspect that such descriptions were the reason why Perez was so diligent in his denunciations.

Sometimes the men shared recipes for cakes or manioc and tapir-stew. The Hungarian, before his madness, dispensed not only pharmaceutical advice, but instructions to make goulash, root-bread, palm-wine, rum.

They also shared their miracles. The snake that bit without envenoming, the knife-blade deflected at the bar fight in Cuiabá, the tree that burst from lightening strike, missing the fragile little station and the agent sleeping inside. In 1898, when Bonplan's second daughter presented breech and two weeks early, all the agents listened as his wife went into labor, and a Doctor was dispatched hurriedly from the Mines. What had happened then was the kind of story that immediately made its way into legend, for it proved there was a benign angel hiding in depths of the forest. As Bonplan later told it, his wife's screams had become so terrible that he ordered his older daughter, then a shade over two, into the garden lest she be forever haunted with the image of her mother's death. Later he would admit what a mistake this was, but that moment, in such raw panic, he wasn't thinking of what might be lurking in the dark. He hammered at the telegraph, begging the doctor to come faster, pleading, Someone, Someone tell me what to do, when the door opened, and his daughter entered, holding the hand of a person, a man or a woman he couldn't tell, bedecked with beads. He assumed she—he—it—had come from a tribe of Indians that migrated through the hunting grounds near his site, but these were shy, and until that day, none had ever ventured beyond the edge of the clearing. Later, the Hungarian said it was a manifestation of the *boldo gasszony*, an old deity who in Hungary helped women through childbirth. Perez said it was the Blessed Mother herself. The baby was a girl. For the rest of the night, none of them could sleep.

These then were his friends: the sinner and the priest, the pharmacist, the good patriarchs Pinto and Bonplan. And, last, of course, was Wilson-Jones. Though they had never met (indeed, Pascal had never *met* any of them, in the flesh), Agent Pascal reserved a special place in his heart for the Englishmen. He was, after all, the only agent other than Pascal to have endured so long alone. Fernandes had Mathilde and Perez had Saint Ignatius, and Pinto and Bonplan had their families, and even the Hungarian had his hallucinations, and yet from the day of his arrival seven years prior, replacing a mutinous Belgian, Wilson-Jones had endured without a single visit back to Cuiabá. Perhaps because of this, Pascal found himself curious about the Englishman. Of the man's life before the Line, he knew virtually nothing. Unlike Szarsaly who betrayed his nostalgia by a seemingly irresistible need to compare the food and weather to that of Hungary, Wilson-Jones had never even uttered the word "England." He neither mentioned wife or mistress, gave no clue as to his prior profession, made no mention of the life he'd led before. He too had simply tumbled there, thought Pascal, who found something immensely reassuring in this company, as if the other's solitude sustained his own. And yet there was something more to his fondness than the symmetry of their conditions. Briefly, at the beginning of his service with the Commission, Agent Pascal, malarial, finding the ants had infiltrated his quinine, had sent a request to the Commission for a resupply, a common request and one not worth remembering, except that two days later, a train, traveling back from the Mines, had stopped at Urupá to deliver a small bottle of tablets, which the porter said had come from "the agent at Canaã." There was no note, no well-wishing, and yet despite this, the act stayed with him for a very long time. Indeed, years later, alone in his hut, or walking out in the right-of-way, staring at the ever-encroaching forest, at the high-wire slung in great loops from the tall poles like beggar's crutches, Agent Pascal found himself marveling at this realization that he could live in the thoughts of another person, a realization that appeared to him no less a miracle than if he had somehow been twinned. Indeed, in his rare moments of doubt—not loneliness exactly, but just a simple awareness of space and distance, of infinity and eternity—not fear, just a brief shiver, a *shifting* in his repose—in these moments, Pascal imagined himself flickering through the thoughts of that other man, two-hundred-and-sixty-two kilometers forward on the Line. Just as he imagined that Wilson-Jones, when he felt *his* head grow dizzy with the space and light, sought comfort in the meditations of *his* friend, Pascal.

He kept the bottle, long after he had eaten all the tablets, though he knew that simple courtesy dictated its return.

What else might he say of his friend? He was stoical, liked flowers, indulged the others with his descriptions of the metallic shimmer of the palm-leaves and the pink that bloomed in fluted starbursts outside his room. He liked to read, and the names of novels filled his requests to Cuiabá. An odd, and futile demand, thought Pascal, for the nearest bookstore was on the other side of the Andes, unless one counted the itinerant peddler who sold the primers to Bonplan's daughters and the moldering magazines to Mathilde.

Once, it occurred to him that instead of returning to Cuiabá for rest and relaxation, he might take the train forward, to Canaã. Then, beneath him, the ground moved, and he did not let himself consider it again.

So the years had passed: the wet heat, the screeching of the insects, the heavy foliage that seemed to fill all space and time. The vines lengthening in their infinite coil. The clouds and trains. The telegraph tapping, each morning, tapping, and each night. So regular was the sound, the code of names and stations, that it felt at times as much a rhythm of his own body as his heartbeat or his breath. He wondered if the others felt it, that same pulse, as if they were all part of a single organism, a kind of a hydra, or a swamp-reed connected at their roots. There was little to distinguish one day from the next, little, even, to mark the direction of time's arrow, save the advance of Bonplan's daughters through their primers, or the slow descent of the pale meniscus on his moustache-oil. He woke and slept with the sun, which because of his proximity to the equator, bisected his hours into equal portions of night and day. By the end of his first year, even his dreams had taken on a similar regularity, recapitulations of his waking life, down to his responsibilities for a dream-telegraph, the taste of dream-melons, the smell of dream-lavender. Indeed, so symmetrical were the hours, that he felt it might be possible to confuse his two lives, though, oddly, in his dreams, the forest was blue and the sky was green. Why this should be was a great puzzle to him, and occupied hours of consideration. In both lives, he was alone.

Mostly alone. There were times, beneath both blue and green skies, that he felt a presence, someone standing behind him and watching as he attended to the signal. And once he had dreamed—yes, certainly he had dreamed, for a soft green light was falling across their faces—that all the men, Pinto and Bonplan, Wilson-Jones, Szarsaly, and the two Argentines, and their wives and children, were walking together, single file, through the cut. In the dream, someone was speaking—words of comfort, though he hadn't known he was afraid. Someone sang. He saw the priest's cassock swaying, and Mathilde holding one of the capuchins, and Bonplan sweep up one of his girls when she grew tired. Although he told himself that it was nothing more than just a group of people walking, there was something about it that was almost painfully beautiful, and he hoped and feared the dream might come again.

In his sixth year, a rumor came that the Mines might close and with it the Telegraph. For two months he waited for a final train to take him back. He could not conceive of leaving the station. If they came for him, he would hide, he thought. Hide and stay there, as the forest closed over that place that he had tumbled to, living on melons and water from the lagoon. *For life*, he thought: because once the *picada* scarred over, there would be no way to return. *For life*, he thought, and then wondered if he was so distant from everything, that even death, loping through the forest with fang and talon, might miss him, might pass him by.

One morning, in the middle of the monsoons of his ninth year, Agent Pascal woke to the sun and the sound of parrots, rose from his hammock, dressed, lit a fire, set his kettle on the fire, and sat down at the table for the morning report.

At 0800, he received the signal from the Depot, followed shortly by a second from the station at Varzea Nova, and then the third, from Juá. Then he answered, "Urupá reports, 0800", waiting for each station along the line to answer in turn: Fernandes at Itiraca, Bonplan at Macunarímbare . . . The morning report would follow: minor variations on the previous day, a fallen pole at Varzea Nova, a call for new provisions, a request for gunpowder, for a resupply of ties. And then he would rise and pour himself his coffee and set about his day.

There was a pause. A second passed, a single beat of his heart. He batted a fly from his face. For a moment, accustomed to Fernandes' delays, he assumed it was coming from Itiraca. But the telegraph lurched again to life. "Repeat, Cuiabá reports, 0801. Calling all Agents."

"Pinto reports from Varzea Nova."

Then one-hundred-and-seven kilometers deeper. "Szarsaly from Juá."

Then sixty-five kilometers along, Pascal answered: "Urupá."

"Fernandes."

"Bonplan."

Then again: silence.

"Cuiabá reports. The signal is not getting past Macunarímbare. Wilson-Jones? Perez? Please reply."

Again silence. Every so slightly, Agent Pascal shifted in his seat, feeling suddenly, in the flow of hours, a sudden resistance, a tightening in the air. A lizard watched him warily from the wall. Behind him, the kettle had begun to boil, but he ignored it. In his mind, he saw the Line as a bird might see it, nestled in the narrow cut that threaded through swamp and forest, past the little stations, the flocks of parrots, the herds of peccary and tapir, the little tribes of men. Anything might have happened, he thought, fingers resting gently on the table. A fallen tree, a sabotage by the natives. The fact that neither Wilson-Jones nor Perez were answering was reassuring, he thought. It located the problem to the line. As long as it was nothing wrong with one of the agents . . .

Tap tap. Cuiabá again, he thought, leaning back, but then the letters formed. One short stroke, two long, one short. One short stroke. One short stroke, one long, one short. One short. Two long, two short. *Perez.*

"Perez reports from the Mines. The Line is open."

"Cuiabá reports. Perez confirms the Line is open to the Mines. Confirm: Canaã, confirm. Agent Wilson-Jones, confirm. Is the line open at Canaã?"

Slowly, Pascal inhaled. On his watch, the second hand swept its depths.

Again from the Mines: "Perez reports. Again, Perez reports. The Line is open. There is no answer from Canaã."

"Cuiabá reports: Perez reports the Line is open. Agent Wilson-Jones confirm."

The kettle rocked in its trivet.

"Perez reports. The Line is open." And then again, as if they all needed to hear it one more time: "There is no answer from the agent in Canaã."

Agent Pascal stood, stroking his moustache. It was then he was aware of a silence, an impossible silence, as if the crickets, the screaming birds, the monkeys had ceased in unison. There is something outside, he thought. But he didn't move. He could hear his breath, fast and deep. There is nothing wrong, he thought, or spoke, for now he heard himself aloud. "There is nothing wrong." Many times Agents had been late for transmissions. The ants had gotten into the telegraph, or prospectors had stolen the wire, or Wilson-Jones had simply forgotten to wind his wristwatch and was returning from his morning bath. Perhaps he had returned to that place he had come from, to the life, the people, of whom he never spoke. Scarcely three minutes had passed.

Again, the telegraph clattered, again the Depot. Again the others answered. Three times this repeated, the answers growing shorter, like ripples settling over water. The telegraph went still. Now in the silence and the shadows, Pascal could see them. The Cuiabá Agent rising solemnly to share the news with the Director. Pinto waiting as his wife eyed him from the hearth. He could see Szarsaly wrap his blanket about him in his fever, and Bonplan's little girls as they ceased in their play, wide-eyed, not daring to ask. Perez in his cassock, finger on the hymnal.

311

And Fernandes, naked on the wooden stool, briefly ignoring the worried questions from Mathilde. All like him, waiting and watching their identical little zinc and copper dragons, waiting for the thrum of life to clatter through.

An agent isn't answering, says Antonio Pinto to his wife in Varzea Nova.

Go back to playing, says Bonplan to his girls, *there is nothing wrong at all*.

Sixty-five kilometers back, the Hungarian rises to decant a concoction for his fevers.

A rivulet of sweat gathers above the clavicle of Mathilde.

Suscïpe Domine, whispers Perez. *Oh Lord, Receive.*

At Urupá, Agent Pascal stood at the open door of his station and stared into the trembling wall of green. I must not worry, he told himself again: Bonplan was right, There was nothing wrong. But now these words found little purchase. He had been a Line Agent for nine years, and this had happened enough times that he knew the ritual that followed: the soldiers sent deep into the forest's maw, the wary descents to silent stationhouses, the Agents found pierced through with spears or arrows, or hanging from a roof beam, or simply resting, slumped against the telegraph, or cocooned in a hammock, already blooming with mushrooms, half-eaten by the ants. Though mostly, he knew, the soldiers found nothing. An empty hammock. A door half-open, a room clean and silent. No footsteps, not even a note. Someone would telegraph the news to Cuiabá, and then later, a new agent would come, and for some weeks, the soldiers would remain there, guarding the station until at last they grew sick of each other, and permission came from Cuiabá to return, leaving the agent there, alone.

On the table, the dragon lurched. "Urupá, confirm," it said, and Pascal realized that for of the others, kilometers away, he too had disappeared.

"Are you there?" asked the Line again, and for a brief moment, alone, Agent Pascal found himself without an answer. Then through the forest came a surge, of something great and wondrous heaving past, and he sat and stroked his moustache and answered that he was.

Nominated by Zoetrope: All-Story

THE LUOYANG POEM

by YE CHUN

from *LANTERN PUZZLE* (TUPELO PRESS)

1.
Gray streets and dim staircases.

We slid down the banister:

often one of us,
in dream or memory, fell.

2.
I fell ill
or feigned illness
to put those heavy school buildings
behind me.

I rode my bike,
breaking through smoke thicker than hair.

3.
New dynasty burned houses of the old.
Red Guards burned 55,884 rolls of sutras at the White Horse Temple.
Twenty factories burned the sky blind.
Families of the dead burned paper horses.
Crematoria burned the dead.
My father burned another fall's leaves.
I burned my diary.

Summer, dusk clouds filled up the sky,
reddening our faces.
We fluttered cattail fans
as if to burn ourselves faster.

4.
Luoyang, your cross
was formed by the highest smokestack
and the train blocking our way.

O those eyes on the train
looked as if they'd seen through
all that is far away.

5.
Our parents were sent here
to build a new nation.
At home they speak hometown dialect,
cook hometown food.

When Du Fu lived here,
all the males in the city
were sent to fight along the borders.

We cursed and spit on the speckled roads.

6.
Before Jian River dried,
my father took me fishing,

and I found my own land of peach trees
before the woods were leveled
and the dirt covered by concrete.

They caught my friend
cheating on an exam and expelled her.
Her sister told me she left the city.

I still see, moments before nightfall,
a velvet sky above the river,

cranes fly over, turn into fairies
and wash their hair in the darkening water.

In my dreams, my friend returns
in different faces, just like in different cities
I often see peach flowers.

7.
That winter, a boy
came riding beside me,
my big coat a dark corner.

We rode past the sweet potato vendor and his stove;
they stood in every winter
like a small lighthouse.

We rode past Chairman Mao
in front of the Mining Machinery Factory,
his marble arm waving at us.

Black flags of smoke blew above our heads.

We rode toward the huge
suddenly blooming setting sun.

Nominated by Tupelo Press

THE PHYSICS OF TURTLES

by JENNY HENDRIX

from ORION

For all the talk about this city's action and energy—"So much to do!" people say, "The best place in the world!"—I've had the feeling, this spring, that there's really very little going on.

Oh, there is, I suppose, a form of energy that's traded around, expended as stress, frustration, rage, or, for the more sensitive, used as a shield against these things. But nothing of significance, I find, truly *happens* here most days. Today, for instance, there is work and rest, and there is dancing and drinking on weekends. There is, twice daily, a walk in the park with the dog, and there is the rush of the subways, the pasta bubbling whitely on the stove. True, there are in between these moments frights and irritations, careless jostlings and accidents and forthright ugly acts—the resplendent oddities and solipsisms so common to city life. Yet I seem to find myself in a state of constant ground-standing against their effects, resisting the impulse to be porous to them. And so I proceed instead under a hard shell, the days passing in a kind of inertia.

I went to sit, one day, on that tree root in the park from which I can watch the turtles heaped up, sunning themselves on a snag that extends laterally into the lake. Hauled out like this, these creatures, common enough, appear petrified and strange; resting above the green murk in the tentative warmth of spring, they are inert as a heap of fossilized clams, chelonian remnants prized out of the Precambrian mud.

Most of them are red-eared sliders, illegally released pets or their descendants that have become naturalized in this lake, displacing the native turtles that once made it their home. Sliders live about as long

316

as we do; on the log, there were a few old females the size of dinner plates, their necks stiffly upraised as they surveyed me. The red slashes beneath their eyes were a kind of challenge, I thought, like the painted cheekbones of warriors from the great western plains. There are sometimes others here too. For instance, I once found a baby snapper, a tiny black, half-desiccated thing with a long, vestigial-seeming tail, attempting to cross the park road on a summer afternoon. There are also map turtles in the area, the kind that like to stack themselves one on top of the other to bask—turtles, as it's said, all the way down.

I stood, and three or four of the turtles toppled with a jerk, falling one by one off the log and into the lake. They just fell, I thought, astonished, with no concern at all as to where they'd land, simply and blithely abandoning themselves to gravity in their uncertainty over the presence of this large upright ape. I watched as a tiny slider, perched on the log's upward curve, abruptly plummeted several feet. A few more followed him in—the sound like popcorn, or fireworks—until only one massive female, the one nearest the shore, remained. Her head turned to eye me above that red slash on her cheek.

It's hard to explain why this had the sensation of an event, of something's having happened indeed that day, for perhaps the first time. Yet it did. Somehow, the sound of falling turtles and the seven wary heads that regarded me from the brown water broke through the day's sense of sameness.

"Every object persists in its state of rest or uniform motion," Isaac Newton wrote, "in a straight line unless it is compelled to change that state by forces impressed on it." That day at the lake, it was the turtles' falling down that provided a force strong enough to shift me from my straight line: their hard-shelled forces—the blithe abandonment, *plop, plop, plop*—managed to tear a hole in my own adopted shell, such that, for just a moment, I could see without protection from the effects of whatever appeared. Look over there! I thought. A white egret has landed on a willow tree!

Nominated by Orion

ETTA JAMES AT THE AUDUBON BALLROOM

by PATRICIA SPEARS JONES

from A LUCENT FIRE (WHITE PINE PRESS)

Someone knocks over a chair (drunk one)
Fight ready, but this vivid sound stops
fists—who let them big black birds
In? Again. This night. What

Flight. Fight. Let's try dancing the blues
to SMITHEREENS. Rustle up those moans and sighs
for the good working Henrys of this world

ready ready ready to block & hustle.
Shit and cuss you out, some where back stage—the money scatters.

Your skin beams sweetness while your voice screams
Where's the fucking fun house?
Your chest blossoms possibilities/ hips thick enough to swing
Which way and oh my
There he stands
In suit sharp as steel and shoes patent leather,
squarish frames/that wiseguy demeanor, the tipped chapeau

You've picked up the high heel shoe you *throwed* down
Then repaired your make up for that second set
The one that promises a better crowd.
Another chair tips back as smoke swarms the littered stage
You're too young for this mess and he'll never grow old.

Nominated by White Pine Press, Kathy Callaway

A LOCAL'S GUIDE TO DATING IN SLOCOMB COUNTY

fiction by CHRIS DRANGLE

from THE OXFORD AMERICAN

At half past ten the guy from the corner mart came into the shelter. Naomi had only seen him a few times, but he had a distinctive look, to say the least. He was young but rugged, with short-cropped hair and broad shoulders. It figured that the most attractive man in town her age was also a triple amputee. It was so hot out that even he was wearing shorts—red mesh ones with a faded Cola High School crest, below which were hi-tech black metal prosthetics inserted in grubby tennis shoes. He walked up to her and rested his elbows on the counter, and from that position looked normal, except for the one hand that was a carbon fiber hook.

"Morning, ma'am," he said.

"Hi," she said. "What can I help you with?"

"I'm here to pick up my dog. I talked to Dennis yesterday?"

"Okay, great. What's your name?"

"Fisher Bray."

"And what's the animal's name?"

"Barbie. She doesn't have a collar or nothing. I take it off at night cause it itches her. She got out two nights ago and somebody brought her here I guess. Dennis said you got her."

"I see. What kind of dog is she?"

"She's a busted-looking Dutch shepherd. Dark brown and orange-ish. One ear missing. Big goofy smile."

To calm a fever, Naomi's mother had once forced her to take an ice bath. It sucked the air out of her lungs and made her skin burn. She felt like that now. The back of her neck prickled. She coughed.

319

"Okay," she said. Her hands were trembling so she put them in her lap under the desk. "Give me a minute. Let me go in back and find Dennis, okay? I'll just be a minute."

"Thank you," he said.

She walked to the staff room. Dennis and Portia were both there. Dennis was marking up a form on a clipboard and Portia was mixing tea. She saw Naomi's face.

"What's wrong?" she said.

"A man is here to get his dog," Naomi said.

"Great," Dennis said. "I haven't finished the list yet. That'll help."

"No," she said. "He wants the shepherd with the missing ear."

"With the limp?" Portia asked.

"Right," Dennis said. "Yeah, that's right, he called yesterday. What's the problem?"

Naomi looked at Portia.

"Holy shit," Portia said.

"You didn't put it down," Dennis said. "You put it down?"

Naomi left the staff room and walked to the kennel office. The lights were off to save electricity and the blinds had been drawn to keep out the heat, and the sun that got through was cut on the wall in long slivers. She opened the top drawer of the filing cabinet and found yesterday's PTS log and roster. On the log, in her handwriting, in the eighth space: *London, Shepherd mix, 92188. PTS'ed.* On the printed roster, halfway down the third page: *92188—intake—shepherd mix no ID.* Penciled in to the right of the entry, in Dennis's childish scrawl: *Update, contacted by owner, DO NOT PTS.*

But she had checked the roster against the log. Had she checked it? She always checked it, that was the system. The water cooler bubbled, a single thunk that sounded like a heavy stone dropped in a lake. It was hard to imagine that she wouldn't have checked the roster, but she didn't remember doing it yesterday, not specifically. She did remember what she did with the dog, and felt like she needed to throw up.

Back in the staff room, Portia was biting her nails and Dennis was stirring the instant tea.

"How did it happen?" Dennis said.

"I don't know."

"This is so fucked up," Portia said.

"Shut up," she said. "No, sorry. Let's just think."

There was nothing to think about. It had been ten minutes since she left the front desk, and Naomi had to go back. Fisher Bray was sitting in one of the chairs. He looked nervous, but smiled politely when she entered the room. Another woman was waiting at the counter, with a fluffy white cat in a hand carrier.

"I've been waiting here ten minutes," she said.

"Someone will be right with you," Naomi said, and turned to the man. "Will you come with me, sir?"

Portia took over at the front desk and Naomi showed him back to the kennel office where Dennis was waiting. She wanted to be anywhere else in the universe. She sat in a metal folding chair on the side of the room. He sat in the comfy chair. Dennis sat behind the desk and began by saying there was some unfortunate news. Barbie—that was her name?—had been put down. Tuesday had been a hectic day, and there had been some kind of miscommunication. With so many animals going in and out all the time, they relied on a set of lists, and somehow Barbie had been put on the wrong one. There were no words to express how sorry they were.

Naomi watched Fisher without breathing. He sat with his back straight, hand folded over hook in his lap. The sandy scruff on his cheeks softened the edge of a granite jaw line. He couldn't be older than twenty-two. Dennis talked, and Fisher had no reaction whatsoever.

The numbers went like this: Slocomb County was home to a hundred and twenty thousand people. The Slocomb County Animal Shelter was the only freestanding shelter in five hundred square miles. The shelter had room to house around twenty cats and ninety dogs, and operated at capacity every day. Although it operated at capacity, there was a constant inflow of new cases. Strays, rescues, walk-ins—some days they got two dozen animals. On the other hand, outflow was sluggish. The last time Naomi had seen national estimates, six to eight million pets entered shelters every year. Three to four million were adopted out.

In addition to numbers there were rules. Most of their funding came from the county, and that came with strings attached. Their contract required that they take every animal that came through the door, plus keep a certain amount of kennel space for humane cases, plus cruelty seizure and bite cases that needed boarding while the courts decided what to do. State law required strays to be held for forty-eight hours. It was like musical chairs, except with two hundred rules, cages instead of chairs, and sodium pentobarbital for the losers.

The day before Fisher came in, she sat in the parking lot before work. The shelter was at the edge of town, on the side of the highway. A squat brick building with a gravel parking lot and a carved wooden sign. Behind it was a cotton field, black hickory tree line in the distance. She breathed slowly and checked the visor mirror. Usually she dressed in blouses and khakis but on Tuesdays, her day on PTS, it was t-shirt and jeans.

Inside the waiting room, Portia manned the front desk. She wore blue eye shadow and golden hoop earrings that would fit around a fire extinguisher. Her hair—jet black this month—was four inches shorter than it had been yesterday. She was removing and reattaching a pen cap with her teeth, and spit it out to talk.

"Hey girl," she said.

"Hey," Naomi said. "New do?"

Portia slapped the pen down and leaned forward gravely.

"It broke off," she said. "Broke. Off. I was like, okay, I guess it's summer outside, I guess we'll go short."

"It doesn't look bad."

"I'll make it work. Cut it into this shag thing. 'Layered,' let's call it."

Portia was in her early thirties, a Cola native who held three part-time jobs. Besides the shelter, she did hair at A Cut Above and tended bar at The De Soto. Her husband was a paralegal with an hour-long commute to Pine Bluff. She had confided in Naomi that she made enough at the bar to quit the other gigs, but the variety suited her. She liked dogs, hair, and beer; the system worked.

"Anyway." She turned her mouth down and arched her eyebrows. "Ready for your Tuesday?"

"Sure," Naomi said. "But it's too hot."

"Yeah. Dennis is in the staff room making the list. Let me know if you want to go drinking later."

"Check."

Dennis, their manager, was seated at one of the staff room's plastic card tables, drinking coffee from a mason jar and glaring at a clipboard. He was in his fifties, tall and portly, with white, Martin Van Buren–style muttonchops and an endless supply of pale blue, short-sleeved button-down shirts.

"Morning," Naomi said.

"Ah," he said. "Morning to you."

She put her lunch in the mini-fridge and poured a cup of coffee for herself, dumped in enough powdered hazelnut creamer to change the viscosity. She stirred and stepped behind him to read over his shoulder.

"Not too bad," he said. "Probably just a half-day's work, if you want to go at it like that."

On the clipboard was a single sheet of paper, a simple black-and-white grid.

"Let me know if you need anything," Dennis said.

She took a pencil and the clipboard to the kennel, a large, rectangular room with a smooth concrete floor and fluorescent lights. The two long walls were lined with tiled enclosures and chain-link gates. A half-wall in the room's center served as a divider, so that the cages didn't look directly into each other. Each cage had a number on a plastic card clipped to the gate.

The PTS list started as a page of blanks—Dennis's calculations produced a number, and a corresponding number of empty spaces for recording the work. The number today was thirteen. Not counting walk-ins—and there were always some—Naomi needed to pick thirteen dogs to put down. She made a casual circuit around the room, considering. The boxer puppies had been there a week, but they were cute enough that she held out hope for adoption. They could spend the day in the staff bathroom—that freed one cage. The elderly gray terrier went on the list. Two mutts, a collie-looking one and another terrier type, went on the list. The well-behaved shepherd mix that had come off the street with old injuries, a bad limp and a missing ear, went on the list. The dachshund with cataracts, who slept all day and had not barked once, was a maybe. The fat cocker spaniel went on the list.

She still thought of it as training, or tried to. That had been the original plan: stay in Cola for a year, get experience at the shelter, then apply to vet schools, where she would need professional composure. Millions of pet owners declined to get their animals spayed or neutered; people were too poor, or lazy, or didn't know better. She didn't like that part of the job, but it was part of the job. Of course it was harder now to pretend she was only training. She had been at the shelter four years.

When all the blanks were filled she went to the kennel office, a closet with a computer and a landline, and spent the morning making useless phone calls. The breed rescues in Jackson and Shreveport were sympathetic, but unable to get anyone to Cola until later in the week. The no-kill rescue groups in El Dorado and Pine Bluff were overloaded. No room in shelters at neighboring counties or their neighboring counties. At a quarter to eleven, Dennis poked his head into the office.

"A guy just dropped off two cats," he said.

"Did you tell him they won't last the day?"

"Yep."

"All right."

"Good news is, there's a young couple here, with a little kid, and they want a dog. I'm about to take them back."

"The boxer puppies are in the bathroom."

"Ah, good call. That's our first stop."

The kid liked the puppies but decided he wanted a snake. The mother refused, the father refused to have an opinion, and the family left arguing. Naomi added the cats to the list and worked out a schedule for the rest of the day. First, update her online dating profile. Second, eat lunch. Third, kill all the animals the shelter didn't have room for.

Part one didn't last long. There wasn't much to add. Naomi Connelly, twenty-six years old, native of Bossier City, graduate of Centenary College. Interested in veterinary science and waterskiing. Likes sushi and Brad Paisley. Transplant to southeast Arkansas by way of a college boyfriend who had grown up in Cola and wanted to move back. That wasn't in the profile. He had begged her to come with him, the shelter had liked her résumé, and it seemed like a decent spot for a layover while she saved money for vet school. They rented a truck, signed a lease—in her name to help build credit, which she later learned didn't work—and made the drive on a Saturday afternoon. Two months later he changed the plan. A Kappa Sig brother could get him in the door at a finance firm in Houston. It was too good to pass up. He loved her, he really did, but this was what he needed right now. They would be in touch. They never were.

And then, what? The job was pretty good, most parts of it. Rent was cheap. She could cover her student loans and still save a little, and living by herself was nice after four years of dorm life. She didn't miss Bobby. She took drives on the weekends, but never back home, though it was only three hours away. She found a good tamale place. She read in the evenings. A year passed, then another.

She had five messages on the dating site. One from a man who had sent the exact same text a month ago, asking for a full-body shot, one an invitation for "no-strings-attached fun," one from a sixty-year-old widower looking for a backgammon partner, and two from bots notifying her of totally free, no-hassle, super hot porn. She hated the Internet.

At noon she got her Tupperware out of the mini-fridge and mixed a pitcher of instant iced tea. Every communal fork was dirty, so she leaned against the counter and ate her Cobb salad with a spoon. Portia came in and used the microwave to heat her own lunch—a tub of macaroni and cheese with bacon bits mixed in. The smell was overpowering. She chewed with her mouth open.

"I'd like to be senile," she said, "and get all my jobs confused. Get the animals drunk, cut barflies' hair, and euthanize people at the salon."

"There's probably a legal defense for that," Naomi said.

After lunch she stepped out for a short walk. It was seven thousand degrees outside. The cotton field behind the shelter was halfway into flowering, the dark bolls splitting around the cloudy blooms. In a month the strip picker would start lumbering down the rows, huge tires and green chassis and bright yellow teeth in front, thoughtless and methodical.

Tuesdays had never been easy and still weren't. But there were the numbers, and the rules, and the necessity. She hadn't cried about it this year, yet. Still the occasional nightmare, but they were less frequent. The way to do it was simply to do it, the quicker the better, and try not to think too much. So she stared across the cotton field until the back of her neck was burning, then she went back inside the shelter and through the waiting room and back to the kennel office.

She checked her list against the log and the roster, as she always did. Updates would have been obvious. She would have noticed any special instructions or changes to an animal's status. Nothing jumped out at her.

In the kennel she took the quiet dachshund with cataracts out of its cage and led it to the room in back. She lifted it onto the metal table and went to the refrigerator. While she put on her gloves and filled the syringe, it sniffed around the edge of the table, looking for a place to jump down, but the table was too high so it sat and waited. She took its left front leg in her left hand, pushed her thumb down on the vein, slid in the needle and pushed the plunger. The dog got sleepy and lay down and was dead in forty-five seconds. She took a heavy-duty plastic garbage bag from the supply cabinet and rolled the dog into it, then carried it to the floor-to-ceiling freezer and put it on the middle shelf.

She did it over and over for three hours. When she took a break to drink more tea in the staff room, Portia and Dennis did not talk to her. An informal custom. After the break she put on new gloves and started again. All the cats went in one bag. The big dogs got their own bags, the smaller ones shared. Before she finished, the freezer became so crowded she had to shove to get the bags to fit, wedging the smaller animals in where she could. Twice she had to take some out and repack. Luckily, Dennis had scheduled a pickup for that evening, so however full the freezer got, it would be empty in the morning. Not that it mattered to her. On Wednesdays, she worked the desk.

The lights were on in the office but the blinds were still drawn. Naomi wanted to open them, to do anything to make this room feel bigger, but she didn't want to move. Fisher sat quietly, without responding or batting an eyelid. Dennis kept talking.

"Sometimes dogs will have a chip," he said. "But we didn't find one on her. So that would've made us hold on to her, but she didn't have one, our records show."

Fisher smiled suddenly. Naomi's stomach did a somersault.

"It was torn out," he said. "She was injured in combat. Barbie's a veteran."

"A veteran," Dennis said.

"Yes sir. First Battalion, 25th Infantry."

They sat in silence. Gravel crunched under tires in the parking lot. The ceiling fan spun above them. A cartoonish ceramic owl sat on the desk. It was painted a dark blue and its eyes were wide and bright. Dennis turned it around in a circle.

"I see," he said. "But you can imagine, we get a lot of strays. Lots of injuries you know, you see these dogs around. Without a chip, no collar, we can't know."

"But I called."

"That's true." Dennis did not look at Naomi. "It's very unfortunate. The lists are usually always cross-checked."

Fisher nodded and looked at the window. The blinds were still closed. He took a deep breath, let it out slowly, and looked up at the ceiling. Head tilted back, he laughed once through his nose. Dennis caught Naomi's eye and bit his lip, but she ignored him. Fisher rubbed his face with his good hand, the hard jaw with neat, light-colored stubble. Then he laughed loudly. They sat quietly until his laughter subsided into giggles. When the giggles had passed, he sighed again, and apologized.

"Sorry," he said. "I'm going to go outside."

"Okay," Dennis said.

Naomi wondered if she should help, but Fisher stood easily, and walked to the door. She searched for something to say and came up with nothing. When he had left the room she looked at Dennis, whose mouth was hanging open.

"Is he coming back?" he said.

She didn't answer. The water cooler burbled. Dennis left to check on Portia and Naomi walked to the window. It was unfair, of course. Was it monstrous? A mistake had been made, but the numbers all but guaranteed mistakes. The sheer numbers. Every system had its failings.

She raised the blinds and saw Fisher out in the cotton field, pacing slowly in the rows with that odd, robotic walk. The first time she'd seen him at the corner mart, she couldn't help wondering how he dealt with the items on the low shelves. Slowly, she supposed, and there was nothing wrong with that. There were no clouds in sight and he used his t-shirt to wipe his forehead. He looked, she thought, like he could use some water. She filled a paper cup.

The heat was worse than advertised. The highway rippled in a mirage and when she reached the field the dirt cracked under her flats. He was facing the distant line of black hickory, shading his eyes with his hand. When she was ten feet away he turned. She had to squint with her entire face.

"You want some water?"

He came forward and took the cup, drank and handed it back.

"Appreciate it."

"We really are sorry," she said. It was not exactly like offering comfort, but what else was there?

He nodded and looked out to the trees.

"Where's the body?" he said. "Can I see it?"

"No."

"Where is it?"

"We have so little space," she said. "And no money. We schedule pickups with freight coordinators. Reefer trucks will take the cargo for free, just stop on the way through town."

"And go where?"

She took a breath. "Wherever they were already going. Lots of hub cities have rendering plants. The plants will buy remains."

Fisher looked at her. He smiled once, broadly, then all expression left his face.

"Rendering plants," he said, and looked off again. "A rendering plant."

The smell of the cotton field had always reminded her of glue. Sweat dripped from under her arms and ran cold down her ribs. She put her arm up to shield her eyes and waited for words to come. When that arm grew tired she switched to the other.

"I'll tell you what," he said. "That takes the cake. And I know what I'm talking about. Not bragging or nothing. Just—I've seen bad, and this is a cherry."

She followed his line of sight into the field, trying to imagine what he saw. Nothing but acres and acres of cash crop, hunched in the light, theoretically on its way to being useful. The cup in her hand was nearly full—he hadn't taken more than a sip. She let a little water spill into the dust at her feet. The ground was so dry the water pooled instead of soaking in. It was hard to imagine anything worthwhile growing here.

"Beer?" she said.

"Oh yeah. Beer."

"I'll buy you one, I mean."

He looked at her. For some reason he didn't have to squint as much as she did.

"How's that?" he said.

"I don't know," she said. "I guess this is wildly inappropriate. I'm just saying, I'm sorry what happened to your dog. I mean, Jesus—I'll get you a beer. This isn't protocol or anything. I understand if you'd rather burn us down."

For the first time she saw despair on his face. A small change at the corners of his eyes. He looked down at his shoes. She wondered if his prosthetics absorbed the heat from the sun, if that was a concern.

"You mean The De Soto?" he said. The only bar in town.

"Sure."

"Okay," he said, and laughed. "I guess."

He walked away from her, deeper into the field. She suddenly felt rude for watching, and marched back to the shelter. Portia gnawed on a pen cap at the desk. After the heat of the field the inside air froze her shoulders. The waiting room was empty.

"How did that go?" Portia asked.

"I don't know," Naomi said. "He's not happy. Doesn't really seem angry. Sad."

"He's not going to kill us?"

"I don't think so." She hesitated. "I'm going to get him a beer."

"What, now?"

"Tonight. At the bar."

"You're kidding."

"What are we supposed to do? 'Sorry we killed your dog, bye.' That can't be it."

"No, you're right." Portia tilted her head like a cat regarding strange human behavior. She raised one eyebrow. "Sure. Why not a beer. If he says okay."

"He seemed okay."

"I'm working the bar tonight, so you know."

"I know."

"In case he chops you up, is what I'm saying."

"I know."

Late in the afternoon, the family with the snake kid came back. The father, apparently, had been forced to take a position, and decided against reptiles. Naomi directed them to Dennis, who again showed them the available animals. Again they deliberated noisily and, again, left without adopting anything. When the door closed behind them, Portia mimed a gunshot to the head.

Naomi stayed after closing to go over the PTS list and roster. She sat at the desk and stared at the documents. Not that it made any difference now, but she hoped some memory might shake loose, and she could be assured that Dennis's note hadn't been there the first time she checked. But she couldn't remember. And she hated Dennis, because although he was a goofy old man with ridiculous sideburns, between the two of them she was more likely to make a mistake.

At home she took a long shower, and afterward laid out a few tops on her bed. She tried them on and narrowed the choices to a green halter that tied at the neck, and a simple black v-neck. She considered appropriateness, comfort level, and whether or not she was going insane.

When Fisher Bray was six, his father, a roofer, moved the family to Cola to take advantage of what would turn out to be a very brief construction boom. He was sad to leave the house in Lake Village, because the dryer on its back in the side yard made an excellent racecar, when his sisters weren't using it as their bakeshop oven. Cola was hot and flat, and though the new side yard had a beech stump good for holding BB gun targets, it was a poor replacement for the dryer.

In middle school, his mother encouraged him to go out for football as a way to make friends. He played offense and defense, as there were seventeen total players on the team. In two years they won three games.

329

He did make friends, and his house became a popular sleepover destination, at least partially because of the two high school girls who also lived there.

That lasted until his father's fourth and final back injury, the result of another, minor, twelve-foot fall. His father sold the work truck and went on disability, and became an affable but spooky presence around the house—the pain meds made him foggy, and he spent the majority of his time sitting in the recliner in the living room, watching the TV whether it was on or not. Fisher stopped inviting his friends over. His mother started work as a gas station attendant to help with the finances. She was qualified for more, but managed her income carefully—a thousand dollars too much would change the family's benefits category, and her husband's medication would cost ten thousand more a year.

In high school Fisher discovered metal and weed. He shot up to five-eleven and let his hair grow into a long ponytail that he tied with rubber bands. He was a mellow, straight-C student, not because better grades were impossible, but because Cs took basically no effort. The girls graduated when he was a sophomore and moved to the capital together, to attend culinary school. Having two fewer dependents did restructure the family's benefits categorization, so Mr. Bray switched from a battery of prescriptions to over-the-counter cocktails. His fog dissipated somewhat and was replaced by pain and anger. He started stealing Fisher's pot, and their fights got progressively uglier until Mrs. Bray intervened, and designated Fisher as the official buyer for his father. She had recently found that four years at the One Stop had lowered her earning potential to the status quo.

His senior year, Fisher attended the Slocomb County High School career fair. He talked to a bait shop owner, a welder, a newspaper ad salesman, a pig farmer, a rice farmer, and a soybean farmer. The rice farmer in particular radiated disappointment, and Fisher, looking at the man's gnarled hands and hangdog face, felt the future closing around him like a fist. Then, in the corner of the convention hall, he was waylaid in his attempt to get a free keychain and ended up talking to an Army staff sergeant for half an hour. The sergeant had perfect teeth, a maroon beret, and a fine white scar on his temple, which he said he got rappelling. He was only six years older than Fisher, but from some other world where people wore polished shoes and knew how to break necks. He had been to thirteen countries. They looked over some forms, just to get an idea. Fisher agreed to take the ASVAB, to see what he might qualify for.

He left for Fort Benning three days after graduation. His mother cried and said she could not be more proud. His father asked where he would get his pot from. His sisters, by phone, said he was an idiot and was going to get killed. On his first plane ride, he was surprised to see how little of the earth was covered by human things.

Basic Training was a shock, mostly because of the routine. He shaved at four-forty every morning, and went to bed so tired he didn't roll over in his sleep for ten weeks. After Basic he stayed in Georgia for Advanced Individual Training—just another four weeks for infantry-men. He was fit, disciplined, and happy. In October, Private Bray crossed the Atlantic on a C-40 Clipper. It was the first time he had seen the ocean. He celebrated his nineteenth birthday a month later, at Forward Operating Base Sykes in dry, dusty, empty Tal Afar. An engineer he knew from training knew a corporal with an acoustic guitar, and someone brought Oreos into the barracks. It was his best birthday since childhood.

Two weeks passed slowly. Companies were being cycled in and out of Mosul, where the fighting was apparently heavy. Fisher's company waited for its first rotation. Part of him was afraid, of course, but he was also confident and excited. He had skills and wanted to use them. No one back home had ever done anything like this.

His two best friends in the unit were Specialist Leonard Ramos, a dog handler, and Leonard's Dutch shepherd, Barbie. Leonard was short, plump, and intensely religious. He and Fisher bonded over a mutual love for Megadeth. Barbie was sleek and lean, with giant up-standing ears, a brownish-orangey coat, and a floppy pink tongue that felt like used sandpaper. Fisher had always wanted a dog, but his father was the one man in Cola who wouldn't allow it. He and Barbie got along so well that Leonard let Fisher throw the tennis ball with her, though playtime was usually reserved for the handler. While the dog fetched, the men talked about combat. They were terrified and eager.

Their opportunity came in December. The company drove to Mosul in a convoy and initiated police operations in an outer district. Fisher's platoon was in charge of a guard post at an apparently important inter-section, a square of brown dirt between four identical stone buildings. They could hear artillery in other parts of the city, but for three days the intersection itself was relatively sedate. Fisher helped man the guard station that checked passing vehicles. Leonard walked Barbie around tires and bumpers, let her sniff compartments and passengers.

One Tuesday the traffic was heavier than normal, and a line formed at the gate. The drivers—Iraqi citizens, other American soldiers, other coalition forces—were irritable and surly. It was early evening and the light was failing. The shadows in the square lengthened and grew darker. The sky glowed a soft purple. Fisher was trying to get through his checklist with a French journalist when he heard barking. He looked up, but it was difficult to see in the increasing gloom. A man was in the square, a dozen meters away. The man was running toward the guard station. Barbie was barking at him. Leonard let go of her and she ran at him. The man saw the dog coming and stopped, and then Fisher's ears blew out and everything in his vision smeared together.

When his eyesight came back, a thick cloud of dust hung in the air, and he was lying on the ground next to the journalist's car. He tried to push himself into a sitting position, but failed because his left hand was gone. He gasped and looked away. It must have been a mistake, because he could still feel the hand, still feel the fingers moving. He looked again but it remained absent. Strange—he would have to figure that out later. Right now he needed to get moving. He tried to stand using only his feet, but that proved impossible, because they were gone too. He screamed, and someone touched his shoulder. It was the French journalist, leaning down from the open car door. His face was bloody but he had all his limbs. He was saying something, probably something important, but Fisher didn't speak French, so he closed his eyes and lay back. He was confused and needed a nap.

Fisher had nine surgeries in Germany. In two months he was aware enough to ask questions and remember the answers, and he learned that Leonard had taken shrapnel through the brain stem. Barbie had survived, and was actually being treated at a veterinary clinic a few miles away. He got phone calls from his family, parents solemn and sisters hysterical. In March he underwent another round of surgery. Whenever he was lucid he made phone calls to administrators at the veterinary clinic. Barbie was getting a medical discharge. Fisher wanted her. The strings were easy to pull.

They did their rehab together at the VA in Birmingham. Barbie had lost an ear and gained a permanent limp, but Fisher's pace wasn't exactly challenging. He did pool therapy and the parallel bars to build strength, and was finally able to use the prosthetics without aid. His walk was slow and ungainly, but after eleven months without standing, it felt like a miracle to look at the world from his original height.

His sisters drove down from Little Rock to bring him back to Cola.

They made a hundred chocolates stamped with a profile of George Washington, the same as his Purple Heart. They brought a three-foot novelty dog bone for Barbie. When they reached home, his father surprised Fisher by sobbing openly, then laughing and asking which of them was the gimpiest now. His mother kept a stern frown and didn't look at his legs.

He got a small apartment in the downtown area, with a tiny concrete patio and a small backyard where Barbie could drink out of the sprinkler. He went to physical therapy twice a week and the psychologist once. After a few months he got a part-time job at the corner mart, stocking shelves. He read in the evenings and barbecued on weekends, usually just him and the dog. He didn't mind the solitude. He knew he was processing, and the doctor said he was doing well.

In July his air conditioner broke, so he left the windows and back door open at night. One morning Barbie wasn't there. She had gotten out before—the latch on the backyard gate was pitiful—but he usually found her sniffing snake holes in the dirt alley just behind the property. He paced the length of the alley but didn't see her, walked a circuit around downtown and couldn't find her. He knocked on his neighbors' doors and asked, then called his parents for some reason. No one could help. He sat at his kitchen table and tried not to panic. All the walking had exhausted him. The shelter—he would call the shelter.

Someone named Dennis answered, and Fisher described Barbie, trying to keep the agitation out of his voice. Sure enough, a dog matching that description had been brought in. She was happily waiting for him to come collect her. Fisher put down the phone and choked once. He had not realized how worried he'd been. He rubbed his eyes and asked Dennis if they could keep her until the next day, when he could borrow a car from his mother. That, he was told, would be no problem.

For the second time that day, Naomi waited for the right response to occur to her. On the other side of the booth, Fisher pulled from his beer and looked up at the crossbeam that traversed the bar's interior, the crusty license plates nailed onto the black lacquer. She had chosen the green halter, and was glad—the paper streamers taped to the vent of the window a/c unit barely floated, and the condensation on her bottle was so thick that the label slipped off in her hand the second time she raised it. The three other patrons sat at the bar watching baseball on a ceiling mounted tube television. Portia cut lime wedges, as if someone might order something that required them. Naomi wrapped the sodden label around her beer again.

"Did she get a medal, too?" she asked. "Like yours?"

"No," he said. "Dogs aren't eligible for military awards."

"You were right about taking the cake. The cherry."

"Like I said, not trying to brag."

He wore a faded maroon polo with the same mesh shorts, sat with his hand on the table and his other arm in his lap. There was a wry expression on his face when he looked at the tacky crossbeam, at the door when it swung to admit another lonely sixty-year-old in overalls, at the saltshaker made from an old hot sauce bottle. But when he directed his gaze at her, it was genuine. Open and even kind. She avoided it.

"I feel like . . . like saying 'sorry' would be an insult. A joke. Like there's not really anything for me to do. Besides go to prison, or get strung up by the thumbs or something. I don't know."

He kneaded the place on his forearm where the prosthesis attached, just below the elbow joint. A strap looped around the upper part of his arm, and he undid and adjusted the Velcro before speaking again.

"You know why this place is called The De Soto?"

She shook her head, worried that now he would think she was the incurious type, who never wondered why anything was called anything. Why hadn't she wondered that?

"It's after Hernando de Soto," he said. "He's buried in the lake here. Supposedly. You know Lake Chicot, right over that way? His men sank the body so Indians wouldn't know he wasn't a god. Native Americans."

"You do what you got to do," she said. "Was he the guy looking for the Fountain of Youth?"

"Just gold, I think."

A man entered the bar, a leathery skeleton of indeterminate age in camouflage cargo shorts. He nodded at Fisher, who nodded back. He took a stool near the TV and Portia grinned and said, "Look at this old rustler, I thought you died." The air conditioner wheezed and sputtered.

"That guy used to work at the corner store," Fisher said. "He got fired for stealing porno mags."

"You do what you got to do," she said.

He laughed and cracked his neck. She was glad to make him laugh.

"Anyway," he said. "What exactly are we doing here?"

"What do you mean?"

"I mean, it's pretty weird circumstances."

"Right."

"But it feels like a date."

"Uh," she said.

"So I'm thinking, how all does this work? Am I trying to score a pity date from the cute woman who put my dog down?"

"It's not a pity date."

"Is it a date?"

"I don't know."

She wanted to look around the bar, in case there was a life preserver in reach, or a convenient method of suicide. But she was afraid to break eye contact with him. His elbows were posted on the edge of the table. He looked at her and didn't speak.

"This is just, I'm getting you a beer," she said. "Like people do when something happens. I know it's stupid and inadequate. If I was you I'd want to kill me. But you seem nice and I feel like shit. So I guess this is a pity party for me."

"Right," he said. "That's about right."

"Right," she said. Her stomach twisted into surgical knots. "And I hoped you'd like this shirt, I guess."

He sat back and finished his beer.

"Do you want another one?" he asked.

"Yeah," she said. "I'll get it."

"I'll get it."

As soon as he turned his back, she took a napkin from the dispenser and wiped her eyes. The window across from her was too dusty to provide a reflection, but the napkin came away clear of makeup. At the bar, Portia was doing a crossword, and Fisher waited patiently until she noticed him. He carried the bottles back to the table in his right hand, and behind his back Portia watched and gave Naomi a questioning eyebrow, her thumb held sideways on the bar. Naomi smiled at her.

"I asked her to leave the caps on," he said.

Still standing with both bottles gripped, he positioned the caps against each other. A quick slam downward sent the upper cap flying. He pushed the open beer toward her and sat down.

"One," he said. "I don't want to kill you. Two, my best friend was a dog, sad as that is, and she died yesterday, so I'm a little down. And I don't blame you, or at least I can tell that I'm not going to, but I do have complicated feelings about it at the moment. Three, I do like that shirt. Can you open this?"

She opened the other beer for him. It foamed over and spilled.

"That's okay," he said. "Four. If you're getting a pity party, I don't want a pity date. I want to get pity laid."

He sipped. His mouth was cast iron and his eyes retained the sadness she'd seen in the cotton field. She waited for a grin, a tell that would alert her to the joke. After three beats she knew it wasn't coming.

"One," she said. "I'm glad you don't blame me. I think it's because you know that I know what a fuckup this is, and you're kind, and you know that I'll still torture myself. Two, I also picked this shirt because it's hot as hell everywhere in this damn town, but I'm glad you like it."

He raised his bottle to her.

"Three, nobody's getting 'pity laid.' Not by me. Not even if your other hand and your head got blown off in Iraq."

His face didn't change. He nodded his head minutely.

"Four. This is a date, if you want. That's basically insane considering how we got here, but you're probably the most eligible bachelor in town, God help us."

"Okay," he said. He laughed.

They talked about the boringness and pleasantness of baseball. They talked about war movies, good ones and bad ones. They tried to remember the name of the Fountain of Youth guy but failed. The old men left one by one until they were alone with the bartender, and Portia brought over gin and tonics on the house, heavily garnished with lime wedges. Fisher recognized her from the shelter. He patted her arm and proposed a toast to Barbie, which he slurred slightly. Naomi supposed that a diminished body weight would increase the effect of alcohol. He apologized after spilling gin on his shirt. Portia laughed at him and left to get a rag. Fisher excused himself to go to the bathroom.

Naomi got up and propped the front door open with a cinder block. Full dark had fallen and she put the air temperature at a brisk eighty-two. She stood in the blinking neon of the window sign and had grand thoughts about how so few things in the world happened the way you expected. Those kinds of thoughts meant she was tipsy enough now to have a headache in the morning. She reentered the bar in time to see Fisher spit a chewed lime wedge back into his glass.

They took her car. In four minutes they reached his apartment, which was modest but clean, with tan carpet and new paint. A breakfast bar separated the living room from the kitchen, and he walked behind it and opened a cabinet. She sat on a corduroy sofa beneath a framed print of that Japanese woodcut where the huge waves are about to swamp the little boat.

"I hope you don't mind," he said. He set a bottle of bourbon on the counter. "I'm just going to make sure I'm drunk."

"Your house," she said. "Your rules."

"Want one?"

"Yes."

When they got to the bedroom she told herself that sex was always strange, between any two humans, anywhere on earth. She waited on top of the covers while he removed his prosthetics at the edge of the bed. Although it was too dark to see—he had made sure—she closed her eyes. After a moment she felt his weight settle next to her, then his fingertips on her clavicle.

"Do I," she said. She put her hands on her knees to stop them from shaking. "I mean, I've never, you know. Just tell me what to do."

"How should I know?" he said. "I don't know either. Should be basically the same, I think. More or less."

It was, more or less. She stayed on top, which seemed easiest, and after a few minutes her biggest worry was the heat.

"Sorry I'm sweating so much," she said.

"It's okay."

"I'm sorry."

"I heard you."

After he came they held each other for a spell, then he rolled away and fell asleep. She watched the digits change on the bedside clock, listened to cars going by on the street outside, and tried to ignore all the different parts of her brain that wanted to make pronouncements on her character, or lack thereof, her future, or lack thereof, and the mysteries of the world in general. The strain or the alcohol finally produced a throbbing headache, and after an hour spent lying awake she slipped from bed and inched through the dark, thinking of water.

In the living room she found the edge of the breakfast counter and circled around it onto the kitchen tile. Without any idea where a light switch might be, she opened the refrigerator, and fluorescent light washed over the cabinets. The cool air felt good on her skin, and the light reached into the far corner where a blue dog bowl sat almost empty. It occurred to her to make a gesture. Though the refrigerator

337

was nearly desolate it did have a filtered water pitcher on the top shelf, and she took it out. The bowl was too far to reach, so she leaned across the kitchen, one hand holding the door open to keep the light on, the other straining to extend the pitcher as far as she could. Her arm shook. She tilted the spout toward the bowl. The water came out in a smooth stream that sparkled in the light, splashed off the lip, and spilled onto the floor.

Nominated by The Oxford American

SPIRITUAL EVALUATION

by TAIJE SILVERMAN

from MASSACHUSETTS REVIEW

> *If You Think You Have Been the Victim of Witchcraft,*
> *Envy, the Evil Eye, or Bad Luck, Come Inside*
> *and Get a Spiritual Evaluation.*
> —*sign on the Church of Jesus Christ in the Lord, Philadelphia*

Did you want this baby?
There are a certain number of questions you may pass over
without forfeiting your score on the test.
Do you understand that metaphors involving hummingbirds
are not useful? Do you understand
that you are in no way related to hummingbirds?
If this baby is the size of an a) eraser or b) apricot
or c) memory, will you be able to determine
whether on the day after the hurricane,
the river was as full as a river can be
without flooding the ramp to the bypass?
Heavy rain has been known
to push hummingbirds into bodies of water,
causing them to drown. Hummingbirds
remember each flower they have visited
and on average they visit 1,000 flowers a day.
Define, in one word, your relationship with the unbelievable.
Do you think you have been the victim of witchcraft?
There is a limited number of questions
you may choose not to answer.
Calculate the amount of water in a bathtub
if one eighth of it drains at one half of the speed
that the water now flows down the river.
You have one hour and nine months.
You have six months. You have the evening.

When you hear the words *count down*,
do you think of the moon? When you picture the moon,
do you see its surface or a not inhospitable orb
that alternates in size according to proximity with rooftops?
This problem is commonly referred to as *moon illusion*.
This theory is generally known as *shape constancy*.
With the shape of your body please prove
that the moon does not generate its own light. Do you like
charades? If this baby is a girl, what.
If this baby is a boy. Do you think
you have been the victim of bad luck?
Describe in five words what this baby will fear
if this baby is an apricot. List everyone it will love
if it is an eraser. Will this baby's smile be like
a) the furniture in your basement or
b) someone dead whom you loved more than you love
the baby. Explain what it means to love someone more.

Nominated by Massachusetts Review

FINDERS KEEPERS

by JENN SHAPLAND

from TIN HOUSE

OBJECTS OF MY AFFECTION

> *For a collector—and I mean a real collector, a collector as he ought to be*
> *—ownership is the most intimate relationship that one can have to objects.*
> —WALTER BENJAMIN, *"Unpacking My Library"*

Here is a list of things you might find in 7B:

1. Suitcases
2. Typewriters
3. Hatboxes
4. Funeral shoes (unworn)
5. Eyeglasses
6. Swizzle sticks
7. Board games
8. Socks (worn)
9. Handkerchiefs (used)
10. Pen refills

A library is not a list. A library is dirty, has smells. I know this because I interned in a special collections library. It's a special collections library that happens to house, along with its First Folios and signed copies of *The Waste Land*, a larger assortment of socks than you might guess.

Personal effects generally arrive at the Harry Ransom Center's loading dock on the University of Texas campus via happenstance. They get stuck into boxes of manuscripts and books for reasons unknown. They're stowaways. That is why I'm so fond of them. Personal effects include items owned or worn that do not necessarily pertain to the recorded work of a cultural figure. They are objects that don't fit comfortably into folders. Working on the seventh floor, where a sign by the elevator warns IF YOU FIND A BAT, DO NOT TOUCH IT, and especially working in 7B, the room that houses the personal effects collections, is not unlike haunting an uninhabited Collyer Mansion or Grey Gardens. It's a place where things are housed, where they come to roost. 7B is a microcosm of the archive writ large.

It was in 7B, before my long afternoons itemizing and categorizing the socks of the dead and famous, that I began to collect certain stories. Stories about wanting and having, giving and taking, even stealing. I learned of a caper by a Texas football scion, which led me to a tale of a multimillion-dollar book heist. Yet as I poked and prodded into what began to seem like the dusty broom closet or unexamined under-the-bed of culture, it was my own relationship to objects that began to feel illicit.

Not long after I finished my several weeks of training, I made a discovery while passing through the personal effects stacks. I don't recall what brought me up there. Perhaps I'd been toying with Anne Sexton's eyeglasses, or taking a peek in Sir Arthur Conan Doyle's cabinet of "apparitions and dreams." (He labeled one of the drawers "apparitions of dogs." Imagine: so many canines from beyond appeared to Doyle that he had to allocate an entire drawer for them.) As my cart squeaked down the aisle, rousing the sleeping artifacts, a large box labeled "Einstein, Albert" came into view. I hadn't heard of any Einstein materials in the personal effects collection. A closer look at the box's label informed me that it contained the physicist's molecular model kit.

I shifted my weight, eyeballed the box, quickly looked both ways. The Center has a set of Einstein's notes on relativity—chicken scratch— that are kept in the vault. The vault, you'll be glad to learn, is in fact a vault. Picture the cartoon lair of one Scrooge McDuck. Okay, smaller than that—more like a locker. Chalkboard gray, iron, with two handles and a pancake-size combination lock. And inside? Some would call it treasure. Others might just see a pile of junk. Old, musty, moldy (sometimes toxically so): other people's junk.

I carried and handled and sifted through this invaluable cultural material, this *stuff*, all day long. When ink rubbed off a manuscript leaf, or when a page's edges crumbled into literal dust that coated my fingers, I found myself thinking hard about the impulse to collect. To keep.

I pulled down the box labeled "Einstein" and began slowly unwinding the threads that wrapped its button enclosures. I was about to ever so gingerly lift the box from its archival housing (boxes within boxes are sort of a conservationist's specialty, it turns out. There is an entire lab devoted to the making of boxes designed to hold other boxes), brazen background soundtrack playing in my head, when I thought I heard someone approaching.

My heart stopped for just a second. It's extremely easy to scare somebody in a library, but why did I so often feel as though I'd been caught in the act when I was alone with a find from the collections? I was allowed full access to these materials, free range, and yet that feeling—it's the same feeling anyone would get when discovered rifling through someone's stuff. Actually, it's the precise feeling I used to get when I snooped around the houses of people I babysat for while the kids slept, or when I snooped around my own house while home alone. Touching, looking became unique opportunities for access. And violation.

I come from snoopers. When I lived at home, my mom would go through my room regularly. She read all my letters and notebooks without permission, then quizzed me on their contents. As traumatic as her invasions of my privacy were, years later, I can't help but understand the impulse behind them, to some extent. Going through other people's stuff, or having it—borrowing clothes, books—makes me feel closer to them.

And then, too, there are the things objects tell us that their owners never would. Secrets. Now I wonder if I snoop in part because growing up queer in a Catholic house in the Midwest was confusing and lonely. I knew I was different but had no idea how or why. "I had no idea what was missing but felt the missing-ness of the missing," to borrow Jeanette Winterson's wording. My snooping has always felt justified, internally. Like research: How to Be a Person, Exhibit A. Our stuff tells on us. In objects lie the hidden habits of how each of us makes a life. I was rooting around in other people's closets for signs of connection, community. Curiosity is itself a kind of stealing: internalizing an experience that isn't yours.

The personal effects collections I processed—sorted, labeled, photographed, housed—contain the belongings of two of the twentieth century's greatest writers, greatest female writers, greatest queer writers, two of my all-time favorite writers: Carson McCullers and Gertrude Stein. I started to fixate on, even to cathect, their belongings as I worked. They're all I talked about in the office, at the bar: Have I told you about Carson McCullers's llama statue? *Yes.*

So I guess this is a story about my obsessions. Obsessiveness. But it's also about a young queer writer coming into her own. Getting close enough to her heroes to relate to their goddamn handkerchiefs. It's about impossible intimacy, and about recognizing yourself.

The curator who interrupted my reverie helped me get the box out of its box and set it up on the table with the requisite velvet cushions to hold the cover open at an unstrenuous angle. All run-of-the-mill procedures for handling materials.

The process seems to be crucial for maintaining the specialness of special collections. Not just for the practical reasons, like protecting the objects from wear and tear, but for another purpose: the cushions and weights and meticulous housings insert an unspoken of but palpable barrier between person and thing. The first question most newcomers to the archive asked was if they needed to put on gloves. Most were disappointed and a bit unnerved when I told them they could use their bare hands. We want tools, gear, layers of dark velvet or pristine white cotton to protect the materials from us. There is a fear, here, of carelessness. But on the flip side, there is *care*. There is a desire to nestle the object into something soft and perfectly sized to hold it. It's not for nothing that those velvet cushions that support a book by its spine are called "cradles."

Before she left me to it, I heard the curator explaining something that sounded important, but I'd gotten distracted by a small blue ink doodle, possibly from Einstein's own distracted hand, etched into the lower corner of the duct tape on the box. A spaceship? A smiley face? Totally illegible. Alone again with the item, I quickly set aside the stack of papers detailing what I presumed to be boring stats on provenance, acquisition, other library inanity, and dug into the model set. But my eyes caught a letter on personal stationery that had sifted loose from the pile.

I picked up the letter and encountered a Dallas woman named Cecilia Hawk, who wrote to the Ransom Center in the late 1980s. In her letter, she writes that after reading about "a missing page from Einstein's papers in the *Dallas Morning News*"—a sheet of handwritten notes had disappeared from under a locked display case—she decided to offer to the Center "something that might be of interest."

Hawk bought the molecular model kit at an auction in Atlanta, Georgia, for reasons unstated. Nothing in her letter makes it clear why it was significant to her, but her personal investment is unmistakable. So moved was she by the case of theft from the archive, just from reading about it in the paper—in my imagination she wears slippers and sits alone on a porch with fan in hand—that she donated her purchase, asking nothing in exchange but a receipt. John Chalmers, a former HRC librarian whom I had until this point never once heard of, wrote back to let Hawk know that the leaf of Einstein's notes had been recovered, and charges had been brought against the "young man who appears to have removed it."

Chalmers's response takes on a sudden and unexpected emotional tenor—this is a librarian writing to a patron, remember—as he confides in Hawk that "during that rather difficult week, the reception of your letter about the molecular model in small measure gave me comfort." He warmly accepted her donation.

Transference. That's the psychological function at work here. It's a combination of projection, ascribing some aspect of yourself—fantasies, desires, imagination—to the object, and introjection, taking some part of it unto/into yourself. For William James, this is the way objects (which, importantly, can also be *whole people*) become extensions of the self. Cecilia Hawk so incorporated Einstein's molecular model kit into her person that her act of giving it to an institution was perceived by both parties as deeply generous. And for Chalmers, the kit was a form of condolence for a grievous loss that not just the institution, but by extension *he*, had experienced.

But the kit wasn't Hawk's to give or Chalmers's to receive, not really. Its entire significance is bound up in its being *Einstein's*. Something was being taken in this scenario; something was being stolen. I wanted to know what, but first I wanted to play with the thing myself. I wanted to open the box and hold its molecules in my hands.

The revelation of the theft left me with a bit of a buzz as I turned back to the kit, which consisted of small wooden blocks—atoms—in different shapes, organized by color. The item had a story and now I was invested. Attached.

One of the provenance letters suggests that Einstein requested extra types of atoms directly from the manufacturer; the basic set apparently did not meet his molecular modeling needs. The pieces had been neatly organized by color, which I instinctively took to be Chalmers's doing; in current archival practice, such rearrangement constitutes a pretty serious breach, but in earlier eras it was common to adjust, fix, arrange, and reconfigure items upon arrival. The pieces in the box are blue, orange, yellow, black, green, dark blue, beige, and brown spherical shapes with rounded and flat sides. Each has several holes in it, into which brass pegs fit. I pulled out several atoms, distinctly aware that the fingerprints of the man who came up with relativity were all over them. I pictured him standing before a classroom, demonstrating the universe's most fundamental truths with wooden blocks.

I was mulling over Cecilia Hawk and the missing notes, and wondering in an abstract way what would possess someone—that phrase—to steal from an archive. In my hand I could feel the weight of the tiny molecule I'd built—I think it was H_2O—its particular heft, its smooth surfaces. My fingers closed around it. It occurred to me how easy it would be to pocket the thing.

I already felt a creeping guilt just doing my job. It was enough of an intrusion to handle these objects. Sliding my arms into McCullers's nightgown sleeves to prop them up with tissue in their new housings? Adjusting the button fly on Doyle's suit pants? Toying with Alice Toklas's jewelry box? I was an intruder. How else could such proximity to traces of the radically ordinary—the dingy bottoms of McCullers's socks, the faint smell of poodle that pervades the Stein collection—feel but radically intimate?

All vicarious experience is a kind of stealing, but living vicariously is a huge part of how we form our identities. We commit undocumented thefts continuously as we form a self. When you think about it that way, biography and narrative, the usual forms of interaction with famous cultural figures, are types of possession. Like unrequited love, unrequited interest and unrequited access are ways to own something or someone that isn't yours. A line keeps coming to mind that I can't track down: that you can understand something only without desiring it. It echoes in my brain, a refrain, but I don't know if I have it right, or if perhaps it's the other way around.

An anonymous tip-off led to the discovery of the single page of Einstein's notes, now slightly water-damaged, creased, and tucked in a photo album, in the duplex of Samuel K. Royal, nineteen-year-old grandson of the late University of Texas football coach Darrell K. Royal. As in Darrell K. Royal Memorial Stadium, the 100,000-seat football megachurch down the street from the Ransom Center. No motive was given.

The district attorney at the time had this to say: "This is an invaluable treasure that belongs to the entire species of humanity and we are delighted to report to you that it has been recovered."

Chalmers, head librarian at the time, had this to say: "This has wonderful elements of mystery about it." He refers to the circumstances of the notes' Houdini-like escape from a locked display case that showed no sign of damage or break-in. Royal was sentenced to five years probation and two hundred hours of community service.

Can anything "belong" to "the entire species of humanity?" The words *belong* and *belongings* share roots with both desire (*longing, to long*) and proximity (*along, alongside*). The funny thing about the Royal case is that the thief put the notes in an album. He made his own effort at preservation and conservation. And he opened them to the public. Ransom Center staff rumor has it that the anonymous tip came from a guest at one of Royal's duplex parties, where he entertained partygoers with his prized Einstein possession.

After learning of Royal's heist, I became fixated on theft, the possibility of items slipping away unnoticed. For a few months I played investigator— maybe I'd been watching too much *Veronica Mars*—and hunted down reports of theft from all the top archives. I came across the Smiley map heist at the Beinecke, the Poe hoarders at the Alderman Library. I found out as much as I could about the HRC's security systems, which are a huge presence throughout the building.

Here is a set of facts and conjectures:

1. The Ransom Center's security system underwent a complete overhaul in 2003, to the tune of half a million dollars.

2. At any given time you will find at least three armed guards on duty downstairs to protect the ca thirty seven million manuscripts inside.

3. The doors to this building are *heavy*.

4. Unlike the special collections at the British Library or at most other universities, the Ransom Center is a public archive. All one needs

to enter is a photo ID and a brief orientation. This is one of my favorite things about it.

5. While one of the improvements to the building's security features was to funnel all building users through a single entrance and exit point, there remain at least two other ways in:
   a. A loading dock entrance to the basement by which materials come into the building.
   b. An entrance to a tunnel—*think about this*—that runs under Austin to the State Capitol Building. Built in the 1930s, the system of tunnels totals six miles in length; public entry to the tunnel system is forbidden due to heightened security since 9/11.

6. In the basement, you'll find several multimillion-dollar walk-in freezers that are used to quarantine collections when they arrive in their damp, crumbling, contaminated cardboard boxes from the garage or basement or attic in which they previously resided.

7. Floors four through seven are restricted.

8. If you ever read *From the Mixed-Up Files of Mrs. Basil E. Frankweiler*, a chapter book about two kids who secretly live at the Met that is, not surprisingly, a long-standing favorite of mine, then you should know right now that it would be impossible to enact such a fantasy here. Which is not to say I haven't thought about it.

9. The elevators to the stacks, which require a key-card swipe, stop running at 4.47 PM precisely. I found this out the hard way.

10. It may also be a violation to list these facts. To conjecture.

I got good enough at playing librarian that I managed to coax a story about theft—something no one seemed eager to tell the nosy intern about—out of the steely ringleader of the Reading Room while sitting at the reference desk. The Reading Room is a glass fishbowl on the second floor surrounded by the writing desks of John Fowles and Edgar Allan Poe, plus a veritable army of busts. The busts are exclusively white male writers and artists whose collections the Center houses, with the exception of Dame Edith Sitwell and her glorious nose. I find her presence (and her nose, which arcs like mine but at an even bolder angle) immensely comforting. The librarian in charge has worked this desk for as long as anyone can remember and wears sweaters that coordinate with even minor holidays. She keeps a collection of windup toys at the front of her desk, which seems at first out of sync with both her personality and the room's aesthetic. They are lined up neatly, but they are dusty.

Throughout the building there are nods to and parodies of the collecting and exhibiting of materials; on the fourth floor, outside the men's restroom, you'll find a locked case full of paper clips across the ages, each type sorted, named, and labeled. Sometimes I'm not sure what the precise difference is between the paper clips, or the windup toys, and the exhibitions downstairs in the galleries. Once we decide objects are worth collecting for reasons apart from monetary value, where do we draw the line?

I could ask myself this question. Sitting on my desk right now are several black binder clips that came home in my pockets after I processed the last installment of David Foster Wallace's manuscripts. I was tasked with removing and discarding all clips, but I couldn't part with them. Instead, I gave some to friends and academic advisors as quirky gifts, and kept the rest. The problem is that I can no longer tell, looking at the pile of clips on my desk, which belonged to him and which are just ordinary—that is, clips that already belonged to me.

The reference librarian told me her theft story in fits and starts as she swiveled around, printing requests, arranging materials to be reshelved, directing the library staff, always with an eye on the patrons. She mentioned several times how embarrassed she had been that she didn't realize why a patron kept asking about the price of each book he requested. These requests included a copy of *The Origin of Species* that he put down his pants and walked out with one afternoon in 1988. As she told me how it was recovered at a nearby rare bookshop, her flinty look momentarily left her. The only thing her blue eyes conveyed was sadness. A sense of betrayal. Someone flouted the rules and to this day it flouts something personal, precious, and cherished in her.

In the Reading Room a kind of magic is at work. A conjuring. It happens every time patrons put in requests, summon materials from above or below to their tables. In my mind it's Matilda-esque, objects flying from their shelves straight into a patron's outstretched hands. It's similar to what some visitors—very easy to spot when they arrive—are up to when they come in to do readings with Aleister Crowley's tarot cards. There's also something sort of erotic about it, all the touching. But there's another kind of intimacy, too. The intimacy of texture. Of odor. Of atoms mingling with each other. In 1988, patrons were still allowed to have whole carts of books beside their tables. Now up to five books are delivered to them by staff. The reference librarian keeps a map behind her desk of where everyone is sitting at a given moment. Intimacy still exists between patrons and the books and papers they summon, but no one's putting anything down their pants these days.

I started to write letters to the personal effects I itemized in 7B. I wrote them on the HRC's yellow paper, on which I was supposed to be recording details about the collection for the finding aid. That's one reason I'm not a librarian. And one reason the librarians started to give me some side-eye. You're not supposed to have all these *feelings* when you're working behind the scenes. Or if you do, I guess you're not supposed to write about them. You're not supposed to commune with the objects. That gradually became clear. It now occurs to me, at the distance of several years, what I brought to this job as a twenty-five-year-old graduate intern, and what gets me in trouble at most of my jobs: unlicensed perspective.

When I arranged an interview with a head librarian to investigate the Center's history of theft more thoroughly, I—amateur gumshoe, life-long snoop, bored intern—found myself in deeper than I intended to go. He met me in a windowless office off the Reading Room that contained nothing but a table, two chairs, and a silenced phone. I took excessive notes. I tried to ask "hard-hitting" questions.

He told me the story of a massive heist. Between three and four hundred books were smuggled from the stacks—the exact number can never be known. Some are still missing.

The magnitude of the theft is shocking, but I was probably even more shocked that no one had so much as mentioned it before. I now understand that its impact resonates in just about every aspect of the Center's day-to-day policies. It is a matter of something more, something deeper than reputation or legacy. It is about possession and immortality, like the archive itself. Libraries, archives, and museums all find themselves at the intersection of materiality and the mystical. Perhaps this is why we're so quiet when we enter them. As I listened to the librarian's story it dawned on me that theft, these actual physical slippages, are just interruptions to the collective body, the assembled self that the archive represents. A collective body that includes not only objects but also the archivists and conservators who care for them.

It was an inside job. Mimi Meyer, a volunteer working in book conservation, began taking books home with her sometime after she started in 1989. She was a trusted member of the Ransom Center's volunteer force, but the librarian was quick to tell me that her skills as a conservator were seriously lacking. And despite everything, this seemed to be her worst offense in his eyes. In 1992, she was fired for a having a book in her office that she had not checked out.

The books she took were no pocketsize paperbacks. They were big books. Old books with signed bindings, gilt covers, calligraphed interiors. She sold most of them to dealers overseas, and the ones she didn't sell wound up stacked all over the apartment she moved into in Chicago after leaving the Ransom Center, an apartment she shared with her boyfriend, none other than John Chalmers, who had remained the head librarian until 1990. They shared $400,000 in a joint checking account when Meyer was convicted. Chalmers was never officially charged with the book theft, but it was, according to the librarian, "inconceivable" that he didn't know what was going on. The books were *in* his apartment. In all likelihood, he directed Meyer to steal certain books and helped to sell them. Yet he remains a member of the Caxton Club, a prestigious bibliophile association in Chicago.

Did the Einstein theft and its "wonderful elements of mystery" inspire Chalmers to make a mystery of his own? I'd like to know what was missing for him, what void he was trying to fill with books and cash. Chalmers had refused indignantly to let the guards check his briefcase on exiting the building each day, a policy that is still in place, a policy I abided by daily. He was fired by the director in 1990 for "incompetence." The police found the books when they raided Chalmers and Meyer's shared apartment in 2003. Meyer was already in prison on drug charges. The current head librarian spent much of his first ten years working with the FBI to hunt down the books and recover them from dealers, none of whom gave the books back readily. He keeps a list of the books that he knows are still missing, but it isn't possible to know with certainty what has been lost. The librarian used the word "skullduggery" to describe the world of rare book dealing; he said this without a hint of irony, but with real anger, masking sadness.

I keep wondering: Was Chalmers's goal simply to make as much money as possible on the black market with rare books? How did Meyer get involved? Or was it her idea? Was the heist a precursor to their romance? Did it fuel it? I think the apartment where they squirreled the books away is significant. The psychology of hoarding is almost indistinguishable from the process of collecting. Hoards are often intentional, organized, and used by their owners. Sometimes they're shared, displayed. The main difference, according to psychologists of hoarding Gail Steketee and Randy Frost, is that hoarders' lives are in some way encroached upon by their collections. "Hoarding is not defined by the number of possessions, but by how the acquisition and management of those possessions affects their owner." The collections start to take over the collector. I think of Cecilia Hawk—that is, the Cecilia Hawk I've invented in my mind—and wonder if, perhaps, Meyer and Chalmers were just lonely. Loneliness is my go-to assumption for people who spend a lot of their time in libraries. Objects provide a kind of company a constancy, that other people simply cannot. If I've learned nothing else from working with librarians, archivists, and *things*, it's this fact. It's what brought me here in the first place.

Throughout its history the Ransom Center, whose name seems more and more significant to me, has been viewed as sort of a renegade in acquisitions. The notoriously snooty British libraries in particular are resentful that the papers of so many of *their* national authors have been sent to Texas (the "of all places" is implied). Profiles on the center's archive and its directors cite the practices of pirates or bandits as apt points of comparison. The Ransom Center perpetuates the stereotype in its promotional materials and its continuous snatching up of valuable collections.

And surely the imperialist motives of museums are well documented; amassing cultural goods is a colonial enterprise. Mary Ruefle, who fell in love with a shrunken head at a museum, an infatuation to which I can seriously relate, explains how this truth unfolds: "I can assure you my school did not teach what I now know to be true—that the museum I wandered in was built on rape and plunder and pillage and oppression and murder, that everything in it was stolen, that the very wealth necessary for such acquisition was stolen, wealth acquired by force of so filthy and unspeakable an evil our heads cannot fathom it and have no single word for it." In Texas, some of the words for it are *oil* and *football*. I wonder if at the Center one of the words might be *loneliness*. From owner to archive to thief to dealer, the playground policy of "finders, keepers" rules the day. Acquisition is driven by power and money yes. But it is also driven by desire for a certain kind of intimacy, a relation. Ownership is a relationship with objects and with the person those objects *embody* in the word's most literal sense.

When trying to convince a writer or her family to sell a set of papers to the Ransom Center, the librarians emphasize, above all, the care those belongings will receive. They promise tireless attention. We will value these things as if they were our own. Watching librarians and scholars handle materials, hearing their stories of loss, witnessing their constant vigilance against the threat of carelessness, affirms my long-held suspicion that research, attention, and careful arrangement—the touch that allows everything to find its right place—are sure signs of unconditional love. There is satisfaction in housing, in placing. The books on their shelves, the manuscripts in their boxes, the personal effects nestled in tissue, and, on a larger scale, the security guards and heavy doors and card swipe elevators—all of these constructs hum with the energy of human devotion.

The clothes are the things that stick most with me. Mentally, that is, spiritually, perhaps, but of course not materially. Sometimes I miss them, miss having them within reach. I can look at the collections on-line, can see the digital photos I took, and I can even call them up in the Reading Room if I want, but I don't. I prefer to remember them as I encountered them, one-on-one. Gertrude Stein's beaded sleeping cap, Carson McCullers's pale green winter coat. In McCullers's collection I found a gold lamé, magenta-lined jacket with the Saks tags still attached. It isn't her typical style—she tended toward neutrals and primary colors, classic menswear silhouettes—and I wondered if the jacket was a gift, or if perhaps she bought it in a moment of trying to be someone else.

Closets are spaces to store our alternate identities. The objects and outfits in 7B expand and confound our oddly complete sense of the *person* behind a given proper name. They contradict what we think we know, surprise us, and in the process help us better relate to these unreachable people. There's something queer in our relationship to objects, or some queer potential in the space of that relationship. A love and an attachment outside the bounds of the normal. And, to me, the

353

quirks, the idiosyncrasies that a person's possessions reveal tend to make them anything but normal. If you look long enough at your own knickknacks or keepsakes, you, too, might start to question the possibility of normalcy.

Ian Woodward, glossing Jean Baudrillard, says we project "our own feelings onto a particular object that we use in order to be who we are," but that our need to do so comes from a psychological lack he describes as "cavernous." In Baudrillard's view it's all very pessimistic, because the objects can never satisfy that need. But what if they can? What if our relationships with objects in fact act on us, make us who are?

On that afternoon I spent alone with Einstein's model kit, I looked up at the personal effects shelves lined with meticulously labeled boxes and felt overwhelmed by the fact that it was all just stuff. And not even the Ransom Center's stuff, but other people's belongings crammed together in a room in the middle of Texas. Everything began to smell. The cold air began to reek of all these strangers'—dead strangers'—skin cells, pipe smoke, decay. The word *ephemera* took on a more desperate meaning. The highly systematized, rigid order the library tries to enforce revealed itself in that moment for the flimsy facade it really is, the shoddy but desperately maintained boundary between culture or knowledge or history and the basic physicality—the bodies—in which these abstract ideas are contained.

Why do we want to have these things? Why do we deserve access to them? Why does the institution want them; why do individuals want them? Why do we preserve them, touch them, catalog them, put them under glass, build gray, elaborate, eerily coffin-like containers for them?

Of course, there's the issue of mortality. We want these figures—the owners of these objects—to live on in some way; we want to preserve materials against the effects of time because it is one of the few ways we think we might control time. Temperature control it, in this case. But I'm more interested in *housing* than in memorializing. An archive is a living thing, a community of imagined people who reside together and interact and change and confound through each new encounter with their belongings. It's a big, strange family, and the people who work there perceive themselves to be a part of it. My strange intimacies with these collections, my daydream of donning McCullers's suit or Stein's embroidered vest—this is why I borrow loved ones' clothes and never return them, the reason I snoop with impunity.

Maybe this desire for communion, for identity—the *longing* in belongings—is what Walter Benjamin means when he says that collec-

354

tion is a renewal, acquisition a form of rebirth. And isn't it funny, the big lie at the heart of the enterpriser. All of this stuff is ultimately just that. No apparatus, no matter how meticulous or expensive or careful, can protect a collection from the inevitable slippages, losses, thefts, whether the perpetrators be people, bugs, mold, disintegration, or time. Acquire it, collect it, steal it, hoard it, conserve it, preserve it, store it, house it, box it, hold it, wear it, but there's just no keeping it.

Nominated by Tin House

HURRICANE SONG

by CECILY PARKS

from *O'NIGHTS* (ALICE JAMES BOOKS)

The pines dizzying for a hurricane, the wind
so hotly twirls their skirts and underskirts,
unnerves their pinecones, ratchets up and up
their branches into needle-spangled, needle-spraying
plumes. The white-running sunlight falls and tumbles
through the meadow, rattling the grass. The meadow
sweeps me up in its arms so that I lose track of east
and feel that little kidnapped thrill that comes with drastic
weather. O almost-wilderness, will the hurricane
hunt this far inland for our green juice? I guess
yes. The meadow guesses wet where it laps up
against the soft remnants of wall. The clouds guess wind
behind the swervy treetops. Blue jays vanish in the orchard's
green. A deer flips herself over and over, white tail-spark,
black hoof-sparks, brown wheel. The clouds
guess again: shadows blooming and wilting in the grass,
latticed branch-shadow mottling the road. The sound
of kisses increases through the forest, switchy sticks.
The forest has loved itself long enough to do this.
Is now when I should love myself into a safer place,
or is this the place where love makes me safe? I guess yes
and yes. Spastic gods, the grasshoppers manifest
on the margins of errant leaves and spring into bright
nothing. Where do they come from, where do they go?
The wild strawberries guess wind. The wind guesses wind.
The grass guesses grass, tossing all of us.

Nominated by Alice James Books

THINGS I KNOW
TO BE TRUE

fiction by KENDRA FORTMEYER

from ONE STORY

I am leaving the library when Miss Fowler stops me, peering through her glasses like they are windows in a house where she lives alone. She says, "Charlie, a patron saw you ripping up books."

"I didn't," I say. These words sound true, but Miss Fowler holds up *The Collected Works of Edgar Allan Poe.* Bits of paper flutter from its edges like snow.

I know a man in that book. He was trapped underground, dying in the dark and the antiquated language. He coughed then. He rustles in the pocket of my windbreaker now.

From elsewhere, Miss Fowler says, "Give me the pages."

"I am going to take him outside," I announce. I *declare. Declare* which is like *clarion call* which is of trumpets. "I am going to take him into the light."

"Look," Miss Fowler says. Her lips blow bubbles of words into the air: crisp, faceted ones like *replacement* and thin-filmed ones like *expensive.* She speaks to me like I am a child. Like *operations* can smooth these cracked, dark hands, like *damages* can topple the twenty-seven precarious years stacked in my name. I try to listen but my eyes jump to the rack of newspapers behind her, the small truths of their headlines swimming up like snakes: CARTER WINS DEMOCRATIC NOMINATIONS IN NY. MONTREAL PREPARES FOR 1976 OLYMPIC GAMES. NORTH, SOUTH VIETNAM PREPARE FOR REUNIFICATION.

Miss Fowler says *last chance*, her eyes blinking behind her glasses like she is drawing the curtains and they are a color she never particularly liked.

She says, "Give me the material or we're revoking your borrowing privileges."

It is the *we* that frightens me, because I can see Miss Fowler, but I cannot see the rest of *we*. They could be anywhere, plural.

Slowly, I draw the crumpled pages from my pocket, the clamshell edges glinting gold.

Miss Fowler waits until I put them in her hand, nose curling. She eyes my blue jacket, careful not to touch my skin.

"Thank you, Charlie," she says.

This is my day: I wake up. I make oatmeal. I eat my oatmeal, and I go to the library. I go to the library because it is full of words, and I trust words. They make things real.

Words like: this is my apartment. Like: I have lived here alone for eight months. Like: it is small, and dark, and the air conditioner is broken, and no one is on the other end to fix it when I call. All true. My sister Linda pays the rent, but we both agree that *this is my apartment*. The same way everyone agrees that *I can't live with Mother*, even though Mother says it's because I'm too grown-up to live at home and Linda says it's because Mother's a selfish drunk and then apologizes and looks exhausted.

Is it any wonder that I prefer words?

There is a list above my bedroom door. I do not remember making it, but it's in my handwriting. This is what it says:

> *These are the things that I know to be true:*
> *1. The past and future exist through stories*
> *2. Stories are made of words*
> *3. Words make the future and past exist*

This means: if I went to the VA clinic yesterday I can say, "I went to the clinic yesterday." Then there it is, in your head, like a real thing: a little image that is *me at the clinic*. I could also say, "I went to the zoo yesterday," and then that would be real in your head instead. You would not know the difference. I might not know the difference. I could believe the words *I went to the zoo* or I could believe the words *I went to the clinic*.

Maybe both are true.

It is some several tens of thousands of words later, on a dark night, a long winter, a little girl losing her mother, a retired detective taking on one last case. There is a body in a dumpster when I feel a touch on my shoulder.

"I thought we talked about this." It is Miss Fowler. Her words are the same but her voice is the word *truncheon*.

"Oh my God," I say. There is a hand lying on top of a McDonald's wrapper. Its fingernails are blue.

"Charlie," Miss Fowler says again. Then I look up and scream, because the hand is *on my shoulder on my shoulder* and suddenly Miss Fowler's face is far away shouting "Charlie! Charlie!" and all of the other faces are turning to see us, like too many small dark moons. The hand is gone from my shoulder and it is waving through the air and it is *attached to Miss Fowler* and I am screaming but the fingernails are pink and there is no dumpster and I am in the library and slowly I am breathing, breathing, calming.

There is a man standing in the doorway of the reading room. He is in a uniform. My muscles flinch to attention, and then down again. It is not the place or time. Linda is always saying those words, ever since I came back home. *Charlie, this is not the place or time.*

Miss Fowler holds a book with a woman on the cover, her face curling at the edges. "I told you, Charlie," Miss Fowler says. "We can't have you damaging any more books."

I look at the man in the uniform. I know the uniform is all I am supposed to see, but I can see his eyes, too, and they are full of pulling away.

"It was the fire," I say to the uniform man.

Miss Fowler asks, "What fire?" There are teeth in her voice.

"Her lover was burning alive," I say. "She couldn't stop it."

Miss Fowler looks pained. "So you tried to put it out."

"I did put it out." I turn back to my book *to the dumpster*, but Miss Fowler closes the book. Her mouth makes a line like a broken-down L. It is not a word whose shape I understand.

"No, you didn't, Charlie. What you did was run a book under the bathroom faucet because you read the word *fire*." She opens the book, points to a page. "Look, Charlie. *Fire. F-I-R-E.*" She rubs her finger on the page, and I wince. The word *smoke* floats past my eyelids and the back of my throat begins to burn. "See? No fire. Just four letters that won't go away, no matter how much water you pour on them."

359

Her fingers are beginning to smoke. I can see her pink nails turning black, and still she stares at me from behind the windows of her eyeglasses. She does not flinch.

"I'm sorry, Charlie," she says. Her hand is beginning to sear and crackle around the edges. There is a smell like bacon. I gag, eyes watering. Miss Fowler says, "I know it's hard for you to understand, but what's in here? It's fiction." The flames are eating her sleeve now. One of her fingernails peels off and lands on the floor where it writhes like an insect.

"Miss Fowler!" I say.

"And what's out here," she says, reaching towards me with a hand that is charred and bone, "is the real world."

"Stop it!" I shriek. "Stop! Stop!" I lunge through the fire that is eating her alive. There are flames dancing on the lenses of Miss Fowler's horned glasses and behind them, something dawns in her eyes. Then my hand is on the book, and I can feel it singeing the pads of my fingertips as it sails across the room, arcing through the stacks like a firefly in the dark. My panic follows the book for a moment *it will burn the library down* but Miss Fowler is standing there next to me, and her skin is blackening and shriveling like a fungus. I know somewhere deep down that it won't do any good *her burns are too bad it's too late* but I tackle her to the ground, beating her with my coat, trying to put out the fire that's everywhere, everywhere. People are shouting. The uniform man has left the doorway. He is beside me now, and he is holding my arms behind my back.

"Miss Fowler!" I howl. "Miss Fowler!"

"All right, buddy, that's enough out of you," the uniform man says and hauls me towards the door.

I don't want to go, but pain shoots through my shoulder and I stumble forward. "Miss Fowler!" I cry.

I hear her voice say, "Thank you, Robert," and I twist around. Miss Fowler looks tired, terrified, bedraggled. But soft and clean and whole.

"You're alive!" I shout to her. The man in the uniform is dragging me towards the door and my shoulder is crying in unwritten language, but I cannot stop staring, marveling at Miss Fowler's wholeness. "I saved you," I say. "You're alive!"

The man in uniform pushes me through the door. "Wait," I say. My feet turn to syrup on the floor, dragging. I do not want to leave this house of words. Miss Fowler watches me go. Her mouth looks like the word *sorry*.

The uniform man does not wait. The uniform man has no pity. He pushes me out into the dazzling sunlight.

Then we get into his car and go to the police station.

I spend one afternoon and part of a night in jail. They make me take off my belt and give them my wallet. There is nothing inside but a library card and a feather I found on a park bench. The feather is blue. The jail cell is gray like bad teeth and the word *granularity*.

There are two men in the cell with me: one in a corner saying quiet, angry things, and another who just sleeps. The angry man rushes the door when I come in, and I fall backward against the uniform who shouts HEY HEY HEY and the angry man backs off, still saying angry things into the air, eyes jumping from one mildew-stained wall to the other. My heart and I stumble over to the opposite side of the cell, where the sleeping man sleeps on the concrete floor. His army shirt is vomit-stained and his beard is scraggly and his skin has been beaten into submission by the sun. I sink down by the toilet, biting the fleshy part of my hand. I try to tell myself this is *jail* instead of *prison* but it's unfurling in my brain like a fire ant sting. The past and future are made of stories *of words* so I tell myself don't give words to this. Don't give words to this. Don't give it any words.

My sister Linda comes down from Richmond, a two-hour drive that takes three with Nixon's new speed limit. She signs her name for my freedom at the maroon desk. Her face looks like it was in the middle of a wash cycle when she got the call—still damp and rumpled, half-wrung out. The policemen give me my wallet and jacket back. Linda has my keys. She makes a face when she sees my windbreaker.

"You're still wearing that ratty thing?" She looks me over, checking face, teeth. "Mom would have a conniption. What happened to that sweater she sent?"

I shrug, zip the coat up to my chin. Cloaked in a windbreaker, I cannot be broken. It smells like safety, and me.

They let Linda take me home. She ties a kerchief around her hair and lights a cigarette before starting her car which is a Dodge Dart.

Her husband Lewis is not with her, which makes me happy because I do not like Lewis. He laughs at things that are not funny, and he makes too much money to be nice. One year on Thanksgiving he brought me some pamphlets that made Linda mad: they said *Institutional Living Facility*. Linda threw them in the garbage. She said, "Dr. Schaefer said he's making progress." She said, "For God's sake, can't you give him some time to recover?" My mother said nothing and only poured herself another drink. Lewis said, "It's been six years." And, "We're paying too much for that damn apartment." And, "He not okay, he's *crazy*." Those words have kept knocking around in my skull. When I try to imagine myself striding into the future, I trip over them like stones.

Linda and I walk through the front door of my apartment. There are library books everywhere—books on the floor, on the sofa, lining the halls like yellowed border guards. Linda wrinkles her nose.

"Can I get you something to eat?" I ask, because I remember that that's what you're supposed to do when people come to your house. I hope she won't say yes because I don't have anything except a can of SpaghettiOs, and I would like to eat it myself. But Linda shakes her head.

"I ate on the road," she says. "Stopped at a McDonald's. Jesus, Charlie."

She starts to laugh, stops, then gives up and laughs anyway. I laugh too, politely, though I'm starting to wish she would leave.

She wipes her eyes. "It's not funny," she says.

"Okay," I agree.

Linda sits on my armchair and digs her finger into the stuffing. Her finger looks like a pink worm that cannot escape from her hand. "Why did you attack that librarian?" she says at last.

"I didn't," I say, feeling uncomfortable. I don't remember attacking anybody. But there are the words: *You. Attack.* "Did I?" I ask, trying to sound casual.

She stares at me. "The librarian at Cameron Village," she says. "Mrs. Fuller."

"Miss Fowler," I say automatically. And then, "She was on fire." Saying this makes me feel better. I think this will make Linda proud of me, but she looks at the sofa instead, at the little worm of her finger. It writhes in the Styrofoam innards of my couch.

"Charlie," Linda says. Her voice sounds tired, like it used to when we were kids and she was tired of playing whatever game we were playing. "I can't drive down here every time you get into trouble."

"Okay," I say.

"The woman's not pressing charges, though Lord knows she could," Linda says. "You got off easy. Not even a fine. They just banned you from the library. All the county libraries, actually."

I blink. I am just banned.

Banned: *officially or legally prohibited.*

Just: *guided by truth, reason, fairness.*

My mind races.

"For how long?" I say in a voice that is tight and high and not mine.

Linda shakes her head. "It's not a 'for how long' type of deal, hon," she says. "That's it. You're out."

My lips work, but there are no words.

The worm disappears from my sofa as Linda rises. She takes me in her arms. Her eyes are hurting for me, and blue.

"I'm sorry, sweetie," she says. "You're just going to have to handle it the best you can, okay?" She rocks me in her arms. She smells like french fry oil and Virginia Slims. "You're going to be okay. You'll find a new hobby. All right?"

It is strange how everything in the room looks exactly the same while my world slides slowly sideways.

I try not to watch as Linda packs up all of my library books. The fat classic editions. The dog-eared paperbacks. The worlds I know so inside and out that no card catalog in the world can make them not mine. I eat my SpaghettiOs and focus hard on all the new words I can make: *flavormouth, redsauce.* I try to make new words, new small truths, because if I do, I can make this moment into one where I am not twenty-seven years old and trying not to cry.

Linda promises to drop my books off at the library on her way back to Richmond. She asks if I want to come and live with her and Lewis, but I shake my head. I wish my sister would stay with me here, and we could move back again with Mother and things would be just like they were before my hands grew cracks, and when Mother could still look at me without flinching away and talking too loud.

Linda presses some money into my hand, but I make my hand limp, and so she leaves the bills on an empty bookshelf before kissing me a kiss that is goodbye.

I wonder if Linda would still come see me if she weren't called *sister*. I wonder if the light would still fade if there weren't a word *night*.

It is a long, cold couple of weeks.

This is my day: I wake up. I make my oatmeal, and I eat my oatmeal. My feet still want to take me to the library at first, and I have to fight them. "We are going somewhere new today, feet," I say, and a little girl stares at me. I pull my blue windbreaker tight and drag my body north.

I walk a new direction every day, until I do not recognize anyone or anything. Only the letters are the same, on street signs and in newspaper boxes, everything everywhere draped in red-white-and-blue. It is America's Bicentennial. Bi, meaning *two*. Centennial, meaning *hundred years*. 1776 and 1976.

The flags in shop windows and lawns twinkle like clues to another world where everything is truer and brighter and nothing is denied to me. Where *Oakwood Ave.* is green like meadows and bobbing in the wind, and *Peace St.* is not a place where car horns wail and men sleep with their feet on the sidewalks. This outside world makes me ill. Nothing makes sense. I come back to my apartment at the end of the day and feel I cannot trust anything.

I have no books left. None: *not any, not at all, not one*. I read what is left: cereal boxes, warning labels, my life delineated into *fat* or *iron*, *blindness* or *death*. I try to read the shapes carved into the popcorn ceiling by the streetlights outside, and everything swims.

My eyes feel like they are starving.

Dr. Schaefer says I should write new stories. Dr. Schaefer says I can choose what is in them. "You get to invent yourself now, Charlie," he says. "Pick the person you want to be. That's what happens in America. You get to start over."

I try to explain to him *go to the clinic* or go *to the zoo*. He smiles enormously with an exclamation point. "That's it precisely!" he exclaims. "Do you want to be Charlie who is sick and sorry for himself, or Charlie who has fun? Tell me, Charlie, where would you rather go?"

I say, "The library."

Dr. Schaefer nods *yes* but his forehead is scrunched *no*. He lights a cigarette. He sucks the end and blows out smoke.

He says, "You don't need the library, Charlie. The library was an escape. Think of this as an opportunity. You've got a talent with words. You could go back to school. Journalism. Maybe advertising. Have you thought about that?"

"No," I say.

Dr. Schaefer reaches for my chart. "The old you is gone," he says. I want to ask how to make the library ban *gone*, but he does not have time to hear what I want. Instead he takes a green, spiral-bound notebook from his desk and puts it into my hands. He says, "Now is the time to write the new story of you."

That night, I try to write the story of myself. I use the green notebook. All of the words jumble in my head, with no order to them. I keep my mouth pursed up in a small *O*, so that only one sound can come out at a time. I write with a ruler, so everything stays straight, but nothing helps. Too many letters, too many lines. Here and there a sentence pokes out, and it is like a small miracle: *This is my day.*

I tear out the pages. Being mine doesn't make a story worth telling.

At night, I dream of paper leaves and trees made of fire.

Once, I forget a word. I am on my way to the bathroom and *I think I am going ____ the bathroom* and suddenly it is gone. The word means: move in the direction of something. Closer. Move at something. I panic, because without the word, how can I move? How can I do what I cannot say? I lie on the floor with my bladder aching and want to cry until there is a whisper in my mind like angels that says *toward*. And I know how to move forward again. This is not the me I want to make.

I have to find new words.

I do not know what day it is, or what time, when I get a phone call from Mother. She says, "Charlie, dear." She calls me once a month, usually. Sometimes she forgets and two months go by but that is okay because she is very busy. It takes a lot of time to have an adult son. There is so much more of me to take care of.

"How have you been?" she asks.

"Fine," I say. This means *small* and *slippery* and *falling through the cracks*.

We talk about her bridge club and her church. We talk about if Linda will ever have children. Then Mother says, "Linda called last week. She told me you're not allowed to go to the library anymore."

Oh. I fiddle with my fingers. They are out of key. "I was banned," I say.

Banned. Brand. A stigma stamped in my skin.

Mother sniffs. "They sent you over there, and now they want you to be invisible. I think it's sick. Denying a man the right to read. But that's what we get, electing a Democratic governor."

I do not know the answer to the questions she isn't asking, but I barely care. My mind is whirling. *A man the right to read.*

"Mother, I love you," I say.

"Thank you, Charlie," she says, and sounds surprised.

We hang up, and I lie on the couch, seeing nothing, mind singing *a man the right a man the right a man invisible the right to read*. And me humming with it, because I figured it out:

If I go to a new library, nobody will know me.

And: If they do not know who I am, they cannot make me leave the library.

I stay up late at night, thinking about this until my head hurts.

I walk the next day to the CAT bus station, and I purchase a 30-day pass. It uses up nearly all of the money that Linda sent with her last letter, but I cannot make myself care. I have never been good with numbers anyway.

I climb on the bus. The bus rattles. Inside of me, my organs rattle. I am afraid of being caught and turned away, but the bus driver doesn't even look at me as I fumble with my bus pass. He looks at the numbers printed on it and finally he says, like he is surprised that I am still there, "Sit down, son." I sit. I am so grateful that I smile at every person on the bus. It is my thank-you to them for being alive on the day that I get my world back.

The new library is in a shopping center. At first I think I am making a mistake, but the driver says no, this is the North Hills branch. The cars in the parking lot shimmer in the heat. By the time I get inside, through the glass doors and into the air conditioning, sweat has stuck my windbreaker to my back.

A librarian looks up when I step into the library, and every nerve in my body shrieks. I duck my head, turn blindly left. I end up in the children's area. A new librarian looks up at me. She frowns. Before she can speak, I plunge left, and left again. I feel dizzy, and the walls lean out at odd angles. *We know you Charlie you are not supposed to be here Charlie you'll hurt us drown us burn us Charlie Charlie Charlie.*

Then suddenly the space opens up around me. I am in a place I recognize: *Reading Room.*

The air is quiet. Other patrons float by like fish, weaving in and out of the stacks in earthy colors. I go to a table. I put down my bag and breathe a soft sigh. Then I go to the stacks like that is exactly where I am supposed to be, and I begin to pull down books.

I know better than to try my library card. If they find out who I am, they will make me leave, and then I will be empty again, my shelves empty, no words left to me and mine.

But now I know how to keep the words.

At my table I take Dr. Schaeffer's green notebook from my bag and begin to copy the first book. Word. By. Word. It is slow going, and my hand starts to hurt, but I don't stop. The library begins to darken and empty, and when the first closing announcement bursts through the intercom, I drop my book and scuttle out the door. In my old library, Miss Fowler used to have to come and make me leave, but here I am afraid of being recognized. So I go home before anyone can lay a kindly hand on my shoulder like a little white bird and sing, "We're closing, Charlie. Closing time."

On the bus I smile the whole way home because my world has come back, and this is so true that one lady even smiles back at me.

I get home with my notebook. I put my notebook on the table and think about all of the things I could do that are not reading my notebook: *Eat soup. Go to the bathroom. Go . . .* but the words get blurred in my head in a kind of hunger, and before I can help myself I have the notebook in my hand.

I open it to the first page, and the paper crinkles a little. My eyes swim for a moment in the glory of words: all the lines and shapes and letters that say a million different things and all belong to me. My own book. I almost do not understand what to do with it.

But then I begin to read, and that is when my heart breaks. Because I know all of these words already. Because I read them all already. When I was copying them down.

There is a dark feeling building and building in my chest, so hard and sharp-edged that it pushes the notebook out of my hands. I bite down on my forearm like they taught us, to *don't make a fucking sound* when you see something you don't want to see, like someone's head blown away or their guts hanging out over their knees. I bite into my own flesh and bone, and in the biting my mouth is full and there are no words and there are too many.

I wake up. I eat my oatmeal and don my blue windbreaker. I go back to the North Hills Branch and do not turn left.

I pick a new book and begin again. When I realize that I am reading the book too much, I begin to hum in my head, to keep my mind completely blank so that my hand can copy now and my mind can read later. I hum a song called the *1812 Overture*. It loops in my mind, all brightness and fireworks and triumph.

I work for a long time at my table and nobody bothers me. I even get up to go to the bathroom, and as I pass by the desk, there are no lingering looks, no pointed questions punctuated "Charlie?" I go to the bathroom and come back to my table and embrace my newfound identity of *nobody*.

On the bus home, two people smile back.

At home I take out my notebook and I begin to read. And there, in my stilted handwriting, a beautiful first sentence: *For a long time, I went to bed early*.

I read until the light drains from the room.

I finish one book and start another. Chapter by chapter, I rewrite myself. In Agatha Christie, in Marcel Proust, in Kurt Vonnegut, in Richard Bach. The covers are luscious, titles cool and ripe on my tongue. I glut myself in ink, stained to the knuckles. Time passes in pages and in dried-up pens.

It is late and what they call a Tuesday. I have been working on *Cannery Row* for the last several weeks, and am nearly complete. I place the period at the end of the second-to-last chapter, close my notebook. My hands are cracked but strong.

I zip up my blue jacket and stand ready to leave, when a voice says, "Excuse me. Are you Charles Harrison?" and I jump.

She has the right soft voice of a librarian. Also the glasses. Also the cardigan sweater.

She has hair that is colored like sunsets and freckles flung in a star scape across the planes of her face.

I have never seen her before. She should not know my name.

"Please," I say softly. I am caught. I want to hide, to go to earth, but I have no earth, just this word: "Please."

"I thought it might be you," she says. "I have something for you. Hold on, I'll go get it, all right?"

I am *banned caught in trouble* tearing into two. Two syllables. Dismay, consent. "Oh," I say, and, "kay."

She beams, a spill of light. "Just wait right here."

I stand a second, a minute, unsure. *She caught me she didn't seem angry how does she know it was me she's pretending she's going to call the police she's going to going to call the police.* My feet drag on the tile. The second hand drags across the clock face.

I will wait. She smiled. It is safe. I will wait.

I wait twenty seconds exactly. Then I bolt out the door.

I lie in bed a long time the next day, trying to find meaning in the bumps and shadows of the ceiling. I am trying not to think about *Cannery Row*, or about the way I feel when I am reading it. Like everything was wrong and now I am in a room full of music and laughter.

I cannot go back to the library. It is not safe anymore.

But.

I climb on the bus and tell myself I am just going for a ride. My pass expires tomorrow. I may as well enjoy it. See the sights. I smile at everyone and it is such a good day that four people smile back and one person says hello. I feel like a true American citizen.

(I get off at the library.)

I duck my head and go straight for the reading room. I find *Cannery Row* behind the plant where I left it, and I keep my head down. I scrawl and I scrawl and I scrawl, waiting at any moment to feel the hand on my shoulder. *Where were you? You ran away! You're a criminal! You've been banned! You can't be here! Security!*

Two pages left. One. I write the final words: *And. Behind. The. Glass.*

The. Rattlesnakes. Lay. Still. And. Stared. Into. Space. With. Their. Dusty. Frowning. Eyes.

I fling my notebook into my bag and dash for the door. I catch a blush of autumn in my periphery, and my steps do not falter. I vanish into the white afternoon light.

You believed me, didn't you? You saw me in your brain, vanishing. Which means that for one minute it was true, and now it exists, and will be true forever.

But what also happened is this:

Doc is washing glasses carefully because there is beautiful music and he is afraid of spoiling it when somebody sits down across from me and puts something on the table. The somebody is the red-haired librarian. The something is a crumpled yellow envelope.

"You ran away yesterday," she says.

"I'm sorry," I say. "I forgot."

She knows I am lying and I think she likes me a little less now. But she gives me the envelope anyway. There is a book inside, so stained and ugly and battered that the title is rubbed off its broken spine.

But I know this book. I would know it anywhere.

I want to push my chair back from the table, but I can't move. I see faces smiling frowning shouting and I see jungle so thick that I'm afraid my eyelashes have grown up over my eyes.

"This book," I say through the jungle, "is gone."

The librarian does not understand. She gives a tentative smile. "I found this Joseph Heller mixed in with a large bundle of returns," she says. "I thought someone had taken notes in the margins. And then I read what you had written and I thought . . . well, I thought you might like to have it back."

She reaches across the table and opens the cover and there is my name in red crayon. Written in my own handwriting. The pages flutter like crazed butterflies. I look down and see through the high whine in my ears that my hands are cracked and through the cracks I see names. Jimmy Metcalfe. Lucas Johnson. I see the way the light reflects on the water where they found that girl bathing. I see the song Joe Crispin played on his guitar in Quang Tri, and how it got stuck in everyone's head for days, and we changed the words so many times that no one remembered the original. And how a month later, out of the blue, Soup came busting up singing *your cheese is straight from hell* and Joe laughed so hard he shot bug juice out his nose. I see C-Rations and finger necklaces curled like shrimp. I see all of us tired, and hot, twenty-one and younger, and breathing Jimmy Metcalfe's farts all morning on patrol, through jungle leaves thick as eyelashes. And I see the way the air gleamed pink after Jimmy stepped onto the mine—the tiny click and then the sky blown apart and the whole world set singing, flashing white in the sun, pieces of flesh against the green like cherry blossoms in the first light of spring: so pink and bright that your heart rips in half at the beauty.

One half says, *the trees are on fire.*

The other half says, *the trees are not on fire.*

Maybe both are true.

I see this book inside Jimmy's pack and then me taking it and writing down these words, a story hidden inside another story. I see the pages fill while the doctors patched up my leg and the skin scabbed over on my arm. I see the hospital bed with the ringing fading from my ears and my leg itching and burning and stinking in its cast. I see the medical review when no one in the room would look at me straight, and the smell in the air from the bed-wetters was so thick you could cut it with a knife. And I see the book on a plane, carried all the way home until I landed on American soil, and that chapter ended and I closed it.

But then, here it is. On the table. In the library. And here I am.

"This book is gone," I say again.

"No," the librarian says, slowly. "It was just misplaced."

I think, *This is not the place or time.*

"How did you know it was me?" I ask.

"We had a regional staff meeting at the beginning of the month," she says. "Your name came up. There was a photo." Simple as that. She does not say: *you are a criminal.* Does not say: *you attacked Miss Fowler.* Just. You came up. Like a flower.

I push away from the table. "I am going to go home now."

"It's okay," she says. "You can stay."

"I am going to go home," I say again, and leave.

I do not smile at anybody on the bus. At the corner, I throw my *Cannery Row* notebook into the trashcan. No matter how hard I read and how hard I write, it seems like I can only have one story, after all.

I try to do everything right. I wait until the sun goes down. I light the lights. I close the curtains, so that the echoes of me are not in the window. I sit across the room from the book that won't let me go and wonder how long it is before the words harden back into truth.

In her last card to me Linda wrote, *Have you thought about keeping a journal like Dr. Schaefer said?* I look at the card, alone on the empty bookshelf. On the front is a chicken wishing me an Egg-cellent Day.

"I can't write me down again," I say to the chicken.

I pretend the chicken can answer. It says, *But you can write any story you want. You can make the words.*

The chicken sounds like Linda. I want to make her happy but I know that I can't. All I want is to be gone, like the book was supposed to be gone. Then I see the list above my door. *The Things I Know To Be True.*

I detach it from the wall and try not to look at my hands.

I write: *Charlie didn't go to war, and he didn't kill anybody.*

And his mother let him come home again.

And his sister lived there too and they went to the movies together.

It was Superman.

And Charlie had a good car.

And a library card.

And he was never hungry again.

I sit and wait for those words to become truth, and my stomach rumbles. I underline, *never hungry*, but it rumbles again and my world blurs. I shred the list into pieces so small that they slip through my fingers like water, spilling onto the bare floor and down over my dry and rootless feet.

This is where the story ends. But.

The sun comes up again the next day. The sun always comes up again. It doesn't know when to quit, maybe because it doesn't speak any language that can tell it *no*.

So I get up. I make my oatmeal. I eat my oatmeal, and I go to the bus stop. The bus driver looks at my 30-day pass and shakes his head at me.

"Sorry," he says to the zipper of my windbreaker. "This expired yesterday. You've got to go get a new ticket. Sir," he says. "Sir?"

But I am not listening. I am looking past him at all the people on the bus, their feet secure in boots, their faces as closed as books on a shelf. The whole bus of unwritten words humming, waiting, sentences strung out in infinite lines across the city. Carefully, I shred my ticket. I shred the expiration date into pieces. Then I find a seat and wait to be carried, like everyone else, into some bright and not-yet-written future.

Nominated by One Story, Nancy Richard

FORGOTTEN SOUND

by MELISSA BRODER

from TIN HOUSE

I pretended the lust was voices
And I wrote down the voices
And sometimes the voices spoke as I had written them
To confirm what I already knew
Which is that I am a child and ready for petting
And sometimes the voices said nothing
To confirm what I already knew
Which is that I am filled with holes
And sometimes the voices spoke in tongues
To confirm what I did not know
Which is that I am a ghost
And the men are real
And going on without me

Nominated by Tin House

AFTER READING PETER BICHSEL

fiction by LYDIA DAVIS

from THE PARIS REVIEW

Last spring and summer, I was reading the stories of the Swiss writer Peter Bichsel. I began reading them in Vienna. The little book—a hardcover, but small and lightweight—was a gift from a German friend at the start of my trip, to provide me with something to read in German, since I wanted to improve my facility in the language. I had brought with me from home a paperback thriller by a very popular German writer, but I wasn't enjoying it: the plot, so far, was tiresome, the main character unpleasant, and the tone sarcastic. My friend thought she could find something better for me, and she was right. I continued reading Bichsel's stories on the train from Vienna to Salzburg, and then in Salzburg, and then on the train to Zurich, and then in Zurich, Berlin, Hamburg, and Cologne, and on each train I took to go from one city to the next.

In fact, Peter Bichsel regularly writes about reading and about train journeys. He will also sometimes begin a story, or remark in the middle of a story, "There are stories that are hardly worth telling," or "There is almost nothing to say about X," and then sometimes follow that with a "but": "But I have wanted to tell this story for a long time now," or "But it has to be told, because it was the first story in my life, the first one that I remember ." He then goes on to tell a lovely, quiet, modest story, a story that glows with human kindness, or love, or some combination of compassion, understanding, and honesty. (Or am I, these days, finding this quality so marked in his stories because I am seeking it?)

I was reading his stories as I traveled, but I was also distracted by all that I saw and experienced, so that I did not often think about his stories when I was not reading them. But then I particularly thought of him and his stories after an experience I had in Salzburg. I wanted to describe this experience, but I wanted to say, near the beginning of my story, that there was not much to tell, because, really, so little happened: there was a scene, one that involved a peculiar character, and later a coincidence.

I had stopped for lunch at a small, undistinguished restaurant that I had picked out earlier in the day, on my way through the town and across the river to find Mozart's birthplace. It looked to me like a reliable sort of local place, without pretensions, not expensive, not particularly attractive to tourists, but frequented by locals. Its entrance was set back from the main street and it was called Café Central. Rain was falling in the street outside, and the umbrella stand inside the door was filled with wet umbrellas. The coat tree was hung with damp jackets and slickers. The colors of the place were strikingly tan, brown, and cream. The first part of the room, where one entered, contained the bar and was partitioned off from the main room to serve bar customers at small tables. A shelf along the top of the partition held stacks of folded newspapers and magazines for the customers.

The place was quite crowded, though not yet entirely full, and noisy, since this was the height of the lunch hour. A buxom, energetic woman who seemed to be the manager or co-owner of the place showed me to a cramped spot in a line of little tables against one wall, but after she went away, and after a moment's hesitation, I got up and walked on back to look for a more comfortable spot. I found a roomier and more peaceful seat in the far corner, at a small table between two tables already occupied. To my left was a large corner table surrounded by banquettes, and to my right, a small table for two, identical to my own.

At the large table were seated a man and a woman, evidently a couple, though for a long time they did not speak to each other. The man was calmly and very thoroughly reading a newspaper, and the woman was sitting completely still beside him and gazing off into the distance with a placid and agreeable expression on her face. I am left with the impression, now, that the man was Asian, though I can't be sure of this. The woman was not. Try as I may to retrieve a more exact image of the man's face, there is no more memory available to me and I cannot do it. It is not relevant to the story, anyway, but this vague impression adds to my sense of the difference or disparity between the two of them, though they seemed comfortable and companionable.

It was the woman at the table to my right who came to interest me the most during that lunch hour, although at first, in my preoccupation with settling into my seat, putting my bag down beside me, bringing out something to read, and looking around to take in the sights and sounds of the room, I did not pay particular attention to her. It was only as I became used to my surroundings, having examined the features of the room, the customers in my part of it—the larger part—and those beyond the partition, having absorbed the particular characteristic sights and sounds of this place and taken note of any more unusual features or occupants, that my attention was more and more drawn to my neighbor.

I had ample time to observe her, as well as the others in the restaurant, because, although the young waitress and the older manager both kept rushing back and forth without a pause among the tables, taking orders and carrying food, my order was very slow in coming—thirty minutes, forty minutes. Since I was tired from my long morning of wandering through the streets of the older parts of Salzburg on this side of the river and across the bridge on the other side, stopping to read plaques and look into shop windows, crossing back over the bridge, I did not mind waiting.

The woman to my right was perhaps in her fifties—it was hard to tell. She was a large woman, though of moderate weight, tall and broad-shouldered, in build like a man, and dressed in such workaday clothes that her purse seemed incongruously feminine: plain pants and sturdy shoes and a T-shirt with some message on it that I eventually identified as pro–European Union. Her hair was short and curly and rather disordered, pressed down in one part and standing up in another. She wore glasses of no particular style, and these gave her a somewhat serious or studious look.

What drew my attention first, and then repeatedly, was the speed with which she was eating. She had ordered some kind of a chicken dish—chicken drumsticks with a pile of white rice. I later decided that it had to be one of the specials of the day, available for a good price. All her motions were quick, perhaps twice the normal speed of a person consuming a restaurant meal, even one at an inexpensive lunch place. She manipulated her utensils, wielded her knife and fork, one in each hand, constantly, industriously, and busily, her elbows out to the sides. She chewed fast and swallowed fast. Some of her motions were neat,

377

as when she cleaned a drumstick of its flesh and piled the bone at one edge of her plate, alongside another bare bone. But sometimes she overshot her aim, so that rice spilled off the edge of her plate. She would quickly reposition a drumstick to present a different angle for cutting and occasionally give the plate a little spin to reach another drumstick or gain better access to the pile of rice. Spin, stab, slice, open mouth, receive forkful of food, chew, swallow; spin, stab, slice, etc.

After I had watched her eat for a few minutes, I noticed that she had, to her right, in front of her, facing her, and increasing my sense of the urgency with which she was eating—or more than urgency, the frantic haste—a small round-faced travel alarm clock. And yet, through the course of her lunch, she did not otherwise seem in a hurry to finish her lunch and leave the place. She paused sometimes to read her newspaper, and later to make a note in a notebook.

Her newspaper was folded and laid on the table in front of her. She looked at it from time to time or picked it up and refolded it. I had my own paper, though it was a different kind of paper, a literary weekly, also folded and laid where I could read it, though I did not read it, being too interested in the people around me. She and I may have been sitting on the same banquette that ran the length of the wall, because I remember that she had room to keep her purse next to her, and so did I. Beyond her, the row of little tables continued as far as the partition.

I noticed her purse because at one point she pulled a notebook out of it and then began searching through it for a pen, again moving hastily, now scrabbling wildly in its depths, pulling it closer to her, lifting it onto the table the better to search. When she did not find a pen, she looked up and around at the people near her, including those in my direction, and asked us all generally if anyone could lend her a pen. I hesitated, waiting for someone else to offer. I had been writing in my own notebook, though I had put it and my pen away. I did not want to lend her a pen, even though I had more than one.

The man who had been reading the newspaper, and who was by then, though still silent, sharing a dessert of palatschinken with his wife, eating from the same plate, lent her his pen, passing it to her by way of the elderly woman who was now sitting across from me. Once she had the pen, my fast-paced neighbor bent far over, bringing her nearsighted eyes close to the page, and began writing, again with quick motions, in her notebook.

The elderly woman across from me had made her way to my little table because the other seats in the restaurant were by this time all occupied. She had asked me if the seat opposite me was free, and I had nodded and said it was. I probably said only, *"Ja,"* because although I could understand some of what was said to me in German, I could not reply in very elaborate or idiomatic sentences.

The elderly woman had ordered her meal, which I saw, when it came, was the same plate of chicken drumsticks and rice as my neighbor to the right. My new tablemate, before her meal arrived, watched soberly and intently as I ate my own meal, which had at last been brought to me, not long after she had sat down. She watched me for a little while and then asked me, still soberly and intently, whether that was a slice of ham or a slice of fish. I said it was fish and then, remembering the words on the menu, I reproduced them fairly accurately, I thought, specifying that it was smoked salmon. She thought about that while she continued to watch me eat, and then she asked, still unsmiling, and not as though she were making polite conversation but rather as though she simply wanted certain information, how did I suppose they smoked the salmon. I barely caught the meaning of her question, and I forgot—though I remembered later—how to say the useful and emphatic phrase I often overheard people saying on this trip, which was *"Keine Ahnung!"* meaning "No idea!" so I merely smiled and shrugged to indicate that I didn't know.

Our conversation died, her meal came, and she in turn lowered her head and tackled her rice and chicken, at a steady speed but in a methodical, tidy manner.

For a time, I felt that we five, in that corner of the restaurant—the silent but contented married couple, who had now finished their palatschinken and returned to their former activities, he reading his newspaper, she gazing at the room; my new table partner with her pale wrinkled face, her little bun of white hair, her somber curiosity; my large-framed energetic neighbor to the right with her firmly planted feet, her wheeling elbows, and her alarm clock; and I—were an odd group, and in our variety reminded me, more than anything, of a group of the more harmless patients on a mental ward at mealtime, each with his or her own difficulty in the face of the food.

In time, the fast eater—who, for all her speed, had not outpaced the elderly woman—was finished with her lunch, and the elderly woman was also finished, and they both paid their bills. The elderly woman handled the transaction easily and decisively, naming the amount the waitress should take—a little more than the price of the meal—and the fast eater in a state of slight confusion, holding the money on her palm and letting the waitress help her to count it out. My elderly tablemate slipped unobtrusively into her beige raincoat, picked up her purse, and left the restaurant quietly while most of my attention was on my fast neighbor.

Her preparations to leave were quite elaborate, especially compared to those of my tablemate. After standing up from the banquette and moving out into the room, where there was more space for maneuvering, she quite openly and unself-consciously zipped and fastened her pants, which she had evidently undone for greater comfort while eating. She then stowed her clock and notebook in her purse—she had earlier returned the pen, passing it to me to give to the Asian man. She next started off down among the tables to return her newspaper to the shelf at the far end of the room but turned back when she remembered that it was her own. Nearly back at her table, she stopped the manager and said something to her and remained standing there waiting. The manager went away and came back with a date book and they conferred over the pages. Perhaps the manager was reserving a table for the next day, though that seemed odd to me in a casual lunch place such as this. Or perhaps they were making some other kind of appointment, though I couldn't imagine what that would be. She then went into one of the restrooms, whose doors were opposite our tables, and came out again. Finally she put on her rain jacket and took up her purse, nodded left and right to her neighbors, saying good-bye, made her way back down among the tables, and disappeared out the door.

I was left wondering about the open datebook, and the appointment, and more generally about her. What kind of appointment? What was she doing? Who was she? Did she live here in this town or was she visiting? She seemed very familiar with the place, she did not seem like a visitor, she was not dressed like a visitor. I thought she was a local person who liked to eat lunch here. And yet the manager and waitress did not seem to know her, as they would have known a regular customer. Or perhaps they knew her but preferred to keep their distance from her.

The quiet couple still sat quietly, now both looking out into space, still blandly pleasant and calm.

After a long afternoon of walking up and down more streets, venturing into the front halls and up the stairs of private houses that interested me because of their age or their conformation, climbing up and then back down the steps cut into the rock face leading to the Capuchin monastery, crossing the river again and walking on uphill through the Domplatz and into the vast Residenzplatz, where a Nazi book burning had taken place, stopping to read the plaque, which included a good quote from Heinrich Heine about burning books, running under a sudden downpour to the archway of the museum of the city of Salzburg, entering the museum to see the famous nineteenth-century painted panorama of the city, buying, in the gift shop, a piece of reddish salt rock from the Salzburg mine, continuing downhill to Mozart's birthplace and visiting every room of every floor of the house, pausing to stand for a while in the room in which he was born, returning over the river to see the larger and grander house in which his family had lived later in his childhood, walking through the vast ballroom of that house, in which dance classes had been held, I was tired as evening approached. The museums were closing, dinnertime loomed, and I needed to make the important decision of where to eat.

Some acquaintances with whom I had been sitting the evening before, late into the night, on a café terrace that looked out over a broad, dark, leafy street of apartment buildings, had made several suggestions, each accompanied by a good deal of discussion, and I had written them all carefully down. But now I was tired, and my mood was not exalted, as it had been the night before, and I no longer had the ambition or resolve to walk back into the heart of the city and find one of those restaurants. I wanted to return to my hotel, which was some distance away in the opposite direction, and I wanted to rest and then stay there.

Perhaps my acquaintances had told me the hotel restaurant was itself quite good, or perhaps when I returned to the hotel, tired, to await the hour for dinner, I looked at the menu posted outside the door to the restaurant and decided it would be good enough. In any case, after resting in my room for a short time, until the earliest moment I could go down, I went back down and into the restaurant.

But there, I found that the main dining room, at the back, had been reserved for a large tour group. I was told, as I stood by the long bar of the restaurant, that I could still eat in the restaurant, but I would have to eat there in the barroom—the ample room in which we were talking. I looked around. It had a mirrored wall, wooden chairs, many wooden tables covered with red-and-white-checked tablecloths, and a row of windows facing the street. It did not seem as calm and comfortable as

381

the room I had imagined, but if I could eat from the regular dinner menu, I did not mind. I thought it might even be interesting. I sat down at a table against the wall and opposite the entrance, where I could see the whole room. I took out the same literary weekly I had had with me at lunch, and I settled down to enjoy the peaceful interval of waiting, first, to order a drink, and then for the drink to come and the food to come, sitting on the comfortable padded banquette and resting my tired legs.

Soon I had my glass of white wine and had ordered the appealing and surprising item I had found on the menu—a fennel risotto. I read my paper, looked at the others settling at their tables, and watched the doorway, where the tour group was now coming in. They were filing across the room toward the door to the main dining room, which was near me beyond a cabinet holding silverware and napkins, and as they entered, almost every member of the group looked straight across the room in my direction and stared seriously and critically at me. I began to wonder—was it something about my appearance? No, I realized, it was not me at all—they were looking at themselves in the mirror above my head.

My risotto was slow in coming because of the service demands of the tour group, who had long since embarked on their own meal, but at last it came, and I was well into eating it, and finding it very good, when two more people entered the room—two women. To my great surprise, one of them was, in fact, my fast-eating neighbor from lunchtime. How could this have happened? What were the chances of this happening? Salzburg was not such a small town. Where had she been all afternoon, and what had she been doing? She had not changed her clothes.

She was dressed just as she had been when she left the other restaurant at lunchtime—in the short rain jacket and the pro-EU T-shirt. This time she had brought with her a younger companion, a woman in a red sweater with a ponytail of dark hair who looked rather glum at first but who, I saw later, though her back was to me, talked animatedly enough during their meal. They found a table not very far from me, settled in, and ordered non-alcoholic drinks and eventually salads and what looked like the same fennel risotto.

The fast eater ate fast again and stopped now and then, as she had during lunch, to blow her nose in a large white handkerchief, with the same loud noise as earlier. But now, while she ate, she was talking in

382

what seemed to be an exuberant and spirited way, though fast, and occasionally laughing.

I asked myself the same questions I had asked at lunchtime, along with some others—did she live here in town? If not, why was she so casually dressed? But if so, why was she eating out twice in one day? Who was her friend? Not a daughter, clearly. The fact that she was in the same restaurant as I, once again, was something I could not explain. Clearly, she liked the same sort of restaurant I liked, but that was not enough to explain the coincidence.

Well into the meal, the two were joined by a stout, older man who gave them each a handshake rather than a kiss. He did not eat but sipped a coffee as the three of them talked. Well, who was he? A friend? A lawyer? The fact that she was eating in a convivial way with two companions made her seem to me less odd than she had seemed at lunchtime, and yet her unusual behavior of lunchtime remained a fact. This evening she did not, at least, have the alarm clock in front of her on the table. She had probably—though not certainly—not unfastened her pants.

I spent some time debating whether to speak to the waitress, who seemed to know several of the customers, and ask her if this woman was a regular customer and if she could tell me anything about her. But I could not think how to do it. I finished my meal well before the fast-eating woman and her companions and left the restaurant, thinking I might still come back down from my room a little later and talk to the waitress. I never did—it would have been too complicated to manage in German, and it would have appeared too strange.

Another coincidence: although my lunch and my dinner that day had been entirely different, my bill was exactly the same, down to the cent.

This was a simple story, and perhaps pointless. But I was still remembering things about the fast-eating woman the next day on the train through the mountains, headed for Zurich. I was reminded of her in part because I was again reading the stories of Peter Bichsel and because of my interest in the way he observes and writes about the people in his world and the way he conceives and constructs a story. I was reading his stories on the train and thinking now and then about this woman, but I was also observing the other passengers, one of them being the white-haired man across from me. He was himself like a character in a Bichsel story, such an avid reader that even as he entered the compartment he carried an open book in his hand, and he resumed reading as soon as he had sunk into his seat, his jacket still on, one foot in the aisle braced against the motion of the train.

Nominated by The Paris Review, Katherine Taylor

IDYLL

by RICHIE HOFMANN

from *SECOND EMPIRE* (ALICE JAMES BOOKS)

Cicadas bury themselves in small mouths
of the tree's hollow, lie against the bark-tongues like amulets,

though I am praying I might shake off this skin and be raised
from the ground again. I have nothing

to confess. I don't yet know that I possess
a body built for love. When the wind grazes

its way toward something colder,
you too will be changed. One life abrades

another, rough cloth, expostulation.
When I open my mouth, I am like an insect undressing itself.

Nominated by Alice James Books

FAIL AGAIN

by DAVID J. UNGER

from THE POINT

There's a little time left before the show is supposed to start, and paying audience members are gathered outside the black-box theater behind the furniture store in Boulder, Colorado. Laura Ann Samuelson, who is in charge here, is worried about the garbage bags. She has passed around a box of them to the dozen or so of us who have arrived early— performers, crew, supporters and pre-performance hangers-on. We've been told to put them on like ponchos. First you poke a small hole for your head in the base of the bag, then you push your head through that hole, expanding it as you move through it. Then you reach your arms up and press a finger into each of the two corners, stretching the plastic seams until they begin to tear. Then you move your arms through each hole. Colin, a friend of a friend who's here to make a documentary, screws it up. He makes the head hole way too big, so the bag is more like a strapless dress than a poncho. I help him fix it along with my other friend, Ethan. We bunch up the bag just below his armpits, bringing the straps up over his shoulders and stretching to tie them together. It works, though I worry it will constrict his blood flow.

The bags function surprisingly well as ponchos, but there is some trepidation as to why we must wear them in the first place, not to mention why black plastic and tape coat the windows, why the back wall of the stage is covered with a semi-transparent tarp, why there is a big bucket of sopping wet tomatoes onstage. Samuelson has something else on her mind, though. She's worried that the bags' false lavender scent will linger on attendees' clothes. "Is that bad?" she asks.

There's no time to dwell on it, so Samuelson continues fast-walking her crew through how all of this will unfold. She makes laps around the tiny blackbox theater, appearing and reappearing amid the rows of fold-up chairs, or near the doors that swing out onto the parking lot behind the boutique furniture store/experimental arts space. Her cropped blond hair can't keep up with her head as she spins in all sorts of directions, throwing her attention to this or that unresolved issue. She's onstage with a pantomimed microphone in her hand, demonstrating how she'll welcome the audience to this, the first night of Boulder's first-ever Failure Festival. Most of her sentences begin with things like "What I think I'll do . . ." or "I don't know what . . ." or "I think I may . . ."

None of us could say we weren't prepared for improvisation. The ads for the Failure Festival read more like warnings:

> FAILURE FESTIVAL is an invitation. An invitation for you to help us engage failure in a public setting. We need you because we don't know how to do it on our own. We don't know whether to barrel towards it, argue with it, or sit on its lap. We don't know if we should give it keys to our apartment, or ask it to apologize. Sometimes we cower in the corner. Sometimes we lie down and try to convince it that we are asleep . . . or dead.

> We want to know what failure reveals about our world that success masks. We do not expect easy answers. We may find none at all. This is a celebration and acknowledgement of the fact that when things inevitably don't go as we plan, somehow, we must adapt. Please help.

Instead of trumpeting career highlights, the performer bios document shortcomings and insecurities (e.g. "Though she has yet to reach wide acclaim within her own family, her brother's girlfriend has repeatedly praised her work"). When I went to order a three-day pass as advertised, there was no option to do so. In at least one message to ticket-holders, there was discussion about whether or not attendees should bring their own chairs. Were I attending any other performance, I would have thought this was going to be a disaster. Since this was the Failure Festival, I couldn't be so sure. Here was a festival dedicated to the opposite of what most festivals aspire to achieve. Over three nights, in a box under the Rockies, men and women would clamor onstage to fail miserably before their peers.

"Failure isn't necessarily given attention, in some way," Samuelson would tell me later. "Well, actually I think that we give it a lot of attention in that we're all fixated in our own quiet way on all of the ways that we're failing all the time. But I didn't know—and I'm really curious—what it means to create a space for failure that is collective."

It's no coincidence that the phrase "Failure is not an option" is so often attributed to Gene Kranz, a man who worked at NASA, on the most American of all endeavors. The sentiment resonates well beyond fixing a broken spaceship. From its inception, America has felt the need to prove itself; mandatory success is a national neurosis passed down from one trembling generation to the next. Shit. What if we're the ones who finally let our fathers down?

In *Born Losers: A History of Failure in America*, Scott Sandage charts the rise of the Great American Neurosis throughout the nineteenth century. Antebellum America was perpetually on the verge of a nervous breakdown amid rapid urbanization and industrialization. The adolescent nation bounced from one economic crisis to the next. Slavery nearly tore it apart. Meanwhile, capital accumulated in a few hands and everybody wrung their hands over "the most imperious of all necessities, that of not sinking in the world," as Alexis de Tocqueville put it. Its status as an experiment, Sandage reminds us, was still fresh in everyone's minds back then, and its success was by no means guaranteed. "Twins were born in antebellum America," Sandage writes. "Success and failure grew up as the Romulus and Remus of capitalism. Failure was intrinsic, not antithetical, to the culture of individualism. 'Not sinking' took both self-reliance and self-criticism, lest a dream become a nightmare."

One hundred and fifty years later, failure is having something of a moment. The *New York Times Magazine* declared as much last fall when it dedicated its annual special innovations issue to failure. Innovation is, "by necessity, inextricably linked with failure," Adam Davis wrote in "Welcome to the Failure Age!" As the speed of human invention has accelerated, so too has the failure rate. "We're now suffering through a cycle of destabilization, whereby each new technology makes it ever easier and faster to create the next one, which, of course, leads to more and more failure." The solution, as Davis would have it, is to establish new and better systems. Systems exist for a reason, after all: to make life safer, better and more efficient. "The only way to harness this new age of failure is to learn how to bounce back from disaster and create the societal institutions that help us do so."

Maybe. Or maybe that's a cop-out. When the *Times* emblazons failure across the cover of its magazine, we'd like to think we're reconciling ourselves with a debilitating fear. But our obsession with success is never far behind. Conversations about losing almost always end up being about winning. We tell ourselves, "If at first you don't succeed, try, try again." "Fail again," Samuel Beckett calls back at us. "Fail better."

The Failure Festival is trying to confront failure on its own terms, apart from the win/fail binary. Failing at a "Failure Festival" makes as much sense as taking the stairs in an M. C. Escher painting. You wouldn't call it a success, but you wouldn't call it a failure either. Does that make it a success?

At this point everyone—Samuelson included—is covered in black plastic. The only outliers are a handful of lithe dancers dressed all in black, with their long legs and shoulders and arms exposed. They wear laboratory goggles too, and stand clustered near the door to the back parking lot, shaking out their limbs and discussing which parts of their bare skin it is OK for the audience to write on with permanent marker. The tomatoes in the bucket are still on the stage, next to a pile of baby carrots. I picture a rifle above a mantle in a Chekhov play.

Now the rest of the audience comes through the big door at the back of the theater. Samuelson is back up onstage. This time she's got a real microphone in her hand, with the cord curving down along her body. She's perched on a black block against the back of the black-box stage, squinting out through the white light at the audience.

"There's sort of a three-part process going on here," Samuelson says, directing traffic. "First, we're putting on our trash bags, which you guys are doing a great job of, by the way. Then, two, we're going over to that corner there, see where the dancers are over there? And we're writing one, or more, failures of our own on their bodies, OK, with the markers there. Someone should have markers to give to you. Christina? Can you make sure the markers are there for people to write with? And then,

389

three, once you've written down your failures, we're all coming up here and sitting onstage together. OK? So, yeah. You're all doing great."

Once everybody has written their personal failures on the bodies of the begoggled dancers, we all hunch cross-legged onstage, our bodies red with proximity. "If you're feeling claustrophobic, it's because there are a lot of things going on that might make you feel that way," Samuelson says, still perched with mic in hand lording over the audience. Her nasal exhaling comes flooding through the other end of the tinny wires and metal speakers. "The trash bags alone . . . and now we're all crowded onstage here. And all I can say is that I'm sorry. I know it feels warm in here, and, well, we're in it here together. That's all I can say."

At least one audience member has fashioned a sort of bandana with his garbage bag, instead of a poncho. "I *failed* the garbage bag," he quips. (He will not be the last person to make this joke; in that respect, it will be a long three days.) Some carrots are now being passed around, along with a fistful of toothpicks. "Take a carrot and a toothpick," Samuelson instructs us, "then use the toothpick to carve one expectation we have about the evening into the carrot—any thing or word that we think might or should happen tonight." Jet-lagged and hungry, I carve "FOOD" into the carrot.

At this point, Samuelson's blond hair is beginning to darken with sweat. I, too, begin to notice a certain dampness. We place our carrots onto toothpicks like hors d'oeuvres at a fancy party and pass them back up to her. Participants begin plopping tomatoes into paper bowls and passing them around. One bowl spills onto somebody's pants, which are not covered by plastic (a troubling flaw in the garbage-bag poncho system). Everyone recoils in gleeful disgust. Several participants get the same idea at the same time and yell "FAIL!" in unison.

"OK, so, we've had our first kind of moment here where, 'This is real,' OK?" Samuelson says. "Does everyone have a tomato now?"

"Yeah!" they yell.

"Welcome to the Failure Festival."

Samuelson, 25, grew up in Boulder and went to Hampshire College, majoring in dance. She stuck around the East Coast after graduating, trying to gain a foothold in the dance scene. It didn't pan out like she expected and she ended up back in Boulder, where she's been teaching, dancing and nannying to help pay the bills. "It's been a really interesting process," she tells me, "of kind of—how do you sort of take ownership of what you want to be doing, and being real about where you are?"

Maybe failure flourishes somewhere between those two points. Everyone has big ideas about who they should be and how that person is different from who they actually are. We think of failure as marking discrete events in time—stuck landing gear, chapter-eleven bankruptcy or the love that got away. But the feeling we're dealing with here, under the Rockies, is more pervasive. In a culture that values success above all else, failure is a turbine that spins all day and all night. It either catches and consumes us, or the thrust of it propels us forward.

Most of us here, at this festival, have got that background application running in our minds that tells us we're subpar. Every day we log on to view the infinite display of our acquaintances' successes, browsing in a state of perpetual relative inferiority. There are always more posts of people's new jobs, new loves, new babies. They are better than us, ad infinitum, ad nauseum. What losers we all are—the lot of us.

I mostly came to Boulder to see my college friend Ethan perform in the festival, but another reason I went was because I used to be a performer too. I did a lot of theater and improv in high school and college, and I imagined that's what I'd keep doing. Others thought the same—at the festival I ran into two old acquaintances who asked me if I was "still doing performance stuff." It's a perfectly reasonable question, but I never know how to answer it. Time passed, I got interested in other things, and performance dissolved into the background. That's one interpretation. Another is that I was afraid of failing.

Now that we've all got our tomatoes in the bowls, we are told to take a seat among the rows of chairs half-circling the Saran-wrapped stage. As we settle in, Samuelson makes her way to the lip of the small stage with the mic cord trailing behind her. "So, just so you know," she says, "should you feel uncomfortable at any point throughout tonight's performance, there will be a stack of catalogs in the back there. And, whenever you want, you can just escape and go and grab a catalog, and, you know," she begins idly thumbing through one of the catalogs, "just flip through a catalog, OK? Look at the things in the catalog."

Samuelson finally introduces the night's first performer: Lauren Beale, a performance artist and dance instructor at the University of Colorado Boulder. "There are so many voices inside of Lauren's head that distract her or convince her that just being herself is not worthy of artistic creation or unconditional love for that matter," Beale had written in her failure bio. "Making choreography is a painful process filled with self-deprecating back talk and self-sabotaging procrastination . . . and so she improvises . . . on stage and in life, because being spontaneously present is a coping mechanism and a strategy for getting out of her own way."

Beale kneels down near the carrots on the block at the rear of the stage. The dancers we tattooed with our failures escort her, blindfolded and begoggled, to center stage. They position themselves at the four corners of the stage. Out of the stillness, the supporting cast begins stomping and running in place while shouting various insults at Beale. When Beale touches her index finger to her body or the floor, the four others sprint to the center. They use their bare palms to push and rub and slap the unseeing Beale all over her body.

They repeat this cycle a few times. Eventually, one of the dancers begins yelling the word "Throw!" It's unclear if we've heard her correctly. "Throw?" There's stomping and shouting and there it is again: "Throw!" More stomping and shouting. Again, "Throw!" And from another dancer, "Throw!" And another, "Throw!" Nervous laughter rumbles through the audience. "Throw?"

Everything about being human in public tells us to leave the sopping tomato undisturbed in the bowl in our laps. But all it takes is for a first shot to be fired. One brave hand dips down into the paper bowl and slings a tomato. And then another and another. Now everyone has permission to throw. And we all do. Tomatoes and their juice and pieces fly everywhere. Many land with a hard splat on Beale's arm or chest or neck or face. The tomatoes that don't hit their target are recovered by the dancers and chucked at her or smushed in her hair or squeezed all over her head and down her chest. She squirms and writhes, doing what she can to protect herself.

Samuelson crouches, folded in on herself, declaiming the words we have carved on the toothpicked carrots. "Getting a nosebleed while giving a blowjob," reads one. "Committing a fox paws," another of the dancers says. ("I think it's pronounced *foh pah*," Samuelson says from her perch.) Dancers gather bits of tomatoes into buckets and resupply the audience with ammunition. The stage is now sopping wet. My greatest concern is that one of the dancers might slip and break their skull open. Already there are some near slips and small spills, which are kind of fun to watch. Everything is a mess of black and red.

At one point, Beale lashes out at the audience. On her knees, she gathers tomato debris into her fists and holds it up in the air, scanning around in her blindfolded and tomato-stained goggles. The audience oohs in a low register, recognizing the threat and daring her to go through with it—not quite believing she actually will. She does. The tomatoes fly blindly out from her clenched fists and splat somewhere in the back. The spectator-performer dynamic has shifted, perhaps irrevocably. The perfect way into three nights of failure—play tinged with violence, on the verge of spiraling wildly out of control.

After the last tomato is thrown, the audience gets a short break and a "limited number of towels." Samuelson tells us we can remove our garbage bags if we'd like. Many do, but some, including Samuelson and me, keep them on. Months later, I would learn that the name of this first piece was "Aim."

After a more subdued video projection by a local filmmaker, we come to the final performance of the night. The piece is about a piece that will never happen. Samuelson tells us about Bhanu Kapil, a Boulder-based British writer whom she very much wanted to perform at the festival. They corresponded over the phone and left one another lengthy voice messages—a few of which Samuelson plays for us through the loudspeakers. Kapil speaks eloquently about the frustrations of life in academia.

"Bhanu Kapil could have been a doctor and married a dentist and written creative nonfiction set in the suburbs of London during the time of riots," she tells us in quiet, British tones. "Instead, she became a creative-writing industry expert, failed to cook a lasagna or ten . . . and wrote experimental prose set in the suburbs of London during the time of riots." Later, she says, "Is Bhanu amazing? No, she is a loser who makes life worth it in radical bursts."

Kapil couldn't be in Boulder for the festival, but Samuelson wants to convey something in her stead. The tension—borne out in Samuelson's stops and starts—is that Samuelson also doesn't want to occupy someone else's space or rob them of their narrative. The violent nature of that narrative adds to the tension. In 2012, a young woman in India was raped, brutally violated and left to die on a highway for forty minutes before being spotted by passersby. Kapil had all sorts of ideas about how to interpret this onstage, which we hear in her audio recordings or because Samuelson tells us about them. One includes giving an audience member a ball of red twine, taking the other end outside and into a car and driving away, allowing the twine to unspool disembodied in the spectator's hands.

Samuelson sits legs straight-out onstage, explaining it using Kapil's recordings and a massive flow chart she has laid piece by piece on the tomato and tarp covered stage. She has lugged onto the stage a bag of potting soil, spools of red twine, bags of rose hips and other earthly elements. The audience is quiet; we are tired, but we are still with Samuelson. Everything comes to the point of lying down, she tells us, poring over the flowchart that stretches out in front of her. Kapil told her to be "a ghost of the intestines" and she is trying, in real time, in front of us all, to do justice to that. After twenty minutes of talking through the various ideas she has had, or is having, Samuelson settles hesitantly on one: "I'm just gonna lie down," she says, telling us she's going to put tape on her mouth and lie down for exactly forty minutes— the same amount of time the woman lay dying on the street in India. She is quick to assure the audience that there is no obligation to stay. All of us are free to leave or watch or join her or do as we feel with the various elements scattered about onstage.

She puts the tape over her mouth and lies down flat on her belly, her arms at her sides and her face turned out to her right, looking just past me. I can see that her eyes stay open. Certain audience members rise from their seats to move about onstage or take photos with their phones. One man goes straight for the tape, puts it across his mouth and lies down with Samuelson. Somebody opens the potting soil and begins pouring it on Samuelson. Others rub handfuls of it in their hair. One approaches other spectators, takes their hands, presses her forehead to them and whispers. A woman takes the red twine and laces it through the hands of others to create a web. Some clamor onstage just to get a closer look at Samuelson's chart—and a few begin to read from it.

Among those readers is a man who has crawled up to the chart on his belly, his mouth taped over. He takes one scrap of the chart—now shredded in various ways from the footfalls—and begins to read, his words and breathing muffled by the tape. Eventually he rolls over onto his back and cakes his neck in the potting soil. He kicks his legs and arms out as if he were making a snow angel, the tarp crinkling under him. He begins to moan and cry out forcefully through the tape. He cries louder and writhes, gargling, "*Mhhmmmmmmmmm! Mrggggggggg!*"

Suddenly, Samuelson, who has been still for the first time all night, leaps up violently—the soil and the rose hips and the twine falling from her back. She rips the tape off her mouth and bends her hands up into the air as if to explain.

"OK, I'm going to stop," she says, the soil still falling from her. "Because something needs to change. I feel like I'm taking a role I wasn't supposed to take. I'm at the center of something I didn't mean to create. So what I'm going to do is I'm going to make an outline just so that we're leaving room for the erasure that's happening and then I'm going to step aside. But you all should keep following what you're feeling because that's what I'm doing—following what I'm feeling."

She kneels down and with her hands clears space on the tarp among the dirt and rose hips and red twine. The writhing man has shut up. She stands up again.

"OK, now I feel better," she says. She leaves the stage, takes off the garbage-bag poncho and seats herself in the second row. I watch her sitting there in total silent stillness, her arm draped across an empty seat next to her, one leg crossed over the other. She sits in the dark like that for the rest of the performance, watching everything unfold, her head silently bowed.

For a while it is silent. Then the man begins to moan again. He rips off his garbage bag and takes off his shirt, which spills soil onto his bare, hairy chest. He rolls over and again reads unintelligibly and at random from the tattered scraps of paper—Bhanu's words, not his—his nude upper body propped up on his elbows. He wears black-and-white pants, and there is a noticeable bulge in the crotch. Suddenly, one of the performers from another act jumps onto the stage, lies down next to him and whispers into his ear. It's hard to make out exactly what she says, but it's clear she's telling him, very politely and reasonably, to shut the fuck up.

She leaves the stage. He freezes for a moment. Then, very deliberately, he gathers soil from around him into a pile under his chin. Then he buries his face in it. The woman sitting next to me reaches out to him and gently pokes him as if to get his attention. After several tries with no response, she converts the poking into petting, then gives up. Later she pulls out a piece of paper onto which she's written her own words and begins to read them aloud. They are addressed to a former lover, and they deal with just barely overcoming the tendency toward suicide that can come with a broken heart. At this point, I slip out to join my friends. We eat gluten-free sandwiches, then go out into the cold November night.

Samuelson was the first to admit something had gone wrong in the Bhanu piece. But it was hard to say exactly what had gone wrong, or how something even could go wrong within the festival's framework of failure. "There's a certain kind of preparation that happens for some things that you expect to go awry, and then there's also the stuff that truly goes awry," she told me later. "And they're not one and the same. There is a way to memorialize, or something. But erasure is not a metaphor. It can't be represented the same way because it's just happening. And so this place of stepping into, or trying to illustrate, I think is where I made a mistake. I filled in the—this space . . . I basically erased—I was the erasing. I was the person that was erasing, in that particular moment."

Samuelson dialed down her involvement for the second and third night. She again offered the catalogs to the audience—but this time it didn't feel like a joke. She also posted a series of emails inside the theater for the audience to consider. It was the back-and-forth between her, the other performers and Kapil, discussing what happened and what went wrong. "The minute I was lying down and people started putting stuff on me, I'd realized that I had put myself right at the center of this thing that was actually supposed to be empty," Samuelson told me.

Bhanu was in India, attempting to put on a similar performance at the exact site where the violence took place, but she ran into the same challenges and limitations. In both instances, she would reflect later, "The male observers were interfering with the kind of attention you think you need to give or extend inside the performance." She continued:

> I don't know how it's possible to have gone so far from everything that you thought was going to happen. But there we have it. There we have it. I am ever-so-slightly alive, and that's something I want to share with others. Not only do I want to share it with them, I want to share everything with them and give them everything that I have, so that I don't have to do all the work of making things happen. I can share with others. And that's what I hope for most of all.

The Failure Festival went on. There were people in red onesies singing pop songs and trying to pitch camping tents. There was a touching improvised dance duet that had been "choreographed" via texts and emails over the course of several months. There were short films that featured skateboarding fails; YouTube clips with zero views; and a man who pretended to hang himself and put it on Chat Roulette to see how others would respond.

On the second night we returned to the black-box theater attached to the boutique furniture store to watch Ethan's performance. He sits center-stage on a wooden stool he had made with his father. He addresses the audience directly and calmly, at times surprising himself when his own words choke him up. He had realized, he tells us, that his greatest failures had to do with relationships and intimacy.

He tells us the story of his first girlfriend. They met in college and grew very close. She was a year younger so he stayed on after he graduated to be with her. Then they moved to New York together and pursued artistic endeavors and all the trappings of hipster youth. Like many intense college relationships, this one did not last. For whatever reason, he went back home and she stayed put. At one point, he felt he had made a terrible mistake, and he flew to New York to try, maybe, to be with her. But it failed.

He moved on with his new life, in the fits and starts that come in lost love's wake. She became a Famous Person, drawing on their failed romance in her writings and films. Failure cloaked in success followed him everywhere. Even as he tells his story, a woman in the audience realizes who the Famous Person is and excitedly blurts out her name.

"Man, talk about 'failure,'" he says to the audience member, and everyone in the room laughs nervously. He is trying to crack a joke but is clearly upset about his story once again being subjected to the whims of an outside party.

It nearly derails the performance. We watch Ethan pause, gather himself and carry on. His story continues: He becomes interested in Feldenkrais, a physical therapy technique, and spends several years learning the practice. He begins teaching classes in Boulder and eventually opens his own practice which he calls "F°Yoga." He unrolls a poster with a manifesto of sorts on it. It reads:

F°Yoga is not exercise. No sweating.
F°Yoga has no postures. Posing is for posers.
F°Yoga is radically subtle pleasure and satisfaction. All the
    feels you want.
F°Yoga increases choices and decreases compulsions.

F*Yoga undoes struggle and strain.
More than flexible bodies, F*Yoga wants flexible brains.

He ends his story by holding up a box of cards advertising the Failure Festival; he was supposed to distribute them in advance as promotional materials but forgot. He shrugs. Instead, he'll pass them around now and people can bring them to his studio to redeem for a free session.

"This is your ticket to new feelings," he says.

Nominated by The Point, Paul Maliszewski

I DREAM OF
HORSES EATING COPS

by JOSHUA JENNIFER ESPINOZA

from NEPANTLA

i dream of horses eating cops
i have so much hope for the future

or no i don't

who knows the sound a head makes when it is asleep
my dad was a demon but so was the white man in uniform
who harassed him for the crime of being brown

there are demons everywhere
dad said
and he was right but not in the way he meant it

the sky over san bernardino was a brilliant blue when the winds
     kicked in
all the fences and trash cans and smog scattered themselves
and the mountains were on fire every day

i couldn't wait to die or be killed
my woman body trapped in a dream

i couldn't wait to wake up
and ride off into the sunset
but there isn't much that is new anywhere

the same violence swallows itself and produces bodies
and names for bodies

i name my body girl of my dreams
i name my body proximity
i name my body full of hope despite everything
i name my body dead girl who hasn't died yet

i hope i come back as an elephant
i hope we all come back as animals
and eat our fill

i hope everyone gets everything they deserve

Nominated by Nepantla

MIDTERM

fiction by LESLIE JOHNSON

from COLORADO REVIEW

Midmorning in mid-October, in the middle of the campus, Chandra stopped in the center of the crisscrossing sidewalks. She pulled the phone from her handbag and pretended to be texting someone; she smiled down at the screen as if someone had texted her back. She felt other students brushing past her on the walkway, but didn't look up at their faces.

She had left her dorm room fully intending to go to class, even though she wasn't prepared. Today in Gender Perspectives they were supposed to be discussing sex slaves in third world nations, a series of articles based on the real-life stories of young women who were prisoners in brothels forced to do disgusting things or be brutally punished. Chandra hadn't gotten the reading done, but she could still go to class, and when it was her turn to speak, she could say it was horrible, she couldn't believe that such things were happening to young, helpless girls in this day and age, and how could she be wrong? It *was* horrible. She *couldn't* believe it. If she read the articles, Chandra figured she would probably feel exactly the same way as she felt now anyway. She wasn't afraid to go to class. The professor was nice. If she could tell that Chandra hadn't done the reading, she wouldn't embarrass Chandra in front of everyone. She might ask in a concerned voice to speak to Chandra after class, though, and Chandra could tell her that she was a little behind because she'd had the flu.

Chandra had spent the last two days in her dorm room, pretending to have it. Not that she really needed to put on a show. Her roommate, Jillian, didn't care. They were not enemies, but they were not friends.

Between her boyfriend and her sorority, Jillian rarely slept in the room and used it mostly for the closet space. When Chandra had heard the key in the door on Monday morning, she pulled the sheet up to her neck and mumbled that she wasn't feeling well. Jillian wrinkled her nose and opened the window between their beds to let the germs out. Chandra had spent the day watching YouTube videos on her laptop. She had an open bag of animal crackers in her desk drawer, with seventeen crackers left inside, and she ate four at a time, every three hours, and threw the leftover one, a walrus, out of the window into the night sky.

On Tuesday, she had the same bad feeling that made her stay in her dorm room. Not sick, but not regular—a feeling like something bad was happening and she just didn't know exactly what it was yet.

This morning, Wednesday, Chandra had awoken with fresh resolve. Enough already. *Up and at 'em*, as her mother used to screech through her bedroom door. She made her way to the dorm bathroom down the hallway. After seven weeks at college, it still felt funny to Chandra to wear shower shoes, which were highly recommended to avoid fungus. She always carried an extra towel with her and hung one on the hook outside the showers and kept one wrapped around her body until she was inside the stall. When she let the towel drop and she was standing there in only her shower shoes, she thought sometimes of those porn girls, naked but still wearing high heels.

This morning she had taken her time, even though she knew there were people waiting for their turn. She closed her eyes and turned her face up to the showerhead and let her hands rest on the sharp knobs of her hip bones, which were her favorite part of her body. She would go to class today, and tomorrow, and then all she had on Friday was math lab. Hump day. That's what her dad had always called Wednesday. And the torture chamber was what he always used to call his job. *Oh, boo hoo hoo!* Chandra could remember how her mother used to mock him when they'd fight at night before the divorce. *You have to talk on the phone and write claims and report to a boss! Poor you! Too bad you can't get work at a plastics factory and breathe toxic chemicals all day and die in your fifties!* Because that was how Chandra's grandfather whom she never met—her mom's dad—had died. From lung cancer, even though he never smoked; they all knew it was the plastic fumes. And she'd started to cry a little, not about her grandfather she never met, but at the memory of her dad's voice saying, *It's over-the-hump day, Sweetie Peetie. Can we do it? Can we make it over?*

Now the walkways were clearing, everyone delivering themselves to their 9:50 classes, and Chandra should have been inside Auerbach Hall, but she remained in the middle of the intersecting sidewalks. She was wearing her hair tied back with a paisley scarf and her brown boots and black leggings and a long corduroy shirt over a purple knit turtleneck. She looked fine. She should go to class. She looked fine.

The campus was still. The red brick buildings, the bright yellow tree-tops shimmering in a crisp breeze. Maybe, she thought, she should get a coffee at the student union. And a banana, maybe. She hadn't eaten yesterday except for some peanuts from the vending machine. She could have a banana, and maybe a Pop-Tart with the crusts cut off.

She hated to go to the cafeteria, but she could do it. She could go in there and get a coffee and a Pop-Tart. She was looking toward the union at the end of the walkway, and suddenly someone was standing under the big maple tree next to the building. A guy. A tall guy wearing a peacoat. Where did he come from? He seemed to be standing very straight on purpose. Was he looking at her? It seemed like he was look-ing at her! Chandra held her phone to her ear and tossed back her head and tapped the toe of her boot on the walkway and laughed, and even though she knew the guy was too far away to hear, she said out loud, "Seriously? Listen, I gotta call you later." Then she dropped the phone into her handbag and walked with purpose on the walkway to the left, toward the union, keeping her eyes on the building, not allowing her-self a glance at the tree or the guy standing under it, but then she did glance, and he was gone. Disappeared. She stopped and looked around, but didn't see him walking away in any direction—not toward the li-brary, not toward Dana Hall. She turned in a slow circle.

"*Hello*."

She jerked her shoulders, taking a breath—more of a stupid-sounding hiccup, actually. With three more steps toward the union, she could see his body lying flat on the ground like a corpse beneath the tree. He propped himself up, one elbow at a time. His reddish-brown hair stuck up on one side; crumbled pieces of brown leaves clung to his coat sleeves. Was he smiling at her? His lips were curled up a little, anyway. Chandra's stomach twisted. "Sorry, like, were you," she mumbled, pushing a piece of hair into her scarf, "were you saying something?"

"I said hi."

He had a patch of acne on one side of his jaw, and his Adam's apple looked weird, like a big walnut inserted for no good reason under the skin of his neck. His eyebrows were bristly, but his eyes underneath them were okay. Greenish-brownish. Looking up at her. She said, "Hi."

"You want to see something?"

Chandra didn't answer, but she didn't keep walking either.

He said, "You have to come closer to the tree to see what I'm talking about." He pointed up at something in the branches of the maple. "From underneath."

Three students came out of the union. One of them was saying *Shit! Shit!* in a gleeful voice. Chandra looked over her shoulder at them, long enough to see them huddle together as one of the girls cupped her hands to help the boy get his cigarette lit in the breeze. Chandra looked back at the guy under the tree. He was sitting up normally now, cross-legged, and so she sat down next to him, with a couple of feet or so between them. "What?" She looked up into the branches, where he'd been pointing. "What were you looking at?"

"I'm looking at a particular leaf, the one on the smaller branch that's attached to the largest branch, right *there*—" He pointed above their heads. "The one that's completely red, the deepest red compared to the ones around it. Do you see the one I'm talking about?"

Chandra craned her neck. The maple leaves were mostly lemon yellow, some tinged orange, their tips transitioning to scarlet. A few mostly red. She tried to spot the guy's perfect red leaf among the foliage. "I see it," she lied.

"I'm watching it until it falls."

"Why?"

"Because. I believe it will be worthy of seeing."

"Hmmm." Chandra saw the three students walking away, their laughter fading. The guy stretched out on the ground again, his hands behind his head, and Chandra extended her legs and leaned back on her elbows. Above her, sunlight illuminated the bright leaves; they trembled like chandelier crystals. She said, "I'm supposed to be in class."

"We're all *supposed* to be somewhere. But I can *choose* to see one red maple leaf come to the end of its life. To see the moment it releases from its branch."

"I guess."

"We see only what we look at. To look is an act of choice."

Chandra let her arms splay, relaxed her head on the ground, gazing up at the canopy of golden-plum. "I guess."

"Have you read Berger? *Ways of Seeing*?"

"I take it you have."

He made a noise, a sort of grunting sound. "I sound like an asshole?"

Without moving her head, Chandra shifted her eyes. His face was a couple of feet away from hers on the ground. "Maybe." She pretended to laugh a little, so he would know she was kidding. He smiled, and Chandra felt suddenly aware of her knees. Why was she wearing leggings? What had made her think this morning that she looked good in leggings? Her knees were too knobby for leggings. They stuck out like knots in the middle of her thighs and calves, like that big bulge on the tree branch over her head where another branch must have broken off in a storm or something.

"Ahhh!" The guy's mouth gaped, his eyes suddenly widening. His face flushed so the acne on his jaw didn't look so noticeable. He quickly rolled and lifted from the ground into a crouching position on his knees. "Did you see it? Did you?"

"I did," Chandra lied again. "I saw it."

He smiled, a big smile showing his teeth, which were large and straight, and Chandra wanted to ask him if he had a retainer from his orthodontist that he still wore to bed at night like she did. She said, "I was going to get a coffee."

He pulled up the sleeve of his leafy jacket. There was a watch on his wrist, the kind with hands and Roman numbers, which made Chandra wonder. Who wore a watch? He said, "Let's wait ten minutes. At eleven we can get early lunch."

We. She felt the veins in her neck start to pulse, the way they did when she got nervous. She took out her phone and scrolled Facebook. She clicked on a video link of someone feeding a doll-sized baby bottle to a squirrel in a blanket. She said, "Wanna see something?"

He held up his arms in an X, shaking his head. "I gave it up."

"What?"

"Technology. Personal technology, that is. I understand that the cafeteria we're waiting to eat in is powered by technology. But you know— my cell phone. My laptop. Even my iPod. That was the hardest, actually. Because I love my music. So much."

"What do you *mean*?"

"I'm unplugged. I disconnected myself from cyberspace and all the gadgets. It's an experiment, right? To see what I discover about myself, living, you know. Without the texts, tweets, sound bites, Instagrams, everything constantly separating us from the life that's happening for real right in front of us. Around us. I'm going to write about it."

Chandra nodded. "Steinmetz gave us that same extra credit, but his was just for cell phones. We were supposed to not use them for a week-end and keep a journal about it. Some people were going to do it, but then he said you actually had to give him your phone for the weekend. He was going to lock them in his desk. So nobody did it."

The guy's mouth twisted to one side. "This isn't *extra credit*."

He looked at his watch again. "You should come with me. After our lunch. Did you know that you're allowed to listen to the rehearsals in Jaffrey Hall? The music students are practicing for the parent weekend concerts, and we can just walk into the auditorium today at 1:10 and listen. I went yesterday for classical. Chamber groups playing Bach concertos. Amazing. When was the last time you actually *felt* the vibra-tion of a cello's strings?"

He stood up, and so did Chandra. He was at least a foot taller than she was. Between the flaps of his coat she could see his gray sweater underneath. He was thin, but not too thin. She could see some extra flesh at his stomach, which she liked. Chandra liked to be much thinner than any guy she was standing near. It made her feel larger somehow, or stronger or something, rather than smaller. Which made no sense, but, she thought, maybe was kind of interesting. Maybe she could put that in the paper she was supposed to be writing for Professor Stein-metz.

He'd begged her not to write about anorexia when they turned in their issue proposals. He was on the young side for an English profes-sor. He wore jeans and sneakers and denim shirts. He was popular with students for the way he'd get all worked up in class. Once he dropped to his knees and begged them to care about a short story by someone named Junot. His forehead would get red where his hair was receding, and Chandra had heard other girls laughing about it after class, but in the way you laugh at someone you think is cute. *Not another eating disorder paper!* He pleaded with her, pretending to be desperate, clutching his hands by his chest. *And not the effect of the media on self-esteem!* She asked Steinmetz why that was a bad topic, and he said it wasn't a *bad* topic, but he'd read so many student essays about it in the last three years that if he got one more, he might break down and start weeping in his office.

The guy was pointing at the iPhone in Chandra's hand. "Try giving it up for just one day—not even a whole day, just till later this afternoon. Just try it."

"I could turn it off for a while, I guess." She didn't turn it off, but she slipped it away, into its spot in the interior pocket of her bag.

He shook his head. "No. It's not the same. You have to be actually separated from it or it doesn't work. Trust me." He looked past her shoulder to the entrance of the union, took a few running steps to it, and returned with a flier he'd ripped off the notice board. "Come on! Give me your phone!"

"So you don't have Steinmetz for comp, right?"

"I had him last year for freshman lit." He rolled his eyes. "What a self call."

When Chandra couldn't think of another topic, Steinmetz had told her that if she *had* to write about anorexia, she'd better make it unique to her own life and relevant to her own generation, or she'd be responsible for making an aneurysm burst inside his skull. But maybe she could write about giving up her cell phone instead, like this guy. Even though she already missed the extra credit, she could probably still write her paper about it. She was supposed to have a rough draft done already and she hadn't even started. As she reached into her bag and handed over her iPhone and watched the guy fold the orange flier around it, she was already forming sentences in her head. *I wrapped my phone in a flier for an Alpha Phi Halloween costume contest and placed it in a hole in a big tree, like that character in* To Kill a Mockingbird.

The guy covered her phone in the tree's hollow with fallen leaves. She said, "What if someone steals it?"

"Look! It's perfectly camouflaged. No one would ever, ever notice it there." He grinned at her. She felt her heart race, like she was being talked into something dangerous.

If she came back to the tree later and her phone was gone, she'd have to email her mom and get a replacement on their Verizon insurance. They'd had to do that once before, when Chandra left her phone at her dad's apartment, but he said it wasn't there. Chandra's mother had wanted to go over and help her look, but her dad's girlfriend, Melanie, wouldn't allow it. It was Melanie's apartment, technically, so she had the right.

"What's your name, anyway?"

"Eli."

"I'm Chandra."

She followed Eli into the cafeteria. There were a few students at the long tables in the dining room, but the food stations were mostly empty. A cafeteria worker in a paper hat was clearing out the pastry case, and another was stocking the salad bar, getting ready for the lunch wave.

Eli moved in long strides to the Grill. Chandra stood a few feet behind him as he ordered a double cheeseburger.

"The grill's gotta heat up," said the bleary-eyed student worker in a stained chef hat. He was separating a stack of frozen patties with a metal spatula. He wore those clear plastic gloves, but Chandra saw him wipe his nose with his gloves on and then start poking at the raw hamburger with the same fingers. She held her empty plastic tray in front of her chest like a shield.

Eli told the grill guy that he'd be back for the burger and pushed his tray along the metal counter to the Chicken Basket, where he ordered nuggets and fries, and to Pizza & Pasta, where he heated up two slices of pepperoni in the serve-yourself microwave. Chandra got a cup of black coffee at the Starbucks counter and a packet of blueberry Pop-Tarts at Toast & Bagels. She peeled apart the foil wrapper and placed one of the Pop-Tarts in a toaster and waited, glancing over at Eli, who'd returned to the grill for his double burger. He waved at her, and she felt herself smile. She hoped her smile didn't look stupid—too big, maybe, or too small.

They met up at the long counter that led to the cash registers. There was no line at all yet. Chandra wondered why she hadn't figured this out on her own, instead of always fighting the lunch crowd after classes let out at 12:10.

"This is like Disney World," she told Eli. "You have to know all the off times."

"Disney World." Eli repeated the word flatly.

"My mom had a book, like a guide book thing, that told you when to go to the rides and restaurants and stuff at the times when most other people *wouldn't*. So you didn't have to wait so long . . ."

She let her voice trail off and turned her face away, began pushing her tray toward the register. Why was she talking about Disney World? God. Why did she have to be so weird? Her neck was red, she knew it, she could feel it getting hotter, and even though she was wearing a turtleneck the redness probably showed on that part of her skin between her throat and her jaw.

"Hey." Eli bumped the edge of his tray against hers, then hooked his finger around its edge. "That's all you're getting?"

"I told you. I was just going for coffee in the first place."

"Well, put your stuff on my tray, then. That's not enough to waste a swipe on."

She watched as he balanced his pizza on top of his fries and cookies on top of the burger's bun, making room for Chandra's coffee and Pop-Tart. He slid her empty tray out of the way, and she walked beside him to the register, where he discussed with the cashier whether it should be two swipes or three swipes on his meal card; Eli said the pizza was a side dish, but the cashier said it counted as a meal.

Eli shrugged. "Whatever."

Chandra walked with him to the condiment counter. "It's barely mid-term. You're going to run out of swipes."

"I'm not worried about it."

He squirted ribbons of ketchup over his chicken and fries; Chandra stirred Equal in her coffee. They sat across from each other at a table by the window with a view of the quad. If she craned her neck, she could see the tree where her phone was hidden, under the leaves in the hollow space of the trunk. What was she *doing*? She should go out there and get her phone while the quad was still quiet, before classes switched again. Put it back in her bag where it belonged.

Her mom had bought her this bag at Urban Outfitters before college, the same day they shopped for bedding and dorm supplies at Target and Bed, Bath, and Beyond. What if her mom was texting her right now? What if, Chandra wondered, something suddenly happened, like what if her dad had a heart attack out of the blue and her mom didn't want to go to the hospital and sit beside Melanie in the waiting room and wanted Chandra to go in her place?

She knew the chance of something happening the moment you randomly think of it happening was probably like zero. Thinking of it probably made it even less than zero, because when things happened it was never when you thought of them. Someone could be texting her about something right now, though, that she would never ever think of in a million years just sitting here thinking about *different* things.

If she had her phone she would know for sure that nothing was happening. She should go get her phone out of that tree.

"So you have the kind of family," Eli said, "that goes to Disney World together. One of those families?" Beneath his curly hair she could see his forehead wrinkle.

"Not really." She stabbed at her Pop-Tart with the cafeteria fork. "We only went once. When I was eleven."

Eli hunched over his tray, feeding himself with both hands, pizza rolled in one fist, his burger in the other.

"We're not rich," Chandra said, "if that's what you mean."

Eli hurried to chew and swallow, wiped at his mouth. "That's not what I meant. It's not the money thing. It's more about these premade experiences society wants you to have, you know? It's like, *Oh boy, the Magic Kingdom!* Prepackaged family fun."

"It's easy, I guess, for the parents. If you can pay for it."

"Exactly! That's exactly it!" Eli's spine straightened and he tilted forward across the table, like a drawbridge lowering. His swampy green eyes blinked slowly and reopened, focusing in on her face, a sudden zoom lens. Chandra tried to remain still, instead of looking away. She'd read that advice in *Seventeen* a long time ago and still remembered it. Eye contact, the article had said—don't underestimate it! No one had looked at her like this, Chandra realized, since she'd arrived at college. Looked closely at her face. Except maybe a couple of her professors, like Steinmetz. Chandra's mother used to stare at her now and then, sizing her up, making her lift up her shirt sometimes to check her rib cage, or inspecting her front teeth to make sure they weren't shifting in their gums after how much they'd paid the orthodontist.

Steinmetz. Chandra tried writing a sentence in her head again: *Without my phone I took the time to really look into the eyes of my friends while I was talking to them instead of constantly checking my screen.* She hoped she could remember it later when she got to the writing lab. What time was it? She reached by instinct for her bag, then drew her hand back. There was still time, probably, to knock out a couple pages of a draft before her 2:05 comp class. Even if they were terrible, at least Steinmetz would give her points for making an effort.

"People," said Eli, "want to buy premade experiences because it's easier. Safer, maybe. I think my parents sent me to camp for every vacation of my whole life. Computer camp, rock-climbing camp, video game–design camp, et cetera, and that's the same thing, right? You pay for it, and somebody has figured out every step of the way for you in advance, and you just follow along and you're expected to love it. And if you don't love it, then what's wrong with you, right?"

Without thinking Chandra picked up a piece of Pop-Tart, and now it was in her mouth, the dry crumbs mixing with a bit of moist filling on her tongue, and she wanted to spit it out on her napkin, but Eli was still looking right at her. She chewed, and her stomach talked to her the way it did, yelling at her, and she took another piece from her plate. "You're supposed to *appreciate* everything," she said.

"So true! Even if you didn't choose any of it. And college is the same exact thing, right? Pay your money and they give you a program and tell you what to think and what classes to take and you join a fraternity and they tell you what parties to go to. You can get all the way through your *college experience*, as they call it, without having one actually authentic experience of your own."

Suddenly, the quad's walkways began to fill from four directions, like faucets turning on, students streaming from the buildings. Classes were changing.

"My mom would kill me," Chandra said, "if she knew I skipped class this morning. She told me that skipping just one college class is like flushing $500 down the toilet, when you figure how much you're paying for tuition each semester."

"Can you put a price, though, on an hour of time? Time from your actual *life*?"

"My mom can. She totally guilts me about it. Just last week she texted me: *Better not be wasting grandpa's money.*"

"That's way aggressive."

"That's what's paying my tuition. A lot of people got cancer from the factory where he worked. My grandfather. This was a long time ago, like twenty years or something. Some lawyers started a big lawsuit with all of them, a class action thing. It took a really long time. My grandpa died, and it still was going on, and then finally they ended up winning. My mom was his only family, so she got the money—my grandpa's lawsuit money—and she saved it. And that's what's paying my tuition. Which she likes to remind me."

She felt a pain blossom inside, deep between her stomach and lungs, thinking about what she would say to her mom when the college mailed home her midterm grades next week. Her mom had made Chandra sign the FERPA agreement that let the school disclose her student information. She had a right to know Chandra's grades, her mom had pointed out, if she was the one paying for them.

Eli was still watching her. Listening to her. She felt herself starting to blush and couldn't stop herself from looking away, out the window. She noticed a girl walking by, someone decent looking, who had the same bag as she did from Urban Outfitters, which made Chandra feel sort of good for a moment. Like she knew how to choose things in an okay way. If someone saw her through the window sitting here at the table with Eli, she thought, that would be okay. She imagined for a minute that her roommate might walk by and notice her and ask her about it later

411

and Chandra would have something to say. *Oh, that guy? He keeps asking me out on weird dates, like to jazz concerts and stuff. But he's kind of interesting. I have coffee and stuff with him sometimes.*

Eli pushed his tray toward her side of the table. "Have a nugget. I ordered too many." There were four ovals of chicken left on the tray, dried ketchup spotted on their greasy tan coating. "Go on. You look like you need to eat."

This guy, Chandra thought—Eli—he was attracted to her. Wasn't he? She picked up one of the greasy chicken pieces and brought it to her lips and waited for a few moments before wrapping it in one of her crumpled napkins.

He pushed back his chair, lifting his arms, palms upturned toward the window. "The day is ours!"

She followed him outside, where a spiral of colored leaves swirled in a sudden wind.

"Do you miss it?"

For a minute she thought he was reading her mind because she was thinking about her old house on Riley Road, where she lived when she was little. Autumn was her dad's favorite season. He liked the leaves. He hated shoveling the driveway in the winter, couldn't stand mowing the lawn in the heat of summer, but for some reason he always liked raking in the fall. He'd build these huge piles, orange and red, right under her swing set and give her pushes while she pumped herself high enough to let go and jump. He'd cover her under the dry crackling leaves, making her disappear. Pretend to start walking away. *Hey, do I hear a squirrel?* And she'd wait, wiggling just a little, waiting for him to reach in and grab her and pull her out.

"Leave it. You can live without it." Eli tugged on the sleeve of her shirt, and she realized they were standing by the tree where her phone was hidden. "*Live* being the key word."

Chandra looped a strand of her hair around her finger, twirled it for a minute before tucking it behind her ear. That was another sign that Chandra had read about that was supposed to hold a guy's attention without words—touching your own hair.

"Let's go over to Jaffrey. The jazz groups are probably starting now." She shrugged.

"You don't like jazz? Maybe you should try it. You might be surprised."

"I didn't say I didn't like it." Her voice came out with an edge, and she saw the way he noticed it. His head drew back a little, his eyebrows lifting.

"I'm tired of sitting," Chandra said, and realized that this was actually true. "That's all college is, mostly. Sitting around and listening to things."

Eli's lips parted. She'd surprised him; she could tell.

"If I'm skipping class again," she said, her voice still louder than usual, "I want to *do* something. I don't want to sit around."

He looked at the watch under his coat sleeve, then grinned. "I know something we can do. Come on!"

He reached out his hand behind him, and Chandra took it, felt the momentum of his larger body pulling hers along. How long had it been since she'd held a guy's hand? She remembered for the second time today that trip to Disney World with her parents when she was eleven, how they'd walked through Fantasyland with the three of them holding hands, Chandra in the middle, her parents lifting her feet off the ground to a sing-song rhythm on every third step—one two *three!*—and Chandra knew she was too old for it but she didn't care.

Eli was leading them forward, past the library and the computer lab, all the way to the sports complex. They practically jogged past the recreation center, and through the glare on the wide front windows Chandra could see students on the treadmills. She tossed her head back and mimed an uproarious laugh, a silent one so Eli wouldn't notice, to let them know, if any of them recognized her dashing by, that she was on her way to doing something unpredictable and hilarious.

When they turned the corner of the building, Eli slowed up and they walked together to a large red door. "This is where the athletes work out," Eli said, pushing it open. She followed him inside to a gray-carpeted lobby with framed team pictures hung in neat lines on the tan brick walls. Smiling faces, bodies in matching red and white uniforms, posed in gymnasiums or fields or courts. The air smelled like a sweet medicine; fluorescent lights hummed overhead. Something she couldn't see was making a steady ticking noise. "Are we supposed to be in here?"

He grinned at her. "This'll be good. I haven't done this for a long time." She followed him down a short hallway to another door, also painted red.

"What? What are we doing?" She whispered, because Eli's voice was hushed too, like they were in the library.

"I was friends last year with this kid on the lacrosse team. He got put on probation, so they moved him out of the athlete dorm into Warner on my floor. We used to do this sometimes."

Eli pressed a series of numbers on the keypad above the doorknob;

the small circle on the pad flickered green. "*Yes.*" Eli opened the door, stepped forward, and gestured like a magician. "Voila!"

She entered a small, darkened room with tiled walls and two small swimming pools, side by side. Eli shut the door behind her. There was a long bench against one wall; on the opposite wall, a freezer and a shelf with stacked towels and a large rolling hamper on wheels. Directly across from Chandra and Eli was a double door made of glass, which led to an adjacent room, also dark, with shadowed shapes of exercise machines.

"Where is everyone?" she whispered. The room felt warm, the air heavy with moisture. "What are we doing here?"

"Welcome to our private spa!" Eli tossed his jacket on the bench. "It's all ours till 2:00. Or 1:45, to be on the safe side. That's when the teams start afternoon practice and the injured guys, or the guys with physical therapy routines, come in here to work with the trainers. But from 10:45 to 1:45, this room is always locked. Unused. Shame to let it go to waste, right?"

He sat down and kicked off his Sperrys, peeled off his socks. He said, "All the athletes have their classes scheduled between 9:25 and 1:30. Then they have afternoon practice, and then dinner and study hall, and then night practice. Like clockwork. My lacrosse friend had to write down everything he did every day and every night while he was banned from the team to prove himself, and then have it signed every week by the team manager."

"Didn't he just make stuff up?"

"Of course he did. And then he would feel guilty and cry sometimes. Actually cry. He told me he felt like a piece of shit for being dishonest and breaking the honor code, like he was in the fucking Navy SEALs or something. And I was like, *Dude, you play lacrosse. For a second-rate conference. Get over yourself.*" He pulled off his long-sleeved shirt. He got up from the bench and padded in his bare feet around the pool. With just his T-shirt on, his biceps looked weaker than she'd imagined.

"People," said Chandra, "are so full of themselves."

"That's right." He pointed at her across the water. "You get it. You know that, Chandra? You so get it."

She was still standing there with her Urban Outfitters bag over her shoulder, sweating in her corduroy shirt. Suddenly, he reached toward the wall, and Chandra covered her eyes, expecting sudden brightness from a light switch, but instead a churning noise started, like a big engine. It was the water in one of the pools, violently bubbling. The smell of chlorine lifted, making her eyes water. Eli pulled off his T-shirt and unzipped his jeans.

"Stop!" Chandra covered her stinging eyes.

"Oh, come on. Your underwear is just like a swimsuit. It's just the same as swimming in our swimsuits."

"What if someone comes in?"

"If someone starts to press the combination on the locked door, we'll hear it and run out the glass door. And if someone comes in the trainers' room from the other side, we'll see them before they see us and run out the other way."

He was wearing boxers. Chandra watched as he sat down by the edge of the pool and lowered both feet in the water. "Aahhh!" He pushed himself off the edge with a splash, standing now in the pool up to his waist, his arms lifted like chicken wings. "And besides," he said, "what if someone did come in and find us? I mean, what's the worst thing that would happen? They'd tell us to leave? We'd get a warning?"

It was dark, Chandra thought. But not so dark that he wouldn't see her body. Could she actually do this? She placed her bag on the bench and took off her shirt. Even though she was wearing a turtleneck underneath it, she felt her heart start to race. She could feel his eyes on her back.

"You said you wanted to *do* something. Get in. Come on."

She balanced on one leg and pulled off her right boot and then the left. She took off her socks. The mats under her feet felt rough and prickly. She curled her arches and moved around the pool toward the shelf of towels with slow, quick steps, like one of those old-time Chinese girls with foot binding that her professor in Gender Perspectives had told them about. She wrapped a towel around her body and tried to figure out if she could take off her turtleneck and leggings and make it to the whirlpool without dropping the towel until she was completely submerged in the dark water.

"Come on. You're wasting time."

The silliness had disappeared from Eli's voice. He sounded annoyed. Pinching the towel at her breastbone with one hand, Chandra pushed at the elastic band of her leggings with the other, trying to wriggle them off her hips.

She heard him suck in a breath of air and then splash underwater, saw the dark shape of him coiling into a mass on the bottom. Quickly she pulled off her turtleneck and covered up again with the towel. He rose up from the bubbling water with a grunt, shaking his head, flinging drops that hit her bare forearms. She pulled her feet free from her leggings and walked to the metal ladder on the far side of the pool, holding on to it with one hand, keeping her towel secure with the other; she felt with her feet for the textured steps leading down the pool's wall, and then the slippery bottom as she lowered in. Hot water from a jet spray pelted her back. The towel swirled up and she held it like a cape at her neck; it floated behind her shoulders as she folded her arms over her stomach, squatting in the pool up to her neck.

Eli's head bobbed above the surface a few feet away. The darkness of the room made his face look older, Chandra thought—handsome, kind of, with his hair slicked back. His eyes looked deeper in the steamy air, which she hoped was making her own face look better, too, more mysterious maybe, and if her mascara was running, hopefully it wouldn't show. The churning water swirled around Chandra like a force field, protecting her body from scrutiny. Eli was moving toward her now. This was happening. If he kissed her, Chandra decided, she would kiss him back. She was doing it. Finally, she was having a college experience.

"I'm so bad, letting you talk me into this," she said, hoping her voice sounded flirty and mocking in a fun way. "This is the *third day* I'm missing classes. I'm so behind."

"That's nothing." Eli laughed, low and abrupt.

She felt his toe slide against her toe underwater. He said, "This is my fifth week."

"What do you mean?"

He grinned, his teeth glinting in the dark. "I haven't been to classes for five weeks."

She felt the space between their bodies in the water get smaller as he moved closer, the pressure of the waves against her stomach building. "But . . ."

"I had it figured out by the second week. That I was going to live by my own rules for a change, you know? Relinquish the façade."

"Can you do that? Just not go to your classes for that long? Haven't they *said* anything to you?"

"Oh, I'm sure my student email account is full of dire warnings from my professors, at least the ones who bother to take attendance. But, as you know, I'm not reading them. Or anything else online. Because I'm choosing to spend my time actually living my life."

"I didn't know you could *do* that. Just never go to your classes."

"*I'm* doing it." His white teeth flashed.

"But for how long?" Chandra felt a twist of anxiety in her chest.

Eli grunted. "A couple more weeks, probably. The midterm grades will all be submitted by next week, and then the week after that they'll probably come get me out of the dorm. And that'll be it."

"They'll make you leave?"

"I'm already on academic probation from last year. So yeah. They'll undoubtedly request my departure." This time his laugh was louder and seemed to echo off the slippery walls.

"Then you'll go home?"

She saw his shoulders shrug, above and below the water's surface.

"Where do your parents live?" she asked.

His body was so close to hers in the whirlpool. If she lifted her hand, her fingers would touch his chest. "I'm not going there," he whispered, and it sounded to Chandra like he was about to cry.

"Eli," she said, "I'll help you. You can stay in my dorm. They won't know where to look for you."

"I'll disappear." He sucked in a breath. "Poof!"

With a sudden *whoosh* he dunked himself under the water, and then his long legs and one of his knees, or maybe both of them, were pressing against her legs and his hands were on her waist, his thumbs on either side of her belly button and his fingertips on her back, and where was her towel? Her towel was gone, she realized, both frightened and glad, and Eli's head was above hers now, he was gulping at the air, and she leaned back in his hands, arching her neck, the crown of her head touching the water. She let her hands reach up to his shoulders and looked into his eyes.

"*Chandra*," he said.

His hands loosened their grip on her waist; she felt the support slip away and had to plant the balls of her feet on the bottom of the pool to keep herself from falling backwards into the water.

"Chandra, your *bones*. Jesus."

She pushed off with her feet and flailed with her arms, moving in slow motion through the water away from him. Her towel, where was her towel? She spotted it swirling in a jet stream near the metal ladder and lunged for it.

"God, Chandra, chill *out*. I just, you know . . . It's kind of shocking—"

"Shut up!" She managed to pull herself out of the pool; the rushing of the whirlpool engine seemed to be right inside her head now.

She grabbed at her boots and bag and her big corduroy shirt by the bench, but then as she ran around to the other side of the pool and tried to pick up her turtleneck and leggings, she lost her grip on the towel again and it dropped to the floor. She started to cry, and she could picture herself standing there like a hunchback, cradling her load. She couldn't bear to turn around to look at Eli, watching her from the pool. She could feel her bare back and her soaking panties clinging to her ass in the horrible invisible air.

"It's sad," Eli said. "What this fucked-up society does to people."

"Don't *say* anything!" She pushed against the glass door and ran to one of the treadmills in the physical therapy room, crouched on the other side of it, and waited for a couple minutes, afraid that he would follow her. But he didn't.

She struggled to pull her leggings on over her wet skin, then her two shirts and her boots. She raked her fingers through her tangled hair. She found her way to a different doorway on the other side of the room, back to the lobby, past the rows of team pictures, all those smiling athletes posing with the Hawk mascot, its cartoonish beak and red wings. Who was the person hidden in that bird costume? Chandra wondered.

As she stepped outside into the October air, the wind wrapped itself around her wet scalp like an icy tourniquet. She held her Urban Outfitters bag against the side of her body and began marching across the campus, headed toward the student union. Had she muted her phone before she let Eli hide it in that hole in the big tree? She couldn't remember! What if someone had texted her, what if her mother had called, and someone walking by heard her Rihanna ringtone—*yellow diamonds*—and found it there. By now maybe Professor Steinmetz had sent her an email about missing class again. To voice his concern. That's how he would say it, or something like that.

Maybe she could write her paper for him about money. She didn't want to write anymore about giving up her cell phone; she had nothing to say about *that* topic. She wished she were smart enough to write an essay about money, about how money could make you hate someone, like the way she guessed Eli hated his parents, like the way her father hated her mother for not giving him her lawsuit money to buy a Sonic burger franchise, which would have been the whole solution to his whole life, or at least that was what he believed. He would have screwed it up, her mother had told her, *guaranteed*, and then where would that have left Chandra, and her college education, and her future wedding, God willing? But Chandra didn't know. She didn't know where that would have left her, or where she was left now.

She started walking faster. The union was still far away, and she wanted to be there. She wanted to start running, but that would look so weird, wouldn't it? She was wearing her boots, the ones with high heels. People didn't run in high-heeled boots. But still, she could feel herself picking up her feet between each quickening step.

She used to run all the time. She missed running. Maybe she could write her paper for Professor Steinmetz about running. It was during that horrible summer when she'd started running, the summer when she was fourteen, after her parents had sold the house and moved into their separate apartments in different towns. She would start at her mother's apartment in Vernon and walk all the way to their old house in Woodlen, on Riley Mountain Road. It was a yellow Cape Cod with a slate-blue door and matching shutters. It took her two hours and twenty minutes. When she got there, she would stand by the mailbox for a few minutes. Sometimes, if no one was around, she would walk onto the front yard and stand there. She didn't know who had bought the house. Her parents never told her, and it seemed somehow too embarrassing to ask them. Shameful, for some reason. When she stood on the front lawn, a trespasser, sometimes she would feel her heart start thumping. She would count to ten, or twenty, or sometimes fifty, and then step back to the street.

And then she would run home. She could slow way down on the upward hills, but she had to keep lifting her feet. If she didn't run home, she told herself, then she couldn't go back. It would be the last time.

That's how it started, Chandra thought. At some point during the summer, Melanie commented on how good Chandra was looking. Chandra remembered the day that Melanie seemed to notice her in a new way, surveying her with a lifted eyebrow. Lean, Melanie had said. Lean and fit, not sloppy like so many teenage girls with their belly shirts and pudgy thighs and boobs bouncing around. When school started at the end of August, Chandra had to stop her journeys to the old house, but she found other ways to test herself. She kept going and going.

Right now, all she wanted was her phone back. As she made it past the computer lab, the union came into view, and there was the tree in

419

the distance, its golden leaves glowing in afternoon sunlight. She could feel her fingers twitching in anticipation. She wanted it back so badly. She would text someone, anyone, just to hear it buzz, just to feel it trembling there in the palm of her hand.

Nominated by Colorado Review

THE RAPTOR

fiction by CHARLES HOLDEFER

from CHICAGO QUARTERLY REVIEW

Cody was the only one to see the raptor descend. What to believe? On the second day of their vacation, Lisa had put Ronny—barely three weeks old!—on the picnic table in his baby seat while she paused to apply sun cream to his soft, wrinkly knees. She'd already greased his face, but those little knees were particularly exposed. She said, "Beautiful day, big boy." Ronny gaped toothlessly at the sky, drooling from a corner of his mouth. His mother had just changed his diaper, and he was unstrapped in the seat, which allowed him greater freedom to experiment with his legs, kicking as if to climb into the expanse of blue. "Happy Ronaldus!" Lisa straightened for a moment to apply some of Ronny's protective cream to her own face. Up here in the mountains you had to be careful, the ultraviolet rays were more powerful.

Cody sat on a nearby rock, looking up at the pines, the fleecy clouds, and a black dot that was growing bigger. He was Ronny's older brother, just three weeks shy of his fifth birthday. His father, Dan, was back at the car, retrieving the ice chest. That black dot was coming straight at the picnic area. Lisa was saying, "Cody, you need to cream up, too. I'll get your hat—"

With a swoop the raptor grabbed Ronny and the baby chair and then began to arc upward, pumping its wings furiously. For an instant it appeared to hesitate. (That was how Cody remembered it when he replayed the moment in his head, countless times over the years). More likely, it was struggling with the unexpected weight.

Lisa heard the beating of air and turned in time to see the flurried form, with Ronny, now more than twice her height above the picnic

421

table. She screamed, and at the same time the baby seat, which had dangled below Ronny by a strap that had momentarily caught on his ankle, came loose and fell to earth, bouncing and skidding across pine needles and pebbles. Now the raptor began to ascend more rapidly, and Dan, hearing Lisa's screams, came sprinting down the path. Ronny and the big bird disappeared around a curve of pines, and Cody, more upset by the sound of his mother's distress than by what he'd just witnessed— it was hard to believe, and he wasn't even sure he believed what he'd seen, yet—let out a guttural moan, surprisingly deep, for one so young.

Even if not for the raptor, Lisa and Dan's marriage might've fallen apart. It's not obvious. But it's true that Dan hadn't entertained the idea of a divorce, nor had Lisa, before that summer vacation in the mountains. He and Lisa and Cody and "Ronaldus Magnus" (the nickname they'd given Ronny, a passing jest after hearing the phrase on the radio) had been a tight young family. The future was something to look forward to. Lisa's second pregnancy was no accident. It was a conscious confirmation of their decision to make a life together.

The police were incredulous; the park rangers surprised but not totally dismissive; while the ornithologist Abby Van Rheenan from the University of California at Davis was sufficiently ambiguous to give credence to what Lisa had partly seen and what Cody had witnessed from the beginning, but had trouble articulating. "A rabbit, sure. Or any small rodent," said Dr. Van Rheenan. "There's folklore about this kind of thing happening but nothing in corroborated research. There is nothing in the literature. Still, it's not impossible, I mean in terms of the practical physics, for weight and uplift. Especially if it were an exceptional raptor."

She said this to Lisa and Dan in a private interview in her office. It bothered them that she seemed so preoccupied with determining the type of raptor, whether a condor ("highly unlikely, but not inconceivable") or perhaps an eagle. Dr. Van Rheenan went on for minutes at a stretch without speaking of little Ronny at all. She repeated her opinion to the police and later, in front of television cameras. Cody, who wasn't present at his parents' private interview, knew the professor's most vivid testimony from a video sequence played to him a month later at the request of his mother's psychiatrist. Cody's manner of parroting Dr. Van Rheenan's hypotheses, word-for-word, when questioned by the police only made investigators more suspicious that something else, less extraordinary and perhaps criminal, had happened to the infant. After all, a body was never found. Park officials who assisted in the search reminded the police that looking for a baby in two hundred square miles of rugged wilderness, full of canyons, cliffs and crevices, was a difficult and borderline impossible task.

The criminal investigation bore no fruit.

Ronny found himself in a nest on a cliff ledge with two baby birds. Still looking up at the blue sky, inhaling the thinner, colder air, his cries competed with the screeks of his companions. Oh, he was hungry! As the blue air turned purple and then black and stars pricked the blackness and constellations whirled in the firmament above, he welcomed the warmth of the bodies next to him, and it was a comfort when the big, heavy body sat on him, with its stronger heat, its thicker feathers.

Ronny tired himself crying and then fell into a doze, feeling the beats of hearts next to his. They beat very fast.

Even if not for the raptor, Lisa might've taken to drinking too much and too often while on anti-depressants. There had been a precedent. Once, when a teenager, she'd been prescribed Sarafem after an emotional crisis involving an ex-boyfriend, and she'd ended up in the hospital for swallowing her pills with a bottle of brandy; but it had happened only once, and Lisa's parents, blinded by their love and hopes for their daughter, never spoke of that ugly weekend and over the years had almost succeeded in willing themselves to forget it, because it was so long ago, and since then Lisa had settled down into a solid marriage with a good fellow, Dan Titus, who straight out of college had been hired for a good job at NatFinance. A year after the raptor had passed, Lisa was on fifty milligrams of desvenlafaxine daily, along with four to eight gin and tonics of varying strengths. She quickly went through two sales jobs before luckily landing a part-time position for the Department of Highway Safety and Motor Vehicles, taking photos for the Drivers' License Division. Faces, so many faces she lined up in a digitized oval on her computer screen, faces often a blur to her eyes, but faces she captured nonetheless with a click of a mouse, a snick and a flash. Once Cody found Lisa passed out after work on the couch with her skirt up and, before turning away, he studied the bristly pubic hair protruding around the V of her panties. This was Cody's introduction to adult bodies.

Even if not for the raptor, Dan might've started cheating on Lisa. He hadn't done so earlier, but six years of previous fidelity was the past, and the future loomed large. He'd always had a roving eye, even when he'd been most in love with Lisa. But he'd always been a looker, not a doer. He would've felt too guilty and the thought of Lisa finding out, of hurting her, was mortifying. So he hadn't cheated on her. Four months after the raptor, though, he pressed his mouth to the lips of a camerawoman from a news crew who'd come to interview him, and when she pressed back, he grabbed her hand and brought it down and began to rub it on his crotch.

Cody didn't know about this but he noticed when his parents shouted and when his father slept on the couch, and he didn't think of the raptor then, but he could tell, he knew, that now something was missing from their lives, and it wasn't only his little brother Ronny.

Ronny had never eaten regurgitated chipmunk proteins before, but he had no inkling that it might be unusual, and, in fact, when feeding time came, he was very pleased. By now the others had pecked off his dirty diapers and consumed the contents. They pushed him around the nest while he struggled to roll back into a more comfortable position. He rocked one way and then another, his back cut by briars.

Lisa and Dan and Cody did not figure in his life, but he was hungry again—oh, he longed for the soothing, warm, and pleasantly filling regurgitation.

Dan accepted a NatFinance transfer to Portland, Oregon, after consenting to the first calculation of alimony and child support proposed by Lisa's lawyer. Dan felt guilty about leaving his family and wanted to settle the matter as quickly as possible. Within months, though, he regretted his generosity and resented the struggle to pay bills in two states.

Cody stayed with his mother and grew up to be a gangly kid who shared her taste for alcohol. He was a starting forward on the freshman basketball team, and, unlike many of his classmates, he didn't smoke dope. But the first time he got drunk, when he was fourteen, was perfect. It felt like falling in love. From then on he got drunk every weekend—it was his preferred manner of dating, and never mind basketball, either. His mother didn't find out about his predilection till he was almost sixteen, for which she scolded him, but she was lucid enough, due to her own dependency, to know that she couldn't force him to stop. Instead, she stressed responsibility, that it was not forbidden for Cody (and soon his buddies) to make use of her supply as long as he (and soon they) didn't get behind the wheel of a car but stayed in the rec room in the basement and got drunk in front of the TV there. If anyone threw up, it had to be in the toilet and not on the rug. "Is that clear?" she said firmly.

Cody respected this in-house policy most of the time. He wasn't a particularly rebellious boy. As he approached his senior year, the situation evolved to the point where Lisa sometimes went downstairs to the rec room and joined Cody and his pals. She'd dated a few men— divorced and tired types who wanted sex and sympathy but were too lackluster to offer her much in return—and sometimes it was actually more relaxing, and certainly more amusing, to spend time with the boys. She liked their humor, their energy, watching their bare muscular arms in cut-off T-shirts as they laughed raucously at action DVDs. Sure, they were immature, and favored rum and Cokes; but at least these fellows had vitality. Instead of being on her own and depressed, it was a boost to walk downstairs and step into a party. "Freshen your drink, Mrs. T?" asked Eddie, a dark-eyed, considerate young man with a husky voice. She might've even let herself be persuaded to dance (just for fun, with nothing funny or inappropriate going on) if the boys had gone in for that sort of thing, but the boys didn't go in for that sort of thing. By now these parties took place on school nights, too; Cody was fully in love and committed to them.

He barely graduated from high school, and both he and Lisa were terribly hungover on the June noon of his commencement ceremony. Still, they covered for each other (an expression of mother and son loyalty) in front of Dan, who'd flown in from Portland for the occasion. Entering the restaurant for a celebration dinner afterward, Dan walked alongside them with a similar, stiff-legged gait—one could almost assume it was a family trait—but in his case it wasn't a question of willed sobriety but because under his shirt his ribs were wrapped with yards of bandage. He complained to Lisa and Cody of a rough fall playing touch football with some friends from work though, in truth, his injury had occurred in an argument with a girlfriend who'd struck him with a garden rake. (Shana, now an ex-girlfriend. It was something he'd said.) She'd swung with all her might and caught him square across the chest. Lucky for him the prongs were facing the other way! "I won't be playing again for a while." He mustered a smile.

They ordered pulled pork and spoke of Cody's plans to enroll at Reiser County Community College, which had accepted him on probation into its culinary arts program. While waiting for their food they clinked together their sweaty glasses of iced tea. "Proud of you Cody," Dan said, and Lisa nodded. "To the future!"

Two a.m. Cody has a test tomorrow that he hasn't studied for, but he's not thinking about it. He's lying in the upper bunk and talking to his dormmate in the bunk below, a chubby kid named Mario who always wears sweat suits and swabs his ears at least twice a day. He and Mario get on pretty well, they play a lot of Xbox, and now with the lights out they've continued talking and told a few dirty jokes and gossiped about other dorm residents, and in their easy familiarity in the darkness, suddenly Cody feels a strong desire to tell Mario about something he witnessed a long time ago when he was a little kid at a picnic site. It's like a need to confess. "One time I was sitting on a rock and—"

Two a.m. Lisa is fast asleep and the phone rings. She gropes for the receiver. "Hullo?"

"It's me."

She's been sleeping deeply, and the call is unexpected, so it takes her a moment to understand. "Dan?"

"Yes. Can we talk? Sorry it's so late, but can we talk?"

"Uh, yeah." She sits up in bed, finds an angle against the headboard. "I'm listening."

Dan looks over his shoulder at the closed bedroom door where a woman named Heidi is sleeping. She's Dan's latest, not nearly as attractive as the other women he's been with since he dumped Lisa, and not as attractive as Lisa, either, but she's not violent and she's very successful. Heidi owns three optical outlets. Dan hunches his back and speaks softly into his cell. "Do you still think about Ronny?"

Although she wasn't aware of it till this moment, Lisa realizes that she's known all along the reason for this call.

"Sure I do. But not as much as before." She sits up straighter in the darkness. "Which is still probably more than you ever did." Lisa is ready for this conversation.

"Sometimes—"

"You just shut everything out," she adds.

426

"Sometimes I wake up and can't go back to sleep and, you know, it's Ronny I'm thinking about. Been almost fourteen years. Remember how you called him Ronaldus Magnus?" Dan chuckles softly.

"You were the one who started that," she says.

"No, it was you."

"Well, if it was me I didn't invent it, it was just a silly thing from the radio."

Suddenly Dan is sobbing into the phone. A surge he doesn't want to hold back. He expects Lisa to sob with him, but she doesn't. Her voice is brittle. "He's beyond our reach now, you know."

Still, she doesn't hang up on him.

Presently he says, "Sorry I woke you. Goodnight."

"Goodnight, Dan."

Mario barks with laughter.

"You expect me to believe that?" He kicks the mattress above him, giving Cody a bounce in the darkness.

The nest was so crowded! There was hardly room to perch. The raptor pecked and pushed, pecked and pushed, and then suddenly, one of the little ones toppled over the edge.

It plummeted and began to beat its wings and, helped by a brisk updraft from the canyon below, managed to climb in the air, awkwardly, before dipping down, and then climbing again, almost all the way back up to the nest, coming to rest, though, on a ledge several meters below. Its hooked beak opened and closed, emitting cries like spasms. Its head turned with sharp jerks from side to side.

The second one pushed out of the nest reacted in much the same way, only it struggled less against the air and managed to glide safely to a granite outcrop further below.

Ronny didn't see any of this. He lay on his back, wiggling his arms, his nostrils and the corners of his mouth encrusted. He was happy, gurgling. Now there was more room in the nest.

The raptor lowered its head and pushed at his side. Ronny cried out when it grabbed his ankle and began to pull. He kicked and tried to roll away. The raptor hopped to the other side of the nest and began to push and peck. Ronny still tried to roll away, and this time he went over the edge.

Lisa was on her exercise bicycle in front of the TV when the phone rang. She hopped off the seat to answer.

"Mom, I've got great news!"

"What is it, Cody?" she panted.

"I've found the Lord and I'm going to dedicate my life to his work."

"What's that, honey? Let me turn down the TV."

The volume was up high because of all the creaking and whirring of the exercise bicycle. She found the remote control and pressed the mute button.

Cody explained that he'd accepted Jesus and received a blessing from the Holy Spirit and he'd never felt so much joy, so much promise, so much love. "I love you, Mom."

"I love you too, Cody."

"I haven't had a drink in nine days. And you know, most of the time I haven't even wanted a drink. I've got the peace which passeth understanding."

"Well—good for you."

Lisa was taken aback, but if she were honest she would have to admit—and this required no reflection, despite her lack of faith—that she was glad for her son, very glad, if he'd found a way to throw off this affliction. She would've even volunteered that she envied him. But then he had to go and spoil it.

"Mom, I want you to join us this Sunday."

"I don't know, Cody."

"Have you had a drink today? You told me you were trying to cut down. Have you?"

"No," she said, exasperated. Here she was, on her exercise bike, trying to do better, and now her son was picking on her.

"Did you drink last night?"

"No," she lied.

"Mom, if only you could know this joy!"

Dan saw the raptor during his colonoscopy. It was supposed to be a routine procedure, but he was scared. You never knew. What if there were polyps? What if they were cancerous? A routine procedure, yes, but it could be the beginning of the end. While under gas, he saw the raptor coming down. The memory startled him with its clarity. He felt a mixture of horror and something almost like elation, watching it swoop through the sparkling sunlight against a backdrop of blue mountains.

Of course, this memory was nonsense. He recalled as much a few hours later as he sat up in bed and ate a solid meal and began to feel normal again. He'd already telephoned Heidi to tell her that she could come and pick him up. No, they hadn't found any polyps. As he ate, he reflected on this experience under anaesthesia. What the hell? The day the raptor descended, he'd been back at the car, getting the ice chest. He wasn't there.

"There was a reason for what happened to Ronny."

"You can't know!" Lisa snaps. "You don't know a thing!" Cody has tried to bring this up before, and Lisa has cut him off. But this time he persists.

"It might've been an angel. It might've been a demon. But whatever it was, it was part of God's plan."

"I don't have to hear this. I don't care what you believe—you're, you're trivializing it when you talk that way. It's disrespectful. I don't want to hear it."

Now Cody's temper flares, too. "I'm not the one who's trivializing. My point is, it's not just about you. It's not just about our family. The world is so much bigger. I can see clearly how you and Dad have always used what happened to Ronny as a reason to go and do whatever you wanted. People choose that, instead of facing what they should do. You're no exception. You've embraced temptation, you just rolled over and gave up after Ronny. Me, too. Even when I didn't know I was doing it. Maybe you didn't always know, either. But it's got to stop! It's not too late to accept the truth, to hear the Word. Just invite the Lord to come to your heart, that's all I'm saying. I want you to know the joy."

"You want to torment me," Lisa says.

Cody clears his throat and announces: "I'm going there."

"Huh? Where?"

"To the park."

"Oh, God. What for?"

"I want to go back. I want to feel the place again. Haven't you ever thought about going back there?"

"No," Lisa lies.

"Maybe on the mountain I'll get a message. Maybe the Lord will have something to tell me there, something that will convince you and Dad."

"Yes, maybe," Lisa says wearily.

"Maybe I'll find Ronny. You know they think they've found Noah's Ark on Mount Ararat. Above the vegetation line."

"Oh my God. Don't do this, please."

"He tells me we're living in sin," Dan tells Heidi. "That's the way he talks now. He's not angry when he says it, but he sincerely means it. And—I don't know, aside from that, he's showing plenty of progress. At least he's serious about school now, he's got a girlfriend, and he told me he's training for a marathon. He always had athletic ability, I'm glad he's picked that up again. He's really doing a lot better."

Heidi lets him ramble on this way; it seems to relax Dan as he chops the food for dinner. Watching him work, though, she's relieved to learn that she doesn't have to meet his son yet. Apparently the boy has postponed his visit to Portland to go on some religious retreat in the mountains.

The wok sizzles. Dan shakes it and then glances back at her. Heidi realizes that he's waiting for a response.

"Well . . . who isn't living in sin?" she asks.

The moonlight was so strong that the tent fabric seemed to glow, even inside the tent. Cody could hear Ashley's steady breathing.

It was the first time they'd slept in the same space, and she'd let him kiss her, but, before things went too far, she suggested that they share a goodnight prayer.

"Well . . . sure," he said.

Ashley was the one who'd brought Cody to the Lord. She was a slim redhead majoring in intelligent design at Carson Christian College. She was nice to him in many ways, so Cody didn't insist too much beyond the kissing, though he couldn't help thinking about possibilities.

Now he got up and unzipped the tent flap, trying not to make noise. She sat up. "What's the matter?"

"Nothing," he said. "Just need to pee."

He stepped out of the tent and closed the flap behind him.

A full moon bathed the mountains. Here, the sky was unpolluted by city lights, and the world appeared silver and soapy, as each rock, each tree stood out distinctly and he could even see shadows from the trees and from himself as he moved away from the tent. Despite the hour, there was no danger of stumbling. The moonlight was that bright.

Next to a tree he pulled down the front of his shorts and began to urinate. His mind raced. Amid those rocks, those round glowing shapes—was Ronny's skull reflected among them? Or those bushes—did Ronny's ribs protrude from the side of the mountain like tiny boat timbers? Or maybe Ronny had been carried straight from this earth, like Enoch who had walked with God . . .

He didn't know the answer, but it was interesting to think about. He finished urinating slowly, with difficulty, because the touch of his hand on his penis provoked a reaction and resulted in an erection protruding out into the chill air. He hadn't sought this effect; probably he was still trying to get over the proximity to Ashley, the kissing in the tent. But there it was. When he released his penis, it no longer fit back in his shorts. It poked out above the elastic band which, when he tried to walk on, pinched and squeezed him with a still-arousing effect. He stopped and reached down to grip it, and then he let it go; he walked a little further and couldn't resist stopping and grabbing it again.

Cody looked around in the silver light. If he went behind that ridge of rock, Ashley would never see him, even if she stuck her head out of the tent. Nobody could see him—except God, who already knew what was going to happen—so he went behind the ridge and lowered his shorts and tugged on his penis which, in this light, glowed silver, too. Soon it pulsed, and Cody came, gasping.

When he fell, rolling into the open air, he felt surprised and, at the same time, affronted. What was happening to him?

Ronny bellowed headlong into a vast and hideous deep. There was no time to think of who could hear him. His heels moved eagerly for traction against the retreating sky. This missing sensation seemed precious, but it was also like an insult to him and to the place from which he fell.

Darkness in a hurtling tract, the rub of cold. His voice split the air, refusing to submit or yield. This much felt right. His will was intact, still untouched, his own.

A cold sweat broke out on the back of Cody's neck and he inhaled deeply several times. He shivered. He was much better now. Presently he was able to tuck his penis back into his shorts. He gazed up at the night, the cavernous sky.

"Thank you, Lord, for your blessings. Thank you for this wonderful world and for having a plan."

Cody turned around and headed for the other side of the ridge of rock. Dry pine needles crackled softly underfoot, and he continued to whisper to himself when suddenly a breeze gusted up the canyon, and he heard a clatter of stones. Cody stopped in his tracks, listening to the air. Waiting. He rubbed his arms. Eventually he let out a low moan and angled in another direction, away from the tent, unable to think of sleep.

Nominated by Chicago Quarterly Review, Elizabeth McKenzie

RESTING PLACE

by KATE LEVIN

from RIVER TEETH

When we arrive at daycare, I step out of the car and close my door gently, hoping not to startle my son awake. As I open the back door to retrieve him from his car seat, I see the bird.

I gasp, but only its stillness is gruesome. Otherwise, it's perfect—round, brown, downy, wedged between leather and metal, tucked into the space where the door opens and closes. A baby; a sparrow, I think. When I was young, we had a Christmas ornament just like it.

There is my sleeping son, and there is the dead bird.

When he was younger, just born, fear overtook me in waves. I could lose him at any time. I could lose him because I had him, and anything I had, I could lose. The logic was airtight, suffocating.

But then I would look at him, breath muscle bones, humming in motion; a system insisting on itself. Who was I to doubt it?

A clean napkin is the best I can do for a shroud. I pluck the sparrow from the backseat, amazed by its lightness and lack of resistance. A few feet away, a thick wall of green shrubbery separates us from the day-care's yard. No one is watching. I reach in and give the bird to the branches. Through the windshield I can see my son, eyes still closed. Beneath a buckled harness, his chest rises and falls, rises and falls, rises and falls.

Nominated by Tim Hedges

THE INVITATION

by BARRY LOPEZ

from GRANTA

When I was young, and just beginning to travel with them, I imagined that indigenous people saw more and heard more, that they were over-all simply more aware than I was. They were more aware, and did see and hear more than I did. The absence of spoken conversation when-ever I was traveling with them, however, should have provided me with a clue about why this might be true; but it didn't, not for a while. It's this: when an observer doesn't immediately turn what his senses convey to him into language, into the vocabulary and syntactical framework we all employ when trying to define our experiences, there's a much greater opportunity for minor details, which might at first seem unimportant, to remain alive in the foreground of an impression, where, later, they might deepen the meaning of an experience.

If my companions and I, for example, encountered a grizzly bear feeding on a caribou carcass, I would tend to focus almost exclusively on the bear. My companions would focus on the part of the world of which, at that moment, the bear was only a fragment. The bear here might be compared with a bonfire, a kind of incandescence that throws light on everything around it. My companions would glance off into the outer reaches of that light, then look back to the fire, back and forth. They would repeatedly situate the smaller thing within the larger thing, back and forth. As they noticed trace odors in the air, or listened for birdsong or the sound of brittle brush rattling, they in effect extended the moment of encounter with the bear backward and forward in time. Their framework for the phenomenon, one that I might later shorten just to 'meeting the bear', was more voluminous than mine; and where

435

my temporal boundaries for the event would normally consist of little more than the moments of the encounter itself, theirs included the time before we arrived, as well as the time after we left. For me, the bear was a noun, the subject of a sentence; for them, it was a verb, the gerund 'bearing'.

Over the years traveling cross-country with indigenous people I absorbed two lessons about how to be more fully present in an encounter with a wild animal. First, I needed to understand that I was entering the event as it was *unfolding*. It started before I arrived and would continue unfolding after I departed. Second, the event itself—let's say we didn't disturb the grizzly bear as he fed but only took in what he or she was doing and then slipped away—could not be completely defined by referring solely to the physical geography around us in those moments. For example, I might not recall something we'd all seen a half-hour before, a caribou hoof print in soft ground at the edge of a creek, say; but my companions would remember that. And a while after our encounter with the bear, say a half-mile farther on, they would notice something else—a few grizzly bear guard hairs snagged in scales of tree bark—and they would relate it to some detail they'd observed during those moments when we were watching the bear. The event I was cataloging in my mind as 'encounter with a tundra grizzly' they were experiencing as a sudden immersion in the current of a river. They were swimming in it, feeling its pull, noting the temperature of the water, the back eddies and where the side streams entered. My approach, in contrast, was mostly to take note of objects in the scene—the bear, the caribou, the tundra vegetation. A series of dots, which I would try to make sense of by connecting them all with a single line. My friends had situated themselves within a dynamic event. Also, unlike me, they felt no immediate need to resolve it into meaning. Their approach was to let it continue to unfold. To notice everything and to let whatever significance was there emerge in its own time.

The lesson to be learned here was not just for me to pay closer attention to what was going on around me, if I hoped to have a deeper understanding of the event, but to remain in a state of suspended mental analysis while observing all that was happening—resisting the urge to define or summarize. To step away from the familiar compulsion to understand. Further, I had to incorporate a quintessential characteristic of the way indigenous people observe: they pay more attention to *patterns* in what they encounter than to isolated objects. When they saw the bear they right away began searching for a pattern that was resolving itself before them as 'a bear feeding on a carcass'. They began gathering various pieces together that might later self-assemble into an event larger than 'a bear feeding'. These unintegrated pieces they took in as we traveled—the nature of the sonic landscape that permeated this particular physical landscape; the presence or absence of wind, and the direction from which it was coming or had shifted; a piece of speckled eggshell under a tree; leaves missing from the stems of a species of brush; a hole freshly dug in the ground—might individually convey very little. Allowed to slowly resolve into a pattern, however, they might become revelatory. They might illuminate the land further.

If the first lesson in learning how to see more deeply into a landscape was to be continuously attentive, and to stifle the urge to stand *outside* the event, to instead stay *within* the event, leaving its significance to be resolved later; the second lesson, for me, was to notice how often I asked my body to defer to the dictates of my mind, how my body's extraordinary ability to discern textures and perfumes, to discriminate among tones and colors in the world outside itself, was dismissed by the rational mind.

As much as I believed I was fully present in the physical worlds I was traveling through, I understood over time that I was not. More often I was only *thinking* about the place I was in. Initially awed by an event, the screech of a gray fox in the night woods, say, or the surfacing of a large whale, I too often moved straight to analysis. On occasion I would become so wedded to my thoughts, to some cascade of ideas, that I actually lost touch with the details that my body was *still gathering* from a place. The ear heard the song of a vesper sparrow, and then heard the song again, and knew that the second time it was a different vesper sparrow singing. The mind, pleased with itself for identifying those notes as the song of a vesper sparrow, was too preoccupied with its summary to notice what the ear was still offering. The mind was making no use of the body's ability to be discerning about sounds. And so the mind's knowledge of the place remained superficial.

Many people have written about how, generally speaking, indigenous people seem to pick up more information traversing a landscape than an outsider, someone from a culture that no longer highly values physical intimacy with a place, that regards this sort of sensitivity as a 'primitive' attribute, something a visitor from an 'advanced' culture would be comfortable believing he had actually outgrown. Such a dismissive view, as I have come to understand it, ignores the great intangible value that achieving physical intimacy with a place might provide. I'm inclined to point out to someone who condescends to such a desire for intimacy, although it might seem rude, that it is not possible for human beings to outgrow loneliness. Nor can someone from a culture that condescends to nature easily escape the haunting thought that one's life is meaningless.

Existential loneliness and a sense that one's life is inconsequential, both of which are hallmarks of modern civilizations, seem to me to derive in part from our abandoning a belief in the therapeutic dimensions of a relationship with place. A continually refreshed sense of the unplumbable complexity of patterns in the natural world, patterns that are ever present and discernible, and which incorporate the observer, undermine the feeling that one is alone in the world, or meaningless in it. The effort to know a place deeply is, ultimately, an expression of the human desire to belong, to fit somewhere.

The determination to know a particular place, in my experience, is consistently rewarded. And every natural place, to my mind, is open to being known. And somewhere in this process a person begins to sense that they *themselves* are becoming known, so that when they are absent from that place they know that place misses them. And this reciprocity, to know and be known, reinforces a sense that one is necessary in the world.

Perhaps the first rule of everything we endeavor to do is to pay attention. Perhaps the second is to be patient. And perhaps a third is to be attentive to what the body knows. In my experience, individual indigenous people are not necessarily more aware than people who've grown up in the modern culture I grew up in. Indigenous cultures, of course, are as replete with inattentive, lazy, and undiscerning individuals as 'advanced' cultures. But they tend to value more highly the importance of intimacy with a place. When you travel with them, you're acutely aware that theirs is a fundamentally different praxis from your own. They're more attentive, more patient, less willing to say what they know, to collapse mystery into language. When I was young, and one of my traveling companions would make some stunningly insightful remark about the place we were traveling through, I would sometimes feel envious; a feeling related not so much to a desire to possess that same depth of knowledge but a desire to so obviously *belong* to a particular place. To so clearly be an integral part of the place one is standing in.

A grizzly bear stripping fruit from blackberry vines in a thicket is more than a bear stripping fruit from blackberry vines in a thicket. It is a point of entry into a world most of us have turned our backs on in an effort to go somewhere else, believing we'll be better off just *thinking* about a grizzly bear stripping fruit from blackberry vines in a thicket.

The moment is an invitation, and the bear's invitation to participate is offered, without prejudice, to anyone passing by.

Nominated by Granta, Jack Driscoll, Joyce Carol Oates

HOSPICE

by JEAN VALENTINE

from *SHIRT IN HEAVEN* (COPPER CANYON)

I wore his hat
as if it was the rumpled coat
of his body, like I could put it on.

The coat of his hair, of his brain, its glitter
he gave it to me, something he'd worn.
He didn't touch his dog, touch was too much,

he didn't let her go.
I felt his hat on my head, like a hand,
though his hat was on the floor, just by my chair.

I went on drinking water
as if there was more water.
I went on living on earth
as if there was still life
on earth

        I remembered
like an islander   my island

like a calving iceberg, air

like jazz
rumpled

like its glitter
worn hand
by my chair

❋

I thought I'd have to listen, hard,
I didn't even swallow.
But nothing from you stopped.

Nominated by Copper Canyon Press,
Jane Hirshfield, William Olsen, David Wojahn

MISTRESS MICKLE
ALL AT SEA

fiction by ELIZABETH McCRACKEN

from ZOETROPE: ALL–STORY

New Year's Eve in a Rotterdam garret, the whole block blacked-out, bottle-rockets rattling the casements: Mistress Maggle, villainess of the children's game show *Barnaby Grudge*, off-duty and far from home, ate a cold canned hotdog in the dark and pronounced it delicious. These were the last minutes of the old year. She'd come from Surrey to visit her half brother, Jonas, whom she'd last seen in Boston just before their father had retired to Minorca. Expatriation was the family disease, hereditary: thanks to an immigrant ancestor, they all had Irish passports. The world was their oyster. An oyster was not enough to sustain anyone.

"This happen off-ten?" she asked. "Blackouts, I mean."

"Off-ten?" he mimicked, then he said, "Nah. I don't know what's going on." His Boston accent was thick as ever, but years in England had bent her diction, and she couldn't decide which of them should feel superior. The blackout was in its third hour. She'd hated the darkness at first but now it had gone on long enough it would be the story of the evening, and so was essential. Let the New Year arrive unelectrified, lit only by pyrotechnics, thought Mistress Maggle.

The Dutch did not wait till midnight to celebrate. Through the enamel tabletop they felt the detonations of fireworks, explosion after explosion in the dark. Life in wartime, if you knew nobody was dying, probably, and the privation would end by morning. She jumped at every salvo. She was a nervous woman. When Jonas fished out a joint she didn't turn him down, though it had been decades. Maybe it would calm her. Last year she would have had a drink but she didn't drink anymore. She was 49, which didn't surprise her; Jonas was 39, a shock.

He had long insufficient blond hair he was trying to drum up into dreadlocks and a thick dark beard he'd trimmed to round perfection. Why couldn't he take care of anything else so well? He was a fuck-up. He said so himself. It was as though fucking up were his religion, and he was always looking for a more authentic experience of it: bankrupted by Scientology, busted for selling a stolen antique lamp, fired from an Alaskan cannery for stealing salmon, beaten up by a drug dealer, that is, a ham-headed college kid who dealt ecstasy but took only steroids himself. For the past six months he'd lived in this garret, renting the space beneath an Irish woman's kitchen table, with access to her stove and sink and toilet and, occasionally, herself. The Irish woman had gone back to Kilkenny, would return tomorrow. Tonight Mistress Maggle was sleeping in her bed. The Irish woman must never hear of this. Jonas's pallet was still spread out under the table they now sat at, his pillow at Mistress Maggle's feet.

At 11:30 the lights came back on.

"Oh good," said Jonas.

"A shame," said Mistress Maggle.

Jonas shrugged. He was a lifelong shrugger. It was the genuflection of the devout fuck-up. "Let's go to the street," he said. "Midnight will blow your mind."

Outside they stood by the murky canal that ran down the street like a median strip. All along the block the Dutch set off bottle rockets, nearly dutifully, and gossiped and smoked. She felt the peculiar calm of not understanding the ambient language, a state she loved: it was like having part of your brain induced into coma. "Just wait," said Jonas. What were they waiting for? O yes: midnight. Mistress Maggle consulted her heart the way she might reach into her handbag for a wallet she was continually sure she'd lost no matter how many times she found it. How was her heart? There, but working? She took her pulse in her neck: steady, fine, though her torso felt percolated. She'd read an article on-line about women's heart attacks, how they presented differently from men's, how nearly anything (it seemed to Mistress Maggle) might be evidence. Was that pain in her chest, or in her back? In her chest or her breast? What bodily border did a pain have to cross to enter another bodily meridian? Insomnia could be a symptom, the article said: well, she had it now. She had all the symptoms, though fly-by-night versions. Intimations of symptoms. Not pain, but twinges. Not racing but a trot.

She was dying, she was making it up, she wouldn't go to a doctor. She had no natural fear of death, and was vain about this: it was what separated her from the rest of dumb humanity. But she was terrified of embarrassment. That's what it would say under cause of death on the certificate: *embarrassment, congenital and chronic.*

In the middle of the street, a small blond boy knelt next to a man with 1970s Elvis sideburns. Not father and son, surely, there was a formality: the man seemed to be the boy's firework godfather, come from far-off to teach him how to light a bottle rocket. The boy must have been eight. The man must have been a ghost. Together they held a twisted smoldering length of paper to the fuse then stepped away. Mistress Maggle felt the rocket's rising shrill at the back of her throat, felt its detonation in her tonsils. It tore itself into three red branches, then faded.

"Fucking *awesome*," Jonas called to the kid.

"Extraordinary," she said, in a four-syllabled, English way. Then, "Yeah, awesome." Already the man and boy were righting the bottle for a new rocket.

"Sixty-five million Euro, according to the papers," said Jonas. "That's what the Dutch spent on fireworks this year. Hey, did I tell you? I'm going to apprentice to a hatter."

"You're too old to be an apprentice," she said. Then: "A *hatter*?"

"Felt hats," he said. "They're the next thing. They're coming back."

"Come and went, haven't they?"

He'd been smiling but his smile slipped. He shook his head then smiled more broadly: that his sister might know anything was something he could only believe for seconds at a time. "No," he said. "Real hats. My friend Matthias. He's, like, a genius."

That perfect round beard: it looked like a hatter's apparatus, come to think of it. A form for the crown of a bowler, a tool to bring up the nap of the felt.

"I'll give you more money," Mistress Maggle told him.

"That's not what I'm saying." He had his hands in his greasy mechanic's jacket; he who had never been a mechanic. "I don't need your money."

"Oh?"

"*No*," said Jonas. "That's why I invited you here. To show you. I don't need you anymore. Your help, I mean. Look! I'm standing on two feet." Then he added, "I think she's pregnant. She *is* pregnant."

"Who? Oh, Irish."

"Siobhan," said Jonas. "Yes."

"So you'll want the money then."

"Listen to me! That's why hats."

"*Hats*," said Mistress Maggle.

Bickering into the New Year. Typical. They'd heard no countdown, but the turning of the calendar was unmistakable: the syncopation of bottle rockets was replaced by the sorts of fireworks that in America would be reserved for the finale of a big city 4th of July. Whumps, thunderclaps, the crackling aftermath: beauty. Ordinarily Mistress Maggle was afraid of both loud noises and house fires, but the fireworks over Rotterdam—no, she realized, *not* over Rotterdam, the fireworks over this particular neighborhood—she goggled at them. Nobody was sighing in unison, as in the States. There was no time to sigh. Every inch of the sky was stitched with firework. Fingers were being blown off, surely, and heart attacks induced, and underneath the explosions you could hear dogs of all sizes bark in all agonized registers—but how could Mistress Maggle not be hypnotized? It was the most astonishing thing she'd ever seen.

She thought of the Invisible Woman at the Science Museum, that mannequin who showed her various systems through her Lucite epidermis: circulatory, nervous, respiratory, reproductive, lit up in turn. The fireworks lit Mistress Maggle up: the blond fireworks her nerves and the white ones her bones, the red ones her heart, the blue ones her capillaries. They were curing her. She was not just fine but better. Soon they'd finish, and she'd be new. But they didn't finish. They kept going. Cured, afflicted, cured, afflicted, cured, until she realized there was no waiting for the end of them. The Dutch would set off fireworks till the dark was done. Maybe Jonas was right, maybe this was the year he'd stand on two feet. She felt hope saturate her.

"It's so good to see you," she said to him. She'd learned through the years that saying it made it so, at least sometimes. "Really, Jone."

"This is going to be the greatest year of my life," said Jonas, and she said, "Yes, it will, I know it."

Not blond, but gingerale. Not gingerale but champagne.

Later, from the Irish woman's bed, she heard a clunk against the roof, and realized it was fallout from some rocket. Ordinarily she would have stayed awake, waiting for the inevitable smell of disaster. Now she thought, Icarus, Newton's apple, David Bowie, impossible beautiful falling things. A rocket set off hours before by the boy in the middle of the street, flown so high it had gone into orbit, circumnavigated the globe, and—like so many flying things—got homesick, decided to plummet back.

Should she throw something to the kitchen tabletop, to give her brother the same exhilaration on his bedroll beneath? Would it work?

The table was still scattered with empty hot dog cans. In the Netherlands, they were called *knaks*.

Twelve hours later, Mistress Maggle—her name was Jenny Early, though 49 seemed to her too old to be Jenny and too late to be Early—boarded a ferry at the Hook of Holland, headed for Harwich, where her car was parked. She'd lived in England for 20 years, working as an actress, more or less, all that time: in an experimental theater company (*experimental* meant foodstuff and nudity, mostly); as a clown in a new wave circus; as a minor recurring character on *Coronation Street*; as the slowest person in an improv troupe; as a reader to the blind; as a voiceover artist in cartoons and, later, video games; and finally, as Mistress Maggle, which involved walking on stilts and wearing a multicolored Victorian dress and yelling, week after week, at an audience of children, from which six players were plucked, who were protected by a young hero named Micah. (The eponymous Barnaby—actual surname O'Malley—had been fired for sleeping with 17-year-olds, which he told the papers was unfair: there were no 17-year-olds in his audience.) Micah was the beautiful child of a Danish mother and Nigerian father and as cheerful off camera as on, though in real life guileless, dumb, incapable of outwitting anyone, never mind a woman so many years his senior. He reminded Mistress Maggle of an alternate Jonas, one whose every slapdash decision raised him up instead of knocking him down. She hated Micah for his good luck (though neither Micah nor Jonas believed in luck: they believed in breezily accepting the day), and for his consistent love of the children, for his youth, for the way the game itself was stacked against her. The children needed to foil Mistress Maggle in her attempts to kidnap them, and even when she managed to land a child and slip him in jail—on stilts! in a hoop skirt!—Micah was always there with the enormous unconvincing cardboard key. They, the children, booed her.

No children waiting for Mistress Maggle on the other side of the journey, nor husband, nor (at the moment) boyfriend, and that was fine.

She liked sex and she liked privacy and it had taken her till her mid-thirties before she'd realized life could offer you both. The time that living with another person took up! The small talk! The politeness! Life alone was banal, too, but at least then the banality wasn't narrated. It was bad for you, to say aloud the minor grievances of the day, the rude bank teller and the gum on the bottom of your shoe. It was terrible to alter your diet because of what another person liked or didn't: the last man she had lived with had hated capers. And so she had given up capers, until she gave up the man. His name was Philip. He was a the-ater director who had made fun of her accent, the way she dropped Ts in the middle of English expressions and words: bee'root. Wai'rose. Whi'bait. Qui'right.

She was an ideal expat. All her life she'd felt foreign. It was a relief to have it as an official diagnosis.

This was a day crossing but she'd taken an outside cabin, with one double bed and one single bed and a surprisingly large bathroom with a toilet, shower, and sink, three thick white towels, more than Jonas had to his name. (What had happened to him, that he lived like that? Shit happens, Jonas would say. Life happens, Micah would say, when you're making other plans. Men!) A little free minibar. She ate both chocolates and the packet of potato chips while the boat was still in port. The strange joy of the previous evening was still in her. She felt calmer than she had in ages. The Irish woman was pregnant. Their family would continue after all! Aunty Maggle! Still stoned, she thought, though she wasn't sure that was true, and she lay down on the single bed, because it was on the right side of the cabin, and the homing device in Mistress Maggle's brain always went right: on busses, trains, in restaurants. There was a little wall-mounted television; she tuned it to the station that showed footage from closed-circuit cameras in the belowdeck ken-nels. She'd like to see a dog about now. Empty. Empty. Empty. Still, the channel suited her. She worked in television: she wanted to watch but she couldn't bear watching. She might see, for instance, an actor in a movie whom she'd met fifteen years ago on a soap: now how did he get that break? She would see young talentless gleaming people. It shocked her, the jealousy of her middle-age, though it only flared up now and then, a trick knee. Lumbago, whatever lumbago was. Spiritual arthritis. As a young woman she was (she believed) mostly generous, entirely sane, and the acting jobs she got, the soaps and re-enactment shows and cartoon voiceovers, had seemed like good fortune. Now nothing seemed like luck, but a conspiracy, mean and purposeful, designed to hurt her, and she knew that there were people she'd worked with who saw her in the piebald pirate-y Mistress Maggle costume on *Barnaby Grudge*, who were filled with jealousy themselves, and this didn't comfort her: indeed, when she stopped to contemplate it, she felt humiliated.

Knock it off, she told herself. New year. She plumped the pillow. It was a real pillow. It was a good ship. That felt lucky right there. She checked her heart. Beating.

No dogs, still.

She never quite fell asleep, but she observed, as though from a distance, obscure outlandish thoughts as they arrived: would Jonas take the Irish Woman's bed, innocent of the traveling Irish Woman, or would he sleep obediently on his mat beneath the kitchen table? Why underneath the table? Oh, to avoid being stepped on. A baby in a hat might crawl by too, now what did that mean, she asked herself in an Irish accent. She felt the sea get rougher beneath her and every now and then a wave lifted the boat up and set it down with a minor clunk and the backroom of her brain thought, *ah the plane has landed*.

She sat up after she thought this for the third time. Not plane, boat. The television still showed a series of empty kennels. It looked like a prison break: I don't know, Sarge, the cells were all full half an hour ago.

Between the beds, a large lonzenge-shaped window. Porthole. A window nobody could spy you through. She regarded the polished green sea cut through with unpolished white foam. She could hear outside her cabin a ululating child run down the ferry corridor: toddler Doppler effect. Other than that, the cabin was the most complete privacy one could imagine while still surrounded by hundreds of people, and delicious. There was nothing she didn't like about the room. How to fully enjoy it? She had an urge to transgress, to drink the pygmy mini-bar red wine, then the white, then the two cans of Heinekin, to strip and press her nakedness against the window.

Who would know? Some unseen sailor with a telescope. Satellites. Aliens. Nobody. Fish.

She didn't drink anymore. Hours to go before Harwich. She needed to get out.

The public areas were on deck 9. She'd been on shitty ferries but this was a nice one. Coffee bars, wine bars, a cafeteria, even a fancy restaurant with a 3-course prix fixe menu. Most of the passengers (there weren't many) seemed to be middle-eastern Muslims, the women in chadors and headscarves, even a pair of tiny girls hidden in floor-length burkhas, the men in blue jeans. Of course, thought Mistress Maggle: everyone else was too hungover on New Year's Day to chance a ferry. You had to be from a non-drinking people to survive. Or Naval: she had Navy on both sides of the family, she never got sick. Still, the roughness of the sea was a low-level prank beneath her feet: three steps fine and then the deck rose up quick. At the far end of the cafeteria a white-haired man pulled a clattering child's toy, a dragon that smacked its jaws as it rolled along. The man wore a round embroidered Chinese hat and pants that showed his ankles, and he tweaked balloons into dogs and handed them to children. She supposed she and he were members of the same tribe, or the same theoretical union. *Keep your distance*, she thought at him.

Where was Jonas? He'd ridden the bus with her to the central train station, bought her ticket to the port. He was going to be a father. (She resolved to believe it.) Fathers should not sleep beneath kitchen tables. Of course he needed money. She would send it happily, without negotiation or expectation.

She walked through a door out onto an open deck at the end of the boat. Not end. Stern. The stern of the boat past the smokers and stared sternly out. The sharp salt air did her some good, though the smokers all looked fucked off with the cold. Why she'd quit: after the ban in restaurants and pubs smoking had become a standing endeavor and she had no interest in smoking upright. She stood at the rail and looked at the water.

She thought—as she often did when she saw an opportunity—of doing away with herself. Wait till the deck cleared so nobody saw her. Jump in. Drown. How long would it take till she was noticed missing? She might be an enduring mystery, like Judge Crater (US), or Lord Lucan (UK). You waited to disappear till nobody saw you go. Otherwise you'd be only a dull suicide.

This was a lifelong habit. It didn't feel suicidal but the opposite, a satisfying of a not-quite-urge. Whenever she moved to a new place, for instance, she looked for the support she'd hang herself from. In her current house, a barn conversion, there were likely beams everywhere, though the best was in the kitchen, with an iron hook. Finding the spot calmed her. She didn't want to kill herself but she did want to think about it. After all, she wasn't afraid of death.

She decided to live forever or as long as possible. She would learn to

449

be a better person, for her niece's sake. (Why niece? She couldn't imagine Jonas as the father of a son, was all.) Today it felt entirely possible. Was this optimism? Was this what Micah and Jonas felt?

The water behind a boat is the deepest wishing well in the world, it has drag and intention. Throw your dreams into it. If they don't pull you in and drown you perhaps they'll come true.

On a table inside she found a flyer. CHILDREN'S ENTERTAIN-MENT, it said. 2:30 IN THE KIDZONE! MAGIC, BALLOONS, OLD-FASHIONED PUNCH & JUDY SHOW. Well, she thought. Why not. The boat felt so empty she imagined nobody else might show up, the sea rough enough that any children were lying flat and sipping warm water. Professional courtesy, one children's performer to another. She would be his audience.

But the *KIDZONE!*, a glassed-in space just beyond the cafeteria, was filled with kids and their parents. A young white woman (English, Mistress Maggle was pretty sure) watched her two-year old wander up to the man in the Chinese hat with palpable delight: how lucky, the mother clearly thought, that the world had the chance to experience her child! A plump red-headed boy clutched a model of the very boat they were on, purchased from the onboard gift shop. Two-thirds of the audience seemed to be one large Muslim family or several families traveling together, kids in the front row, a couple of men leaning against the far wall, four young women in matching robin's egg blue headscarves who were young enough it was hard to tell whether they were mothers to the audience, or older sisters. Not all the teenage girls wore head-coverings, so probably they weren't all related. They were different strains. *Denominations.* The God of one allowed you to show your neck and the God of another allowed you to wear slacks.

Where were they from? Somewhere in the middle-east. Even if she heard them speak, she wouldn't know. She had a bum ear: probably why the height of her acting career was a villain on a children's game show. Dutch sounded like German to her, and Portuguese like Spanish. Were they traveling from Iraq, or Yemen? Then one of the teenage boys sighed and said to a teenage girl, in a voice of dread and Birmingham, "This is taking for*ever*. I wish we had flown."

"Fly, then," said his sister. "Go ahead."

Going home. At sea with the English, as per usual.

450

One elderly woman, tucked in a porthole frame, clapped impatiently at a small boy who'd stood up and started to wander. (She was from elsewhere, surely, the original cutting on the family tree.) (They were at sea, they were all from elsewhere.) The boy was little, in elasticized jeans with prominent belt loops. Mistress Maggle wanted to set him in her own lap, whisper in his ear, *Shh. Let's watch the show,* lay her cheek against his hot head. She did feel tender towards some children, little ones: it was only that they'd been taught by television to hate her. The boy's older sister, a girl of 6, knit her already comically serious eyebrows and grabbed him by the waist and pulled him back and gave him a good slug on the arm. Then, as though overcome with love, she seized and kissed him.

Mistress Maggle sat on the floor by the door.

The man in the Chinese hat turned to the audience. He held up to the light three balls filled with glittery fluid. Wordlessly he began juggling. Three balls was relatively easy, Mistress Maggle knew from her years with *Circus A Go-go,* and then thought: but hard on a pitching boat. With a military *hup* he popped the third ball, then again, again, till all the children in the audience were looking.

"Hello," he said. "I am the Magnificent Jimmy." He had a London accent and London teeth, despite the Chinese hat and Moroccan slippers. Then he said, more firmly, "Hello!"

"Hello," the audience answered, the way you might a friendly lunatic in the park.

"That's rubbish, that is," said the Magnificent Jimmy. "*Hello!*"

"Hello!" the children said, loudly this time. He gave a satisfied nod.

At juggling he was fine, he was acceptable, he was *delightful*: she had forgotten what a good audience member she was. How she liked *looking* at people who only wanted to entertain, no matter how talented they were. That was why she'd wanted to act in the first place, to be regarded by strangers the way she did them, a kind of open narrative love that made up stories. Where had he come from? Had he done this all his life? Did he live on board? No: he lived in a bedsit in Harwich. He'd wanted to be a famous magician but had never thrown that first leg over the gate of success. His elderly mother was still alive. He took care of her.

The toddler girl threatened the Magnificent Jimmy's knees as her mother watched in admiration; the redheaded boy kept trying to go back of him, as though the Magnificent Jimmy himself were a trick the

451

boy wanted to get to the bottom of. "Here we go," said the Magnificent Jimmy, "keep your eye on the green ball," and then the green ball got away from him. It rolled towards the little antsy boy, who caught it. "Thank you mate," said the Magnificent Jimmy, "toss 'er here," and the boy did. "You're a very naughty green ball," the Magnificent Jimmy told the green ball. "Don't ever leave me again."

His balloon animal skills were terrific, balloons inside balloons, all blown up by himself, no tacky hand pump. "I'll do this in one go," he said, and he did, filled a green balloon with one long breath. "I like to do it to annoy the smokers. Not bad for 67, eh?" An alien in a helmet. A dachshund who'd swallowed a meatball. A yellow jellybaby. "All my dogs are green poodles," he said. "Reason being: when I was 11, I painted the neighbor lady's poodle green, and my father laughed. First good response I ever got from the man. Therefore, poodles."

She hoped he made balloons for everyone. She felt nervous for the children who didn't have one yet. When you were a child you believed yourself special, deserving, and every piece of evidence to the contrary broke your heart. When you were an adult the same was true, you'd just sustained larger heartbreaks as well. She hated when magicians asked for child volunteers, as the Magnificent Jimmy did: she felt swamped by the longing that rose up from the audience. Little kids put up their hands, 18-month-olds, they didn't know they didn't have a chance.

And yet Mistress Maggle loved the Magnificent Jimmy. It was a condescending love, she knew, she was Mistress Maggle, on television, you could buy a doll of her; he was the Magnificent Jimmy, 67 and performing on a ferry. Perhaps he could appear on *Barnaby Grudge*. Or some other CBeebies program: she would take to them. She would change his life. He had the melancholy edge of a man acquainted with the dark thoughts of the back of the boat, someone whose life had not quite panned out. Maybe she would invite him back to the excellent privacy of her cabin. Her heart scuttled, a sign she was actually considering it. Today she might do anything.

"All right," said the Magnificent Jimmy, "this doesn't work for everyone but it does for some." He pulled out a large black and white disc on a stick, and set it spinning. "Stare at the center. The very center. Keep staring."

Was he hypnotizing them? She hoped so. She wanted to be changed. She would stand up and do anything the Magnificent Jimmy commanded. For once in her life, she would be *susceptible*. So she concentrated, the good student, on the gyre of the disc. It seemed to go on for hours. "Stare. Stare. Stare—now look at me!"

Gasps. Laughter. A teenage girl said, "Oh! Look at his head!"

For Mistress Maggle, nothing.

"Now, some people would have seen my head getting bigger," said the Magnificent Jimmy, and she was stabbed with jealousy, she wanted to snatch the vision straight out of the heads of the undeserving children. "Did you see it?" he asked the girl with the serious eyebrows. The girl nodded, looked thoughtful, and opened her mouth—to vomit, it turned out.

She was only the first. The sea had gotten rough but nobody had quite noticed. You could tell the mothers from the sisters then: the sisters giggled and flinched, the mothers leapt forward, hands open—for what?

"Oh, sweethearts," said The Magnificent Jimmy. "Poor things. There's your mother, darling. All right, all right, she'll take care of you."

But what about *me*? thought Mistress Maggle. And then she stood, and threw up, and fled.

She should have gone back to the cabin—to the shower, the clean towels, her suitcase full of clothing—but she had an idea that she shouldn't be sealed in a box. She needed to be near other people just in case. So she threw her coat over her dress (not an awful mess: she had thrown up directly into a pool of other people's vomit) and stumbled to the open air. The cold felt good and she felt a flare of the day's joy. Then it passed and she felt doom.

Throw yourself in. Who would care?

Over the years, she'd always gone through the list: her parents (they'd get over it), Jonas (him, too), various lovers (who would mourn her or not, but their lives would not be ruined). Her soap opera character (if she were currently playing a character) would be gently written out of the show, if she were consequential enough for her absence to matter.

Wait. Wait now.

No writing Mistress Maggle out of Barnaby Grudge. Was it the water or the realization that made her anxious? The wind boxed her ears. She drew her shoulders up to shield them. Short of breath she was.

How would they explain it to the children? Would they simply hire another tall woman with a deep voice and the ability to walk on stilts? Would they offer young actresses her corset like Cinderella's slipper?

The parents of those children: they would be the ones who'd hate her. Who would be furious: What happened to Mistress Maggle, mummy? They put her in jail for good, the heartless bitch.

"Ahoy!" said someone behind her. She turned. The Magnificent Jimmy had put on an enormous orange Michelin-man down coat, but his ankles were bare to the wind, and his little velvet slippers horrid, splattered. "You all right?"

She nodded. She didn't feel all right but she couldn't say so. "Quite a finish," she said. "Was that arranged?"

He laughed. "Never had a show end like that before! A chundering ovation. Where's your child?"

A reasonable question. She looked around for her child before she remembered. "I don't have one."

"Oh," he said, puzzled. Then, "Me neither."

She'd always thought it was good for a children's performer to be childless. Otherwise, you would meet children thinking, Not as smart as mine. Or worse: smarter than mine, lovelier than mine. She judged every piece of art that got sent in to *Barnaby Grudge*: Martin, age 6 of Sussex, you drew that with your foot. Penny, age 7, of Walthamstow, that's the worst fucking fairy I ever saw: it looks like a wingéd footstool.

"I hate children," said Mistress Maggle, with the force of a religious confession. It echoed the same way. "Never wanted them."

The Magnificent Jimmy looked stricken, and cold. "Oh. Pity. I did. We did. Wanted them. But it did not happen for me and the wife."

Mistress Maggle felt dizzy. Her whole back ached. Panic. She should say something. Ask for help. Then, "You were great. You were really great."

"Thanks very much," he said, but he was turning away, going back in. "You all right then?"

"Listen," she said, "I can get you work."

"I've got work."

"No, I mean—I'm—"

"I know who you are," he said, and went back in.

She sat down in a chair and pulled her coat around her and threw up again and then without knowing it was going to happen, without a single premonition, she shit her pants, it was the most awful and strange feeling, the warmth of all the matter in her digestive system against her cold sodden skin. Mistress Maggle was dying. Jenny Early was dying. Not of embarrassment after all, though embarrassment was here too.

She was afraid.

454

Of death? Yes, she felt the edge of it, like a metal box buried in the dirt of the yard that's worked its way up. All those years she wasn't brave about death but incredulous. On the most fundamental level and despite all the evidence to the contrary, she didn't believe in it. She might have believed when her parents died, right then—her father of a heart attack, her mother of liver cancer—because she did grieve them, missed them. Then she cheered up, and it didn't feel as though it was time healing all wounds, but an incorrect assumption made correct. They weren't dead, they were elsewhere. Of course she'd had her mother cremated, she'd gone to the memorial service arranged by her father's second wife. She'd seen neither parent for years, of course. But there was no part of her that believed in their permanent absence. That's why heaven. Heaven was invented not because people believed but because they didn't.

She could feel the boat of people behind her. They were in the wine bar or the cinema. They were wiping the brows and mouths of their children. She, she was facing all they'd sailed away from. Jonas in the garret, the Irish woman home and coming up the stairs, everywhere the tatters of fireworks. Her money would go to Jonas. Her nice house. It would save him or ruin him. The ferry was an hour from Harwich but she'd never see Harwich again. The crew would find her body an hour after docking.

She tried to say something to the air. She felt like one of those Rotterdam dogs, barking and barking while the humans laughed and set off explosions. Don't you understand, I'm not unhappy, I'm warning you, I'm telling you this is wrong, dangerous, calamitous: the sky will fall around your ears at any moment. Stop looking up and laughing. It isn't cute. It isn't beautiful. It's the end of the world.

And then—how do we know this? reader, we have it on the highest authority—the ocean came calm and smooth, and Mistress Maggle's heart did likewise, and she felt entirely better, and safe.

Nominated by Zoetrope: All–Story

LAIKA

fiction by SARA BATKIE

from NEW ORLEANS REVIEW

Babette came to the home the same week we got a television. They arrived three days apart, both dropped unceremoniously at the front door. Madame Durance never bothered much with the girls but was very put out by the lack of paperwork for the strange machine. "We need to keep track of these things," she said, nudging the box with her sensible shoe. "What if it makes us all sick?" Hollis the orderly had it hooked up within an hour. It was 1957, the year Khrushchev looked up to a stardrunk sky and found a new world to conquer. We were all hankering for the unknown, though that could be hard to find in Nebraska.

Babette, however, was left to dawdle in the hall, regarding her new surroundings gingerly. She had a stooped posture that made her appear smaller than she was, the sack dress she wore so thin it seemed in danger of dissolving with each breath. But her hair fell in Grimm-golden ringlets that anointed her in a light that seemed both suspect and enviable. She could as easily have come from Hollywood as Omaha.

"Babette," Madame Durance repeated when she asked who she was. I could see her mulling it over, the name that sounded at once Biblical and lewd. "You'll bunk with her," she said, nodding towards me. All the new ones did.

It was an unspoken rule that the girls not ask each other what brought them to Durance Home. It was simple enough to guess some of their troubles, the ones with space pod bellies already in orbit. They'd grow big, disappear for a day or two then return with bodies evacuated of their heroes. Nothing left but tears.

The rest were dragged in by their mothers. I was brought by my

456

brother, the only family I had, my slippery fingers having found their way into one pocket too many. He bought me a chocolate malted on the drive, the last ice cream I would taste until adulthood. The woods around the home were filled with brocade trees. Deer flashed past like hoaxes. When we pulled up to the gate with its jack o'lantern teeth, it was blocked by ogling boys that Madame Durance shooed away. Like pigeons. When he left my brother kissed my cheek, his whiskers leaving little cat scratches on my skin. That was 1954. I was ten. He died eleven years later in Vietnam; I remember the look on Madame's face when she told me about him. But Babette, far as anyone could tell, arrived alone.

Televisions were made of tubes in those days. There was enough time between turning the knob and the light snaking through its electric guts to wonder what exactly you were going to see. After Hollis finished plugging everything in, we all stood around the squat brown cube, observing its bulging poker face, the insectile antenna. Nobody wanted to be the first to touch it. We had heard of them, certainly, but if anyone had been in the presence of one before, she didn't say so.

"Step back," Madame Durance shouted, "I'm not paying for your medical bills if you all get cancer."

Then she leaned over and switched on the knob. The screen flickered, fuzzed, a low hum agitating the air. We waited silent, fingers in mouths, breath held. Madame Durance thwacked the side once and then the image caught, stilled. An old man, caterpillar-lipped, hair combed in white peaks, was seated at a desk, looking straight at us while he spoke. We all flinched in one great wave and then we started to listen. Someone named John Glenn had set a new transcontinental speed record, flying a supersonic jet from California to New York in three hours, twenty-three minutes, and eight seconds. We all looked up as if he were still above us, as if we could see something other than the ceiling.

"Only one hour a day," Madame Durance said, fixing small padlocks over the knobs. But we could still be carried into sleep on visions of staticky life.

Later that year, the Soviets would launch its two Sputniks into space. The first was just a satellite, a shiny metal sphere elbowing its way through the constellations. But the second had a dog in it. Laika. Russian for "barker," the old man in the television would say. A stray from the streets of Moscow. They showed a blurry image of her in her flight

457

harness. The tips of her ears flopped down. The fur of her face was dark, kissed with ashes, except for one white line that ran from her forehead down her snout. Before she was shuffled into her own metal sphere, she turned back to the cameras and smiled like a starlet.

At night in our house on that little hill, when there were no lights for miles and the only sound was the breath in Babette's nose like the cooing of a dove, I would dream about Laika and what she saw up there. That sky so big it could swallow you. Keep you safe and warm.

Though Madame Durance did not pay much mind to how the girls arrived, she carried a different tune when it came to how they left. We were not prisoners, serving out a stay, but we were not quite wards either, kept confined until our eighteenth birthdays when we were left to the whims of the world. We were there for our betterment, a betterment that was decided upon by Madame, and once it was reached, a mysterious transaction was performed and a parent or guardian showed up to take us home. This was a process we accepted rather than observed. One day, a bed was empty, a girl was gone, and we were left knowing that she had learned something but not what it was.

By the time Babette arrived, I had been in the home for three years and was losing interest in bolstering the sort of behaviors that would get me out. I was not a pretty girl. My hair was the same color whether dirty or clean. I was solid as a tree trunk. I had the complexion of curdled milk. I wasn't made for much more than scrubbing floors, which was also my daily task at the home, lacking the parents to pay my keep. Still, Madame saw something in me. To this day I cannot name it. But a trust of sorts had built between us. During my first few weeks at the home she would leave things out for me: a pencil case, a snow globe, a silvery thimble. A test to see if I would steal them away. Sometimes I did. But I grew to anticipate the tilted smile she gave me when I left something untouched. I recognized the glory in giving things away and became her confidant.

Most of the other girls were incessant talkers and boasters, having just recently recognized they were interesting, if only to one another, though they quickly learned to hold their tongues around me. Once they realized how their secrets reached the ears of Madame Durance I was promptly snubbed. A room change was requested; another newcomer was installed. But I couldn't help myself. The rest of them chattered away to anyone in earshot but Madame truly listened. It seemed the source of her power. And I knew what to tell her, which seemed the source of mine.

But Babette was also a quiet girl and thus a figure of great curiosity for everyone else.

"I was led here by the Lord," she'd answer.

Every night before bed Babette knelt at the window and prayed. When I wanted to know why, she said it was because she was closer to God that way.

"Does that mean your prayers get to Him quicker?" I asked.

She laughed, a bright, trickling sound I never quite recovered from.

"Come," she said, patting a spot on the floor beside her. "We'll see who He answers first."

I sat down, mimicking her pressed-hand pose, bending my forehead to my fingertips. But I had never asked God for anything but forgiveness, forced into the darkness of the confessional to recite my litany of petty crimes to a man I couldn't see. "You lie" was the only thing I had ever gotten in return.

"I don't know what to do," I mumbled into the hollow between my thumbs.

"You don't have to do anything," Babette whispered. "Just let your thoughts wander where they need to go. He'll follow you."

I thought about Laika, looked up at the sky above us, the impossible cradle that carried her. I imagined her passing through the stars, being accepted as one of their own, each small bright ball leading her gently along her path. I thought of her smile flashing across the television screen, all the hope she held in her, and I wished her safely home.

The mystery of Babette's troubles revealed itself soon enough. About six weeks after she arrived, she started getting sick.

"She's sitting too close to the television?" Madame Durance said. But we all knew what it was.

Another week later Babette and I were called into her office. Madame Durance sat behind her desk, hands knit in a neat fist. Her hair mirrored her hands, a high, tight bun coiled so close to her head it surely required pins to hold it though I never saw any. She had the same stern look of that man on the television, but she wanted to know the news rather than to give it.

"You've been here a month and a half," she began. "Do you want to tell me how long you've known?"

I watched Babette in the nosy way that children are allowed to look at one another. She was calm in front of Madame. Most girls cowered, confessed before they were accused, or fought back viciously. Babette simply sat there with the same bemused expression of someone taking entertainment.

"I need to know when it happened, Babette."

She shook her head but the gesture was so small that it seemed she was neither refusing nor denying.

"I need to know if it happened here."

Babette remained silent.

Madame Durance turned to me. "Have you noticed anything unusual happening recently? Somewhere on the grounds? Perhaps even in your room?"

I shook my head knowing full well the long, withering look that would follow. But what else could I do? It was the truth.

"Babette," she said, "whom have you been having intercourse with?"

"Nobody," she replied the way a mother might cut off an argument with a troublesome child.

"I beg your pardon?"

"Any baby in me was gifted by the Lord," she said. "Like Mary."

Now it was Madame's turn for private amusement.

We were both dismissed but Madame found me later in the third floor latrine up to my elbows in soapsuds. "There's something off about that girl," she said, "I don't trust her. It happened here, I just know it. She needs looking after. And I need you to do it."

It was a test of a different sort, the first order Madame had ever given me, and one that in the days after the revelation I found difficult to follow. There was no reason to believe Babette of course, except that all of us did.

"What's it feel like?"

"What did you see?"

"Did He speak to you?"

One girl even asked for a lock of Babette's hair, as if holiness was something you carried on you, not in you.

Madame's skepticism seemed ugly in comparison or, at least, unfair. She fired Hollis. She had to, she explained, to set an example for the other girls. It was a mistake to hire a man in the first place. Through it all Babette remained peaceful as a river, suggesting things at work just underneath.

Every girl has something she never quite got over. For some it was the first time they heard Bob Dylan. For others, it was the sight of Paul Newman striding on-screen in *Hud*. For me, it was Laika. Though there was little available at the time, in the years since I've been able to learn much about her. The Russians only had four weeks to build the space-craft for her flight, but they made many provisions for her. There was an oxygen generator and a device to absorb carbon monoxide. An automatic fan was installed to keep the interior cool. Enough food was stored for a seven-day flight and Laika was fitted with a bag to collect her waste. Monitors of all sorts kept track of her movements, her heart. She was estimated to be about three years old. Vladimir Yazdovsky called her "quiet and charming."

She was trained with two others, Albina and Mushka. To adapt the dogs to the confines of the craft's tiny cabin, they were kept in progressively smaller cages for periods of up to twenty days. Such captivity caused them to stop urinating or defecating, made them twitchy and weak. The train-ers tried giving them laxatives. But only by prolonging the internment could anything come of it. Later they were placed in centrifuges that simulated the movement and noises of the spacecraft during launch.

Their pulses doubled; their blood pressure increased. They came out with the addled velocity of the elderly.

Before the launch, Dr. Yazdovsky took Laika home to play with his children. "I wanted to do something nice for her," he would later say. "She had so little time left to live."

Every once in awhile, if it had been a long time since an incident, we were taken out into the world for a field trip. Madame Durance rented a bus and those of us who were allowed to go piled in for the drive. Boys ran alongside, blowing kisses, leaving damp prints on the windows. This was the only touch of a boy I'd ever known: partitioned, ghostly, and quick to fade. I liked it that way.

The year Babette was with us we went to the town's art museum. It was a small, modest place whose walls were usually adorned with roll-ing hillsides and farmers forking hay. But that fall a painting was on loan from New York City, touring the country like a band or a play.

It stood alone on a far wall, a rope mounted around it to prevent anyone from getting too close. Most of the girls studied it for a full minute or two before moving on in the unfamiliar space as if the sludge of their locomotion could slow down time, could keep them there. But I was transfixed by what I saw: in the foreground a woman in a pink dress, dark hair in a low bun. She was sprawled out on an open field, her fingers gripping the half-dead grass. Her face was turned away, looking toward a gray house on the horizon, a place that I would never see her reach. Her name was Christina, so the plaque said. Though suffering from polio, she refused the use of a wheelchair. The artist was inspired to paint her after watching her crawl across a field from a window in his house.

It must have taken her hours. What sort of person could just stand by and observe something like that? But it was a hopelessness there's no helping. Like Laika. Like all of us, I suppose. Perhaps capturing it was all that could be done, was, in its way, the only chance of honoring it.

The noise of the other girls brought me back, the tumble of their laughter, the scuff of their shoes on the floor. I blinked, glanced around, felt color creeping into my cheeks though nobody had taken any notice. They burbled with hidden mirth, danced figure eights around one another, and it dawned on me that Babette was not among them. She had disappeared.

Fear like hunger pangs filled me, doubled me over. Everywhere I looked were faces I knew but couldn't comprehend. My lungs twisted into strange balloon animal shapes. When Madame turned to reprimand a group of tittering girls, I slipped out the door and into the courtyard, gasping for new air.

Only one of us had ever tried to run before and she came back: Corinne, the girl who wanted to hold onto holiness. A friend posing as a brother had come to visit and smuggled her away. She was gone five days before her mother returned her, dragging her in by her hair as she kicked up a feral dust. "Goddammit Corinne," her mother had cried, "why would you leave this?" She glanced at those of us who'd gathered, a wall of widening eyes. "This place is better than home." The bewildered look on her face as she said this is one I've never forgotten. But I knew Madame's response to my failure would be even more enduring.

Once my breath caught up with me, another sound made itself known. It was Babette, her hands making tiny arcs across her stomach, sitting on a bench beneath the bosom of a wilting tree. From a distance she appeared to be shivering but as I drew closer I heard the lamb bleats of her distress.

"It hurt," she said as I sat beside her.

"Are you okay?" I asked, looking her over for cuts and bruises, thinking one of the girls had done something to her. "Do you want me to get Madame?"

Her head gave a violent shake. "When it happened. It hurt. Why didn't He tell me?" she said. "What if He made a mistake? Choosing me?"

As startling as it can be to hear such doubt from an adult, I've come to believe over the years that it's more frightening from a child. It seemed my duty to comfort her in that moment. Perhaps even my destiny.

"No," I said, less because I believed it than I wanted her to, "God doesn't do that."

She took a deep breath, wiped at her tears, and when I looked at her again there was a calmness in her eyes that dwarfed her age.

"You sure you're okay?" I asked.

But Babette smiled, just like adults did.

Laika died on the fourth day of the flight. Though she succeeded in her mission her machine failed her. The Block A core of the satellite didn't detach as planned. She overheated in orbit after the thermal insulation tore loose, raising the temperature in the cabin to over 100 degrees.

The Soviets had always planned for her death. They had hoped to euthanize her; her seventh serving of food was poisoned. For forty-five years the scientists offered conflicting reports on the mission, a deception that allowed the Russian, and eventually the American, programs to continue their march towards successful human spaceflight. Laika's true demise was not revealed until October 2002 when one of the scientists presented a paper at the World Space Congress in Houston, Texas. "It turned out that it was practically impossible to create a reliable temperature control system in such limited time constraints," he said in the news clip.

About five months after the launch, on April 14th, 1958, Sputnik 2 disintegrated upon reentry into the Earth's atmosphere, carrying Laika's remains with it. By then everyone else had moved on. Other, greater missions lay ahead.

A few months passed. There was a cold spell and a new year. We grew older, grew bigger. Some of us grew less bad and left.

Then on a Tuesday in February Babette's brother Luther came to visit her. She didn't seem surprised to see him but then again she never seemed surprised by anything. Though Madame Durance eyed him over suspiciously, the Beat poet hair and mudlashed pants, she let him in. I was put in charge of watching them.

Though Madame usually sat right at the table with visitors, I chose a seat a bit more removed. I wanted to have a good view of any cracks in Babette's manner. And though she did not meet the hand her brother offered her, she treated him with the same dreamy courtesy as anyone else I'd seen her with in the home. He seemed pained by this, wincing as if from countless invisible blows.

"Nice place here," he said.

She nodded, waited, resting her arms on her belly. How strange to watch families interact this way, as if a new place also made them new to each other.

"You're big," he said.

"Yes," she smiled. "The Lord has blessed me."

Sourness passed over his face. "Too late then," he said.

"The Lord has blessed you too."

"I don't want it."

"You can't talk like that."

"You don't want it neither," he said. "I know."

I didn't feel so good then, like my whole body was caught in a shiver that wouldn't stop. It was how he was looking at her. Like she was the bone his teeth kept gnawing.

"All babies are blessings," she said.

"You got the devil in you."

She took his hand and pressed it to her lips then to her stomach. He jumped like lightning. But when he pulled his hand back and held it up as if to hit her, she was never anything but calm.

"I forgive you," she said.

But when I told Madame what I had heard she looked at me with the narrowed eyes of a skeptic. "Her own brother?" she scoffed. "Why would you say something like that?" It seemed there were limits to the badness even Madame would believe.

"Madame," I said, panic and protest rising in me at once, clouding my eyes with tears. She hated this sort of blubbering even more than lies.

"You should know better," she said. "Perhaps Durance Home has done what it can for you. There are other places girls like you can be." Then she went back to the papers on her desk, not even bothering to dismiss me.

These words came back to me later that night when I heard our bedroom door click open, the soft rustle of someone wanting not to be heard, and then a cry muffled by a swift clamp. I felt a curl of sickness in my stomach. Sweat flocked in my pits, my heart slashing me like a razor. But I stayed still, kept my breathing steady, even when I heard her bite his hand and grunt out something. The start of my name, I think. I knew the places Madame spoke of. My brother and I had been shuffled in and out of them for years before Durance Home. So I shrank from the sounds of their struggle, the violence I didn't want turned on me, until the door shut behind them, leaving me alone in the smothering silence.

As the terror of the moment began to subside, another stranger feeling began to build in me: relief. I would be blamed for it, I knew, but I would be believed. I would be safe.

Fifty years after her remains incinerated in the sky, Laika was memorialized in a statue and plaque, unveiled on April 11th, 2008, in Star City, Russia, not far from the military facility where she was trained. The statue is an iron dog standing on top of an iron rocket.

Though few in Russia spoke out about the controversy of the mission before the fall of the regime, Oleg Gazenko, one of the scientists who worked with Laika, has since said, "The more time passes, the more I'm sorry about it. We shouldn't have done it . . . We did not learn enough from this mission to justify the death of the dog."

I have thought about Laika often over the years and Babette too, turning them over in my mind like a Rubik's Cube. Laika's story is known though not well recorded, which is its own kind of tragedy. But I have wondered what became of Babette, if there was any joy in the life she was dragged back to. Even now some nights I dream of her and Luther in the bed beside me, limbs writhing together like a den of snakes, my name like venom on her tongue. I wake up screaming loud enough to be heard in other rooms, and other years.

A girl appeared here not too many months ago, the same blonde hair,

465

the same smile. A granddaughter perhaps? But no. She was no child of God, that one. I've been at Durance Home for close to sixty years now. I've taken care of it myself for thirty though I have never thought to change the name. The girls call me Miss, but I know behind my back it's Sister. In a way the slur makes sense; I'm performing a penance of sorts.

I haven't left the grounds since Madame died. Even before that, I rarely wandered very far. It took time to rebuild Madame's trust, but we both knew I didn't belong anywhere else. I didn't have the schooling for college or the manners for a husband. I understand the cruelty of the young better than most. But there's no respect in these girls now, no fear. They tussle with one another and cuss and scream. They see nothing worth learning in my lessons. I'm ruining their lives keeping them here, not keeping them from ruining themselves. I want them safe; they wish me dead. The woods around us have grown bald but sometimes they still disappear into them.

Perhaps I have been wrong to think of Laika's death as a tragedy. After all, if she had been able to return, what kind of life would she be coming back to? A hero's welcome, surely, but then what? To eke out her remaining years manhandled by some ignorant child, dreaming of another orbit? And there was no sorrow in being chosen in the first place, saved from a street-wandering squalor, to be fed and if not loved then trusted. Some of us are meant to bear the glory that the rest of us merely share in. At least she was allowed that moment of awe when the stars were surrounding her, and the moon, still so far from reach, was looking at her, wondering what she was doing there.

Nominated by Seth Fried

THE CARNATION MILK PALACE

fiction by MELISSA PRITCHARD

from ECOTONE

> *Was she beautiful, or was she only someone apart?*
> —Edith Wharton, "New Year's Day"

Fourteen-year-old Charlotte fished the invitation from between unpaid bills—PG&E electric, her dermatologist, Dr. Gass—and a lapsed subscription to *Ladies Home Journal*. On the engraved card, cartoon bubbles fizzed from a champagne glass, bumped around the words: JOIN GLEN AND STIBSY! RING IN 1964!

The Haldens were the richest people her parents knew.

She slid the invitation back in with the more-ordinary mail on the antique sewing machine her mother had turned into a side table by painting it avocado green. The Masseys couldn't afford new things, so her mother had made a domestic career of slapping one of two popular decorating colors over everything in sight. Mr. Massey joked that one day he would wake to find himself painted harvest gold.

The Haldens lived two suburbs over, in the Republican stronghold of Hillsborough, in a mansion her father liked to call the Carnation Milk Palace, like Daly City's indoor arena, the Cow Palace. Jack Massey and Glen Halden had been students at UCLA's law school when Glen came into an early inheritance, something to do with Carnation Condensed Milk. Charlotte knew those milk tins, red and white with ruffled, pink carnations; it was her job every Christmas to puncture the squat cans with the church-key opener when she and her mother made marshmallow fudge. Still, it was an unfathomable distance from tins of sweetened yellowish milk to the Haldens' estate with its ironwork gates, circular driveway, two-tiered fountain, multistoried house, Olympic-sized swimming pool with a blue and white striped cabana. "Filthy rich," Charlotte's father, a probate attorney, would say of his old college friend. "Observe how the stinking rich half lives."

Charlotte had visited the Carnation Milk Palace once when she was ten, a time when a mansion with opulent rooms unfolding in every direction and a green, wandering estate still meant the pleasure of discovery and eluding the vague, condescending gaze of grown-ups. She remembered sitting beneath a broad valley oak, small moths cupped and panicking in her hands, the dark gold dust from their wings leaving smudges on her white palms and party dress. She couldn't remember if she had been alone or with other children.

The Masseys attended the Haldens' New Year's Eve party every year, and for two to three days afterwards, Charlotte's mother boiled over with rage. Compared to the Haldens', her life came up irredeemably short, and she took it out on everyone and everything around her. Even the ivory invitation displayed on the mantel would be ripped in half and thrown out, along with its matching envelope and green foil lining. The sight of it sparked a sick envy in Mrs. Massey even as it lent status, a status she suspected derived more from nostalgia than equality.

Years later, one week shy of Mrs. Massey's eighty-first birthday (did one never stop learning uncomfortable things?), she began confiding secrets to her daughter, small burdens of conscience Charlotte supposed her mother didn't want lugging to her grave. Glen Halden, for instance, whose untimely death years before in a boating accident had put an end to the New Year's Eve parties and to Stibsy Halden's charmed life, had once been madly in love with her mother. For an entire college year, every Friday, he'd had scarlet tea roses delivered to the modest bungalow where she lived with her parents. One Christmas Eve, he proposed beside the unlit fireplace with its cold brass andirons and single stocking dangling from the mantel. Scissored from red felt, the stocking had a green sequined cuff with her name, Hazel, looping in green glitter down to the toe.

Clouding the whole of her mother's adult life was regret, self-recrimination. Who might she have been, what sort of glamorous life might she have led, as Mrs. Glen Halden? She had refused one of California's most eligible bachelors and married poor Jack Massey. (Actually, she had been pregnant with Charlotte's sister, Evelyn, the elopement a forced, hasty affair with a ceremony held in the cluttered parlor of a Methodist minister in Yuma, Arizona, a secret Mrs. Massey did take to her grave—or thought she did. Before either of them became mothers,

Evelyn and Charlotte easily guessed the truth of Evie's illegitimacy.) When Charlotte, freshly aware of the odds of her own birth, asked why her mother had married her father in the first place, Mrs. Massey said she supposed it had to do with Glen being too decent. "Dull as a post. His flowers were predictable, expense meant nothing to him, and my parents' dining room reeked of roses. Almost a blight—they turned me against the color red. Your father, on the other hand, was the best dancer at UCLA. He won all the contests, was blond, tall, elusive. Sex appeal, you'd say now. He didn't have two nickels to rub together, but all us girls went after him."

Charlotte recalled her father's morning ritual—inspecting his smooth-shaven cheeks in the bathroom mirror while declaring, "You handsome devil, you!"

"To this day, I don't understand why I married your father, Charlie. We eloped, two crazy kids, and it took Evie's birth for my parents to speak to me again. It's awful to think Jack's gone—sometimes I still think I'll find him sitting in the next room."

Charlotte's father had died of an aneurysm, alone and, according to the coroner, painlessly.

The day the Haldens' card arrived, Charlotte came home from school with an invitation of her own, hoping her parents might be relieved she had somewhere to go. Her one friend, Moira Duffy, had asked her to sleep over on New Year's Eve, adding that Mr. Duffy could drive Charlotte home before mass the next morning. Charlotte was not Roman Catholic—she was not anything, not even baptized. Sending her to the Convent of the Sacred Heart had been a calculated, costly decision on her parents' part. Many of the girls in the private school came from old California families; every season, there were debutantes. The President of Mexico's twin daughters were boarders at the school and stuck together, inseparable. In the back of the convent's old-fashioned classrooms, they sat behind heavy oak desks, buffing one another's fingernails, giggling, whispering in Spanish. Yawning with moist, ripe, red mouths, they reminded Charlotte of languid tropical blooms.

"No." The word, clipped, dry, was muffled by the evening newspaper, a print wall raised before her father's face.

"But . . ."

"No." This time more vehement, so the thin pages of the paper shook a little.

"Why not?" On thin ice, asking.

At this show of defiance, demonstrating precisely why he didn't want his daughter going over to that girl's house—these days disrespect was as contagious as poverty—Mr. Massey lowered the newspaper to his lap.

To avoid having to look at her father's crew cut, his new, pencil-thin mustache that so upset her mother, the squint of his eyes, Charlotte stared down at her saddle shoes, their dingy laces. Her father rarely allowed her to do anything, saying only that while she was under his roof, it was his job to protect her from "the real world."

"Boys, that's why not. Boys." In that one word lay his daughter's potential defilement, her ruin.

Charlotte knew two boys. Werner Leipzig, oldest of nine, attended Woodside Priory, a small, exclusive boys' school. The Leipzigs permitted him two activities: babysitting his siblings and maintaining his status as the top student in his school (valedictorian of his class, Werner would go on to Stanford with a full scholarship). Charlotte had seen him on three occasions, two supervised—the Fall Tea, where they'd met in a fussily furnished, salmon-colored parlor next to the school chapel, and at the winter dance, heavily chaperoned, in the school's Little Theater. The second boy, Owen Harmon, was Werner's best friend. Owen spent holidays in Manhattan with his mother, a Jungian analyst, and the academic year with his father, a popular liberal columnist for the *San Francisco Chronicle*. Emulating his father, Owen was a left-leaning political animal. He wore rumpled corduroy jackets with leather elbow patches and got away with wearing his unruly, fawn-colored hair too long. Being the only child of divorced parents gave him cachet, as did his parents' wealth, a portion of which, it was rumored, kept the priory afloat. Charlotte, Werner, Moira, and Owen had gone on one double date—to a pizza parlor in Menlo Park with black painted walls and strobe lighting. Afterward, when Werner accidentally scraped the tires of his father's green and white VW van against the curb in front of the Masseys' ranch-style house, Charlotte's mother was caught peeking through the kitchen café curtains, a pink plastic bonnet covering her giant sponge curlers. That night, Charlotte had fallen in love, not with morose, lantern-jawed Werner but with his friend, Owen. A creeping, unfair revulsion toward Werner had taken hold as she'd studied the teasing ringlets of Owen's hair falling over the back of his russet corduroy collar, listened to him go on about his father's lead article on the Civil Rights Movement in the *Catholic Worker* and express his own defiant opinion about the criminality of the Vietnam War. This was after the March on Washington, which Owen's father had taken part in, just three weeks before the assassination of the first Roman Catholic president. At Charlotte's house, no one ever mentioned what was going on in the larger world. Watching the nightly news, the black-and-white footage of race riots and marches, a jungle war and faraway atrocities, her parents sat impassive in their matching wing chairs. To speak one's mind, to take exception or to openly disagree over war, religion, or race, was so far outside Charlotte's experience that she naturally fell headlong in love with this radical messenger, his news of the world, his curling, Byronic hair.

On the night of the Haldens' party, Charlotte found her mother in her parents' pink and black tiled bathroom, doing her makeup, or as Mr. Massey liked to say, "spackling on her party face." Charlotte was not yet permitted to wear makeup, only a bit of lipstick, and Vaseline on her lashes, for special occasions.

If her father laid down the rules and her mother embellished them, Charlotte preferred to hole up in her bedroom, burning black cones of Chinatown incense and writing poems that Mother Lussier, to Charlotte's mortification, occasionally read aloud in class.

"Last year, at least Evie was home." A freshman at a girls' college back east, Charlotte's older sister rarely wrote or called her family. When an overweight, defiant version of Evie flew back for a visit that spring, nightly arguments erupted like blood sport between her and her father in the living room. When Mr. Massey put his foot down, refusing to let Evelyn return to her private college, ostensibly because she had let herself run to fat but actually because he could no longer afford the tuition—a local community college would do—Evelyn retaliated. She eloped.

Mrs. Massey pressed her eyelash curler against one eye, clamping and squeezing. "You won't be alone, didn't your father tell you? You'll be with us. There will be loads of people. Friends of Glen Jr.'s and Anne's too, if they haven't gone back to school yet." In the stage-lit mirror, she narrowed one free eye on Charlotte, who sat on the toilet seat with its black shag cover. "Wear your royal-blue wool trapeze dress with your new black Capezio flats. And Charlie, do pull your hair back like I showed you. You have such a little peanut face, why must you hide it with all that hair?"

Charlotte's parents worried about a number of things, not the least being Moira Duffy, a social nullity contributing nothing to their hopes for Charlotte. Not only did her bursting-at-the-seams family exemplify the enthusiasm to overbreed, then accept handouts from more practical members of their faith who covertly practiced birth control, Moira was rebellious, shifty-eyed, a smart aleck whose bohemian tendencies were fast putting her on perdition's low road. According to Mr. Massey's city sources, a Free Love movement was underway. The Duffy girl seemed doomed by her own reactionary character to become part of it. A hippie. A flower child. God only knew what.

Both Duffy girls, Bridget and Moira, had full scholarships to the convent. Charity cases, Charlotte's mother sniffed. Every Thanksgiving and Christmas season, funds were quietly collected from the wealthier school families, and bags of food delivered to the dilapidated white clapboard house in Menlo Park's low-income, slightly seedy neighborhood. Charlotte had been to the Duffys' once, riding her bike over after school. In the kitchen, Bridget was shooing various dogs and cats in and out past the screen door, shoving a tuna casserole in the oven while a marmalade kitten with mange and one bloodied eye cowered inside a large cardboard box, two of the Duffy boys handling it so roughly that Charlotte felt sick and couldn't watch. Bridget was a top student in her class, and for the talent show had played her guitar and sung "Oh, Danny Boy," an Irish lament that caused mothers in the audience to weep and see themselves abiding "in sunshine or in shadow" as their children grew up, grew past them, were gone. Bridget's ethereal voice surprised everyone that night, lofting out of her squat body, plain-as-an-old-shoe features, and square, dustpan haircut. While Bridget won academic prizes and slaved for her six brothers and sisters, Moira leapt about, imagining herself a dancer, a revolutionary living at a formidable distance, far, far away.

Charlotte had never seen Mrs. Duffy, who lived up a set of steep, toy-raddled stairs with cheaply framed photographs of Pope John XXIII, John F. Kennedy, and Jesus nailed along the wall. She was on bed rest, doctor's orders, until the eighth baby was born, and on the day Charlotte visited, she twice heard her thin, querulous voice calling down for something, once for peace and quiet, another time for tea. No one paid any attention.

Staying for dinner, Charlotte had been shocked by the meager portions scooped onto each of the seven plates, eight, including hers. When, out of habit and appetite, she held out her empty plate (pale green, heavily scratched melamine) for a second helping, she saw too late the scraped-clean casserole dish. At the Massey home, platefuls of food, tightly wrapped in foil or Saran, got tossed after a day or two, at the first whiff of staleness.

After dinner, Mr. Duffy, a wordless man with an air of defeated elegance, hefted Charlotte's bicycle into the back of a battered old station wagon and drove her home. In the kitchen, she opened the refrigerator, reached around her mother's perfectly stacked cans of chocolate-flavored Metrecal ("liquid chalk," Mr. Massey called it), and fixed herself a second dinner from that night's leftovers, stroganoff and rice.

Charlotte had been permitted to invite only two school friends over for sleepovers. Coral Lynch, from Baltimore, had bushy, liver-colored hair, protuberant eyes, metal braces on her teeth, and a snoring affliction that had kept Charlotte awake all night, ready to pitch things at the second twin bed where Coral was indelicately lodged, sawing. Her second guest had been Mariko Takahashi from Osaka, a pretty girl with downcast, thick-lashed eyes, a convert who, upon graduation, elected to be swallowed up forever in a cloister in Belgium. Years later, when Charlotte had become a middle-class wife and mother of two girls, she and Mariko began exchanging annual Christmas cards. It was a thrill to Charlotte, diminished by domestic tasks and tempted to have an affair with someone, anyone, to find Mariko's envelope among the ordinary holiday cards, with its foreign stamps and featherweight, blue airmail stationery, the cloister's French address penned with cobalt ink in Mariko's impeccable, personalityless hand. The Masseys had approved of Coral's plainness and Mariko's courtesy, but had they known, neither would have cared for the Osaka girl's obsession with Jesus. In the tidy, secular darkness of Charlotte's bedroom, Mariko confessed she was, in her heart, already a bride of Christ. Charlotte envied her friend's devotion; in her own home, religion was contemptible, a superstition. She ached for an outsized fate, some operatic destiny as sacrificial and epicene as Mariko's. Although she was outwardly docile, Charlotte's inner life teemed, and when Mother Lussier read her villanelle aloud in class, the nun's praise distancing her from her classmates, Mr. Massey read that same poem and said Charlotte must have copied it from a book. What book? his wife asked. Mr. Massey didn't know.

By contrast, Moira Duffy's inner and outer lives were interchangeable. A willful bloom flashing up from the parched, rocky soil of her family, she intended to be a famous dancer in Paris or New York. Not ballet, deformity disguised as grace, but free, natural movement, modern dance. Her heroines were Isadora Duncan and Joan of Arc. Both, she told Charlotte, suffered unforgettable deaths, both stood for something. With untrammeled confidence, Moira persuaded Reverend Mother Flanagan, head of the convent school, to let her organize an after-school dance class. Borrowing a record player from the school's music teacher, a clarinet-playing spinster named Pinky Hoare, Moira swept out a practice space in the ill-lit, mildew-smelling basement. The class was a substitute for physical education, held after school on Mondays and Wednesdays, when one could choose tennis or soccer, gawking about with a racket or a stick in the convent's gym uniform, a bilious mint-green one-suit with short, square sleeves, elasticized waist, and knee-length triangular shorts. Instead, Moira wafted defiantly about the basement, barelegged in a short-sleeved black leotard, a hand-me-down so worn the fabric shone in places. Her one pupil, Charlotte, wore a still-new leotard, tights, and slippers bought for a YMCA ballet class she had dropped out of after two lessons, since the class only exposed how discomfited she felt in her own body.

Angular, pointy-nosed, histrionic, Moira wore her gruel-thin hair parted down the middle. She plugged it behind her big ears, which made them stick out more, and let it fall, a limp, yellow, dispirited banner, past her bottom. Charlotte believed she was learning a great deal, being Moira's friend, but was never quite sure what. Confidence? That it was possible to convince a stern old knacker like Reverend Mother Flanagan that modern dance was an acceptable substitute for soccer? That while Moira's older sister might labor, saintlike, at home, wiping the snotty noses and dirty bottoms of the Duffy brood, Moira could soar, swanlike and free, through that dingy, untidy household? That, she, Charlotte, might one day soar, too?

In dance class, Moira whipped her limbs like pale tentacles around the shadowy humid basement, Charlotte trailing in her wake. They danced to the only record Moira owned, Miles Davis's *Kind of Blue*. When the janitor limped down the cement stairs at 5 p.m. to switch off the lights, the two dancers, sweaty, liberated, pedaled their bikes past

474

the convent's black iron gates into the golden, cooling dusk, pumping off in different directions, Moira to her crummy neighborhood, Charlotte toward homes whose owners aspired to affluence through elbow grease, cutting corners, painting over.

Because she was possessed of an eerie, eruptive self-confidence and was Bridget Duffy's sister, Moira was uneasily respected by her classmates. On poetry day, standing in front of the class, she recited E. E. Cummings's "i like my body when it is with your body," until a beet-faced Mother Lussier, who may or may not have known the poem, stopped her after the lines, "i like kissing this and that of you, / i like, slowly stroking the, shocking fuzz / of your electric fur . . ." There was something uncompromising, hinting of heroism, even principled martyrdom, about Moira; everyone left her alone. She openly mocked the President of Mexico's phlegmatic daughters, wrote an essay about her class ring (paid for by donations from other families), calling the gold heart of Jesus in its ruby setting an "orbit of power." She was the first to use tampons, refusing the "bloody saddles" other girls wore, telltale maroon stains on the backs of their uniforms. Out of earshot of the nuns, she peppered her speech with "damns," "hells," "*merdes*," and "double-*merdes*," and on sidewalks, flashed peace signs at complete strangers driving by in cars. In Shakespeare class, she raised her hand to declare the word *nun* a slang word for *prostitute* in Shakespeare's time, and that when Hamlet told Ophelia to "get thee to a nunnery," it was a clever insult, because what Shakespeare really meant was that Ophelia should get herself to a brothel.

By throwing in her lot with Moira Duffy, Charlotte ensured her own social exile. Taking her cue from Moira, she first pretended not to mind, then didn't. On occasion, they conformed. Accepting a classmate's invitation to be in the annual talent show, Moira and Charlotte performed a soft-shoe routine with top hats made of black papier-mâché, swinging orthopedic canes and singing "Here Come the Beatnik Cats." They took modest roles in the school play, *Mary, Queen of Scots*. As a lady-in-waiting, Charlotte proffered a single curtsied line, "Your Majesty, the Lords of the Council are here," while Moira, one of many Lords, said nothing. On the whole, however, they preferred the periphery, the fringe.

At the last minute, Mrs. Massey changed from fuchsia Capri pants, a matching blouse knotted at the midriff, and turquoise flats to a conservative black peplum sheath with a slim rhinestone belt and black satin

475

pumps. Charlotte and her father waited in the foyer, next to the avocado sewing-machine table. "Your mother's got your old dad cooling his heels again, right, Brunhilda?" (When had he started calling her Brunhilda? She hated it.) Mr. Massey had on his best sport coat and tie, and smelled of Old Spice. He had shaved off his mustache and looked himself again. Itching in her blue trapeze dress, Charlotte wore the same black cotton tights she'd worn earlier that day in the school basement where, attempting splits on the concrete floor, she'd ripped a hole in the crotch. Twin flaps of hair, pulled forward, hardly concealed her acne, impervious to Dr. Gass's ultraviolet treatments. She had put on pink lipstick, borrowed her mother's mascara. Her father was shaking his keys. "Time to shove off, Haze! *Eins zwei drei!*" On cue, as if she were an actress, her mother swam out of the dark hallway, perfumed, alight in achieved beauty. After two Jack Danielses, Mr. Massey was prone to refer to his wife as "the old goat," but he had not yet had his first drink, so was silent about her appearance. In fact, he was already out the door, leaving Charlotte to tell her mother she looked nice, which wasn't the same thing, of course.

In the red Mustang he'd bought last summer, an exorbitant birthday gift for himself, Mr. Massey took note of his wife's attractiveness with a short, earthy grunt of approval. Mrs. Massey reciprocated, complimenting her husband for doing away with his "horrible lip caterpillar." Otherwise, the half-hour drive was tense with anticipation on her parents' part, dread on Charlotte's. She felt exposed, dressed up. In her convent uniform—a glaucous-blue circular skirt, white blouse, and matching vest, dreamed up by some clothes designer in Cairo, Egypt— she could be invisible.

They drove through cool, bracing, coastal darkness. Giant pin oak and eucalyptus trees hung close over winding roads as they passed increasingly large estates, jewel-bright mansions tucked deep inside the properties. Eschewing the turn signal, Mr. Massey swung his car neatly into a long, tree-bordered driveway. In the distance, a tall ship of blazing lights, the Carnation Milk Palace floated, miragelike. Anticipating Glen Halden's showcase of expensive liquor, Jack Massey smiled indulgently at his wife. This is when Charlotte liked him best, her father, when he was enigmatic but not unkind, with a minor hint of male charm.

"The cars, Jack, so many!"

"Same ones every year, Haze. Same rich lunkheads."

"The valet. Did you bring money for a tip? Charlie dear, do put your hair behind your ears. Let people see your face. Charlotte's turning into a beauty, Jack."

The car's interior was stifling, ripe with Old Spice, Eau de Joy, and the icy, naphthalene odor of mothballs from the black Persian-lamb coat her mother wore on special occasions. The coat had belonged to Charlotte's grandmother. Charlotte had worn it for dress-up, tottering about in her mother's heels, swinging a tiny patent-leather purse, empty but for a copper coin, the coat itself, animal-like, dragging on the floor behind her.

Standing in the entryway, a lean, rectangular woman wearing a black dress, a white apron, and a pleated paper cap like a nurse's greeted the Masseys. Throughout the Milk Palace's vast first floor, men and women in uniform hovered around the guests with a trained air of imperturbability, formal neutrality. They were all what her parents would call "Negroes," and what Owen, echoing his father, would call "black people."

Whenever she belittled someone for putting on airs, for acting "high and mighty," Charlotte's mother would say, "Look who's all *hoity toity*." Now Hazel Massey was *hoity toity*, standing exaggeratedly still so one of the uniformed men could slip the Persian lamb with its tight, glossy black curls off her bare shoulders, letting a second man wait as she chose a glass of chilled champagne to take from the silver tray, took an appraising first sip. Mr. Massey had ducked off to find more substantial drink.

In the marble-floored foyer, Charlotte shrunk to a speck, listening to the sounds of the party down the hall somewhere, the live band music, and the hot, insect hum of conversation. She was beginning to panic when a man with a head of high, snowy hair emerged from a room off the hall and came toward her, smiling. Wearing a Scotch plaid vest and giving off a florid, patrician heat, Mr. Halden took up each of her freezing hands in his own and kissed them. Her disloyalty was swift; she wanted this man for a father. But having greeted her, a gold watch winking out from his starched shirt cuff, Mr. Halden quickly left, to be smoothly replaced by his wife, Stibsy, columned in cerise velvet, a ropey glitter around her taut, dusky throat. *Diamonds*, Charlotte heard her mother say. *Real diamonds*. Above their cruel gleam, Stibsy Halden's face was rugose, creased from long summers of sailing her yacht. How delighted she was to see Charlotte, how terribly pretty and grown-up she'd become! As she swept Charlotte up in an embrace that smelled of Dove soap, Charlotte's disloyalty, fed by fury at her parents for not letting her stay at Moira's house, redoubled. She wanted these people, so kind, permissive, solidly rich, for her parents. If the Carnation Milk Palace were her home, she would stay up late reading book after book, ride her bike everywhere, have all the sleepovers, even boyfriends, she wanted. She and Moira would drape themselves, lithe serpents, over the banisters, perform brilliantly in plays, do underwater handstands in the pool at night. It would be a place where almost anything was acceptable and everyone, especially Charlotte, would be loved.

Stibsy Halden, pan-rumped, flat as a playing card, firmly guided Charlotte down the long main hallway toward the party, dropping her at the entrance to the ballroom with a word to someone standing nearby—"Take care of our lovely young friend, will you? Doesn't she just remind you of Debbie Reynolds? I must dash back . . . other guests . . ."

Pressing her back against a wall of beveled oak paneling, Charlotte lifted a glass of champagne from the tray held by a man (black, not Negro) with an elegantly cut, disdainful face. Raising the glass to her lips, champagne fizz tickling her nose, she peered from between thick blinders of hair. Everyone in the room was her parents' age or older. There must be a library, a rose garden, some better escape than the refuge she had found during a debutante ball in Atherton her mother had once wrangled an invitation to. After one dance with a boy more tongue-tied than she was, Charlotte had shut herself up in a beige toilet stall, reading a Mother Stuart religious tract over and over until nine o'clock, when she found a pay phone and called her father to come get her. At least the Carnation Milk Palace, sumptuous, fragranced, reflecting the affable personality of its owners, promised some better sanctuary.

When the waiter with the silver tray stopped in front of her again, Charlotte exchanged her emptied champagne glass for a new, full one. At the far end of the ballroom, the band played her father's favorite music from the Big Band era. On the tightly packed, dimly lit dance floor, couples circled, while along the perimeter, guests sipped cocktails, drifted about, conversed. A dark knot of men huddled in one corner laughing, no doubt telling off-color jokes (Charlotte had seen her father at the center of these groups, and overheard, half-comprehending, his dirty remarks). But he was on the dance floor, whirling a meaty woman in a bursting taffeta sheath as if she were gossamer. The dance ended, he glided over. By his breath, Charlotte guessed he was on his third or fourth drink. He was usually still pleasant between the second and third. "How about a spin with your old dad, Brunhilda?" As the band launched into one of her father's favorite swing tunes, "Let's Dance," the same waiter took her emptied champagne glass, his expression contemptuous.

Her father was lubricated, limber, in perfect control. Charlotte twirled the wrong way twice, stepped on one of her father's long, polished shoes, banged into another couple, tripped again. Frowning, her father pulled her closer. *Relax, follow the man's lead, you're too tense.* But she was flustered, all mistake. Worse, she'd humiliated him. Before the dance was over, he walked her to the edge of the floor and pulled from the sidelines a pert, blond woman in olive slacks who kept up with his every move. Dancing with women was what her father did best. He receded from Charlotte, absorbed back into a blurred kaleidoscope of dancers.

Lifting the microphone, crackling, from its stand, the DJ called everyone out on the floor to dance to a new song topping the nation's pop charts. Hired to humor wealthy, middle-aged Republicans, the band, bored and dutiful up to now, came crashing to life with Chubby Checker's "The Twist." *"Come on baby, let's do the twist! Come on baaaby . . ."*

A woman standing close to Charlotte cupped one hand to her mouth, shouting, "I'm afraid this is our exit, dear. We're much too old for twisting. Walt will twist his lower back right out!" Walt bared short, yellow teeth in a goosey honk, and the couple vanished. Charlotte seized a third glass of champagne and avoiding the face of the man holding the tray, gulped it down. She could at least tell Moira she had gotten drunk. *"Come on, baby, let's do the twist, come on baby, let's do the twist . . ."* The music was deafening, off-key. Mothers with bouffant, teased hair, wearing sleeveless holiday shifts, fathers, jackets off, shirt sleeves rolled up, gyrated, twisting their thickening waistlines side to side, up and down. Flushed with drink, one couple hustled over to Charlotte, pounced. "You're the only teenager in the whole damned room, c'mon, show us!" The woman took her empty glass, the man towed her onto the dance floor, everyone closing in, singing, clapping. Charlotte began to twist. (Moira said it was the easiest, stupidest, most *merde* dance ever.) They imitated her, the mothers and fathers, loosening up, catching on, then quickly forgetting her. No one noticed when Charlotte ducked out, threading her way through the twisting couples, the sickening reek of sweat, alcohol, perfume. Out in the silent hallway, hoping for a bathroom, Charlotte pulled on the nearest door. It opened into a cold, forbidding room. Farther down, she tried a second door. It opened into the library she had hoped existed.

They looked like a magazine advertisement for cigarettes or the perfect brassiere. A reed-thin woman in black, seductively arched against a room-length bookcase, bare arms outspread, a young man pursuant, closing in. The woman's face sparkled, her pelvis tipped against his, a provocative pose. Pelvises were depraved, important. (She'd learned other words from Moira—*crotch, twat, pussy*, and the funniest—*beaver*. "Down there," her mother called it. Her father remained silent on the subject, though Charlotte, sneaking around in his den one day, had unearthed a deck of playing cards, naked women coyly posed on the glossy face of each one.)

The young man was no one Charlotte had seen before. Seeing her daughter, Mrs. Massey immediately straightened up, reached casually for her drink.

"Charlie, darling, don't hang back! Come meet James, he's a medical student at Stanford, a budding cardiologist. We're chatting, looking at books while we're still stuck here in 1963."

Forced to shake his warm, flaccid hand, she saw James was half her mother's age, much nearer her own.

"I saw you," he smirked. "Dancing."

"Charlotte? Dancing?" Her mother sounded intoxicated, flirty, asinine. She never read books.

"Considering it was music from—apologies—another generation, she did great."

"Her father gave up trying to teach her. She and her little hippie friend are doing some sort of modern dance now. No proper steps, no skill, all flopping about."

"Really? Are you a hippie, Charlotte?" Insolence corrupted his mouth, his handsome features. He smiled, but his eyes held a brooding look, melancholy, as if he felt cheated of something.

"No, I'm not. Excuse me, I need to find a bathroom."

James politely held the door for Charlotte as she edged out of the library. Slipping off her flats, holding them in one hand, she tiptoed up the stairs, her feet soothed by the plush, white carpet. Everything was spinning.

"Want to have some fun?"

His hand caught her waist.

She wondered what Moira, always bold, would do now. What Moira would urge her to try. She felt slightly sick.

Upstairs, he held Charlotte's hand, opening doors until he found the room he wanted. In the unheated darkness, he pulled her beside a bed hilled with guests' winter coats, thrust his thick rough-grained tongue in her mouth, bleak and sour from champagne. (Werner had kissed her once, a timid, dry peck she nearly hadn't bothered to record in her diary.) Pushing her onto the perfumed, uneven layer of coats, he shoved her dress above her hips, awkwardly pulled at her black tights until they were down past her knees. His hair, cut short like her father's, bristled against the naked skin of her thighs.

He raised his head. "What's the matter with you? You're shaking like a leaf."

Charlotte lay trembling, wool dress bunched around her waist. Her back hurt.

Brushing a hand over the top of his hair, he shook his head as if to clear it, stood up.

"Hey, sorry. I was out of line just now. I had the wrong idea about you." On his way to the door, he turned back, spoke as if he could see her. "You're a beautiful girl, you know that? And way too innocent. You need to watch out for assholes like me."

When she was sure he had gone, Charlotte stood, pulled up her torn tights, straightened her dress. Sitting back on edge of the bed, the room still whirling a little, she reached with her fingertips, among the richly textured coats, mink, camel's hair, velvet, until she felt the cool, tight coils of black Persian lamb.

The party had moved farther off, a faint congregation of voices . . . *seven, six, five, four, three, two, ONE! Happy New Year!* . . . drunken shouts, the blat of cheap party horns, a banal, forlorn-sounding noise, dying off.

Coming downstairs, Charlotte held her mother's coat, lined with its fraying silk moiré, over one arm.

They stood by the front door, her parents, talking with another couple waiting for their car. Her mother turned. "Heavens, Charlie, you missed ringing in the New Year! We were about to send out the troops."

Her father ignored her.

Bringing their car around to the entrance, the valet swung each door

481

wide, waited until they were settled inside to wish them a happy new year.

On a densely wooded, unlit road, less than a mile from the Carnation Milk Palace, Mr. Massey missed a curve, running the Mustang off the road into a shallow ditch. Mrs. Massey calmly offered to drive but, at her husband's look, drew her coat tighter around her and stared out the window. Craning his head back, one arm gripping the top of the front seat, Mr. Massey gunned the car so violently it leapt from the ditch and landed at a sharp angle on the road. Charlotte, in the shadows of the back seat, started to cry.

"What? What the hell's the matter? We're all fine here."

"Jack."

"You too, Hazel. You made a pretty wide ass of yourself tonight with that college brat."

Mrs. Massey opened her car door. "That's it. I'm walking home."

"Simmer down, Haze. Get back in the car. I didn't mean it."

Yes, you did, thought Charlotte. You meant every word.

She trailed her father toward the house as he cursed his way up the porch steps, then turned to help her mother, still in the dark car, head bowed, shoulders small inside her coat's secondhand glamour.

Later, in bed, Charlotte imagined ways to tell Moira about the New Year's Eve party—the Haldens, the Milk Palace, the champagne, the stupid dancing, her mother's embarrassing flirtation with a college boy who would follow Charlotte up the stairs into a dark bedroom, his French-kissing her, half-undressing her, then leaving her, respecting her or saving himself, who knew, but the first boy ever to tell her what she most wanted to hear, that she was beautiful.

She would not tell Moira what she now suspected, that terrible things happened all the time, secret, violating things. And she could hardly know, not yet, that this foul prince would be the first of many to lead her to his own pleasure, poisoning the pure ideal, the sweet well of herself, before reviving her with a cold word like *beauty* and, later, *love*.

Nominated by Ayse Papatya Bucak, Joyce Carol Oates, Maura Stanton

CROSS YOUR FINGERS GOD BLESS

fiction by RON CURRIE JR.

from WIG-LEAF

Because she was not a superstitious person, in the days leading up to her solo hike in the thickly wooded ridges Annie ignored several warnings proffered by the universe regarding what was about to happen.

Because she did not believe in premonitions, she was not given pause when she flipped open a magazine at her podiatrist's office to a two-page spread about staying safe while hiking, and in particular staying safe from wildlife attacks.

Because her notion of existence made room for nothing but the banally palpable, on the long drive to the trailhead she failed to register a roadside sign that read "**BEAR** Collision Specialists."

Because she was raised in a rational age that had little use for the supernatural and/or extrasensory, when the cosmos—practically screaming at her now, and Annie's third ear as deaf as you like—threw a wooden carving of a bear from the bed of the pickup truck in front of her, she simply slowed, drove around it, and continued on her way without a second thought.

It was only later, trapped in the envelope of agony her body had become, rendered incommunicado by both morphine and the tube in her trachea, that these things came back to Annie and she recognized them for what they had been, saw them gleaming in the haze of consciousness like lodestars, suddenly the only true things in existence.

And so then her world became nothing but Ouija and omen, good winds and bad vibes. She left the hospital with a face pieced together just well enough that people could stand to look at it. For months, she drank her meals. She gave much thought to buying a veil. She wore customized shoes designed to accommodate the new difference in the length of her legs. But she was not unhappy. She passed the time mostly alone, turning over tarot cards and remembering the first glimpse of the bears as she reached the end of a long turn in the trail: the mother, huge, black, wet-snouted, and the two cubs, harmless and helpless as stuffed playthings. Which, of course, explained the mother's fury in protecting them.

Annie didn't blame her a bit.

As that first winter came on her old friends fell away, some gradually, some all of a sudden. One might have imagined that grief drove them off, or else that they found her too difficult to gaze upon for more than a few seconds, let alone the amount of time necessary for a cup of coffee or, God forbid, dinner. But that wasn't it. Not really. They, like her, had been raised in a rational age. Many of them held degrees in the physical sciences or mathematics. They never attended church. The only invisible thing they believed in was the air in their lungs, and so what cleaved them from Annie was, in fact, her new credulousness, her good cheer, her refusal to be saddened by the illusion of this new, teeth-grinding circumstance. She struggled to explain the unseen, and her old friends looked at her ravaged face and the violent hitch in her stride and felt the brand of pity that the well reserve for the crippled. They imagined that the only possible explanation for her rapture was that she'd been rendered daffy by trauma, poor soul. And so one by one they left her, backing away and speaking pleasantly to cover their unease, much as one is supposed to behave when encountering a wild animal in the woods.

Nominated by Wig-Leaf

THE TRADITION

by JERICHO BROWN

from POEM-A-DAY

Aster. Nasturtium. Delphinium. We thought
Fingers in dirt meant it was our dirt, learning
Names in heat, in elements classical
Philosophers said could change us. *Star Gazer.*
Foxglove. Summer seemed to bloom against the will
Of the sun, which news reports claimed flamed hotter
On this planet than when our dead fathers
Wiped sweat from their necks. *Cosmos. Baby's Breath.*
Men like me and my brothers filmed what we
Planted for proof we existed before
Too late, sped the video to see blossoms
Brought in seconds, colors you expect in poems
Where the world ends, everything cut down.
John Crawford. Eric Garner. Mike Brown

Nominated by Ellen Bass, Karla Huston

BLUE OF THE WORLD

fiction by DOUGLAS W. MILLIKEN

from GLIMMER TRAIN

May 24th, 1965

Walked the orchard line with the boy today after the service, from the house to the north end of the property. All the blooms had blown off the limbs, so just a foamy wash of white or dried-up yellow petals were left here and there on the ground. Very many small green apples have started, few much bigger than the head of a nail. The trees looked good. I do not much fear a late frost ruining everything that's begun. But in this, I've been wrong before.

The land very slightly inclines to the north here, so it was harder going up than coming back. We collected blowdowns as we followed the single straight file of trees, stacking them on a sledge the boy pulled. I brought a saw in case we needed to clear a split limb from a live tree. We needed the saw twice. Mules grazed nearby with the jack donkey in the pasture east of us, and after a spell, were joined by the quarter horses. We'd been discovered. Just post and board fence between us and them, them following as we worked the orchard line. We must have been good fun to watch. I suggested we hitch the sledge to any one of them—it's easy work for a horse and not work at all for a mule—but the boy said no.

The pasture west of the orchard has grown meadow-sweet and fallow with tall grass. If I can mend the fences on that side of the trees, I will swap the beasts over there. But I'm not certain I have that ambition yet this year.

At the northern boundary line where our land meets the Finnegans', we rested and ate sandwiches and shared cold coffee from a jelly jar. We agreed, the coffee was not as good as it used to be. Something missing, or the ratios wrong. It's hard to enjoy a thing when your memory of it is sweeter. Toward the faraway hills, men were standing the first girders of a new weather tower. The sight of it makes me hate. We finished our lunch and coffee and headed back south to the house, looking for anything we missed along the way. The horses followed.

May 25th, 1965

Taught the boy how to mend the leather of a stirrup torn free from its fender. He is still too short to work at the bench with ease.

May 28th, 1965

John Henneker has called every day for the past two weeks, begging me to bring a sire out to rut his dam Dilly, and only just yesterday offered to pay me for this service. Being neighbors entitles us to nothing of each other. He must have just got the news. He named what he could pay and I told him what that could buy him. He didn't seem too picky. Chose a young painted stud, barely more than a colt. Never been sired. Quick and leggy. Rambunctious and maybe a little dumb. It all sounded fine to John. All he asked is that it be pretty.

The Henneker farm is a twenty mile drive or more, but only fifteen if one draws a straight line between our two places, and anyway they weren't expecting us at any particular time, so the boy and I saddled up our Ghost and Coyote before dawn and led the paint by a rope from the team. Among the wild parti-colors of quarter horses, there's a wordless rare something in riding tall milk-white Saddlebreds. It's best in the dark before sunrise, when you're the only white thing in the world glowing like a moon. It's good to feel you're a rare riding thing sometimes, even if you aren't. We took turns holding the paint's rope: when we crossed a property, we'd switch. Headed north along the orchard line and crossed onto the Finnegans' land, down their pasture and through the wooded way and along the west shore of their wide, muddy cattle pond, then up the grassy slope and across a dirt road onto the Halls' land, where things flatten and dry out nicely. It's a piece of land that'd be more at home two hundred miles west of here, in Interior or

Kadoka. No good for pasture or growing much more than pigweed and morning glory and really, given the rockiness, not the safest riding. A horse can twist an ankle on a loose stone as easily as a man can. But it feels correct. The sun was still low, so the earth looked more purple and blue than anything else. Now and then a spooked rabbit would dart off ahead of us and disappear. It was ghostly, that flash of rabbit. Far away, we could see the big hills rolling. The boy had once said they looked like someone lying with a blanket pulled up over her face. But he didn't say anything today. Told him, back east, people called these mountains. He said he knew, I'd told him that before.

We took the horses easy on that sweet flat piece, then watered them at Cane Brook. That marked the boundary between the Halls' and Hennekers' lands. But we still had a ways to go. We traded the paint's rope and crossed the brook, up a rock bank under a canopy of cottonwoods, then into a pasture that'd grown wild with disuse. The Hennekers, I believe, have more land than their cattle can manage for them. John needs to up his herd. Or let some bison in. Then again, I should not be so quick to advise unasked, as much of my land to the west looks just the same as this. That pasture—though I guess it's really straight reclaimed prairie—ran all the way to the farmhouse. There were eventually beef cattle grazing who'd look at us curiously as we passed. Great black and crimson cows. The grass was shorter near the farm.

The younger two Henneker boys met us at the gate and took Ghost and Coyote into the barn, their little sister chasing along after. I believe she was intent on brushing them. It was beginning to make sense to me why John wanted his dam foaled so bad. A girl child had lit a fire under his ass for something pretty to ride. He didn't give a damn what kind of horse he fostered as long as it was a horse. I felt fine with my choice of sire. John Henneker came along a moment later, worrying his fingers with a dirty red rag, then shook my hand and the boy's hand and admired the paint entirely on its color and shape. He did not look at its teeth, and I was glad. It's always a favor when folk don't pretend to know something. I explained to him the horse was not really a Paint, just painted. He looked at me like I was a moron. John's wife Evelyn came out after that and asked if we'd like something to eat or drink. We did. We had coffee and cold lunch in their kitchen and when we were done, we took the sire to a paddock where Henneker's bay draft horse Dilly was waiting. We let the two of them figure it out from there.

We stood there leaning against the wood fence, watching. Me and the boy and John Henneker and Evelyn. I was prepared to leave the paint for a day or more to give them time to adjust to one another, but they proved to make pretty fast friends. The two horses circled and sniffed each other, then the dam lifted her tail and pissed and the sire sniffed the piss, then sniffed its source and climbed on. He was a solid three hands shorter than she and just about fell off on his first attempt. But it's a lesson each of us eventually learns. It wasn't long before they got it all worked out.

John paid me after that. You could tell he'd made a special trip to the bank just for this. Crisp new bills still bound in a paper band. While we shook hands, John's youngest two—one boy and one girl—led out our rides by their bridles. Both horses looked well brushed. The girl was leading the boy's horse. She knew it. It pleased the boy and she knew that, too. We mounted, then led the sire by his rope out the gate, and he seemed a little more frolicky than usual. The rutting has put some pep in him. Trotted out of the used pasture, then galloped when we hit the disused part. Everyone seemed happy for the speed.

Heading back, we took a different route home. The sun was angling lower, making everything bright green and golden. The horses shook their heads and made sounds, as if they found it pleasing to try an un-trod path. Once on our own land, we cut southwest past the orchards into a pasture grown tall and wild. We rode until we reached our cold water pond, big flat rocks and silt at its edges. Narrow creek nuzzling out of the shallows, acting casual, sneaking southwest to join up with its friends and rush wicked into the Missouri. In its middle, you could see the pond's face purling where the spring boiled up underneath. I can remember a time when the boy would ask where the water came from, how come it was always there. I know as much about it now as I did then. We tied the horses to a bone-dry and uprooted cottonwood root, then took off our clothes and swam. The boy was laughing. He could slice through the water like some silvery, brown-eyed fish. He did not learn this from me. I am all mammal in water, built to push through it, get to the other side. Have to remind myself that this is not a job. But the boy needs no reminding. Dive to the bottom and come up with rocks, little white twists that might be ancient bone. He's teaching me what is fun. I'd crouch in shallow water up to my chin and he'd balance his feet in the stirrup of my hands. Then I'd stand up quick and launch him.

June 1st, 1965

Every morning, there's a great revival of birds singing all at once in the orchard trees and pastures. See them lined up on the crossbeams of our tin-can scarecrow in the garden. Watch them slice shapes in the air. They never stop singing when they fly. They will light on the backs of sleeping horses and sing. I do not know if they understand what the other birds are saying, or if they even understand themselves.

I have never known the name of any bird other than a crow. But the boy knows. He is learning. There's a library book with colored pictures, and a record of the songs they sing. It's one of the things he studies. He'll put on the record and page through the book. Our house filled with the songs of singing birds. He knows the names that people use and the Latin names used only by doctors and poets. He feels it is his inheritance and responsibility, the naming of all the birds, when there's no one else here who can name them anymore.

June 2nd, 1965

Drove the boy to the library. He's a collector now of everything. Engine design and Iron Age wars and big books of maps, places I never heard of. Asked him on the ride home if he minded that I'd taken him out of school for so long. He said no, he didn't mind, but by fall he'll want to go back. He knows what this is about. I hope I'll be ready by then.

June 4th, 1965

Today came the man from the big Montana ranch with his two trucks hauling long gooseneck trailers. We had spoken on the phone. This was expected. Sort of waddled when he hopped down out of his truck, but the other driver didn't even turn off his engine. Without these deals now and then to big ranches, an operation small as ours would go under in a season. It saves us. Even still, it saddens me to see so many animals gone in one day. I feel a closeness to these things. Quarter horses and mules. Strange animals like great dogs with hooves, both sweet and wild. The Montanan had the specs of his order, and it'd have been easy enough for the boy and me to gather in his horses—they are familiar with us and don't worry when we cull any one of them from the team— but the Montanan wanted to have a physical role in their selection. Which made it a true culling. They ran. We spent the morning chasing them in circles, cutting horses out one at a time. It was a waste of time, and it scared the beasts. But the Montanan felt very proud of his efforts and his active hand in the choosing. The work was a joy for him because it was his choice to work. The boy kept arrowing glances my way, like he wanted me to say something, stand up to this pot-bellied rich man. I couldn't rightly tell him then that this one sale would spell easy sailing for the rest of the year. So I held my tongue and cut the horses one by one, and later forgot to explain. So I guess he still sees me more as a coward than a businessman.

For letting him pretend he was a cowboy, the rancher threw in a bonus. Then he took his sixteen head of skittish horses and went back to Montana. The boy said he wished that lost sixteen luck. I take that to be his way of saying that he was not fond of the fat man. It was long after dark when what was left of my team finally lost fear and grew still.

June 5th, 1965

I let the boy sleep more lately than I did when he went to school. There really isn't enough work now for two men. I can do the rote chores in the morning while he sleeps. Save the more interesting work to tackle later on as a team. But even with these dawn chores, I'm learning to take my time. This morning I went out onto the porch with my coffee, thinking I'd watch the blue world take on all its colors with the sun, but as soon as I stepped out, I saw on the deck boards a little gray lump. A big black beetle was rolling the lump around. Sometimes burying its head into a softness. And as it moved the lump around, I realized what I was seeing was a very small, very dead bird. I do not know what bird it was. It hadn't any feathers to speak of, just the moldy fuzz of a hatchling. The beetle unfolded the bird's bunched-up neck and articulated its clenched legs. I know the beetle was just feeding, but it seemed it was trying to reanimate the bird. As if by exercising its limbs, it could bring it back to life. I crouched there on the porch watching the beetle work to resuscitate this little rotten thing. Then I went back inside. Without my noticing, the blue of the world was gone.

But a curiosity was in me now. Took the little ash shovel down from its place by the wood stove and went back outside, scooped the bird and beetle up. Set them on a stump behind the house where I once had

491

to cut an old rock elm down. Figured they'd be safe over there. Keep an eye on them now and then without worrying the boy might find them. I don't know how he'd react to this sort of thing. I'm not sure how I'm reacting myself.

June 6th, 1965
Thought I saw you hanging laundry today. Wind whipping the white sheets to snapping at your heels. But it was just the boy. Doing the job you used to do.

June 8th, 1965
The boy went out to pick alpine strawberries (or as my ma used to call them, *fraises des bois*) with the Hautenot girl this morning in the Kelloggs' fields south of here, so I took the truck into town. I needed nails and coffee and thought maybe I'd see what else they got at the store that we've never tried before. I think it's good for the boy to try new things. I do not like being in that house all alone. Went to the hardware store and got some nails and a new leather punch, as mine has mysteriously grown bent (a mystery I'm sure the boy knows the solution to) then talked to Henry for a spell and had an RC Cola because business was slow for Henry and I was in no hurry. He didn't have anything worth saying to say. At the Hy-Vee, got the coffee and a box of pancake mix because I can't make them right from scratch—there is something I'm missing that I cannot get right—and nothing else looked interesting, so I bought a giant southern watermelon. It was shaped like a box. I suspected the boy would get a kick out of that. The girl working checkout was pretty and smiled at me a lot. But I couldn't really smile back. I'm not ready yet for that kind of attention, it does no good for me now. So I didn't look at her at all. I hope she understands.

Driving home, waiting at a red light, I happened to notice a little orange butterfly flying circles round above the pavement. It was new tar macadam there. It was black. The butterfly kept circling the same patch of road like there was something there it liked. But there was nothing there. Then a worrying thing happened, as I started feeling a sort of panic tightening up in my throat. Just off the shoulder, there were flowers growing in the grass, and not far past that, fields of flowers. So why was this butterfly circling hot tar? Maybe there wasn't

492

anything there where it was circling, but there used to be. Maybe it was remembering something that was long gone, paved over and buried. What I understand is that butterflies are always heading somewhere, either to or from some breeding ground in Mexico. But this one wasn't going anywhere. Just circling where something used to be. I was scared it might die by this choice. Get burned up on the sun-hot tar or hit any second now by a car. The world is too much for an animal so small to make choices that aren't only survival. The light had turned green but I hadn't noticed. Then someone behind me leaned on their horn. I wanted to save that stupid damn bug. But I couldn't. I couldn't even try. I drove through the light and brought the melon home to our boy.

June 10th, 1965

The dead bird moves a lot in the night. If it lay along the northeast rings of the stump at dusk, it'll be in the southern rings by morning. It's as if the beetle is passing coded messages, divining the weather, spelling good omens I hope. And too: there is a dead spider on the stump now as well. I don't know what killed either of these things. Only know they are gathering here.

June 13th, 1965

Ronald Haskell called about renting one of the mules to pull a load of wood he aims to fell in the back quarter of his property. Told him for an extra two hundred dollars, he could have a mule and keep it. It was a good deal for him, but I don't think he wanted it. I felt like a bully, sticking so firm to my offer. All mule or no mule. He came and got his animal before suppertime.

Later, the boy and I took Ghost and Coyote out in the west pastures. Sometimes trotting the horses and sometimes letting them run. It was aimless, the paths we took. Mostly let the beasts decide. The sky was liquid bright with colors, but the dark lay low to the ground, almost black, everything just an outline of a shape. Shape of the boy. Shape of a tree. Far out, we saw some scavenger birds cutting circles in the air, so we rode out to see what we'd find. Dead doe splayed out in the grass, its hindquarters mostly ate off. A look of permanent terror fixed on its eyeless face. It stank. Ghost and Coyote stamped in the grass and threw their heads. They hated it.

Heading back, the boy pointed out the weather tower, getting taller. But I didn't want to see it. I spat.

June 14th, 1965

We were stripping an old saddle down to its tree when the boy asked me if we were ever going to talk about it. Didn't seem to me there was anything to talk about. But I didn't even say that. I showed him where the skirt tied into the tree. Then I cut the seam.

I believe he's beginning to resent me. He didn't like learning that Ron Haskell had taken the mule for keeps. He's been spending more time with the Hautenot girl. That scrawny whippet with all the teeth. Over dinner, he stressed to me how much he was looking forward to starting school again in the fall. We both pretended like school wasn't still in session for everybody other than him.

After the boy went to bed, I stood out in the yard awhile, listening to the wind and the horses and the rattle of the tin cans hanging in the scarecrow and what I assume was an owl calling, though it wasn't how I imagine an owl ought to sound. Then I went inside and found a lantern and headed off west past the orchards, tall grass hushing around my knees. I did not light the lamp until I got to our pond. I followed the horse paths there. Took off my clothes and folded them and set them in a pile beside the lantern on a flat rock. Then I went for a swim. The half-moon was high and set the water sparkling, and I swam to the far side and back three times, and on the fourth pass stopped and treaded water in the center. There was nothing else out there. Just me and the water and the moon and the lamp. The lamp was only there so I could find the shore again when I was done. You couldn't see the far hills. Just prairie in all directions forever. But nothing felt far away. It was all right there with me. In the water or close to shore. The moon and lantern and the cold spring beneath my feet. Everything right there with me. I stayed as long as the cold water would let me. Then I swam to the light and got dressed and walked home, the lantern now dark in my hand.

Across the distance, I saw the kitchen light was on. You were sitting at the table when I walked in, playing solitaire and drinking a glass of ginger ale in your hospital gown. It's the last thing I'd seen you wearing. Two moths fluttered about the yellow light above your head. There were eyes of wet on your glass. I smiled and took my boots off and said

494

hello, and you smiled at me and waved and said nothing. Your skin was very gray but your eyes were still cool like wet slate. Mouth tight and twisted like you were holding back a laugh. You gathered the cards and shuffled. I found a dusty bottle of Canadian Club in a high cupboard shelf and poured myself a glass and poured a splash in yours. I sat across from you at the table and you dealt out the cards. I wanted very badly to touch you. Your blond hair was stringy and kept falling in your face. I wanted to tuck it behind your ear, touch the hollow where your jaw bends to meet your neck. But I didn't. I knew that was against the rules. There were dark bruises inside your elbows and on the backs of your hands where the I.V.s had gone in. There was still a paper bracelet around your narrow wrist. A bird's wrist. We played a few hands of rummy, matching runs and pairs. Then you asked me where I've been and I told you I went for a swim in the pond. But you shook your head and said that's not what you meant. I could see your knee peeking beneath the edge of your hospital gown and without thinking reached to touch it with the tip of my finger, the acre of my palm, but you shook your head again. Then you were gone.

I sat for a long time in the kitchen beneath the moths spinning in the light, my hair still wet from the pond. It was cold. Even with the night still and the wind far away, this house creaks like old bones. The unseen motions of ancient things. I turned out the light and went to bed.

June 18th, 1965

The boy told me today that I am stupid for selling the mule. We were weeding our small garden, culling the little shoots of jewelweed and pigweed and plantain from among the potato mounds and pea vine and bush beans. He said that I was getting it all backward. Said we ought to have lent the mule to the Haskells for free as a favor, and only charged him if the beast got hurt or took ill. He insisted that favors are worth more than dollars, as the price of gold goes up and down but a favor is always a favor. At the very least, we should have traded services, as the Haskells raise good hay and oats, and they needed the mule to haul wood, all of which are things we will need come wintertime. But regardless: we should not have sold the mule.

I said to him that I suppose he thinks we ought to have let our paint rut with the Henneker's dray for free, too. And I should fix every saddle and bridle and harness for whoever comes begging at our door. He agreed the leatherwork ought to cost, but to charge to let an untested colt plow a draft horse for no other purpose than to make an animal whose only job will be to be an animal? He thought it was a pointless and mean thing, asking money for that.

I reminded him that what we ran was a horse farm. Then he did something that surprised me. He was squatting down in the potato mounds, but he'd stopped picking weeds. He was looking at his hands in the cool, dark earth. Then he said that people's sympathy for me was wearing thin. He said I was eating up our neighbors' goodwill by being a greedy fly.

I told him sympathy was another name for cancer. I'd be happier when it was gone.

The boy stood up and chucked a clod of rotten seed potato at me. It sailed over my shoulder and struck the line of tin cans strung to our scarecrow crucifix. Then he marched out of the garden. Headed south. I suspect to go play with that homely Hautenot girl.

I finished weeding my row of peas. I worked in the barn on a new bridle and traces set. I stood in the orchard and listened to the nicker of horses, the scream of birds. I did not go into the house. I stood with the wind pushing my shoulders and tugging at my clothes. Then I got into the truck and drove. I didn't go anywhere. There was nowhere I wanted to go. I drove the dirt roads between farms and fields and looked out at the cattle standing still and chewing. I watched the sun melt off in the hills and the silver flint of moon rise up. Stars and the occasional mercury lamp burning cold over a closed barn door. I drove until very late before turning and heading back. I could smell the sweet dust gusting off the road as I passed along. Hoped the boy would be home when I got there.

June 20th, 1965

Afternoon clouds got dark all at once and a warm wind blew in hard and wet from the south. An uneasiness breathed in by the weather. I'd been sleeping but something woke me. Like a cool hand tracing down my neck. Looked to see what it was but saw nothing. Then I saw what was happening outside. Looked for the boy but could not find him so called, but he wouldn't call back. The scarecrow's tin cans banged together like the drums in an Indian's dance. In the pastures, the horses were running hard, making noise, being beasts. The mules faced the wind and were mules. I saddled Circle, as she hadn't been rode in some time, and took to the fallow pastures at a steady beat, and found the boy up in a box elder southwest of the farm. It was a squat arthritis tree with the pale undersides of its leaves turned up. It was the only tree around. Just a lot of tall grass lying flat beneath the wind. The boy's face was all wet and he wouldn't look at me. This was nothing I'd thought him liable to still do, to run away and to cry. I wasn't sure how to react to that. I did not like him in the tree. As he was on a low branch and I was on your horse, we were just about on a level with each other. I reached out and patted his shoulder. But I felt like a little league coach doing that, consoling a batter after striking out on an unimportant play. I suspected that sentiment was incorrect. He didn't look hurt, so I assumed it must be the other thing. The wind was getting worse and there was some deep animal sound coming from the clouds. It was a mean thing to say, but I told him to stop that now. Then I reached out and put an arm behind his back and pulled him onto Circle ahead of me on the saddle. He was too old for that kind of thing. But we had to move. I put the heels to your horse and we rode hard and fast back to the house. The quarter horses were acting like horses again, calm with the wind whipping back their manes. The jack donkey was chewing oats. They didn't care. They could handle themselves. We disrobed Circle and set her and Ghost and Coyote loose in the pasture with the others. Three white horses among varnished sorrels and blue roans and charcoal blacks, underneath an evil marble of storm. Then we went inside, and first it hailed but then it rained in dark ribbons, so you could see it wind like snakes through the air, while far to the south, though we couldn't tell how far, we watched a black tornado touch down and ride.

June 21st, 1965

The bird is less lump and more skeleton now. No sign of the beetle. Where'd he go?

June 22nd, 1965

A full month or more after all the others had passed, the last late dam foaled today. I'm sure she had her reasons, but as they're horse reasons,

I wasn't made privy. The boy'd been feeding sugar cubes to the quarter horses when he saw what was happening and ran back to the house. In his excitement, he forgot he wasn't talking to me. Put in the call to Dr. Vining, then saddled Ghost and Coyote and culled the dam real easy from the team. Put her in a paddock behind the stables. There was just a pale blue bubble, like a misplaced balloon, swelling out from her sex. But in the balloon there were hooves. She circled the paddock's dusty edge once slowly, then laid herself down in the shade.

It wasn't much longer after that, and with little more to do but to watch. Dr. Vining showed up and waved his hat and took up alongside us at the fence. Had only called him in in case there was trouble with the afterbirth. There wasn't. The dam passed the foal and licked off its blue membrane, then passed the afterbirth and ate that too. She nuzzled the foal until it found its feet and wobbled and had its first feeding. The dam was all chestnut with white showing on her ribs, but the foal was buckskin, pale on its underside with a diamond between its eyes. After it fed, it gamboled a bit, ungainly but excited, like it'd been looking forward to this chance to finally stretch out.

Dr. Vining refused any payment. Said he was happy to have been useless in the presence of such an easy birth. An uncommon twitchiness meanwhile was torturing the boy. He does not normally get worked up over new foals, but today on all accounts is an exception. Said he'd like to ride out and fetch his friend, the Hautenot girl, so as to show her the new foal. So maybe his excitement was on loan from her. Girls and horses. As she'd be riding back with him, I suggested he bring Circle along. They'd then each have their own ride. This seemed to please him, too. I hope he remembers this, that I am not always so contemptible. Saddled up Circle and mounted Coyote and took off with both horses across the southern fields. Watching them go, Dr. Vining laughed and said what a hell of a boy, and I laughed with him and agreed, though I could only suspect what the doctor was commenting on. It didn't matter. Maybe I was starting to feel some of this contagious animal excitement, as it was with a sudden burst of good feeling that I asked the doctor if he'd like to stick around for a spell, have a coffee or take a quick ride. Said he wished he could but duty called. He did not say what duty, though. He said my name and started his pickup and in a moment he was gone, and very suddenly the farm felt emptied. I was still smiling in the yard, but there was nothing to smile at. All at once, I was alone.

Went and checked on the foal and dam, and found them sleeping in the dust, bellies rising big with deep, sleepy breaths. It's always made me uneasy, seeing horses sleeping but not standing, lying on the ground like they're dead. In the pasture, the mules and horses had gathered as close as they could to watch. Looked at their black eyes all pointed at me and could not know what they saw. Walked through the stables, sweet with the faint hay and manure smells, but vacant for the summer so feeling abandoned and forgot. The few slit-eyed barn cats here and there did not ease this deserted feeling. My brief flash of excitement was gone. People take it with them when they go. Stood out in the dooryard looking west, wondered what to do with myself while I waited, saw the weather tower far out and almost complete, putting its mark on the horizon, and a stomach-sour anger took me. I'm sick of that thing and it has only just arrived. My feeling anything won't make it go away.

Keys were in the house but there's a spare in the shop. Started the truck and drove south to the first crossroad. Drove west.

The tower was farther out than I expected. Seemed it got bigger the longer I drove, but not any closer. That worsened the sourness in me. Forty or fifty miles out, hit a crossroad where I could see more traffic had been going—there was caked mud and dust on the pavement—so turned in that direction and soon found a dirt scratch cutting through the prairie toward the tower. From the road I could see two cranes and a job trailer and all these stacks of material, and it was all up on a small rise, but when I got there there were no men working. The site was empty. Just machines and material. Got out the truck and took a few steps toward the thing. Then I just kind of stood there. It was likely two hundred feet tall. Just four long legs and metal X's zipping up in between. It looked like it should all lead up to something. But at the top, there was just a red glass lantern. Like a lighthouse in the prairie.

I stood there awhile feeling helpless. Scooped up a rock and threw it, but the rock sailed right through, missing the legs and braces and landing in the dirt with a poof. I suppose this is what impotence feels like. They take everything away and bury it behind some church some-where, and leave you nothing but the world stretching wide all around you. But they won't even leave you that. They build a lighthouse where there is no water, just something to remind you that even this they've taken away. You can't even look upon a goddamn sunset without being reminded of some lost time that was better. It grants no mercy to us trying to forget.

I do not remember driving home. The boy and his ugly girl were fawning over the foal. They waved when they seen I was back. Somehow, seeing that made everything worse. Went into the workshop and for the first time in years, shut the door.

June 23rd, 1965

Over dinner asked the boy if he'd like to ride the fences with me and repair what needed repairing. Not just the far side of the orchards. The whole back forty. The boundary lines and interior partitions. We could harness a mule and load the cart with new fence posts and boards. We could pack tools and food and bedrolls, take it easy and camp out when we had a mind to. Take a few days. Make an adventure out of it. I asked him if he'd like that. But he didn't say anything.

I told him the best thing to do when you see a rattlesnake is to pretend you don't see a rattlesnake. Just walk the other way. Let it be. I asked him, does that make sense?

I waited for him to answer. Then I told him: we are going to repair the fences. We will harness a mule and load the cart with provisions. We will work as a team and sleep in the fields. I didn't try to make it sound fun this time. Made it sound like the work it was. I asked him, did he understand?

The boy responded with a very slow nod. When I asked him to say it, he said he understood. There wasn't any life in his voice or in his eyes. He stared at his plate awhile then got up and left the room. He put on his record of bird songs.

He does not understand yet that a kind person can be hard sometimes and still not be a mean person. Just as a cruel person can sometimes grant favors and still not be generous. All he sees is me being firm or silent or pushing, and that makes me a bully or greedy or unfeeling. He isn't curious about the why. Or he's already made up his mind. And what he's made up is wrong. If it was just me here now, I wouldn't give a damn. I'd likely let all the horses go and get wild on their own. Or I would lead them to someplace greater than this. Take nothing else and ride north. Manitoba or Saskatchewan. What we think is big is small up there. What we call empty is full. I would lead the horses until they chose to lead themselves, tear their hooves away from me in some unending Canadian prairie. I would leave them and ride up where I could be so small that I wouldn't even exist. That would be a solution to all things.

It is for the boy that I do not do that. Instead, I do everything else. He's too much of a child to understand.

June 24th, 1965

I have let the issue of repairing the fence slide.

The boy's gone over to the Hautenots' for supper. He still is not talking to me. He's taken Coyote along but it's a long pasture ride to take in the dark. I do not suspect he will be back tonight. I had hoped this time would bring us closer together. I know it is something we both need now. A proximity not just of flesh. But I feel instead that we're driven apart. There is no question that I am to blame. He sees me as stubborn and maybe a little cold in my heart. How can I know if he's wrong? With only two of us here, there is nothing else to contrast me to, no other voice to provide context. And maybe I am different now. In our solitude, I've become something I was not before. I would not need defending if it weren't just he and I. There'd be nothing to defend. I hope in his adulthood he does not look back on me with resentment and disappointment. I would rather he hate me, as hate is close to love. But disappointment is an open gate to not caring. I do not want him to learn to not care about his father. But he probably will.

Alone, I saw no point in cooking supper. I worked on a saddle the Fensters had left me to repair. I checked in on the beetle and spider and bird. When the sun was aiming to set, I headed westward from the house, just so far as to put the orchard at my back. I wanted an unimpeded view of the grasses and far hills and the sun. The clouds spread the light around so the whole sky was hot and waxy. There was wind. There came a point when everything was red. The sun red. The prairie red. The Missouri River which I cannot see and the faraway hills and the Badlands all red as a liquid and beating heart. In the weather tower, now complete, a single red light. If I looked at my hands, they'd have been red too. But I did not look at myself.

I asked if you were far away.

You said, "I am."

I asked if I was making a mistake.

You said I am.

But you would not tell me what it was.

I know there will be a time when this distance is not so great. When

I am allowed to touch you again. But that time is so far away. I asked if I would get this right but already, you were gone behind the hills, and everything in the world was blue.

June 25th, 1965

The bird and beetle are gone.

Nominated by Glimmer Train

DRITTER KLASSE
OHNE FENSTERSCHEIBEN

fiction by STEVE ALMOND

from ECOTONE

In the spring of 1889, Kaiser Wilhelm II visited Constantinople for the first time. He was enchanted—by the Topkapi Palace, the promontories of the Golden Horn, and in particular (as the rumor went) the exotic gyrations of the Sultan's harem. The German Emperor, then at the height of his power, became convinced that the destiny of his kingdom resided in the expansion of its frontier into what he whimsically called "the Sultan's forlorn flank."

The discovery of vast oil reserves beneath Iraq ratified this notion and led to the conception of the so-called *Bagdadbahn*, a railway intended to connect Berlin to the Persian Gulf. Using the Ottoman Empire as a fueling station and trade depot, Germany would challenge the imperial dominance of Britain and Russia.

Historians may debate to what extent these ambitions contributed to the First World War. This much is known: in 1912, the Deutsche Bank transferred Wilhelm Geist, a Jew of modest birth and steadfast manner, from Berlin to Constantinople to oversee the project.

Herr Geist brought with him an elegant young wife, an infant daughter, and the conviction that progress required the imposition of will upon the feckless. He quickly discovered that this view did not suit what he had come to regard as the Oriental attitude. If he hoped to recruit a syndicate to fund construction, and to obtain permissions, the parade of minor caliphs who oversaw the regions in question would have to be entertained, fed lavish meals, handed cigars and silver pocket watches.

His wife Eva oversaw these operations.

She was the youngest daughter of an aristocratic Jewish family from a small city outside Munich, a woman who found her deepest sense of self in the assembly of parties: menus, flower arrangements, the hiring of a string quartet. Frau Geist was not a handsome woman but took pride in her appearance. It pleased her enormously to have posed for the German edition of *Vogue* magazine. She was tall, slender, a skilled conversationalist who understood her husband's aims and limitations.

Constantinople lay at the intersection of Europe and Asia, two oceans, a dozen trade routes. Greeks and Romans, Crusaders and Turks had slaughtered one another upon its seven hills, battled for its shipping lanes, laid siege to its monuments. As in all cities of frantic human industry, the dead nourished the delusions of the living.

Wilhelm Geist knew war was on the horizon, but he regarded such matters as temporary disruptions, inefficiencies in a system destined to assign value in a civilized manner. He read the diplomatic cables about Gallipoli, the naval engagement at the Dardanelles. He took note of the German garrison dispatched to guard Dolmabahçe Palace, which housed the remnants of the enfeebled Ottoman government. In the main, he turned his concerns south and east, to the bandit regions of Mesopotamia, the rocky wilderness through which he would forge a steel path to the Promised Land.

As the war turned against Germany, a climate of anxiety settled over the city. British and French forces advanced from Megiddo to Damascus and Beirut. The men and metal necessary to construct a railway were diverted to military campaigns. Geist wrote ardent dispatches to his superiors in Berlin. His parties became an extravagance that seemed to mock the prevailing food shortages. Frau Geist was heard to lament the quality of the liverwurst.

The girl, Leah, was raised by servants. She saw her mother at supper, her father on Sundays and holidays. Only once was she ushered into his sanctuary. Beside the mahogany desk stood a giant glass bulb that expelled a strip of paper with tiny letters and numbers, which her father held by his fingertips and inspected devoutly.

Her gaze traveled to the vast survey maps tacked to the walls. Herr Geist, who had marked completed sections of track in red ink, pointed to the spot where the color ended. "We shall have to use explosives to make a tunnel in the Taurus Mountains," he explained rather formally. "What do you think of that?"

Leah did not know what to think. At age four, she had never heard the word *explosives*. Her father was nearly a stranger to her. "Why must you spend all day making a train?" she asked softly.

The governess, stationed just outside the door, stiffened. The girl, sensing the magnitude of her transgression, stood very still. Geist himself looked stunned. His blue eyes swam in a sudden innocence. For a moment, he noticed the beauty of his daughter's face, its delicate, undisguised disappointment. He clutched the edge of his desk. "Dear child, don't you understand? I do this work for the Fatherland."

Her mind would circle back to this scene for years, as if to affirm a truth that had been, at the time, only a vague intuition: he had wanted a son.

Leah remembered the gnarled olive trees in the courtyard, the illicit sensation of stomping the black fruits, the oily stones squirming against the balls of her feet, the governess scolding her in primitive German. Once, the pantry maid (who relieved the governess on Sundays) took her by carriage to the fish market, where piles of anchovies flashed upon the docks. A boy shyly waved to her from a boat moored to the dock. She remembered the gauzy fog of autumn and the pale yellow walls of her room. The crystal doorknob she was not allowed to touch. Her playmates, the offspring of German diplomatic officers, disappeared one by one.

In the summer of her fifth year, the Turkish cavalry began to stage maneuvers at the end of her street, spurring their sullen underfed animals over berms of dead nettle. She listened to the rhythmic scraping of the half-empty artillery boxes lashed to their belts. At dinner, she watched her mother for clues as to what was happening. Her mother looked up from the soup, as if ready to confide, then called for more salt.

In October 1917, the Kaiser paid his final visit to Constantinople. His reputation on the world stage lay in shambles. His cousins, the Tsar Nicholas II and King George V, had united with the French to stymie the German army. His generals treated him as a prop: the glamorous relic of a diseased monarchy. He surveyed the city's naval fortifications, visited a military hospital, then traveled to a small field where cavalry troops conducted a parade while local dignitaries stood about anxiously.

Wilhelm Geist was among them, his wife and daughter at his side. To the shock of his retinue, the Kaiser paused in front of Geist. "I am told you are the man who will advance our cause to the shores of Persia."

"That is my devout hope, your majesty."

"One doesn't speak of hopes to an emperor," the Kaiser snapped. "One speaks of deeds."

Geist lowered his head. A moment of strangled silence passed. The Kaiser bowed to Frau Geist, then to Leah. "This must be your daughter," he said.

Leah had been informed, in the most urgent terms, that she was to meet the Emperor. But the emperors in her illustrated fairy tales were elderly men in beards and robes. This emperor looked more like a mechanical soldier. He wore a helmet with a golden spike rather than a crown. A dozen braided cords ran across the front of his uniform, in and among large buttons and ribbons. Some hidden manipulation of these cords, Leah felt sure, governed the Emperor's mincing steps.

The Kaiser now did something wholly unexpected: he grasped the cane employed to conceal his withered left arm from public inspection, leaned down, and kissed Leah on the brow. It seemed to those on hand a gesture of spiritual import, evidence offered, amid a dimming German fate, of the mysterious whim by which history touches the common.

There are simpler explanations. Leah Geist was the only child among the assembled witnesses. Behind her left ear, she wore a stunning pink blossom plucked from the Judas tree. Her presence may have arrested the Kaiser, provoked some flickering suspicion that his instigation of war—a war by now collapsed into ruin—held at its center a fragile and immaculate beauty. This theory is supported by the single word he murmured to Frau Geist, who stood beside her daughter perspiring under a woven veil. The word was *Jungfräulich*.

It meant maiden, and also virginal.

The episode haunted Leah Geist: the lurid face swinging into view, its black mustache turned up at both ends (as if in fright), the breath of spoiled lamb and pipe smoke. In the bath, she waited for the governess to turn away, then scrubbed at the spot his lips had touched. Two unwelcome thoughts seized her mind: That this man was the "father" her father had spoken of in his study. And that he, the Emperor, was running out of hope.

The war made itself known in stages: as a rumor, a news report, a commercial disturbance, a curfew. Gallant men in gilded uniforms sauntered through the drawing rooms of homes like the one owned by Wilhelm Geist. Then those men were gone. Puffs of smoke appeared, faint pops like kindling, sirens. The local cavalry troops, summoned to Aleppo, trotted their mounts into formation and marched south, happy to let the world gaze upon them. At last the business of war—which is, after all, mass murder with a dash of plunder—arrived in Constantinople.

It was the winter of 1918. The cook disappeared, then the pantry maid. The governess kept getting dust in her eyes and having to stop the lesson. One evening, after bathing Leah, she led her to the drawing room. Her father sat near the fire, his reflection in the black window. Her mother perched on a divan. The air smelled of rosewater and ash.

Leah paused on the threshold. She had a child's instinct for conspiracy. The governess touched her shoulder. "We have some good news," her father said. "You will be returning to the Rhineland with your mother."

"On the train!" Frau Geist said. "It's time your grandmama saw what a big girl you've become. We can celebrate your birthday with her."

"I shall come afterward," Herr Geist said.

"Papa must finish his train," Frau Geist added brightly. "We'll have a fine time, just the two of us."

Leah turned to seek the reassurance of the governess; she had vanished. Her parents, whom she had seen together only at the supper table, or in the presence of esteemed guests, joined hands and leered at her with benign intent. Leah flinched, so as to restrain herself. She wanted to scream or tip a lamp, to disrupt the eerie choreography. "We are moving?" she said finally.

"There is nothing to worry about," Frau Geist said.

Snow fell on the city the next morning. Frau Geist appeared in a mink and climbed into the auto while the remaining servants dashed about piling luggage cases into the trunk. The Bosphorus chopped. Minarets spiked the horizon. Herr Geist showed his wife the tickets, which were embossed and threaded with silver. He recited the amenities he had purchased for them. As they drew closer to the city center, the road knotted up with carriages. When beggars launched themselves at Geist's car, the liveryman warded them off with a steel-tipped cane. But a boy in a tiny fez crouched just below the window. He smiled mischievously at Leah, who smiled back. Then he reached up suddenly and touched her on the cheek. Her eyes were lovely in their astonishment. Then the steel cane came down, cutting his cheek in two.

At the station all was chaos; the grand concourse was packed with soldiers disgorged from military transports, others ranked for departure, and scattered amid them, the few remaining foreign citizens, *civilians* now, soft creatures, prey, if not to the soldiers themselves, then to the jewel merchants, money changers, pickpockets, and mountebanks whose vital task is to exile wealth from the wealthy pursuing exile.

Wilhelm Geist stood with his wife and daughter on the platform. They were to travel north, by way of the Balkans, then Vienna. Snow settled onto his hat. Geist, in accordance with his own upbringing, recognized deep emotion as a form of betrayal. His daughter wore a little muslin cape with a pearl clasp and white stockings. For a foolish moment his chin trembled.

A bit later, wife and daughter waved to him through the frilled curtains of their compartment. The engine released a hissing belch of steam. The slow roll of the wheels began. Herr Geist clasped his hands behind his back and stared at the snarl of tracks that met under the yard's sooty roof. One set of them stretched all the way to the Tigris. But there it stopped, five hundred miles north of Baghdad. He had made a foolish wager, a whole series of them. They were all he had now.

In the middle of the night, a conductor roused Frau Geist. He tried to explain the situation delicately: the couchette had been "requisitioned" by a group of Austrian officers.

"Nonsense," she whispered. "We purchased tickets."

"Yes, you see, the terms of service no longer—"

Further explication was rendered unnecessary by the Austrians themselves, who burst into the compartment and tossed the conductor into the hall. Frau Geist rose to her full height to address them. "I shall thank you to leave at once. My daughter is sleeping below."

The officers stank of apple brandy. They regarded Frau Geist wearily. A few glanced down at Leah and blinked in confusion, called back to an obedience learned in peace time. Their tiny captain wore a patch. His left eye had been torn by shrapnel in a skirmish outside Damascus. He pulled a box of matches from his shirt pocket. With an elegance borrowed from the cinema, he lit a cigarette and said, in careful German, "Listen to me you rich mule. You have one minute to gather your daughter and your clothes and get out." He inhaled, then blew the smoke slowly into Frau Geist's face.

To observe that Frau Geist had never been treated in this manner fails to capture the enormity of the shock visited upon her. She knew that wealth had insulated her from less desirable aspects of human behavior. But her understanding of this fact resided at the level of abstraction. Not so the smoke in her face, the rough thumb at her hip. She looked to the corridor. The conductor had fled; a daughter she barely knew, a kind of bright human ornament, clung to her in confusion. These experiences formed a fault line between what her life had been and what it was now. She struggled to find balance, a foot on either side.

"What's happening?" Leah asked.

"We're making a little game," she answered. "We must find another couchette. Will you help me look?"

Frau Geist seized a valise in one hand, her daughter in the other, and hurried down the aisle. The blackness smelled of camphor. Blasts of frigid air met them as they passed to the next car, where the rousted conductor, a sweet, pig-faced Romanian, leaned against the grate of a boiler.

Frau Geist removed the tickets from her mink stole, but the conductor shook his head. "This train has been requisitioned by the Ministry of Defense, madam. All but a few civilians have been removed. You are quite lucky after all."

"This is absurd. How are we to sleep?"

The conductor took note of Leah and bowed nervously. "You may follow me, please." He led mother and daughter through a dozen cars, all filled with soldiers, veterans now, wiry farm boys from Mistelbach and Weiz who had signed up to serve the Kaiser, to make men of themselves, and had learned that war held little regard for personal valor. In dream, they pawed the air.

Leah kept tripping over their boots and landing on her bare knees. The soldiers cursed. Her mother yanked her wrist. She began to cry, a sound swallowed by the roar of the train. She missed her room. She missed the governess, who rapped her knuckles then fed her sugared figs.

They arrived at the rear of the train, cramped and shabby as a trolley car. The conductor shoved a huddled figure aside and gestured with satisfaction at the resulting slot.

Frau Geist presented her tickets a third time. "I must repeat myself. My husband, Herr Wilhelm Geist, purchased first-class passage. He works with the Ministry—"

The conductor plucked the lovely billets from her hand and tore them savagely. He was not an unkind man. He would become, in time, a doting father to four daughters. But the war had shown him the truth of the world, and his place in it. He understood that cruelty was in certain cases the best means of quelling panic. "Another word, madam, and I shall be obliged to put you off this train." After a moment, he added, "There is an additional surcharge for civilian passengers."

Frau Geist pulled Leah under her mink and whispered, "You see? We've found a cozy place to sleep!" Thick bodies resettled themselves against her, seeking warmth. She smelled the putrefaction of their wounds. The stars whistled and zoomed.

As dawn filtered into the car, Frau Geist surveyed the pine benches, the filthy water closet. Daggers of ice dripped from the window slots. Her shoulders jerked silently. Leah heard her mother murmur a single phrase with such bitterness it was as if the words were a poison released onto her tongue. "Dritter klasse ohne fenstercheiben."

Third class without windows.

It would take many years for Leah Geist to recognize this moment as one of liberation. She had spent her first six years marched through rooms and dressed for meals, an anchoress in a petticoat. Now the world was upon her. Yellow light raked the windows. The mountains wore dainty caps of snow. Strange men in uniforms spat and moaned. Her mother *wept*. Leah stretched her arms and took in the thrilling stink of unwashed bodies. Her fellow passengers, Hungarian infantry-men, regarded her and her mother with drowsy bemusement.

A conductor strode past and Frau Geist inquired as to the location of her luggage. She took a few steps after him, then felt herself dragged down by the collar. A soldier with a bloody bandage across his ear

510

barked in fractured German, "Your evening gowns are gone! Shut up and let us sleep, you ugly Jew. Only fetch your little princess there. She can be my playmate."

A phalanx of soldiers managed to wrest Frau Geist from the man's grasp. She returned to her seat, removed her jewelry in silence, and instructed her daughter to do the same. "We are Germans now," she whispered. "Nothing more. Do you understand?"

Leah watched decrepit barns hurtle past, grain silos hacked open, the outskirts of towns half eaten by mortar. Refugees looked up from cook fires and rushed at the train in doomed tides: women in head scarves, a bearded skeleton wailing ancient prayers. One boy, lost to the madness of hunger, leaped at the stepladder to a coal car and disappeared. A magic trick. She began to understand her father's fascination with trains. They marked the division between progress and loss, between the rescued and the damned.

At considerable expense to her pride, Frau Geist petitioned German soldiers for provisions. Leah dined on black bread and old cheese. A weepy corporal, reminded of his sister, pressed a disc of peppery salami into her palm, which she savored until the fat dissolved on her tongue.

In the water closet, Frau Geist endeavored to relieve herself, a procedure requiring an arduous disassembly. Beneath her dress, the Frau wore an overslip, an underslip, a bra, stockings, garters, and a whalebone girdle. Leah, who had never seen her mother in anything less than evening wear, watched through the door slats as these items fell away to reveal the pale disorganization of her flesh: the sagging belly, angry welts where the straps dug in, spidery veins behind her knees. From the dark sash of her sex, her mother produced a velvet drawstring pouch and inspected its contents. Then she perched on the commode morosely and struggled to defecate. Several dramatic gaseous events ensued, culminating in the desired outcome. This accomplished, the Frau vomited delicately into the sink.

In the foothills of the Carpathians, outside Bucharest, Leah woke to stillness. Though nobody onboard would have known why, the car had been uncoupled from the rest on orders from the German High

Command—to hasten the return of soldiers to Berlin for redeployment. Such was the state of the war.

The Hungarians were furious. "It's the Jews who started this bloody mess," howled the one who had accosted Frau Geist. "Germans and Jews. Jews and Germans." He suggested an obscene form of restitution.

"Shut up, for God's sake," his neighbor said. "She's got a girl there."

These negotiations were conducted in Hungarian, but to Frau Geist their meaning was apparent. She reached into her undergarments for the velvet purse, from which she withdrew the sum of her worldly wealth: a large diamond ring, emerald earrings, three strands of pearls, eight gold coins. These she held out to the most gallant of the Hungarians, a tall sergeant with a toothbrush mustache.

"We are not thieves," he said quietly.

A platoon of soldiers set off toward the nearest village with four of Frau Geist's gold coins. They returned at dusk with a cured ham, a bushel of tart winter plums, flagons of brandy, and a cord of kindling. An hour later the stars appeared. Leah sat by the fire with her mother, gobbling plums and slices of ham while the drunk soldiers—which is to say all the soldiers—serenaded her with folk songs about brave shepherds and lost maidens. In this way Leah Geist spent the final hours of March 3, 1918, her sixth birthday.

The car joined a military convoy and arrived in Budapest two mornings later. Frau Geist stepped off the train. She had no idea what to do, having never arrived in a city without an attendant. A clean-looking cripple in a worsted suit approached her and insisted, in decent German, that his cousin operated the finest hotel in the city. She was thus relieved of two more gold coins.

At the pension, Leah surveyed the boulevards lit by petrol lamps, the buildings streaked with ash. She accepted solitude without complaint. In the alley below her, a young couple pressed their bodies together, as if to hold something precious in place. Behind her, Frau Geist lay on a straw mattress, denouncing the vermin that infested their room.

They arrived in Berlin on a Sunday. Gray threads of rain plashed the awnings. A siren rang madly then fell silent. Red trolleys wobbled down the Kaiserstrasse. Frau Geist closed her eyes and bid her farewells: to the hellish train, to the vulgar spices of the Turks. Germans understood the order of things. The world was composed mostly of servants. If you gave them enough money they became *your* servants.

She located a jeweler willing to purchase her gold, and a telegram office where she sent a cable apprising her husband of the dangers and indignities to which she, and their daughter, had been subjected, and for which (there was no need to specify this) he would be held to account. She had in mind a grand estate, perhaps in the Schwartzwald.

She brought her daughter to a delicatessen, where they devoured a plate of watery sauerkraut, then a second. Frau Geist began to rhapsodize about the swimming pool behind her parents' country home, the apricot tree that dropped fruit into the water, the afternoon a hummingbird buzzed the flowered print of her bathing suit. Leah tried to imagine her mother in a bathing suit.

At the station counter, Frau Geist ordered two first-class berths to Munich. The attendant explained that service to the Rhineland was suspended.

Frau Geist demanded to speak to the manager.

"The track has been torn up," the manager said kindly. "The Kaiser spoke on the radio—"

Frau Geist shrieked triumphantly. "I have met the Kaiser! He kissed my daughter just a few months ago!" She grabbed Leah and hoisted her up to the window. "Tell them, Leah!"

The girl, taken aback by the violence of her mother's grip, whispered, "It's true."

The light shifted just then in such a manner that Frau Geist caught sight of herself in the glass. It's true what they say, she thought. I am a mule. How is it that my daughter should be blessed with beauty? Her pride, chipped at bit by bit, now collapsed entirely. She slumped to the pavement.

Mother and daughter went to stay with distant cousins. The Kaufmans were an elderly couple, orthodox Jews who had lost a son in the war. It was silently observed that neither mother nor daughter knew the blessing spoken over meals. Jews of this variety, with their high-born manners, were strangers to God.

In the privacy of the small study where she and her daughter slept, Frau Geist grew listless. She stared at the cracked leather spines of Herr Kaufman's books. She stopped appearing at meals.

Leah tried to revive her mother's spirits by asking about the swimming pool with the apricot tree. Her mother's voice, when she finally responded, sounded like an ancient radio transmission. "The apricot tree is dead," it said. Outside, the starving pigeons of Berlin patrolled the eaves in bickering spirals.

Later that night, Frau Geist suffered some kind of fit. Leah would remember, in particular, the sound of her mother retching, the long yellow jaw shivering in moonlight. Her mother kept asking, "Why did you bring me here?"

Frau Kaufman appeared and led Leah away.

In the morning, the day bed where her mother slept had been stripped bare, its soiled cushions and sheets flung onto the back stoop. The house was empty. A bowl of stiffened porridge sat upon the table. Leah ate it all. She gazed at Berlin in its winter coat. The streetcars looked like petit fours; the cathedral was frosted in sugar. She thought: *I've done something to make my mother disappear.*

Leah was told her mother had contracted influenza, the best available lie.

Mother and daughter were reunited in Bavaria eight weeks later. Frau Geist refused to discuss with her family the journey from Constantinople or her subsequent illness and recovery. She allowed her daughter's care to revert to servants. The traumatic events that had briefly bound them were a closed book.

News of Herr Geist's death arrived that autumn. The word "accident" was used with Leah, though the official cable described the episode as "unresolved." Herr Geist had traveled to Ankara, hoping to direct several tons of rail from a Chinese foundry to the idle crews in Mosul. Here the record becomes unclear. It is agreed Geist asked to inspect the local rail yard and that his torso was crushed beneath the wheels of a transporter wagon. In a final letter to his wife, he bemoaned the state of his project. "And what if I never make the track connect? I shall be considered a dreamer and a fool."

In delivering the news, Eva Geist grasped her daughter and uttered a line she had clearly rehearsed: "We shall have to continue on without Papa!" Leah closed her eyes and tried to remember him, but the image

514

that arrived was of a red face swinging toward her beneath a golden spike.

On November 9, 1918—two days before the Armistice—Kaiser Wilhelm II abdicated his throne and crossed into the Netherlands by train as a private citizen. Forty-one rail wagons followed with his belongings. In a colorful letter to his former field marshal, Wilhelm blamed the Jews for his downfall and advocated pogroms in the Russian tradition. "They are a nuisance humanity must get rid of some way or other. I believe the best would be gas!"

He gave no thought to Wilhelm Geist, whom he had entrusted with his dream of a new German frontier, nor to the thousands who had perished in loyalty to his throne. Many years after the war, while strolling the grounds of his estate in Doorns, the Kaiser thought absently of the girl he had kissed once in Constantinople, as a commendation for her beauty. He decided that he was seeking to alleviate her sorrow.

Leah Geist remained lovely. Photos taken between the wars capture a girl with large somber eyes and a sensual mouth. In 1935, she came to New York to study child psychology. Her intention was to be free of the past, which offered her little direction or comfort. She married the first man to accept her silences, an ambitious researcher more like her father than she would have cared to admit.

At the insistence of an older sister, Frau Geist left Germany in 1937. She spent the early years of World War II overseeing the construction of a lavish home in Bergen, New Jersey, a monument to her fine taste, where she lived with her sister and brother-in-law. She did not read newspapers or listen to the radio. It was understood and accepted that her nervous condition would require summers in the country. Some months after the war, a young émigré, invited for tea, mentioned the atrocities of the camps. Frau Geist gestured to the gardenias ranked around them and said, pleasantly enough, "Perhaps you will find me old-fashioned, but I prefer to speak of beauty."

Frau Geist remained a brittle and demanding woman to the end. She refused to travel, and learned very little English. Every few years, Leah flew to her mother's estate from her home in Chicago to present her children for inspection. There were four in all, born over a decade.

Leah held no expectation that her mother would "love" the children in any sense beyond formality. She herself struggled to feel affection for them. Often she was repulsed—by their entitlement, their grubby hands and tantrums, the tender venoms with which they poisoned any scene not to their liking. There were dire moments when she imagined harming them, drowning one in the bath, tossing another from a moving car. She knew she would never succumb to these wretched urges. They were an affront to the idea she held of who she was. But they sustained her. They kept her from retreating into the wilderness of her own disappointment.

The children grew into Americans: informal, ironic, restless for amusement. They teased her about the habits of her upbringing, her tendency to dress for dinner, or to speak indirectly in matters of conflict. None of them learned German. It was, as one of them put it, "the language of murder."

On the eve of her youngest child's departure for college, Leah presented her with an emerald brooch passed down from her mother. The girl, who had drunk with friends earlier, burst into tears. It took some minutes to calm her down.

"What's gotten into you?" Leah said.

With a sudden insolence, the girl cast the brooch onto the rug. "You must be glad to finally be rid of us."

In the end, it fell to Leah to attend to her mother. She could have left the old woman in the care of her staff. But to do so struck her, obscurely, as a form of surrender. Instead, she moved her mother to a retirement community near her home. Frau Geist filled her suite with antique furniture, monogrammed silver, Dürer prints. Leah had stared at one in particular as a child—a winged woman with a baby hovering above her and a lamb at her feet—and puzzled over the baleful expression on the heroine's face. Wings, a baby, a lamb: what more could any woman desire?

Her mother refused to sit with the other residents at meals. She complained incessantly and with relish. She treated the orderlies like servants. It was an embarrassment. But Leah felt toward her mother what was, at times, an abject gratitude. At last she had someone with whom to speak German, someone who understood what had come before.

Leah arrived one afternoon to find that her mother had unearthed the ancient photo of herself in *Vogue*. Eva Geist stood at the top of a winding staircase wrapped in a gown of organdy. She wore gloves, a cloche. Her exposed shoulder stood out like a dab of chalk.

"How lovely," Leah said.

Frau Geist regarded the photo fondly. "It was the most subtle shade of green. An Italian shade. I've looked for it ever since."

"It's a shame you can't see the cut more clearly," Leah said.

"Yes," Frau Geist said. "They took so many photographs. And then they chose one from the bottom of the stairs, you see, because of the unfortunate angles of my face."

"Nonsense, mother."

Frau Geist looked at her daughter and smiled. "I've looked like this my whole life, dear. Those brutes on the train were only saying what I'd heard in school a hundred times. Children can be cruel. It's how they protect themselves, I suppose."

Leah was too stunned to speak.

"But you weren't cruel." Frau Geist looked directly at her daughter, something she was not in the habit of doing. "It's true what the Kaiser said. He found you beautiful."

"That's not what he said." Leah picked up one of the anise biscuits her mother had set out with tea. It crumbled on her tongue. All women are hostages, she thought suddenly. They believe themselves protected by beauty or wealth or powerful men. But in the end the world takes hold of them and they are left to protect themselves.

And then there was the evening Frau Geist tried suicide. Six sleeping pills with sherry. She was transported to the emergency room, but spared the stomach pump because of her frailty. Leah assumed the attempt had been triggered by an episode (shared with her by a sympathetic attendant) in which her mother's wig fell off in the common room.

The victim herself evinced no interest in discussing her motives. She said only one thing of consequence to her daughter—"It's done! Your father finally finished the damn thing!"—a statement Leah took as an indication of her drugged state, or perhaps incipient dementia.

A few days later, she visited her mother at the retirement home. On the way out, she passed the facility's main gallery. It was unlike her to tour the exhibits. She had done so once, as a courtesy to the visiting artist, whose watercolors were heartbreakingly plain. In this case, her eye was caught by a flash of silver. Acting on what would later seem to her a queer instinct, she turned around and entered the hall.

A display of model trains ran the length of a raised table. Some lonely enthusiast had painted each car and arranged their route with meticulous care: around the base of a mountain covered with twisted trees, into a rock tunnel, through a stretch of desert, and finally into a station where a dozen figures in tiny military uniforms waited on a platform the size of a dollar bill. *Baghdadbahn.*

At the end of her life, Frau Geist complained of a draft through her windows, though they were locked tight and her room was sweltering. She hoarded food and began to harangue the woman who came to wash her. One found her rubbing at her favorite blouse, which she had neatly folded into the little stainless steel sink in her kitchenette.

Her attendants were accustomed to such erosions of the mind. Or, more precisely, the mind's inevitable reversion to the degradations of the past. It was hard for Leah. She had come to cherish her mother, the way one cherishes a difficult child whose absurd dignities are, in fact, a form of seduction, an expression of smothered need. She was there at the end, as she had been at the beginning. They held hands and spoke the language of Goethe, of terror and beauty.

Frau Geist said, "Have you seen such tickets ever?" And, "Stop fiddling with your pinafore." And, "What station is this, with such flowers?" Leah wondered which flowers she was supposed to remember. Her hand traveled to her mother's brow. She felt for whatever warmth might persevere. They remained in this delicate arrangement until Frau Geist died.

Nominated by Ecotone

CLEANING THE GHOST ROOM

by TATIANA FORERO PUERTA

from HAWAII PACIFIC REVIEW

Mami made me dust
the ghost room as she swept
the kitchen downstairs, washed the fruit-
shaped porcelain dishes.

I objected, tearing up and shaken, clutching
to the dust rag, heart pounding. She said,
it builds character of high caliber, camaraderie
with the spirits. You want the dead on your side.

Invisible Mr. Traynor, passed only three weeks,
rocked his wicker chair. I held the
can of Pledge, an old sock rag, and
antagonism for my mother–

She knew I had to wipe
the mirror clean to reflect my
fear up close– I had to dive
into its center, see myself in its pupils.

If I hadn't, as a kid, dusted the accruements
of the departed, the disheveled
libraries of sepia-toned photographs with
serrated edges and dated newspaper pages;

If I hadn't disinfected the debris
of the deceased until I swallowed
that innate foreboding for the long-gone,
phobia for the remnants of the lingering,

Then today I may not be able to polish the rust
off the roses—embossed in the bronze of Mami's urn.

Nominated by Hawaii Pacific Review

SAFE HOME

fiction by DANIEL PEÑA

from PLOUGHSHARES

Cuauh always greases the landings. If the winds are strong, he lands in the desert north of Obregon, on a sand strip outlined by burning tar barrels, desert oak, and split saguaro cut lengthwise to catch the neon sun. But if the winds are calm, Cuauh lumbers his aircraft, an aging M20J, onto a neighborhood street in Lomas de Poleo just inside Ciudad Juarez. All of the homes abandoned. Everyone gone from the drug wars.

The neighborhood landing always warrants thirty degrees of flaps, the elevators popped low with the shimmy damper extended full to the hook and bolt, no further slack to give. The flexing tension of the wire pings up and down the length of the aircraft as it descends. You can hear it ringing like a bell in the sky from both sides of the border: From one hill the Ejército—the Mexican military—gazing up with silent admiration for the pilot who can grease such a landing. From the other hill, the Americans looking down into the city with a fixed gaze, as if willing the cartel plane to crash.

Cuauh dives in at an angle, on a slipstream, with his left rudder pushed full to the carpet and his ailerons turned fist-over-lap so the plane falls fast and loud, the up-gush of wind roaring high through the idled propellers, the plane like a screaming vulture descending crooked into the remnants of the neighborhood. Five hundred feet, four hundred feet, and he'll kick out the rudder to right the plane just before impact. He'll land it clean and free onto a street named Nahual where the crumbling tar-gravel and rock splatter up against the nickel-plated underbelly of the plane behind the thrust of the cooling twin flat-eight Lycoming piston engines still revved to a thousand RPM.

The wingtips, forty-eight feet from one tip to the other, scrape along the thresholds of the houses on either side of Nahual Street. The power lines roll up and stretch over the bump of the cockpit. All the birds move to either end of the line, unimpressed by the smoking four hundred and fifty horsepower engine threatening to suck them in. The driver, too, waits unimpressed at the end of the road.

The driver is always the one asking questions. The driver is both Cuauh's ride home and his interrogator, his friend and his enemy. *How was the flight? Any messages to be relayed? Any peculiarities along the way? Are you sure? Are you sure?* he'll ask. Cuauh knows the routine, and he knows better than to incriminate himself on what he did or did not see from the skies.

The driver is always different but more or less a variation of the same man. Mid-thirties, severely overweight, reeking of Delicados and cheap sex and Tommy Hilfiger cologne. Probably named Chuy, which is short for something. Cuauh can never remember.

From his cockpit, Cuauh can see the driver sitting back in his pleather-covered seat, drumming his nicotine-stained fingers on the steering wheel of the truck. He listens to the American radio pouring in from the station atop the hill. He hates Ke$ha. He loves Katy Perry. He checks his watch and waits for the engines to cut. He checks his hair in the mirror, perfectly lacquered with Tres Flores pomade. He cracks his spearmint gum. His breath smells like Swiss cheese.

Cuauh purges it all from his mind before his boot even touches the ground. He forgets the bloody road leading up to San Miguel. He forgets the private strip in Sweetwater, Texas, called Fraley, where he made his drop, cocaine by the smell of it—it had no smell. He purges his memory of looking down on Interstate 20 running east of El Paso. Those burning cars. Hot, greasy, diesel smoke pouring black up into a plume that screened out the sun and painted the whole scene wispy in shadows of smoke. That familiar burnt-orange Ford Lobo—the one he'd ridden in so many times before from the airstrip—gushing from the undercarriage. Blood and oil and gasoline in the sand. A body pouring out from the driver's side wearing purple boots. Cuauh knew, even from the sky, who those boots belonged to. He purges that name from his mind too.

He plants his foot on the running boards of the white Dodge Durango at the end of Nahual street and climbs into the passenger seat.

"Any peculiarities?" the driver asks him, cracking his spearmint gum. Cuauh glasses him over. They've never met before. "No," he says. Cuauh keeps a stolid face, but his hands give him away, his finger pulling at the long, puckered scar on his left arm where it was cut the night he was deported from Texas, the night he was kidnapped and forced to fly cartel planes.

Cuauh says nothing as he eases his body into the passenger seat of the car. He turns down the radio and clicks it to the AM band. Texas High School Football. Westlake vs. Copperas Cove. He takes the driver's Stetson from the dash and drapes it over his sun-wearied eyes.

"I can't understand English," the driver says.

"I know," says Cuauh softly and lowers the brim.

The engine turns over and the driver pulls out onto a side road. The driver expertly weaves through the boulders strewn pell-mell about the streets that keep the police from navigating the neighborhood and keep the military out too.

Cuauh closes his eyes and feels his neck fuse with sweat to the hot pleather headrest. His mouth is dry. His bones are aching. The driver takes Cuauh the long way to the safe house, which looks like all the other safe houses in Juarez. A squat, pale-brown one story. Bad foundation. Meandering cracks in the walls that split jagged in the cold months like sweeping bolts of lightning.

Desert wasps make their home in the seams where the warmth escapes. They breed and die. They shred up the adobe with their lives until the house takes on the fragile look of a cracked egg, or like tempered glass about to shatter.

Cuauh eases his aching body from the comfort of the pleather. He moves to turn off the radio but it's already off. He walks around the fender and slaps the numbers tacked on the wall of the house just for kicks. 410. All the safe houses end in 10—2810, 510, 4510. Cuauh commits every safe house address he's tried to bring down with the slap of his palm to memory.

The door opens. Darkness pours out from the threshold. A wiry little man with ropy muscles lays out the flat of his hand. Cuauh and the driver hand over their chirping Nextel phones like they do every time.

The little man puts them in an oversize Ziploc bag and says, "I hope all is well." Cuauh's eyes adjust to the musty darkness inside so he's nearly blind. He can only feel the little man's words on his neck now, a plume of smoke that cools just above the shirt collar and hangs there at the volume of a whisper. The driver follows behind.

"All is well," says Cuauh to no one in particular and the door shuts behind him.

Inside, there's the too-sweet smell of perfume and sweat. There's the honeyed sound of women's voices, soft, like heather—the lilt of beauty queens or beautiful liars who say they're beauty queens. There's the knock-knock-knock of their heels against the tile, tiny women who seem almost weightless as they glide.

They appear to Cuauh behind the iridescent patches of light that burn away from the center of his gaze, his pupils fully dilating in the dark. All the women look the same to him. He wonders if he's met any of them before.

On the long table in the living room are silver bowls of cocaine, an RCA universal television remote, a polished pistol reeking of Hoppes 9 oil, a sweating beer, a half-finished ham torta sandwich with a bag of Sabrita potato chips.

"All is well?" asks the little man again. Cuauh takes a bite of the sandwich and a swig of the beer and repeats, "All is well."

The man with purple boots lies unconscious in the safe house tub, his hair still tinged with the sulfury smoke of burnt diesel. His hands are smoked black and his eyes are two fiery coals peering out with a thousand-yard stare. His name is Lalo and he's barely breathing. He's soaking wet in his clothes: a blue pearl-snap shirt, a pair of Wranglers, a pair of purple Larry Mahans that have all but cracked the fiberglass wide open. Along the inside of the tub are long, black arcs where the heels have scuffed in the struggle. The leather of his boots bloats about the same time his skin does. His fingers turn white and slough off their outer layer into the water.

Cuauh's face turns ashen at the sight of Lalo—this man he'd purged from his mind only thirty minutes ago. A million thoughts course through Cuauh's brain just then but none louder than the questions.

"What happened? What's going on?" says Cuauh. He acts just as surprised as he should be, though of course he'd seen this coming from way down the pike.

There's a doctor sitting on the toilet in a white coat, R.M.P. embroidered on his lapel. Across from him there's a boy with blue tattoos up and down his arm, these beautiful Chinese dragons with red eyes. The boy is wearing jeans rolled up to his calves and a plastic green rosary that dips in and out of the pink water of the fiberglass tub. He seems to be holding Lalo down or at least guarding him.

The doctor checks Lalo's pulse, consults his watch, and then produces a capped needle from his breast pocket. He plunges the needle through the denim into the fleshy part of Lalo's thigh. Lalo's eyes spring open, the black of his pupil spreading like ink to chase the green of his iris away.

"I only fly planes," says Cuauh to the little man staring up at him. The little man rubs his eyes and says, "We need to know who else. We know you were close. We need to know who."

"I only fly planes," says Cuauh. He says it again and again. He keeps repeating it as if it might change something.

Of course, Cuauh knew these things happened, but he never dreamed he'd ever be part of it. He knows what's coming and Lalo knows too. Everyone looks down on Lalo in the tub. The air is static. Lalo refuses to look anyone in the eye or speak for that matter.

"I need you to tell me where it's at," says the boy with blue tattoos into Lalo's ringing ears. He grabs Lalo by the neck. Lalo coughs deep and raspy from the diaphragm. He looks at Cuauh finally. Cuauh looks away.

"Where's the money?" the boy asks Lalo, tired and aggressive as if he's asked him a thousand times before. Lalo swallows his own voice. "Where's the money? Where is it? Who has it? Tell me," says the boy with a cool, unnerving calmness. A whisper. A plea. "Tell me. Where is it? Where is it?"

Lalo's eyes stay open even beneath the water. They only close right before a giant, pink glug escapes his lungs and clouds the tub with a rolling boil. Lalo's hands grasp the sides of the tub. His index finger points at the boy, then the ground, then Cuauh standing by the doctor.

The doctor waits a beat or two and then raises his hand. "That's enough," he says. The body is still.

The doctor rubs his eyes and puts a plastic device over Lalo's mouth that makes him puke up water until his teeth chatter, until the color returns to his lips.

"You'll get us those names," says the little man. He leaves the bathroom and Cuauh and Lalo are left alone. Everyone knows what Cuauh knows already.

Lalo's eyes are still dilated wide, the adrenaline in his veins faster than the cortisol.

"Don't say anything," says Cuauh to Lalo, and Lalo nods his chattering head. Lalo points his index finger to the mirror over the sink, and Cuauh looks up at it. Presses his thumb to the glass to check if there's a space between his thumb and its reflection. It's flush. It's a two-way mirror.

Cuauh turns off the lights and lights the votive candle over the toilet with the single match left in his ruddy matchbook. Saint Rita. Cuauh places the candle between him and Lalo.

He produces two crushed Faro cigarettes from a soft pack in his breast pocket and puts one behind his ear, puts the other at the corner of Lalo's face, the bent cigarette jumping up and down, up and down with Lalo's chattering jaw. Little flecks of tobacco fall from the end of the cigarette and rest on the surface tension of the water.

"How long has it been since you ate?" Cuauh asks.

"Long," says Lalo.

"What do you want?" Cuauh says. He rubs his eyes.

"Please," says Lalo.

"Chinese food?"

"Please"

"That's good," says Cuauh lighting his own cigarette from the flame of Saint Rita's candle. The smoke casts shadows on the wall. "That's good," he says again and takes Lalo's cigarette by the filter to light it with the cherry of his own.

He places the cigarette back into the corner of Lalo's face. It's wet, so it burns better at the top than it does at the bottom. Lalo takes quick puffs to keep the fire from going out. His mouth fills with hot smoke. He coughs and coughs, unable to get a breath.

To Cuauh, it's the saddest thing he's ever seen.

Some people said Lalo was a queer, but others said he was just like that—purple boots, those games he used to play. That one he used to do with a ten-dollar bill.

He'd stick it in a urinal, a cantina urinal, and then go back to the bar and drink with Cuauh and watch, observe, take note of everyone who stepped inside to take a leak.

He liked to take bets with the bartender: who'd be the one to reach in and fish it out? The thought of it amused Lalo to no end, his little giddy chuckle amplified by the half-emptied cantina glass at his lip that made him look retarded.

Every so often a patron—a nice elderly woman or a vaquero or someone—might pat Cuauh on the shoulder and say, "So nice of you to take your brother out. He looks better every day," or "Lucky him to have a brother like you. How is he doing as of late?" to which Cuauh would say, "fine, fine," and end it at that. Lalo would take little swigs and then laugh again to himself. He taught Cuauh to laugh in those days. Cuauh would laugh only when Lalo was right about who'd take the bill from the urinal.

Almost always, somebody would pay the bar with the piss bill and the bartender would know (Lalo would smell just for proof) and the matter would be settled. If the bartender won, Lalo would cover 5 percent of whatever the cantina was paying the cartel that month in collections. But if Lalo was right, the bartender would pay 5 percent to Lalo on top of the standard fee. It was usually a wash, the odds favoring the bartender if anything, which is why the bartender kept betting with Lalo.

For Lalo, the kicks were enough, and when he won, he'd always split the earnings with Cuauh, which is how they got talking about money in the first place.

This was in the beginning, when Cuauh was freshly deported. The new pilot from Texas who'd once been a crop duster. He was kidnapped in Nuevo Laredo, right after he'd walked the bridge, and ever since, he'd been lonesome in that briny way—sulking, scared, stone hopeless. For all the lore he'd heard growing up in Texas about the Zetas and Sinaloa and El Golfo, with all their evil ideas and all their evil ways, he'd never expected a narco to look like Lalo, who was more silly than scary and a little bit stupid too.

But Lalo, like Cuauh, was also an outcast within the cartel—one of those men who were kidnapped and not recruited—and that made them brothers in a way. They were both paralyzed by their circumstances. Their loneliness hurt and throbbed like a bruise. It was only when Cuauh thought of escape, of going home, that his body felt at ease. Cuauh could sleep when he dreamed of escape. He ate, he breathed, he laughed knowing that everything he did, every cent he made in this line of work, would all be put to use someday—not too far from now—when he'd leave Mexico and go back home to Harlingen. He decided, from the day he was kidnapped, to dedicate his life to returning, and he and Lalo mostly talked about that. How Cuauh planned to go back to his old farm in the orange groves and dust the crops until he bled black in the nose. He told Lalo about June bugs and cicadas that come every so many years and the smell of all that chlorpyrifos raining down from under his plane like the tang of urine. He told him of other smells too. The smell of his mother's posole stew boiling hot on the kitchen stove. The smell of tobacco drifting in off the breeze from the grove master's cigarillo, wet like rain but sweet like autumn.

"Work on a farm like a fucking slave?" Lalo would say to Cuauh. His lecture was always the same. "That's your big dream?"

"Maybe," said Cuauh to Lalo.

"That's the problem with paisanos, Cuauh. We're still slaves. Even in Texas, Tucson, wherever. We make El Norte run and we bring this country to its knees. But at least there's some dignity to destruction. Some dignity in living here. It's nice for a little while, don't you think? But eventually, I'll leave this too. We'll both leave it, you and me."

"How?" he asked Lalo one time. And Lalo looked at Cuauh almost surprised, as if he didn't expect that question or at least the audacity of it. It was only one word—*how*—but between them both it was the most dangerous word. It was the bridge between dreaming and doing. *How* connected them at the brain. *How* was the end but also the beginning of everything. And suddenly, it was out that they were both planning, scheming against their captors. They would both leave their cartel, escape it, which, of course, carried its own dangers, especially for those who were kidnapped. The cell chiefs kept names and addresses of relatives. Even if they couldn't find you they would find your brother or your parents. It was the thing that kept Cuauh from simply taking his plane and flying off into the north. It was the fear of it that kept him coming back, day after day, to the desert strip or the little road in Lomas de Poleo.

"Out with it, then," said Cuauh, as excited as ever. "How? How?"

Lalo's answer was simple. "A lot of cash."

"How much?"

"A lot."

"From where?" asked Cuauh.

"From everywhere," said Lalo, and he explained how he kept his money in one place but never on him. He kept it in the base of the aluminum-lined false steering column in that burnt-orange Ford Lobo he'd drive across the border into Texas, that hollow space where drugs were kept and stored. Safe from the prying eyes of X-rays, gamma rays, whatever rays reflected off the aluminum sheet inside the steering column. Other drivers drove that pickup too, but the money was still safe. Everyone knew that to steal from the cartel was a death sentence. And of course, everyone talked about the stash in that steering column, but nobody knew who it belonged to, so nobody dared take it. The other drivers assumed it was a test of sorts, of loyalty or something. And Lalo got a kick out of that.

He loved the idea of his money traveling to all the places drugs went, the places he might go some day after this—Houston, Wichita Falls, Oklahoma City, Tuscaloosa, Raleigh, New York, Montreal.

"Come with me," Lalo would say, and they'd make plans together. They dreamed of fancy hotels, fancy dinners, Buchanan's Single Malt Scotch, never having to work again.

Lalo told him that when it was his turn to drive the Lobo, he always checked on his money and it was always there, packed against the back of the column down by where the Freon hit the A/C vent. The bills were always cold and he liked to fan them in his face. The smell, like plastic.

Cuauh remembers Lalo telling him all of this. And he remembers asking again, "But how? So, you have a lot of cash. But what do you do with it?" Cuauh remembers that crooked index finger on Lalo's hand and how it waved the bartender over with just the tiniest motion that night in the bar, the cold of the January wind slapping hard against the window panes.

Lalo took a hundred-peso bill from his wallet, looked off toward the Cantina bathroom, and said to Cuauh, "Let me show you what honest men will do for money."

In the bathroom, Lalo busts his chin on his way toward the porcelain lip of the toilet. He hurls and hurls, his voice splattering echoes inside the toilet bowl that rattle out at the tiled corners of the ceiling and ping with a long whang like the tight, coiled racket of a kicked doorstop. Nothing comes up. A beaded string of spit arcs from the fleshy part of his lip to the clear water below.

Cuauh hooks his arms under Lalo's and pulls him up so he's kneeling. His chin sluices bright red. It meanders in streaks like jagged lines that dry maroon, brown, black, and then stops at his collarbone. He looks as fragile as an egg and just as pale. That incredible voice, that incredible noise.

"Don't talk," says Cuauh, "don't speak," and he takes the Chinese food from the ledge of the bathtub and places it on the floor. "Don't eat," he tells Lalo, who tries his best to be a good sport about the whole thing.

They look at the mirror and then look at each other. They see themselves. Lalo, the boy he used to be. Cuauh, the man he might become—the bloody mess, that pulp of a person. He looks at Lalo the way you might look at a car wreck, the way you might observe it and rubberneck because you don't want it to happen to you. He observes Lalo begging. Cuauh swears when it's his time that he won't beg.

"Please," says Lalo shivering in his cold clothes. "Please," he says reaching for the food, and Cuauh lets him have it.

He nibbles at the breaded chicken. He can't keep anything down.

Inside the tub the ashy cigarette from Lalo's lips, snuffed and bloated at the filter. It spins slow under the drippy faucet.

Cuauh takes off his shirt and ties it like a scarf around Lalo's neck. He pats him dry with the tail of it. He grabs him by the shoulders and blows out the candle.

The sodium lamps pour in through the window and light up half the tub orange. In the dark the other half is blue. Lalo's skin is yellow, his torso cut in half. The water is green, the same shade of green Cuauh remembers so well from his childhood.

He eases Lalo's head into the water and closes his eyes. Lalo wraps his legs around Cuauh, and Cuauh lets his mind drift back in time. The warmness of Lalo's escaping breath. Like Texas heat in the summertime.

Cuauh lets his mind go elsewhere. He imagines walking barefoot in his old backyard or what he considered his backyard at one time. It's where he played anyway, him and his little brother. It's still teeming with sounds. The tick of the heat in his ears, the tick of the insects flapping pell-mell from one tree to the other, ruining everything he's ever worked for.

Behind his closed eyes are the cicadas too, seventeen-year-old cicadas humming pitch perfect in the shade of the orange-tree branches. You can't see them but they're there. And they'll die eventually, like all the other critters and crawlers and men and women in the grove—all poisoned by the pesticides.

Lalo moans and Cuauh brings his toes to a point. He's flexing his calves, he's bringing his body up two or three inches to the tree. He pulls down a switch and plucks a cicada from the branch. He pinches its humming legs between his fingers and dangles it away from his face,

530

as far as his arm can reach, staring at its molting body. The cicada feels the same way it did when he was seven—the last time he handled a cicada—like a sliver of metal but undeniably alive.

He remembers how they'd make them fight, him and his brother. How he'd clip their wings and set them off against each other in a dirt ring like oversize ants. Being flightless made them hostile. They circled for a long time before they attacked one another. They made them carnivores, him and his brother.

It was always a quick death. He remembers how placidly his little brother watched as one cicada would split the other open, the broken one's exoskeleton sloughing off like flaking bits of fish food. And they'd talk over it just like teenage boys might talk over cigarettes or old men might talk over dialysis at the Harlingen Scott & White down the road—what is the worst way someone can die?

His little brother would always come up with the funny deaths: ants, getting killed by a hooker, getting killed by ants and a fire and a hooker at the same time.

When it was Cuauh's turn, all he could think about was shriveling to death, sloughing away like that bug—molting, beautiful and iridescent like that cicada drying in the dirt.

What a slow death, he thinks. How cruel children can be.

He thinks of the cicada and thinks of the drivers and thinks of Lalo and thinks of himself. Disposable, just like everything else. He'll molt under hot dirt eventually, somewhere in the world. In his mind he can see their skin sloughed off by zip ties or bullets or fire. He's suddenly conscious of his own scars all over his body: the puckered red blips of skin around his wrists from when he was zip-tied and kidnapped in Piedras Negras; the pink laceration over his arm when he was made to fight gladiator-style at midnight; the serrated bead sutures across his clavicle from when he crashed a plane for the first time with his brother.

He opens his eyes and sees that face underwater. Perfectly still. Perfectly at peace. He imagines plucking each scar from his body to lay them over himself. He thinks he can remember what it felt like to be flawless at one time.

Nominated by Ploughshares

BLOODLINES

by LAUREN SLATER

from THE SUN

I.

We have been married for twenty-two years. Everything was fine until, twelve years into it, we had kids. Our children changed us. They brought out in B. a love so fierce, so focused, that I fell off the edge of his world, plunging into some sea where, no matter how much I flounder and flail, he fails to toss me a line. My children often seem to be apparitions, floating forms, people of poured glass, ghostly and beautiful and beyond my reach.

I recently told my husband that if we want to save our marriage—in which whatever common ground we had has long since eroded into rubble and slid down some steep slope—then we need to spend time together without the children. It works like this, I told him: The husband and wife are a team of two. That team has to be the priority, or the family collapses.

It works like this, my husband told me: We need to do more things together as a family. If I would join them when they play Scrabble or Clue, then our marriage would improve.

I don't see how Scrabble could possibly restore the romantic bond that drew B. and me together way back when: him with his strawberry-blond hair and pale-sky eyes; me with my mahogany hair and hands the size of starfish. We made our own wedding invitations, taking pictures of our faces and cutting them in two and then pasting half of his face to half of mine and xeroxing the image one hundred times. I found a copy of the invitation the other day, and I can see now that the joined faces look rather like some kind of crash, and if you peer at the paper closely, you can see the ragged rift between the half husband and the half wife, a subtle seam between us.

Right from the start my husband and I were radically different people, and over the years our differences have deepened. He is an engineer and a committed rationalist, approaching every problem by breaking it into its component pieces and searching for a solution in a process utterly devoid of emotion, which B. says clouds the mind and obscures the necessary steps. I approach problems by listening for their emotional undertones in an attempt to find the hidden issue, peeling back life's layers, lifting lids to peek inside. In his youth my husband did drugs and holds dear his memories of special LSD experiences in which he saw whatever it was he saw. I am terrified of drugs and believe that I lack the mental stability to endure a psyche-shattering psychedelic trip. While making dinner or driving, my husband listens to lectures on genomics or history. While washing the dishes or walking on my treadmill, I listen to country music, which he can't stand. "Headphones," he tells me. "Get headphones."

Six months or so ago, my husband brought home two boxes that he laid side by side on the counter. The labels were printed with a stylized image of an x chromosome beside a company's logo. "We spit into the test tubes," my husband said, tapping the top of one box, "and then send it off, and in six weeks we'll get back our genomes, completely analyzed."

I told him I didn't need to have my genome analyzed. I already knew that I am Jewish, that my people come from eastern Europe, and that breast cancer and diabetes both run in my family.

"You might find out something you never knew," my husband said. "You might find out that you are not as Jewish as you think. You might find out that you are at high risk for a disease you can do something about."

"Yeah," I said, "and I also might find out I'm at high risk for a disease I *can't* do anything about, like Alzheimer's. If I know that's in store for me, it will ruin whatever time I have left."

My husband said he was going to do it—for the kids. They deserved to know what they'd inherited from us. And right then and there he tore open the package, the x chromosome ripped in half. Inside, packed in wadded cotton, were a test tube and a little instruction booklet, which he thumbed through. Then, snapping open the top of the tube, he began to spit. And spit, and spit, and spit. The tube had a red line about a third of the way up, indicating the fill point.

"My God," my husband said after several minutes. His saliva, which had a strange pinkish tinge, barely filled the bottom. "I never realized how hard it is to salivate."

The instruction booklet said that rubbing your cheeks would stimulate your salivary glands, so he put down the test tube and started massaging. "Let me," I said, and I massaged his cheeks—the first time we'd touched in who knew how long. His face was covered with stubble, a barely there beard the color of a sunset, russet orange and wiry but also soft. I pressed in, imagining his salivary glands filling with viscous liquid, his mouth starting to moisten. "Now," he said in a burbling sort of way, and he spit again, this time producing a big bubble that hovered over the vial and then burst, dripping down the sides. After about twenty minutes he finally reached the red line, the spit frothy and still with its strange pink hue, like a magic fluid. And indeed it was. From this liquid the scientists at the chromosome company would uncoil my husband's DNA. I pictured them separating the strands with long knitting needles, the code tumbling onto the table with a rattling sound: A, C, G, T—adenine, cytosine, guanine, thymine—the basic building blocks of DNA, four letters that, in near-infinite combinations, make us who we are. I envisioned the scientists assembling and interpreting, pressing their ears to each consonant and vowel as if to better hear its history. And once they had completed their task, they would send B. the results, his whole life's script, complete with a cast of characters and plot points where disease might dwell.

Later that night, alone in the bedroom, my husband asleep on the couch downstairs, I massaged my own cheeks and spit into my hand. My spit did not have a pinkish hue. It was just a milky dab of wetness on my palm, seeping into my lifelines, darkening them, deepening them. What, really, did I know? I knew that my great-grandmother's name was Mindle, and that she'd been a seamstress in Minsk. But my whole long line, lush with possibilities—that I did not know. Did I want to know? The chromosome company's pamphlet said that the genetic testing would reveal my ancestry going back tens of thousands of years, back to a time when two species of humans roamed the earth: *Homo sapiens*, who survived and thrived and at some point about ten thousand years ago discovered the power packed inside seeds and started the agricultural revolution; and the Neanderthals, who lived in Europe and Asia during the most recent ice age and eventually died out. If I spit into that tube, I might find out that part of me comes from a land of snow Or the opposite: I might find out I have Sephardic Jewish ancestors, that my lineage winds through red deserts and over crumbling cliffs. I might find out I have a bit of African in me, Caribbean color snuffed out by the pallor of my Caucasian covering. And there was a practical side to this, too. In all likelihood I'd get back a report that would be useful to my children. I'd know, for instance, whether or not I carried the genetic mutations for breast cancer, a disease for which I'd already undergone a bilateral mastectomy ten years earlier. Breast cancer can be entirely unrelated to genes, or it can arise from a DNA code gone wrong, a major misspelling in the sequence that I could have passed on to my daughter or my son. I looked up at the ceiling, which seemed to spin. Then I went downstairs to retrieve the second, un-opened, kit from the kitchen counter. I broke the band around the box, lifted the lid, took out the test tube, peered into its slender chute, touched the red fill line, and felt my mouth begin to water.

I went and told my husband that I was going to take the test. He massaged my cheeks for me, kneading the sides of my jaw, which was continually clenched, even in sleep. (I was often awakened by the sound of my own grinding.) It was past midnight. The children were dream-ing. The moon's light came trickling through the kitchen windows and cast long shadows on the floor, shadows that looked like liquid, shadows we stood ankle deep in, B. moving his fingers around my cheeks and I lowering my head and aiming into the tube, my spit suddenly coming fast and furious. Within minutes I had hit the fill line. My husband then took the tube from me gently, carefully, treating it with a reverence that made my heart ache, for he'd once held me the way he was now holding my saliva. He capped the tube, slipped it into a preaddressed envelope, and said, "I'll send it out in the morning." I nodded. I could still feel his fingers on my face. My flanks burned. His eyes looked sunken, sleepy. He usually crashed on the couch while I slept alone in what our children called "the big bed."

"Come upstairs with me," I said, extending a hand.

He shook his head. "You're going to read," he said, "and I need to get up early."

Why didn't I tell him that I wouldn't read, that as soon as we slipped between the sheets, *our* sheets, I'd snap off the light? Why didn't I insist, persist? Habit, I suppose, and also the terrible fact that I prefer to sleep alone with books piled high around me, as if to form a wall with words.

Between my husband and me stretched a long, flat plain of silence and arguments unresolved. We argued about who'd said what and when. We argued about who did the dishes and who did more of the child care and why I wouldn't play Monopoly with them and how we spent our money. Each argument was small and inconsequential on its own, but they accumulated like the debris that got in our gutters.

Now, though, something had shifted. B. and I had embarked on a joint venture, a project involving test tubes and spit. The very next day he rose before dawn and left for work, taking the test tubes with him. Four hours later he called me from his desk to say that he had mailed them in. And five days after that, we each got an e-mail message in our separate inboxes: "Congratulations! Your sample has arrived at our lab." I pictured our test tubes lying side by side, surrounded by smart strangers who would study our spit, drawing from that sticky lubricant the long loops of our DNA, which tethered us to people in a past we had never known. My husband and I were experiencing a shared state of anticipation: A little fear. A little hope. On the outside nothing had changed, but between us was a simple string, attached to him and to me. We didn't discuss the string, but it kept us connected across minutes and miles, in dreams and in daylight: two people, hitched and here.

II.

B. got his test results back before I did. The envelope came in the mail on a Friday in March, hand addressed, the letters lacy and elegant. I studied the handwriting closely, as though its form or style might reveal something about the contents. A hand-addressed envelope from a big company suggested significant information, findings that required softness, a personal touch—which could have been good or bad. Perhaps the company was writing to tell him that he came from British royalty; or perhaps he harbored some dreadful disease, and the company wanted to ease the pain by personalizing its response. The thick white envelope was completely opaque, even when pressed right up to a light bulb. Finding that the seal had puckered in places, I used my pinkie to try to pry the flap open, stopping only when I made a tiny tear: evidence of my snooping. I knew better than to rip open that envelope. B. was a deeply private person. I'd once asked him about his most erotic fantasy. This was many years earlier, when we were still lovers and lying naked in bed on a warm evening in June, the skylight propped open, a silver plane crossing the band of blue sky. I had already told him mine. He thought for a long time and then said, "Eating red, ripe strawberries with whipped cream."

I turned to him and looked into his eyes, because the eyes always reveal the lie, even a harmless one. "That couldn't really be your most erotic fantasy," I said.

"Red and ripe," he replied. "And fresh whipped cream."

I pressed and prodded but could get nothing more. Frustrated, I moved away from him then, opening a space on the sheet between us, and into this space fell the shadows of oncoming night. I'd revealed to him a deep and dark and personal secret about myself, and he'd responded with a low-calorie dessert. I knew it wasn't true. I knew he wanted what everyone wants—or some version of it, anyway: to hold or be held, to hit or be hit, to be entered and exited and turned inside out with lust and longing. But he wasn't going to admit it to me and maybe not even to himself. Years later, in a rageful attempt to crack the opacity that cloaked my husband, I prowled through his closet while he was at work and found the proverbial stash of porno magazines: girls with enormous breasts, women with their bottoms thrust into the air. We'd been married well over a decade by then. Sex between us had slowed to a trickle but hadn't stopped. I didn't mind the magazines. In fact, they were heartening. In a way they brought B. home to me. Here he was, a man like any other, full of desire. For days afterward it seemed I could see the red haze of his heart beneath his chalk-white chest: a complex, coiled muscle beating in its niche. I wanted to ask him why he'd said strawberries when what he really liked was ivory asses hoisted by high heels, the aperture barely visible in the v where the taut thighs met. I wanted to ask him why he couldn't tell me his real fantasies and desires, but that was a conversation I didn't know how to start. It also would have required me to admit that I'd been spying. And so we continued on as before. A marriage can be many things. Ours was a series of secrets and small betrayals, little lies that poison you like an odorless gas you don't even know you're breathing until you stop.

Standing there holding B.'s envelope, thinking of the pinup girls and their breasts pouring out of bustiers, I considered simply tearing open the flap so I could read his results and know him before he knew himself. I thought of the scientists patiently decoding my husband, how he'd offered up his body to them in a way he so rarely had with me. Our sex, before it had stopped, had typically been with the lights out and his eyes clamped shut—the kind of sex that leads to loneliness, if that's possible. Sometimes during sex with B. I would imagine I was someplace else. I'd think of the enchanted doorways in children's books, three upright planks of wood in the middle of a grove of evergreen trees, the children approaching and then, in a big rush of courage, walking through into another world of blue pools and fruit trees and big birds with crimson beaks and eggs that gushed gold when you broke them. I have always loved doorways and cupboards and windows for their fairy-tale possibilities, and thus my excitement when, last year, I discovered that the wall in our hallway was hiding a set of shelves. With the sharp point of a pry bar I tore into that white plaster, feeling it give way with a soft crumple, and there they were: three shelves hidden all this time in our house, so deep you had to stretch to touch their backsides, and I imagined that I pushed through and found still more cubbyholes giving way to more cubbyholes that grew into rooms, our whole house unfolding and giving up its gifts. I wandered through those rooms, looking for B., who appeared at a distance I could never seem to close.

In real life B. was angry that I'd taken down the wall, and he did not find the cubbies I'd revealed whimsical or useful. "I wish you'd asked me first," he said. Such a reasonable request. *I wish you'd asked me first.* Like the letters that compose our DNA, B.'s seemingly simple statement was in reality a coded message that, if opened up, would have revealed years of animosity between us. I was often making changes to the house, rearranging the furniture so that, when he came home at the end of the day, nothing was where it had been. Or, worse, I would hire contractors to take apart the bathroom and lay the tile I had found and fallen in love with, all without asking him first. In my defense, B. appeared to care little about his surroundings, leaving a trail of dust and debris, of smelly socks and popcorn boxes wherever he walked. It was easy to find him: just follow the dirt. So why was it, then, that I could never find him?

And now here I was with his envelope in my hands. I picked up the phone and called him at work but got his voice mail. "Please leave your personal data after the beep," his message said. I did not leave my personal data. I hung up and called back: voice mail. I hung up and dialed a third time, listening to the tinny ringing and the click when he finally answered.

"Hi," I said. "Your test results have come in. I have the envelope right here. Want me to open it and read to you what it says?"

"No!" he said without a moment's hesitation. "I'll read my results when I get home."

"I'm curious," I said.

"Don't," he said, and then he paused. I could practically hear his memory working, calling up images of me tearing down a wall or ripping up the carpet in search of the planks beneath, always wanting to explore and expose. "Lauren," he said, "don't touch my mail."

His tone was so serious that I dropped the letter and watched it land on the countertop. "OK," I said, "I won't touch it," and we hung up. Out of childish anger I flicked his letter to the floor and let it lie there. Then, with a sigh, I slowly bent down, one hand at the base of my back, as if I were a hundred years old, and retrieved the envelope.

The day darkened, the children arrived home from school, and then B. from work. "Where's the letter?" he asked. No *Hello*. No *How are you?* Just *Where's the letter?* I pointed to it. He swept it up and, kissing each child on the crown of the head, disappeared into his study.

I expected he'd be in there for some time, reading and digesting the information, but not more than three minutes had passed when the door flew open and B. marched back into the kitchen, where I'd started to slice an onion for a recipe. He paused, thrust out his chest, pounded it three times with a fist, and said, "I'm pretty much pure Viking."

"Pure Viking," I repeated, not knowing what, precisely, that meant.

He said his ancestors were all from northern Europe—Norway, Iceland, those countries.

I nodded. The envelope that contained his results had been quite thick. I asked what else the report had said.

"That's pretty much it," he said. There were no health risks he might have passed on to our children.

"The report looked really long to me," I said.

B.'s eyes turned to slits. "How would you know?" he asked. "You didn't read it, did you?"

"Was the envelope opened?" I said. "Isn't it obvious that I didn't read it?"

He then declared that I was in one of my "moods" and said he was going to play with the children instead. "Come on, kids," he called as he retreated from the kitchen. "Let's make a movie." I heard our son and daughter thudding down the stairs and B. unpacking the video camera in the living room and snapping the tripod legs into position. What would their movie be about? I should have gone in there and joined them. I should have put down the onion, turned off the stove, and plowed into the center of the group. How had I come to stand so outside of my own family? Had I been exiled, or had I exiled myself? The children adored B., and he spent all his free time with them. I was the parent who made the dentist and doctor appointments, who sorted through clothes and closets, who registered for schools and camps and kept vaccination histories in a file. I didn't doubt that my offspring loved me, but I knew I did not enchant them the way B. did. Right from the beginning he'd been able to enter their worlds, reading aloud Greek myths, *Grimm's Fairy Tales*, and all seven Harry Potter books. During car rides he would tell the children about his travels before he'd met me, when he'd wandered the globe as a free man, eating goat's-head soup in Indonesia and drinking the blood of a cat in Africa and meeting wise men in India who'd given him amulets and charms he still has today—silver pendants with ruby rocks blazing in their centers, an emerald-green bead of glass. B. kept these treasures, along with assorted treasures from other countries, in a cardboard box in his office closet. Once, I'd walked by his door— usually closed but this time ajar—and seen him holding up a Tibetan tapestry. I'd stopped and stared. He was just admiring this piece of exotic cloth, sewn with seed pearls and flecks of glitter, embroidered with glowing scenes of elephants and forests. He gripped the translucent textile in two hands, stretching it so he could see it better. I studied him studying his past, the travels he'd taken long ago, and I imagined he was wondering: How had settling down come to claim him so completely? By what means does a relationship erode, and what do you do when even the erosion—which is itself a form of movement—stops, and everything stands still, stuck? How do you find your way out of that fairy-tale forest?

In the living room where they'd set up the camera, B. began to tell the children tales of Viking warriors. "You descend from people who conquered the true north," he told them, "who came to Iceland in boats they made by hand, strong people, fierce people." B. told the children about the old Norse gods: Odin, the Allfather, a war god and a poetry god; and Thor, the thunder god who battled the World Serpent and tossed him back into the sea. On and on my husband went about Freya and Loki, communicating to the kids that this was their heritage, when the fact of the matter was that our children were half Jewish, and thus were also inheritors of another set of ancient tales.

It wasn't long after that when I decided that our family should have a Passover Seder. It was time the children learned their *whole* heritage, not just half of it.

One night at dinner I announced that this year we were going to celebrate Passover.

"Cool," said B., chewing thoughtfully. Then he put down his fork. "What exactly does Passover celebrate?"

"The Jews," I replied, and I looked at our two kids across the table. "The Jews, which both of you are, were once slaves in Egypt, and Passover celebrates their escape from slavery."

The children continued to eat, clearly unmoved by the fact that their ancestors had once been slaves.

"You are," I said, my voice rising in a way I did not like, "part of a tiny, tiny tribe of people, a people so persecuted that it's a miracle Judaism even still exists." I explained how the Jews had wandered for forty years in the desert before finally reaching their promised land. I tried to make my story as colorful and compelling as possible: Moses. The burning bush. The parting of the Red Sea. The Ten Commandments handed down from on high. A land of milk and honey and unleavened bread. Blood on doorways. Plagues of locusts and toads. But it had been so many years since I'd practiced Judaism that the pieces of the Passover story didn't cohere, and my tale fell flat. "What matters," I said to the kids, "is that you know you're Jewish, that you understand you come from this tribe of people who survived against all odds. You have Jewish blood in you."

B. said there was no such thing as Jewish blood. "Judaism is a religion, not a bloodline."

"It's both," I said, the kids drifting away as we faced off.

"That's what the Nazis thought," B. replied. "They thought that Judaism was a bloodline, when in reality it's a set of beliefs and practices that have nothing to do with the way we, in this house, live our lives."

I insisted that you didn't have to practice Judaism to be a Jew. "Judaism is something you *are*; not something you do."

"I disagree," B. said, "but I'm happy to have a Seder."

In the days before Passover it would have been easy enough to go online and reacquaint myself with the great Old Testament stories, but I didn't. Why not? Did I need to see my genome-analysis results before I could claim the traditions and tales that I knew were mine, and therefore also my children's? I remembered enough from my childhood to know what it was to be a Jew: the haunting call of the shofar, that polished horn the cantor blew in temple; the names of the dead read aloud as congregants sang Kol Nidre and rocked back and forth. But I didn't do it, because I feared boring my children. I feared I could not compete with B., who had a storytelling flair he rarely showed in ordinary conversation, his tone undulating, his voice strung with suspense. I am a writer, not a storyteller. When you tell a story out loud, you put yourself at the center of attention; you are the sun, and the audience is drawn by your gravitational pull. In our family B. had the pull. I stayed off to the side with my solitary activities: reading, writing, daydreaming of doorways in forests. My temperament was solitary and often melancholy, whereas B.'s, despite his love of data and his engineering inclinations, was bright and elfin.

Still, I hadn't expected that B. would respond to the scientific analysis of his self with this set of stories from thousands of years ago. I would have thought he would meet science with science, and the fact that he hadn't was evidence that he could still surprise me. At this thought a small flame flickered somewhere in my middle, in a hollow that once hadn't been hollow. It hurt, this place, not just sometimes but all the time, a burl of grief for which I could not find any tears, though I longed for them. I wanted to cry in front of B., to cry *with* B., both of us mourning what we had lost: How he used to call me "pie" (short for "sweetie pie"). How we used to go to movies and eat Thai takeout straight from the boxes, stabbing the fragrant mangoes with chopsticks, holding back our heads and popping the bites into our opened mouths. How, when we made love, I could smell him, a smell so particular it was like an olfactory signature: a little grass, a little sweat, a little sadness—a complex scent that told me I was home. I missed these things and badly wanted them back. B. often said they would come back once the kids were grown and we found ourselves alone again. Until then, however, there was no room.

"Aren't you lonely?" I'd asked him once.

"Yes," he'd said. "Very."

With my marriage at a standstill so complete even the smallest shift felt seismic, that flame inside me flickered again.

III.

About one week into April, when the buds on the magnolia trees were still in a fetal furl, I received my results: a colorful array of graphs and pie charts and percentages that, at first glance, made my mind swirl. It was Friday, and B. was home, helping our daughter with her biology homework, explaining covalent bonds and how they break. Part of me wanted to call him into my study so he could help me sort through the document, but another part of me wanted to figure it out on my own and then announce to my husband precisely who I was, where I'd come

542

from, and, most important, the places where our genomes overlapped. After staring at the screen for some time, I came to understand that 3 percent of my genes come from the Neanderthals (the average person of European or Asian descent has between 1 and 4 percent), which means that, hundreds of thousands of years ago, during that time when two distinct species of humans coexisted, there was crossbreeding. This fact made me feel oddly happy and full of possibility: if Neanderthals and *Homo sapiens* could find enough common ground to mate, then surely B. and I could, too.

On the second page of my report was my lineage, traced back thousands of years. While B.'s ancestors came from Iceland and northern Europe, mine came from eastern Europe and were 100 percent Ashkenazi Jewish. I do not carry a gene for Alzheimer's, nor for Parkinson's, and, more significantly, I do not carry any of the mutations for breast cancer. So if my daughter ever gets the disease, it will not be because of the DNA I have passed on to her. My report told me that I am at significant risk for deep-vein thrombosis and high cholesterol, that I have wet earwax, and that I am genetically prone to like sweet and salty foods. For the most part it was a bit of a dud. Who cares about earwax? And I didn't need to spit into a test tube to find out what tickles my taste buds. But the report confirmed what I'd secretly been fearing: that my husband and I have absolutely no crossover in our bloodlines. He is from one people, I am from another, and that's that. The two genome reports, if laid side by side, described two vastly different human beings with two vastly different heritages, people whose differences extended past the surface and went straight down to the cellular level. Whatever optimism I'd been harboring since the start of spring vanished.

That night B. and I had a huge fight about money. Our bank account was, once again, dangerously low. We'd have to dip into our savings to pay our bills. He blamed my horses.

"The whole purpose of buying this property," I said, "was so that I could have horses."

"They are a purely discretionary expense," he said. "And it appears you care more for them than you do about our kids' college education."

"Untrue!" I shouted, and I shot back that he spent too much on computers and refused to do a budget with me.

He claimed a budget wouldn't change the fact that we were not rich enough to afford horses.

"How can you say that," I asked, "when we haven't even looked at the figures?"

"I'm tired," B. said. "I didn't get any sleep last night."

I felt slapped. The night before, I had awakened from a nightmare and gone downstairs to find B. asleep on the couch. Waking him, I'd explained that I'd had a bad dream and asked if he would sleep with me for the rest of the night. Without answering, he had risen and followed me upstairs and climbed into bed beside me. But then, rather than hold me, he had turned his back and pulled a pillow over his head. Still, we were under the same covers again. It was a start.

And now here he was telling me he could not get a good night's sleep in our marital bed.

"Why not?" I asked. "I was completely quiet."

"I just couldn't," he said. "In fact, you thrash around."

I had an image of myself struggling to stay afloat in a giant ocean, the horizon gray, rain falling from the sky. I was swimming and swimming and could not get any closer to the shore.

My husband walked out of the room, headed for who knows where. I sat down in a chair. I couldn't get enough air, as if my lungs were stuffed with wadding. I thought of the basics of genetic code, the letters A, C, G, T. I vaguely remembered reading about a man who had transcribed his genome onto paper, and it had filled three one-thousand-page books—impressive, for sure, but still too small, I thought, to hold the whole of a human being.

The house was oddly quiet. Darkness fell. The headlights of passing cars swept over the walls and the woodwork and also my feet, my two bare feet on which I could have risen and walked out of there for good if I'd wanted. I heard the horses whinny and pace, whinny and pace. Animals know when storms are approaching; they smell it on the breezes blowing past. I sat there in a straight-backed chair and listened to the heartbeat of the house. The children were not home. I could hear my husband shuffling in his office. I wanted to burst through his closed door and say something, anything, but what? *Please*, I might say, and nothing more. I could not go to him and kiss him, because too great a gulf had formed between us, and it would have been as inappropriate as kissing a stranger. But I could say, *Please*.

I stood up and headed down the hall to his office. The hall was darker even than the rest of the house, because it had no windows. My footsteps echoed. I saw the crack of light beneath his door, heard the sound of a clicking keyboard. I was going to walk in there and say, *Please*, and see if that monosyllabic plea could somehow restore us to a state of union. The closer I got to his office at the end of that long, narrow hallway, the more I smelled a familiar and pungent scent. The smell had body to it. It felt physical, palpable—not a bad smell but a ripe one, as if someone had left out a plate of fruit for a few days too many, the browning bananas and apples with their black bruises. I was getting closer to the door with its line of light and also to this strangely comforting odor, whose source I discovered right outside my husband's office: a wicker laundry basket piled high with his sweaty T-shirts and crumpled clothes. I put my hand on the mound of dirty laundry, then lifted my palm to my nose and took in the scent of him. I felt happy because, well, here he was, the man I'd married, his scent the same now as it had been twenty-odd years earlier when, after the wedding ceremony, we had headed to our hotel room to make love; the same as it was whenever he came close to me—the smell of a fall garden, of musty mathematical equations in a dank but beautiful book. There, with my hand on his pile of clothing, I recalled an experiment I had once read about: A group of men wore simple cotton T-shirts for a couple of days, perspiring in them, sleeping in them, and finally peeling them off and giving them to the researchers, who then asked female test subjects to select the T-shirts that smelled the best to them. The researchers found that each woman consistently rated highest the T-shirts from the men whose immune systems contained important components that hers lacked, thus ensuring that any offspring they produced would have a robust defense system. In other words, women are drawn to men who have deep genetic differences from them—immunologically, at least. Why would this be? Because evolution does not want us to pick mates with genomes that are the same as ours. Evolution wants diversity; the more, the better.

I think of evolution as a kind of god. It is the primal force that decides which species survive and which do not. It creates adaptations and mutations that allow certain species to flourish while others fail. It guards against incest and drives us toward mates whose genomes differ from ours, because divergent genomes make for healthier children. I don't doubt this for a minute. But, as a psychologist, I also have read studies showing that couples who share interests are more likely to have successful marriages than those who don't. Thus we are caught in a complex bind when it comes to marriage: we are drawn unconsciously toward partners who deeply differ from us in order to create healthy offspring, but once the offspring have sprung, so to speak, we are left with a partner who may be more foreigner than friend. What is one to do in such a situation? Say, simply, *Please*, and hope that single, simple word ferries you and your spouse to some single, simple place where you can stitch your relationship back together? Obviously that won't work. So, really, what is one to do? B. and I have had our children, and thus the force that drew us together has done its job. We have procreated. We have produced two sturdy, intelligent beings who I'm sure have benefited from the divergent genomes of their parents, and who are fast growing up and entering a world where those parents will be less and less relevant. One day soon, as B. has reminded me, he and I will be the solitary pair that we once were—only he's leaving out an essential piece of the equation. What if, after the kids have left the nest (soon now, soon), we find our differences insurmountable? B. will forever be a man whose ancestors sailed the seas in boats they'd carved by hand, whereas I'll forever be a woman whose ancestors were seamstresses and rabbis who cultivated small, bookish lives in crowded conditions. I will always be a woman of words, a writer, and B. will be an engineer with big ambitions, ready to conquer whatever world he steps into.

I carried my husband's laundry downstairs to the basement and emptied it into the huge washing machine, stopping to smell his T-shirts as I did. Sure enough, that little flame in the hollow I wished were not there flared and flickered before settling down to its soft and steady burn. The laundry detergent was deep blue and viscous; I drizzled it over the clothes, watching it pool here and there, and then I slammed the lid shut and started the machine.

Feeling the need for light, I flicked on switches as I ascended the stairs. Where were the children? Should I have worried? It was nearing 6 PM, and only my husband and I were home. They must have made plans; I remembered as much in a haze. I turned on the hall lights and heard the telltale *ping* of a burned-out bulb. In the kitchen I flicked every switch, and the lights burst on almost theatrically. In the living room I rolled the dimmer all the way up until the furniture seemed to pulse with light: the couch pillows still holding the shape of the last person who'd sat there, the socks strewn in corners, the swirl of a cobweb up by the ceiling. I continued to make my way through the house, illuminating every space, ending in the master bathroom, where I turned on the shower, took off my clothes, and stepped under the spray. The steam rose up my legs and wound around my torso; the soap bubbles were slick on my skin. *My skin.* For how long could it go without touch? I ran my hands over my navel, my shoulders, my armpits, my neck, feeling the taut tendons, reaching behind myself to touch the vertebrae, hard knobs strung with fibers of nerve. I took the cake of soap between my palms and rubbed, creating a sweet-smelling froth, which I used to wash my chest, my hand passing between the two saline implants that are now my breasts and then lifting each sac and washing beneath.

And that is how I found it. I was scrubbing the skin under the left breast, digging in so hard I could feel bone, when I came across a nub of hardness, a little knot, a tight-pressed piece of gristle like a bur. Ten years earlier I'd had my breasts taken off and whisked away as if they were appendages one could simply unsnap from the body and send sailing down a dark river, never to be seen again. I woke up from my mastectomy in a dim recovery room, where there were many beds and many other people also waking up, stirring and groaning, and a machine beeping arrythmically, and a nurse standing over me saying, "Breathe, breathe," which scared me, because she made it sound as if maybe I weren't breathing. And then B. was there, flowers blazing in his fist, and the wheels of my bed were unlocked, and I was rolled through the labyrinthine hospital to my room, which overlooked the Charles River from the tenth floor: sails on the water and tiny people walking still-tinier dogs on leashes that looked like pieces of string. The pain—well, the pain I was not prepared for. My whole chest was on fire. They had to peel off the blood-soaked bandages, and I looked down and then regretted that I'd done so, my chest a train wreck of angry wounds and big black stitching and fresh pools of blood, as if a bomb had gone off in my heart, leaving me with only shreds of skin. And pain. They brought a morphine pump, and I pumped that juice into my body and felt the pain take its teeth out of me and walk across the room, where it hunched, waiting for a chance to bite again. I kept pumping. The next morning a gaggle of medical students came to observe the bomb site, again unwrapping the crusted bandages. (This time I had the good sense not to look.) It took me many weeks to heal from my mastectomy, but not once did I regret it, even when it became obvious that the plastic surgeon had botched the job, giving me two asymmetrical mounds with no nipples.

"If you want nipples," the plastic surgeon told me in a postoperative visit, "we can take some tissue from your tongue and create them."

No. Enough was enough. I'd go without.

And so I had, and fairly happily, been freed from mammograms and breast exams and MRIs and worry, until now with this little knot, this bur beneath my skin.

I stepped from the shower, my heart beating so fast I looked down to see if it was visible. I said B.'s name, then called it again, louder. I didn't bother wrapping myself in a towel, which was unusual, because, in our estrangement, we had become shy and no longer showed each other our unclothed bodies. But the bur, the knot, had changed that. B. came to the doorway of the bathroom, his eyes widening as he saw me standing there naked.

"I found a lump," I said.

We both knew that a recurrence after a mastectomy would be a very bad thing. The oncologist had told us, after she'd sent my breasts sailing down the dark river, that women rarely have recurrences after a bilateral mastectomy, and when they do, it's usually in the bone and comes with a poor prognosis. My legs wavered like skinny stems in a high tide. "What's wrong?" B. asked, as if he hadn't heard me the first time, and I said again, "I found a lump," and then the tears I'd thought I'd wanted for so long burbled up, and I wondered whether you could analyze a genome using tears instead of spit.

"A lump," B. said, still standing on the other side of the threshold, on the other side of the world, and I said, "Yes," and then I rode on that little raft of a word across the tiled floor and almost—but not quite—into his arms. "Feel this?" I asked, and I lifted the pathetic saline sac, and he extended his hand to knead the flesh around my ribs, touching the hollow where my heart beat. "Over to the left," I whispered, and his fingers landed right on the spot, massaging, measuring, contemplating, and pressing as if to assess what he could not—the danger. And though I thought I was in danger, endangered, about to be extinct, as B. touched me, I felt something unwind like a piece of twine between us, undoing years of rigid posturing. My knot gave way to an opening, and we went through it.

With his free hand B. wrapped me in a towel—I was shivering—and together we stepped through a door, back into a time when I'd first been diagnosed and B. had cupped my breasts the night before the surgeon had sawed them off. Later, when B. had seen the botched reconstruction job, he had found the heart to say, "It's not that bad," and when I'd asked him to touch them, he'd said, "Of course I can touch them," and then he'd gingerly caressed my prosthetic no-nipples breasts, cradling first one and then the other, his thumb circling the spot on each where a nipple should have been. And even though I knew it wasn't possible for me to feel his touch—the saline sacs had no nerves in them—I nevertheless experienced a tingle when he rounded what

would have been the areola. Mine had been huge and, in pregn⸻
had darkened to a mahogany color with nipples a deep, burnished
topped with the golden goo of colostrum. All gone, that. And here my
husband was, touching what was left—or, rather, what had been added,
like two new rooms, so to speak—and then he had kissed them and said,
"Welcome."

And even though you can't go back in time, even though time is not a
knot that can unwind, as he wrapped me in a towel and steadied the reeds
that were my legs, I nevertheless imagined his voice saying, *Welcome*.

IV.

There's a story I particularly like of a Zen student who complains to his
master that focusing on his breathing during meditation is boring. The
master grabs the student and plunges his head into a stream and holds
him under for some seconds, then yanks him back up into the shining,
abundant air and asks, "Still boring?" Illness—or, more specifically, the
threat of death—has a way of putting an edge on everything, of bringing
bounty where before there was none. It's not a question of making
lemonade with lemons or anything like that. It's a question of having
the film pulled back from your sticky eyes, the bandages removed, the
blinders ripped off so you can take in the view, which is filled with light,
light, light. The kind of light you don't want to linger in, because it has
an ominous, heavenly quality. The kind of light that illuminates even
the most delicate details, so you can see everywhere the scratched and
the marred. There was a time when I thought that I might die, when
death seemed imminent, and I moved through a world that was bril-
liantly lit with this light and beautiful in its flamboyant decay. And then,
when I learned I wasn't about to die, the light left me, but not the
memory of its glow.

We are all, no matter what our genome or genetic differences, wired
to die. And we know this. And this knowledge perhaps makes us more
alike, in the end, than different. This knowledge means that we all
share a personal pain that is common across cultures and continents
and that provides a bridge to every other human. Some of us deal with
the fact of our deaths by writing books or having children to preserve
our genomic signature into centuries beyond. Others do things that to
me seem strange, like cryopreserve their bodies in the hope that some-
day scientists will figure out a way to reanimate the dead. What the

knowledge of death did for me this time around was get me to make an appointment with my oncologist, who put me in a CAT-scan machine that clicked and whirred and then finally stopped.

"Well?" I said, sitting up, clutching the flimsy paper robe around my vulnerable body.

"A bone spur," she said, smiling. "It's just a bone spur."

I was beyond relieved that my latest brush with death had turned out to be just that: a brush, a drive-by. But, nevertheless, seeing my horizon—and knowing that, sooner rather than later, I would shoot past it—had altered my psychology once more, however briefly. In that moment of reprieve, even pancakes seemed sacred, and a grilled veggie burger was like a gift from some god—Thor or Yahweh, no matter.

"I'm fine," I said to B. when he came home. "It was just a bone spur."

"A bone spur," he said, more to himself than to me, a look of genuine relief on his face, and it occurred to me that maybe he didn't want to lose me, that he might miss me after I am gone, although I am still not sure why. Perhaps, even for radically different couples, even for estranged couples, there exists some kind of connection built of shared memory, of the once-was love. The genome results showed that B. and I have deeply divergent bloodlines, that our DNA is different, but those differences are actually quite small compared to the thousands of similarities that the whole human species shares. We all have neurons in our brains that recognize the softness of a smile; we are all capable of laughter, terror, loneliness, love; we all feel hot and cold, the tenderness of a touch and the severity of a slap; we all know right and wrong; we all sleep, and every one of us dreams.

I have a hunch that B. and I will find a way to stay together, despite the distance between us, despite the fact that we share neither bedroom nor bed, despite the fact that we have not kissed in years. I think that something, I don't know what, will pull us through, which may not be for the best. God knows, there are good-enough reasons for us to separate, especially once the kids are grown. But perhaps we can draw on the history that we have together, a history belonging only to us: a wedding, a wedding night, pregnancies, the blood of birth, affections and nicknames and sex that meant something, once upon a time. In the end maybe we can call on those thousands of similarities in all humans to forge a path wide enough for both of us to walk on.

Nominated by The Sun, David Jauss, Jennifer Lunden

SPECIAL MENTION

(The editors also wish to mention the following important works published by small presses last year. Listings are in no particular order.)

FICTION

George Matteson — An I for An I (Ep;phany)

Justin Carroll — Homecoming (The Pinch)

Erin Osborne — If This Chandelier Were A Woman (Noon)

Alejandro Zambra — Family Life (McSweeney's)

Nathan Oates — Natural Succession (Barrelhouse)

Roxana Robinson — In Naples (Southampton Review)

Porochista Khakpour — Something With Everything (Conjunctions)

Kiik Araki-Kawaguchi — Dissolving Newspapers, Fermenting Leaves (Pleiades)

Joyce Carol Oates — The Nice Girl (Boulevard)

Amy Yolanda Castillo — Sister Almas's Divine Revelation (Berkeley Fiction Collective)

Vincent Scarpa — We're All Here Because We Love You (Story Quarterly)

Erika Krouse — Wounds of the Heart and Great Vessels (Crazyhorse)

T.Y. Lee — My Name Is Manuel Vargas (Harvard Review)

Siân Griffiths — Sk8r (Georgia Review)

Lydia Conklin — Pioneer (Mud City Journal)

Kirstin Valdez Quade — Night At the Fiestas (Southern Review)

Ted Kehoe — The Children's Kingdom (Ploughshares)

Toni Jensen — In The Time of Rocks (Ecotone)

Janice Obuchowski — Sully (Gettysburg Review)

Michael Sheehan — September (Conjunctions)

Susie Mee — The Goldfish (A Public Space)

Tatyana Tolstaya — Smoke and Shadows (Iowa Review)

Richard Burgin — Don't Think (Hopkins Review)

Laura van den Berg — Volcano House (American Short Fiction)

David Huddle — Golden Gloves (Georgia Review)

Gloria Whelan — The Fourth Miracle (Notre Dame Review)

Marie-Helene Bertino — Exit Zero (Epoch)

Jessamine Chan — The Mansion District (Tin House)

Kate McIntyre — The Moat (Copper Nickel)

Jamie Quatro — Wreckage (Ecotone)

Molly Giles — Assumption (*All the Wrong Places*, Willow Springs)

David Szalay — Youth (Paris Review)

Emil Ostrovski — Pulse, My Electric Heart (New Orleans Review)

Michelle Hart — Spit (One Teen Story)

Pamela Painter — Deck (Five Points)

Bette Howland — A Visit (A Public Space)

Brian Turner — Smoking With the Dead and Wounded (Georgia Review)

Matthew Baker — Rites (One Story)

Jaimy Gordon — Mysteries of Lisbon (Mississippi Review)

Wendell Berry — Dismemberment (Threepenny Review)

Malerie Willens — Gropius Falls (Agni)

Janet Kim Ha — The Reunion (Iowa Review)

Jack Driscoll — The Goat Fish and the Lover's Knot (Georgia Review)

Austin Smith — Friday Night Fish Fry (Narrative)

Douglas Trevor — Faucets (Midwestern Gothic)

K. Brattin — Pods (Fjords)

David Watson — The Vanishing Mr. Klein (Mid-American Review)

Absolom J. Hagg — Someplace South, Anywhere Warm (Sixfold Fiction)

J. Robert Lennon — Something You May Not Have Known About Vera (Gigantic)

Katherine Conner — Mummy Baby (Pembroke Magazine)

Micah Dean Hicks — Flight of the Crow Boys (Salt Hill)

Rebecca Makkai — The Miracle Years of Little Fork (Ploughshares)

Philip Connors — Confirmation: Love and Basketball (n + 1)

NONFICTION

Elizabeth Benedict — What We Talk About When We Talk About Money (Salmagundi)

Robert Boyers — Fifty Years of Salmagundi (Salmagundi)

Brian Doyle — The Manner of His Murder (Timberline Review)

Kenneth A. McClane — Secrets (Antioch Review)

Lisa Wells — All Across the Desert Our Bread Is Blooming (Believer)

David L. Ulin — Freeway Jam (*LAtitudes*, Heyday)

Elizabeth Stoker Bruenig — Why We Confess (Hedgehog Review)

Fatima Bhutto — Psychic In Reykjavik (Catapult)

Andrew Cohen — Ronaldo (Missouri Review)

Camille Dungy — A Shade North of Ordinary (New England Review)

Joe Fassler — Wait Times (Creative Nonfiction)

Morwari Zafar — A Thousand Splendid Stuns (Granta)

Christian Wiman — Kill The Creature (American Scholar)

Georgina Nugent-Folan — Samuel Beckett: Going On In Style (Southern Review)

Cataline Ouyang — Spillings (River Teeth)

Mara Naselli — Bodies in Motion (Agni)

Gregory Bright — Twenty-Seven and a Half Years (The Sun)

Mariya Karimjee — Damage (The Big Roundtable)

Peter Trachtenberg — Inside The Tiger Factory (Virginia Quarterly)

Shawn Wen — A Body Later On (Iowa Review)

Jess Row — No Crying (Boston Review)

Alison Townsend — The Scent of Always . . . (Southern Review)

Andy Martin — Nausea in New York (Raritan)

Jack Conroy — The Fields of Golden Glow (New Letters)

Adina Talve-Goodman — I Must Have Been That Man (Bellevue Literary Review)

Amy Butcher — Reenacting (Iowa Review)

Judith Kitchen — Breath (River Teeth)

Matthew McNaught — Yarmouk Miniatures (n+1)

Jacqueline Kolosov — Pilgrimage to St. Ives (Sewanee Review)

David Wojahn — Can Poetry Save Your Life? (Blackbird)

Emily Geminder — Coming To (Prairie Schooner)

Aisha Sabatini Sloan — D Is For the Dance of the Hours (Ecotone)

Sheila Kohler — In A Woman's Kingdom (Agni)

Chris Stowe — One Summer Night (O-Dark-Thirty)

Zsolt Láng — Ping Pong (World Literature Today)

Eva Saulitis — Man of Letters: An Elegy (Alaska Quarterly Review)

Judith Pulman — On The Death of A Difficult Parent (Water-Stone)

Joni Tevis — What Looks Like Mad Disorder . . . (*The World Is On Fire*, Milkweed)

Lewis Hyde — Forgetting Mississippi (Tin House)

Dave Mondy — How Things Break (Iowa Review)

Gary Ferguson — Obliquity . . . (Georgia Review)

David Graeber — The Bully's Pulpit (The Baffler)

Ben Shattuck — He's-At-Home (The Common)

Samuel Autman — Invisible Nails (Ninth Letter)

Maureen McCoy — Smile: Your War Is Over (Gettysburg Review)

Jeannie Vanasco — What's In A Necronym? (The Believer)

Rachel Toor — The Old Town (American Chordata)

Peter Birkenhead — The Man Who Jumped Out of A Window (The Big Roundtable)

Kristofer Lenz — Stendhal Syndrome (The Point)

Ana Maria Spagna — Hope Without Hope (Ecotone)

Liz Falvey — Ultimate Gifts (Fourth Genre)

Russell Banks — Notes On Literature and Politics (Salmagundi)

John Landretti — Blessings (Orion)

Eduardo Halfon — Oh Ghetto My Love (Electric Literature)

POETRY

Robert Pinsky — The Foundling Tokens (The American Scholar)

Rajiv Mohabir — Ortolan (The Journal)

C.K. Williams — Mantis (Threepenny Review)

Robert Wrigley — Impeach Reagan (River Styx)

Johannes Göransson — The Heart of Glamour (Denver Quarterly)

Nick Lantz — Posthumanism (Pleiades)

Cate Marvin — High School in Suzhou (New England Review)

Ocean Vuong — To My Father / To My Unborn Son (New England Review)

Laura Eve Engel — Memorial Day (Copper Nickel)

Kathleen Ossip — Innocence: A Memoir (The Rumpus)

Denise Duhamel — Reproduction Pantoum (The Cossack Review)

Albert Goldbarth — Whole Imagining (River Styx)

Katy Didden — C Train Concerto for Two Cellos, with Cavafy (Ecotone)

Noah Warren — Automatic Pool Cleaner (Agni)

Cedric Tillman — The Flag (Rove)

Shaun Robinson — American Men (QWERTY)

Marsha de la O — Antidote for Night (BOA Editions)

Camille T. Dungy — Frequently Asked Questions: 10 (Poetry)

Chen Chen — Tale of the Heart & the Knife (Porkbelly Press)

Lynn Emanuel — The Angels of the Resurrection (Verse Daily online)

Joseph Fasano — Genesis (The Meadow)

Jameson Fitzpatrick — On 5N (Springhouse)

Julian Talamantez Brolaski — in the cut (Nepantla)

Robin Estrin — Bubbe (Chinquapin Literary Magazine)

Jacqueline Woodson — How To Eat To Live (Yarn)

Melissa Stein — Racetrack (The American Poetry Review)

Afaa Michael Weaver — Spirit Boxing (Field)

Jaclyn Dwyer — For Sale: Positive Pregnancy Test, Used (Iron Horse)

Matt Hart — from Radiant Action (Arroyo)

Kay Ryan — Sock (Believer)

Stephen Burt — Esprit Stephanie (The Awl)

Kaveh Akbar — Palmyra (The Offing)

Alejandro Escudé — The Moth (The McNeese Review)

Reggie Scott Young — Back\Strokes (Louisiana Lit.)

Marilyn Nelson — Weeping Baboons (upstreet)

Arseny Tarkovsky, translated by Philip Metres and Dimitri Psurtsev — Ignatievo Forest (Cleveland State University Poetry Center Press)

Billy Collins — Helium (Five Points)

Danusha Laméris — Reading My Valentine's Poem to Frank X. Gaspar (America Poetry Review)

Alice Friman — The Interview (The Southern Review)

Rachel Richardson — Drowning Doesn't Look Like Drowning (The Georgia Review)

Jim Peterson — Second Sight (from *Original Face* / Gun Powder Press)

D.M. Aderibigbe — Pink (Hobart)

James Arthur — Ode to an Encyclopedia (Academy of American Poets)

Xi Chuan — Mourning Problems (Paris Review)

Alberto Ríos — Looking Across the Line (from *A Small Story About the Sky* / Copper Canyon Press)

Safia Elhillo — Watching Arab Idol with Abdelhalim Hafez (One Throne)

PRESSES FEATURED IN THE PUSHCART PRIZE EDITIONS SINCE 1976

A-Minor
The Account
Adroit Journal
Agni
Ahsahta Press
Ailanthus Press
Alaska Quarterly Review
Alcheringa/Ethnopoetics
Alice James Books
Ambergris
Amelia
American Circus
American Letters and Commentary
American Literature
American PEN
American Poetry Review
American Scholar
American Short Fiction
The American Voice
Amicus Journal
Amnesty International
Anaesthesia Review
Anhinga Press
Another Chicago Magazine
Antaeus
Antietam Review
Antioch Review

Apalachee Quarterly
Aphra
Aralia Press
The Ark
Art and Understanding
Arts and Letters
Artword Quarterly
Ascensius Press
Ascent
Aspen Leaves
Aspen Poetry Anthology
Assaracus
Assembling
Atlanta Review
Autonomedia
Avocet Press
The Awl
The Baffler
Bakunin
Bamboo Ridge
Barlenmir House
Barnwood Press
Barrow Street
Bellevue Literary Review
The Bellingham Review
Bellowing Ark
Beloit Poetry Journal

Bennington Review
Bilingual Review
Black American Literature Forum
Blackbird
Black Renaissance Noire
Black Rooster
Black Scholar
Black Sparrow
Black Warrior Review
Blackwells Press
The Believer
Bloom
Bloomsbury Review
Blue Cloud Quarterly
Blueline
Blue Unicorn
Blue Wind Press
Bluefish
BOA Editions
Bomb
Bookslinger Editions
Boston Review
Boulevard
Boxspring
Briar Cliff Review
Brick
Bridge
Bridges
Brown Journal of Arts
Burning Deck Press
Butcher's Dog
Cafe Review
Caliban
California Quarterly
Callaloo
Calliope
Calliopea Press
Calyx
The Canary
Canto
Capra Press
Carcanet Editions
Caribbean Writer
Carolina Quarterly

Cave Well
Cedar Rock
Center
Chariton Review
Charnel House
Chattahoochee Review
Chautauqua Literary Journal
Chelsea
Chicago Quarterly Review
Chouteau Review
Chowder Review
Cimarron Review
Cincinnati Review
Cincinnati Poetry Review
City Lights Books
Cleveland State Univ. Poetry Ctr.
Clown War
Codex Journal
CoEvolution Quarterly
Cold Mountain Press
The Collagist
Colorado Review
Columbia: A Magazine of Poetry and Prose
Conduit
Confluence Press
Confrontation
Conjunctions
Connecticut Review
Copper Canyon Press
Copper Nickel
Cosmic Information Agency
Countermeasures
Counterpoint
Court Green
Crab Orchard Review
Crawl Out Your Window
Crazyhorse
Creative Nonfiction
Crescent Review
Cross Cultural Communications
Cross Currents
Crosstown Books
Crowd
Cue

Cumberland Poetry Review

Curbstone Press

Cutbank

Cypher Books

Dacotah Territory

Daedalus

Dalkey Archive Press

Decatur House

December

Denver Quarterly

Desperation Press

Dogwood

Domestic Crude

Doubletake

Dragon Gate Inc.

Dreamworks

Dryad Press

Duck Down Press

Dunes Review

Durak

East River Anthology

Eastern Washington University Press

Ecotone

El Malpensante

Eleven Eleven

Ellis Press

Empty Bowl

Ep;phany

Epoch

Ergo!

Evansville Review

Exquisite Corpse

Faultline

Fence

Fiction

Fiction Collective

Fiction International

Field

Fifth Wednesday Journal

Fine Madness

Firebrand Books

Firelands Art Review

First Intensity

5 A.M.

Five Fingers Review

Five Points Press

Florida Review

Forklift

The Formalist

Four Way Books

Fourth Genre

Fourth River

Frontiers: A Journal of Women Studies

Fugue

Gallimaufry

Genre

The Georgia Review

Gettysburg Review

Ghost Dance

Gibbs-Smith

Glimmer Train

Goddard Journal

David Godine, Publisher

Graham House Press

Grand Street

Granta

Graywolf Press

Great River Review

Green Mountains Review

Greenfield Review

Greensboro Review

Guardian Press

Gulf Coast

Hanging Loose

Harbour Publishing

Hard Pressed

Harvard Review

Hawaii Pacific Review

Hayden's Ferry Review

Hermitage Press

Heyday

Hills

Hollyridge Press

Holmgangers Press

Holy Cow!

Home Planet News

Hudson Review

Hunger Mountain

Hungry Mind Review
Ibbetson Street Press
Icarus
Icon
Idaho Review
Iguana Press
Image
In Character
Indiana Review
Indiana Writes
Intermedia
Intro
Invisible City
Inwood Press
Iowa Review
Ironwood
Jam To-day
J Journal
The Journal
Jubilat
The Kanchenjunga Press
Kansas Quarterly
Kayak
Kelsey Street Press
Kenyon Review
Kestrel
Lake Effect
Lana Turner
Latitudes Press
Laughing Waters Press
Laurel Poetry Collective
Laurel Review
L'Epervier Press
Liberation
Linquis
Literal Latté
Literary Imagination
The Literary Review
The Little Magazine
Little Patuxent Review
Little Star
Living Hand Press
Living Poets Press
Logbridge-Rhodes

Louisville Review
Lowlands Review
LSU Press
Lucille
Lynx House Press
Lyric
The MacGuffin
Magic Circle Press
Malahat Review
Manoa
Manroot
Many Mountains Moving
Marlboro Review
Massachusetts Review
McSweeney's
Meridian
Mho & Mho Works
Micah Publications
Michigan Quarterly
Mid-American Review
Milkweed Editions
Milkweed Quarterly
The Minnesota Review
Mississippi Review
Mississippi Valley Review
Missouri Review
Montana Gothic
Montana Review
Montemora
Moon Pony Press
Mount Voices
Mr. Cogito Press
MSS
Mudfish
Mulch Press
Muzzle Magazine
N + 1
Nada Press
Narrative
National Poetry Review
Nebraska Poets Calendar
Nebraska Review
Nepantla
New America

New American Review
New American Writing
The New Criterion
New Delta Review
New Directions
New England Review
New England Review and Bread Loaf
    Quarterly
New Issues
New Letters
New Madrid
New Ohio Review
New Orleans Review
New South Books
New Verse News
New Virginia Review
New York Quarterly
New York University Press
Nimrod
9X9 Industries
Ninth Letter
Noon
North American Review
North Atlantic Books
North Dakota Quarterly
North Point Press
Northeastern University Press
Northern Lights
Northwest Review
Notre Dame Review
O. ARS
O. Bl k
Obsidian
Obsidian II
Ocho
Oconee Review
October
Ohio Review
Old Crow Review
Ontario Review
Open City
Open Places
Orca Press

Orchises Press
Oregon Humanities
Orion
Other Voices
Oxford American
Oxford Press
Oyez Press
Oyster Boy Review
Painted Bride Quarterly
Painted Hills Review
Palo Alto Review
Paris Press
Paris Review
Parkett
Parnassus: Poetry in Review
Partisan Review
Passages North
Paterson Literary Review
Pebble Lake Review
Penca Books
Pentagram
Penumbra Press
Pequod
Persea: An International Review
Perugia Press
Per Contra
Pilot Light
The Pinch
Pipedream Press
Pitcairn Press
Pitt Magazine
Pleasure Boat Studio
Pleiades
Ploughshares
Poem-A-Day
Poems & Plays
Poet and Critic
Poet Lore
Poetry
Poetry Atlanta Press
Poetry East
Poetry International
Poetry Ireland Review

Poetry Northwest

Poetry Now

The Point

Post Road

Prairie Schooner

Prelude

Prescott Street Press

Press

Prism

Promise of Learnings

Provincetown Arts

A Public Space

Puerto Del Sol

Purple Passion Press

Quaderni Di Yip

Quarry West

The Quarterly

Quarterly West

Quiddity

Radio Silence

Rainbow Press

Raritan: A Quarterly Review

Rattle

Red Cedar Review

Red Clay Books

Red Dust Press

Red Earth Press

Red Hen Press

Release Press

Republic of Letters

Review of Contemporary Fiction

Revista Chicano-Riqueña

Rhetoric Review

Rivendell

River Styx

River Teeth

Rowan Tree Press

Ruminate

Runes

Russian *Samizdat*

Salamander

Salmagundi

San Marcos Press

Santa Monica Review

Sarabande Books

Sea Pen Press and Paper Mill

Seal Press

Seamark Press

Seattle Review

Second Coming Press

Semiotext(e)

Seneca Review

Seven Days

The Seventies Press

Sewanee Review

Shankpainter

Shantih

Shearsman

Sheep Meadow Press

Shenandoah

A Shout In the Street

Sibyl-Child Press

Side Show

Sixth Finch

Small Moon

Smartish Pace

The Smith

Snake Nation Review

Solo

Solo 2

Some

The Sonora Review

Southern Indiana Review

Southern Poetry Review

Southern Review

Southwest Review

Speakeasy

Spectrum

Spillway

Spork

The Spirit That Moves Us

St. Andrews Press

Storm Cellar

Story

Story Quarterly

Streetfare Journal

Stuart Wright, Publisher
Subtropics
Sugar House Review
Sulfur
Summerset Review
The Sun
Sun & Moon Press
Sun Press
Sunstone
Sweet
Sycamore Review
Tab
Tamagawa
Tar River Poetry
Teal Press
Telephone Books
Telescope
Temblor
The Temple
Tendril
Texas Slough
Think
Third Coast
13th Moon
THIS
Thorp Springs Press
Three Rivers Press
Threepenny Review
Thrush
Thunder City Press
Thunder's Mouth Press
Tia Chucha Press
Tiger Bark Press
Tikkun
Tin House
Tombouctou Books
Toothpaste Press
Transatlantic Review
Treelight
Triplopia
TriQuarterly
Truck Press
Tupelo Review

Turnrow
Tusculum Review
Undine
Unicorn Press
University of Chicago Press
University of Georgia Press
University of Illinois Press
University of Iowa Press
University of Massachusetts Press
University of North Texas Press
University of Pittsburgh Press
University of Wisconsin Press
University Press of New England
Unmuzzled Ox
Unspeakable Visions of the Individual
Vagabond
Vallum
Verse
Verse Wisconsin
Vignette
Virginia Quarterly Review
Volt
The Volta
Wampeter Press
War, Literature & The Arts
Washington Writer's Workshop
Water-Stone
Water Table
Wave Books
West Branch
Western Humanities Review
Westigan Review
White Pine Press
Wickwire Press
Wigleaf
Willow Springs
Wilmore City
Witness
Word Beat Press
Wordsmith
World Literature Today
Wormwood Review
Writers' Forum

Xanadu
Yale Review
Yardbird Reader
Yarrow
Y-Bird

Yes Yes Books
Zeitgeist Press
Zoetrope: All-Story
Zone 3
ZYZZYVA

THE PUSHCART PRIZE

FELLOWSHIPS

The Pushcart Prize Fellowships Inc., a 501 (c) (3) nonprofit corporation, is the endowment for The Pushcart Prize. "Members" donated up to $249 each. "Sponsors" gave between $250 and $999. "Benefactors" donated from $1000 to $4,999. "Patrons" donated $5,000 and more. We are very grateful for these donations. Gifts of any amount are welcome. For information write to the Fellowships at PO Box 380, Wainscott, NY 11975.

SPONSORS

Altman / Kazickas Fdn.
Jacob Appel
Jean M. Auel
Jim Barnes
Charles Baxter
Joe David Bellamy
Laura & Pinckney Benedict
Laure-Anne Bosselaar
Kate Braverman
Barbara Bristol
Kurt Brown
Richard Burgin
David S. Caldwell
Alan Catlin
Mary Casey
Siv Cedering
Dan Chaon
James Charlton
Andrei Codrescu
Linda Coleman
Stephen Corey
Tracy Crow
Dana Literary Society
Carol de Gramont
Nelson DeMille
E. L. Doctorow
Karl Elder
Donald Finkel
Ben and Sharon Fountain
Alan and Karen Furst
John Gill
Robert Giron
Beth Gutcheon
Doris Grumbach & Sybil Pike

Gwen Head
The Healing Muse
Robin Hemley
Bob Hicok
Jane Hirshfield
Helen & Frank Houghton
Joseph Hurka
Diane Johnson
Janklow & Nesbit Asso.
Edmund Keeley
Thomas E. Kennedy
Sydney Lea
Stephen Lesser
Gerald Locklin
Thomas Lux
Markowitz, Fenelon and Bank
Elizabeth McKenzie
McSweeney's
John Mullen
Joan Murray
Barbara and Warren Phillips
Hilda Raz
Stacey Richter
Schaffner Family Foundation
Cindy Sherman
Joyce Carol Smith
May Carlton Swope
Glyn Vincent
Julia Wendell
Philip White
Eleanor Wilner
David Wittman
Richard Wyatt & Irene Eilers

MEMBERS

Anonymous (3)
Stephen Adams
Betty Adcock
Agni
Carolyn Alessio
Dick Allen
Henry H. Allen
John Allman
Lisa Alvarez
Jan Lee Ande
Dr. Russell Anderson
Ralph Angel
Antietam Review
Ruth Appelhof
Philip and Marjorie Appleman
Linda Aschbrenner

Renee Ashley
Ausable Press
David Baker
Catherine Barnett
Dorothy Barresi
Barlow Street Press
Jill Bart
Ellen Bass
Judith Baumel
Ann Beattie
Madison Smartt Bell
Beloit Poetry Journal
Pinckney Benedict
Karen Bender
Andre Bernard
Christopher Bernard

565

Wendell Berry
Linda Bierds
Stacy Bierlein
Big Fiction
Bitter Oleander Press
Mark Blaeuer
John Blondel
Blue Light Press
Carol Bly
BOA Editions
Deborah Bogen
Bomb
Susan Bono
Brain Child
Anthony Brandt
James Breeden
Rosellen Brown
Jane Brox
Andrea Hollander Budy
E. S. Bumas
Richard Burgin
Skylar H. Burris
David Caligiuri
Kathy Callaway
Bonnie Jo Campbell
Janine Canan
Henry Carlile
Carrick Publishing
Fran Castan
Chelsea Associates
Marianne Cherry
Phillis M. Choyke
Lucinda Clark
Suzanne Cleary
Linda Coleman
Martha Collins
Ted Conklin
Joan Connor
J. Cooper
John Copenhaver
Dan Corrie
Pam Cotney
Lisa Couturier
Tricia Currans-Sheehan
Jim Daniels
Daniel & Daniel
Jerry Danielson
Josephine David
Thadious Davis
Maija Devine
Sharon Dilworth
Edward DiMaio
Kent Dixon
A.C. Dorset
Jack Driscoll
Penny Dunning

John Duncklee
Elaine Edelman
Renee Edison & Don Kaplan
Nancy Edwards
Ekphrasis Press
M.D. Elevitch
Elizabeth Ellen
Entrekin Foundation
Failbetter.com
Irvin Faust
Elliot Figman
Tom Filer
Finishing Line Press
Susan Firer
Nick Flynn
Starkey Flythe Jr.
Peter Fogo
Linda Foster
Fourth Genre
John Fulton
Fugue
Alice Fulton
Alan Furst
Eugene Garber
Frank X.Gaspar
A Gathering of the Tribes
Reginald Gibbons
Emily Fox Gordon
Philip Graham
Eamon Grennan
Myrna Goodman
Ginko Tree Press
Jessica Graustain
Lee Meitzen Grue
Habit of Rainy Nights
Rachel Hadas
Susan Hahn
Meredith Hall
Harp Strings
Jeffrey Harrison
Clarinda Harriss
Lois Marie Harrod
Healing Muse
Tim Hedges
Michele Helm
Alex Henderson
Lily Henderson
Daniel Henry
Neva Herington
Lou Hertz
Stephen Herz
William Heyen
Bob Hicok
R. C. Hildebrandt
Kathleen Hill
Jane Hirshfield

Edward Hoagland
Daniel Hoffman
Doug Holder
Richard Holinger
Rochelle L. Holt
Richard M. Huber
Brigid Hughes
Lynne Hugo
Karla Huston
Illya's Honey
Susan Indigo
Mark Irwin
Beverly A. Jackson
Richard Jackson
Christian Jara
David Jauss
Marilyn Johnston
Alice Jones
Journal of New Jersey Poets
Robert Kalich
Sophia Kartsonis
Julia Kasdorf
Miriam Polli Katsikis
Meg Kearney
Celine Keating
Brigit Kelly
John Kistner
Judith Kitchen
Stephen Kopel
Peter Krass
David Kresh
Maxine Kumin
Valerie Laken
Babs Lakey
Linda Lancione
Maxine Landis
Lane Larson
Dorianne Laux & Joseph Millar
Sydney Lea
Donald Lev
Dana Levin
Gerald Locklin
Rachel Loden
Radomir Luza, Jr.
William Lychack
Annette Lynch
Elzabeth MacKiernan
Elizabeth Macklin
Leah Maines
Mark Manalang
Norma Marder
Jack Marshall
Michael Martone
Tara L. Masih
Dan Masterson
Peter Matthiessen

Maria Matthiessen
Alice Mattison
Tracy Mayor
Robert McBrearty
Jane McCafferty
Rebecca McClanahan
Bob McCrane
Jo McDougall
Sandy McIntosh
James McKean
Roberta Mendel
Didi Menendez
Barbara Milton
Alexander Mindt
Mississippi Review
Martin Mitchell
Roger Mitchell
Jewell Mogan
Patricia Monaghan
Jim Moore
James Morse
William Mulvihill
Nami Mun
Joan Murray
Carol Muske-Dukes
Edward Mycue
Deirdre Neilen
W. Dale Nelson
New Michigan Press
Jean Nordhaus
Celeste Ng
Christiana Norcross
Ontario Review Foundation
Daniel Orozco
Other Voices
Pamela Painter
Paris Review
Alan Michael Parker
Ellen Parker
Veronica Patterson
David Pearce, M.D.
Robert Phillips
Donald Platt
Plain View Press
Valerie Polichar
Pool
Horatio Potter
Jeffrey & Priscilla Potter
C.E. Poverman
Marcia Preston
Eric Puchner
Osiris
Tony Quagliano
Quill & Parchment
Barbara Quinn
Randy Rader

Juliana Rew
Belle Randall
Martha Rhodes
Nancy Richard
Stacey Richter
James Reiss
Katrina Roberts
Judith R. Robinson
Jessica Roeder
Martin Rosner
Kay Ryan
Sy Safransky
Brian Salchert
James Salter
Sherod Santos
Ellen Sargent
R.A. Sasaki
Valerie Sayers
Maxine Scates
Alice Schell
Dennis & Loretta Schmitz
Helen Schulman
Philip Schultz
Shenandoah
Peggy Shinner
Lydia Ship
Vivian Shipley
Joan Silver
Skyline
John E. Smelcer
Raymond J. Smith
Joyce Carol Smith
Philip St. Clair
Lorraine Standish
Maureen Stanton
Michael Steinberg
Sybil Steinberg
Jody Stewart
Barbara Stone
Storyteller Magazine
Bill & Pat Strachan
Julie Suk
Summerset Review
Sun Publishing
Sweet Annie Press
Katherine Taylor
Pamela Taylor
Elaine Terranova

Susan Terris
Marcelle Thiebaux
Robert Thomas
Andrew Tonkovich
Pauls Toutonghi
Juanita Torrence-Thompson
William Trowbridge
Martin Tucker
Umbrella Factory Press
Under The Sun
Jeannette Valentine
Victoria Valentine
Christine Van Winkle
Hans Vandebovenkamp
Tino Villanueva
Maryfrances Wagner
William & Jeanne Wagner
BJ Ward
Susan O. Warner
Rosanna Warren
Margareta Waterman
Michael Waters
Stuart Watson
Sandi Weinberg
Andrew Wainstein
Dr. Henry Wenkart
Jason Wesco
West Meadow Press
Susan Wheeler
When Women Waken
Dara Wier
Ellen Wilbur
Galen Williams
Diane Williams
Marie Sheppard Williams
Eleanor Wilner
Irene Wilson
Steven Wingate
Sandra Wisenberg
Wings Press
Robert Witt
David Wittman
Margot Wizansky
Matt Yurdana
Christina Zawadiwsky
Sander Zulauf
ZYZZYVA

SUSTAINING MEMBERS

Stephen Adams
Betty Adcock
Agni
Dick Allen

John Allman
Altman/Kazickas Fdn.
Dr. Russell Anderson
Renee Ashley

Alec Baldwin Fdn.
Ellen Bass
Ann Beattie
John Blondel
Brain Child
Jim Barnes
Big Fiction
Bomb
David Caldwell
Mary Casey
Alan Catlin
Linda Coleman
Stephen Corey
Lucinda Clark
Suzanne Cleary
Martha Collins
J. Cooper
Pam Cotney
Lisa Couturier
Daniel & Daniel
Catherine and C. Bryan Daniels
Jerry Danielson
Josephine David
Nelson DeMille
E.L. Doctorow
Dan Dolgin & Loraine Gardner
A.C. Dorset
Jack Driscoll
Penny Dunning
Elaine Edelman
Maureen Mahon Egen
Ekphrasis Press
Elizabeth Ellen
Entrekin Fdn.
Elliot Figman
Finishing Line Press
Alice Friman
Ben and Sharon Fountain
Fourth Genre
John Fulton
Alan Furst
Frank X. Gaspar
Ginko Tree Review
Robert Giron
Mary Ann Goodman & Bruno Quinson
Myrna Goodman
Beth Gutcheon
Jessica Graustein
Susan Hahn
Clarinda Harriss
Jeffrey Harrison
Tim Hedges
Michele Helm
Stephen Herz
Kathleen Hill
Jane Hirshfield

Rosellen Brown Hoffman
Helen Houghton
Karla Huston
Mark Irwin
Diane Johnson
Don Kaplan
Sophia Kartsonis
Peter Krass
Edmund Keeley
Wally & Christine Lamb
Linda. Lancione
Sydney Lea
Stephen O. Lesser
Dorothy Lichtenstein
William Lychack
Maria Matthiessen
Alice Mattison
Tracy Mayor
Robert McBrearty
Rebecca McClanahan
Rick Moody
John Mullen
Joan Murray
Neltje
New Michigan Press
Celeste Ng
Christiana Norcross
Joyce Carol Oates
Osiris
Daniel Orozco
Pamela Painter
Plain View Press
Horatio Potter
C.E. Poverman
Randy Rader
Elizabeth R. Rea
James Reiss
Juliana Rew
Stacey Richter
Ellen Sargent
Valerie Sayers
Maxine Scates
Schaffner Family Fountain
Alice Schell
Dennis Schmitz
Cindy Sherman
Grace Schulman
Lydia Ship
Charline Spektor
Maureen Stanton
Jody Stewart
Sun Publishing
Summerset Review
Warren & Barbara Phillips
Elaine Terranova
Susan Terris

CONTRIBUTING SMALL PRESSES FOR PUSHCART PRIZE XLI

(These presses made or received nominations for this edition.)

A

A Public Space, 323 Dean St., Brooklyn, NY 11217
aaduna, 144 Genesee St., Ste. 102-259, Auburn, NY 13021
Able Muse Review, 467 Saratoga Ave., #602, San Jose, CA 95129
Accents Publishing, P.O. Box 910456, Lexington, KY 40591-0456
The Account, 408 Washington St., Las Vegas, NV 87701
The Adroit Journal, 1223 Westover Rd., Stamford, CT 06902-1037
Aerogram, PO Box 591164, San Francisco, CA 94159
Agni Magazine, Boston University, 236 Bay State Rd., Boston, MA 02215
Airlie Press, P.O. Box 82653, Portland, OR 97282
Alacrity House Publishing, 695 Main St., Sanford, CO 81151
Alaska Quarterly Review, 3211 Providence Dr., Anchorage, AK 99508-4614
Alexandria Quarterly, P.O. Box 1148, Taos, NM 87571
Algonquin Books of Chapel Hill, 225 Varick St., New York, NY 10014-4381
Alice Blue, 4019 NE 39th Ave., Vancouver, WA 98661
Alice James Books, 114 Prescott St., Farmington, ME 04938
Alligator Juniper, 220 Grove Ave., Prescott, AZ 86301
Alyss, 5946 Alpha Ave., St. Louis, MO 63147
American Chordata, PO Box 797, New York, NY 10163
American Literary Review, 1155 Union Circle, #311307, Denton, TX 76203
The American Scholar, 1606 New Hampshire Ave. NW, Washington, DC 20009
American Short Fiction, PO Box 4152, Austin ,TX 78765
Anomalous Press, 3930 NW Witham Hill Dr., #95K, Corvallis, OR 97330
amomancies magazine, 203 Amy Court, Sterling, VA 20164
Anaphora Literary Press, 2419 Southdale Dr., Hepzibah, GA 30815

Animal, 264 Fallen Palm Dr., Casselberry, FL 32707

Anthropoid Collective, 714 Pinehurst, Midland, TX 79705

The Antioch Review, PO Box 148, Yellow Springs, OH 45387-0148

Antrim House Books, 21 Goodrich Rd., Simsbury, CT 06070

Aperçus Quarterly, 423 S. Ash St., Redlands, CA 92373

Apogee Journal, 418 Suydam St., Apt. 1L, Brooklyn, NY 11237

Appalachian Heritage, Berea College, CPO 2166, Berea, KY 40404

Appalachian Heritage Literary Project, P.O. Box 5000, Shepherdstown, WV 25443

Apple Valley Review, 88 South 3rd St., #336, San José, CA 95113

Aquarius Press, P.O. Box 23096, Detroit, MI 48223

Arcadia Magazine, 1314 S Denver Ave., #2, Tulsa, OK 74119

The Ardent Writer Press, P.O. Box 25, Brownsboro, AL 35741

Arizona Authors, 6939 E Chaparral Rd., Paradise Valley, AZ 85253-7000

Arlington Avenue Books, 927 Prospect St., #333, Honolulu, HI 96822

Arroyo Literary Review, C.S.U. 25800 Carlos Bee Blvd., Hayward, CA 94542

Arsenic Lobster, 1830 W. 18th St., Chicago, IL 60608

Asian American Literary Review, 1110 Severnview Dr., Crownsville, MD 21032

Askew, P.O. Box 559, Ventura, CA 93002

Aster(ix), Univ. of Pittsburgh, 5200 Cathedral of Learning, Pittsburgh, PA 15260

Asymptote, #84, Section 1, Zhongshan North Rd., #13-7. Taipei City 10444, Taiwan

At Length, 716 W. Cornwallis Rd., Durham, NC 27707

Atelier26 Books, 4207 SE Woodstock Blvd., #421, Portland, OR 97206

Atlanta Review, PO Box 8248, Atlanta, GA 31106

Atrocity Exhibition, 3236 Washington School Rd., New Cumberland, WV 26047

Atticus Review, 39 Longview Ave., Madison, NJ 07940

Augury Books, 305 E. 12th St., Apt. 1, New York, NY 10003

The Austin Review, 4700 Hilwin Circle, Austin, TX 78756

Autumn House Press, 87 ½ Westwood St., Pittsburgh, PA 15211

Autumn Sky Poetry Daily, 5263 Arctic Circle, Emmaus, PA 18049

Avignon Press, 41 Shearwater Place, Newport Beach, CA 92660

Awst, P.O. box 49163, Austin, TX 78765-9163

B

The Baltimore Review, 6514 Maplewood Rd., Baltimore, MD 21212

Bamboo Ridge Press, PO Box 61781, Honolulu, HI 96839-1781

Banshee, 18 Pacelli Road, Naas. Co. Kildare, Ireland

Barbaric Yawp, 3700 County Route 24, Russell, NY 13684

Barrelhouse, 793 Westerly Parkway, State College, PA 16801

basalt, Eastern Oregon University, 1 University Blvd., La Grande, OR 97850-2807

Bat City Review, 1 University Station, B 5000, Austin, TX 78712

Bayou Magazine, U.N.O., 2000 Lake Shore Dr., New Orleans, LA 70148

Beachwood Review, 350 W. 53rd St., #4, New York, NY 10014

Beecher's 1445 Jayhawk Blvd., Lawrence, KS 66045

The Believer, 849 Valencia St., San Francisco, CA 94110

Bellevue Literary Review, NYU Medicine, 550 First Ave, OBV-A612, NY, NY 10016

Bellingham Review, MS-9053, WWU, 516 High St., Bellingham, WA 98225

Beloit Fiction Journal, 700 College St., Box 11, Beloit, WI 53511

Beloit Poetry Journal, PO Box 1450, Windham, ME 04062

Belt Magazine, 1810 N. Humboldt Blvd., #2, Chicago, IL 60647

Berkeley Fiction Review, 102 Hearst Gym, MC #4500, UCB, Berkeley, CA 94720

Berkeley Poetry Review, McNichols, 2727 Haste St., Berkeley, CA 94704

Best New Writing, 311 N. Linden Ave., Annapolis, MD 21401

Beyond Baroque Books, 681 Venice Blvd., Venice, CA 90291

Big Big Wednesday Journal, 13 Monroe St., #1, Northampton, MA 01060

Big Muddy, SMSU, One University Plaza, Cape Girardeau, MO 63701

Big Roundtable, Columbia University, 2950 Broadway, New York, NY 10027

Big Table, 383 Langley Rd., #2, Newton Centre, MA 02459

Bigfoot Books, P.O. Box 11553, Honolulu, HI 96828

Birch Brook Press, P.O. Box 81, Delhi, NY 13753

bird's thumb, 701 S. Wells St., #2903, Chicago, IL 60607

Birmingham Poetry Review, English Dept., UAB, Birmingham, AL 35294

BkMk Press, UMKC, 5100 Rockhill Rd., Kansas City, MO 64110-2446

Black Clock, CalArts, 24700 McBean Parkway, Valencia, CA 91355

Black Fox, 336 Grove Ave., Ste. B, Winter Park, FL 32789

Black Lawrence Press, 326 Bigham St., Pittsburgh, PA 15211-1463

Black Poppy Review, 1022 Hisse Dr., San Jacinto, CA 92583

Black Rose Writing, P.O. Box 1540, Castroville, TX 78009

Black Warrior Review, University of Alabama, Box 870170, Tuscaloosa, AL 35487

Blackbird, P.O. Box 843082, Richmond, VA 23284-3082

Blink Ink, P.O. Box 5, North Branford, CT 06471

Blood Pudding Press, 1150 Chapman Lane, Unit 7, Medina, OH 44256

Blue Cubicle Press, P.O. Box 250382, Plano, TX 75025-0382

Blue Fifth Review, 267 Lark Meadow Circle, Bluff City, TN 37618

Blue Heron Review, N66W38350 Deer Creek Ct., Oconomowoc, WI 53066

Blue Mesa Review, UNM, MCS 03-2170, Albuquerque, NM 87131-0001

Blue Monday Review, P.O. Box 34452, Kansas City, MO 64116

Bluestem, English Dept., Eastern Illinois University, Charleston, IL 61920-3011

BOA Editions, 250 North Goodman St., Ste. 306, Rochester, NY 14607

Bodega Magazine, 454 Court St., #3R, Brooklyn, NY 11231

The Boiler, 119 Peach St., Denton, TX 76201

Bomb, 80 Hanson Pl., #703, Brooklyn, NY 11217-1506

Bona Fide Books, PO Box 550278, So. Lake Tahoe, CA 96155

Book Ex Machina, P.O. Box 23595, Nicosia 1685, Cyprus

Booth, English Dept., Butler Univ., 4600 Sunset Ave., Indianapolis, IN 46208

Bop Dear City, 212 Wildoak Dr., Birmingham, AL 35210

Border Crossing, LSSU, 650 W. Easterday Ave., Sault Sainte Marie, MI 49783

Boston Review, P.O. Box 425786, Cambridge, MA 02142

Botticellii Magazine, 5982 Goode Rd., Powell, OH 43065

Bottle of Smoke Press, P.O. Box 66, Wallkill, NY 12589

Bottom Dog Press, P.O. Box 425, Huron, OH 44839

Boulevard, 7507 Byron Place, #1, Saint Louis, MO 63105

Boxcar Poetry Review, 3508 NE 158th Ave., Vancouver, WA 98682

Brain, Child, 341 Newtown Turnpike, Wilton, CT 06897

Brainchild, Kent State Univ., P.O. Box 5190, Kent, OH 44242-0001

The Briar Cliff Review, 3303 Rebecca St., Sioux City, IA 51104-2100

Brick, P.O. Box 609, Stn. P, Toronto, Ontario, M5S 2Y4, Canada

Brick House Books, 306 Suffolk Rd., Baltimore, MD 21218

Brick Road Poetry Press, 513 Broadway, Columbus, GA 31901

Bridge Eight, 11 E. Forsyth St., #1605, Jacksonville, FL 32202

Bridge To Somewhere, 3731 Westover Rd., Fleming Island, FL 32003

Brigantine Media, 211 North Avenue, St. Johnsbury, VT 05819

Brilliant Corners, 700 College Place, Williamsport, PA 17701

Broad River Review, PO Box 7224, Gardner-Webb, Boiling Springs, NC 28017

Broadkill River Press, P.O. Box 63, Milton, DE 19968

Broadstone Books, 418 Ann St., Frankfort, KY 40601-1929

The Broken Shore, 15 Sandspring Dr., Eatontown, MJ 07724

Brooklyn Arts Press, 154 N. 9th St., #1, Brooklyn, NY 11249

The Brooklyn Rail, 845 Hancock St., Brooklyn, NY 11233

Buffalo Almanack, 606 E Sheridan St., Laramie, WY 82070

burntdistrict, 2016 S. 185th St., Omaha, NE 68130

Burrow Press, P.O. Box 533709, Orlando, FL 32853

Busy Signal Press, 16642 Shinedale Dr., Canyon Country, CA 91387

Butcher's Dog, 17 January Courtyard, Gateshead, NE8 2GL, United Kingdom

C

Cactus Heart Press, 31 1/2 A Lyman Rd., Northampton, MA 01060

Cadence Collective, 4763 Deeboyar Ave., Lakewood, CA 90712

Café Irreal, PO Box 87031, Tucson, AZ 85745

Caffeinated Press, 3167 Kalamazoo Ave., SE, Ste. 104, Grand Rapids, MI 49508

cahoodaloodaling, 2681 Conejo Canyon Ct., #37, Thousand Oaks, CA 91362

Caitlin Press, 8100 Alderwood Rd., Halfmoon Bay, VON 1Y1, BC

California Quarterly, 23 Edgecroft Rd., Kensington, CA 94707

The Canyon Country Zephyr, P.O. Box 271, Monticello, UT 84535

The Caribbean Writer, UVI, RR 1, Box 10,000, Kingshill, VI 00850

Catamaran Literary Reader, 1050 River St., #118, Santa Cruz, CA 95060

Catapult, 1140 Broadway, Ste. 704, New York, NY 10001

CCLaP Weekender, 4157 N. Clarendon Ave., #505, Chicago, IL 60613

Central Avenue Publishing, PO Box 254, Point Roberts, WA 98281

Chaffey Review, 5885 Haven Ave., Rancho Cucamonga, CA 91737

Change Seven, P.O. Box 562, Hamptonville, NC 27020

The Chattahoochee Review, 555 North Indian Creek Dr., Clarkston, GA 30021

Chatter House Press, 7915 S. Emerson Ave., Ste. B303, Indianapolis, IN 46237

Chautauqua, UNC Wilmington, 601 South College Rd., Wilmington, NC 28403-5938

Cheap Seats Ticket To Ride, P.O. Box 249, Empire, CO 80438-0249

Chicago Literati, 1017 Pine St., St. Charles, IL 60174

Chicago Quarterly Review, 517 Sherman Ave., Evanston, IL 60202

China Grove Press, 4927 6th Place, Meridian, MS 39305

Chinquapin Literary Magazine, 504 Cayuga St., Santa Cruz, CA 95062

Chiron Review, 522 E. South Ave., St. John, KS 67576-2212

Chronogram, 314 Wall St., Kingston, NY 12401

Cider Press Review, P.O. Box 33384, San Diego, CA 92163

Cimarron Review, Oklahoma State Univ., 205 Morrill Hal, Stillwater, OK 74078

Cincinnati Review, Univ. of Cincinnati, PO Box 210069, Cincinnati, OH 45221-0069

Cirque, 3978 Defiance St., Anchorage, AK 99504

Citron Review, 57 Centre St., Natick, MA 01760

Cleaver Magazine, 8250 Shawnee St., Philadelphia, PA 19118

Clementine Poetry Journal, 855 York Rd., Carlisle, PA 17015

Clerestory, 755 N. 11th St., Laramie, MY 82072

Cleveland State University Poetry Center, 2121 Euclid Ave., Cleveland, OH 44115

Clockhouse, 352 9th St., Brooklyn, NY 11215

Clover, 203 West Holly St., Ste. 306, Bellingham, WA 98225

Coach House Books, 80 bpNichol Lane, Toronto ON M5S 314 Canada

Coal City Review, English Dept., University of Kansas, Lawrence, KS 66045

Coda Quarterly, P.O. Box 257, Thetford Center, VT 05075

The Collagist, Warren Wilson College, PO 9000, CPO 6205, Ashville, NC 28815

Colorado Review, Colorado State Univ., Fort Collins, CO 80523-9105

Columbia Journal, Columbia Univ., 116th St. & Broadway, New York, NY 10027

Comment, 185 Young St., Hamilton, ON L8N 1V9, Canada

Compass Flower Press, 315 Bernadette Dr., Ste. 3, Columbia, MO 65203

Concrete Wolf, P.O. Box 1808, Kingston, WA 98346-1807

Confrontation, English Dept., LIU/Post, Brookville, NY 11548-1300

Conium Press, Gapinski, 124 Nw 22nd Place, #4, Portland, OR 97210

Conjunctions, Bard College, Annandale-on-Hudson, NY 12504-5000

Consequence Magazine, P.O. Box 323, Cohasset, MA 02025

Constellations, 127 Lake View Ave., Cambridge, MA 02138

Copper Canyon Press, PO Box 271, Port Townsend, WA 98368

Coppernickel, University of Colorado, Campus Box 175, Denver, CO 80217-3364

The Copperfield Review, 8828 Elk Grove Way, #101, Las Vegas, NV 89117

Cosmonauts Avenue, 4 Glenwood Ave., Apt. A, Northampton, MA 01060

Cossack Review, 15810 Cherry Blossom Lane, Los Gatos, CA 95032

Court Green, 600 South Michigan Ave., Chicago, IL 60605-1996

Cowfeather Press, P.O. Box 620216, Middleton, WI 53562

Crab Creek Review, P.O. Box 247, Kingston, WA 98346

Crab Fat Magazine, 5485 Woodgate Dr., Columbus, GA 31907

Crab Orchard Review, SIUC, 1000 Faner Drive, MC 4503, Carbondale, IL 62901

Crazyhorse, College of Charleston, 66 George St., Charleston, SC 29424

Creative Nonfiction, 5501 Walnut St., Ste. 202, Pittsburgh, PA 15232

Crisis Chronicles, 3344 W. 105th St., #4, Cleveland, OH 44111

Cross-Cultural Communications, 239 Wynsum Ave., Merrick, NY 11566-4725

Cultural Weekly, 215 W. 6th St., #801, Los Angeles, CA 90014

Cultured Llama, 11 London Road, Teynham, Sittingbourne, Kent ME9 9QW, UK

Cumberland River Review, 333 Murfreesboro Rd., Nashville, IN 37210-2877

CutBank, University of Montana, LA 133, Missoula, MT 59812

Cutthroat, A Journal of the Arts, PO Box 2414, Durango, CO 81302

D

Dalkey Archive Press, 6271 E 535 North Rd., Mclean, IL 61754

Daniel & Daniel Publishers, P.O. Box 2790, McKinleyville, CA 95519

Deadly Chaps, 673 Classon Ave., #1R, Brooklyn, NY 11238

december, P.O. Box 16130, St. Louis, MO 63105

decomP, 726 Carriage Hill Dr., Athens, OH 45701

Deep Water, O'Reilly, 34 McCurtain St., Fermoy, Co. Cork, Ireland

The Delmarva Review, PO Box 544, St. Michaels, MD 21663

Denver Quarterly, English Dept., 2000 E. Ashbury, Denver, CO 80208

Diagram, New Michigan Press, 8058 E. 7th St., Tucson, AZ 85710

Dialogist, 14172 Sacramento St., Fontana, CA 92336

District Lit, 2016 N. Adams St., #312, Arlington, VA 22201

The DMQ Review, 16393 Bonnie Lane, Los Gatos, CA 95032

Dos Gatos Press, 6452 Kola Court Northwest, Albuquerque, NM 87120-4285

drafthorse, Lincoln Memorial University, P.O. Box 2005, Harrogate, TN 37752

Dragonfly Press, P.O. Box 746, Columbia, CA 95310

Driftwood Press, 8804 Tallwood Dr., #24, Austin, TX 78759

drunk in a midnight choir, 4416 NE 10th Ave., Ste. B., Portland, OR 97211

Drunken Boat, c/o Mena, 353 29th Ave., San Francisco, CA 94121

Duende Literary Journal, 5153 Haydenbend Circle, Grapevine, TX 76051

E

ELJ Publications, P.O. Box 904, Washingtonville, NY 10992

Ecotone, UNCW, 601 S. College Rd., Wilmington, NC 28403-3201

Ekphrasis, PO Box 161236, Sacramento, CA 95816-1236

Electric Lit, 1140 Broadway, Ste. 704, New York, NY 10001

Eleven Eleven Journal, 1111 Eighth St., S.F., CA 94107

Empty Oaks, c/o Cummins, 4 Hill Crest, Knowle, Bristol, BS4 2 UN, England

Empty Sink, 2330 Boxer Palm, San Antonio, TX 78213

Encircle Publications, P.O. Box 187, Farmington, ME 04938

The Enigmatist, 104 Bronco Dr., Georgetown, TX 78633

Enizagam, Oakland School for the Arts, 530 18th St., Oakland, CA 94612

Ep;phany Literary Journal, P.O. Box 2132, Sag Harbor, NY 11963

Epoch, 251 Goldwin Smith Hall, Cornell University, Ithaca NY 14853-3201

Escape Into Life, 108 Gladys Drive, Normal, IL 61761

Evansville Review, Creative Writing, 1800 Lincoln Ave., Evansville, IN 47722

Event, PO Box 2503, New Westminster, BC, V3L 5B2, Canada

Exile, PO Box 308, Mount Forest, ON N0G 2L0, Canada

Exit 7, 4810 Alben Barkley Dr., Paducah, KY 42001

Exit 13, Box 423, Fanwood, NJ 07023

Expound, 5824 N. Campbell Ave., Chicago, IL 60659

F

Fablecroft Publishing, P.O. Box 915, Mawson ACT 2607, Australia

Fabula Press, 752 A/2, Block P, New Alipore, Kolkata, West Bengal, India
700053

The Fabulist, 1377 5th Ave., San Francisco, CA 94122

failbetter, 2022 Grove Ave., Richmond, VA 23220

Fairy Tale Review, English Dept., University of Arizona, Tucson, AZ 85721

Falling Star Magazine, 1691 Tiburon Ct., Thousand Oaks, CA 91362

Faultline, English Dept., UC Irvine, Irvine, CA 92697-2650

Feathertale, PO Box 5023, Ottawa, ON K2C 3H3, Canada

Femspec, 1610 Rydalmount Rd., Cleveland Heights, OH 44118

The Feral Press, P.O. Box 358, Oyster Bay, NY 11771

Fiction International, English Dept., SDSU, San Diego, CA 92182-6020

Fiction On The Web, 441 40th St., Brooklyn, NY 11232-3442

Fiddlehead, Box 4400, Univ. New Brunswick, Fredericton, NB E3B 5A3, Canada

Field, 50 North Professor St., Oberlin, OH 44074-1091

Fifth Wednesday, P.O. Box 4033, Lisle, IL 60532-9033

Finishing Line Press, P.O. Box 1626, Georgetown, KY 40324

Firewords, 29 The Crescent, Durham DH6 1EJ, United Kingdom

The First Line, PO Box 250382, Plano, TX 75025-0382

Five Oaks Press, 6 Five Oaks Dr., Newburgh, NY 12550

Five Points, Georgia State University, Box 3999, Atlanta, GA 30302-3999

Flapperhouse, 31 Ocean Parkway, #5J, Brooklyn, NY 11218

Flash, University of Chester, English Dept., Parkgate Rd., Chester, CH1 4BJ, UK

Flash Frontier, 267 Lark Meadow Cr., Bluff City, TN 37618

Fledging Rag, 1716 Swarr Run Rd., J-108, Lancaster, PA 17601

The Flexible Persona, 4582 Kingwood Dr., Ste. E-172, Kingwood, TX 77345

Flint Hills Review, Dept. MLJ, 1 Kellog Circle, Emporia, KS 66801

Flycatcher, 5595 Lake Island Dr., Atlanta, GA 30327

Flyway, English Dept., 206 Ross Hall, Iowa State Univ., Ames, IA 50011

Folded Word, 79 Tracy Way, Meredith, NH 03253

Folder, 344 Grand St., #2K, Brooklyn, NY 11211

Foliate Oak, University of Arkansas, 562 University Dr., Monticello, AR 71656

Fomite, 58 Peru St., Burlington, VT 05401-8606

Foothill, 165 E. 10th St., Claremont, CA 91711

Fordham University Press, 2546 Belmont Ave., University Box L, Bronx, NY 10458

Forge, 1610 S. 22nd, Apt. 1, Lincoln, NE 68502

Four Way Books, P.O. Box 535, Village Station, New York, NY 10014

Fourteen Hills, Creative Writing, 1600 Holloway Ave., San Francisco, CA 94132

Fourth Genre, 235 Bessey Hall, East Lansing, MI 48824-1033

The Fourth River, Chatham University, 1 Woodland Rd., Pittsburgh, PA 15232

Frank Martin Review, 2421 Marian St., Columbia, SC 29201

Free State Review, 3637 Black Rock Rd., Upperco, MO 21155

F(r)iction, 13999 County Rd. 102, Elbert, CO 80106

Front Porch Journal, Texas State Univ., 601 University Dr., San Marcos, TX 78666

Fugue, University of Idaho, 875 Perimeter Dr., MS 1102, Moscow, ID 83844-1102

G

Gargoyle Magazine, 3819 13th St. N., Arlington, VA 22201-4922

Gemini Magazine, PO Box 1485, Onset, MA 02558

The Georgia Review, University of Georgia, Athens, GA 30602-9009

The Gettysburg Review, Gettysburg College, Box 2446, Gettysburg, PA 17325

Ghost Ocean Magazine, 612 W. Magnolia St., #B, Fort Collins, CO 80521

Ghost Town Literary Review, 1516 Myra St., Redlands, CA 92373

Gigantic, 1140 Broadway, #704, Brooklyn, NY 10001-7504

Gigantic Sequins, 209 Avon St., Breaux Bridge, LA 70517

Gingerbread House, Gaffney, 378 Howell Ave., Cincinnati, OH 45220

Gingko Tree Review, Drury University, 900 N. Benton Ave., Springfield, MO 65802

Gival Press, PO Box 3812, Arlington, VA 22203

Glassworks, Writing Arts, Rowan Univ., 201 Mullica Hill Rd., Glassboro, NJ 08028

Glimmer Train Press, P.O. Box 80430, Portland, OR 97280-1430

Glint, Fayetteville State Univ., 1200 Murchison Rd., Fayetteville, NC 28301

Gnarled Oak, 9412 Billingham Trail, Austin, TX 78717

Gobshite Quarterly, 338 NE Roth St., Portland, OR 97211

Gold Man Review, 22218 Elkhorn Pl., Cottonwood, CA 96022

Golden Foothills Press, 1443 E. Washington Blvd., #232, Pasadena, CA 91104

Good Men Project, 252 Marcia Way, Bridgewater, NJ 08807

Gothic and Main Publishing, 29 Butler Place, Northampton, MA 01060

Granta, 12 Addison Ave., Holland Park, London W11 4QR, UK

Graphic Arts Books, P.O. Box 3225, Durango, CO 81302-3225

The Great American Lit Magazine, 11621 Deerfield Dr., Yucaipa, CA 92399

great weather for MEDIA, 515 Broadway, #2B, New York, NY 10012

Green Dragon Books, 2875 S. Ocean Blvd., Palm Beach, FL 33480

Green Mountains Review, Johnson State, 337 College Hill, Johnson VT 05656

Green Writers Press, 34 Miller Rd., West Brattleboro, VT 05301

The Greensboro Review, UNC Greensboro, Greensboro, NC 27402-6170

The Greensilk Journal, 221 Shenandoah Ave., Winchester, VA 2260

Grist, 301 McClung Tower, Univ. of Tennessee, Knoxville, TN 37996

Guernica Magazine, 112 W 27th St., Ste 600, New York, NY 10001

Gulf Coast, University of Houston, Houston, TX 77204-3013

Gulf Stream, 3000 NE 151st St., ACI-335, North Miami, FL 33181

Gyroscope Review, 1891 Merrill St., Roseville, MN 55113

H

Haight Ashbury Literary Journal, 558 Joost Ave., San Francisco, CA 94127

Hamilton Arts & Letters, 92 Stanley Ave., Hamilton ON, L8P 2L3, Canada

Hamilton Stone Review, P.O. Box 457, Jay, NY 12941

Hampden-Sydney Poetry Review, Box 66, Hampden-Sydney, VA 23943

Hand Type Press, P.O. Box 3941, Minneapolis, MN 55403-0941

Happa Pappa Press, PO Box 27401, Oakland, CA 94602-0901

Harbour Publishing Co., P.O. Box 219, Madeira Park, BC V0N 2H0 Canada

Harvard Review, Houghton Library, Harvard Univ., Cambridge, MA 02138

Hawai'i Pacific Review, 1060 Bishop St., Honolulu, HI 96813

Hayden's Ferry Review, P.O. Box 870302, Tempe, AZ 85287-0302

Headmistress Press, P.O. Box 275, Eagle Rock, MO 65641

The Healing Muse, 618 Irving Ave., Syracuse, NY 13210

Heavy Feather Review, 803 N Front St., #1, Marquette, MI 49855

Hedgehog Review, Univ. of Virginia, P.O. Box 400816, Charlottesville, VA 22904

Helen, 6650 S. Sandhill Rd., #231, Las Vegas, NV 89120

Hevria, 450 Montgomery, #1, Brooklyn, NY 11225

Heyday, P.O. Box 9145, Berkeley, CA 94709

Hidden Charm Press, 246 South Huntington Ave., #9, Jamaica Plain, MA 02130

Hidden Clearing Books, 6768 Real Princess Lane, Gwynn Oak, MD 21207

High Country News, P.O. Box 1090, Paonia, CO 81428

Hinchas de Poesia Press, 11932 Venice Blvd., Los Angeles, CA 90066

Hip Pocket Press, 5 Del Mar Court, Orinda, CA 94563

Hippocampus Magazine, 222 E. Walnut St., #2, Lancaster, PA 17602

Hobart, PO Box 1658, Ann Arbor, MI 48106

Hold, c/o SPD, 1341 Seventh St., Berkeley, CA 94710

The Hollins Critic, P.O. Box 9538, Roanoke, VA 24020-1538

Hot Metal Bridge, Univ. of Pittsburgh, 4200 Fifth Ave., Pittsburgh, PA 15260

The Hudson Review, 33 West 67th St., New York, NY 10023

Huizache, UHV University Center, #301, 3007 N. Ben Wilson, Victoria, TX 77901

Hunger Mountain, Vermont College, 36 College St., Montpelier, VT 05602

Hypertrophic Press, P.O. Box 423, New Market AL 35761

I

I-70 Review, 5021 S. Tierney Dr., Independence, MO 64055

Ibbetson Street Press, 25 School Street, Somerville, MA 02143

Ice Cube Press, 205 N. Front St., North Liberty, IA 52317

Idaho Magazine, 1106 W. State St., Ste. B., Boise, ID 83702

The Idaho Review, Boise State Univ., 1910 University Dr., Boise, ID 83725

IDK Magazine, 5412 Black St., Pittsburgh, PA 15206

If and only If, 4030 Park Blvd., Oakland, CA 94602

IFANCA, 55 W. Van Buren St., #220, Chicago, IL 60605

The Ilanot Review, English Dept., Bar-Ilan University, Ramat Gan 5290002, Israel

Illuminations, College of Charleston, 66 George St., Charleston, SC 29424

Illya's Honey, PO Box 700865, Dallas, TX 75370

Image, 3307 Third Avenue West, Seattle, WA 98119

Immagine&Poesia, C. Galileo Ferraris 75, 10128, Torino, Italy

Indiana Review, 1020 E. Kirkwood Ave., Bloomington, IN 47405-7103

Indiana Voice Journal, 3038 E. Clem Rd., Anderson, IN 46017

Indianola Review, 1616 West Salem Ave., Indianola, IA 50125

Inlandia, 4178 Chestnut St., Riverside, CA 92501

Insomnia & Obsession, English Dept., University of Akron, Akron, OH 44325-1906

Intellectual Refuge, 1343 McCollum St., Los Angeles, CA 90026

Intima, 43 Bruckner Blvd., #3, Bronx, NY 10454

Into the Teeth of the Wind, Creative Studies, UCSB, Santa Barbara, CA 93106

Intranslation, 85 Hancock St., Brooklyn, NY 11233

Inverness Almanac, PO Box 712, Inverness, CA 94937

Invisible, P.O. Box 539, Marmora, ON K0K 2M0, Canada

The Iowa Review, 308 EPB, University of Iowa, Iowa City, IA 52242

Iowa Source, 108 W. Broadway, Fairfield, IA 52556

Iron Horse, English Dept., Texas Tech Univ., Lubbock, TX 79409-3091

Ishaan, Collin County College, 2800 E. Spring Creek Pkwy, Plano, TX 75074

Isthmus, PO Box 16742, Seattle, WA 98116

J

J Journal, 524 West 59th St., 7th fl, NY, NY 10019

Jabberwock Review, MSU., P.O. Box E, Mississippi State, MS 39762

Jacar Press, 6617 Deerview Trail, Durham, NC 27712

Jaded Ibis Press, English Dept., FSU, 100 State St., Framingham, MA 01702

Jam Tarts, 294 Arroyo Ave., San Leandro, CA 94577

Jane's Boy Press, 219 Arlington St., Watertown, NY 13601

Jelly Bucket, 521 Lancaster Ave., Case Annex 467, Richmond, KY 40475

Jellyfish Magazine, 235 South St., #2, Northampton, MA 01060

Jellyfish, Mediterania Garden Residences D15KE, TJD, 11470 Jakarta, Indonesia

Jerkpoet, 217 Central Ave., #3, Brooklyn, NY 11221

Jersey Devil Press, 1507 Dunmore St. SW, Roanoke, VA 24015

Jewish Fiction, 378 Walmer Rd., Toronto, ON M5R 2Y4, Canada

Jewish Women's Literary Annual, 40 Central Park So., #6D, New York, NY 10019

The Journal, Ohio State Univ., 164 Annie & John Glenn Ave., Columbus, OH 43210

Jubilat, 482 Bartlett Hall, Univ. of Mass., Amherst, MA 01003

JuJuBes, 604 Vale St., Bloomington, IL 61701

Juked, 3941 Newdale Rd., #26, Chevy Chase, MD 20815

JuxtaProse, 339 West 2nd South, #204, Rexburg, ID 83440

K

Kaleidoscope, UDS, 701 S, Main St., Akron, OH 44311

Kelsay Books, 24600 Mountain Avenue 35, Hemet, CA 92544

Kelsey Review, MCCC, 1200 Old Trenton Rd., West Windsor, NJ 08550-3407

Kenyon Review, Finn House, 102 W. Wiggin St., Gambier, OH 43022

Kerf, College of Redwoods, 883 West Washington Blvd., Crescent City, CA 95531

Keyrelm Books, 713 Park Ave., Woodbury, NY 11797

Kind of a Hurricane, Press, 1817 Green Place, Ormond Beach, FL 32174

Kindred, PO Box 80142, Baton Rouge, LA 70898

Knot Magazine, 721 E. 8th, Springfield, CO 81073

Koehler Books, 210 60th St., Virginia Beach, VA 23451

Kolob Canyon Review, 351 W. Center St., Cedar City, UT 84720

Kore Press, PO Box 42315, Tucson AZ 85733-2315

Korean Expatriate Literature, 11533 Promenade Drive, Santa Fe Springs, CA 90670

Kudzu House Quarterly, 1019 NW 10th Ave., Gainesville, FL 32601

Kweli Journal, P.O. Box 693, New York, NY 10021

KY Story, 2111B Fayette Dr., Richmond, KY 40475

KYSO Flash, P.O. Box 1385, Marysville, WA 98270

L

La Vague Journal, 7809 Estancia St., Carlsbad, CA 92009

Labello Press, Unit 4C, Gurtnafleur Business Park, Clonmel, Tipperary, Ireland

The Labletter, 3712 N. Broadway, #241, Chicago, IL 60613

The Lake, 11 Durbin Rd., Chessington, KT9 1BU, UK

Lake Effect, 4951 College Drive, Erie, PA 16563-1501

Lavender Review, P.O. Box 275, Eagle Rock, MO 65641-0275

Leaf Press, Box 416, Lantzville, BC, V0R 2H0 Canada

Light, 1515 Highland Ave., Rochester, NY 14618

Lime Hawk, 10 Cross Highway, Redding, CT 06896

Limestone Journal, English, 1215 Patterson Office Tower, Lexington, KY 40506

Lincoln Center Theater Review, 150 West 65 St., New York, NY 10023

The Lindenwood Review, 209 S. Kingshighway, St. Charles, MO 63301-1695

Lines + Stars, 1801 Clydesdale Pl., NW, Ste. 323, Washington, DC 20009

The Linnet's Wings, 30 The Park, Lakepoint, Mullingar, Co. Westmeath, ROI

Lips, P.O. Box 616, Florham Park, NJ 07932

Literal Latté, 200 E. 10th St., Ste. 240, New York, NY 10003

Literary House Press, Washington College, 300 Washington Ave., Chesterton, MD 21620-1197

Little Fiction, 24 Southport St., #353, Toronto, ON M6S 4Z1, Canada

Little Patuxent Review, 5008 Brampton Pkwy, Ellicott City, MD 21043

Little Star, 107 Bank St., New York, NY 10014

The Lives You Touch, P.O. Box 276, Gwynedd Valley, PA 19437-0276

The Lonely Crowd, 62 Kings Rd., Pontcanna, Cardiff, CF11 9DD, Wales

Los Angeles Review of Books, 6671 Sunset Blvd., Ste. 1521, Los Angeles, CA 90028

Lost Horse Press, 105 Lost Horse Lane, Sandpoint, ID 83864

Lotus-Eater, Via F. Coletti 2, 00191 Roma (RM) Italy

Louisiana Literature, SLU 10792, Hammond, LA 70118

The Louisville Review, Spalding Univ., 851 South Fourth St., Louisville, KY 40203

Loving Healing Press Inc., 5145 Pontiac Trail, Ann Arbor, MI 48105-9279

Lowestoft Chronicle Press, 1925 Massachusetts Ave., Cambridge, MA 02140

Lucid Moose Lit, 1386 E. Hellman St., #1, Long Beach, CA 90813

Lumina, 1 Mead Way, Bronxville, NY 10708

Lunch Ticket, Antioch University, 400 Corporate Pointe, Culver City, CA 90230

M

The MacGuffin, 18600 Haggerty Rd., Livonia, MI 48152

Madcap Review, 3030 Verdin Ave., Cincinnati, OH 45211

Maine Review, P.O. Box 373, Cape Neddick, ME 03902

Malahat, University of Victoria, Box 1700, Stn CSC, Victoria BC V8W 2Y2, Canada

Manhattan Review, 440 Riverside Dr., #38, New York, NY 10027

Map Literary, William Patterson Univ., 300 Pompton Rd., Wayne, NJ 07470-2103

Marathon Literary Review, 362 Dupont St., Philadelphia, PA 19128

Marin Poetry Center, P.O. Box 9091, San Rafael, CA 94912

Massachusetts Review, Photo Lab 309, 211 Hicks Way, Amherst, MA 01003

Masters Review, 1824 NW Couch St., Portland, OR 97209-2119

Matchbook, 9 Dana St., #1, Cambridge, MA 02138

Math Paper Press, 1223 Westover Rd., Stamford, CT 06902

Mayhaven Publishing, P.O. Box 557, Mahomet, IL 61853

Mayo Review, Texas A&M University, PO Box 3011, Commerce, TX 75429

The McNeese Review, MSU Box 93465, Lake Charles, LA 70609-3465

McSweeney's, 849 Valencia St., San Francisco, CA 94110

The Meadow, English Dept., VISTA B300, 7000 Dandini Blvd., Reno, NV 89512

Meerkat Press, 3123 Woodwalk Trace SE, Atlanta, GA 30339

Memorious, c/o Frank, 118 College Dr., #5037, Hattiesburg, MS 39406

Meridian, University of Virginia, P.O. Box 400145, Charlottesville, VA 22904

Miami University Press, English Dept., 356 Bachelor Hall, Oxford, OH 45056

Michigan Quarterly Review, 915 E. Washington St., Ann Arbor, MI 48109-1070

Michigan Writers, P.O. Box 2355, Traverse City, MI 49685

Mid-American Review, Bowling Green State Univ., Bowling Green, OH 43403

Midway Journal, 77 Liberty Ave., #10, Somerville, MA 02144

Midwestern Gothic, 957 E. Grant, Des Plaines, IL 60016

Military Experience & the Arts, Inc., PO Box 821, Morgantown, WV 26507

Milkweed, 1011 Washington Avenue So, Ste. 300, Minneapolis, MN 55415

The Millions, 701 Highland Ave. NE., Atlanta, GA 30312

the minnesota review, Virginia Tech, ASPECT, Blacksburg, VA 24061

MiPOesias, 322 E. Micheltorena, #32, Santa Barbara, CA 93101

Misfit Magazine, 143 Furman St., Schenectady, NY 12304

The Missing Slate, 29 Disbrow Lane, New Rochelle, NY 10804

Mississippi Review, USM, Hattiesburg, MS 39406

Missouri Review, 357 McReynolds Hall, Univ. of Missouri, Columbia, MO 65211

Mobius, the Journal of Social Change, 149 Talmadge, Madison, WI 53707

Molotov Cocktail, 1218 NE 24th Ave., Portland, OR 97232

The Mondegreen, 641 North Highland Ave., NE, #7, Atlanta, GA 30306

Monkeybicycle, 611-B Courtland St., Greensboro, NC 27401

Moon City, English Dept., MSU, 901 South National Ave., Springfield, MO 65897

Moonpath Press, P.O. Box 1808, Kingston, WA 98346-1807

Moonrise Press, 8644 Le Berthon St., Sunland, CA 91040

The Morning News, 234 Meserole St., #3, Brooklyn, NY 11211

Moss, 30 Columbia Pl., #A00F, Brooklyn, NY 11201

Mothers Always Write, P.O. Box 282, East Greenwich, RI 02818

Mount Hope, Roger Williams Univ., One Old Ferry Rd., Bristol, RI 02809

Mouse Prints, 43200 Yale Ct., Lancaster, CA 93536-5375

Mouse Tales Press, 19558 Green Mountain Dr., Newhall, CA 91321

Mud Season Review, 1283 Snipe Ireland Rd., Richmond VT 05477

Muddy River Poetry Review, 15 Eliot St., Chestnut Hill, MA 02467

Mulberry Fork Review, 95 County Rd., S21, Hanceville, AL 35077

Muse-Pie Press, 73 Pennington Ave., Passaic, NJ 07055
Muzzle, 262 State St., #3, New Haven, CT 06510

N

N + 1 Magazine, 68 Jay St., #405, Brooklyn, NY 11201
NANO Fiction, 2630 Bissonnet, #5155, Houston, TX 77005
Narrative, 2443 Fillmore St., #214, San Francisco, CA 94115
Narrative Northeast, 384 Bloomfield Ave., Verona, NJ 07044
A Narrow Fellow, 4302 Kinloch Rd., Louisville, KY 40207
Nat. Brut, 5995 Summerside Dr., Unit 796032, Dallas, TX 75379
Nat'l Federation of State Poetry Societies, 22614 N. Santiam Hwy, Lyons, OR 97358
Natural Bridge, English Dept., One University Blvd., St. Louis, MO 63121-4400
Naugatuck River Review, PO Box 368, Westfield, MA 01086
Nepantla, 579 Franklin Ave., Apt. 3, Brooklyn, NY 11238
Never Mind the Press, P.O. Box 8106, Berkeley, CA 94707
New Directions, 80 8th Avenue, Floor 19, New York, NY 10011-7146
New England Review, Middlebury College, Middlebury, VT 05753
The New Guard, P.O. Box 5101, Hanover, NH 03755
New Issues, MS 5463, 1903 W. Michigan Ave., Kalamazoo, MI 49008
New Lit Salon Press, 513 Vista on the Lake, Carmel, NY 10512
New Madrid, FH Suite 7C, Murray State University, Murray, KY 42071
New Millennium Writings, 4021 Garden Dr., Knoxville, TN 37918
New Native Press, P.O. Box 2554, Cullowhee, NC 28723
New Ohio Review, Ohio University, 360 Ellis Hall, Athens, OH 45701
New Orleans Review, Loyola Univ., 6363 St. Charles Ave., New Orleans, LA 70118
The New Orphic Review, 706 Mill St., Nelson, B.C. V1L 4S5 Canada
New Pop Lit, 400 Bagley, #1953, Detroit, MI 48226
New Rivers Press, 1104 7th Ave. S., Moorhead, MN 56563
new south, Campus Box 1894, Georgia State Univ., Atlanta, GA 30303-3083
New Southerner, 375 Wood Valley Lane, Louisville, KY 40299
New Verse News, Les Belles Maisons H-11, Jl. Serpong Raya, Serpong Utara, Tangerang-Baten 15310, Indonesia
New World Writing, 10 Rachel Vincent Way, Buffalo, NY 14216
Newfound Journal, 6408 Burns St., #209, Austin, TX 78752
Newtown Literary, 61-15 97th St., Rego Park, NY 11374
Night Ballet Press, 123 Glendale Court, Elyria, OH 44035
Nightblade, 11323 126th St., Edmonton, AB T5M 0R5, Canada
Nightjar Press, 63 Ballbrook Court, Wilmslow Rd., Manchester M20 3GT, UK
Nimrod, 800 South Tucker Dr., Tulsa, OK 74104

918 Studio, PO Box 820, Le Claire, IA 52753

Ninebark Press, 3 Central Plaza, Box 356, Rome, GA 30161

Ninety-Six Press, Furman University, 3300 Poinsett Hwy, Greenville, SC29613-4100

Ninth Letter, 608 S. Wright St., Urbana, IL 61801

No Tokens, 300Mercer St., #26E, New York, NY 10003

Noon, 1324 Lexington Ave., PMB 298, New York, NY 10128

The Normal School, 5245 N. Backer Ave., M/S PB 98, Fresno, CA 93740-8001

North American Review, Univ. of Northern Iowa, Cedar Falls, IA 50614-0516

North Carolina Literary Review, ECU Mailstop 555, Greenville, NC 27858-4353

North Dakota Quarterly, 276 Centennial Drive, Grand Forks, ND 58202-7209

Northampton House Press, 7018 Wild Flower Lane, Franktown, VA 23354

Northwestern University Press, 629 Noyes St., Evanston, IL 60208-4170

Notre Dame Review, B009C McKenna Hall, UND, Notre Dame, IN 46556

O

O-Dark-Thirty, 5812 Morland Drive No., Adamstown, MD 21710

Obsidian, Illinois State Univ., Campus Box 4241, Normal, IL 61790-4241

Ocean State Review, U.R.I., 60 Upper College Rd., Kingston, RI 02881

OCHO, 2542 35th St., Apt. R, Astoria, NY 11103

Off the Coast, PO Box 14, Robbinston, ME 04671

Ofi Press, 94 Matamoros, Tlalpan Centro, Tlalpan, D. F., C.P., 14000, Mexico

Old Mountain Press, P.O. Box 66, Webster, NC 28788

OMG! Press, 482 40th St., #6, Oakland, CA 94609

Onager Editions, P.O. Box 89, Ithaca, NY 14851-0849

One Story, 232 3rd St., #A108, Brooklyn, NY 11215

One Teen Story, 232 3rd St., #A108, Brooklyn, NY 11215

One Throne, P.O. Box 1437, Dawson, YT, Y0B 1G0, Canada

Ooligan Press, PO Box 751, Portland, OR 97207

Oregon Humanities, 921 SW Washington St., #150, Portland, OR 97205

Origami Poems Project, 1948 Shore View Dr., Indialantic, FL 32903

Orion Magazine, 187 Main St., Great Barrington, MA 01230

Orphios, 1035 Pike Dr., Colorado Springs, CO 80904

Osiris, 106 Meadow Lane, Greenfield, MA 01301

Otter Magazine, 218 W. Colorado Ave., Unit D, Trinidad, CO 81082

Outer Banks Magazine, P.O. Box 10, Nags Head, NC 27959

Outpost 19, 301 Coleridge St., San Francisco, CA 94110

Outrider Press, Inc., 2036 North Winds Drive, Dyer, IN 46311

Oxford American, P.O. Box 3235, Little Rock, AR 72203-3235

Oxford Magazine, 356 Bachelor Hall, 301 S. Patterson Ave., Oxford, OH 45056

Oyez Review, Roosevelt Univ., Literature & Languages, Chicago, IL 60605-1394

Oyster Boy Review, P.O. Box 1483, Pacifica, CA 94044

P

P.R.A. Publishing, PO Box 211701, Martinez, GA 30917

Pacific Coast Poetry Series, 313 N Avenue 66, Los Angeles, CA 90042

Painted Bride Quarterly, Drexel Univ., 3141 Chestnut St., Phila., PA 19104-2875

Parcel, 6 E. 7th St., Lawrence, KS 66044

The Paris Review, 544 West 27th St., New York, NY 10001

Parody, 4609 N. Gantenbein Ave., Portland, OR 97217

Passages North, English Dept., N.M.U., Marquette, MI 49855-5363

Paterson Literary Review, 1 College Blvd., Paterson, NJ 07505-1179

Pebblebrook Press, P.O. Box 1254, Sheboygan, WI 53082-1254

The Pedestrian Press, 1727 10th St., Oakland, CA 94607

Pembroke Magazine, P.O. Box 1510, Pembroke, NC 28372-1510

Pen Women Press, 650 Diamond Leaf Lane, Houston, TX 77079-6105

Perihelion, 133 Akron St., Rochester, NY 14609

Permafrost, Univ. of Alaska, P.O. Box 755720, Fairbanks, AK 99775-0640

Perugia Press, PO Box 60364, Florence, MA 01062

The Petigru Review, 4840 Forest Dr., Ste. 6B, PMB 189, Columbia, SC 29206

Phantom Drift, P.O. Box 3235, La Grande, OR 97850

Phoebe, George Mason University, 4400 University Place, Fairfax, VA 22030

Phoenicia Publishing, 207-5425 de Bordeaux, Montreal QC H2H 2P9, Canada

Phrygian Press, 58-09 205th St., Bayside, NY 11364

The Pickled Body, 54 Manor St., Dublin7, Ireland

Pilgrimage, Colorado State University, 2200 Bonforte Blvd., Pueblo, CO 81001

The Pinch, English Dept., 467 Patterson Hall, Memphis, TN 38152-3510

Pine Mountain Sand & Gravel, 6203 Erie Ave., Cincinnati, OH 45227

Pinwheel, 733 Summit Ave. E., Seattle, WA 98102

Pinyon Publishing, 23847 V66 Trail, Montrose, CO 81403

Pirene's Fountain, 3616 Glenlake Dr., Glenview, IL 60026

Pithead Chapel, 1300 S. 23rd St., Apt. A, Lincoln, NE 68502

Pizza Pi Press, 194 Winthrop St., Medford, Ma 02155

The Places We've Been, 1305 S. Michigan Ave., #1510, Chicago, IL 60605

Plain View Press, 1101 W. 34th St., Ste. 404, Austin, TX 78705

Pleiades, Univ. of Central Missouri, English Dept., Warrensburg, MO 64093-5069

Plentitude Magazine, 3023 Grauman Rd., Roberts Creek, BC V0N 2W1, Canada

Ploughshares, Emerson College, 120 Boylston St., Boston, MA 02116-4624

PMS, poemmemoirstory, University of Alabama, HB 217,1530 3rd Avenue So, Birmingham, AL 35294-1260

Poecology, 109 McFarland, #418, Stanford, CA 94305

Poemeleon, 5755 Durango Rd., Riverside, CA 92506

Poet Lore, 4508 Walsh St., Bethesda, MD 20815

poeticdiversity, 6028 Comey Ave., Los Angeles, CA 90034

Poetry Box, 2228 NW 159th Pl., Beaverton, Or 97006

Poetry, 61 West Superior St., Chicago, IL 60654

Poetry Northwest, 2000 Tower St., Everett, WA 98201-1390

Poetry Pacific, 1550 68th Ave. W., Vancouver, BC V6P 2V5 Canada

The Poetry Porch, 158 Hollett St., Scituate, MA 02086

Poetry South, MVSU 7242,14000 Hwy 82 West, Itta Bena, MS 38941-1400

The Poet's Billow, 6135 Avon St., Portage, MI 49008

The Poet's Haven, P.O. Box 1501, Massillon, OH 44648

Poets and Artists, 604 Vale St., Bloomington, IL 61701-5620

Poets Wear Prada, 533 Bloomfield St., #2, Hoboken, NJ 07030-4960

The Point, 2 N. LaSalle St., Ste. 2300, Chicago, IL 60602

Pole to Pole Publishing, 5312 Brandy Dr., Mount Airy, MD 21771

Pond Road Press, 221 Channing St. NE, Washington, DC 20002

Pool, 11500 San Vicente Blvd., #224, Los Angeles, CA 90049

Porkbelly Press, 5046 Relleum Ave., Cincinnati, OH 45238

Port Yonder Press, 6332 33rd Avenue Dr., Shellsburg, IA 52332

Posit, 245 Sullivan St., #8A, New York, NY 10012

Post Road, Boston College, 140 Commonwealth Ave., Chestnut Hill, MA 02467

Potomac Review, 51 Manakee St., MT/212, Rockville, MD 20850

Pouch, 4186 Beryl Dr., Bellbrook, OH 45305

Prairie Journal Trust, 28 Crowfoot Terrace NW, P.O. Box 68073, Calgary, AB, T3G 3N8, Canada

Prairie Schooner, UNL, 123 Andrews Hall, Lincoln, NE 68588-0334

Prelude, 589 Flushing Ave., #3E, Brooklyn, NY 11206

Presa Press, PO Box 792, Rockford, MI 49341

Press 53, P.O. Box 30314, Winston-Salem, NC 27130

Pretty Owl Poetry, 4133 Windsor St., #2, Pittsburgh, PA 15217

Prick of the Spindle, P.O. Box 170607, Birmingham, AL 35217

Prime Number Magazine, 1853 Old Greenville Ave., Staunton, VA 24401

Prism International, UBC, Buch E462 – 1866 Main Mall, Vancouver BC V6T 1Z1, Canada

Prism Review, University of La Verne, 1950 Third St., La Verne, CA 91750

Prodigal, 18082 Grassy Knoll Dr., Westfield, IN 46074

Profane, 7600 Heatherstone Dr., Lot 9, Athens, OH 45701

Progenitor, A.C.C., Campus Box 9002, 5900 S. Santa Fe Dr., Littleton, CO 80160

Prospect Park Books, 2359 Lincoln Ave., Altadena, CA 91001

Provincetown Arts, 650 Commercial St., Provincetown, MA 02657

Provo Canyon Review, 4006 N. Canyon Rd., Provo, UT 84604

Proximity, 6316 Morrowfield Ave., Pittsburgh, PA 15217

Prufrock, 201 Herald Pl., 2 Tamboerskloof Rd., Tamboerskloof 8001, South Africa

Puddingstone, 113 Cross Keys Rd., #C, Baltimore, MY 21210

Pulp Literature Press, 8336 Manson Ct., Burnaby, BC V5A 2C4, Canada

Puritan, 179 Gilmour Ave., #2, Toronto, ON M6P 3B2, Canada

Purple Passion Press, 15466 Los Gatos Blvd., Ste. 109, Los Gatos, CA 95032

Q

Qu Literary Magazine, P.O. Box 195, Alderson, WV 24910

Quarterly West, 554 Portland Ave., St. Paul, MN 55102

Quiddity, Benedictine University, 1500 N. Fifth St., Springfield, IL 62702

Quiet Lightning, c/o E. Karp, 734 Balboa St., SF, CA 94118

Quill and Parchment Press, 1825 Echo Park Ave., Los Angeles, CA 90026

Qwerty, UNB Fredericton, P.O. Box 4440, Fredericton, NB, E3B 5A3 Canada

R

r.kv.r.y literary journal, Lockport, NY 14094

Rabbit Catastrophe Press, 147 N. Limestone, Lexington, KY 40507

Radar Poetry, 19 Coniston Ct., Princeton, NJ 08540

Radius, 65 Paine St., #2, Worcester, MA 01605

Raleigh Review, Box 6725, Raleigh, NC 27628

Rappahannock Review, 426 N. 32nd St., Richmond, VA 23223

Rare Bird Books, 453 South Spring St., Ste. 302, Los Angeles, CA 90013

Raritan: A Quarterly Review, Rutgers, 31 Mine St., New Brunswick, NJ 08901

Rat's Ass Review, 3035 Chimney Ridge, Perkinsville, VT 05151

Rattle, 12411 Ventura Blvd., Studio City, CA 91604

Rattling Wall, PO Box 6037, Beverly Hills, CA 90212

Raven Chronicles, 15528 12th Avenue NE, Shoreline, WA 98155

Recovery Diaries, 1500 Locust St., Ste. 1801, Philadelphia, PA 19102

Red Bridge Press, 667 2nd Avenue, San Francisco, CA 94118

Red Dashboard Publications, 4408 Sayre Drive, Princeton, NJ 08540

Red Dragonfly Press, 307 Oxford St,, Northfield, MN 55057

Red Fez, 304 W. 15th St., Georgetown, IL 61846

Red Hen Press, PO Box 40820, Pasadena, CA 91114

Red River Review, 4669 Mountain Oak St., Fort Worth, TX 76244-4397
Red Savina Review, 409 Florence, Silver City, NM 88061
Red Wheelbarrow, Weisner, 528 Windham St., Santa Cruz, CA 95062
Redactions, 604 N. 31st Ave., Apt. D-2, Hattiesburg, MS 39401
Redivider, Emerson College, 120 Boylston St., Boston, MA 02116
Referential Magazine, 21B Morton Rd., Bryn Mawr, PA 19010
Rescue Press, 605 Center St., Iowa City, IA 52245
Rhino, 5007 S. Dorchester Ave., #2S, Chicago, IL 60615
Ricochet Editions, USC Dornsife, Taper Hall #404, Los Angeles, CA 90089-0354
The Riding Light Review, 5142 Hollister Ave., #42, Santa Barbara, CA 93101
Right Hand Pointing, 3433 Old Wood Lane, Birmingham, AL 35243
River Styx, 3139A South Grand, Ste. 203, St. Louis, MO 63118-1021
River Teeth, Ashland University, 401 College Ave., Ashland, OH 44805
Rock & Sling, 300 W. Hawthorne Rd., Spokane, WA 99251
Rogue Agent, 2715 Murray Ave., #717, Pittsburgh, PA 15217
Room Magazine, P.O. Box 46160 Station D, Vancouver, BC V6J 5G5, Canada
Rose Books, 64-49 60th Rd., Maspeth, NY 11378
Rough Beast, 88 College Road West, Princeton, NJ 08544
Rove, E. Barnett, 435 E.70th Terrace, Kansas City, MO 64131
Rum Punch Press, JCHS, 101 Elm Ave., SE, Roanoke, VA 24013-2222
Ruminate, 140 North Roosevelt Ave., Ft Collins, CO 80521
The Rumpus, 1810 N. Humboldt Blvd., #2, Chicago, IL 60647
Rust + Moth, 2409 Eastridge Court, Fort Collins, CO 80524
The Rusty Toque, 2-680 Shaw St., Toronto, ON M6G 3L7, Canada

S

S & H Publishing, P.O. Box 456, Purcellville, VA 20134
Sadie Girl Press, 4763 Deeboyar Ave., Lakewood, CA 90712
Sakura Review, 1727 Sena St., Denton, TX 76201
Salamander, 41 Temple St., Boston, MA 02114-4280
Salmagundi, Skidmore College, 815 N. Broadway, Saratoga Springs, NY 12866
Salt Hill, Syracuse University, English Dept., Syracuse, NY 13244
San Pedro River Review, P.O. Box 7000-760, Redondo Beach, CA 90277
The Sand Hill Review, 1076 Oaktree Dr., San José. CA 95129
Santa Monica Review, 29051 Hilltop Dr., Silverado, CA 92676
Saranac Review, SUNY, 101 Broad St., Plattsburgh, NY 12901-2681
Sastrugi Press, 2907 Iris Ave., San Diego, CA 92173
Saturnalia Books, 105 Woodside Rd., Ardmore, PA 19003
Science Thrillers Media, P.O. Box 601392, Sacramento, CA 95860-1392
Scribendi, MSC06-3890, 1 University of New Mexico, Albuquerque, NM 87131
Seattle Review, Box 354330, Seattle, WA 98195-4330

Seminary Ridge Review, 61 Seminary Ridge, Gettysburg, PA 17325

Sensitive Skin, 216 Laverne Ave., Mill Valley, CA 94941

Sequestrum, 19439 E. Mann Creek Dr., Unit E, Parker, Co 80134

Serving House Journal, P.O. Box 1385, Marysville, WA 98270

Seven CirclePress, 744 N 114th St., Seattle, WA 18133

Seven Corners, 1011 N. Walnut St., Normal, IL 61761

SFA Press, P.O. Box 13007 – SFA Station, Nacogdoches, TX 75962-3007

Shabda Press, 3343 East Del Mar Blvd., Pasadena, CA 91107

Shadowgraph, 418 Alamo Dr., Santa Fe, NM 87501

Shanti Arts, 193 Hillside Rd., Brunswick, ME 04011

Sharkpack Poetry Review, 17 Deerfield Rd., Medway, MA 02053

She Writes Press, 1563 Solano Ave., #546, Berkeley, CA 94707

Shipwreckt Books, 309 W. Stevens Ave., Rushford, MN 55971

Sibling Rivalry Press, P.O. Box 26147, Little Rock, AR 72221

Sierra Nevada Review, 999 Tahoe Blvd., Incline Village, NV 89451

Signature Books, 564 West 400 North, Salt Lake City, UT 84116

Silver Birch Press, P.O. Box 29458, Los Angeles, CA 90029

Sinister Wisdom, P.O. Box 144, Riverdale, MD 20738

Sixfold, 28 Farm Field Ridge Rd., Sandy Hook, CT 06482

Sixpenny Magazine, 1825 Buccaneer Dr., Sarasota, FL

Sixteen Rivers Press, 23 Edgecroft Rd., Kensington, CA 94707

Sixth Finch, 95 Carolina Ave., #2, Jamaica Plain, MA 02130

Slapering Hol Press, 300 Riverside Dr., Sleepy Hollow, NY 10591

Sleet Magazine, 1846 Bohland Ave., St. Paul, MN 55116

Slice, P.O. Box 659, Village Station, New York, NY 10014

The Sligo Journal, Montgomery College, Takoma Park, MD 20912

Slippery Elm, University of Findlay, 1000 N. Main, Findlay, OH 45840

Slipstream, Box 2071, Niagara Falls, NY 14301

Smallberry Press, 64 Berberis House, Highfield Rd., London TW13 4GP, UK

Small Print Magazine, P.O. Box 71956, Richmond, VA 23255-1956

Smartish Pace, P.O. Box 22161, Baltimore, MD 21203

SmokeLong Quarterly, 5708 Lakeside Oak Lane, Burke, VA 22015

Smokestack Books, 1 Lake Terrace, Grewelthorpe, Ripon, North Yorkshire HG4 3BU, UK

So To Speak, 4400 University Dr., MSN2C5, Fairfax, VA 22030

The Sockdolager Quarterly, 826 43rd St., #16, Brooklyn, NY 11232

Solo Nova, 744 Islay St., San Luis Obispo, CA 93401

Solstice, 38 Oakland Ave., Needham, MA 02492

Solstice Publishing, 614 Wal-mart Dr., Ste 209, Farmington, MO 63640

The Song Is..., 523 N. Horners Ln, Rockville, MD 20850

Sonora Review, English Dept., University of Arizona, Tucson, AZ 85721

South Dakota Review, English Dept., USD, 414 E. Clark St., Vermillion, SD 57069

The Southampton Review, 239 Montauk Hwy., Southampton, NY 11968

The Southeast Review, English Dept., Florida State Univ., Tallahassee, FL 32306

Southern California Review, 3508 Vinton Ave., #7, Los Angeles, CA 90034

Southern Indiana Review, USI, 8600 University Blvd., Evansville, IN 47712

Southern Poetry Review, 11935 Abercorn St., Savannah, GA 31419-1997

The Southern Review, L.S.U., 338 Johnston Hall., Baton Rouge, LA 70803

Southwest Review, PO Box 750374, Dallas, TX 75275-0374

The Sow's Ear Poetry Review, 17748 Cave Ridge Rd., Mount Jackson, VA 22842

Spank the Carp, 203 Lombardy Lane, Oswego, IL 60543

Spider Road Press, 1135 Allston St., Houston, TX 77008

Spillway, 11 Jordan Ave., San Francisco, CA 94118

Spirit Wind Poetry Gallery, 735 E. 14th Ave., #2, Eugene, OR 97401

Springwood Press, 302 Fairmount Dr., Madison, IN 47250

(the) Squawk Back, 17-15 Greene Ave., #1R, Ridgewood, NY 11385

St. Julian Press, 2053 Cortlandt, Houston, TX 77008

Stanford Court Press, 5255 Stevens Creek Blvd., #233, Santa Clara, CA 95051-6664

Star°Line, W5679 State Road 60, Poynette, WI 53955-8564

Still, 89 W. Chestnut St., Williamsburg, KY 40769

Still Crazy, 271 Chriswood Ct., Columbus, OH 43235-4624

Stillwater Review, Poetry Center, Sussex County College, Newton, NJ 07860

Stirring, 328 W 8th Avenue, Apt. #409, Spokane, WA 99204

Stone Canoe, 1897 State Route 91, Fabius, NY 13063

Stoneboat Literary Journal, P.O. Box 1254, Sheboygan, WI 53082-1254

Storm Cellar 212 Ames St., Northfield, MN 55057

Story Quarterly, English Dept., Rutgers, 311 N. Firth St., Camden, NJ 08102

Storychord, 66 West St., #2, Northampton, MA 01060

Storyscape, 407 S. 51st St., #1, Philadelphia, PA 19143

storySouth, 3302 MHRA Bldg., UNC Greensboro, Greensboro, NC 27402-6170

Strange Days Books, Chimaras 6, 74100, Rethymno, Crete, Greece

Structo, Groenhazengracht 3, Leiden 2311 VT, Netherlands

subTerrain, P.O. Box 3008 MPO, Vancouver, BC V6B 3X5, Canada

Sugar House Review, PO Box 13, Cedar City, UT 84721

Sugared Water, 5046 Relleum Ave., Cincinnati, OH 45238

The Summerset Review, 25 Summerset Dr., Smithtown, NY 11787

The Sun, 107 North Roberson St., Chapel Hill, NC 27516

Sundog Lit, 626 Dekalb Ave., #1341, Atlanta, GA 30312

Sundress Publications, 114 Newridge Rd., Oakridge, TN 37830

Superstition Review, 14610 S. Presario Trail, Phoenix, AZ 85048-1823

Sycamore Review, Purdue University, 500 Oval Dr., West Lafayette, IN 47907

Synchronized Chaos, 602 Boyer Ave., #C2, Walla Walla, WA 99362

TAB: The Journal of Poetry & Poetics, Chapman University, One University Drive, Orange, CA 92866

Tahoe Writers Works, 3170 US Hwy 50, Ste. 2A, Tahoe Paradise, CA 96150

Tahoma Literary Review, 6516 112th Street Ct. NW, Gig Harbor, WA 98332-8697

Tampa Review, 401 W Kennedy Blvd., Tampa, FL 33606

Tar River Poetry, East Carolina University, MS 159, Greenville, NC 27858-4353

Tell-Tale Inklings, 246 South Huntington Ave., #9, Jamaica Plain, MA 02130

Telling Our Stories Press, 185 AJK Blvd., #246, Lewisburg, PA 17837-7491

Ten G Publishing, 557 W. 140th St., Apt. 1A, New York, NY 10031-7054

Terrain.org, P.O. Box 19161, Tucson, AZ 85731-9161

Texas Christian University, TCU Box 298300, Fort Worth, TX 76129

Thank You for Swallowing, Flat 9 Rickman House, Grove St., Deptford, London SE8 5RB, UK

Third Coast, Western Michigan University, Kalamazoo, MI 49008-5331

Third Wednesday, 174 Greenside Up, Ypsilanti, MI 48197

32 Poems, Washington & Jefferson College, 60 South Lincoln St., Washington, PA 15301

Thomas-Jacob Publishing, P.O. Box 390524, Deltona, FL 32739

Thorny Locust, PO Box 32631, Kansas City, MO 64171-5631

Thoughtcrime Press, 9750 SW Marjorie Lane, #3, Beaverton, OR 97008

3: A Taos Press, P.O. Box 370627, Denver, CO 80237

Three Rooms Press, 561 Hudson St., #33, New York, NY 10014

Threepenny Review, PO Box 9131, Berkeley, CA 94709

Thrush Poetry Journal, 889 Lower Mountain Dr., Effort, PA 18330

Tiferet, 211 Dryden Rd., Bernardsville, NJ 07924

Tiger Bark Press, 202 Mildorf St., Rochester, NY 14609

Tikkun, 2342 Shattuck, #1200, Berkeley, CA 94707

Timberline Review, 2108 Buck St., West Linn, OR 97068

Timeless, Infinite Light, 4799 Shattuck Ave., Oakland, CA 94609

Tin House, 2601 NW Thurman St., Portland, OR 97210

The Tishman Review, 4540 Hummer Lake Rd., Ortonville, MI 48462

Torrid Literature, P.O. Box 151073, Tampa, FL 33684

Transition Magazine, 104 Mt. Auburn St., #3R, Cambridge, MA 02138

Tree of Knowledge Press, PO Box 4564, Deerfield Beach, FL 33442

Trestle Creek Review, North Idaho College, 1000 W. Garden Ave., Coeur d'Alene, ID 83814

Triptych Tales, 8 Shaw Court, Kanata, ON K2L 2L9, Canada

Truman State University Press, 100 East Normal Ave., Kirksville, MO 63501-4221

Tuesday, PO Box 1074, Arlington, MA 02474

Tule Review, Sacramento Poetry Center, 1719 25th St., Sacramento, CA 95816

Tulip Tree Review, P.O. Box 787, Sterling, CO 80751

Tupelo Press, P.O. Box 1767, North Adams, MA 01247

Turnip Truck(s), Tina Mitchell, 305 Cleveland St., Lafayette, LA 70501

The Tusk, 1477 Bedford, #4, Brooklyn, NY 11216

Twelve Winters Press, P.O. Box 414, Sherman, IL 62684-0414

Two Cities Review, 1 Hanson Place, Apt. PHA, Brooklyn, NY 11243

Two Lines Press, 582 Market St., Ste. 700, San Francisco, CA 94104

U

U.S. 1 Poets' Cooperative, PO Box 127, Kingston, NJ 08528-0127

uHlanga Press, 201 Herald Place, 2 Tamboerskloof Rd., Tamboerskloof, Cape Town, 80001, South Africa

Umbrella Factory Magazine, 2540 Sunset Dr., #125, Longmont, CO 80501

Unbroken Journal, 109 South Gallaher View Rd., Rm 108, Knoxville, TN 37919

Under the Sun, Tennessee Tech U., English Dept., Box 5053, Cookeville, TN 38505

Undertow Publications, 1905 Faylee Crescent, Pickering, ON L1V 2T3, Canada

Unicorn Press, 1212 Grove St., Greensboro, NC 27403

University of Arizona Press, 1510 E. University Blvd., Tucson, AZ 85721-0055

University of Hell Press, 0524 SW Nebraska St., Portland, OR 97239

University of Louisiana Press, P.O. Box 40831, Lafayette, LA 70504-0831

University of New Mexico Press, MSC05 3185, Albuquerque, NM 87131-0001

University of Nebraska Press, 1111 Lincoln Mall, Lincoln, NE 68588-0630

University of North Texas Press, 1155 Union Circle #311336, Denton, TX 76203

University of South Carolina Press, 1600 Hampton St., Ste. 544, Columbia, SC 29208

Unsplendid, University at Buffalo, 306 Clemens Hall, Buffalo, NY 14260-4610

Up the Staircase Quarterly, 716 4th St., SW, Apt. A, Minot, ND 58701

upstreet, P.O. Box 105, Richmond, MA 01254-0105

Utah State University Press, 5589 Arapahoe Ave., Ste. 206C, Boulder, CO 80303

V

Vagabondage Press, PO Box 3563, Apollo Beach, FL 33572

Vallum, 5038 Sherbrooke West, PO Box 23077 CP Vendome, Montreal, QC H4A 1T0, Canada

Valley Voices, MVSU 7242, 14000 Highway 82 West, Itta Bena, MS 38941-1400

Verto Publishing, 9118 Cox Ct., Apt. 2, Louisville, KY 40241

Vestal Review, 127 Kilsyth Rd., #3, Brighton, MA 02135

Vine Leaves Press, Konopisopoulou 31, Athens, 11524, Greece

Violet Book, 73 Farringdon Rd., London EC1M 3JQ, United Kingdom

Virginia Normal, 1 Hayden Dr., Petersburg, VA 23806

The Virginia Quarterly Review, 5 Boar's Head Lane, P.O. Box 400223, Charlottesville, VA 22904-4223

The Volta, 1423 E. University Blvd., ML445, Tucson, AZ 85721

W

Waccamaw Journal, Coastal Carolina Univ., P.O. Box 261954, Conway, SC 29528

War, Literature & the Arts, HQ USAFA/DFENG, 2354 Fairchild Dr., Ste. 6D-149, USAF Academy, CO 80840-6242

Washington Square Review, 58 W. 10th St., NY, NY 10003

Water~Stone Review, MS A1730, 1536 Hewitt Ave., St. Paul, MN 55104-1284

Water Wood Press, 47 Waterwood, Huntsville, TX 77230-9671

Watershed Review, CSU, Chico, 400 West First St., Chico, CA 95929

Waxwing Magazine, 220 S. Humphreys St., Flagstaff, AZ 86001

Wayne State University Press, 4809 Woodward Ave., Detroit, MI 48201-1309

Weasel Press, 4214 Norton Dr., Marvel, TX 77578

The Weeklings, 43 N. Manheim Blvd., New Paltz, NY 12561

Wesleyan University Press, 215 Long Lane, Middletown, CT 06459

West Branch, Stadler Center for Poetry, Bucknell Univ., Lewisburg, PA 17837

West Marin Review, P.O. Box 1302, Point Reyes Station, CA 94956

The Westchester Review, Box 246H, Scarsdale, NY 10583

Western Humanities Review, University of Utah, Salt Lake City, UT 84112-0494

Whale Road Review, 3900 Lomaland Dr., San Diego, CA 92106

When Women Waken, 133 Sharp Top Trail, Apex, NC 27502

Where Are You Press, 504 NE Dekum St., Portland, OR 97211

Wide Awake Poets of Los Angeles, 313 N Ave. 66, Los Angeles, CA 90042

Whistling Shade, 1495 Midway Pkwy, Saint Paul, MN 55108

White Dot Press, 707 Carl Dr., Chapel Hill, NC 27516

White Pine Press, P.O. Box 236, Buffalo, NY 14201

Wigleaf, University of Missouri, 114 State Hall, Columbia, MO 65211-1500

Willow Springs, 668 N. Riverpoint Blvd., 2-RPT- #259, Spokane, WA 99202

Winter Anthology, 5400 S. Harper Ave., #201, Chicago, IL 60615

Winter Tangerine, 3820 E. McCracken Way, #4, Bloomington, IN 47408

Wisdom Publications, 199 Elm St., Somerville, MA 02144

Wising Up Press, P.O. Box 2122, Decatur, GA 30031-2122

Witness, Box 455085, 4505 S. Maryland Parkway, Las Vegas, NV 89154-5085

WMG Publishing, 1845 SW Highway 101, Ste. 2, Lincoln City, OR 97367

WomenArts, UMSL, MC226, One University Blvd., St. Louis, MO 63121-4400
The Worcester Review, 1 Ekman St., Worcester, MA 01607
Word Works, 1337 County Rd. 59, Cambridge, NY 12816
Words Without Borders, 2809 W. Logan, Chicago, IL 60647
Workers Write! P.O. Box 250382, Plano, TX 75025-0382
World Literature Today, 630 Parrington Oval, Ste. 110, Norman, OK 73019-4033
World Unknown Press, 2223 Gunderson Ave., Berwyn, IL 60408
World Weaver Press, 215 W. Lake St., Alpena, MI 49707
The Writing Disorder, P.O. Box 93613, L.A., CA 90093-0613
Writing Knights Press, 324 Cleveland Ave. NW, Canton, OH 44702
Writing on the Edge, Writing Program, UC Davis, Davis, CA 95616
Wyvern Lit, 462 Shawmut Ave., #2, Boston, MA 02118

X

Xavier Review Press, Xavier Univ., 1 Drexel Dr., Box 89, New Orleans, LA 70125
Xenophon Press, 7518 Bayside Rd., Franktown, VA 23354

Y

Yarn, 26 Hawthorne Lane, Weston, MA 02493
Yellow Chair Review, 5606 Fairview Dr., Waco, TX 76710
Yellow Flag Press, 224 Melody Dr., Lafayette, LA 70503
Yellow Medicine Review, English Dept., SMSU, 1501 State St., Marshall, MN 56258
Yemassee, English Dept., USC, Columbia, SC 29208
Your Impossible Voice, KJP, 1081 E. Dunedin Rd., Columbus OH 43224
Yucca, P.O. Box 97, Gila, NM 88038

Z

Zephyr Press, 400 Bason Dr., Las Cruces, NM 88005
Zoetrope: All Story, 916 Kearny St., San Francisco, CA 94133
Zone 3 Press, APSU, P.O. Box 4565, Clarksville, TN 37044
Zoo Cake Press, 123 Frosting Way, Animal City, USA, zoocakepress(at)gmail.com
ZYZZYVA, 57 Post St., Ste. 604, San Francisco, CA 94104

CONTRIBUTORS NOTES

STEVE ALMOND has written several novels and works of non-fiction. His story collection, *God bless America,* (Lookout Books, 2011) won the Paterson Prize.

SARA BATKIE received an MFA in fiction from New York University. She lives in Brooklin and recently completed work on a novel.

CHARLES BAXTER has appeared many times in this series. He is a winner of the Rea Award for the Short Story and many other citations.

T. C. BOYLE has published fourteen novels and over one hundred short stories. He lives in Montecito, California.

MELISSA BRODER is the author of several books. She lives in Venice, California.

JERICHO BROWN's first book, *Please,* (New Issues, 2008) won the American Book Award and his second book, *The New Testament* (Copper Canyon, 2014) was named one of the best books of the year by *Library Journal.* He teaches at Emory University.

YE CHUN is the author of *Lantern Puzzle* (Tupelo Press, 2015) and *Travel Over Water* (Bitter Oleander Press, 2005). She teaches at Providence College.

DOUG CRANDELL has published two memoirs and four novels. He lives in Douglasville, Georgia.

PAUL CRENSHAW has appeared in several anthologies. He teaches at Elon University

RON CURRIE JR. lives in Portland, Maine. His fourth novel, *One Eyed Man*, is forthcoming.

LYDIA DAVIS has won six previous Pushcart Prizes. She lives in E. Nassau, New York.

ALEX DIMITROV is the author of books from Copper Canyon and Four Way Books. He is Senior Content Editor at the Academy of American Poets.

CHRIS DRANGLE earned an MFA at Cornell and is a recipient of a Stegner Fellowship at Stanford. He lives in the Bay Area of San Francisco.

EMMA DUFFY-COMPARONE teaches at Tufts University. Her work has appeared in *One Story, American Scholar, Mississippi Review, The Sun*, and *Pushcart Prize XXXIX*.

STEPHEN DUNN's eighteenth collection of poems, *Whereas*, will be published by Norton in 2017. He lives in Frostburgh, Maryland with his wife, the writer Barbara Hurd.

JOSHUA JENNIFER ESPINOZA appears in this series for the first time. She lives in Riverside, California.

TARFIA FAIZULLAH's *Seam* was published in 2014. She co-directs Organic Weapons Arts Chapbook and video series with Jamaal May.

KENDRA FORTMEYER's debut novel is forthcoming from Little, Brown in 2017. She is a writer, youth librarian, and prose editor for *Broad*.

JENNY HENDRIX is a freelance writer and critic. Her essays have appeared in *The Believer, Slate, Paris Review daily* and the *Boston Review*.

CATE HENNESSEY'S essays and book reviews have appeared in *River Teeth, Gettysburg Review, PANK* and *Tinderbox Poetry Journal*. She teaches at West Chester University.

DAVID HERNANDEZ lives in Long Beach, California. His new poetry collection is *Dear, Sincerely*, (University of Pittsburgh, 2016).

RICHIE HOFFMAN received a Ruth Lilly Poetry Fellowship and is co-editor of Lightbox Poetry.

CHARLES HOLDEFER lives in Brussels. His story is from a collection in progress titled *Rapt*.

PATRICIA SPEARS JONES authored three poetry collections and four chapbooks. She is a lecturer at LaGuardia Community College, New York.

LESLIE JOHNSON lives in Coventry, Connecticut. This is her first Pushcart Prize.

JAMES KIMBRELL has published three volumes of poetry with Sarabande Books. He has received a Discovery the Nation Award, a Whiting Writer's Award, the Ruth Lilly Fellowship and a Bess Hokin Prize from *Poetry* magazine.

DAVID KIRBY has appeared in three previous volumes of this series, most recently with "Skinny Dipping with Pat Nixon" (PPXXXII).

VLADISLAVA KOLOSOVA was born in 1987 in St. Petersburg, Russia. She now lives in Berlin, Germany. This is her first published work.

JANE LANCELLOTTI is associate editor at *Narrative*. She received an MFA in fiction from Sarah Lawrence College in 2015.

KATE LEVIN teaches at the University of Southern California. Her work has appeared in the *New York Times*, *Boston Globe* and elsewhere.

BARRY LOPEZ is the author of fourteen books of fiction and nonfiction. He received the National Book Award for *Artic Dreams*, and lives in Blue River, Oregon.

REBECCA MAKKAI is the author of two novels and a short story collection, *Music for Wartime*. She has taught at the Iowa Writers Workshop and Northwestern University.

SALLY WEN MAO is the author of *Mad Honey Symposium* (Alice James Books, 2014). She was writer in residence at Singapore Creative Writing Residency (2015) and a fellow at the New York Public Library's Cullman Center (2016).

DAVID TOMAS MARTINEZ's debut poetry collection, *Hustle*, was released in 2014 by Sarabande Books. He has been a Breadloaf and Canto Mundo fellow.

DANIEL MASON is a clinical assistant professor of psychiatry at Stanford University and the author of two novels: *The Piano Tuner* and *A Far Country*.

ADRIAN MATEJKA's The Big Smoke (Penguin, 2013) was a finalist for the National Book Award and the Pulitzer Prize. His new book, *Collectable Blacks*, is due in 2017.

ELIZABETH MCCRACKEN's most recent book is *Thunderstruck and Other Stories*, winner of the 2015 Story Prize. She lives in Austin, Texas.

SHANE MCCRAE teaches at Oberlin College. His most recent books are *The Animal Too Big To Kill* (Persea Books, 2015) and *The Language of My Captor* (Wesleyan, 2017).

ERIN MCGRAW has won two pervious Pushcart Prizes. She lives in Sewanee, Tennessee.

MARTIN ESPADA previously appeared in *Pushcart Prize XXVIII*. He lives in Amherst, Massachusetts. His new poetry collection is *Vivas to Those Who Have Failed* (Norton, 2016)

DOUGLAS MILLIKEN authored four books including the novel *To Sleep As Animals*. He lives in Scarborough, Maine.

KALPANA NARAYANAN was born in New Delhi and now divides her time between New York and Atlanta. Her work has appeared in *Boston Review*, *Granta* and *The Millions*.

CHRIS OFFUTT is the author of several books, most recently *My Father, The Pornographer*. He lives in Oxford, Mississippi.

CECILLY PARKS teaches at Texas State University. She is the author of two poetry collections and editor of the anthology *The Echoing Green*: *Poems of Fields, Meadows and Grasses*.

DANIEL PEÑA teaches at the University of Houston. He is a writer, blogger, book reviewer and journalist.

DOMINICA PHETTEPLACE has been published in *Asimov's*, *Clarkesworld*, *PANK*, and the *Los Angeles Review*. She lives in Berkeley, California.

MELISSA PRITCHARD is the author of eight books of fiction, an essay collection and a biography. She lives in Phoenix, Arizona.

TATIANDA FORERO PUERTA is originally from Bogata, Columbia. Her work has appeared in *Juked*, *Moon City Review* and elsewhere. She is a graduate of Stanford University and New York University.

LIA PURPURA is the author of eight collections of essays, poems and translations. She won Guggenheim, NEA and Fulbright Fellowships and teaches at The University of Maryland.

MONTE REEL is the author of *The Last of the Tribe* and *Between Man and Beast*. He lives in Evanston, Illinois.

ELIZABETH SCANLON is editor of *The American Poetry Review* and the author of two chapbooks. She lives in Philadelphia.

TAIJE SILVERMAN is the author of *House Are Fields*. She teaches at the University of Pennsylvania.

EMILY SKILLINGS is the author of two poetry chapbooks and the forthcoming collection *Fort Not* (Song Cave, 2017).

JENN SHAPLAND lives in Austin, Texas and teaches at the University of Texas.

SEA SHARP lives in England and is the winner of the 2015 Prairie Seed Poetry Prize.

LAUREN SLATER is the author of *Prozac Diary* and other books. Her new book of nonfiction is due for 2017.

JANE SPRINGER is the author of two poetry collections. She has been honered with a Whiting Writers' Award, an NEA Fellowship, and a MacDowell Fellowship. She teaches at Hamilton College.

MICAH STACK graduated from the Iowa Writers' Workshop. His work has appeared in *Juked*, *Gemini Magazine*, *Fiction Advocate* and *The Rumpus*. He teaches at the University of Nevada, Reno.

MATHIAS SVALINA is the author of five books, most recently *The Wine-Dark Sea*. He lives in Denver.

LISA TADDEO has just complete her first novel and is at work on a debut nonfiction book about desire and sexuality in America.

ELIZABETH TALLENT is the author of a novel and a short story collection. She teaches at Stanford.

DEB OLIN UNFERTH'S is the author of three books and a fourth is set to appear in 2017. She lives in Austin, Texas.

DAVID UNGER is a writer and reporter based in Chicago. Previously he wrote and edited articles about energy transistion for the *Christian Science Monitor*.

JEAN VALENTINE has appeared in two previous edition of this series. "Hospice" is from her collection *Shirt In Heaven* (Copper Caonyon).

ALLISON BENIS WHITE is the author of three poetry collections, most recently *Please Bury Me In This* (Four Way Books). She teaches at the University of California, Riverside.

ERIC WILSON's work has appeared in *Massachusetts Review*, *Epoch*, *Carolina Quarterly* and *O'Henry Prize Stories*. He lives in Santa Monica, California.

SHELLEY WONG lives in Oakland, California, Her poems have been published in *Vinyl*, *The Normal School*, *The Collagist* and elsewhere.

JAMILA WOODS is a poet, singer and teaching artist from Chicago. She is the Associate Artistic Director of Young Chicago Authors. Her first solo is just out.

ANGELA WOODWARD is the author of *Natural Wonders* (2015), winner of the 2015 Fiction Collective Two Catherine Doctorow Innovative Fiction Prize. She lives in Madison, Wisconsin.

ROBERT WRIGLEY is the author of eight poetry collections. He won the Kingsley Tufts Poetry Award in 2000. He lives in Moscow, Idaho and teaches at the University of Idaho.

LIZ ZIEMSKA lives in Los Angeles and describes herself as "A writer of slightly strange fiction."

INDEX

The following is a listing in alphabetical order by author's last name of works reprinted in the *Pushcart Prize* editions since 1976.

603

604

606

614

615

618

619

620

621

625

627

629

635

DEC, 2016